Make A Wish

Tina Ray

Make A Wish

ISBN 978-0-615-39031-4 (Ubiquity Productions)

Printed in USA

Dedication

I dedicate this book to all those who know and understand that they live a life projected by circumstance…yet have risen above them. I dedicate this book to the naysayers' who knocked the reality of the pursuit of my dream. Last but not least…I dedicate this book to me, myself and I, for it is a true labor of love and a testament to the only true belief one can have…and that is of self.

Acknowledgements

I would like to thank my wonderful cipher of family and friends who have encouraged me along the way and held my hand as I strived to make the production of this book a reality. First and foremost I would like to give thanks to the Great Wankan Tanka for his guidance and assistance in maintaining my resolve through some very rough waters in my life. I would also like to thank my Mom and my siblings Gordon, Lisa, Francine, Jeannita, Sidney and Niece-Tereese for always loving and accepting me just as I am. I also appreciate the support of my nieces, nephews, friends and family members who also supported me with their belief. I would also like to give thanks to my extended sisters Aisha Belfield, Alicia Boone, Paula Boone, Tamantha Ramsey, Takimah Rein; your existence in my life has made it that much rewarding. A special thanks goes out to my book club sisters past and present, Aisha Belfield, Shakeerah Belfield Terry Belfield, Tiecher Belfield, Alicia Boone, Jeannita Brown, Lisa Brown and Dishreen Riddle for being patient for this production. I would also like to acknowledge those who had to read my chapters and gave me feedback even when you didn't want to. And I must absolutely thank my man-child Isaiah Brown for giving me pointers on my formatting and editing them for me. Love you much. A very special thank you goes out to Katrina A. Kelly our very own family graphic arts designer who designed the book cover for Make A

Wish…marvelous…simply marvelous. I'd like to take the time to give a special thank you to my brother Divine who has proven to be a true friend that always has total confidence in me and my well being. I appreciate all the patience and words of wisdom you shared with me in some of my darkest hours.

And last but not least…to my father Sidney Alexander Brown who left us way too soon. You instilled in me the virtues that a true man is comprised of. You taught by example as to what I should seek in my quest for togetherness. Respect, consideration, honesty, integrity, tenacity and one who has a total belief in love for his woman, his family and his self.
I love you always daddy

That quest for togetherness…I'm still looking.

I want to give total thanks to my Famous Best Friend. I spent many years trying to decipher the methods of your very unconventional lessons. The lessons were hard...the lessons were long and most often confusing. Yes...it took a minute but there are no time restraints on learning, as both time and learning are infinite. As you schooled me I learned how to convert the negative to a positive and utilized that energy as fuel to replenish my mindset. So...Thank you for being exactly who you are, as it allowed me to see exactly who I needed to be.

And for that...I will always love you.

Make Wish A Wish is a total work of fiction and depicts no actual events and/or dialogue of any of the characters named of either real or fictitious nature.

Introduction

In regard to the issue of men and their relentless challenge and pursuit of women, a wise man once told me that yes…men in their primal pursuit may elect to have the attention of many. Like wheels on a vehicle that he can rotate, deflate and even store in the trunk as a spare. The wise man went on to inform me that in this process of wheel rotation, it is usually the squeaky wheel that gets the oil. So essentially, in translation, the woman who voices her discontent, and then tracks, monitors and regulates her demanded needs for attention will be the one constantly attended to. I thought about it, and yes…I had to admit that what he said bears much truth. I mean…I see that happening around me, all day…every day. But you know I have to ask…am I wrong…or wouldn't a wise man know that a wheel that truly matters would never have to squeak?

Part I

March 2008 – July 2008

Chapter 1
It All Started When...

JT

I'm watching as they glide down the escalator after disembarking the plane, stepping right into a den of reporters and paparazzi. My baby looking like the divine angel that she is...tempting angel; I think as I laugh out loud to the very thought. And my big little brother Murad...so in charge, so protective, yeah...he's on the job with our girl. Our girl...what an oxymoron. She's supposed to be my girl, but the actual is...she's "our" girl. No disputing that fact. My God...just look at them together....they are glowing. Both adorned in semi matching fur jackets, jewelry banging, hair meticulous. The chemistry is so evident between them, it's like everyday is the 4th of July. Yeah...that hot. They depict the ultimate couple. Look at her....so unsuspecting...just being her. Murad...arm around her waist...holding on to her like she belongs to him...and she fitting there so perfectly. Ain't no point in denying it...them two are made for each other. Damn...what am I gonna do when they both realize it.

Nubina

Damn look at all these hounds up in here. Can a sista get a chance to breathe? This fame is quickly becoming challenging, but I wouldn't trade it for the word I'm thinking as I laugh out loud to my surroundings. Where's JT?

"Nubina...Nubina...can you tell us now that you're back in your own hometown, will you be appearing here anytime soon?" Wow...I'm so busy looking for JT I'm not paying attention, let alone prepared to answer the reporter. But Murad...who is always hot on me like a shadow was up on it.

"Nubina has a tight schedule, but I'm sure we will be looking into accommodating NYC, no doubt" he answers for me with that infamous million dollar smile. Murad is PHINE...yep phonetically...lol. I can't remember the last brother I've known as fine as him. He's got to have one of the most gorgeous faces this side of heaven. I quickly averted my attention back to my immediate cipher, leaning into Murad flashing and smiling, while internally glowing inside with the knowledge that Murad was my rock, always there to guide me and keep things on track. I'm so glad he's in my life....don't know where I'd be without him. But where is JT? I wonder as I sneak furtive peeks around the area to locate him.

Murad

Wow...more paparazzi here than I thought. Aight...let me see how soon I can maneuver us thru this nonsense.

"Nube"...man...she ain't even paying attention. Probably checking for my dry ass brother JT. Man...something gotta give. Butter here is growing on me... everyday live. I ain't never felt for no female the things I'm starting to feel for Nube. I mean, I know I'm her manager and all, and she with my brother, but his faithfulness don't even know what to do with all this. Damn...I'm sounding like I'm sprung as hell. Hold up...what this trick reporter here talking about. Nube ain't even listening. As I began to pick off this reporter with my answer, I feel her swing into me, and I wrap my arm around her a little closer. Aww...now this shit right here feel right. At that same precise moment, I spot JT eyes upon us drinking it all in. I toss him a nod with a 50/50 notice of intent. Half of me is feeling like relax man ain't nothing grimey going on here, while the other 50 percent is saying "yeah choir boy...you already know." I release my self from his gaze and direct my eyes to where they truly wanna be. She still wrapped up in my arms, sending my blood flow all haywire and don't even know it. And just as she flashes that sexy-ass smile up at me...my blackberry buzzes on my hip, letting me know that either jump-off number 1,

2 or 3 been watching the news and knows that I'm back in town. I let it vibrate...

Chapter 2
Keeping The Ball Rolling

Nubina

OMG...I can't believe this is all happening. My work is getting noticed, and things are jumping off. I never thought so many people would be feeling what I'm saying...feeling me. This feeling is so awesome.

"Rod can you believe this?" I blurt out as he maneuvers the Escalade in and out of traffic down 7th Ave.

Of course he doesn't answer me immediately, he's on his blackberry. I swear that thing stays glued to his ear. I side slap him upside the head and whine, "Rod...you not listening to me."

I hear him say "Aight man...I'll catch up wit ya later," as he slides the phone closed.

"What Nube...I heard you?" he replies with a feigned smile of bothersome.

"Man...you ain't heard one thing I said. I'm over here gushing bout all my work poppin off and you got that darn Blackberry glued to your ear." I shot back in a playful mood.

"Listen," he said, "I heard you ...I heard you. Don't worry, I've got it all taken care of...we gonna celebrate Friday night at Sarafin's in South Orange. Some people coming thru...a few from the industry and it's gonna be all good. You know I'm gonna make sure the light stay shining on your spot, cause if you eat...then we all eat," he laughs out loud.

"You know what," I say, slapping him upside the head again.

"Yo, watch it Nube...I'm trynna drive. You do want us to get home in one piece right?' he answers, "Besides, I'm just playing Nube. You know you mad hot right now...stone killin them all over the planet. You talented girl...really talented. Seriously...I'm glad I'm here with you making this journey...keeping these snakes in order, cause what you do is real. It's from the heart."

Wow I'm thinking as he's talking. Always good with a comeback that nobody can argue with. In another life time Murad could have been a politician. Still in all…he ain't never lied.

"So a party huh?" I respond, "When did you decide all this?"

"Girl…I'm always on my grind. You don't know? While you out there grinding…I'm grinding. Don't worry, it's gonna be all she wrote, and we gonna be knobbing with the right people so we can get a feel on how they operate, ya know. We don't want to have to be screening every person coming at us with a hustle, so we gonna limit who we screen to the cream of the crop. Got it?" he tossed me a look as if looking for my approval.

"It sounds like a plan Rod," I said, hearing him sigh with relief. I know that he's very careful in what he plans and who he lets have dealings with me. I'm sure that the event will be productive; it's just that JT probably won't come to Sarafin's since it's considered a night club.

Just at the time JT and I started talking with one another, he decided to pursue the Ministry. He's trying to be an apostle to the church or something Christian like that. Don't get me to lying…I have no use for organized religion at all let alone be up on the newest trendy Christian positions. He had been thru some traumatizing events in his life, and I am no stranger to trauma either; so I came to the realization that it is every individual's choice in how they revitalize themselves from their trauma. I can't discount his good soul, just because he chooses to be involved in the church. And oh my…it don't hurt none that he bears some of the same phine as his brother Murad, just on a much quieter, toned down level. But this serving God getting myself together thing is getting in the way. I'm just saying at this stage of the game, I want to get on with doing what I'm doing romantically. I understand the working out of issues…I myself have many issues to contend with, but I just don't feel that Christianity is the answer to fix yourself internally. I feel you do best serving yourself if you wanna see positive results. The Creator is only here to guide you, as you are one of his magnificent creations. I don't feel that it was meant to put all of your burdens upon him, merely for you to just draw strength from his existence to propel yourself forward. He's far to busy contemplating the demise of the earth's resources to be piddling around in our self imposed dramatic lives. I love the fact that JT is doing something in regard to his troubles and issues, but I hate an organization that holds you restrained to all kind of conditions that's supposed to test your strength in what....belief?

But as I said...who am I to judge...I just know that all the trying to live in God's eye are crossing my own up. I need him to be sure that what he decides to give of himself to me is his choice, and not prescribed under some guideline that his "religion" dictated for him. I need him in so many different ways. I need him to mentally believe in me, I need him to sometimes accompany me in my arena. I do sacrifice as much as I can with my schedule and go with him to special church events, but he doesn't feel that my venue is of a true Christian atmosphere, so he doesn't attend with me. I need him to sometimes just be around to scratch my head, my back, rub my feet, catch a movie....but those times are far and few between. Whenever I'm home off the road, he's busy with his ministry classes and such, and don't want to be tempted away from advancing in his studies. I'm patient and don't believe in jumping the gun, but a sister could also use some loving as in sexing. How many kisses, shoulder rubs and squeezes can one girl take without trying on the "real thing". Its shit like that could make a girl wonder. If I didn't know better....hmmm....

Chapter 3
Observations and Explanations

JT

Tania has been home for 2 days now, and I haven't been able to spend any time with her. Well Nube as she's better known, short for her stage name Nubina. It's funny that she created that name, because it so reflects her inner beauty. I just sure wish I could get past this conflict I'm having with honoring my faith. She's been so understanding and hanging tough with me all the way, but I know a woman of her creative, loving spirit is full of passion, and very much in need of releasing it. Oh...don't get me wrong, I wasn't always a man of the book...something inside me would love to bend her over and make her scream my name...but those are choices from yesteryear. And choices like that have led me down a bumpy road...so I will continue with my choice to refrain from secular activities until my mind and soul are complete with God. I just hope that the two can coincide sometime in the near future. I guess I'll try her on her cell phone this time. Called the house and she was not in. I know she had an appearance on Live at 5 this morning, and she and Murad are scheduled to attend a ceremony uptown in order to raise money for a Women's Shelter.

I have to say, she is keeping her word in sharing her knowledge and inner thoughts within her community, and doing her part to uplift those that she can. That's what I love about her so. She is so genuine in her care and concern for others, so honest to a fault, it's unreal. I wish that I had known her at the time that I was out conceiving a child without a damn clue. I wouldn't have been forced to deal with the antics of my son's mother, and I 'm sure he would have had a much better chance at self progression if Tania was his mom. But...who's to say what would have transpired. At that time in my life, I myself was not the brightest bulb in the pack, so I suppose things happen they way they do for a reason. Tania would never have deserved having to deal with the man I used to be. I was weak...not in the sense of weak for women, or running and hustling; but weak for not standing strong in my own convictions; or for even attempting to practice my convictions, and strive for my goals. I let others choose and decide for me, which led me to the misery I've encountered for most of my adult life. I let my son's mother wrangle me into a relationship that I was not interested in being, I let her coax me into having unprotected sex, believing her lies about not being able to get pregnant. And I also believed that the child was mine, although a car accident when he was 16 and a need for blood resigned the fact that I was not.

At that point in our lives, Kane and I were so tight that nothing could separate our bond, and nothing has. In spite of our undying love as father and son, the fact that he was not mine delivered a severe blow to my self-esteem. I lost all trust and faith in women as well as in my self and just started practicing all kinds of irrational behavior. I mean I never really became an alcoholic, but I started downing a six pack every other day, and sleeping my time away with different women the other days of the week The utter chaos and drama of the compilation of the many miserable souls in and out of my life led me to lose my job, my home, and the majority of my sanity. It was actually Kane who came to my rescue, and set down with me and talked me back to reality. He explained that trust in any human being is so hard to find, and is such a gift when you do come across it. He let me know that I was his gift to him, and the inner vision of a man who he has looked up to all his life. He then told me he was not going to sit by and watch the insecurity and issues of another human being destroy the spirit of the one most person on the planet that he loves without a doubt. I listened to this man-child expel nothing but the simplicity of his version of the truth and I sat there and cried my soul clean. He sat with me, and held me until I was thru, and told me thank you. Can you actually believe the promise within this child? He thanked me he said for being in his life despite the lies of his mother, and showing him what being a man is all about. If I have to say so myself...he turned out to be pretty damn good.

So I guess things happened just as they were supposed to. Kane went on to graduate high school, and attend Brown

University where he is currently in his second year. I in turn turned to church and Christ and decided to live my life resurrecting myself to be a man that not just Kane would continue to be proud of, but a man that I myself could be proud of. Tania became an interest in my life about 2 years ago. She is a longtime friend to one of my female cousins, and I'd seen her around here and there over the years. I'd never really paid too much attention to her before, as I was busy being led thru the nose by the many nemesis of my life, and not for nothing, she was jumping thru her own hoops and dealing with her own situations. But at some point, she began to develop her talent and passion for writing poetry and speaking out in a positive nature and got herself noticed by a friend of my brother Murad, who dibbled and dabbled in entertainment/promotions. Kason saw a vision in her, when she recited some of her work at one of our annual family cookouts, and started buzzing in her ear about where he could take her with it all. My brother Murad, the stone hustler and master of ceremonies was not about to be shut out of an opportunity, and proclaimed himself the overseer of her, carrying her under his wing, while she was dealing with Kason.

It started out as a pure business venture for Murad, but somewhere along the way, he got serious, took a positive interest in her work and what she does, and became her manager in a massive way. He began to secure projects and deals that only benefited her interest to the utmost and secured her top dollar as well. He cut all the leeches out of the operations, including Kason and has done nothing but lead her continuously to success. He put in mad hours and made sacrifices that elevated her to the levels of Oprah, Larry King, and venues all over the country. She spoke and performed at colleges, high school graduations, community events, sporting events and even political events. You name it...any positive venues that existed, Murad secured them. He even put a deal in motion to get her work on a CD that became the licensed theme song for several different TV shows, and one track that was included as part of a movie soundtrack. No doubt...a part in an actual movie was next. Yeah...Tania was doing big things...great things...all at the hands of Murad. So ironic... for Murad never respected a single woman his entire life.

Chapter 4
This Be The Bull

Nubina

Well this is sure proving to be a challenge. Me and Rod over here at the mall cause I want to shop for something to wear to this networking, celebration thingy we got going on Friday night. He keeps trying to convince me that we can bring on a stylist/personal assistant and let her handle all those things, but I still want to have my hand in it, so for now...it's still on me. After 4 stores, and several try-ons, I finally settled on 2 choices. Right about now Rod started grumbling about being hungry, and needing to get something to eat.

"Okay big baby. Let's go get you fed, cause I don't want your cranky ass around me the rest of the day." I told him.

"Yeah...you don't," he answered back, "Let's make some moves on over to this food court. A brother is starving."

On the way to the food court, I eyed an accessory store, and remembered that I could use a necklace with one of the outfits, so I veered off, and called out, "Rod...I'ma go over here to check something out. I'll be done in five."

"Nube, girl come on...I'm hungry," he shot back.

"Five minutes Rod...I promise. In fact go ahead...I'll be right there," I told him.

"Aight, but don't be playing round..." his words were cut off by the ringing of his blackberry.

"Uh-huh...yeah...just like I know." I said to him and spun around on my heels towards the store.

"Five on five Nube," I heard him call out before he turned his attention back to his phone call. I laughed to myself as I entered the store. That man...always got some kind of negotiations going on one way or another. Well let me hurry up, I'm kind of hungry too, and we still have to do a studio session tonight, so. Oh...look at this one...this might work. Let me see what it's looking like on me. I attempt to pull the necklace around my neck when I heard a distinctive voice ask “Would you like some help with that?” and a strong set of hands grab the clasp and secure the necklace around my neck for me. I grabbed one hand and whirled around in utter confusion spitting and stuttering, “Trey?”

“Peace Beena,” he replied.

I stand there transfixed as though someone has glued my mouth and my brain together.

“Is there a problem?” he responded to the complete look of confusion on my face. “I saw you were having a little trouble, so I came over to assist you.”

“Trey,” I repeated again. “What...where...I guess...well ain’t this original. You have got to be the LAST person I was ever expecting to run into. Especially here...today. Wow....I’m at a lost for words. Sooo....”

“Sooo....what?” he questions me, cocking his head to the side and raising them eyebrows just the way I used to love. And oh...no he didn’t just flash them frigging pearly whites he used to dazzle me with.

“So, is there something I can help you with?” I push back, coming up out of my daze. With that statement, I unknowingly unleashed a fuse of negative energy that sufficed as the key that unlocked a Pandora’s box... one that I didn’t even know existed.

Murad

“Yeah...I’m up at the mall...yeah with Nube. What you mean...we taking care of business. Yeah I’m scooping you up Friday night. What...hold on” I took one last turn around to the store in where Nube stopped to cop her jewelry and I’m seeing something real unfamiliar. Some midnight ass dude is wrapping something around her neck, and now Nube done backed up...but she talking to him. I need to go handle this.

“Yo Jazz, I’ma hit you later...what...naw gotta take care of something. Yeah...I’m sure...later,” I said and hung up the phone. I started to take 10 strides at once and stomp over there like King Kong and shit, but something told me to slow my roll and check out the situation first. I mean she talking to him, so she know him, and...I'll be damn...that gotta be that Trey dude that broke her heart. Yeah, who else that's darker than 2 nights in a row could it be. Shit...she don't need this mutha fucka back up in her space. He is so all about nothing but game and I oughta know. I'm going over there...I'm diffusing this bullshit right here, right now.

On my way over, I hear Nube asking dude, "Is there something I can help you with?" I walk right up behind her and before they both realize I'm there, I relay the question to him a second time.

"Is there something you need some help with?" I interject and they both turn towards me.

"Rod, I thought you was getting something to eat," Nube responded.

"Well I lost my fucking appetite," I snapped back. I see a quick slice of pain slide across her face, and I feel low for hurting her and all, but I rise right back to the occasion when his lame ass had to chime his two cents in.

"Excuse me...my man," he said, "I don't mean no disrespect. Beena and I are... old friends. I was just in the process of seeing how she living right now."

"Beena?" I asked all twisted for no reason.

"Rod," she finally speaks up, "This is Trey."

"Oh I know who he is," I jumped in and cut her off, "And what's his issue?" I throw back at her.

"Rod...he just wanted to talk...we haven't seen each other for a minute, and I'll be done in a few." she said to me giving me the screw face.

"Nube...he ain't talkin bout shit you need to hear," I tell her. "I ain't too comfortable with this situation," I added on.

"Rod," she answers me in that short, tight voice, "It's all good...I'll be done...in...a...minute."

The sound of the irritation in her voice is something that I never experienced from Nube, and that shit hit me like a brick in my stomach. At the same time, I just realized that I don't own her...not in that way. I need to back up, let her handle whatever the fuck she think she need to handle. But just in case, I gently grabbed her face in my hand and turn her till we meet eye to eye and simply say, "Nube." I twist my head with a final gesture that I know she understands, and she answers me back the same.

"No problem," I state, "I'ma be right over there," I say pointing to a bench directly across from the store she and Trey are standing in front of. I'm feeling like a piece of runned over dog shit as I turn my back to go have a seat. Something just happened here, and I don't know the fuck what. But what the fuck I do know is...I'm getting dude PI'd on the next tomorrow. That's a fucking promise. I sat down on the bench, and proceed to dial that shit into reality.

After 2 rings my phone came live with, "Holla." Without a moment of hesitation I was on it, "Yo...I want this mutha fucka on surveillance like yesterday morning. What for? Nigga, cause I said so. What? ...no his ass rubs me the wrong fucking way. That's why. Trey...I think Wilson or Wilkerson. Check them both. Oh...I'm not concerned with all that. That shit will be on him. Look Dame...I ain't ask you for your opinion, slick. Just do what I asked you. Can you do me that? Then cool...no further discussion needed. I'll check you later. Peace." What this silly ass mutha fucka talking bout? I'm trynna make sure Nube is secure in a safety sort of sense. Ya know? She starting to get really popular, I just can't be letting nukkas' run up on her whenever they feel like it. Hell naw....we ain't havin no parts of that nonsense!! I mean we business partners, I've got interest in her, and I need to protect my damn interest. It's what any man in his right fucking mind would do. But sheeiit...that right there is getting to be a problem though. I'm not in my "right" fucking mind right now. In fact, I'm outta my damn mind...feenin over Nube.

Chapter 5
The Best Thing I Ever Had

Trey

"Wow...he's a little intense. Is that your man?" I asked.

"His brother," she replied, "He's my manager, and...why am I explaining to you. Trey this is not about me. What is it you thinking you wanna say?"

"Beena, it's always been about you."

"How you figure Trey?" she came back with, "Was it about me when you jumped off with ole girl? That nasty...fat nasty skank you just had to have. And somewhere between God and Luchipher lies the answer to how many other skanks you been with in the last 3 years."

"Seriously Been...that was some phase I found myself regressed in," I replied. "You know I'm so much more than that...just couldn't shake unhealthy desires. I lost prospective somewhere along the way and compromised my integrity. But at some point I hit rock bottom and it took that to make me regain my insight to the total understanding of self worth."

"Oh," she counter replied giving me a round of applause, "Is that the latest scene from your ongoing production of Victims Never Cease? Would this be Act 1, Act 2 or a special VIP performance? If so...you can stop right there, cause I'm not purchasing a ticket this time around."

I sensed quite a bit of anger, and decided to give her that one; I wasn't out to get myself strung up today. I took a deep breath, and then responded.

"You know what... I deserved that and anything else you got coming...but I just wanted to let you know that I'm not that man anymore. I've divested in myself, and operating on a level of mental consciousness to always live, breathe, and practice respect. And me living my life this way can assure that only those of a respectful nature will cross my path."

"Oh yeah," she says with the sourness of a lemon, "you are the newly appointed Global Ambassador of respect. Don't know how the world would ever progress without you. In fact I'm sure the Council of Respect is busy revising the newest policies so that you can go out and begin the World Tour of Respect for 2008. I can't believe you! You know how many times I walked to hell and back because of you? And you say you were going thru a phase? Do you know the months...days...years I doubted myself because you had to satisfy your unhealthy phase? Save it Trey, that was just the real you that you couldn't contain anymore. I called you...I texted you. No response. I wrote you letters pleading with you to not cut me out of your life, and to this day I don't recall an answer. So don't come at me with all that knowledge, wisdom and understanding shit you spit on a regular. Cause with all that damn knowledge you had, you should have had the wisdom to know that there could be no understanding of the foulness...that you...dealt me. I have long since concluded that I was just one of your unhealthy desires. Why don't you try and see if you can respect that?"

Damn...something about her is new, different. Or either the true internal she is beginning to peak...I don't know. But whatever it is...I'm feeling that shit in a big way. Her personal level has definitely grown; she ain't beat for the nonsense at all, she's much more confident and secure. Ironically she's probably on a level now where we can finally build something together. I wonder if she would be interested in re-exploring coming to that understanding. I was just about to let her know that I'd like to hook up and have this conversation in great depth, when her "bodyguard" stormed over firmly took her hand in his and with a slight tug said, "Nube, we gotta go." I could tell that she was not too happy being blindsided for the second time today, but was probably too overwhelmed with the situation and relented.

"Trey, I need to go," she said and allowed herself to be led away.

I don't know what possessed me to put myself out there, but I didn't hesitate for a moment and called out in the most seductive voice I could find, "Beena."

She stopped and turned around to face me giving me a look somewhere between curiosity and defeat.

“Call me,” I said, releasing the hopeful into the universe. She looked at me one last time...this time it appeared to be a look of disgust, and as she turned her back on me to walk away, I heard her utter, “Puhleese.”

I stood there with nothing else to say, as she and the angry bodyguard made a bee line for the exit, leaving me in a zone. As I turned to start walking to my destination, I thought...what method or resources I could use to get her to consider being “us” again. What would it take to secure us in an unbreakable union and set us on a path of forever? How in the world could I convince this woman that our true time is now, and that now is ripe with reason. And by the time I reached the driver side door to my car I wondered...how I could convince myself of the same.

Chapter 6
The Aftermath

Nubina

As I'm being led hand in hand by Murad from the mall to the car, I find my mind twirling with the chain of events that have just taken place. Trey...Trey...I haven't seen him in 3 years!!! And I'm not understanding what the heck I'm feeling right now. I mean...I'm not goo-ga happy, but something is not letting me hate on his ass like I need to be. Doesn't help none that I didn't have a minute to absorb it all before Murad came storming over. And just look at him now. Like a missionary, who's accomplished his task and bringing home the bounty. He is mad like that. Genuinely swoll...really what is all this to him? I kept my mouth shut as he led me around to the passenger side of the truck, opened the door and deposited me inside with that "get yer ass on in there" attitude. I watched him stride around to the driver's side, get in and shut the door, proceed to put his seat belt on, and then... I let him have it.

"Rod," I started, "What the hell was that?"

"What the hell was what Nube," he answered. "You up in the fucking mall cheesing it up with Midnight and shit like things gravy between you and dude. That mutha fucka need to get on with the bullshit. Take his gaming ass somewhere on to somebody that gives a shit."

"That mutha fucka?" I got back with him raising my voice an octave, "What makes him that mutha fucka to you? You don't even know shit about him Rod? How you fixing your mouth to talk shit bout something you don't know?"

"Bullshit Nube, bullshit," he yelled, "That corroded bastard is the one that broke ya shit all down, and left you out there exposed. All that nukka is about is crushing asses and then tossing when he done. He don't want fucking nothing except to see when he can get you back up into rotation again."

"Oh what the fuck," I yell instantly steamed by what I know is the truth, "You of all people, talking bout crushing and rotations? Seems to me like you two are reading pages out of the same damn book. All them raunchy whores and rats you got on your roster, and you calling him out?"

"Yeah right Nube," he answered me, "and I know game when I see it. That bastard there ain't about shit, and I don't want you associating with him. You got too much going on for you right now, and WE got big things bout to pop off. We don't need no fucking dream stompers up in our camp. Then ole boy gonna open his mouth like he think he might wanna flex and shit. His sorry ass don't want no fucking parts of this right here, I kid you not...I will rip his fucking head off!"

As Rod goes on with his rampage of rambling, I zoned off for a few thinking where is all this coming from. What does he know about Trey? I never really sat down and told him nothing about my past relationship. I mean he knows we were together, and he's the one that had me all twisted, but where did he get any information other than that. Hmm...Jayson? Well they are brothers; maybe it came up in discussion or something. But Murad and Jayson don't even really chill together like that, and especially now that things have blown up for me, they don't even have the time to get together. I don't know. My private thoughts are interrupted by Murad asking me a direct question.

"What?" I query back at him highly irritated.

"I said what the fuck he want anyway?" he came back just as irritated.

"Oh no," I answered, "What we not gonna do is make shit a habit of me...explaining to you...who I talk to and what we talk about. First of all...you ain't my man. His name is Jayson Tillman, not Murad Tillman. Is that what this is all about...you keeping tabs for your damn brother?"

Fuck...Double ouch...Nube's words hit me right upside the head like a runaway baseball knocking me out of my madness. Yo...what the hell am I doing? I'm like mad blacking out over dude, and she ain't even my lady. This is JT's girl, and not only that she a grown-ass woman. She worldly, the whole nine, and quite capable of handling her own. I exhale like I'm chiefing, and pull the car over.

"Nube," I began, "Look...I'm out of line. It's just that I seen some dude next to you...at the time, I didn't know him, didn't know what his deal was. And even now that I do know...I'm not liking it. Nube...I don't know a whole fucking lot about Trey, but what I do know of him is that he ain't good for you. He wants to be next to you for your goodness, then he sucks that shit right out of you and leave yer ass all dried up and lethargic. You priceless Nube, you got mad shit going on for you right now. You came up...you blossomed, and built your dream without him. He serves no purpose for you Nube. You think that nigga ain't seen your shit blowing up all over? Ain't seen or heard about your work? He don't fool me none Nube, he just want to get back on and ride for free. I don't want him upsetting what you got going on right now, and bringing salt to the game."

"So you had to interrupt me and march me off like a naughty child?" she replied. "Murad, it's true that I've come up. I've been all across the country, in the presence of dignitaries and celebrities alike...hell you've been right there by my side with me. You of all people should know that I am very much in control of handling myself. You know my work and my ability first hand; I find it very disappointing that you don't trust that I can effectively deal with an ex-boyfriend. Especially one who has been my ex for quite some time now. I mean come on Rod...you know me, you and me are tight. I'm not gonna do anything to jeopardize our projects, or our bond. We work good together, we are a phenomenal team. I don't think anyone else out there could have solicited the deals for me that you have. You believed in me, and you've proved that to the fullest. You think I would let some ex-boyfriend who gave me nothing but grief ruin all the work we've both put in?"

"It all depends on the size of his dick Nube...the size of his dick," I heard a voice filter thru the car, "You wasn't hanging on to dude all that time for nothing." Once I heard the second sentence in the air, I realized a second too late that it was me talking. Can't say what I was thinking, this shit was just hanging around up in my mind. And for some strange reason, it felt that it needed to be voiced so it bypassed the check point of common sense and just fell right on out of my mouth.

The silence in the air after that snafu of a statement was enough to hear the other shoe drop all over the world. I watched Nube as her eyes blinked twice real fast and cringed as I knew she was trying to stuff down the pain of what I'd just said.

"Nube..." I started, "Nube, I ain't..."

"Murad," she said cutting me off instantly with such an icy tone that I was sure that I could visually see the icicles forming in the air, "I need you to not say another thing to me, and just drop me off at JT's."

"But Nube, we've got that studio session set up for tonight and we need to handle that before the opportunity slips away," I told her.

"You know what," she started, "You'll figure everything out, just drop me off at JT's. I'm done." The pain in her voice was so evident; I didn't even know how to come back with anything else, so I just put the car in gear and pulled off. The ride from the mall to my brother's house was about 30 minutes, and we drove the majority of it in silence. She'd hit JT up on her cell, when we first pulled out and told him she was stopping by. She mumbled a few other words and then got off the phone. Yet after that phone call, she did not utter one word the whole way.

Damn...what is wrong with me!!! What could I have been thinking to say some foul shit like that to her? I caught myself sneaking looks over at her from time to time, trynna see if she was crying or something, but I didn't want her to see me checking on her, so I gave up and just drove on in silence. I don't know...shit just ain't giving like it need to. I've got to get real with myself on this one...I'm wilding out about Trey cause I'm jealous. Jealous cause that bastard had a chance with Nube and fucked over her, and here he come popping up like it's all good. Mutha fucka talking bout call me. Puh...his punk ass ain't got no shame in trynna get her back in his line-up. If I see that nigga hovering around her plotting and scheming, shit ain't gonna be pretty when it's all said and done. Then on the real...how I'm tripping when Nube ain't even my lady. She knocked me upside the head with that piece, and she right...she right. Her man's name is Jayson Tillman. As my mind began to envelope that reminder, I decided that now would be a good time to tune out all the madness in my head before I find myself having another wild out session. I hit the button for the CD player, selected Play 1 and let Jaheim - The Makings of a Man-track 6 serenade my brain as we cruised the rest of the way home.

Chapter 7
Well Almost...Kinda...Naaaww

JT

I jetted over to the door as quickly as I could once I heard the chiming of the bell. Tania was pressing on the bell with such intensity that I just wanted to get there so that I would not serve as an addition to any more intensity. Once I opened the door, she stormed in, stomping and ranting about Murad and tossing her bags.

"I don't know what his damn problem is. He must have lost his damn mind. Who does he think he is?" I didn't know which one to answer first, or if I was even supposed to answer at all.

"Jayson, what's wrong with him?" she turned and asked me specifically, "Sometimes I just don't know if he thinks I'm just a stock commodity or profit venture for him. He don't own me...we supposed to be in this together."

"Tee...calm down," I finally answer her. "What happened exactly?" I said to her as I came over and wrapped her up in my arms.

"Well, we were at the mall," she started, trying to get me something new to wear to this networking affair Friday night, and he got all intense and started flexing and what not just because...uugghh!!" She stopped mid-sentence, then just burst out, "You know what...forget about it. I'm not going to let Murad ruin our time together. Enough of him. Let me bring it down a notch and breathe...whew...So...What's going on Jace?" she asked as she wrapped her arms around me returning my embrace.

"You, sweetness...you. You're what's going on," I answered her while wrapping my fingers up in her curly hair. Tania was the proud owner of her own natural curly wavy-like hair that she always had styled very similar to Oprah's curly do.

"Just look at you," I continued, "Little Ms. Nubina, doing it up big time traveling all across the country, right here, right now, putting in time with Mr. Nobody." My words had barely escaped my lips when she leaned into me and devoured my mouth in such a seductive, breath taking kiss that I had no choice but to swing with it. After a good 10 seconds, I gently pulled back and asked her, "Whoa Tee...what's that all about?"

"Just missing you Jayson," she answered, "What ...is there a problem? Do you need me to leave?" she playfully baited me.

"Not at all," I said, "Not at all. Come on in here and take off your coat and relax. I've got a few plans in place for us. I ordered your favorite fish and chef salad from Noonies and after that we gonna curl up and watch us a little telly, DVD's or chill to some music. Whatever you prefer Sweet, cause tonight is all for you." I watched as she sauntered into the living room and draped her jacket onto the couch. She seemed a little pensive, and I could tell that wheels were spinning up in that pretty head of hers, so I walked over and gave her another hug and told her, "Relax, I've got you tonight," and gave her one of my own tender kisses for reassurance. It seemed to lift her spirits a bit, and she happily announced that she'd be right back and went to use the bathroom.

Wow...she and Murad must have gone thru something really heated; she is so put out with whatever happened. I've got to talk with him later and see what happened between them. I generally try to stay out of their business arrangement, but I'm sure this part here classifies as my territory. I'm saying, she's my lady and she's pretty upset about whatever went down. I definitely got to get to the bottom of this. By the time Tania came back from the bathroom, I had dished our food out on plates, and proceeded to get our drinks. I filled 2 large glasses with Coke and crushed ice then she and I got busy on the food. The food was awesome, or either we were very hungry cause it hit the spot just right. After dinner we got squared away up on the couch and proceeded to watch Def Jam Comedy. I didn't know it still came on, but I guess it's a new version. They had some talented young people on the show, and we laughed till our sides ached. It sounded so good and so right to hear Tania laughing and enjoying herself; especially after her big upset with Murad earlier today.

Once Def Jam went off, we switched to the VH1 video soul channel, and started watching some old school videos. I guess we both fell asleep, because I remember briefly waking to stretch out my legs, and she was cuddled up under me. I guess I went back to sleep, because the next thing I know I'm hearing soft sighing, and feeling her fidgeting. I wake up to see Tania sitting up on the couch in a funky mood and close to tears.

"Sweet," I called out, "What's going on?"

"Jace," she started, "Jace, baby I'm aggravated. I can't believe what went down today. I didn't want to mention it earlier, because I didn't want you to read anything more into it than what it is but...Jace...I ran into Trey today at the mall."

"Trey?" I asked like it was impossible.

"Yes Jace..Trey. The one...the only...Trey. Can you believe it? I tell you I was like...speechless. I never expected I'd ever have to cross paths with him again."

"Well is that what's got you so upset, you seeing Trey?" I asked, not sure if I really want to hear the answer.

"I doubt it...well, I don't know," she said, " I used to think about what I'd do if I ever came across him, but when it actually happened, things that I thought no longer mattered seemed to bubble up within me somehow and...Oh I don't know. Then Murad comes busting up like the FOI looking to do some damage. I just felt as though things were so out of my control. Jace...I don't owe Trey nothing...but I was handling it and Murad just came over yelling and cursing at me, he put me on the spot, and I felt so disrespected. I mean...I just can't believe the way he spoke to me. You know...his tone Jace...like I disgusted him."

And with the last set of words she broke out crying and shaking as if the entire world had come to an end. Oh man...I can't stand to see her hurting like this. There has to be an explanation; Murad is big on Tania, something ain't right. But in the meantime...what the hell did Trey want? It is so not a good thing for him to be coming back into her life right now. As much as I hate to admit it, a pang of jealousy swept over me for the moment and distracted me from the immediate matter. Trey was that son of a bitch...you know the one that every girl has had in her life. He was that one she would follow to the end of a never ending sunset. That one that she had envisioned her happily forever after with. He was also that one, who didn't share the vision with her, yet helped himself and shared the goodness of her soul without reciprocating. He was that one that would butter both sides of the bread then informs you that you have greasy fingers. Yeah, that one who....

The sounds of Tania crying and rambling brought me back to the right now and I reached over to pull her in my arms yet again in one night.

"Sweet, don't cry," I told her, "No one is worth you being in pain, no one is worth your tears, Sweet. Trey is Trey, and Murad...I'll find out from him what the problem is."

"But Jace, you had to hear him, his tone. I have never heard him speak to me like that before Jace, I'm shook," she replied accompanied by another round of sobs.

"Look," I told her, "we are not going to feed into any of that tonight...I'm here for you and everything is going to be alright." I began to place a number of delicate kisses on her face, her forehead and eventually her eyelids. I kissed her nose, her chin, her throat and finally her lips to which she responded to like a moth to a flame. We found ourselves feeding ever so greedily on each others mouths, so much so as if we were trying to create new smiles for one another.

This was the point where I should have regained my composure, and gotten things under control. But my senses must have been compromised by her tears, and I found myself caught up. My hands began to explore places on her, and she readily complied and started her own explorations. It began to get so hot and steamy in the room and it must have fogged my brain, cause the next thing I know, my hands were massaging her breasts and my fingertips expertly teasing her budding nipples thru her blouse. I tell you, this sex thing is like riding a bike, no matter how long you've been off, you never forget how to ride. As I felt them grow and rise beneath my touch, I realized that my other hand was going for the gold in her pants. It wasn't until I actually touched my hand to skin that I realized where I was headed. Amidst her pleasurable gyrations and the soft sweet moans, I came to a sudden halt. With her moans subsiding she opened her eyes to look and me, and whispered, "Jace...baby...what's wrong. Don't stop Jace...baby please don't stop."

"Tania," I said lamely, "I can't...my studies...I've gone too far already."

"Oh Jace...baby...pleeaaase," she whined, "I don't wanna hear about no damn studies. I want to keep feeling like you want me, feeling like you care for me."

"Tania," I came back, "I can't jeopardize all the progress I've made. I need to be so right with myself before I can bring intimacy to someone else. I promise you when things are right, we will make love all day... and all night if you want. Sweet...I promise."

My explanations were lost on a fresh torrent of tears, and her attempts to get up from the couch.

"Sweet wait...wait," I called out to her.

"Move JT, let me go...let me go. I'm tired!" she cried out, "I'm tired of men who don't want me. MOVE...I'll make it truly easy for you. You won't have to make a choice between me and your blessed studies."

But I couldn't let her go, couldn't let this let down of my manhood take place. I pulled her back onto the couch and pulled her in my arms where I titled her back and kidnapped her lips with mine. As I snaked my tongue back and forth thru the sweetness of her mouth, my hand found its former spot between her legs and began to dive in to finish the job I started. I began to work with intensity because Tania was still protesting her hurt. I began to place pressure of my middle finger directly upon her magic button and massaged it back and forth until she had no choice but to respond. I then took the same finger and dipped inside the wetness of her interior, and brought the wetness out to the exterior. I worked the wetness around the folds, and listened as the slurping sounds began to make her gyrate and pump on my fingers. I released my mouth from hers, and listened out loud to the moans that were held in place by my tongue.

"Aahh...uh...uh...ahh..," came to my ears ever so lightly and gave me the incentive to proceed.

Sitting myself up, I used my other hand to lightly caress her breasts, squeezing them as if I was selecting fresh fruit for a recipe. That reintroduction of stimulation made her burst out in full fledged moans and accolades of pleasure.

"JT...Baaaby...ah...aww...ah JT. Baby it feels so good. Oh...JT," she sang out, "But ...baby...you...just...doing...this...cause...you..." she started, but I cut her off with a dip of 2 fingers inside and a comeback.

"Naw Tee...I told you tonight was all for you. This is all about you. How my baby feeling right now? You like it?" I asked her as I slid the fingers out to rotate the button, then slid them back in. My response was a quick jerk and then a rise of her hips about 2 full inches.

"Aw Jace," she cried out, her sweet voice egging me on, "You driving me crazy Jace...ah...ah..."

"Well you about to take crazy over the edge, cause I'm not gonna stop till my baby is floating," I replied.

"Jace," she started, "Jace...I'm ready baby...give me the real thing."

As I wrapped my head around what she just said, my brain began to freeze.

"Jace...baby please...give me the real thing...make love to me Jace. Give it to me."

The actual plea for sexual intercourse brought me back to reality and what I was up against if I went thru with it. I struggled with my inner thoughts. If I don't go thru with this, she'll think I'm a punk. Yet if I give in to my carnal desires...I will have sacrificed all that I've worked to accomplish on a Godly level.

But wait... that damn Trey dude about to be looking her up again, I know it. He didn't just resurface for nothing. How did he just happen to bump into her at the mall of all places? How come he just...Oh man what am I doing? What am I thinking, Tania don't want him. Awww...I'm feeling so tormented right now!!! In the meantime...Tania is all hot and sexed up and ready and I'm sitting here folding under pressure.

So I did what any other immature minded man would do...I ignored her. Instead of responding to her pleas, I tuned her out. In fact, the more she kept begging the more I kneaded, massaged and caressed her. It wasn't long before she got to her place and I'm sure that her long time abstinence of sex played its part in bringing her to a climax as soon as she did. I continued to lightly rub and massage her while she gently shook and regained her calm. I reached over and hugged her and lightly kissed her head, her face and rocked her gently until she fell asleep.

As she slept, I continued to hold her and rock her in my arms and pondered on the many thoughts running thru my mind. Trey back around, up in the mall trying to push up on Tania while Murad intervening and wilding out about it. I wonder what Trey had to say to Murad? No doubt he had to think that Rod was her man with the way that he was acting. Wow...that would have been some kind of tussle. Murad definitely got skills; used to box Golden Gloves all thru high school and beyond. He technically has a 3rd degree black belt in martial arts, but was kicked out of the class due to his temper, just weeks before the actual certification ceremony. Now I can't speak for Trey, but as grimey as he's been, I'm sure he's been in a scuffle or two. And just what is it that Sweet was so upset about? She's a brilliant woman, I'm sure she could see that Murad was just trying to protect her from that snake Trey. Why would she be upset to the point of tears? This situation has got to have some other parameters....DAMN!!! What's wrong with me?

Why am I running circles in my mind, when it's so obvious? Whether they know it or not Murad and Tania are beginning to realize that they've got more going for them than a business arrangement. Subconscious feelings are being manifested thru this controversial incident. Especially since the point of controversy is another man. It's happening, it's moving forward. I don't know if this is the inevitable or just the consequences of a fast paced life style. Aww man...I don't know what it is, but whatever it is...I'm not ready for this to go down. I can't even begin to think on whether or not this is the will of God. This woman here is my salvation right now, and the reason that I keep striving. Uggh...I'm going to need some help on this one. I need a plan, some prayer, some reasoning. I've got to handle this somehow, someway. As I continued to rock Tania in my arms, my mind kept spinning as if it was in sync with the Earth's rotation. And as it swiftly passed over the great peaks of the Tibetan mountains, I came to the conclusion that I would indeed be in attendance of this pretentious affair on Friday night.

Chapter 8
Mama Ain't Raise No Fool

Nubina

As I proceeded to lather myself down in the shower, I had no choice but to think back to last night and JT. Mr. Jayson Tillman gonna have to come one better if he think I don't know he just blew me off when I asked him to put it on me last night. I mean things were so hot, we were all up in the moment, and then the wrath of the good Lord hit him. What's up with that? Some stone player hating on the part of the Lord, if I must say so myself. Ha...ha...ha...okay, that's enough of cracking myself up. Jayson...I'm not understanding what part of the bible does it say that you can't slide it to your woman. Oh...okay, it must be that fornicating part. Don't get to asking me, cause I don't even know. I just think this whole "I can't do the sex thing right now," is something deeper than what it is.

Somehow, somewhere, something is not being said. Oh well...I'm not sure that I can go the distance catering to some issues that I'm not even privy to. It's not like he's planning on becoming a pastor or something. As a matter of fact, I don't even know what it is exactly that he is trying to accomplish. I do know that he wants to advance himself on a personal level under the maintenance of Christianity, but other than that I can't say what the ultimate goal is. I really don't know. Maybe it's me and my inability to effectively communicate. Perhaps I wasn't quite paying attention when he was explaining his whole situation to me back when we first hooked up. My silly ole' self was probably entranced with his good looks and well spoken manner that I couldn't concentrate on a word that he was saying. Well what does it all matter...we're here with this religious infused issue now. I've got to somehow get him to open up to me and tell me what's the real reason he's hiding behind his religion.

In the mean time... Murad...and oh no...Trey!!! I can't believe either one of them. Trey really has it in his twisted mind that it would be nothing but a thang for me to call him. He has the audacity to think that because I didn't cuss him out and make a scene, that I've forgotten all that he's put me thru. And Murad...that one still blows my mind. He was so steamed; I didn't know that he disliked Trey so much. Didn't know that he knew so much about him to even dislike him; yet the way he was stomping around and pacing the floor over Trey you would think that he was the brother that I am dealing with. You would be almost sure that Murad is the one that has feelings...for ...me?

Wow!! Does Murad have feelings for me? I can't say that I have paid that much attention. I mean our bond is tight, we get along famously and it shows in our productiveness. But Murad...and me? I mean I'm with his brother, his real brother JT. Naw...I'm going to let that one go. Murad is so not thinking about me like that. I am hardly his type, I'm a little naturalistic, slightly rustic, kinda kooky round the way kind of girl. Besides, he has a never ending supply of cookies in his cookie jar. No way he's looking to nibble on a brand new flavor like me. Let me rinse this soap off and get out of this shower. The main person I need to contend with is in the other room, and oh yes...I do intend to deal with him. As I lean back into the spray of the water to rinse the soap from my back, I can't but help but think in the far corners of my mind... Murad has feelings for me? And as I turn to the left to rinse the under arm, I can't help but notice how that thought is making me tingle more intensely than I did last night.

Chapter 9
When Levels Cross

JT

I'm sitting here on this bed with my mind reeling this morning while Tania's in the shower. I still can't wrap my head around the events that took place yesterday. I mean Trey resurfacing, Murad and Tania going at it. Then me...I let myself engage in a sexual manner that I've been trying to contain for my own self-betterment. I don't know what came over me. It's just that she is so innocently sweet, and full of refinement that I am drawn to want to protect and please her all at the same time. She's got such a unique vibe, and I'm finding it increasingly harder everyday not to succumb to temptation. And after witnessing a preview of Tania in sexy mode, I doubt that she or I will be able to keep a lid on this much longer. She is more than ripe for the real thing, and I am no where near ready to give it to her. Then I have to contend with Trey showing up. From all that she's told me about their past history, I'm sure that he will find a way to infiltrate her life now that he's relocated her. That man is a clown, toying with the emotions of such a wonderful creature all for the sake of pleasure. It would not be a good thing for him to have any correspondence with her at all. The last thing I need is Mr. Put it Down himself reconnecting with my lady. She didn't personally tell me that herself, but in previous conversations we had during her soul searching, she did reveal how she questioned herself many times whether she put up with his nonsense for so long because of the intimate attachment. Well in a man's world...that equates to pipes being professionally laid, and I don't need no perfect pipe fitters around my lady right now; not when my own tool bag is out of commission.

Just as I'm about to contemplate another scenario, I hear Tania emerge from the bathroom and turn to watch her saunter in the room. Imagining what's under her robe, is kind of messing with my psyche, and I tried hastily to verbalize something, anything to change the pace of my thinking.

"Hey baby…you hungry?" I asked her for the lack of anything better to say.

"I suppose," she replied kind of low keyed, "What have you got in the kitchen to eat?"

"Girl your guess is as good as mine," I answered slightly chuckling, "Let's see, I should have some eggs, as well as some veggies and cheese in the fridge. Perhaps I can whip us up some omelets. Interested?"

"Yeah," she replied, "Go on and get started and I'll be in there to make us some of my mocha drink."

I got right up to go in the kitchen, glad for an excuse to get away from the calm before the storm, cause I was sure that I could feel one brewing in regard to my non-compliance of sexing her last night. I got busy getting together all the ingredients for our meal, and in no time was flipping omelets in my gourmet cookware. Oh yeah…Jayson Tillman is one gourmet cooker…no doubt. I was always amazed by different foods and aromas, and sat in the kitchen watching my mom more often than I played sports. The end result is many years of culinary expertise under my belt and a degree in food preparation. I am currently the head chef at a large pharmaceutical corporation and enjoy my career immensely. Today is Thursday and just so happen that I've got the next 2 days off. So ironic that Tania would fall into my timeline without prior planning.

As I slid the omelets onto 2 plates, and pop two English muffins into the toaster, Tania appeared in the kitchen looking so innocently ravishing in some sweats and an old T-shirt of mine. Her curly locks were swept up to the top of her head and pinned up with a bob pin. A few of the curls had spilled loose from the twist and framed the left side of her face just right. My heart started to melt all over again, and I hoped that she wouldn't be adamant with me about anything, cause I could see myself falling for whatever she presented.

"Hey, that smells delicious," she said reaching into the cabinets for the organic mocha mix she keeps at my house. She's somewhere between a vegetarian, fish-atarian, healthy eater, and she strives to find all kinds of organic and natural comps to her food vices.

As she warms the water in the tea kettle and spoons the mixture into our cups, she gives me a sly sideways glance and says, "Soooo…Jayson, any chance we can get some clarification on what went down last night? I mean you had a sister singing acapella, and she's wondering why she couldn't get the whole choir to join her, if you know what I mean."

I purposely stuff a forkful of the omelet into my mouth to stall for a minute and get a grip before I answer her. Wow…what do you tell a dynamic queen about holding out on the goods, when you're afraid of the ramifications your answer will bring forth. I took a few more seconds, swallowed and began to answer the eminent.

"Tania," I started, "First of I would like to apologize. I've been preaching to you about evolving into my spiritual self, and abstaining from intimate contact, and yet I've put us both in a compromising position. I physically led you on when I knew those actions were going against my personal vow to abstain, as well as risking my own spiritual achievements by tempting myself with indulging in your pleasures. Tania, there are things that happened in my past that I'm not too proud of that all stemmed from unwise sharing of my physical person. I got involved with situations and people that did my mental such a disservice and I've now vowed to remove myself from the enslavement of physical pleasures until I can revise my heart and mind to act in unison." I took a breather to observe her response to what I'd said thus far, and noticed a terse yet even look on her face as she fed off the omelet and sipped her cocoa.

After the second sip, she responded to me, "Jayson, I can totally respect your process and I want to truly understand your reasoning for abstaining from sex. I mean, I myself have not been sexually active for quite some time now, but I know that I have come across someone that I can share that very special part of myself with and that person is you Jayson. We are such good friends, and provide such motivation of peace and spirituality to one another. I can't think of any better way to express that appreciation of each other than to intimately merge with one another. I listen to you and converse with you on all kinds of levels, and I know that you have grown tremendously on a personal realm. I honestly feel that sex is not going to impede any further progress on your part."

"You have made some very good points," I answered, "but you have not walked the same roads that I have before our paths crossed. I know that I can't ask you to understand what you know not, but I hope that you will understand my need to be complete within myself before I become one with another." I watched her face after this last delivery, and my heart kind of sank with the look that I received.

"I'm not sure how I feel about all that's been said here Jayson," she said, " I mean I have no choice but to respect where you're coming from, yet at the same time, I'm feeling that we are both there, both ready, but something in particular is holding you back from going all the way. Whew...I don't know Jayson, I don't know. I need...I need that physical piece to complete this yearning of self validation that I've been longing for, for a minute. Sometimes I am so lonely. Lonely in a mental sense, that the men that I care for don't share the same personal needs that I do. And so they confuse the need of tangible affection and couple it together with sex to fulfill the void. I haven't been with a whole lot of men physically either because of this issue, but it's something that I really long for...a true combination of the mental and the physical that I feel we can really pull off. Jayson, I need you to want me just as much as I want you, and the longer you keep yourself from me, the more I'm starting to view this as an excuse of a nature that I don't know about."

I sat rooted to my chair unable to respond to Tania's last point of view. As usual, she was on the mark, as the queen that she is and laying the truth out at my feet like a royal carpet. The only thing for me to do now is acknowledge the gesture by walking the carpet, or continue to side step and risk the opportunity of a happy kingdom. As she sat sipping the cocoa, eyes pinned on me, siphoning my thoughts invitro; I remained silent for a lack of anything concrete to say. She got up from her seat, pushing herself away from the table.

"So Jayson," she said, "I will take your silence as a non-compliant answer. Maybe we have entered upon something that's bigger than we both are, and this is not the time in our lives for us to handle it." With that she walked from the kitchen into the living room, and my mind kicked into overdrive.

I'm not sure exactly what she meant by her last statement, but it sounded too much like she was contemplating leaving me, and I really am not ready for that to happen right now, so I got up to follow her in the living room. As she began to gather her packages from last night, I came up behind her and embraced her, sniffing her sweet delicate scent trying to erase the uneasiness I was feeling at the pit of my stomach.

"Tania," I started, "I understand you, believe me I do. I can't ask you to remain with me until I get my self together, and I can only respect your choice if you chose not to, but Sweet...can you just think about giving me just a little more time? I know that I want you in my life, and I don't want to give up on what we have right now. I know it's a lot, but I'd like to try and maneuver in your world and share the joy and happiness you're experiencing in your current success. I know I can be tight sometimes, you know... that real corny dude, but I'm willing to lighten up and weigh the options of our paths joining. Please don't let the chance of an opportunity of us terminate itself before it's born. Please....Tania?"

She turned to me with a soft look of resignation and replied, "Jayson, baby...I want so much to believe in the "us," trust me I do. I know that you're a good man, and if nothing else I can sure give it all some more time. I just don't want this to turn into a thing where you will regret having invested your time in me cause I don't meet your religious expectations."

"Oh no Sweet, never that," I quickly responded, "Cooking is not my only expertise; I know my gems when I see them and you are top of the line. So rare a diamond, you carry all the shades, blue, pink, canary yellow and brilliant white. A beautiful rainbow of reflective lights, and I would never let anything overshadow that. I will be here for you, whatever you may need, no matter whatever happens between us. Please know that."

"Aww...Jayson," she replied and grabbed me up in an embrace to which I gladly succumbed. I felt such a flood of relief to know that I was going to be extended within her life. As I once again took in her lovely scent, I whispered gently in her ear, "I love you," to which she tightened her embrace....and nothing more.

Chapter 10
The Cat Is Out Of The Bag

Murad

These last two days have been something out of the twilight zone, I'm thinking as I slide into my jacket and proceed to put the finishing touches to my outfit in order. I've had to reschedule our studio session with Coca Cola at the last minute, and Nube still isn't speaking to me. I called over to JT's and she wouldn't take my call, even though I told him to let her know that it was about business. In fact I was feeling some kind of shade thru the phone from the both of them. JT did ask me what happened between me and Nube, and what was I supposed to say, "I'm feeling your lady, and jealous of her interaction with Trey, and oh by the way...can you set her free so that she can be over here where she supposed to be?"

Yeah that would have gone over real well. So I told him that I was just being a little over protective and I do apologize for anything offensive that I said to her. He seemed as though he accepted my apology, but Nube still didn't want to come to the phone. I tried to play the transportation card, and get the information I would need to get the car to come pick her up, but they shut my shit down when JT announced that he would be attending the affair and escorting her in his own vehicle. So I guess I'm just ass out on this one for now, and just have to try to find a way to deal with it. As I gave myself the once over in the mirror, I tried to boost my spirits by acknowledging that at least I would get a chance to see her tonight.

"Yeah son," I told myself, "She'll be there with her man and ain't shit you can do to change that." I turned to grab my car keys and walked out the door to go pick up Jazmine.

Oh my, we are running a little late. Imagine my surprise when JT announced that he would be escorting me to the networking party tonight. I was so pleasantly surprised although I played it down a little. I need him to make real on his efforts to merge our worlds and accelerate his soul searching. And I think this first step was phenomenal given his religious restraints, but I'm not about to let him think that I'm so comfortable with his first effort and give him the implication that this would be enough. Because it's gonna take so much more than that first step and I need him to keep up the pace. Any who...his gesture to attend has put me in such a good mood, that I can feel myself glowing from within. As I spray the oil sheen onto my hair, I watch him thru the mirror as he advances from the bathroom. He is gorgeous in his black suit and tie, a little conservative but gorgeous nonetheless.

"Hey handsome," I playfully call out.

"You not too shabby yourself, Ms. Nubina. Not bad at all," he replies. "This is a new look for you missy," he says giving a slight tug to my hair.

"Yeah, I figured I could use a change of pace, you know mix it up and keep the masses guessing," I laughed.

"Well there won't be the need for too much guessing Ms. Nubina, your beauty surpasses that of any other woman in attendance tonight, and I haven't even seen the others yet," he says. Wow is he laying it on thick, I'm thinking as I laugh in my head. But a girl could get used to these high quality compliments.

"Why thank you Mr. Tillman," I tell him, "Thank you very much. We shall be the spotlight couple tonight won't we?"

"Sure thing Ms. Nubina, sure thing," he says laughing lightly with his response.

"Well in that case, we'd better get a move on. I know it's fashionable to be late, but on a business tip, people are coming thru to meet me and I need to respect that. So come let's we go Jace. It's time to hurt their eyes with our loveliness."

And as he laughs at my last statement, he grabs the car keys and replies, "That we shall do Sweet...that we shall do."

JT

Needless to say, I was a little nervous about going to this type of affair with Tania. I'm not used to being in that type of arena with entertainment types, and media spotlighted venues, but I need to support my lady and broaden my own prospective some. Besides her mood tonight is so upbeat and refreshing that I'm not feeling flaky about this at all. I'm feeling good with us being together tonight, and actually kind of looking forward to showing the world that I'm the man of her choice. I mean she's always up in the presence of Murad and other men in the business that it will be good to take my place at her side for a change. Yeah...I'm glad that I'm here tonight, I'm thinking as I wheel the car into the parking lot to the club. I step out and hand the valet my keys as I walk around to the passenger side and open the door for my queen. I hold my hand out to her and help her out of the car and instinctively closed the door. As the car rolls away, I extend my arm and we walk thru the doors of the club like royalty. I didn't know then that a changing of the guards would take place just on the other side.

As we walked in thru the corridor leading to the main room, we received a small amount of fanfare, as supportive fans, and other noted persons acknowledged Nubina's arrival. There were a few flashes from some cameras as industry photographers were on duty to duly capture the events of the evening. The corridor led out to a platform with a large bar area to the right and a set of cascading staircases on each side that led down to the main ballroom of the club. Once we reached the platform the buzz in the place had accelerated as more and more acknowledgments of her arrival were proclaimed. The owner of the club Minks came over to greet us, and gave Nubina a hug and kiss, and gave me the complimentary handshake. He insisted on personally taking our drink orders and signaled for an usher to come and collect our coats. Once he had our drinks on order and exchanged his pleasantries he went on to greet a few of the other guests.

"He's cool people Jayson. Really cool," she said to me. And as we both turned around to survey the scene below us...the whole world stopped spinning, taking time and the din of the room with it; for down below mid-center to the room stood Murad. At the very precise moment that he noticed her, she noticed him.

As if in slow motion, he reached up to remove the black and mild from his lips and an indescribable surge of energy encased the moment as Murad and Tania's eyes fused in connection and delivered one self projection. Somehow…by some kind of prophecy of the universe, they were dressed to the hilt in the same color schemes. Murad was sporting an impeccable pair of winter white wool gabardine slacks with a cuff. He had on this sea green pastel kind of cashmere blend sport jacket that only Murad could rock and be properly hated on for it. He had on a silk viscose crew neck top that was a light iridescent opal and an ascot in the jacket pocket of the perfect green, brown, opal, and mother of pearl to tie the look into his brown belt and chocolate brown imported leather dress shoes. Tania had on the same exact sea green pastel color asymmetrical form fitting, side zip knit top that was bare shouldered on one side and tied to a perfect leaf bow on the other. She sported a pair of winter white wool gabardine palazzo pants that fit her better than a glove and a platinum necklace with stones that highlighted the same brown, green, opal and mother of pearl to tie in the strappy brown elegant evening shoes. Her perfectly manicured nails and the new found hairdo was doing its part in illuminating her vision of perfection and Murad was no match for what lay before him.

I was the first to step outside of the trance. And as I did, I noticed that there was a second pair of eyes witnessing the interchange with the same observational conclusion that I had; yet we were both too overwhelmed by it to interrupt it. Jazmine, Murad's date, held her drink to her mouth mid gulp and let the glass camouflage her disappointment, anger and jealousy to say the least. I could not see Tania's eyes, so I watched Murad's whose reflection somehow let me know that the adoration that I saw in his eyes only mirrored what was in Tania's. This speaking of the souls was something that I had only heard of, but now I am here to say that I have witnessed it. For whatever went down between them, I could tell that it was all being absolved between this meaningful glancing session they were currently engrossed in. As I continued to watch Murad, I saw a meltdown in his eyes and they began to twinkle as he restored the black and mild to his lips. This action somehow ruffled Tania and she started blushing and nervously hugged herself as she came up out of the trance. The world once again began to spin and the audio of our surroundings resumed its volume. As she turned to face me, all kinds of circumstantial evidence of a woman in love screamed "guilty" and put my mental in a mode of containment.

As she stumbled for words for something she couldn't herself explain, I offered her my arm and said, "Come my Queen Nubina, it's time to go down and mingle with your royal subjects. That is why we're here right?"

She simply took my arm, smiled and said, "Let's do this."

Chapter 11

No Turning Back

Murad

Look at this shit here. It's almost 9:00 and Nube ain't here yet. I should have blazed on JT and insisted on sending the car for her. We got business to attend to here. People came out to meet her and talk business. Both of them over there feeling some kind of way and we ain't got time for no bullshit attitudes. I don't know how long Nube gonna hold this against me, I've apologized so many times, I ain't about to be...I was cut off mid-sentence by my own self as the vision of Nubina presented itself head on at the top of the balconied platform. It was as if somebody hit me up with a tazer as I took in the full glimpse of her. She and I were dressed in a matching color theme. Damn...I can't believe her top is the same exact color green. And her winter white pants are exuding the utmost in sexy, yet defining nothing but class. And her hair...she rocking it out of the ordinary. She must have gotten it flat ironed and that shit is straight hanging down her back. She is bangin hot like I've never seen her before. The necklace...the shoes...all a perfect match. She's definitely top shelf tonight, but that is not even the kicker. It's feeling like there's no one else in the room but me and Nube. I can't see anyone else, I don't hear anyone else, and she's holding me magnetized within her gaze. All the things I've said in the past few days, and all the feelings that I've been going thru for her I felt transmitted as we stood there, and the strange thing about it was that she was transmitting the same to me. All the things that I've been feeling for her these last few months were suddenly being relayed right back to me thru her gaze. The need and desire to continue our connection became evident and the admission of being missed all took its claim in those few magical moments.

I don't know how long I was going to be able to stand there receiving all of these new found revelations without playing myself out, so I took a hit on the black and mild to bring me back to reality. She finally let me go from her gaze and thank god, cause I couldn't contain myself too much longer. Well here comes some reality for sure, cause now JT is leading her downstairs and we somehow gotta get past whatever's going on and work this night like we supposed to. Damn...let me get ready for the whatnot. As I take a sip of the Hennessey to brace myself for the face to face, I feel a hint of evil bearing down on me. I look over and notice that Jazmine is glaring at me with heat waves hotter than a George Forman grill. As I take another sip of the Hennessey, I hit her back with a look of my own that tells her...ain't no comparison.

Nubina

Okay now, pull it together. You are Nubina, you're here for a purpose tonight and that's your priority. Oh, but how can I settle the butterflies in my stomach? They appear to be on a rampage and endangering me from having a productive night. First of all, it was strange that JT is escorting me tonight when this is considered a den of secularism, and that is against his religious guidelines. Secondly, Murad and I are fabulously coordinated without a prior consultation and it's blowing my mind. And the third and most eerie thing is this strange aura that just developed between us that I cannot explain. I was feeling no apprehension on seeing Murad tonight; in fact I had planned on tuning him out for the most part as I was still nursing my wounds from his comments. But once I set eyes on him tonight, something just came over me giving me the sweetest sensation and a warm glow, that there was nothing else I could do but stand there and bear it. The feeling that exuded from his eyes let me know that he was indeed unhappy with the things he said to me. I also derived from the moment that my revelation I had in the shower was revealing itself to me tonight. Yes...Murad has feelings for me other than a business venture! That glow, that warmth that was emanated, clearly stated that to me tonight. I felt it within the core of my soul, and it's got me in a tizzy right now. How come I never noticed this before? How could I not see this...we are together all the time. I had no clue. And what about JT? Did he notice? Is he upset? It doesn't appear that he is, but he is such a gentlemen; he would never display himself in an improper manner. He would wait for what he felt would be an appropriate time.

Well, I can't worry about all that right now. We are approaching an ensemble consisting of Murad, Vernon Tiner, and Austin Phillips who were both executives in the recording industry. As JT and I approached the group, Vernon was the first to acknowledge us.

"Nubina," he said extending his hand to me. As I returned the extension he deftly embraced my hand and delivered a kiss, and stated, "It's really good to see you again. Austin and I both were looking forward to mingling with you this evening."

"Nubina." Austin said with a nod of his head. That was his version of a formal greeting.

"So now that you're here," Vernon picked up, "Let me wet your palette, so that I can brief you on some new ideas we've got brewing down at Nuroscope Records."

"Don't you think brief is kind of a strong word Vee," Murad interjected, "After all, Nubina is not on your payroll as of yet."

"Oh yeah," Vince bellowed out accompanied with hearty laughter. He threw both hands in the air as in a gesture of surrender and said, "My apologies. I'm getting a little ahead of myself. Murad...why don't you and your lovely better half join Austin and I for a discussion of new developments. There is that much better?" he jokingly asked.

"Lot's better my man, a whole lot better," Murad answered him all smiles. Underneath it all, I knew that those smiles were a façade of Murad's when he was about to spin some serious business conversation.

As the group proceeded to retreat to a reserved VIP table, Murad turned and gestured that I accompany him. Instinctively I reached out for his hand, but midway remembered that I was still locked arm to arm with JT.

JT immediately released me and passed me on to Murad saying, "It's fine Tania, go on. This is your season, this is your night. You go and do you. I'll be okay... I'll catch up with you a little later."

"Are you sure?" I asked him.

"Absolutely," he replied, "It's cool." I gave him one last are you sure look, and he nodded and turned to accept our original drink orders that Mink had sent down to us. Believing that he was going to be alright, I turned to accept Murad's hand and once again the world stopped as the surface of our skins met. He took his thumb and traced small circles within the palm of my hand and held me in his gaze.

"I'm sorry," he silently lip synced with a sincerity that melted my heart.

"Me too," I answered copying the lip sync mode, and immediately recognized that the butterflies had settled. As we stood in the moment, a series of quick flashes of the photography crew brought us back to the right now.

Before we could make our way back to our intended parties, we were sidelined with, "Can we get a few shots of the dynamic couple together? Your coordination is astounding!!! Murad, Nubina...this way please. What's next on your itinerary?"

So we stopped, posed and they picked us off with several promotional style photographs together. It felt so real...so right to be here, now in this moment with Murad. I couldn't stop myself from glowing inside out as we posed ceremoniously for all the shots. I was floating so high; it was all that I could do to keep my feet upon the ground. Murad and I finally joined our intended group in the back and involved ourselves in working out an arrangement. Not once since I took Murad's hand that night did I look back. Cause if I had, I would have seen JT find a seat and make himself comfortable... at the loser's table.

Chapter 12
You All Ready Know

JT

As I take a seat in the empty chair, I exhale as my mind needs a minute to take this all in. I came here with Tania...my lady, and somehow I just delivered her to my brother Murad whose been notably tagged as her better half, and they are now being photographed as "the super couple." I don't understand what just happened . As I watched Murad led her over to another set of people and make introductions, I began to feel a certain déjà vue. The disembarkment of the plane from their Minnesota trip played fresh in my mind, where I'd gone to meet them at the airport. The crowd of fans and media surrounding them as Murad held her in his arms, and she fitting up under him so perfectly. She smiling up at him, he down on her, while I stood below looking on while he held the prize. It's funny cause tonight, for just a small minute, I was in his shoes. I was standing at the top of the platform, and she was in my arms...but it seems that destiny knows our positions better than we do ourselves. Destiny let me savor for a hot second, and then she directed Tania back to her original spot...on the arm of Murad. I can't question the actions of destiny, and it's not like I wasn't forewarned. Them two are made for each other echoed in my head, and I remembered that I was the one who bared the warning.

As I watched while they negotiated an impromptu performance, I noticed the extra delicate way Murad touched her, and the fluid way in which she responded. Yet at the same time, their interaction seemed to be all in a day's work. I tried hard to remember if I had noticed these things before, when I realized that I couldn't have noticed as I never attended many of her events. I was always conveniently studying and getting my mind right when she would ask me. As I start to gather my mind on the fact that I enabled this thing to happen, perhaps I falsely accused destiny, as it appears that I may have had a bigger part in it than she. Perhaps it was my issues and my fears that held me back from exploring the many bright lights of Tania the jewel. Perhaps it was me who was afraid to be an accessory to this great gem of a woman, for fear that she would outshine me. Maybe I was the one who kept putting up detour signs for fear that I couldn't carry enough insurance on an investment so rich as Tania. Whatever the true reason behind my failure to maintain, I'm in no mood to speculate and assess what went wrong. But what I do know to be a fact is...I couldn't maintain what I thought to be mine, when she was truly never mine to begin with. I listened as déjà vu replayed for me the look Murad gave me as he stood on the level 2 airport mezzanine that day with Tania so secure in his arms... "Yeah choir boy...you already know."

Jazmine

I can't believe this shit right here. I knew something was going on with Murad and that bitch Nubina. I knew it!!!! She walk up in the fucking place and time just stands still. I seen them checking for each other, no doubt dropping hints and shit. She running all over the damn country spitting out her positive woman, love bullshit and underneath she ain't nothing but a nasty ass. Murad is a man and a man gonna be a man, but him and JT is brothers. How skanky can you be? I knew something was up...I knew it. The day they came from Minnesota and they at the airport so busy getting paparrazied down; I seen the bitch smiling up in my man's face. I tried to put a stop to it then, but he wouldn't answer my call. Well I'ma tell you what...she got a whole lot more options than I do, and I'm not letting Murad be one of them. He can have a 40 mix of whatever females he want as long as he don't bring it in my face, but I'm #1 and I ain't about to give up my spot to that bitch Nubina. I will be pulling the plug on her ass as soon as I can get a hold of her cord...just watch!!

Chapter 13
The Closing Act

Nubina

Good evening all, and welcome to Sarafin's tonight. I really appreciate your love and support for me tonight, and I'm sure Minks appreciates the tabs at the bar...lol...So enjoy yourselves, but drink responsibly. LOL....yeah...I'm going to hit you up with something real nice right about now...let me set it up. You ever been to that place...that place on the way to love, but not quite there? Where some days things were so hot, and on other days it was so, so empty and cold? Well I know a little sumptin', sumptin' about that spot, so let me share a little something with you. It's all about Canary Fires:

Canary Fires... simmering hot, lucent, conditioned to the rise of the storm
Canary Fires...bringing soak-spent nights, hallowed out by the warmth and overflowing with satiation.
Canary Fires...transporting the inevitable, indexing conclusions to solutions not yet proposed.
Canary Fires...caressing the unimaginable while alluding to the sensation of a never ending comfort zone.
Canary Fires...burn till they become stone cold embers of illusions, forged as templates by the blacksmith of reality

As I closed on the last line, I was met with a robust applause that mingled with the jazzy interlude that had accompanied my recital. Dog calls, whistles, and the ruwf, ruwf, ruwf resounded with "Yeah Nubina...Nubina. Much love to you Queen. Peace" I was slightly overwhelmed by the response as usual, and just took a couple of timid bows for the lack of anything else to do. For some unknown reason, I took this moment to scan the crowd to see if I could locate JT, and instead found myself staring straight into the eyes of Murad. As we once again became magnetized, someone from the audience yelled out, "Sexy, sassy, can you hit us up once again?"

I searched Murad for the answer and he gave me the nod with a gesture of 1 finger letting me know that 1 more piece was all that I was to do. I smiled and nodded back as I began filtering my mind to find something to fit the mood.

"Okay, okay...let me hit you up with the second part of that story. You know how you come to the realization that things are just best that you let go...and you've settled up with yourself that it's all for the best? Or is it? I call this piece "Although":

Even though you besiege my mind
Unfolding thoughts of you every day
Standing guard to the gate...keeping others from entering
I still await your call

Even though promises of me have long left you
Your thoughts anew of another each day
Cleaning your plate from my taste I have left you
I still await your call

Even though my mind knows better
Would never accept a you and a me
Even though we worked it right down to the letter
It's still your call I wish to receive

Even though respect is now lacking
My visions, my dreams you no longer see
Turmoil, disappointment is all that I'm knowing
Your call I await so feverishly

Even though my thoughts are now settled
And over the grief you've given to me
Although I now stand on the level above you
My heart swells as I check my caller ID

Again as I close out the last line to the piece, I'm met with a thunderous applause, hoot, hollers and the whole nine. Minks comes out to the mini stage, and takes the mic and gives me a hug.

"Give it up again for the one and only Nubina who graced us with that eloquent on the spot performance. Keep your eyes on this prize, cause big things are happening with her. Check out her theme songs on UPN's sitcom "Just Us", and Fox5's hit show "Rainy Days." Our girl here is fierce and on the rise. So once again... thank you Nubina, for gracing us tonight. You are always welcome here at Sarafin's. This is home."

With that, the spotlight faded, the DJ resumed to spinning and I turned to walk off the stage. On instinct I looked for Murad, and he was right there stage left waiting with an open hand. No sooner than I grabbed it, people were starting to approach me for autographs and questions. I signed a few, and answered a couple of questions before Murad spirited me away to a private section of the club. Once we were away from the noise and crowd, Murad let out a sigh of relief.

"Whoa Nube...that was off the chain Ma. You blazed them again tonight as usual." he said.

"Was it Rod...did I get that off?" I asked squealing like a little child.

"Girl pleeeaze," he said, "That shit was so on, I don't know how I'm gonna handle all the positive fallout. We gonna have mad requests and what not." He laughed and came back on a flirtatious note.

"And look at you Nube," he began running his fingers thru my hair, "This new hair...it's fire...gives you that hot...on it look. I likes...I likes, a lot. And the outfit is slamming, not to mention some of my favorite colors," he says taking my arms and spinning me around, smiling devilishly.

"How did this come to be? Ain't no way you could have known what I was wearing... I'm still trippin on that...but we are rocking it. The best looking couple...in...the house," he finished off haltingly; his words changing the elements in the air around us. We were standing face to face now, minus the laughter as he laced his fingers within mine.

"Nube," he started, "I need you to know from the bottom of my heart that I never meant to hurt you... never that. It's just that I've grown real close to you, and need to protect all that you are and all that you be Nube. You are one of the realest, most beautiful people I know out here, and I was just feeling some kind of way about nukkas running up on you who have hurt you in the past. I've been having some thoughts about you for a minute now, and I just..."

"Murad," I said cutting him off, "what are you saying?"

"Nube...I don't know what I'm saying. I just know that tonight was synonymous with things I've been feeling for a while. I know that I was not liking the fact that I couldn't speak to you or see you for 2 days. Shit just wasn't right. I felt out of control or something. I also know that tonight spoke on something that we both heard loud and clear...there's feelings here Nube. I mean...I know that I've got feelings for you, and tonight I felt that there's some feelings here for me too. Am I wrong?" he asked as one hand returned to its place in my hair.

"Am I?" he asked as our bodies became drawn to one another, and our lips were near to brushing.

"Murad...I..." started off.

"Feel the same damn thing," he said squashing my reply by closing his mouth upon mine. The passion he felt spilled forward thru his kiss and mingled in with the sweet taste of the Hennessey and a black and mild. And I responded. Oh my god I responded!! As if thinking on the same note, he twirled us around to a little niche in the room behind a display case to keep us out of eye view and prevent an uproar. I was so intoxicated with the moment that I just held on for dear life and savored every sweet nibble of his lips and thrust of his tongue. The kiss started to escalate from sweet passion to slightly intense, and that's when reality kicked in.

"Rod," I said coming up for air, "Rod, I don't know what happened here tonight, but I do agree that something has been put down before us. Something that we must deal with...something we must handle. You...me...we definitely feeling "it." We need to figure out if we are supposed to do anything with "it." I'm with JT and you've got...uh... who you got, and we in business together and ...."

"Nube," he said stopping my rambling, "I know all this... I know this. But shit between us is not to be ignored. We owe it to ourselves to put this in prospective and see what's up."

"I'm not disputing you Rod," I said backing up continuing to hold hands.

And not a moment too soon, because just as I did, Jazmine peeks her head around the corner and...

"Well, if it ain't the dynamic couple. What's that you say about a dispute Nubina? Y'all two got things to be disputing about? I would think everything is perfect in paradise after your duo performance tonight"

"How are you Jazmine," I greeted her. Murad said nothing and just gave her a non-descript stare, all the while continuing to hold my hands within his. "Murad and I were just discussing some very detailed issues of concern in regard to our partnership," I told her; which was not a lie, "At any rate it is getting on the late side, and I need to get home for some rest. So if you will excuse me," I said breaking free from the hand embrace.

"Murad," I spoke matching him eye to eye, sensations still tingling between us, "let's review this again at a better time. Hit me up tomorrow so that we can get a fresh itinerary for next week. I have a couple of personal appointments to fit in. Alright?" He didn't verbally answer, he just gave me a head nod and that Murad eye twinkle that put goose bumps up and down my arms.

"Jazmine," I said, "It's been good seeing you again. I hope you enjoyed yourself. Good night." I turned to walk away not waiting for an answer, not wanting to realize the fact that his "woman" just convoluted the moment and drew an X on our new found revelation. I don't know what I was going to do with the components of tonight. Don't know where or how I'm going to sort them out or where I should store them. But what I did know is Murad means to play for keeps...and so does Jazmine.

Chapter 14
Putting On The Ritz

JT

I sit here watching as Tania prances over to the table towards me. Our last interaction for the night was when I first handed her over to Murad. I'm watching her now as she approaches and, I'm having mixed feelings on the evening, as well as the direction of our relationship. It is evident that she is still under the trance of the evening, although her glow is somewhat subdued. I wonder if she even remembers at all that I accompanied her here tonight. Oh man…what am I saying? She is no more responsible for tonight than Murad is. In the matter of them two…destiny definitely has her hand in it.

"Jayson," she says as she reaches the table, "I am so sorry…I apologize. I haven't spent one moment with you tonight."

"Don't worry about it Sweet," I responded, "Tonight was your stage, and you were amazing." I leaned over to give her a kiss and she pulled back slightly. The most I got was a light peck. Ouch…that cut a little deep. Did this evening escalate the inevitable? I looked upon her face to see if I could see the answer, but all I saw was confusion etched on her face.

"Jace," she said, "Can we break out? I'm more than a little tired, and I have some appearances next week. Tomorrow may be my only day to chill."

"Not a problem Sweet, not a problem," I replied, "Let's get you home."

We walked up the stairs to retrieve our coats, and came across Murad and Jazmine as they were also leaving. I could tell that tensions were running high between the two of them, so I just greeted them a pleasant good night and kept it moving. The coolness of the night air seemed to relieve some of my own tensions, and cleared my mind just enough for me to make a decision. I decided that I would drop Tania off at her place, but would not stay the night with her as planned. Instead I would go on home, as I had a quite a few things to settle in my mind.

Tonight was going to be a full night of prayer, as I am truly feeling some kind of way, so it's best that I be alone tonight.

"Jayson," she said to me once we were in the car, "I apologize tremendously. Here you are coming out to support me tonight, and I didn't even get to spend an ounce of time with you. I didn't expect it to be such a whirlwind of networking, hand shaking and photo taking." Deep down inside I wanted to say... "It appeared that you enjoyed it all," but I didn't feel that I had the right to rain on her parade, just because the night had rained on me, so I just replied,

"Don't worry about it Tania. You had to do what you had to do. This is your big come up...so don't you leave not one stone unturned. Don't worry about me, I was fine. I just sat and did some observing since I'm not usually involved in these events. But anyway that was quite ironic that you and Murad were donning the same color scheme. How did that happen?" I threw that in fishing around to see if anything of the evening would be revealed.

"Yeah...imagine that," she said, "I can't explain that one. I had no clue what Murad was planning on wearing. It was so eerie to step in there and see us coordinated so perfectly as if a stylist arranged it all. I guess there was something bigger than us both going on there tonight." As she said this, she looked out the window at the passing landscape as if she wanted to lose her thoughts amongst them.

My time for observing tonight was not over, as I thought of her last comment, and the way she pulled away from my kiss. It also had not passed by me that the stingy kiss that I was able to secure faintly tasted of Hennessy, and I know Tania does not consume strong alcohol like that. Hmmm.... I think its best that I stop with the thinking now, before I think myself into thoughts that will not serve anyone well at all.

"Jayson...Jayson," I heard pulling me from my reverie, " I was just wondering if you didn't mind if we just went straight to bed, cause I'm beat. Maybe we can go out for breakfast in the morning?"

"Oh," I replied, "Tania...I think that I'm gonna just drop you off and go on home tonight. I just realized something that I need to attend to and I need to kind of have my space to do so. Maybe we can hook up next week. Okay?"

"Next week Jace," she answered me in a questioning manner, "Next week...who knows what my schedule will be like. You know we have to steal every moment we can."

"That's true Sweet," I answered, "And one day, us stealing moments of time won't be an issue. But I need to handle this right now...tonight. I hope you won't be too disappointed."

"You know what," she replied, as she suddenly slipped into a new zone, "That's fine. That's fine. I can't deny your need for space. I'm just glad that you accompanied me tonight. Thank you again."

"Don't even sweat it Sweet," I answered, "No problem at all."

It was another 15 mins before I reached her townhouse and as I pulled up to the gate, she turned to me and said, "Good night Jayson, give me a call tomorrow if you want to do breakfast. Okay?"

And with that said she leaned over and gave me a real kiss. I returned the kiss, then watched her as she walked up to the front door, slid the key in the lock, then went inside. I waited until she flicked her bedroom light that signaled me the all clear before I pulled off. And then and only then did I realize that tonight I had clearly lost. Lost a fight that I had never even had a chance to enter into. Tania and Murad were on to something. Something bigger than the both of them, as she so put it. In my heart I knew it to be the truth, yet it did nothing to ease the pain that was beginning to make its way within.

As I drove on towards home, I knew that tonight would be a lengthy one of prayer, as I knew letting her go would be the best option for all. There's no way that I can compete with what has been destined to manifest. Without a doubt I love her so, and loving her would be to release her. I need to set her free so that she can be where she truly needs to be. Yes... in my validation of love for her, I will just get out of her way. That is my final decision, I concluded as I bit down on my lip as I often do when frustrated. And as I turned the car into my parking space at my complex...the faint taste of Hennessey sealed the decision into place.

Chapter 15
Over And Done

Murad

Oh here we go, I'm thinking as I pull away from Sarafin's. Jazz up in here feeling some kind of way, and my head is not keyed to hear no riffing right now. I'm still in a zone over tonight and what transpired between me and Nube.

"Oh so you just not gonna answer me Murad," I hear her say up over my thoughts. "I asked you what was going on back up in the cut with you and Nubina?"

"Yo Jazz, chill with that nonsense," I answered, "I ain't in the mood for all that right now."

"Right now Murad? What you mean right now...like we gonna discuss this at another time? Cause I need an answer Murad. You gonna bring me out for the night, and then you flossing all over the club with her on your arm. I need to know something," she said.

"Listen, it's all about business, Jazz. Nube and I are partners, we making shit happen, and that's what tonight was all about. If you gonna be all insecure and uncomfortable, then you can eliminate all that by you staying ya ass home," I replied. She was starting to annoy me, cause she was fucking with my high for the night.

"Oh I gots to stay home?" she came back with, "Since when this bitch make first string over me? You gonna tell me it's just business, and now I got to stay home?"

In the interest of keeping things polite tonight, I just gave her a look and kept on driving. I guess she tried her best to contain herself for the next 10 minutes or so, but I know Jazz, she just couldn't hold it back any longer. She turned in her seat to face me and said, "Go head Murad, why don't you just say it. You fucking her right? You and her got shit going on?" Man what this silly ass have to go and say that for.

"Let me explain something to your ass right now," I told her as we pulled into her driveway, "You ain't got shit to say on what the fuck I do. I ain't never told your ass you was the one. In fact, I ain't never told your ass that we together. I'm a free agent...don't nobody hold the deed to this here. You must have lost your damn mind thinking you calling me out on some shit. And for the record, Nube ain't nobody that I would ever be "fucking"... that's something that I reserve for you. And while we on it...don't ever... as long as you know me... ever call Nube a bitch again."

Her whole persona changed as she sat there stone faced and shocked, and then a look somewhere out of fear crept onto her face.

"Murad," she started, "I wasn't trying to disrespect her or you either, but my feelings was kind of hurt tonight, and I just thought..."

"You thought what Jazz? That you had my shit on lock giving you the amenities of wifey, you ain't even close to wifey. How you figure you could rip me about another woman? You know what, I just did me some fucking thinking right now, and I think you need to just get on out my car. You home now, safe and shit...so git on. I don't even feel like dealing with this nonsense."

"Murad," she said near tears, "Listen, I wasn't trying to upset you. And I know I need to contain my jealousy...I know, you told me time and time again. But Murad we have good times together, and I just don't want things to be this way between us. I promise I'm gonna do better, I promise..."

"Jazz, get out the car," I told her, now highly annoyed. I don't want to be forgiving and compassionate right now, I just want to go home and be alone with my thoughts about Nube.

With her head hung low, like a child she opened the door and proceeded to get out of the car.

"Well can you at least come in and get the insurance papers you asked me to get for you," she stated, "I made sure to pick them up because I thought you would be coming back thru here tonight after the show and...."

I just looked at her pitiful ass and figured the sooner I comply with her; the sooner I would be done with her ass. So I got out of the car and followed her into the house.

"They're in there on the kitchen counter," she said once we entered the doorway. I walked the familiar walk over to the counter and saw my intended object. As I picked the envelope up to view the addressee, she ambushed me from behind.

"Murad…Murad," she crooned; rubbing her hands all over my chest and down my thighs. "I'm so sorry Murad, I'm sorry…I just get a little crazy when I think of you and other women."

"Jazz," I answered shortly, "Get the fuck off of me."

"No baby…no baby," she replied trying to be sexy. "You need to let me make you feel better, and get your head right for you. I don't like seeing you upset." And with that she made a quick beeline straight to my pants and grabbed my dick.

"Girl…what is you doing?" I screamed out. "Take your hands off me Jazmine."

As I backed up to get away from her, she followed with her hands intact on my dick like it was the bridal bouquet thrown at a wedding.

"I'm gonna make you feel good Murad…so good like only I know how to do," she said to me. By now, sensations were starting to make their way downstairs, and shit was rising in spite of my annoyance.

"Jazz, I'm telling you." I started.

"Telling me what Daddy…telling me that I'm right," she said as she yanked on my already hardness.

"Look Jazz, I ain't come in her for all of that," I said.

"I know baby…but you gonna be leaving with something better," she said pushing me up against the counter, and unbuckling my belt. I should have clocked ole' girl and got the hell on out of there, but by know the frustrations and tensions of the night had all come down on me like a heavy weight and I just didn't feel like tussling with any more mental decisions. In fact, the need to take out some aggressions were starting to surface and I felt that this was just as good a time as any.

"Okay Jazz," I said, "You wanna make me feel better? Then get on your job…do what you do." And with that said I commanded her to her knees and finished the job of extracting my dick from my pants. Once I was all out and standing at attention, I told her, "Paint it Jazz. I want that shit painted with 2, 3 coats at a time. Get busy." And that she did. She started off with small tender kisses, and nipping and circling the tip. I didn't want any intimacy to it, didn't want to have any emotions attached to it at all, so I barked out, "Paint it Jazz...lick it with long wet strokes, paint it sloppy wet like I told you. I don't want that prissy shit; I need you to go hard Jazz...go hard."

And go hard she did. She licked, sucked and stroked like she was Picasso. Got to admit the shit was feeling good, but I was not about to give in to any sensations just yet. Something inside of me wanted to make her pay for her disrespect of Nube, and her overbearing jealousy every time we go out. So I continued to hype her, while holding back from me releasing anytime soon.

"Hit that shit girl...do that...paint it Jazz, paint it. You missed a spot on the left...the shit need another coating."

And she complied, and licked and slobbed for another 10 minutes, and once I thought she had enough, I grabbed her by her hair and pulled hard.

"Keep painting, keep painting," I yelled at her while I slowly started to stroke in and out down her throat. The momentum was building so I grabbed her head with both hands and sexed her mouth like it was the prize. And just as I was about to come, she grabbed me around the waist, so that I could not pull out.

"Yo, Jazz....girl," I started, but the words were lost in my climactic euphoria. I looked down and she was swallowing my shit like a kitten lapping up sweet cream. That shit was bugging me out. I've done a couple of splash offs before, but I ain't really into chicks drinking my shit. Reminds me of some straight up porn shit and besides, it just don't seem all that healthy.

As she finishing up with her slurping and sucking, it's putting a damper on my feel good, so I slowly start to retract myself, careful not to scrape myself on her teeth. Once I'm out I just look at her sitting on the kitchen floor on her knees, shit dripping and hanging from her mouth, and instead of feeling appreciative for the wonderful work she just put in, I'm feeling turned off. Now I know we can't all be Saints and I for one am not even considering applying for the position, so I grabbed a kitchen towel off the counter, wiped myself clean and rearranged myself back into my clothing. I picked up the insurance papers, handed her the towel and told her, "Lose my number."

She sat there on the floor, mouth open with shit running out the sides as I made my way out her front door.

Chapter 16
It Don't Always Make Sense

Nubina

I released the curtain to my bedroom as I watched JT pull away. I don't know if I was imagining things, but I was getting the feeling that JT was acting different, kind of pensive. Hmm...Oh well, look who's talking. I'm as pensive as they come right now. Wow, what the hell went on tonight? It was mystical, magical and something like heavenly, until...borders became crossed, Jazmine busting up private moments, and JT blowing me off for the evening. And you know what...it's probably all for the best. Because in spite of it all, nothing else pretty much matters right now, except for the fact that somehow I'm feeling Murad. It's like someone turned on a light switch that illuminated him in a reflection that I have never seen before. I have been working close to him for what...like going on 2 years now? I've seen him in all kinds of mode, but I never looked at him as someone I could ever be with. I mean...he's into women, he's flashy, he's materialistic, he's...and he's what girl? ...what am I saying? In this past year I have come to learn that he is smart, has a great head for business, he's a go-getter, he has stamina, he has great visions for me, as well as shares mine. He believes in me...believes in what I do. He is supportive, he's there by my side no matter what, he's protective, respectful of me, and my god....he is so damn phine!! Why did this not occur to me before? I guess I probably never thought a man like Murad would go for a chick like me. He is so up on what's hot and vested in all the right circles. I just assumed he always wanted them video girl and hood fab femmes like Jazmine on his arm. Now Jazmine ain't the caboose to the train by no means....she kinda put me in the mind of an Alicia Keyes when it comes to looks. But somehow the "hood" still exudes her persona. I figured that was probably the attraction for him, as it is for many men in our community...could I possibly be wrong?

So exactly what would be his attraction to me? I mean he and I do sit up all night and talk at times. Actually, topics that I was surprised that he had any knowledge of. And he opened a few doors of exposure for me with things that I'd never explored; like he showed me how to play pool, and even a little bit of kick boxing. Said he wanted me to be able to fend for myself if necessary...yeah...I'm laughing out loud on that one. And then there's that added plus that he always reads my new pieces whenever I ask him to. It's like he's really interested in doing so. I guess things between us has been something like we're the coolest best friends going, you know the someone you can hang with, and try new things with... and the one who can understand your yapping. I just never thought in a million years that I'd be someone to catch his eye. Well who knows...catching an eye ain't hard to do. It would really be great to catch a heart...for real...not just for the moment.

Oh...I don't know what's going on with me? How can I even be sitting here considering anything about Murad when he and JT are brothers? That is such a taboo. JT...JT...just where does he really fit in my life? Well, hell...if I just take note to all the quality time I just summed up between Murad and I, it's apparent that JT has been on the outside looking in, and very comfortable with his outside position. Yes...we have our times, and our promising, spiritual conversations, and yeah...we shared that one night of "almost" intimacy...but that venue of restraint is always present with him. It's like a cloak of insecurity or fear that he wears to ward off he and I moving forward to becoming "us." I tell you there's something more to it than religion. I so wish that he would share with me whatever went wrong in his life. It would be such a plus in me knowing if he and I can truly exist. I don't know if we would ever have anything as fabulously famous as Murad and I but....Damn!! Did you just hear yourself Ms. Nubina.? You probably just secured the answer to the "decision" that bears no true need to be presented. Hmmm....

Chapter 17
Sacrifices Of My Soul

JT

Awwww man…my head is booming; consumed by a tirade of thoughts and emotions that prayer and meditation would not extract from my mental. Although I said that I would release Tania from our relationship, I'm having trouble actually coming to terms with what the inevitable will bring. I know that she and Murad belong together. I've taken their unsolicited actions as a sign from God that they have indeed been pegged to explore the opportunity of building a union together. I have witnessed their ability to work together fluidly side by side, making the task of work seem effortless. I have witnessed the chemistry they share between them that allows them to project positive energy and great productivity. I also have to bear witness to the fact that Murad treats her like a queen, as well as respect and protects her at all cost. With Murad by her side, there was never a day that I worried for her safety when she was out on the road.

And there's no way I can ignore how her inner soul spills forth and bathes her in all her absolute beauty whenever she's with Murad. I mean there is no wrong way to look at those two. No matter which angle you seeing them from, the view exemplifies love. I can't fight that…it's just not a battle to be won. Murad and Tania got what it takes to see happily ever after, and I refuse to be one of the obstacles on their journey. Cause yes Lord…despite them possessing all the makings of one of the worlds greatest romances, obstacles will still be a sure fire debt along their journey. Man…The more I rationalize…the more it makes sense, but this rationalizing is doing nothing to quell this pain. Maybe if I could have had made love to her just one time…just indulge in the sweetness just once. But no…Had I engaged in such, I probably would never have been able to step aside and let the wonderful workings of God take its course. Perhaps in his infinite wisdom, he intervened that night and stopped the total exchange of our flesh, because he knew it was the wrong set of brotherly hands pilfering the treasure. Perhaps you have steadily pressed your influence on me Lord, to keep me from ever crossing the line because you are the master of all plans. I know and accept your wisdom, as well as your will Lord, but can you see fit to spare me just a bit of pain?

Oh...the phone. Man...Not now, I am in no mood to speak to anyone. Not even gonna look and see who it is. I'll check the caller ID and get back with them later.

Nubina

Well that's strange...I was more than sure that JT would be home this morning. I wonder why he's not answering his phone. Well maybe he's just in the bathroom. I'll call him back in a few. I can't even say for sure what our topic of discussion will be today. Although Murad and last night is still on my mind, my first priority is to Jayson and my relationship with him. There is a need for he and I to really sit down and discuss what direction this is all going in. My analyzing and running a comparison last night clearly put JT in the runner up position. I mean it's become as clear as a bell that Murad and I have a balance of trust and belief in one another that fortifies the foundation of a great friendship. I know and understand him in ways that allow him to know and understand me. We never operate on pretentiousness no matter what venue we're visiting. He accompanies me everywhere with the patience of Jove, and he is strict as well as wise in his business negotiations. And just look at me. I mean...I don't mean to come off like I'm the president of the Murad Tillman fan club, but all these aspects I'm conveying should be aspects between Jayson and I. Jayson should be understanding of me enough to accompany me, at least half of the time. Jayson should be looking out for my well being, and keeping my business sense straight. Jayson should eagerly review new works and writings with me, or at least ask to see them. Instead he always brushes me off like the words on the pages will burn his soul and condemn him to hell or something. And not for nothing, he sometimes acts as though he is so out of element when he and I are out together in public. Almost as if he's embarrassed or...oh...I don't know.

Let me don't start beating up on Jayson just cause Murad put wind beneath my wings. It was one kiss...just one kiss. Let me slow my roll. Besides, Murad has his hands full with that ratty-ass Jazz, so I'm not sure I understand where I'm supposed to fit in with him, or what his purpose is for revealing his feelings to me. Oh man...now what the hell am I saying...getting myself all twisted cause I admitted the very same thing to him. Whew...what a big twist of uncertainty this has become. I need to talk to somebody, Murad...Jayson...Jazz...somebody. I guess in actuality the very first person I need to speak with is Jayson. He is the one to whom I have committed myself to a relationship with. The fact that it is not very viable right now does not give me permission to disrespect him or the relationship. I've got to get a hold of him and sort this out. I am off to Chicago the day after tomorrow and don't know when I'll get a chance to see him again. Let me try once again. He should be out of the bathroom by now. As I dialed the number I recognize a little melancholy settling over me. Would it be enough for me to be with a man in whom I could always see eye to eye with...or be with the man who possibly shares the eyes to my soul?

Murad

Yo...this chick is mad stressing me out. She's been blowing up my phone...hell all 3 of my phones. I can't deal with her and her nonsense right now. I'm still zoned out over last night. Nube admitted that she feeling something...she admitted that something is there. I can't even begin to get my hope up and shit, cause I also know that she isn't no joke and a true woman of her word. She not about to take her relationship with JT lightly, to just up and be with me. I mean we are brothers. But...somehow...this is different. There's a different dynamic between Nube and I for some reason. The fact that JT is my brother just comes off as irrelevant...and I don't know where that shit is coming from. I ain't never crossed that line before with any of my family or my boys over no female...but it's like I'm doing some out of body shit, all in slow motion, and I can't do nothing but stand by and watch it happen. It's like somebody planted some subliminal directives in my head while I was sleep a couple of months back, and the shit has been growing ever since. Damn...if that's the case, I wish they could have planted the same up in her head; it would have made things a whole lot easier. But what am I saying...that's the very reason I feel as strong as I do for Nube...her realness and her ability to always operate in the actual. She don't spare no change in expressing herself to the fullest. She's not going to mince words on the matter, or mince words on how she truly feels. I'm just hoping that the vibe we felt last night will be the same vibe that bears her true feelings....cause if it's one thing I know, Nube will always go with the truth.

Damn it...that phone don't stop ringing. I don't want to turn them off, I got business to handle. I'm just not going to answer it at all...I really don't have anything else to say to Jazmine. That shit is so over and done regardless to my outcome with Nube. Jazz got the game twisted and shit; she think cause she got that tropical flair going on for her with the Rican skin and hair that that shit is her ticket. But what ole' girl don't understand is that she ain't about nothing. Walking around all tagged down and mall hopping looking for ballers just puts her in a sub-category for me. Females like that is good for the V-spot and nothing else. Should've left her ass at the mall where I found her. Aww...man, let me snatch a shower so I can get up out of here and pick up our plane tickets for the Chi-town trip. Nube is speaking to a group of teen girls at a group home for wayward youth. The program is sponsored by the NAACP, and boasting attendance by local electoral candidates for various municipal and state positions. I am mad proud of Nube. She is getting her word out to the right set of people and making her messages count. My baby on a quest to elevate the world...lol...yeah and she gonna be on a mission until she succeeds. Yeah that right there could take a couple of hundred life times. Well let me get ready, gotta get the tickets and meet Dream. Little nigga must wanna borrow something...don't call unless he need something. As I walk across the bedroom floor and cross the threshold to the bathroom I stop and realize that I referred to Nube as my baby...yeah...don't the fuck I wish.

Chapter 18
So This Is It?

JT

There goes the phone again. Guess it's best if I just go on and answer it. Could be important. Perhaps Deacon Watters is trying to contact me about next month's home service. "Hello," I said not bothering to check the caller ID.

"Hello JT," her voice rang out like a classical symphony taking me by surprise. I wish that I'd checked the number, cause I have no idea what or if I wanna deal with Tania right now. Making the choice to separate yourself from someone and actually telling them is two completely different things.

"What's the deal JT? I tried calling you earlier to see about having breakfast, and I got no answer. Were you in the bathroom?" she inquired. Feeling like a trapped animal, I did something that I have never done before with Tania...I lied.

"Oh...I went out for a run...had to clear my head on a couple of things," I told her, then immediately felt guilty.

"I guess you don't remember my comment about our possibly having breakfast huh?" she answered.

"Actually...I do Sweet. I just didn't think that I could handle seeing you this morning," I answered in an attempt to relieve the uneasy feeling of having lied, "Attending the affair with you last night put some things in prospective for me, and I was not ready to share them with you. But I guess now that I've got you on the phone, now is as good a time as any."

"A good time for what JT?" she answered.

And although I detected a note of defensiveness in her reply, I pressed on anyway, "A good time to inform you that I'm going to fall back on the you and I thing. I really got a chance to see the total process of your lifestyle and I just don't feel that you and I are at the right times in our lives to handle the differences. The hob-knobbing and the night life that defines your world just doesn't fit into the realm of who I am and where I'm trying to go. I think it would be best that you and I demote our relationship to one of a platonic friendship. I don't want us to keep trying to maintain a relationship while waiting on me to reach the level of obtaining my total self. It just would not be fair to you Sweet."

"So for you and I to continue would not be fair JT?" she finally cut in, "Exactly to whom are you trying to extend the act of fairness to? I've been more than fair with respecting your religious differences and the controversy it sometimes brought to our union. I have been completely fair when I gave total understanding to your personal need to abstain from intimacy even though my soul was crying out for comfort. And I have been nothing but fair to endure your absence of support in my career in the name of your Godly self betterment. I threw nothing but support your way in your self elevation while you on the other hand couldn't see past the glitter to support mine. I too delve in self elevation Jayson. My poetry, my spoken word, speeches and songs are all key elements in the process of my self-betterment. Simply because it is not governed by a religious group or set of ideas doesn't make it any less significant. I'm angry Jayson; we just discussed this the other morning at your place. I relayed to you how I felt about putting in my time with you only to have you spin your "my religion...my studies" thing on me as a barrier. There is something else behind all this that you are just not sharing with me, or perhaps not in a position to share with me, but Jasyon I can't help but feel some resentment. You just asked me to continue this relationship as you were going to put in more effort to embrace my world...what happened in the last 2 days that veered you off course? What is the real problem Jayson?"

I now thank God that I am having this discussion on the phone, cause I truly would not want to witness the look of disdain and confusion I know is present in her eyes. I sit on the phone with my mind swirling like a oceanic whirlpool. How do I propose to tell her that I bear witness to her crime...one that she has no control over committing? How do I let her know that I have circumstantial evidence against her, composed of her Hennessey laced lips, compliments of her co-perpetrator? How could I ever tell her that she is right as usual in realizing that something bigger than us all is taking place? I don't want to be biased to my own self revelation, nor do I want to be an ally to her statements of truth, so I feign concern, and side step her pressing question.

"Tania," I replied, "This is not something that transpired in 2 days, but the last 2 days has brought me to that conclusion. It's pretty much an unfair waste of time on our parts to try to consider upholding the inevitable any longer."

"Jayson…Jayson…just stop," she came back with, "You correct me if I'm wrong Jayson, but this is all about last night isn't it? You were not comfortable with the club scene and Murad and I doing our thing. Is this all because of some feelings of you being slighted Jayson? Did my networking last night really set you off down this road?"

"Last night just gave me a clear picture into what would be many more to come," I replied, "I am not being fully supportive in my role as your man, and the differences in our religious views pose a threat that I will never be able to support your world. Tania, please let's not forget that I love you deeply, I will love you always, and I am not extracting myself from your life. I'm just taking a different position in regard to our relationship. And you're right…you have been more than fair in your allowances towards my goals, and now it is my turn to reciprocate. Trust me Tania, this decision of mine is the most fair thing that I have proposed in my life thus far, and the outcome for us both will be most rewarding…all in due time."

"All in due time?" she answered, "That's all good Jayson…but what is it that we do about time overdue? You know what…don't even worry about it. I'm so feeling some kind of way right now…I've got to go. I guess I'll call…uh, talk to you… uh later. Good-bye."

"Tania wait," I called out, but she'd already hung up the phone. Such a good thing that we did not have this conversation in person, cause I wouldn't have been able to tolerate seeing her resentment and disappointment in me. I most certainly would never have been able to separate myself from her while being consumed by all of her beauty. And face to face she most definitely would have no choice but to see… this grown man crying.

Chapter 19
All That Feels Good –Ain't Good For You

Nubina

Ahh...that Raspberry Tea feels good going down. I'm sitting in one of my favorite spots down here at the local book shop with some of my favorite friends surrounding me. Yes...books are my very best friends. They are always available, informative, and don't catch attitudes over differences of opinions. Books always present themselves in a presentable manner, and know how to hold your attention. They can be brash and bold at times, and sometimes demure and understanding. Yes books are my number one companions, because most importantly... books never leave when the going gets rough. They stay right where you set them down until you are ready to pick them back up again. The level of loyalty just don't come no higher than that.

I had to get out and get away for some me time after JT delivered his bombshell, and this spot has always been able to soothe my soul. The soft lighting and big comfy plush chairs provide just the right ambiance for me to sort thru this emotional "thing" I've been thrust into. Just 2 days ago he was up in the kitchen cooking for me and proclaiming his need for me in his life, and now the events of one night has changed it all. There has to be something else to this...and JT knows that I know better than the excuse he's given me. Better yet, he probably picked up on the vibe that was present between Murad and I. And I'm sure the picture taking and flossing all night just had him up in his head thinking. I am more than positive that he knows nothing of the kiss; since we were well out of sight from anyone. So I can't say. Well not for nothing...I need to admit to myself that feelings were bouncing off the walls that night between Murad and I. I suppose anyone that had a clue or care would have been able to pick up on that. But if that be the case, why not admit to that being the issue, instead of telling me our differences in lifestyles are not going to work.

You know what...let me stop being rude and visit with my friends, cause after all that's what I came here for. Oops...let me get a grip. I'm up in here knocking over books and what not... damn, all the way off the far side of the table. As I walk around the table and bend down to pick up the book, a flash of deep chocolate bends down to pick up the book for me, and as I glance up to thank them, I am greeted by the most unexpected....

"Trey," I utter.

"Beena," he says. "Well... the universe really does work in the most mystical ways."

"How are you?" he says as we both stand; he holding the book having won the clutch-off.

"Oh yeah...Trey...I'm good, I'm good. You gonna have to stop sneaking up on a girl like that...I never expected to see you here...I mean again...uh...so soon."

"Oh, come on now Beena," he said, "you know I share the love of books. You and I used to come here all the time...back in the day when the world revolved around us."

"Yeah, that was until you decided to bring forth Armageddon first hand," I got in.

"See now...there you go," he responded and flashed them beautiful pearly whites that set so magnificently within his smoldering midnight face. This man has got to be one of the earth's most gorgeous men to adorn God's darkest and richest hue with such ownership.

His beautiful, smooth black skin is so intense that it is hypnotizing. I used to never get enough of watching him as he slept, just taking in and admiring the beauty of him.

"Whatever Trey," I muttered, "How did you come to be in my neighborhood? On the prowl and ran out of fresh territory?"

"I told you Beena, that's not a part of my life anymore. I'm looking to improve the quality of my life, not deter my growth," he responded, "But just to satisfy your curiosity, I've been looking for a particular book on Epicurus...a volume that has more accurate documentation and info then his usual works. You remember when we were reading them, how we found them kind of monotonous and repetitive since they were compiled of letters and false translations. I remembered this place in the back of my mind and decided to give it a try. And what brings you here? I'm surprised you're not out on the road spreading the word."

"Actually I will be leaving out for Chicago, day after tomorrow. Just wanted to get in some me time before I head out." I answered him taking a seat on the plush sofa.

"Oh, and what...without your body guard?" he said looking around the shop, playfully peeking under the table and over his shoulder before sitting down next to me, "I'm surprised that he let you come out by yourself."

"Well you know," I started back, "somebody's got to protect the hens from the hounds. I don't see nothing wrong with a brother looking out."

"Speaking of brothers... would that not be his brother's job? Cause his brother is your man...am I right? Why is that he's not vested in his role as your protector?" he asked.

"Just so happens, that is water under the bridge. Right now I'm on a quest to fulfill my passion, and not bog myself down with uncertainties in my life," I responded. Oh boy, I realize as I think to myself...that was just a little bit too much information, especially for him. But oh well...I've never been the one to hold back on truth.

"So ole' boy couldn't man up and secure your status huh?" Trey said, "Either that or your "body guard" chased him away."

"Trey what are you talking about?" I said slightly irritated giving him the screw face, "No one has chased no one away. Sometimes things just don't work out. You oughta know."

"Yes Beena...I do know," he said, "and I also know that releasing you from my life was the **biggest** mistake I have ever made. It took me a minute, but I've come to the realization that you represented everything that I called myself striving for, but the intensity of it intimidated me, and I feared losing the me that I was confident with. I didn't want to give up my valiant position by partnering up with someone who had a boat load of valor herself...so I defaulted to dibble and dab with the less than, so that I could continue to be impressive. I now know that concept kind of falls in line with the cliché of "taking candy from a baby."

There's nothing at all impressive when you get your shine on with those who are "less than." There's nothing to measure your development by when you are always on the top. After awhile, you begin to succumb to your environment and that becomes regression on your part. If I could have known then what I know now...I would have never let you go. I would have taken the stance to fight everything put before me that posed a threat on me leaving you alone. But I guess I was supposed to follow the trail of events as they went down so that I would be able to be as reinforced within myself as I am today."

"Well," I said, "I see that you still blitzing sisters with snowstorm conversations. That was the very thing that got me so hooked on you. I used to love lying up under you in bed, sniffing your armpits and hearing your heartbeat as I listened mesmerized as you orate on the sun, the moon and stars to me. But I guess...that was just one of the things that was dear to me and only me. It obviously meant nothing to you. You don't give a damn who's laying in bed with you, just so long as you've got a warm body there for the pleasure."

"Awwww Beena," he responded, "you are so wrong. They were many things about you that were special to me."

"Oh really?" I answered sarcastically, "Please enlighten me on one or two, cause I sure could never tell."

"Well, let's see," he said, "I remember that you always went the extra mile to make me feel comfortable about being a black man in this twisted society. I remember that you cared to listen to all my personal outcomes, be it work related or family issues. Oh and let's not forget the beans."

On that note I had to burst out laughing as he rolled his eyes to the ceiling,

"Them beans were kind of....well...you gave it a try. I can't really be on you about that. Then again...you did your thang on some other dishes. I must say...you were on to something. And on a more sentimental note," he started, his smile receding, and a softness glazing over his eyes, "I remember the way you would trace the features of my face as we lay in bed after making love, then thank me for the pleasure when the pleasure was truly all mine. And even more special...I can remember how our hearts would explode in fireworks, and our eyes light up every time that we set eyes on each other. It didn't matter if we happened to be mad at each other, or we were busy breaking up and then making up. Coming together or improvising on our situation was never a problem with us...I never despised you at any time, and I know you never despised me. Fireworks Beena, true fireworks...in fact...just like the fireworks that are going off now."

As he finished the last statement he gently cupped my face in his hand and met me eye to eye.

"Beena," he said, "I know now that you and I belong together, and I want to take this opportunity to express that to you. You are the other part of me and I want us to start over again...the right way. We will work to get our minds right with no physical intrusion. I want us to learn and grow together and be so totally on point and attuned to one another before we implement sex. I want to practice true respect and responsibility in committing to us. I want to put in hard work and tangibly see my efforts. Beena...I want to show you all that I've learned about true love, and give back to you the appreciation I received when I was a part of your life. I never stopped loving you Beena...I just didn't know how to accept that you... loved... me."

I just sat there speechless while tears started to roll freely down my face. I couldn't have stopped them if I tried since the tickling sensation was the only clue I had that they were flowing.

"Do you know how long I waited to hear those words from your lips Trey?" I finally managed to say, "Those beautiful, beautiful lips of yours...how I prayed for the day to watch those very words fall from those lips. And now that, that day is here, my ears are hearing you like sweet, sweet music. And my mind Trey...my mind is definitely rejoicing with glee at the knowledge it has just received, but my heart ...she can't feel you. She waited and waited for 3 years for an answer, a reply or a response...but it never came Trey. She would hype herself up every once in a while, somehow giving in to them sweet sensations and tingles she experienced when she reminisced over you. She put in mad effort to be that ride or die kind of heart, you know... and wait it out until you came to realize that she belonged only to you. She convinced herself that you must be aware that she lived only for you, and that you'd come back and claim her...for sure.

But you know just as well as I... that time is the dictator of all things...and time whispered in her ear that she had been discarded pretty much as you would a gum wrapper, and how you did not look back as the wind carried her down the street in the opposite direction. Time also revealed to her the understanding of the value of a heart as precious as she, and the recognition of worthiness that she as a heart deserved. And time with its infinite power prompted her to barricade herself so that she wouldn't have to suffer any further damage and breakage and give herself ample time to heal from her wounds. So Trey...she can't hear you. She's bubble wrapped and sound-proofed herself exclusively for you. These tears are not for me...and they're not for you...these tears are for her. Cause now that the day she's longed for is finally here...time has deemed her mute...and that is truly sad."

As I finished my proclamation, I watched as he leaned over to hold his head in his hands. He seemed to be in emotional pain, and I was feeling so uncomfortable about it all. The tears on my face began to itch as they started to air dry, so I reached for my purse to get some tissues. My movement caused him to look up, and I could see the anguish in his face. Now I don't know if it was there because he truly felt bad about the way that he'd let things deteriorate between us, or was his anguish provoked by the fact that I did not respond favorably to his request. What I do know is that I can't assess what it is exactly that I'm feeling right now, but I've got to get control before my sucker-ism kicks in. A small little part of me wants to make things right for him again, but my heart is still feeling like she took a beat down, and is not even thinking about coming out of her cocoon for him.

"Beena," he said, "There was a time in my life where I would not have cared about your feelings...would not have been moved at all by your tears. But the man you see before you here today is devastated to know the magnitude of pain I have caused you. I mean I'm sure somewhere in the back of my mind I had an idea that you were hurting...but I pushed it away, and neglected to respond when you reached out to somewhat avoid an encounter such as this. It hurts me to know that I've hurt you so bad...and yes all out of selfishness. Tell me what can I do to rectify it Beena? What do I have to do to reclaim you?"

Some of the bubble wrap on my heart began to pop...pop... pop. So in a mechanism of self defense, I answered, "Trey...I can't answer you on how to reclaim the expired ticket to my heart, but what you can do is help me carry these books to my car. I really need to get back to the house and make some arrangements. I'm sure Murad is looking for me since..." I stopped mid sentence realizing that I subconsciously committed to accountability to Murad. I sneaked a peek at Trey's face and immediately knew that he noticed it too.

At any rate he answered, "Sure Beena...it's not a problem."

As I collected my things, and paid for 2 new selections, he held me in an uncomfortable gaze. My heart was beginning to race so my mind stepped in to comfort her with "take it down, take it down...breathe." She listened, slowed her pace and I even managed a smile as I said, "You ready?"

"Never been more ready for you in my life," he answered. I didn't respond to him, instead I made idle chit chat to occupy the time of the short walk to the parking lot.

"Hey...so how has your mom been? Still baking those cheesecakes?"

"Yeah something like that," he answered me, "It helps to keep her busy and out of trouble. She is one nosey woman." We both laughed at his last comment, and the sweet musical mode of his laughter tore a hole in the bubble plastic. His melodic laughter was also one of his attributes that kept me under a spell and I was glad that I'd parked close to the entrance and my car was now 2 feet away.

"Let me pop the trunk and you can just place the stuff right on in there." I called out over my shoulder as I walked ahead to the driver side of my car.

I opened the door, and popped the trunk so that he could place my stuff inside.

"I see you are still driving the same old Betsy," he said adding a little chuckle to it.

"Sure am," I replied. "She serves her purpose. No need for something new, now that I'm hardly at home. Anyway...you know that I'm so not like that at all. I really doesn't matter much to me."

"Yes Beena," he responded, "I do know…one of the very many things I love about you. So real…so unpretentious…yet you deserve the world." His voice became low…almost seductive as he reached down and closed the trunk for me. "Beena…I can respect all that you've said here today, yet I believe in universal energy. This was no chance that we happened to come together today…it was predestined so that we could fulfill a mutual prophecy. I know that in your heart, despite all the barriers, you understand the relevance of it all. I know that you share the feelings of love that I do, cause love that is as strong as what we had doesn't die."

"Trey," I started to cut in.

"Yes Beena…I know," he said, "I know. It's a lot that's been said here today, and I need to give you some space on it. Despite all the wrong I've done, I want you to keep in mind that a love like ours only happens once in a lifetime."

And as if to solidify the reality of his statement, he leaned over and gifted me with a kiss. He gave me one of his sweet ones…in fact one of the best he had in stock. I couldn't forsake one of the sweetest kisses this side of heaven, so I let him get that off, but he tried to embrace me, and I had to retrace the boundaries. I broke off the kiss, backed him up and studied his handsome face. I took my two fingers and kissed them, placed them to his irresistible lips, and as he returned the kiss to my fingers, I voiced to him softly, "Next life time Trey…next life time."

I walked around to the driver side of my car and got in. As I sat down and put on my seatbelt I thought to myself damn…this man's winning record is 0 to infinity as I noticed a seeping moistness in my underwear. As I backed out of the spot and pulled away, I looked over to him and threw him the peace sign, then made a right turn onto the boulevard…and into the rest of my life.

Chapter 20
It Is What It Is

Murad

"Yo...Dream the Scream...what up boy," I saluted my little brother as he hopped into the front seat of the truck. Behind my smiles I had to acknowledge that my little brother did me proud. His name is Desmond, but we've been calling him Dream the Scream since Jr.High school on account of all the little girls screaming over him. Of all my mother's 10 kids, Dream and I favor the most. Nube told me that I resemble a Blair Underwood, mixed with Christopher Williams as far as looks, so I guess that describes Dream as well. He's about an inch shorter than me at 6'2" and I'd say about 10 pounds lighter. I guess that's the benefit of being 8 years younger as well. Looking at him as he settles into the front seat, I have to think that Nube is pretty accurate with her assessment. Not bad coming from Christina Milian mixed with Lark Voorhees and throw in a little bit of Tatiana Ali....that's my version of Nube. In my opinion she kinda got a Dominican or Cuban thing going mixed with an East Indian flair. She blew me off for my assessment of her...but man...she just don't know.

"Hey Rod," he answered giving me dap, "what's new playa? What we getting into today?"

"I gotta run over to Main St. to pick up these tickets for me and Nube," I answered pulling out into traffic, "We heading up to the Chi for a speaking presentation. Then we back home for 2 days, and then off to LA for some recordings and negotiations for a guest appearance on CSI-NY."

"Daayum," he said, "You and Little Bit just bum-rushing the U.S. huh?"

"Yeah, as long as she up to it, we gonna storm the nation till Nubina is running thru they dreams at night," I replied. "So what's new with you Dez? How's the internship going?"

"Everything is straight...I'm on a project now that's been slated for the 2010 Architectural Expo, and word is if things go well, there could be a permanent appointment."

"My man," I followed up with, "You make sure you keep blazing them stuffed shirts...show them we grow true talent where we come from. How's my little man doing?"

"Man...that little nukka is straight crazy," he answered me laughing in reference to his 4 year old son. "He took that crazy gene from his damn mama. Shame he couldn't have taken after me cause..." I looked at him, and we both just bust out laughing,

"Naaww...that gene came from you...you know ain't nobody crazier than you," I told him.

"Well you know...it's funny you should say that, cause crazy seems to be floating around these days," he said to me his laughter fading, "Let me ask you something if you don't mind."

"Speak," I answered, sensing a strange vibe in the air.

"Well...what's going on with you and Jazmine? She done called me like 4 times since last night talking bout you dogged her out...and you and Nube been fucking around behind her back...and how she played herself for you, and always treated you like a king and gave you everything you ever wanted, or asked for. I mean...after a while I was like... sitting there holding the phone looking at it like what you want me to do. I told her she needs to be having this conversation with you, and not me, but she said that you won't answer your phone. So what up Rod...What ole' girl talking?"

Damn...I never imagined Jazz would reach behind the walls in my circle with this nonsense...but yeah...her cousin and Dream was involved there for a minute, so I guess she trynna play all her cards. "Look Dez...me and Jazz was never an item. One of many bruh...nothing special at all. I haven't really had much time for her lately and whenever we do get a chance to hook up, she all up on a brother's collar with her jealousy nonsense. All she care about is if I'm gonna bring her something back, and who that on the phone, where you been, and where you going. I ain't beat for her bullshit no more, and I'm just done," I told him.

"Yeah...well that's true...you ain't never been the one to get hemmed up by no female," he said, "But...what is she talking bout with you and Nube fucking around...I know that shit ain't true." Damn...it's been put out there...it's not true...but an element of something is happening and I don't feel like keeping this shit to myself any longer, so...here goes.

"Well Dez...Nube and I are not fucking around. We are business partners and happen to spend an enormous amount of time together. I would be less than a man if I sat here and did not admit that feelings have developed between us as a result. We just recently spoke on it, but neither one of us has taken any action on it. Nube is a real stand up classy lady...if anyone is over the top with it Dream, it's me. I'm feeling her in such a major way...and I really don't know what to do about it," I released and waited for the response.

"Awww man...Rod...not you...come on," he answered me completely shocked, "You know the fucking rules Rod...7 cousins and 7 brothers...everybody keep they ho's to themselves...no pushing up on my ho...no exchanging ho's, no store credits, all sales final."

I blew out thru my mouth, trying to remind myself to be patient, but something inside of me was not going to allow my passion for Nube to be degraded.

"Yo Son," I shot back at him, "first of all, this ain't about no Ho...I'm speaking about Nubina, one of the most beautiful persons I know to grace life, and the..."

"And the what Rod?" he said cutting me off in a hostile tone, "Okay...okay... so we talking about the Queen Nubina, and not a skank...but she is still JT's girl...what the hell ?"

"I know Dez...I know," I screamed out, "You think I don't think about that shit everyday. But this is something different Dez, something out of my control. This thing started back in Bryce's backyard 2 years ago. She was doing her little spoken word thing, and honestly that's the first time I really paid any attention to her. I mean, she and Sumira have been friends forever. But on this day...I thought that she was a little cute and refreshing, so when Kason got his ass up in the mix talking about promoting her, I knew that he was grimey as all hell, so I stepped in to be her manager, and took it as my chance to see what she was all about. After rolling with her and really getting to see first hand what she's about and what she wanted to do with it, I had a new found respect for her. I really listened to the things that she was writing and speaking about and it touched me in a way that I've never known. In the meantime...I didn't know that Sumira had hooked it up for her and JT to start dating, and by the time I wanted to admit to myself that I'd caught feelings, things were off and running with her career as well as off and running with JT. This shit has been eating my ass raw everyday for like 3 months now Dez. I'm with her constantly and yet she constantly checking for JT. I mean we spend mad time together. When we out on the road, we shop, check out the hot spots, hit up all the infamous dining spots, we share our food...the whole nine. And then, we talk...I mean real talk, we hang out and shoot pool together and I even showed her how to play cee-lo. When we on the road we watch each other's backs. Man....she has even screened females for me when we on the road, you know...giving me the heads up based on her womanly vibes. We just tight like that. She is just an amazing person, and she got this sexiness going on for her that she don't even know about."

"Yo Rod," he said cutting me off again, "Kill that nonsense with that sexy shit you talking. You ain't even supposed to be thinking all that about your brother's lady. Just stop and take a minute Rod...think about what you just said...you admitted yourself that women is your thang, so how do you conclude whether or not Nubina is just another conquest for you, or if this in fact is some kind of conquest against JT? Think about it Rod...you been with a lot of females...is Nube really that different?"

As I sat silent, I let Dez's words marinade in the air before I responded.

"Dez," I started, "I guess I can't really expect you to understand this. You still young bruh...you have had no where near the number of experiences that I have. I know a damn pot of gold when I see it, and something beyond me is telling me to go for it. I understand it's a camp full of us dudes all related, and we set up the rules to never shop in each other's store, but there is something I can't put my finger on with this one. Something is nagging at me to not let this one get away."

"But mutha fucka...she ain't yours!" he screamed back at me. Wasn't shit I could come back with at that one, nothing at all. We drove a few minutes in silence before he started fumbling for something to say. Dez has always looked up to me...I guess the look-alike was our connection, and he could never handle if he thought I was mad at him.

"Yo Rod," he started, "Listen...I know that you not the one to be purposely scoping on another man's woman...and I know that you damn sure ain't in no short supply of women either...so maybe something 'else' as you say is going down. I can't see it...but you my hero Rod...I ain't gonna riff about it with you no more." Mentally I accepted his version of an apology, but I had to admit that he had said nothing wrong...nothing at all.

"Don't sweat it Dez," I answered him, "She not the type to swing with 2 brothers anyway. I guess I'll have to digest this shit and move on. Here...sit in the car while I run in and get these tickets."

As I stepped out of the truck, I let the fresh air filter thru my mind as if it could help clear the fog there. Damn...Dez just checked me on my shit, something I usually have to do with him. Fucking tables is turning every where I look. JT got the woman that was meant for me, I got knocked down a few pegs on Dez's ladder, and I washed my hands of Jazmine. Which way do I turn now? As I walked up into the spot to cop these tickets, the little devil on my left shoulder said, "Fuck um all...anyway that opportunity presents itself son...you jump on it...literally." And with that, the little angel on my right replied "Sheeeiittt...you ain't said nothing but a mutha fucking word."

Chapter 21
Be Careful What You Wish For

Dame

Man...this shit here is nonsense. Rod tripping...got me wasting good time following dude. Money don't do shit but the regular! Work, home, b-ball, and the damn food market. I don't know exactly what he need me to see, but dude here is straight. He done went up into the bookstore and I'm parked out here like 45 minutes already... for what? I'ma have to let Rod know that this here is a wash. Whoa...hole' up here he come out now with what... a box of books and ....what the shit!!!...that's Nube. What she doing here? I didn't see her go in there...I guess she was already here. Wow...did they meet here or what? Whatever...I'd better get to snapping. Damn....Rod ain't gonna be too happy with this shit here...Damn!!!

Murad

I climbed back into the truck, knocked off the hazards and pulled out. Dez was on the phone finishing up a call, so I made a decision to swing us around to Crockett's Fish Fry up in Montclair. I know that Dez goes there often and I' m sure he's with it to grab a bite to eat. He finished up his phone convo, slid the phone closed and let out a sigh.

"This chick here gonna drive me insane," he started off, "She really trynna play her baby momma card to the fullest. I just bought little Dez some spring clothes, now she here talking bout he needing a new outfit for some bullshit affair...I don't know. Rod I'm telling you...keep your shit wrapped up. This baby thang and being a daddy ain't all that it's cracked up to be."

"What the fuck you talking Dream," I said laughing, "That's what the hell I told you when you was out there running around dipping raw. You don't need to preach that shit to me...I ain't got no income tax dependents that I can rely on every year."

"Oh hell...tell me about it," he came back with, "Every year we go thru the same thing fighting about whose claiming him. I'm so glad that shit is coming straight out of my check, so that I have proof that she is receiving income from me. Otherwise her slick ass would be trying not to report that she's receiving child support. You right Rod...as usual, I should have been double wrapping my shit and waiting for the right woman. Is that what you doing?"

His last comment put a little tension in the air given our previous conversation. At the same time, it touched on a topic that I had not visited in quite awhile. I had made a vow once I left high school to never...never...never have unprotected sex and bring a child into this world before my time. Needless to say in my first year of college, I broke my own rule once and suffered dearly when the girl of my dreams got pregnant and aborted the baby without telling me a thing. I actually found out later from her girlfriend who was trying to push up on me, and thought letting me know would score her some brownie points. From that day on I have never had sex without wrapping it up. Besides...too much new shit out here going around. I enjoy dipping and splashing just as much as the next man...but not to die for it. And just to keep my self secure...I get an HIV test annually. That shit can be passed more ways than one. But come to think of it...the more projects and offers that started coming in for Nube, the less time I had for sex, and I sure wasn't maintaining at the level that I used to. I haven't had time to think about no kids lately...but if I got with Nube...oh most definitely...no doubt. I wasn't about to voice that to Dez so I just gave him a general answer, "Yeah...I guess some day. The timing right now is a little off, but I guess some day."

I could tell that he knew that was a blow-off of an answer but he accepted it anyway and quickly changed the subject.

"So where we rolling to now, all spla-dowed up in the big boy? Riding up in this joker sure feels good. Smooth and quiet as hell."

"I was feeling my stomach to my back so I figure we could stop up here at Crockett's and grub." I answered him.

"Whoa," he screamed out acting silly, "See that's what I like about yo' ass. A nigga with the know how. Making moves, pressing on to the Fish Fry. Who said that Murad Tillman don't know how…"

"See there you go wit ya loony ass," I said laughing, "You talking bout little Dez. The apple ain't fall far from the damn tree…that's all" Lucky for me there was a parking spot right out in front and I slid the truck right in and pumped on the remote lock as we headed in to the eatery. The place is not all that big, and a moderate crowd was all ready forming.

"Damn…it's like that up in here?" I asked Dream.

"Yeah but if we stay here and eat it, you get your food faster," he replied.

"Aight then," I told him feeling a vibration on my hip. "Go head and put our order in. I'm gonna get us a seat."

As I went and sat down, I pulled out my side-kick. I had a message that some photos were being sent to me, and to put in my pass-word in order to retrieve them. I punched in the code and pressed the button to download the pictures. While the pictures were downloading, my other phone began to ring, so I pulled it out and answered it.

"Yo Dame…what up kid…yeah…they downloading. What you mean…Nube…what the fuck you talking bout? Yo…hold on… they coming up now." My eyes stretched like elastic as I saw a picture of Trey trailing Nube carrying a box of something. The next one just showed them standing at the back of her car. The next on was the one to change the rest of my life…Nube and Trey was kissing.

"Yo Rod…Rod," I heard Dame in the distance. My mind just blanked out as I sat staring at the picture. "Rod…so Rod…what you want me to do?" I heard Dame asking.

I just took a deep breath and said, "You know what…it's cool…I'ma deal with this. You can knock off on the surveillance."

"You sure?" he asked.

"Yeah…I'm sure…thanks…I'll git with you later." As I hung up the phone, I kept staring at the picture with my mind swirling and my thoughts running out of control. Dez came back with the food, and I just let him do all the talking while I picked at my food. I had lost my appetite and really couldn't wait to be done with this outing, so I could be alone and figure out what was going to be my next move. So I smiled, grinned, got off a joke or two and bided my time. All the while my insides felt as if they were being sucked right up…in a Dirt Devil M350.

Chapter 22

Now Or Never

Murad

Once I dropped Dez off, I just rode around with no particular place to go. My phones were ringing…side-kick buzzing, but I was in no mood to deal with anyone right now. I rode out to the park and parked my truck and just sat there listening to music and trying to settle my mind. Try as I might; I could not erase the visual of Nube and Trey sharing a kiss. Especially not when I just shared one with her…I was having a hard time digesting that shit. I reached in my inner pocket and pulled me out something to blow on for a minute…not really trynna get blazed, but I needed some reinforcement right about now. I was trying not to lose my mind over something that really is none of my business. Nube is with JT…JT is my brother…me trying to infiltrate was foul. I gotta forget this shit and let it go…Let it go like Dez told me. 7 brothers and 7 cousins, shop in your own store, no refunds, no exchanges, no store credits, and all sales final. Yeah…that's the right thing to do. I sat and smoked…bumped some Jay-Z and just chilled for about an hour. And just as I settled up in my mind that I was straight with the whole thing, the little angel on my right shoulder said, "Yo Rod…they never said anything about using a Gift Card" And the little devil on my left shoulder said, "Yeah mu' fucka…go get your present."

Nubina

As I finished oiling my body after my shower, I couldn't help but to thinking and just wondering what's going on here with me today and men. JT has dusted himself off from me, and Trey walking behind me trying to catch the dust. And I…I don't know how I'm feeling about all this. I mean the minute that I'm freed up from a man that I've been trying to come together with for 2 years, the man that has eluded me for 3 years appears with promises to make things "right" for me. There's no doubt that I'm being tested right about now...I don't know by whom or the exact reason why...but it's almost as if decisions are being taken out of my control and decided for me by destiny. I mean...JT don't want me no more...Trey talking bout he wants me forever...and I can't forget that I still have to evaluate the revelation Murad and I admitted to last night. Speaking of which, I need to get in touch with him on a business tip. I want to get his opinion on a new angle I want to take with the girls.

As I reach for the phone to dial his number, my phone goes off and it's Rod.

"Hey Rod," I say slightly amused, "We must be vibing on the same wave tonight, cause I was just getting ready to call...I mean phone in hand as we speak. So what's up Rod?"

"I need to speak with you Nube," he said, not sounding exactly like himself.

"Well...okay, that's cool...I need to speak with you about some things too...one of them in regard to the Chicago presentation. I was thinking that I could come at them just a little different than..."

"Nube open the door," he said cutting me off.

"Open the door...what the...?" I said walking to my front door. When I unlocked it and swung it open, there was Murad standing at the other side, eyes glazed frostier than an iced chilled mug. He stood there for a minute with the phone still up to his ear, as did I.

"Nube...I need to...Oh," he said disconnecting the phone, dropping the call on my end as well, "Nube...I got shit to say and I really want to be right about how and what it is that I'm going to say. So can I come in?"

"Since when do you need an invite into my home Rod," I answered him looking at him side ways, stepping to the side so that he could pass thru the door. He was in some kind of a mood and I was a little apprehensive as to what I was about to encounter. As I closed the door...I do believe that I smelled a whiff of weed. Rod only plays the weed card on "very special" occasions, so something of a whole nother nature must have set him off. Guess I may as well get right into it.

"Would you like something to drink?" I asked him walking to the kitchen.

He followed me responding, "Naw…I'm straight."

I proceeded to get myself something, and went on and jumped into it."Rod," I started, "Something serious seems to be on your mind, cause right about now…your ass is blazed. You wanna talk about it?"

Murad

Oh… so do I want to talk about it, she asks me. She has no idea how much I wanna "talk" about it.

"Well then Nube," I said, "Let's get it all on the table. Where you just playing with me last night? I mean is it just your thing to kiss men and hype them by telling them you got feelings for them?"

"Rod…I don't know what has gotten into you," she answered me, "But you of all people know that I don't even operate like that. I'm not in the business of saying things I don't mean. If I said it…I meant it. Why would you ask me something like that?"

"Yeah," I answered, "I'm well aware that you only say and do what you mean. That's why it's really hard for me to stuff this shit here down," I said sliding my phone open and scrolling to reveal the frame of her and Trey sharing a kiss.

Her eyes bucked open wide, and she snapped her head up to meet me and said, "Rod, what the hell is this? You were following me today?"

"Nube…get real," I answered, "I got way too much on my plate to be following you. My boy Dame just happened to be in the vicinity and peeped you and Midnight and snapped some pics then shot em' over to me."

"Well okay…and what?" she asked me. I couldn't believe the response I just heard.

"Okay and what?" I shot back at her.

"Yeah…okay and what?" she answered me.

"Nube," I said, "What's the deal with you and Midnight?"

"I don't appreciate your line of questioning Murad," she said.

"My line of questioning," I came back with, my temper starting to flare, "Nube...you kissing on me last night...you fucking kissing Midnight today, and what...tomorrow you'll be kissing JT? What gives Nube...what's going on with you?"

"What's going on with me?" she said, now in an irritated tone of her own, "Let us understand something here tonight Murad. I'm a grown ass-woman and I don't have to regulate to nobody what I do. Although I can fully explain any and all of my actions, who are you to force the issue?"

"Who am I Nube?" I yelled, now heated, "I'm the one that's been walking behind you sniffing the scent of your ass just hoping that you would notice that I'm there. I'm the one that's been hanging by your side supporting you, while your so called man gets off on his "Jesus Walks" pass. I'm the one that sits around watching while you run behind a man who has more love for his church congregation than the greatness of his woman. I'm the one that keeps pushing and striving for you, cause I know your full potential, while his ass ducks behind his religious studying. I'm the one Nube. I'm the fucking one that wanna see you smile for me...I want to see you checking for me the way that you check for JT."

"Oh is that right," she cut in with, "I sure as hell can't tell with you being the sole owner and CEO of the World Wide Punani Federation."

"What the hell you talking about Nube," I came back with, "You been listening to too many of Sumira's stories."

"Oh have I now," she said, "How bout all the times we were out on the road and you chose to indulge in your share of the services of the Friendly Neighborhood Groupie's Association. You forget Rod...I was right there. And all the time you got Jazz, and whoever else back here keeping home base warm. So what Rod...what is it you've got to say about that?"

Damn...this wasn't going well at all...I forgot for a moment who I'm dealing with here. My blaze now long gone...I took a minute to mull it over and came back with, "Nube...stop for a minute...think about it...you have been doing mad projects like non-stop for over a year...and I'm right there with you...when do I have time for other women? Not only that...every woman I hooked up with or went out with don't mean I slept with her. I haven't been with another woman since Jazz. All that shit you going on about is past history. That's some shit I don't even do no more."

"Well okay," she said, "but that's my case in point right there. Jazz is here...Jazz is now, and Jazz didn't waste no time in letting me know in her own little way last night that you belong to her."

"I don't belong to NO fucking body," I came back with, "I never led Jazmine on and told her we were a couple. I never let any woman on about my situation. Up front they know... it is what it is."

"And is that right," she answered, "Then what is it for me Murad? You think that I was skinnin-grinnin happy about you going home with Jazmine last night? Although my acknowledgment of my feelings for you is new...I have never liked it when you had all kinds of women in your cipher. I have always wanted more for you in that way Rod. More than just you bouncing around in different sexual trysts. You better than that Rod...and even if I never caught feelings for you I still would want the same for you...because it's what you deserve. So like I said Murad...up front...what is it for me?"

"What you mean what is it for you Nube? I wanna elevate me and you to a different level. I want to bring shit full circle and start something new, I want..."

"Oooh Rod," she yelled out, walking into the living room, "you stressing me. I can't be happy that you talking this shit to me today, and just last night you was with Jazz."

"Oh and what the fuck...you think I get a discount on stress?" I yelled back following her, "You think I'm happy knowing that JT is loving and holding the woman that I'm consumed with. You think I'm fucking happy with Midnight slobbing you down at the bookstore. In fact...I can't handle this shit no more Nube...I can't. No matter how hard I try...the thought of you and other men kissing and touching you is slowly leading my ass to the point of no return."

"Well what you want from me Rod?" she said now passing angry tears down her face. "You men are so damn selfish. I can't believe the day I've had today. First JT done kicked my ass to the curb. Yeah, that's right," she inter-responded to the raise of my eyebrows. "And no sooner than I brush myself off, Trey comes around like the street sweeper and want to sweep me back up into his arena...all to satisfy his frail ego. Now here you come...questioning my integrity as a woman and hounding me about what I'm doing with other men. You know what...mentally I'm spent," she said slumping down on the carpet against the wall. "I'm done...I'm just done. I'm not explaining anything else here tonight."

I took a look at her and thought about the shit she just laid down to me. Damn...I really think that I handled this all the wrong way.

"Nube," I started, and as she gave me the look of a stone killer, I put my hands up in surrender, "you know what...I'm wrong. I came here knocking you in the head with shit that I know is not your character and I apologize for the way I handled things." I took a seat on the couch and asked, "But may I please just get this off my chest?" She gave me that "go head" nod, so I stretched back on the couch took a deep breath and began.

"I am really at a point in my life where you have become the most important reason that I get up every day. There's no way in the world that I can cease to work side by side with the one person in the world who is responsible for significantly changing my mindset and my views on life, the world, and relationships. I can't begin to tell you how lost I was as a soul, meandering around, so untrusting of all women yet at the same time flossing and showcasing them. You have no idea the perception I had of women before you were interjected into my life. I had my own set of views and ideas on what I felt that love between a man and a woman should be and I just always felt that no woman could ever understand my line of thinking on it. So I just let things fall wherever when it came to relationships, and I swore myself off of getting involved on any kind of serious level. I just didn't think that there was any woman out here that could meet and match my expectations. That is until I heard you recite your work at Bryce's cookout. You struck a chord within me that vibrated and constantly urged me to engage myself further in you and see if possibly you could understand me, the way that I've always wanted to be understood. I became infatuated with your words, your ability to convey the actual and the soul stirring truth of any matter…and then the positive spin that you put on it all. I fell in love with the spoken word of Nubina, and as time passed and our time together expanded, I fell in love with Tania…the woman. You are everything to me Nube. You give me the incentive to make moves, to press for success and all the while encourage me to remain true to myself in the process. I know that it's wrong…but I've come to depend on the fact that you are in my life on a regular and I at least want the opportunity to explore if this thing between me and you is the right choice. It's an opportunity that I'm asking for Nube…an opportunity I feel that I would never have the courage to ever pursue again. I can't make you see things my way so…if you decide to pass on the opportunity…as impossible as it's going to be…I'm going to have to find a way to wake up every morning and just exist."

Nubina

I'm frozen…I can't move. Murad just pierced my soul with Love's bow and arrow. The words he just revealed to me have gone on to pop all the remaining bubble wrap surrounding my heart. My heart is out there now…exposed. She's been wrapped up for so long that she doesn't know what it is she should do at this very moment. Murad is looking at me as though he's waiting for a response. The longer I sit there, the more and more the image of rejection is reflected on his face. When I failed to make a move, Murad just slumped down on the couch with his head thrown back in defeat and let go a deep sigh. That tender gesture of emotion put me into defrost and I got up from my spot on the floor. I walked over to the couch and climbed up into his lap cross-legged Indian style facing him. I took him by the chin and raised his head until we were face to face. I took my two fingers and pointed to my heart, then took the same two fingers and placed them on his heart. And as I held them in place tapping his heart, I looked him in his eyes and told him, "Always"…and then I sealed the deal with a kiss.

Chapter 23

Where Do We Go From Here

Murad

Now I'm the one who's frozen. Nube just promised to forever have my heart and to forever give me hers. As her words began to marinade within my brain, I think I started to hyperventilate, and grabbed her up in a forceful hug of appreciation as well as reassurance. I mean I couldn't believe that everything had come to a head, and released itself in my favor. I silently thanked her over and over again in my head as I continued to hold on to her for dear life. Okay Murad I'm thinking...now that you've got the green light, where you gonna take it from here? As if literally reading my mind Nube raised up and asked me straight up, "So...now what?" Something about her tone of voice struck me as comical and I just bust out in deep laughter.

"What...Murad...what's so funny?" she asked me starting to laugh as well.

"Oh I don't know Nube," I answered her, "just something in the way you said that, sounding like you 7 years old or something."

"Well today kinda got me stripped down to little girl status," she replied, "I been put thru the ringer by men all day." I guess she interpreted some kind of look on my face, cause she came back at me to hit the nail on the head.

"Murad," she started still sitting up in my lap, "I know you...and I know that you seeking some clarification before we attempt to move on with our thing. For the record, I was at the bookstore seeking some solace after JT dropped his bombshell on me to discontinue our relationship. I wasn't there but a half an hour before I bumped into Trey. He and I used to frequent the bookstore, and he came there to check on a specific book. It was mere coincidence that we were both there on this day. I'm sure you know he got to talking and the topic somehow got around to he and I starting over new."

I knew that I was expecting to hear exactly that, so I don't know why my eyebrows did an involuntary rise on their own.

"And Murad," she began again, "I can't lie. I was touched by the things that he had to say...I mean...I had been waiting for 3 years to hear them Rod. When he and I was together I was so ready to do whatever it took to remain with that man but he just never had the presence of mind to see things my way. I guess he just wasn't ready. To finally hear the words that I was longing to hear softened up a spot in me. I mean...I pulled myself together and cut him short and just asked him to help me to the car, and of course he continued his campaign outside. As I was about to leave he felt really lucky and stole himself a kiss. Again...I won't lie Murad. It felt good that someone who discarded me and left me craving for his kiss was now the one in need of a kiss to validate himself. So yes...I let him get that kiss...but it all ends there. Travelling down the road with Trey again is no longer an option." I was uncomfortable with the tone of her voice as it trailed off as well as the slight tilt in her head downward, so I voiced, "Nube," in a tone that commanded that she look at me directly. I took her chin in my hand and twist my head to the side. She knows exactly what I mean and verbally answers me, "Yes Murad...I'm sure."

Nubina

I just finished clearing the air for Murad, but this nukka better know this here is a 2 way street. He looks at me and gives me a little smile.

"Relax Nube," he says to me, "I'm ahead of you on this one. I cut things off with Jazmine last night. I won't lie to you as well...a little something kind of jumped off last night, but all it did was confirm to me that shit with her needed to be over. Now...she's been blowing up my phone all day, and even trynna drag Dream into it and all, but I'm finished with her and anyone else for that matter Nube. I need this to be all about you and me...and no one else. I feel deep within my soul that I'm at that place where I wanna make real all that I've dreamed a relationship can truly be...and I want to explore that shit with you Nube."

Wow...I can't even tell you the swirling that's going around in my head. I mean, I know him...this man...I've known of him for a while, and I've known him closely for 2 years now, but I don't know him in a romantic way, and I'm kinda scared to take this all on. My exact sentiments must be etched on my face, and he responded to the look by asking me, "What's wrong Nube? I can tell that something ain't sitting right with you. I can assure you...I am done with Jazmine"

"Well it's not just Jazmine," I responded, "It's kind of everything about you."

"Everything about me?" he said puzzled, "What are you talking about Nube?"

"Murad," I started once again, "Do you know who you are? You are Murad Tillman. **The** Murad Tillman of the Oranges... Essex County...in fact, the whole eastern seaboard. You are the man to know, the one to rub elbows with, the financial wizard with investment savvy. You have book smarts, street smarts, physical strength as well as physical beauty. You have your own outstanding sense of fashion, business finesse, and a phenomenal aura that coerces attention from everyone in a room. Every woman wants to be with you and every man wants to be like you. Everywhere we go, woman are jocking you, drooling over you, trying to push up on you. You are like every woman's dream come true... sista's have been waiting on line to be with you since the 9th grade Murad. How am I supposed to compete with all of that?"

"Nube...baby listen," he responded. "Do you know who **you** are? You are Nubina...Queen Nubina, the poetess, the writer, the great philosophical narrator. You are the orator of all truths big and small. The songwriter, the storyteller, the humorous diplomat and lately an aspiring actress. You are a beautiful insightful person and friend to anyone lucky enough to be in your cipher. You have kindness and understanding to all things and all situations. And your aura...it doesn't coerce...it engulfs anyone in the immediate vicinity. Nube you carry an internal beauty that projects in your physical beauty. You possess the most tantalizing honey colored skin tone that compliments one of the most gorgeous faces of the millennium. And not for nothing Nube...your physique is slamming. You take sexy to a whole nother realm. Do you know how many comments I had to let pass over my head in regard to you. Nigga's commenting directly and indirectly about how they would love to have one night with you. Some of the grimey bastards would actually pull me aside before a meeting and ask if you were available for the evening, as if I would pimp you out to benefit securing the deal. Yes Nube," I responded to the look of disgust on her face, "How you think I got pegged with my wild man reputation, for negotiating? I had to smack some of them fools up, and hemmed the rest of them up by the collar and shake the fuck out of them. And shit...that's when you was with JT! How you think I'm gonna handle the insensitive and disrespectful comments now, and we about to be together? Then you got the innocent ones that are just so blown away with you and can't help but fawn all over you. How do I handle the fact that there's not a man on this planet that wouldn't take you from me if given a chance?"

I sat there, still in his lap just blown-away about all that he thought of me, and all that he just hipped me to about people in the business.

"Murad," I started, "I'm not sure if what you just said has helped or hindered. I will admit to you right here, right now...I'm scared. First off I'm intimidated by the "you" that you are, and secondly I am beginning to realize that this choice we've made is not going to be all peaches and cream. Not only that, on the real...I'm just coming off of a 2 year stint of rejection by your brother of all people. I'm a little fragile and delicate right now Rod. I mean...I've come to terms that my feelings for you are real and present, but I just don't want to be hurt again. And I know...I know...you have been the one there for me thru thick and thin the last couple of years, you have put in hard work and a vested interest for my well being on all levels and yes...you have been the one that had no issue at all with expressing your deep emotional desire for me; but in the end...you're a man Rod and in all my past experiences....men have always changed their minds on me. Murad...I couldn't stand the rejection from you...it would empty my soul."

With her last set of words, I had to realize that she is right...this is going to be a decision that we enter into with seriousness and awareness. JT is my brother, and he just cut her loose for whatever reason. There is going to be some other residual fallout from our families and what not. And I'm hearing her on the fact that her track record with men has not been on a winning streak, but you know what...It's not like I'm trynna be the one to add to her misery. She needs to understand that I'm at a place where I'm so ready right now and I'm willing to do whatever it takes for us to be together.

"Nube," I started, "Listen...yes I am a man...I get that. And yes, I was one of "them" men if that's what you wanna call it. I was only in it for the right now, or the "it is what it is" thing. But I am so over and done with all that negative nonsense. After awhile it all becomes one in the same, just dished up in a different body. But you Nube, you have brought so much clarity and understanding to me about where I'd like to be on an emotional level with a special someone. You uplift me in ways that I wasn't even aware of. And I know that you believe deeply in spiritual connections so I'm hoping that you can sense that I am above board with you and not seeking some kind of challenge just for the fun of it. I also know that you have experienced a lot of circumstances with men in the past, and I can't just discount your fears on us being together, but Nube...baby...I won't steer you wrong, if you give me a chance...give us a chance, you will never regret your choice...I promise you that."

She looked at me sideways with them sexy brown eyes, sighed and said, "You know what...I'm just sitting up her hemming and hawing, just making all these admissions of fear, and excuses, when I really need to admit one last thing. I need to admit that for whatever reason...almost beyond my control...I am motivated in the most exhilarating way to explore another facet of Murad Tillman. No matter what happens...there is no way that I can let this segment of history in my life pass by without including you. As long as you are sure Rod...then I want this...I want you and I to take that chance." My girl, I'm thinking to myself; going with her internal instincts and vibes. Yes...yes!! I can't help but just stare at her knowing that it's all a done deal and there is a blank slate before us on which we can build something special. I guess me looking at her was making her feel uncomfortable.

"Rod," she said blushing, "why are you staring at me like that? You making me feel like a little girl again."

"Is that right?" I finally answer her. "Well okay...then we gonna do this up in true fashion here. Tania Baynes," I said taking her right hand into mine, "Will you go with me?"

She bust out in sweet laughter and smiles and said, "Oh my God...what is this like... the 6th grade?" I shook my head yes, then gave her that head twist that I give when I expect an answer.

"Yes," she said answering me between laughter, "Yes Murad Tillman. I will **go** with you." And as she leaned in to me to bless me with those sweet lips she added in..."Anywhere."

Chapter 24

Just One More Thing

Murad

That shit is official. Nube and I are together!!!! I'm thinking as I pull off down the street. I don't know how things have all come to swing my way...but a brother is not gonna question Destiny at all. I told Nube that I had to leave to take care of something and I promised her that we could go over her presentation tomorrow. She didn't protest at all, I know her...she probably wanna sit around and let this all marinade. I could use some marinade time myself but there's just one more thing I've got to handle. I hit the button #5 on the car phone and waited for an answer. "Hello," I heard after the 3rd ring.

"Yo...JT," I responded, "I'm coming thru...be there like 10 on 10."

"No problem," he said and we both hung up. Yeah...I need to handle this.

JT

Well that's no surprise. In fact, I'm surprised he wasn't stomping over here any sooner. I knew given how close them two are that my news this morning would be shared without a doubt, so you could say that I am somewhat prepared for this. I don't know in what context he wants to take this all, but actually, I've got things I need to relay to him and hopefully it will all go over smoothly. Today was one for the books; I released an angel from my world that had somehow been misguided when she was put into the midst of the Tillman clan. Apparently she took the wrong fork in the road on her way to romance. I am sure in my belief that it is Murad that she was sent here to partner with. There is something demanding in his soul that only Tania can resolve. God only knows my depth of pain for my loss, so I sure hope Murad is not going to be over the top with whatever he has to say, cause I honestly can't say how I'll react. I guess I'll leave it all in God's hands.

Murad

Damn I hope this shit remains sublime I'm thinking as I ring the doorbell. I guess he was waiting on me cause he was at the door in 30 seconds flat.

"Murad," he acknowledged, opening the door.

"JT," I answered back walking in past him.

"Look," I started, "I didn't come here to cause no trouble, I need to say what I came to say...possibly get some feedback from you and then leave you to the rest of your evening."

"Okay shoot," he replied.

"Well I'm sure you know that I just left Nube," I began again taking a seat in the nearest chair as he took a seat on the couch facing me, "and she and I both revealed some interesting things. First off...me...as a man, I feel I need to let you know that I have developed very deep feelings for Nube. Feelings that I can no longer contain, and have since expressed them to her. She in turn has admitted that she has feelings for me as well, and we have made a mutual decision to pursue our feelings for one another and enter into a relationship. And yes...I am aware that I have betrayed the family pact, but this connection I feel is so strong, that it voids any prior agreements... and I'm willing to just bear the consequences my decision will bring." I took a pause from speaking to watch his face for a response or a reaction; but he just sat there looking at me, which he knows is pissing me off.

"So...like you wanna contribute to this conversation," I ask him a little annoyed, "cause if the shit don't mean nothing to you, I could just be out and...."

"Murad," he finally says cutting me off, "Slow your roll little brother. I was just giving you your space to verbalize, and actually...you ain't telling me nothing I don't already know. I have had the premonition for awhile now that Tania was meant to be with you and not me. I meditated on it and I prayed on it, and Friday night's events just brought the conclusion full circle."

"So you saying you knew this shit here for awhile JT?" I questioned him still annoyed, "Then why the fuck did you string Nube on for 2 years? Do you know how frustrated she's been about you not wanting her and not being able to participate in her arena? She was always trying to get me to schedule things so that you could be included, and you sitting over her playing God with her heart."

"First of all Rod...let's not get things twisted here," he responded, "I'm still a man...all day long, and I would gladly have stayed in a relationship with her. I love Tania, I will always love Tania. It was not like I intended for things to go on for 2 years. In fact I was hoping that I could come to terms with myself mentally and see our relationship become vested, but it came to my attention that God has other plans for me in regard to Tania, and being her man is not one of them."

"So I'm saying JT...You couldn't have let her know any sooner than today?" I asked him, "She adored you."

"Oh did she?" he answered me right back on the cusp. "Respect me yes...but how could she adore me, when she adores you? Yeah...that's right, she adores you Murad. She's adored you for awhile and hasn't even been aware of it. Friday night brought it all to the surface when you guys saw one another for the first time in two days. That 2 day separation touched off some subconscious elements within her and I can't fault her for what she feels. She's going for what makes her blossom as a woman and what infuses her creativity. I can't argue with the universal order of it all...Tania has been within the Tillman midst for years and her designated partner is you and not me. I guess destiny was waiting for you to be ready Murad, waiting for you to evolve and step in to play your position. And while I've been sitting on the sidelines knowing that this was inevitable, what I want to know now is....are you ready Murad? Are you ready to embrace her for the treasure that she is and fulfill all that's been set before you by God?"

Damn...JT is killing my brain with all this spiritual jargon...BUT...I have to be real...it ain't nothing but the truth. I wasn't necessarily expecting a response of this nature, and for the shit to be turned back on me, but...

“JT,” I came back with, “first off, I feel you on everything you saying. And yes…I’ve been ready for a minute now. Nube is the woman that I’ve been wishing would come my way since forever. I am more than ready to show her nothing but true love and provide her with whatever she needs to continue her dream. And I know you, like everybody else is gonna be holding my past against me and keeping tabs on my performance and whether or not I mess up, but this shit here is the realist thing I’ve got going in my life for me, and I’m going to be on top of my game to ensure that it remains that way.”

“Well Murad,” he replied, “Just to expound on one of your statements…don’t waste your energy worrying on what others perceive of your choice. If it’s a solid choice that you’ve made from your heart, things will fall into place. Now if it so happens that somewhere I’ve read wrong in between the lines and your choice was made haphazardly, then you need only worry about one person surveying your performance or lack thereof…and that’s me Murad. With the help of God and everything I am as a man within me, if you hurt her Murad…I will hunt you down.”

Oh shit…choir boy done laid down the law to my ass!! Threatening me and what not. If this wasn’t as serious a topic as it is…I would be laughing my ass off at his threats. But I came here to this man’s house …my brother no less, to let him know that I was entering into a romantic relationship with the woman he’s been with for 2 years.

“Jayson,” I answered him by his full name; something he knows that I don’t do unless I’m serious, “This time around I’m playing for keeps bruh…and besides…I think I understand just as well as you do the preciousness of this woman. Don’t forget I’ve worked side by side with her for the same 2 years that you all were dealing with each other. In fact, I gamble to say that I probably know her better than you do. So although your concern for her emotional well being is much appreciated, your threat is not something I need to take under advisement. Hurting Nube is the last thing on my mind.”

“Well then okay Murad,” he replied standing as if to signify that this conversation was over, “the ball is in your court.”

“And you ain’t got nothing to worry about,” I answered standing up to meet him, “cause I intend to take that shit to the hoop.” I gave him the nod, greeted him peace...then turned and saw myself out the front door.

Chapter 25

Time To Get Ourselves In Check

Nubina

As I'm standing before you this morning, I'm looking at some faces that society has designated as trouble, as well as some faces that society has labeled unworthy And as I link the combination of the two, I've come to the realization that these are also the faces that society has turned their backs on. Now as I'm looking at these faces some of them look concerned, some of the faces look straight up bored, and a couple of the faces are like sending negative vibes in my direction. I guess the faces in a sense are saying, "What the hell does she know about me?" And I guess if you want to get technical...I really don't know a damn thing about you except for what I've been told. I don't know the immediate circumstances to what led you to be placed in this group home. Don't know what conflicts you've endured in your life that helped to commit you here. But what I do know to be true for each one of you...you and only you are responsible in doing your part to get yourselves up out of here....

Needless to say, Nube and I did not get the chance to review her presentation, we spent all day yesterday acknowledging and revealing different aspects to our previous relationship, and how we were going to currently move forward. We both agreed that we would not rush anything physical and give ourselves time to get used to one another under this new prospective. Got to admit that this shit is kind of weird. Now that I have the right to touch what I want, I'm kind of gun shy about it all. I mean...she's someone who I have just dreamed about form afar and I don't plan to treat her like just any woman, yet at the same time, most of my experiences have been with just "some" woman. I don't want to mess up, nor do I wanna play myself. So I figure I'll just fall back, let the body language guide me and just be patient for shit to develop in its own time. Besides, I'm about due for my annual HIV testing; I think I'll have old Doc just test me for every damn thing while he at it. Yeah...that would give me a sound peace of mind. As I listen to her speak to the girls I wonder if this is the original concept, or if she's free-stylin...

In life there's going to be incidents that take place that are unpleasant or things to set us back. Some of them will be within our control and some of them not. And as I mentioned before, regardless to how you got where you are today, you have to be the one to remove yourself from the negative enslavement... And I know that society and the quoted "system" views you as a failure and feeds your insecurity to progress, but in all actuality if you fail in progression then you have joined sides with the very ones who you feel are against you. I'm saying... if you think those here in authority are non-supportive...don't harbor resentment or ill feelings toward them cause actually, how much support were you expecting from them anyway? The first step in self elevation is, you supporting you. First have faith and belief in yourself and what it is you want for yourself and don't let anyone or anything dissuade you from it. Don't feed into the possible negativity of any of your peers who may not have strength enough to be in the same place that you are as you strive to uplift. Don't resort to aggressive behavior and violence to resolve the obstacles placed before you...you can do much better than that...

I can't help but think back to all of the words and conversation since Friday night. I mean I had words with Nube, words with JT and words...although very little with Jazmine. In such a short time frame, shit has just done a complete 360. I'm wondering if all the spiritual talk that JT and Nube go on about is the real deal. Well it certainly seems to be, cause situations and circumstances just seemed to converge out of nowhere and delivered Nube and I a whole nother reality. A reality I must say that I am perfectly content with. I don't mind being cautious and going slow on this new level, cause even though it may be a little premature of me to say... if I have it my way...this right here is my final destination.

Pay no heed to "they" of society with their twisted conception of priorities. Why should you cower down to judgment of a society who glorifies the troubled actions and antics of Britney Spears as daily headlining news rather than highlight and feature the need for funding and grants of educational bearing. Why should you entrust your worthiness to a society who has devoted television shows to stalk and highlight celebrities in their day to day lives, hoping to slip up and irritate them into an incident they can showcase, rather than showcase the many civic and humanitarian efforts and gestures that celebrities are involved in. In fact, what do you owe a society that garners on building revenue by instigating and pot stirring like some 5th grade bully? Yes ladies...the effort to release yourself from this enslavement and your need to improve yourself should not be blown off with excuses of why should I...and they think that I...and what's the use they...and what will it all mean, cause they, and they ain't got no where for me to go. The only conclusion and answer to it all is you...you are the only one that matters and you are the only one responsible for getting yourselves out of here. Cause if you've been paying attention to all that I have said here today... "They" don't even have a clue.

As I stand in the backdrop, I listen to the thunderous applause delivered by the audience, and I feel a sudden charge of internal warmth that can only be diagnosed as pride. Every time I hear Nube speak, and put the simple and natural things in prospective, it gives me a brand new high. Her oratorical abilities have come to be the constant turn on that feeds my emotional attachment to her. I just can't imagine what reason any man in the world would have for letting her go, or any reason to go outside of their relationship for other physical satisfaction. Perhaps they were mesmerized by her light, and not able to relegate any feasible action. I don't know...but whatever the case...I owe them clowns a thank you...cause they cleared her path so that I could attempt the journey. And let me tell you...I'm coming equipped with everything I'm gonna need to make the journey a success. I so want this to have a forever ending. I listen as she goes thru her question and answer phase, then inform them that she does have material on CD's that can be ordered. I watched as she scanned the group of about 25 to 30 young ladies, and then cringed as she announced that she would give a free copy to each one of them. They responded with thank yous and another round of thunderous applause. The director of the facility got up and acknowledged Nubes' act of generosity as well as thank her for her appearance. She also thanked some of the dignitaries for their attendance, and then closed the program out. Nube was immediately mobbed for autographs, so I made my way over to the crowd to maintain some control. I waited as she signed most of them, and just as I was about to prepare us to break out, my blackberry beeped. Without checking the number, I answered and was greeted by the tone of Jazmine's annoying voice.

"Murad…baby…don't hang up…please," she said.

"What do you want Jazz?" I answered her in a huff, turning my back from the crowd.

"Murad, I just want to know what I've done so bad that you won't speak to me?"

"Jazz…it ain't about what you've done, it's about what I'm unwilling to do, and I don't want to continue the nonsensical cycle with you anymore. I'm moving on and that's all there is to it."

"It's about her isn't it? Isn't it?" she replied, her voice on the edge.

"The truth is Jazz, that it's more about me. It's about what I wanna do and where I wanna be. And yes, if you want to know the truth…Nube has a lot to do with it." I answered.

"But what Murad," she angrily voiced, "What can she do for you that I can't? What can her little stuck up ass do when it's time to put it down? Can she match me move for move in bed? Can she swallow like a champ…the way that I can.? Hell nah…she probably don't even swallow. Can she hold…"

"Jazz, get a life," I told her hanging up and not dignifying her nonsense with a response. I'm going to have to remember to look at the caller ID until I can make a point to block her number.

As I slide the phone closed, I see Nube talking to a tall mature man in a suit. She holds out her hand for me to come over as she noticed that I am done with my phone conversation.

"Murad," she says as I walk over to them both, "This is Kenneth Reagan, the associate director of Inner City Youth programs run by the Chicago chapter of the NAACP. And Mr. Reagan, this is my manager, partner and better half Murad Tillman."

"How you doing," I respond shaking his hand.

"Your lovely Nubina has struck a mighty chord here today," he said, "And I was just asking her if we could get in touch with her to perhaps speak at another engagement in the future? The young ladies really seemed to be engrossed with her message, and I myself was equally impressed."

"Well if you could give me a call with the details, I'll most definitely check to see the feasibility," I answered giving him one of my business cards.

"Okay then young man, that sounds like a plan," he said shaking my hand once again, "Nubina...thank you for your inspirational words to the young ladies, as well as your generous gift. I'll be getting back to you no later than the months end to set something up."

"We'll be looking forward to hearing from you," I answered. As he walked away I put my arm around her and started to exit the building.

"That was awesome as usual Nube," I told her, "Just the right set of words with the right attitude supporting it. I'm sorry that we didn't get the chance to preview it."

"Aww...it's cool," she answered, "I had started a preliminary draft and then just supplemented what I needed to say once I got here and peeped the atmosphere. The girls are so troubled and just need someone to really believe in them."

"Yeah Nube," I replied, "You was believing in them extra hard...up there giving away freebies. Girl...do you know how much loss revenue that is?"

"Murad," she said giving me the eye, "Don't be like that. I'm sure you'll find some way to write that off, or include it as an expense."

"Perhaps," I answered, "But next time you wanna give shit away...we gonna deduct it from your share of the profits."

"Rod," she called out laughing and hitting me in the arm.

"Hey watch it," I responded to her playfully, "No damaging the merchandise."

"Oh no I wouldn't want to do that," she said, "I've just started my investment in the property, and I really want to see it prosper in equity."

"Really?" I asked her leaning in close for a kiss.

"Oh most definitely," she responded and obliged me with her lips. We lingered there for a sweet moment before separating.

"Well look Nube," I said as we made our way out to the main lobby, "How bout we go check out the city, and hit up that spot they be talking bout with the good Caribbean food?"

"Deal," she replied, "Let's do it. I'm starving."

"You know," I stopped her, and pulled her close to me again, "I'm proud of you Butter."

"Butter?" she quizzed me. Damn...I can't believe I let that slip.

"Well yeah Nube," I started explaining, "It's kind of my pet name that I secretly call you in my mind. It's short for Butterfly. Your ability to remain free in spirit reminds me of the freedom that a butterfly possesses. Always flying around so beautiful, so carefree and not letting anything trouble you. So I kind of called you that to myself...back when I first started catching feelings for you. It was just my little secret...and now... you know."

"Oh Murad," she blushed, "that's so sweet. So Butter huh? That's my pet name?" she said smiling at me innocently, not knowing that the smile was being translated as seductive from my point of view.

"Yeah Nube," I responded, "you my Butter for life girl...all day." With that we both started laughing, and continued on our way to the parking lot on our quest to satisfy our hunger.

Chapter 26
The World Premiere

Murad

It's hard to believe that 3 months have passed since Nube and I have been officially together. We have indeed taken our time in getting accustomed to our new status. On the road, we continued to maintain separate but adjoining rooms, but most of the time spent the night up talking and whatnot in only one room. I used to have flowers delivered to her room in the past from time to time, but now that we're together I made sure to have flowers delivered to her room every time we go away. It warms my heart over to see the appreciation in her eyes every time she discovered the flowers, and it didn't hurt none that her kisses were getting longer and stronger each time. But in all of the 3 months since we decided to be together, we have not yet elevated to the physical. I guess things were moving at the pace that they were supposed to be, and you know...honestly I was kind of enjoying this relationship with a lot of specialness going on without any pressure. It seemed to heighten my level of appreciation for her and gave us both the time to mutually develop our communication skills. Once Nube had found out that I was getting myself tested for STD's, she suggested that we go together and share the results. Not a problem...we did...we passed...and we are all ready...set...go. Just haven't gotten with the "go." I don't know if we're both a little scared or just want to savor the quiet before the storm, cause everyone knows once you add sex up into the mix it changes the game dramatically...one way or another.

Nubina

I'm on my way to the New York premiere of Finders Keepers, an African American romantic comedy to which I have completed my first acting debut. It's a small part in which I play a "spoken word phenom"...ooo...what a stretch I laugh at myself. In the movie I recite a poem at a local night club that ignites a spark between a guy and a girl, who in turn have to come back at the end of the movie in hopes of hearing another poem to rekindle their magic. In all I have about 3 scenes, and trust when I say that was enough. The acting thing is a lot of work. Not so much the actual acting then the re-takes for small directorial indifferences with the staff and actors. Then there's the hair, the wardrobe and makeup rituals. And oh man...its hell when you've got a 4:30 am call to the set. But it was a challenge that I tried to take head on, and I just hope that my efforts paid off. I think that it would come off as supreme to know that I could hold my own against the other A and B list actors of the movie. Not trying to take anyone's spot by a long shot, I'm actually hoping that my presence added to the movie rather than take away from it. I'm a little anxious and I wish that Murad was here with me now. He had a spontaneous meeting and had to be in the city at 2:00 pm. It's an early premiere; I suppose it was scheduled early so they could have successful red carpet preliminary activities. Being that this was NYC, space was limited for a true set-up, and traffic is a thorn, so an early event would make life easier. It worked out well for us, because Murad has an after party planned back at Sarafin's so the earlier we get back to Jersey the better. The premiere actually starts at 5:00 and it is now 3:30. Murad sent the car service for me and promised to meet me on the red carpet. I hope he's done with his meeting...he said it wouldn't take long and I'm just really hoping not. I'm a little scared, nervous, all that...and I'm really feeling the need for him right now.

Murad

Damn...it's kinda hot out here in the sun. Glad that meeting was short and to the point, I want to be here at the exact moment the car gets here with Nube. This is her first acting debut and I know this premier is important to her. Let me hit her on the cell and see where they at. Look at this crowd I'm thinking as the phone rings...don't these people have day jobs.

"Hello...yeah Nube...where you at?"

"We coming up on 7th Ave and like 35th Street, we should be pulling up soon," she answered me.

"Oh well, tell him they got like a line set up to the right for drop off. He's gonna have to get in line, and they have coordinators escorting people out and maintaining the line to the red carpet. I guess I'll make my way down to meet you. It's kind of hot just standing here anyway," I told her, "I'll see you in a few."

As I make my way down the street, I feel a couple of eyes on me and note the whispers going on. It's so amazing how people are so intrigued with celebrities and their lives. I guess I shouldn't complain, because that interest along with the fan base is essentially the foundation to many a financial enterprise.

"Murad" I heard someone call out. Who the hell knows me, I think turning around. "Murad…it's me," a female voice called out, "its Shante…we went to school together."

"Oh…hey, how you doing?" I answered her, trying not to be rude, cause actually I don't remember her ass at all.

"You here with Nubina?" she asked me. I'm like duh…what the fuck she think. "Uh…yeah…I'm bout to meet up with her right now, so I'll see you around," I said excusing myself. Not interested in holding no conversations right now.

"I heard they together…are they together?" I heard her girlfriend ask her as I began to scan the line of cars.

In the meantime I do believe I see Chuck's huge head in one of the vehicles a way's down, so I advance toward the car. It's just as well cause the ropes leading to the red carpet premiere line start on that end. Yeah…that's them…I'm glad I was here in time. As the car pulled up in the line, I walked over to open the door for her and help her out of the car.

"Yo Chuck, what's good," I called out to our driver.

"Nothing man, just this crazy traffic," he answered, "So do you guys need me to remain in the city?"

"Naw, you can take it on back in," I replied, "I drove in so we won't need a ride back. Thanks."

"No problem," he said, "I'll see you guys tonight at the after party."

"Cool," I said as I helped Nube out of the vehicle.

"Murad," she said in a low voice. I didn't answer her right away...I was just staring at her. She was looking red carpet stunning with a beautiful azure blue silk chiffon pleated trapeze dress...I think that's what they call it, and accentuating silver jewelry that just set off her beautiful honey colored complexion. She was sporting her curls today, but they were twisted up in a sexy up-do, and she topped the look off with a pair of sexy strapped sandals.

"This way please," I heard one of the coordinators say, gesturing for us to step up behind the ropes that started the red carpet. "Do you have your passes?" he asked, "I mean...I recognize you two...you Jersey's royal couple...I just have to ask as a matter of policy"

"Sure, it's not a problem," I said flashing him our passes. Hmmm...Jersey's royal couple, is that the word on the street I'm thinking as I took Nube's hand and proceeded to the end of the line which was moving along rather swiftly. As I took her hand, then and only then did I get that little vibe from her, and I turned to see her looking at me with her pretty brown eyes.

"What's going on Nube?" I asked her. She didn't answer, she just looked at me with them eyes of hers. "You know what," I told her, "Don't even do it to yourself Bae...you blazed as usual...don't even trip. I promise you, once the movie's over and the credits start to rolling, the world will have witnessed yet another quality attribute of Nubina."

"Murad," she finally opened her mouth to speak, "I love you."

Awwww damn...she just melted my heart like a Mr. Softee's cone on the hot cement. I didn't have time to respond as the line moved up and we were next in the spotlight on the red carpet. Paparazzi flashing, questions being fired away, posing for pictures. In between it all I took my thumb and traced little circles in her hand. We answered all the questions for My9 News, and BET then proceeded on down the line taking pictures all the way. We met up with her co-stars, directors and other industry folks along the way, and gave our share of acknowledgments and greetings before we actually took our seats. The executive producer of the film took the stage to thank everyone for coming out to support the premiere and to thank the cast for what he noted would be a box-office hit. And as the lights went down and the theme song started to roll, I placed my arm around her, turned to her and gave her the most sensually tender kiss I could give. And as she leaned into me to watch the movie, I whispered to her, "I love you too Nube."

Murad

What can I say...Nube nailed that shit like a construction worker. The movie was a hit and the audience gave a standing ovation at the end. I was filled to the brim with pride and admiration. I was also glad that her confidence was restored after viewing the entire movie. I guess it is natural to be apprehensive your first time out in a new venue. But my girl aced that shit and then some. We spent the better part of an hour chatting, accepting and giving congratulations to everyone present. Of course there was more picture taking, especially of the movie cast. I waited patiently...no problem. Besides the movie being a success, I was on a mental high...Nube told me she loved me. I mean we been so busy being tight with one another all this time, it never occurred to me before that we have never verbally expressed a confirmation of our feelings to one another. "Murad..I love you" she had said. Man...that shit keeps running thru my mind. She has no idea how much that means to me, or how much it meant for me to reciprocate the same "I love you too Nube." I have never told a woman that I loved them before. She's the first. Not that I never have...loved before...I once did...but circumstances just got in the way of me letting her know. This time around I'm positive, and I'm ready to tell Nube I love her every day...all day. I can't help but stand here and smile as she poses once again with her cast members. She gave an awesome performance. So surreal...so unique...my girl. Damn...that's my girl!!

Nubina

Wow...I am like in shock. I'm so amped about the movie. We got that off...I mean I got that off too. I mean...I'm so overwhelmed by my own performance. I can't believe that was me up on that screen. And all the picture taking, mingling, and getting accolades from the actors who do this as a craft. It's very uplifting to say the least. And as if the movie wasn't enough, did I mention that Murad loves me? He said he loves me!!! You know how many times in the past I've heard those words from a man; too many times to even count. But somehow coming from him, I feel like it's the real thing. Perhaps it's because I've known him for so long on a completely different level. I've seen him operate in many arenas, but it's come to my attention that we've got our own private arena and it operates under our own accord. So yes...I believe him...and I'm feeling like tonight should be the night we cross our last threshold. I'm looking at him from the corner of my eye as we take this last picture. Standing there so patient and supportive, not to mention looking like his own version of a movie star. You know Rod...always immaculate in his attire. Jewelry flashing, rocking them Louis Vuitton Millionaires and that gorgeous Tillman DNA speaking for itself. He is so damn appealing to me right now, I could cry. Even though I'm enjoying this all, I'm so ready to be done with this and just go be alone somewhere with him. We've had a lot of busy days prior to the premiere and I'm sorry to be thinking so selfishly, but I could pass on this after party and go straight home and lock us both in for 2 days. Gee...two whole days locked up with Murad...what the hell else could a girl ask for. Hmmmm....reminder to myself...have him pencil that in on the schedule. "Yeah," I say as I laugh out loud.

Chapter 27
The After Party

Nubina

The music is banging...liquids flowing, congratulations and hugs left and right. Yeah...we at the After Party. Although I just wanted to be alone with Rod...this promotional thing kinda comes with the territory. I can't disappoint the people that were coming out tonight to support me, and I sure as hell can't disappoint Murad. He wants this for me tonight...so I'm here. And you know what...it's cool. I'm seeing a lot of people I haven't seen for a minute, and it feels good to know that they are here for me tonight. My sister Lani, and Sumira are here as well as Chanda, Kira, Donnella, Kiyma, Bree and...hell...the whole crew. The majority of the Tillman fellas are all coming thru tonight as well, so tonight is definitely going to be one filled with adventure.

"So girl," Lani asked me as we sat in the reserved VIP section, "How does it feel to have an after party in your honor?"

"Yeah," Sumira kicked in, "Look at you, all famous and whatnot. We had to put up with all your damn talking all them years, and now here you is busting up making movies and thangs."

"I'm still in shock," I answered them, "I can't believe I was in a real live movie. Y'all wait until you all see me up on the screen. You gonna be surprised to see me...it's likes its me...but watching a whole nother me. You'll see. Murad's gonna get a couple of VIP passes for the nation wide opening next week, and I'll make sure you guys get passes."

"Make sure you don't forget mine," Chanda said, "I'm gonna need like 10."

"Oh girl, I don't know about all that," I replied, "I don't even know how many he's getting." She was always trying to get more bounce for her ounce...she got issues. But tonight was my night, I ain't letting nobody get me in a funk.

"Listen missy," Kira said, "Tell me something. Word on the street is that you and Murad have been a little more friendly than business partners. Is the word correct?" Wow…I hadn't even realized that I had not submitted my decision to the "board" for approval. Guess I've been really busy cause I usually do share, but what the hell, I'm my own woman.

"Yes m'am, the word is speaking the truth this time. Murad and I are together." I answered her.

"Tania," Sumira vehemently stated, "Murad…since when? What the hell…what about JT? I don't believe this."

Damn…I'd forgotten that JT and I was Sumira's dream hook-up. She had wanted us to be together for a long time, so she was so proud of herself when we decided to take a chance at it.

"Well actually, it's been about 3 months now," I answered.

"3 months Tania," Lani said, "I'm your sister and you ain't even put me up on it." I thought about that and replied,

"We'll 3 months since we made that choice, but we have grown incredibly close in the last 2 years and…"

"Tania…they brothers," Sumira cut in, "And we talking about Murad…Tania, you know how Rod get down. He ain't nothing but a whore, girl, with a capital H. How you gonna be with him? I mean…be with him for what Tania?"

"Listen Mira," I said, "I know that I've made mistakes in the past when it comes to men, but I'm telling you this time I honestly feel that I've made the right choice. Yes Murad has had his share of women, but he's probably no more of a whore than the next man. His actions are just amplified because of who he is and his popularity in the community. And even given that…it's all in the past now. Murad hasn't had time for other women since he's been managing my career. We are together about 80% of the time and the other 20% he's on the grind negotiating new deals for me…for us…so there is very little time for women."

"You know what…" Bree said, "She's kinda right. They're always away together on trips; traveling and working. When does he have time for women, and when did she have time for JT?"

"Bree," Sumira answered still hostile, "They brothers…what kind of way is that?"

"Well personally," Chanda chimed in, "I ain't mad at her, cause even though all them Tillman men look good…Murad is the finest mutha fucka going…so hell…I say do you girl."

“Oh yeah, I can expect that coming from you.” Sumira responded to her.

Chanda looked at her sideways and said, “What’s that supposed to mean?”

Knowing how things can get between them two, Kira intercepted, “Sumira…perhaps Murad has changed. Like they said, he’s making moves, he’s boosting her career, he’s taking her places in life.”

“Ain’t nobody hearing me when I’m talking,” Sumira said, “They are brothers!!”

“Mira,” I stepped in, “first of all…things are not always as they appear to be. Yes JT and I started off trying to make a go of things, but we never really elevated within the relationship, he was very busy with his religious studies and he couldn’t attend a lot of my functions and…”

“Cause he is a Christian man,” she replied cutting me off, “he is doing positive things for himself and living under the Lord”

Okay…now she aggravating me. “Sumira…you know what…not that I have to explain my choices to you, but for the record, JT dumped me.”

“ Oooo…What?” came all the exclamations from the group.

“That’s right…he decided that the path I was taking was not one that his religious background could support, so he broke things off with me. So before you go pass judgment on me and Murad, maybe you, JT and the Lord need to go have a conference and see if you all can come up with a reason why I deserved that after 2 years of loyalty to him.” I got up from the table, sorry to have broken my own vow to remain funkless tonight.

“Listen guys, I’ll be back thru a little later,” I explained to them all. “There’s a couple of other people I need to see before the night is thru. Keep it warm till I get back and the drinks in VIP are on the house…so enjoy.”

I quickly left in search of a fresh atmosphere, so that I could restore my prior mindset. This is supposed to be a damn night of celebration. Damn…how she got the nerve to give me attitude. Well…I guess it does look a little shady from the outside looking in, but people need to understand that life’s perceptions all depend upon what side of the fence you on. Let me take a walk out on the back patio. I could use some fresh air. As I stepped past the bar on my way to seeking refuge, I feel a gentle grip on my elbow, pulling me in and I turn to see who bears such audacity and...Trey. Okay...I'm thinking, what else is this evening going to bring.

"Hey Superstar," he said hugging me.

"How are you Trey...surprised to see you here," I answered.

"Well you remember Bryan right," he said indicating his friend sitting next to him.

"Oh...hey Bryan," I acknowledged his buddy.

"Well his company happened to have complimentary tickets to the premiere, and he had the wisdom to know that I would appreciate being one of the first to view you on the big screen," Trey finished off holding on to my hand that he failed to release after the hug.

"The movie was great Tania," Bryan said, "You did your thing."

"Why thank you Bryan," I replied.

"Yes Beena," Trey interjected, "You gave a stellar performance. I always knew that your special attributes would prevail."

"Well that's nice of you to say Trey," I responded, not trying to get into too much of a verbal exchange. I really just wanted to get out to the patio and get some fresh air.

"Listen," I said, "I've got to catch up with an old friend before she leaves, so I'll holla at you later. Cool?"

Before letting my hand go, Trey threw in, "I hope that you have given some consideration to our conversation at the book store." When I didn't reply to that statement he went on to say, "Well...any chance you'll save me a dance tonight?"

"No problem Trey...you got it," I said releasing myself and walking away. Who is he kidding? I used to beg that man to dance with me to no avail. Guess he had to say something for a lack of anything else better to say. Hope I can make it outside before I run into anyone else. Hmmm...I haven't seen Murad for a minute, maybe I'll look him up once I finish with my breath of fresh air.

Chapter 28

It's About To Go Down

Dream

Now this is whas'up. This right here is the place to be. "Yo Rod," I said up over the noise, "This is Aight. This place look like it's the spot and shit is poppin. This is perfect for an after party."

"Yeah...I know how to make it do what its' supposed to." Murad kicked back to me, "Nube is well respected here, and word of mouth is all it takes to get the crowd to come out and show support. I am so damn proud of her, ain't no telling how far she gonna take all this." I had to turn and give my big brother Murad a look. There was no fake to his funk on this, bruh here is serious.

"So you really do care about Nube huh?" I asked him.

"Man...like I ain't never cared for nobody or anything ever before," he responded, "I mean...I could see me stopping right here." And as if to emphasize his point he stopped dead in his tracks. "I see me and Nube going for the long haul... shit is that crucial for me. You know what I mean?" he asked me with this deep far gone expression on his face. I'm standing here speechless; I mean I can't call it. Rod has always been the MVP of all players, with a roster of over the top honey's signed up on his home team. I had never expected to see him zoned out over NO female...let alone a female that used to be his brother's lady. I still don't know how I'm feeling about all that right now, so I just reply to him, "Wow...shit is that serious?"

"Mutha fucka...don't make me say it again," he said laughing and punching me in the arm.

"All right...alright," I replied laughing with him.

"Yo...I'ma bout to hit up this bar. You want something?" he said to me.

"Yeah...sure...why not," I answered, "Let me see how smooth the drinks go down at Sarafin's."

"Hey...they go down smooth as hell, when you not paying for them. I'll get your first round," Murad said.

As we made our way to the bar we stopped several times for handshakes and people to acknowledge him. Some throwing in a plug or two, with promises to hit him up later. Murad played the part...did his thing, and finally we made our way to the bar.

"So what you having?" he asked me.

"Let me get a Sour Apple martini." I replied.

"I'll get the order in just as soon as."…. For some reason his words stopped in mid-air, and he was gazing off to the left with a twisted look on his face.

"Yo Rod...whas' up? Something wrong?" I asked him.

"This clown," he replied.

"Who...what clown? What...something bout to go down?..Let me know."

"Naw," he said, "That fucking Trey dude is up in here."

"Trey?" I'm thinking out loud, "Who the hell is Trey?"

"Ole' scheming ass bastard Nube used to be with," he answered. Now my mind is really swirling. What the hell..Trey...she used to be with JT, now Murad. What's this chick packing?

"Well when"….I started, and he cut me off with, "Don't even go there Dream, she ain't been with him in over 3 years."

"Oh, cause I was about to say..."

"About to say what?" he sliced with his tone daring me.

"Nothing Rod...nothing. I'm checking myself right now. No...judgment... here. So what's the deal with him? You two got beef?" I asked.

"Not really...long as dude understand his status and stay the fuck away from Nube. Other than that, that nigga can bounce off of my shine forever."

Damn if as soon as the words were out of his mouth, Nube walked in from the corridor, and as she passed by the far end of the bar, Trey reached out and grabbed her gently by the elbow. He pulled her in for a hug, and she responded with a quick pat, and quickly released herself. He held on to one of her hands and cheesed and chatted with her for a minute or two before she excused herself and moved on. The whole time Rod stood there with a tight face and them demonic eyes. I had a feeling in my gut that something was about to go down and the shit wasn't gonna be good.

"Excuse me Dream," he said, "I got some shit to take care of." For a minute I just stood there, and then I figure, let me trail him cause Murad can be vicious with his. I watched as he slid right up next to dude by the bar, and put a drink order in, leaned in on the bar with his elbows as he turned to this Trey dude and acknowledged him.

"Whas'up?," he kicked off to him.

"Nothing," Trey dude shot back at him, "My man Bryan got some VIP tickets to the premiere, and we just came out to support Beena."

"So you came to support Nube," Murad answered correcting him, "Okay...that's cool and all, support is good. But Trey...I just need to clarify this for you this one time, cause I'm not in the practice of revamping shit I say once I've spoken...you need to stay away from Nubina. I do believe things have long expired between you two and it ain't gonna go down good at all if you continue to "conveniently" pop-up in her space."

Trey raised backed with a look like this mutha, and asked, "So just so that I'm understanding you correctly...uh...Mr. Bodyguard, are you like threatening me?"

"Well apparently you have misunderstood me," Murad said, "Cause I don't threaten nor do I promise...I'm just giving you the actual. Whether you have the capacity to understand it or not...is on you."

"Fine...well let me give you some actual," Trey answered back. At this point I stepped a little closer cause I need to be within wailing distance if thangs start to pop off.

"Tomorrow ain't promised to nobody and neither is Tania. She's a beautiful woman, as pure as beauty comes. She's more than capable of deciphering her wants and her want not's all by herself," Trey finished.

"That she is...that she is," Murad started, nodding his head as if recognizing a truth, "But that shit's a little stale coming from your monkey-ass. Where was all this insight, when her beauty was upon you? You wasted her precious time and beauty while you ran around beating up on every ass moving."

"Okay," Trey responded, "You got that...But...What I'm kind of not understanding is... how is that your concern? Cause from what I can understand...she was dealing with your brother...was she not? Are y'all into passing or something?"

That last comment from Trey yielded no response. Murad slowly raised up off the bar, took off his watch, took off his rings and put them in his pocket. When he looked up, that demonic look was back and I could just smell ugly in the air.

"Damn," I muttered to myself. I was quite sure that I would not be able to do a damn thing about the wheels that were set in motion. God must have been feeling my tension cause at that precise moment, Nube walked up and hugged Murad from behind totally unaware of what had just went down. Murad tensed and exhaled heavily to release his disappointment in being deterred from knocking this cat out.

"Hey Rod," she said coming up from behind him taking his hand, "I've been looking for...you. Rod...what's going on?" she asked as she noticed his lack of response and seeing Trey, Bryan and myself standing there all bull faced. She looked back and forth from Rod to Trey and asked, "Trey?"

"Hey...you need to speak to ole' boy," Trey answered, "I don't know what set him off... but he is tripping."

"Nube," Murad finally responded in a low even tone, "I need you to slide to the far left."

To my surprise she said "Alright." Before she stepped, she tip-toed to whisper something in his ear, kissed his cheek, then she backed away slowly releasing his hand as she left. "Trey...Bryan, you all enjoy the rest of your evening. And Dream...I'll see you later."

Murad stood there for a minute, exhaled then said, "Trey...I can respect the fact that you a man to recognize the truth. You right...I'm tripping."

What...I screamed in my head. What the fuck is going on? Murad...back down from a fight. What the...what the shit that girl done said to him...I mean what the shit has she done to him...what?

As I stood there with my mouth open I heard him go on to say, "Although I prefer to drop kick ya' ass, as soon as look at you...and I'm still bulls-eyed with you staying away from Nubina, you are a guest here tonight. Please accept my apology, and as my lady said...enjoy the rest of your fucking evening." With that he picked up our drinks from the bar, turned his back and said to me, "Boy...close ya damn mouth before I drop a nickel in it." I did just that and followed him stage right.

Trey

"Did he just say his lady?" I asked Bryan as I stood there watching them walk away.

"Uh...yeah," he answered me, "And from the way she was all on him...I believe that to be a true statement."

"But she told me that she was dealing with his brother, and The Bodyguard was just her manager," I responded to that fact.

"Well either you misunderstood, or things have changed," Bryan said.

"Yeah...but Beena ain't the kind of woman to get down like that. I wonder what that's all about?" I verbalized my puzzlement out loud.

"Well...it may be a mystery as to which one she's with, but we both know who she ain't with...you. And for that...your ass is stupid. You fucked up Trey," Bryan said ripping me.

"Yeah B," I answered as I fell into a zone, "Tell me something I don't know."

Chapter 29
Just A Matter Of Instinct

Nubina

I had just gotten back in from getting my breath of air...I wasn't even out there but 10 minutes, when I decided to just on and look for Murad. It hadn't taken me but a minute to locate him right at the bar where I'd just obviously missed him. Now I don't know what I had walked up into between Murad and Trey...but I do know Rod's temper, so I just gave him a little reminder that essentially we were still at work, Trey is a guest, and he was gonna have to be real professional about it all and fuck him up at another time. I'm saying the last thing we need is a write up in the media about how the manager of the newly acclaimed movie star was thumping on people at the After Party of the movie premiere. Anyway I doubt anything that was said was worth tussling about. I left them to work it all out, and since I didn't hear anything thing jumping off as I walked away, I went on to visit the ladies room.

Thank God I thought as I walked in to find it empty. I'm really not in the mood for anymore one on one conversation tonight. Someone entered while I was in the stall, and I hoped that they'd be in there for awhile, cause I planned on checking my appearance when I came out. I flushed and went on out to wash my hands, and fix my hair. As I was re-pinning some of the curls, the occupied stall door opened and who steps out of the stall but Jazmine. I'll be damn...I need this shit here like I need a hole in my head.

"Well, well, well," she just had to say, "If it ain't the Queen of Brotherly love."

"Good evening Jazmine," I replied keeping my cool.

"Good evening my ass Nube!! Do you know how long I've been waiting to give you a piece of my mind," she shot back.

"Well apparently you've been holding on to that piece for quite some time cause I haven't seen you since like what...April?' I answered her.

"Don't give me none of your smart ass intellectual bullshit Nube. I ought a fuck you up for coming between me and Murad," she angrily stated.

"Well Jazz," I started, "I don't know what to tell you, cause if you think I'm gonna stand here and trade insults and comments back and forth with you over a man then you are sadly mistaken. That's something that I just don't do. I am well beyond that. Now if you have some unresolved issues with a man then you need to take that up with him. I cannot compensate you for any wrong doing on some man's part."

"What the fuck you talking bout some man...you know good and well I'm talking about Murad," she spit back, "Murad pulled some fucking foul ass shit on me...and it's all because of you. We was fine until you started getting up into his head and what not trying to play shit off like you so innocent. And then to top it all off, your nasty ass was fucking JT and now you up and fucking Murad." Okay... people up in here tonight on a roll, thinking they got shit to say to me. I think I've taken enough verbal abuse for the evening...I'm done.

"Jazmine," I replied to her tirade, "I'm sorry you feeling some kind of way but really...I don't need to stand here and be disrespected with your verbal tantrum. So...I'm gonna leave you to get yourself together and...I guess I'll see you around."

As I turned to leave she called out, "Oh hell no bitch...I wasn't thru wit you," and grabbed one of the ties on the back of my top. I think I heard the sash rip away from the fabric, and that sound just threw me into instinct mode. Now Jazmine is kinda taller than me at 5'8" so I threw up a nice high kiyah kick to the right that caught her just between the chest and armpit area. She let out a gasp, and her big ass came tumbling forward toward me. I didn't want her falling on me so again...instinctively...I hauled off and popped her in the eye, and she fell backward onto the bathroom floor holding her eye screaming.

"Oh you bitch...you fuckin' bitch," she yelled, "I'ma get you...oh my eye." Damn I'm thinking...I guess I kinda hurt her huh?

"Jazmine," I said, "Are you okay? Do you need some help?"

"Fuck you Nube," she answered me, "I got something for your ass...you just wait."

"Well okay," I said, "It's not like I wanted things to go down like this, it's just that...you put your hands on me...and...I can't go for that. Besides the only hands that are authorized to un-do any clothing from my body belong to **my** man...Murad Tillman. So if you don't need any further assistance in here, like I said, I'll see you around."

As I turned to walk out of the bathroom, another young lady entered and cried out, "Oh my God!!! ...is she alright?"

"Well I asked her if she was okay and she told me to leave her alone," I answered, taking one last look in the mirror, "She'll be okay...she's just suffering from a little green eye. It'll pass. Oh and tell her when she gets up...she needs to wash her hands, cause that's what's nasty." And with that I then turned and walked on out of the bathroom leaving Jazmine on the floor and the other young lady helplessly staring down at her.

Chapter 30

Still More After Party

Nubina

My night of celebration was beginning to have the effects of a nightmare. My promises not to get into a funk tonight have all but been obliterated. The hell with this...this is my damn night...this is my After Party...I'm going to find my man...my baby and we gonna celebrate got-damnit!!! We worked hard for this...no one else. So let me get myself together and go make this happen. I went in search of Murad, and was sidelined by just a few more well wishers. I made my conversations short, cause a sister was on a mission. I want to be next to him...all up under him; I wanna feel him and celebrate in my own way. Something stemming from earlier today is moving like a driving force within me, and I am craving the hell out of him tonight. I made my way back to the outdoor patio area and Bingo...there he was leaning up against the flowerbed wall, on the phone. He spotted me and gestured for me to join him. I was more than glad to oblige him and stepped right into his embrace. Ahh...I can't even explain the yearning sensation that overcame me as I leaned into him while he finished his conversation.

"Yeah...most definitely...most definitely," he said, "I guess I can get that in to you early next week, and then we'll make a date to come down and seal the deal. Yeah...I'm sure. You got it...later."

"Yo Nube," he said to me holding me at arms length, "Guess what big time rapper from the ATL wants you on a hook for his next single."

"Atlanta...and we talking somebody that I would work with? Does his name start with an L?"I asked him.

"The one and only Nube," he answered me laughing.

"Wow...me...he wants to work with me. Ahh...this is hot...this is great," I replied giddy with the thought.

"Yeah girl...you blazing left and right. I told you Nube...you all that," he responded.

"Wow," I answered back, "something else to put in our cup to celebrate. And that's what I came to do Mr. Tillman, so let's go get our celebrate on. Our people are waiting for us in VIP...let's go rock it out."

"You got it," he responded as he leaned up off the wall trailing me inside as I lead the way holding on to both of his hands. I was not separating from him anymore for the night. In fact if I have my way...we'll wake up together in the morning.

When we reached the VIP area, all the Tillman's, friends and fam were present and already revved up.

"Ho," they shouted out upon our arrival. "They in the building. Congratulations y'all."

"Hey Princess," Lonnie came over and hugged me, "I heard you took it out girl. What you know about acting?"

"Awww Lonie, it was a challenge, but I did it. Someone I know had a lot of faith in me," I said looking to Murad, "And I didn't want to let him down."

"Girl you could never let me down," he answered me giving me a sultry look that I wanted to bottle up and display as a keepsake.

"So Rod," Sharief asked, "When you gonna hook us up with the movie passes, so we can check out Lil Bit's acting debut."

"Oh for sure," Rod said, "I'm supposed to get them Fed-Exed on Monday. I got you...don't worry...that shit's a given."

"Yo Rod," Brick called out, "Whas good nigga...this party is banging!" Oh boy...Brick done had too much too drink. His wild side is coming out.

"Yo B," Rod answered him, "Everythang is everythang. I see you enjoying yourself," indicating to the young lady Brick had cuffed up under him.

"You know it...you know it," Brick responded, "Listen I gotta holla at you about something later."

"Aight," Rod answered, "Hit me up tomorrow. I'll be home for a few days."

I chatted with my girls for a minute or two; I noticed that Sumira was still in a huff. Oh well...I'm not going to try and placate her. She's got her own ideas on the way things should be and I'm going to leave that for her to deal with. In the midst of the mingling and celebrating, the DJ got into a zone, and threw on some old school. I'm talking bout "Move Your Body." *Gotta have house music all night long...*The crowd went wild and everybody got up to dance. Rod grabbed me up and pulled me onto the floor along with everyone else.

"Yeah party people," the DJ rocked, "Welcome to Club Sarafin's. This is the After Party ...and we doing it up royally tonight. We got them both... here with us tonight...give it up for our royal couple, Murad Tillman aka King Midas, cause everything he touches...turns to gold, and not to mention... the one...and only...Queen Nubina!!!" The club responded favorably to the shout out, with our little VIP section taking the lead, as Rod and I were highlighted by the house spotlights.

"They doing big things and tonight we out to celebrate and support the acting debut of Queen Nubina...Big ups to her. She just did her thang in the new smash hit "Finders Keepers." Make sure you check out our girl...representing for Jersey. The movie opens nationwide next weekend." The crowd continued to rock it out and then the DJ pulled out the ultimate master mix and threw on "Without You."

My life is so empty...like a puzzle you're the missing piece. It's hard tryin to make it without you..oooo...oh. You're the missing link yeah...like one and one makes twoooooo...I just can't go without you...got to get you back into my life. I don't know what I'd do...without you....oooooo. As the opening line to the song filtered thru the club, the place went bananas. I love that song, and just started to let loose and get into it. Murad was right with me and we were finally caught up in celebrating which is what we came to do. He held my hands upward as I danced with my back to him. Ahhh...our vibe was on the money, and must have shifted itself up to the DJ, cause he got back on the mic.

"Yeah...New Jersey...this is the Club Sarafin's After Party. And we got Jersey's royal couple here tonight. They killing it people...they killing it," he goes on returning the spotlight to us. As we danced I turned to face Murad looking up at him smiling and he looked down at me returning the smile. As he pulled me into him, I wrapped my arms around his waist as he draped his across my shoulders.

"Murad," I started, so caught up in the moment I barely heard the voice of the DJ in the background.

"Yeah...this is Sarafin's...the After Party. And yes...the royal couple is here...with us. The body language is speaking volumes and I wonder if we can put them rumors to rest tonight," he went on," Could it be...could it be?"

"Murad," I start again as the DJ drones on, "Baby...I was thinking tonight...well I need...I'm saying...can we..."

"Tonight Nube," he said rescuing me from my anxiety.

"Tonight Murad?" I asked raising my voice an octave in surprise.

"Tonight Nube."

"Are you sure?" I asked him leaning in reaching for his lips.

"Tonight Nube," he replied resting his lips upon mine.

And as we stood there in the middle of Sarafin's confirming tonight's appointment with our nonstop kiss, the DJ put us on blast, "Yes...it's official...this is a Sarafin's exclusive...remember people...you got it here first...King Midas and Queen Nubina are a couple. Word on the street has proved its worth...they are together!!! Congrats and much love to the royal couple!"

There was a mixed reaction of hoot's, hollers and congratulations, as well as some what...when...really. But I was in no position to acknowledge who felt what, cause I just stood right there in Murad's arms, lips locked and swaying to the music. So as the music played on and the lyrics bounced off the walls...I missed the hasty retreat of Trey as he left the club sullenly, only to bump into Jazmine on her way out in a tiff, who were both almost run over by Sumira...as she stormed out in a rage.

Chapter 31
At Last

Nubina

It's 2 a.m. and it's been a long day. Murad and I are trying to leave the club, but we're still being sidelined by guests and well-wishers. Then of course there's the issue of appointing designated drivers, as Brick and a few others were now under the influence and not able to drive. Murad helped get them all squared away, so that we would not be roped into dropping anybody else off. After all…we had a pending date that we were both anxious to keep. He walked me around to the passenger side of the truck and helped me up into the seat. He retreated to the driver's side to get in, and once he closed the door, he took my hand and kissed my fingers. "Where to Beautiful?" he asked me.

"My house," I managed to get out. I mean…the thought…the scenario that's been running thru my mind since this afternoon was about to become a reality. I was going to get my chance to be alone with him, and I was so ready for us to put the icing on this cake. He has no idea of the emotional stage that I've been in all day, nor the sensual feelings that I've been suppressing. Ooohhh…I'm nervous, I'm tripping, yet at the same time…I'm thinking he can't get me home fast enough.

Murad

This has been one long day of numerous events…but I'm getting ready to partake in the most important event of my life. Nube and I are all sexed up and ready to put it down. We taking this party to her place and I'm trying not to show my excitement as I make the drive over there. I can't believe that I'm nervous. I've been with a lot of women in my life, so it ain't like this shit is new…but damn…this is Nube. I can't tell you how many times I've imagined what this night would be like, and now that it's here…man…I can't call it.

The ride to her house was not long at all, so there was little time for a reprieve. I pulled up into her driveway and turned off the ignition. I could tell that she was nervous...but she don't even have a clue...I'm just as nervous. Being the man in this situation...I prefer that she be at ease, and I just have to handle my feelings accordingly. So once again I took her hand and kissed her fingers, "Nube...are you okay with all this?" I asked her.

"I will be, once we get inside," she answered.

"Well aight then" I smiled at her and winked, "let's take it inside."

I climbed out of the truck and came around to get her from the other side. I took her hand and helped her out then closed the door behind me. The touching of our flesh set off another sexual surge, and we just came together again and resumed our kissing. Ahhh man she got me going and just don't know it.

"Murad," she said heavily after a good minute had passed, "I need to get inside."

"Okay," I answered her just as heavy. So we backed up all the way to the door, and as she turned to put the key in the lock, I embraced her from behind kissing her neck. She semi-moaned and swung the door open. Once we entered, and closed the door...it was on.

I don't know what came over the both of us but we were on each other non-stop. I nibbled her lips, and explored her tongue all the way to the beginning of her tonsils. My hands involuntarily felt the need to touch something...anything, and they decided to cup her full breasts. She let go a small whine on contact and that raised the temperature in the room a few degrees. She started to unbutton my shirt as I backed her up into the wall. I needed to feel some skin so I began to undo the ties on the back of her blouse. One of the ties came off...oops...but I just kept going. Once I got them all loose I slid the top down and bam...they were right there all voluptuous and waiting for me. I cupped up the left one and took it in my mouth sucking and teasing the nipple and Nube went crazy. She moaned out loud, and proceeded to unbuckle my belt and undo my pants. She succeeded in getting the zipper down and reached in to visit ole boy. He was already poised and ready, and the touch of her smooth soft hands put him on high alert. I wasn't ready for the reaction from her touch and moaned out loud…

"Ahh shit." This was not how I envisioned our first time, but for some reason we just could not help ourselves.

In response to her touch, I too needed to get possession of something below the waist and grabbed a hold of both cheeks squeezing firmly as she squirmed beneath my touch. I ceased the squeezes to reach around the front to unbutton the buttons on the sailor pants she had on. There were four buttons on both sides and as I got them loose, she made a point to unbutton my shirt at the cuffs and relieved me of the shirt altogether. She pulled the remaining t-shirt up over my head to reveal my bare chest where she began to deliver delicate teasing kisses. In the meantime I returned to the pants and proceeded to get her out of them. In the process of getting them down, I slid my hand up in the V-spot and she all but screamed, "Ahh…Murad."

"Damn Nube," I said in surprise, "You ready like that?" She was dripping wet and my fingers were just slip sliding all over the place…and damn that shit felt good.

"Murad," she breathed out heavily stepping out of her pants and sandals, "Baby…I can't wait…I can't Rod…not another minute."

"Nube, baby," I answered her kissing her neck while squeezing her breasts, "you don't wanna go upstairs?"

"Ooohhh Rod," she moaned, "I can't…just…Rod." I looked around to review my options and decided that the desk we were standing next to would have to do. I lifted her up on the desk and the slanted French doors served just right for a back rest. Kicking off my shoes and stepping out of my pants, I leaned over to once again tease her nipples with my tongue and she once again hit a high note.

"Ooohhh Rod…please…now," she said. "Nube …we don't have a con…"

"Murad…" she pleaded cutting me off. I positioned myself right at her front door, but before I entered I said, "Nube," giving her the head twist, and she responded, "Please…yes." So with them sexy eyes egging me on…I entered.

On the first few inches in we both matched each other in notes of Ahhhhh. Damn...I'm thinking...this is it. As I proceeded to go the remaining way, she gave off an Uunh...instead. It was unusually tight and I must have been hurting her.

"Nube," I said in alarm, "Baby...am I hurting you?"

"Rod...don't worry...about it," she answered, "Just... don't... stop."

"You sure?" I asked her forging my way slowly.

"Yes," she breathed out. "Then relax Nube...relax. I'll be easy. Okay?" Damn...I didn't figure her to be this keyed up about it, so I took my time slowly moving in and out as a precaution. I leaned over and gave her a sumptuous kiss to calm her nerves. Things started to loosen a little and I rose up to watch my delivery. The reflection of the moonlight coming in thru the window allowed me to see her pretty little face enjoying it all. As things started to feeling good, she began to make the most beautiful noises and moans to match the strokes. I just kept it coming and watched her react. We couldn't have been at it more than 2 minutes when her reactions started to escalate. Her breathing became shorter and shorter as I continued to deliver, and as she wrapped her legs around my waist she called out my name.

"Murad," she called out softly..."Murad...I'm bout to come."

"Already Nube...you sure?" I asked her just as softly kissing her neck.

"I'm sure," she answered, "You... just...don't know...Murad. Ahh...I...."

"Baby its okay," I answered her, "It's okay...do what you gotta Nube ...do what you gotta," I told her continuing to kiss her neck.

"Awww...Murad...Murad...Baby...ahhh...ahhh....aaaaaaah," she screamed out as she clung to me and spilled her sweetness all over me.

"Ooohhh Murad," she said as she nestled her face into my neck, "I'm sorry."

"You sorry for what Nube?" I asked continuing to kiss her neck.

"For just bum-rushing and killing the moment," she said.

"You ain't got nothing to be sorry for Nube. Now I'd be sorry if you plan on us stopping...cause you know I'm not done with you," I told her kissing her mouth, sucking on her bottom lip. I picked her up from the desk and sat down in the accompanying chair, keeping us intact. As if inspired by the new position, she moaned low, and returned the intense kisses. I could feel that she was ready for another go round. So I switched the kisses from her lips, to down her neck and settled back on her breasts. As my lips latched on to one, I let my fingertips play with the other. She responded with an "aahh" and began to move herself slowly back and forth.

As I concentrated on her breasts, Nube began to put in some serious riding. She had grabbed the back of the wing tip chair and with her feet braced flat on the floor; she began to slide herself up and down the length of me. Wow...I shuddered, not expecting the feeling to overtake me like that, and I released my lips to give off an involuntary groan of pleasure. My audible expression seemed to move her and she increased her movements. Daaammnn...she was working me and I was overwhelmed with the feeling. First off she was still good and tight, and it seemed as if she was grabbing my shit with each stroke. Yeah...stroking...that's what was going down...Nube was stroking me and working my ass up something good. Shit was so good I forgot all about the breasts and grabbed both of her cheeks and massaged them to the tempo of her motions. I guess she was turned on with the feeling cause she was practically on her feet now, putting in mad work...working that arm action like an amped up Viking rowing on a Norwegian sail boat.

"Aahhh... shit...Nube," I said, "baby...you working me over girl...you bout to make me lose it. Slow down Nube...Nube... Aahhh"

"Murad...baby," she answered me, "I can't help it...ahhh...you feel so good Murad, you feel sooo damn good baby."

And feel good...indeed. I can't remember the last time I physically felt so good. I guess for one thing, we was going at it raw, so the skin contact was banging. All this feeling good was going to bring me to a first time thing that I didn't want to encounter, and I sure as hell didn't want that shit on my record, so I decided to make a move to bring her there first; I took my middle finger and tickled the spot right where the two cheeks meet, and Nube went wild…mission accomplished…or so I thought. Cause that move prompted her to look me dead in my eyes as she came projecting her intense ecstasy, while her internal spasms just started clenching on me like little jelly fish and delivering small sensations of suck-ulation to a point which I could no longer contain myself.

"Aaaahh Nube…daaayuumm baaaaaabbby," I gave off, as I let go of everything I had and then some. Ahhh shit, I'm thinking as we sit face to face in the chair holding on to one another as we get ourselves together, she done tarnished my record and turned me into a 2 minute brother for the first time in my life!! Damn!!!

Nubina

Oh…My…God. I just had sex…sex with Murad no less. Oh…my…god…that shit was sooo damn good. Oh man…I know I rushed it all, but I couldn't help myself. It's been so long. And not to mention he don't fall short at all, he feel so good sitting up in me…all 99 inches. I could just sit up here like this all night. Okay…I'm exaggerating, but however many inches…that shit is alright with me.

"Nube," he nuzzles in my ear, "Can you believe what just took place?"

"Are you kidding me, I'm still trynna believe it," I replied. "I mean I guess it's true since we sitting here all glued together."

"Ah yeah, and I'm feeling some kind of way right now. I mean…things were a little quick and spontaneous, but as far as feel good…girl that shit was on fire…I'm still smokin'," he said.

"Oh Rod, I'm sorry," I apologized again, "It's just I was really anxious today with the premiere, and what not, and just a whole lot of emotions going on inside me, Bae…you just don't know how much I really needed you. How much I need to feel you intimately. Not to mention, I still can't believe that we together…oh my god…and we just had sex. You…me…us Murad…how did this happen? All those years we were around each other…but never really around each other, I don't know…passing each other by…I mean…I don't even think you even used to speak to me."

"Aww...go head Nube. I used to speak to you. You used to be sitting over there with Sumira giving me the evil eye and shit, so I stayed in my lane," he said.

"Uh-huh," I answered, "The fast lane...you know the one where all the fast mami's was running in."

"Well you know what," he said, "It don't even matter, cause we speaking now, and I'm liking everything you've got to say." He complimented his statement with a prize winning kiss, which stirred something up in me again.

"Oh Murad," I replied starting to wiggle around.

"Oh Murad hell," he said. "Girl we taking this adventure upstairs before you turn my ass all black and blue up in this chair." We both bust out laughing, and I reluctantly raised up off of him. Ahh man I didn't want to. He felt soooo good up in there, I could just cry for real.

"Well then let's go King Midas," I said to him, grabbing my things and heading upstairs "I'm ready to see what other golden adventures you possess."

"Hey...look girl...I'm right behind you...believe that," he said.

As I ventured up the stairs, I tried to remember whether or not I'd cleared all the mis-decisions of clothes off of my bed before I came back out to the After Party.

"Nube," I heard him call from the hallway, can I just get a wash rag from the closet and stop in the bathroom?"

"Sure, go head," I answered him, "Bring me one too." When I got in the room, a barrage of clothes on the bed met me, so I proceeded to put them away, while he used the bathroom. I was just about finished when he stumbled into the bedroom.

"Ouch...damn Nube," he called out stepping on something, "what you got in the floor here?" he asked me turning on the light. As I turned around I saw him bending down to pick up my sandal that I'd dropped on the way in. I guess he stepped on it.

"Sorry," I called out as I bent over to pick up a belt from the floor that I had missed. "I guess that I dropped it..." I said turning around to find him staring at me with his mouth open.

"Do that again," he said. And as I stood looking at him confused, he said, "Nube, turn around...please." As I obliged him I heard him say, "Daaayyuuumm...Nube...baby. That ass...it's mesmerizing...so beautiful. Wow...so perfect...so delicious looking. Nube...wow baby," he said approaching me, "This shit here is outta limits...so tempting. Damn I could just..." And he stopped talking and got on his knees and started giving me sweet little sensual kisses on my butt.

"Aww Nube...this is my first time peeping your goods...seeing what you packing, and this ass here is...oh man," he said continuing to kiss and nibble it.

"Murad," I told him breathing heavily, "You getting ready to get something going. Ohhh...Rod...you about to aaaawwww...."

I didn't finish because he reached between my legs and took his fingers and slid them inside me as he continued to kiss and nibble my cheeks. I was held in a suspended animation of pleasure, so I just stood by the side of the bed while he nibbled me, and internally teased me with his fingers. Aaaahhh...I was feeling so good , I didn't even know where I was as I stood there in total ecstasy. He worked them fingers in and out and all up on the right spot. I was a little embarrassed at just how much I was creaming, just running like a faucet, but it was feeling so good, I know I'm about to wake up my neighbors. The more excited I got...the more he pleasured me. At last he said, "Nube...baby...can I bend you over?"

"Oh please do," I answered as he got to his feet and tipped me at the waist. Now actually I've only heard about this, and I ain't about to play myself out trynna touch no toes, so I bent over and placed my hands on the floor, spreading my legs similar to that of one of my yoga positions. As he stood behind me, I heard him say "Nube...awww Nube...this shit is ridiculous," as he rubbed my cheeks softly, as if he was feeling velvet. He then he grabbed a hold of both cheeks, and slid himself inside. I moaned loudly in pleasure and he moaned back just as loud.

"Aww Nube...damn Nube," I heard him say as I know he was getting great pleasure out of watching his own action. I was so in my own space, savoring the feeling of him sliding in and out of me while I was down in this precarious position. Things were not quite as tight as they were downstairs, and he was really getting a chance to offer me more of him; and I took it. The sensation was tripping me out. I really started to get into it and starting rocking back so that I could meet him stroke for stroke.

Murad

Got-damn this girl is off the hook! Who would've ever thought little Nube had a body like this and bedroom flava to go with it. She is bent over like a pro and shit. It's gotta be that yoga...yeah that yoga that she do. She fucking rocking that shit back to me...damn.

"Nube...baby," I started, "You working it bae...you doing it girl." Shit was feeling so damn good. She had opened up a little more, and I was able to get up in there and make shit count. Damn...she feel so good...I can't believe it. I looked down and watched as she worked her legs and kept bringing that ass back to me. She was doing a good job so I stepped it up a notch and went in just a little deeper. She started making her sweet noises again and I knew that I was scoring points. The sweeter her noises, the more intense I took it. But she hung on in there and in order to keep her leverage, she got up on her toes and balanced herself on the balls of her feet and rocked that shit back to me without missing a beat. Now I know that's some of her damn yoga moves, but that shit was escalating my excitement. I had to restrain myself from going hard, cause that ain't how I want shit to be between us. Nube is my sweetheart...my lady...and she deserves nothing but a class act all across the board. But if she keep working me like this, we gonna have a problem. I keep shit coming and she keeps it coming back. I keep hitting it, and she keeps hitting me back. Finally she must be close, cause she takes her noises to the next level and them back body rocks are intensifying.

"Murad," she calls out, "Murad...baby...ohh...ohhh."

"Yeah Nube...you got it girl...if you feeling it...come on with it. Come on Butter...it's all for you girl," I answered her.

"Oh...Murad...baby...oh...oh...I'm...baby," was all she managed to reply. I kept giving it to her and she kept taking it, until finally she took a look backward to watch me in motion. I guess watching me drive shit home must have done it for her and led her down the road to "there." She let out a crazy moan, sounding like a cat in heat. Kinda wild and crazy, but somehow that shit was sexy in a weird way. As she came...she kicked it back to me like a wild cat, and sent me scrambling to keep from losing it. The weird sexy moaning was doing something to my mental, and the next thing you know I had grabbed her by the waist and poured all my pleasure into her shaking and bucking myself. As I managed to bring it down to a less spastic level, I grabbed her around the waist and toppled us over onto the bed on our sides, still intact and breathing like two heavyweight prize fighters.

"Awwww man Nube, what was that?" I asked her trying to recoup.

"I don't know Murad," she answered catching her breath as well.

"You taking me places I ain't never been before. I was just trying to keep up with the flow."

"Nube...I'm blown away," I told her, "I never expected our first time to be like this...so aggressive...so intense."

"Well me either Murad," she replied, "I was so nervous about being with you...worried about disappointing you and all."

"Disappoint who?" I said, "Girl...ain't no disappointment going on with me on any kind of level. Actually I'm looking at you sideways. I would have never pegged you with this bedroom persona."

"Well," she said turning around to face me, releasing us from one another, "My bedroom persona is only as good as my bedroom partner. So if you liked what you was getting, it's cause I liked what you was giving."

"Is that right?" I answered, kissing her lips.

"Oh, that's exactly right, King Midas," she answered me smiling.

"Well tell me something, Queen Nubina," I replied. "Are you always so moist and ready, loud, crazy, sweet, sexy, hot and blazing like you were tonight?"

"I am when I've got the sweetest, most gorgeous, sexy and irresistible specimen of a man sensually provoking me," she said.

"Well I'm good at provoking," I told her, "As a matter of fact...I'm sure that I could schedule it to provoke you on a daily basis."

"Alrighty then," she answered, "I think I could go for the provocation every damn day and then some. For real." We both laughed lightly.

"Besides Rod...we celebrating. This was a night for our cup running over in celebration." she said.

"Yeah...you right," I added, "You put it down in the movie, and you hooking up with one of hip-hops most notorious. That is definitely worth celebrating"

"Not to mention celebrating our love tonight Murad," she added, "Ever since I revealed loving you this afternoon, I've been waiting to be with you this way all day. I mean...I had never allowed myself to say it out loud before today, and today I just felt like I needed to let you know. And once you told me the same...I couldn't keep this suppressed any longer if I tried."

"Yeah Nube," I told her, "you straight on point with that girl. I've been feeling like we've been taking our time crossing that finish line, and something about today, and verbally acknowledging our love had me feeling like tonight was our due date. So trust me...I was on the same page with you back at the club...I was feeling the same way. And I'm glad Nube...I love you, and I want you to be secure with that. I want this night to be the beginning of the many different ways that I express my love for you. "

"Damn...thank you Murad," she told me, "thank you for being so real with me, and always looking out for me. Thank you for loving me, cause this is so new to me. I'm also celebrating the end of 3 years and 8 months of celibacy. And for me to end it encompassed in love is that much more rewarding, so thank you for that as well"

"Oh Nube, you don' have to thank me," I answered, "being with you and loving you is more than I've been waiting for since... What did you say?" I stopped in the middle of my thoughts.

"I thanked you for loving me Rod...the way that a true man should, and in a way like I've never known."

"No Nube...what the hell did you say about 3 years and 8 months of celibacy?" I asked her now sitting up in the bed.

"I've been celibate Murad...for 3 years and 8 months," she answered leaning up on her elbows.

"Nube, baby...how is that possible," I asked her now totally confused, "If my math is correct 3 years and 8 months is longer than the 2 years you and JT were together. Explain to me how that shit adds up?"

"Well Murad...JT and I never had sex," she said. I just sat there...I looked at the ceiling...I looked back at her...then I looked at the ceiling and said, "Nube...shut the fuck up."

"Muuuurad," she whined.

"What?" I answered, "Aight...I'm sorry baby. I don't mean to be crass...but you was with him for 2 years Nube, and you all didn't have sex. Two years Nube...what the fuck was ya'll doing?"

"Well, he was going thru some emotional trauma, and he was not ready to engage in a physical relationship, so we refrained, and built more on a spiritual level."

"But we talking 2 years Nube...2 fucking years," I said totally blown away.

"Yes...and he was not ready to delve on a physical side. He said he didn't want to forsake his religious studies and work he'd put in on his personal self elevation with sexual deviations," she offered.

"Religious what?" I said all annoyed.

"His religious endeavors Rod," she explained, seeming a little bit in a tiff.

"What the hell does religion have to do with it?" I responded, "I'm saying...what religion in the world dictates no sex? People got to procreate and what not, regardless to what religion they follow. That right there sound like some of his own sucker-ass nonsense."

"Well not everybody needs to validate themselves in that way Rod. Perhaps something that went down with Kane's mother affected him to that point. I can definitely understand trying to rebound from deep personal grief," she said.

"I wouldn't give a damn what she did to him," I came right back with, "Ain't no way in hell you gonna be my lady for 2 years and I wouldn't be hitting you off with all the loving that you can handle and then some. Fuck all that grieving nonsense. So you guys just never?"

"Never, Rod," she said.

"Never Nube...he ain't never want to?" I had to question her again.

"I just can't sit here and say that he never wanted to," she answered me.

"But...never Nube?" I came back with.

"Well...,"she started.

"Well what?" I jumped right in on the end of her reply.

"One time...we almost."

"You almost what Nube?" I quizzed her starting to feel some kind of way.

"One time we kind of got into something."

"Something like what Nube?" I pushed on.

"Look Murad," she replied, "this kinda ain't right. The past is the past, and I have not, nor do I intend to quiz you on what you did with who ever from your past. How did we get here?"

"Cause he's my fucking brother...and cause... he my brother," I stated knowing full well that I was dead wrong, but I just had to know.

"Well damn it Rod," she said, "You knew that before we got all into this. Does it really make that much of a difference now?"

"Hell yeah," I shot back, still knowing that I'm wrong as two left shoes.

"Well what is it you wanna know Murad?" she said a shade irritated.

"I wanna know what happened between you...I wanna know." I stated.

"Oh...you wanna know?" she said. "Okay, Murad...it was actually the night that you and I had the fight at the mall about Trey. I was very upset, hurt and I was crying, so he was trying to comfort me. He started off kissing me to calm me down, and then I guess things advanced to touching."

"And?" I busted in asking her as she seemed to pause.

"And nothing...he did manage to get me excited...I asked him for it...but he stopped and said that he couldn't go any further. He didn't want to deflect from his religious...personal progress."

"Okay back up, back up...let's rewind that shit." I told her. "You trying to tell me that ole choir boy never sexed you...as in intercourse?"

"No, Murad." she stated flatly.

"You have got to be kidding me."

"Actually...no I'm not," she said softly sounding a little dejected, "I guess if you and I would have never had that fight, I never would have even gotten that."

I thought about what she said, and decided that maybe I should lighten up a bit. After all, I was willing to be with her before this revelation came about, so exactly what am I tripping on. Besides...she might be feeling a little put down by his reluctance to be with her in that way.

"Alright...but I'm saying Nube," gesturing with my eyes all up and down her body, " You trying to tell me that he could look at all this here and not commence to indulge?"

She looked at me, with them brown eyes going soft and said, "JT has never seen me naked." I had to get the fuck up out the bed on this one.

"Nube!" I all but roared. "Shut the fuck up Nube...shut the fuck up!" She looked up at me, and instantly I knew that I had come off over the top.

"Okay...look Nube...I'm sorry," I told her. "It's just that I'm having a hard time digesting what you telling me."

"Well you wanted to know Rod. For me it was better left in the past. It's not like I'm proud that his religion and self attainment took precedence over me for 2 whole years," she said kind of slipping into a zone.

"Baby listen," I told her kneeling down on the bed, "You ain't gotta worry about none of that lame shit...I'm your man now, and you ain't never gonna have a reason to doubt that physically...mentally or otherwise. And don't you **ever** go doubting yourself over the actions of no man in your life...past or present. You are more woman than any real man could ever want. You just needed the right one presented to you...and I'm telling you here tonight...I plan on filling them shoes and wearing them for a very long time."

She came out of her zone and cracked me a smile and said, "No wonder they call you King Midas...cause them words right there just touched me, and now I'm feeling like a million bucks."

"Well that's what I do," I told her as I got up from the floor, turned off the light and got a throw to cover us as I slid back up onto the bed with her, "But Nube...you didn't need no assistance from me...you're already a treasure."

"Wow...your Majesty" she said, "I sure hope loving you will always be this easy."

"As easy as the sunrise Nube...as easy as the sunrise," I told her as I wrapped her up in my arms and just laid there with her. As I savored the softness of her skin up against me, and them banging body curves teasing me, I just had to ask...just had to know.

"Nube," I started. "Just one more thing...I promise baby. You said he's never seen you naked...so the kissing and touching...how...?"

"We were both fully clothed Murad," she answered softly, "The kisses were on the lips only, and he touched what he could...how he could."

"So baby...he never?" I asked one more time out of disbelieve.

"No, Rod...never," she replied on a sleepy note.

"Damn Nube...shut the fuck up. I can't believe this shit here," I told her once again.

"No, Murad...you shut the fuck up," she whined. "It's 4:30 a.m. . I been thru a lot today. I need my rest."

"You right Bae...you right. Get your rest Nube...you due." I told her kissing the back of her neck.

"Besides," she answered me in a sexy, sleepy tone, grinding that perfect ass into me. "I need to recharge so we can do this shit again in the morning."

"No problem, little Butter," I told her smiling my ass off in the dark. "No problem at all."

Chapter 32

The Analysis

Murad

I got a few things on my mind right now, as I prepare breakfast while Nube's in the shower. Needless to say, we didn't make it till the morning with reinventing our pleasures. I think we fell asleep for like an hour and a half and then somehow awoke and just lapsed into a new mission of satisfaction. I guess if you want to look at it...it's been a long time for us both. I mean it hasn't been as long for me as it's been for her, but on the real...I haven't had actual intercourse myself in like 6 months. I guess that would explain the insatiable mode we were both in. Not to mention JT and his bullshit. I can't believe his sorry ass. I don't know whether I want to fuck him up for neglecting Nube as a woman and hurting her feelings, or if I want to shake his damn hand for not dipping his stick into my pot of honey. I mean...I know Nube was trying to be diplomatic by telling me he touched what he could, how he could. I believe I'm gonna interpret that to mean, he gave her the old high school finger action. I'm not gonna trip on that, cause after all I had originally concluded that much more had taken place since they were supposed to be together. It's pretty funny how that slipped his mind to give me that piece of information when he was grilling me about my intentions a couple of months back.

I can't understand Jayson and his status in life. He's always so comfortable and laid back, and just lets circumstances dictate for him. At what point in life is he ever gonna stand up and act like a man? He don't seem to be no further than when we were kids. His punk ass let me fight 3 guys by myself while he ran home to get my father. I've always been taller than him and had more build, but still at the time...11 and 14 years old...he was supposed to be playing his role as my big brother. Yeah, I took that beat down by myself, and that was the last one I'd ever had to endure. After that I had my dad sign me up for martial arts, and I got into boxing myself during high school. I was determined that I would never be physically taken advantage of ever again all because some niggas was hating on me for no reason.

People don't understand at times, it's hard to be so called handsome, gorgeous or fine. I just want people to understand that first and foremost I am a person, a pretty good person, and I have no control on what was genetically bestowed upon me by my parents. Being good looking does not exempt you from having feelings. And I sure can't help that people out here are so dissatisfied with their own lives that they need to aggrieve me for mine. People are so quick to pass judgment on me, based on what they see, and real quick to talk shit about me. But fuck it...I've learned to rely on myself to get the things that I want, and just limit my trust of others in the process. This way I ain't gotta take into account how nobody is coming at me, cause I'm gonna keep all my bases covered at all times, from all angles. And keeping that pretty little lady upstairs satisfied is top priority on my list. She is the one person in my life that I can count on to uplift me and keep me going. I know that I can be pretty volatile at the drop of a dime, but she always seems to be able to give clarity to any situation, and put me back on track. I love her...I trust her...implicitly.

Nube

Ahh...I feel like the fat cat that just swallowed the canary. Rod and I woke up and went at it again at the crack of dawn. I can't even begin to explain how different I feel in body...my senses...are like...so alert. I feel like the most alive woman in the world. Every time I think of the moves and the pleasure he gave to me, I start to get wet. Oh boy...that ain't no good at all. I'm gonna have to squeeze in an extra load of underwear washing a week at this rate. With that in mind...might as well stock up on some extra Tide and get the washing machine cranked up, cause there will be no cutting back in that department. Every ounce of loving he wants go give me will be graciously accepted. I can't remember ever feeling this good with a man. Well, I haven't had many...but if he had been my first...he would have been my only. Damn...that man got skills. Will I be able to keep up, I ask myself as I make my way downstairs.

As I came around the corner into the kitchen, I spotted him shirtless, wearing some sweatpants that he keeps in my guest bedroom. We both kind of have a small stash of clothing at each other's house as a result of traveling together so much. Many times we would get back in late, and rather than have the car service make 2 stops we would just crash wherever was the closest or the most convenient. Once he spotted me he looked up and smiled at me, not knowing that his semi-nude presence was causing chaos in my underwear again. And damn...I just put these on. I'm gonna have to learn some self control...immediately...lol.

"Good Morning Beautiful," he said as I approached him, holding me in his gaze and giving me the chills. He leaned over and gave me a kiss that just brought on a fresh gush of wetness and had me wiggling in place.

"Good Morning your Majesty," I said backing myself up and trying to regain my composure. "What do we have going on up in this kitchen?" I playfully asked.

"Well," he responded, "I did some eggs, and some kind of potato things you got up in here. You know you got all this organic stuff going on, so I did the best I could do with what you had. Hope I didn't mess things up too much...JT I am not."

"Oh, I'm sure you did just fine, King Midas," I answered him. "You got that magic touch...for sure." I winked at him, feeling myself in a flirtatious mood.

"Well here goes," he said scooping a mound full of eggs on my plate and then some potatoes.

"Well it smells good," I told him. "And hey...not too bad," I mumbled with a full mouth of my first taste.

"What you want to drink?" he asked looking in the fridge.

"Just whatever juice I've got in there will be fine." I told him. As he poured two glasses and sat down to eat, I asked him, "Where did the King Midas title come from? That was the first I heard it last night."

"You and me both," he answered, "In fact, yesterday was a day full of comments from folks whispering whether or not we were together and calling us Jersey's royal couple. I don't know...people kind of come up with their own images and tags and titles to go along with it I suppose. But I guess thanks to DJ Slick, it's common knowledge to everyone at this point."

"Yeah I thought I heard him saying congrats and something else," I replied. "Although…I had some preliminary opposition to the announcement."

"How so Nube?" He asked me as he tasted his own food.

"Well," I started in between bites, "Early on in the evening, I was in VIP with the girls and Bree brought up that she heard we were more than friends, and I gave them the news that we were, and Sumira and I kind of got into some words over it."

"Yeah" he answered, "That right there don't surprise me none."

"Well Rod," I came back with. "You know we talked about expecting shade from the family."

"Yeah but Sumira always got a stick up her ass about something," he said. "It don't take much to get her on her soap box."

"So had you told anyone about our decision? Cause when it came up, I realized at that point that I had been just too busy to make public announcements." I queried.

"Not really," he stated. "I mean…I had spoken on it with Dream before I'd even made a decision to come to you with my feelings. And of course I went to JT with it. So unless they shared with other family members, then no…I also let it slip my mind."

"Well maybe we both subconsciously wanted to hold on to our own special secret for as long as we could. And with good reason…cause now that it's all out the bag…no telling what's gonna be thrown at us by whom." I told him.

"Well they can throw whatever they want," he came back with. "Cause this here is all about us and nobody else. The only acceptance I'm looking for I've already obtained, and that was from you. So I'm good."

"Well men tend to handle things much different from women," I told him. "I mean you should have seen how tight Sumira was the rest of the night. All swoll about it and what not. And then not to mention your girl."

"My girl?" he asked, "What you talking bout?"

"Well I went to the ladies room, and was so glad that it was empty when I walked in. But by the time I finished my business and washed my hands someone else had come in. Before I could leave out, they came out of the stall and it was Jazmine."

"Jazz…what the fuck was she doing there?" he stated.

"What you think Rod…hoping for a minute to get next to you," I answered him.

"Well…go on and spill it, cause I know her….ain't no way she ain't open up her ignorant mouth," he said.

"Ignorant is right," I started. "She proceeded to tell me that she's been wanting to tell me off for a while, and that I took you from her, and I was a nasty ass for sleeping with two brothers and all." He just looked at me and gave me the head twist.

"Well let me finish," I told him. "Now you know I don't argue over men, and I let her know that. Of course I became a bitch and the whole nine, so I just turned around to leave and she reached out and grabbed my blouse and ripped one of my ties."

"She did fucking what?" he raised his voice.

"Not to worry Bae…I paid very close attention to all that you taught me." I told him, "She got all of 5 seconds to herself before I gave her a high body kick, and then I kind of popped her in the eye when she came tumbling towards me."

"Nube," he bust out laughing. "Baby…no you didn't. You gonna sideline me about wanting to knock Trey the fuck out, yet you up in the ladies room taking people down. Damn girl…you too much." He continued to laugh, shaking his head at me the whole time.

"Well I wasn't trynna be physical or nothing, but she put her hands on me first Rod. I mean I asked her was she okay and all. She told me fuck you…so I left her on the floor." I finished off the story with a shrug.

"Nube," he said continuing to laugh. "You gonna put her on her ass and then ask her if she alright?"

"Well yeah," I answered. "It's not like those were my intentions. I was just acting on instinct."

"On instinct?" he asked getting down from his stool and coming over to me.

"Yes Rod," I answered him as he picked me up from my stool and set me on the counter.

"Well what are your instincts telling you now?" he asked as he began to kiss my lips, slowly pulling in on the bottom one.

"They telling me that we gonna need to put this food in the microwave and..." I never finished my response cause he scooped me from the counter, laid me out on the kitchen floor and took me on a return trip to bliss.

Part II

July 2008 – January 2009

Chapter 33
The Apple Don't Fall Too Far From The Tree

Nubina

Everything is all right in my world. Murad and I are growing and building more each day and I am so loving the whole thing. He has proved to be the epitome of everything I dreamed about in a partner, and whenever we have down time, we hole up at my house so I can cook for him and just pamper him in any way that he wants or needs. We up in the supermarket now, picking up some things for a special dish I'm making. I had passed the spice aisle and Rod had gone back to look for the Cumin for me.

I was rolling the cart absentmindedly scanning the aisles for a specific rice when I heard a familiar voice say, "Well hello Tania." I looked up right into the face of Mrs. Wilkerson…Trey's momma.

"Oh, hey there Ms. Dee, how you been?" I asked genuinely surprised to see her. She'd never wanted me to call her Mrs. Wilkerson…didn't want to seem like an old lady, so being that her first name was Delores, I called her Ms. Dee out of respect.

"What you think you so big time now, I can't get a hug? You better get over here and give me a hug," she reprimanded.

"Oh, not at all Ms. Dee…just really surprised to see you around here," I answered as I hit her off with a hug.

"Well, just look at you," she said rearing back from the hug giving me the once over, "You looking good…every bit the part of a celebrity."

"Naw," I answered her. "It's just still the same ole me. Nothing's changed."

"Oh, please chile," she responded. "Trey done told me how you travel all over and got so many things in the works. He told me he went to see your movie premiere."

"Oh cool," I gave back. "Did you get the chance to go out and see it?"

"Well...if it ain't too embarrassing...oh shoot girl...you know I got it on the bootleg. Ha...ha...ha...I ain't ever been the one to spend no whole bunch of money at the movies," she told me.

"Naw, Ms.Dee," I responded facetiously. "We all know you wouldn't want to go and do that."

Now see how we do? Our folk are so predictable...always complaining about not enough blacks getting credit in the industry, but instead of supporting they go out and defile us with the bootleg action. People...

"But you did good, real good," she came back with. "Me and Lorinda sat down and watched it last week. I have to say that I am proud of my almost daughter-in-law." Wow I thought, what prompted that statement.

"You know Trey still loves you," she interjected my thoughts with.

"So I've heard...so I've heard," I replied.

"Well now...how do you feel about that?" she quizzed me. Oh boy... here we go I'm thinking. I remember that she was very "involved." Okay...let me just say it...nosey; and I should have known this lineup was coming.

"Well Ms. Dee," I started. "Trey and I had a lot of turbulent water between us, and I've never been an avid swimmer, so I've kinda moved on to more peaceful waters."

"Tania chile...what is it that you trynna say?" she asked me.

At that moment Murad came around the corner and down the aisle.

"Nube," he called out. "Is this the right one?" he asked, slowing his pace once he noticed that I was not alone. As he walked up to us both, Ms. Dee let out an, "Oh my!"

"Murad," I started off. "This is Ms. Dee...Trey's mother, and Ms. Dee...this is my man...Murad."

"Well...oh my," she said again. "Huhn...you said your man?" she asked as Murad peeled off a, "How you doing?"

"Oh...I'm doing fine...yes...yes indeed," she responded eyeing him up and down. One part of her was overwhelmed by his good looks, while the other part was trying to find something of a blemish to substantiate Trey as the better man.

"Yes Ms. Dee. He's my peaceful water," I said smiling up at him giving him a wink. He gave me back a smirk with a lip nod that said, "I'm feeling you, sexy."

"Well...he's a tall drink of cool water...I must say," she replied to my comment. "Y'all happy?" she asked.

I'm looking at her like...Ms.Dee...that's rather forward of you. But you know what...

"Yes m'am, never happier," I answered her reaching out to put my arm around his waist, as Rod went with the flow and put his arm around me.

"Well...you make a very nice looking couple indeed; although you and Trey looked good together too," she threw in. Oh see...now she pushing it.

"Well," I started so I could break off this conversation. "We have to go. We've got to get back...I have a special dish I'm putting together tonight."

"Special dish huh?" she asked.

"Yes Ms.Dee...for Murad."

"Okay...okay then, I won't keep ya," she replied. "But listen...I have been meaning to have Trey ask if you could come by and speak for our Ladies Auxiliary group down at the church. A lot of people have come to know you in the community and I'm sure you would draw a large crowd for us...oh...as well as bring us some positive words."

"Well," I said looking up at Rod, the look on his face was like here we go, "Murad is also my manager and I guess we'll have to get back to you on that one. Perhaps you can take his card, and get in touch with him on the date and the subject theme of your program, and he'll let you know if we can fit it in our schedule or not." As I gave Rod a discreet elbow to his side, he reluctantly reached into his wallet and produced a business card that he handed over to her.

"Oh my," she said taking the card he handed her. "Such a beautiful card...so professional. You two really into all this huh?"

"Uh...yeah Ms.Dee...this is the real thing," I answered smiling and leaning into Rod as she watched.

"Okay now, I'm gonna let you two get on, so you can get his special meal on," she said. "And I'll get back to you with the details Mu...Mu," she stammered.

"Murad," he finished for her, extending his hand out to her. She took it to shake and he lifted it to his lips and graced it with a light kiss.

"Nice meeting you Ms. Dee," he said, accentuating the bass in his voice, then released her hand.

"Uh...uh....oh my!" she gave off all flustered. "Good seeing you again Tania," she said finally taking hold of her cart and departing at breakneck speed into the next aisle. I looked at Rod, and he looked at me and we both bust out in suppressed laughter.

"Rod," I whispered in between laughter. "what you doing getting his mama all riled up for?"

"Well, I figured I'd give her nosey little ass something to go back and share with her nosey ass son," he answered me. "You know she can't wait to get home and let him know she saw us."

"Oh yeah," I laughed back. "This you know. Trust and believe she gonna call you ASAP for a date and such for her church group."

"Well is that something you wanna do?" he asked me.

"Well Rod...if my schedule is free...I don't want to snub a community offer like that. The people are the ones who I really do all this for. You know...enlightenment...is that a word?" I asked as I answered him.

"Enlightenment...I don't know," he said, "But I sure wish her and her nosey son would be enlightened on the fact that he is out the picture and stop making reference to what's going down between us."

"Awwww, Rod, it's harmless," I told him. "She and Trey both know that it's a done deal between us."

"A done deal between who Nube...you and I being together, or you and he being over?" he asked.

"Both Murad," I answered. "Both." He looked at me and just gave me a look and twisted that head like "really Nube" and I nodded back with a look that told him, "I'm sure Murad...I'm sure."

Chapter 34

Word Is Bond

Nubina

Sure to my word, Ms. Dee took no time at all contacting Murad with the needed details. After checking with me and giving me the subject theme, we agreed that I would appear probono. Well pretty much...I agreed. You know Rod would prefer to charge them top dollar or not do it at all. But the theme the group is promoting is the self betterment of black women, and I just can't put a price on that one. Besides...I never had anything against Ms. Dee, I can do her this one. So 2 weeks have passed and I am here today about to engage in my presentation. Rod is here, although not in too fanciful of a spirit, and oh lord...Trey is here too. He on the other hand seems to be floating on cloud 9. I don't know what his expectations are here today, but I'm here to do this thing and then I'm out. No dilly-dallying around. Murad and I want to get back home and make good on some free time before we leave for Atlanta. As I prepare to step out onto the stage, I feel a strange vibe that I can't put my finger on, and I have no time to analyze it as I hear Ms. Dee announcing my name, "Here with us today is...Nubina." I entered onto the stage amongst a round of applause.

"*Good Afternoon everyone,*" I began, "*I am here to welcome you today on a presentation about us...as black women...and how we can alleviate some of our everyday hassles and rise above. Now I'm sure you know that...*"

Murad

Maaaan...listen. I truly don't feel like being here today. But Nube didn't want to turn this gig down. I mean...I'm feeling her on the community issue, and the betterment of women, but...this Trey and his momma just bring me bad vibes. They both better be glad that I love and respect everything about her enough to trust her choices, cause this is most definitely one I would have passed up. Not only that...we get here and this clown up in here cheesing like he just copped his first piece of ass. I guess the fact that a lot of his mom's friends, and his sister and her girlfriends are all blowing up his head with comments about him and Nube and their prior history. As usual speculation is just running rampant. I'll be damned glad when this is all over. I usually love to hear Nube speak, but today is a whole nother ball of wax, as my dad used to say. Damn if I don't miss him. I sure wish that he was still here. He's probably the only other person to get me to see clarity in a situation besides Nube. I'm sure he would have loved her, if he'd known her. She has such a giving spirit, what's not to love. My thoughts are interrupted by Nube's voice as she shares her concept on the romantic needs of the black woman.

"*And sisters, I know that it's hard to stay within your reasoning and logic when it comes to men. I know how the sound of the right voice, on the right man can manipulate your senses, and have you counteract all the hard work you put in for sustaining. And yes...I know all about how the longing of a touch or caress will lead you to make the un-wisest of choices in seeking intimacy. But you have to be strong in your resolve to ensure you don't pay a hefty cost from your soul. You have to be sure that you are not bringing dangerous energy into your space as well as endangering your sexual health. We have to be cautious in how we deal with sharing ourselves and to whom we are sharing with. We have to know and understand that love looks out for love first, and you have to maneuver your way thru her many fickle changes. We need to strive to practice every day the good sense that resides in us all. Don't relinquish your power for well being to any man.*"

I took a glance around the room and noticed that just about everyone was hanging on to her every word, giving Nube their full attention. Moments like this make me proud, and feed my belief in her dream. Especially since I know these are her true feelings, and not some scripted group of words she puts forth to make a name for herself in the industry. I may not have originally supported Nube's choice of speaking for Ms.Dee, but I guess I have to admit, she is coming off with a mean message for the ladies. It kind of tugs at my heart that she is most likely speaking from experience. As I survey the room once again, I notice Trey leaning against the wall totally enamored with the vision of Nube while some young lady is leaning into him trying to engage in a conversation to which he is totally absent from. I stuff down some ill feelings, and think to myself, that not for nothing...those very same words applied to me at one time. Yeah ...I'm glad Nube and I have come together. My days of sifting thru chicks and tricks is a thing of the past. I can sense that Nube is ready to close out, and listen as she introduces the piece she wants to recite.

"*I truly believe in the power of women, and I just want to share with you today, a tribute to all women. I call this piece Womanism.*

There are many reflections of a woman
Her beauty, her essence, emerging through
in times of hardships, struggle, grief and pain.
She can bear many storms and still come out victorious.
She knows the art of sacrifice, proficient in it as no one else can be.

Plagued with the task of soothing the sorrows of others,
while hers remain on the back burner to simmer.
She can stifle a cry of anguish so severe as an avenue
to ward off fear threatening her loved ones.
She can selflessly endure the worst betrayal and still carry forgiveness in her heart.
She can march pass degradation and humiliation with a deaf ear in order to sustain her piece of mind.

She will take on and accept the flaws of her offspring,
lending an understanding to the situation, as no one will.
She has time and patience for one last chore,
even when the clock has ticked into the 13th hour.
She knows not the words, "I can't," because she must; she has no choice.

She is virtuous, loving, respectful and kind although it is seldom reciprocated.
She moves on thru life unaware, yet totally aware that
she is being worn down by the daily abrasions of life.

So totally in control, yet so unacknowledged, she remains the true core to the cycle of life.

I would in my next lifetime...be her again.

The crowd rose to their feet in thunderous applause and amen's, hallelujah's and all that. Nube humbly accepted her accolades and thanked the audience. I watched as Ms. Dee climbed up on the stage to embrace her taking the mic and addressing the crowd.

"Amen sister, amen...give it up for Nubina. She most certainly shared some powerful words with us today. I have to say that I am so blessed to have had her in my life ever since she and my son Trey were together. Trey come up here," she said cropping up some new bullshit, and leading it to???...I don't know where. Of course he obliged her and came up on the stage and gave Nube a hug, holding onto her like he drowning and shit. Okay ...see...they tryna milk this here for all it's worth.

"Ladies, this is my handsome son Trey, and he and Nubina have a lot of history together. I have always wanted things to work out for them, and I'm still praying," she announced to the group.

"Your prayer is welcome in our circle sister. There's power in prayer...amen...power in prayer," someone called out.

I took a deep breath, cause you know I ain't got the patience for the bullshit. I took a quick glance at my watch before I looked Nube up on the stage. She was trying to be every bit the diplomat as she sought me out and gave me an apologizing look. I hit her back with a look with a raise of the eyebrows and a head nod that let her know, I'd be outside till she's done. She just nodded and let me know with her eyes that she would wrap things up and be out shortly. I spun on my heels, and made my way out of there. I'ma go out here and see if I got me a black out in the truck.

I made my way to the truck in the back of the parking lot. I opened the door and climbed in searching as my blackberry went off.

"Yeah," I responded as I located a black in the console compartment.

"Yo King Midas...whas' good nigga," I heard Brick"s voice come thru.

"Hey B...not a thing...not a thing. Whas' good with you? I thought you was supposed to be getting up with me after the After Party? What you forgot?" I asked.

"Naw," he replied, "Just got a little caught up an' all. Look...I been meanin' to ask you about possibly getting my own shop. You know...break out from Bryce and be in charge of my own shit and what not. I mean, I got a little stash, I was hoping that you could flip it for me...or invest it or whatever the fuck you do."

"Wow B...you sure you ready for operating daily on the total business tip?" I put to him.

"Naw, I'm not sure," he answered me, "But I'm feeling like I'm a grown-ass man, and I need to establish something of my own...you know what I mean? I ain't tryna get no more bids up under my belt and shit. I'm about to be 36 years old man...time to kill all the nonsense."

"Well it all depends on how much you stashed away, and how soon you ready to break out," I told him, "I could do a minimum 6 month investment, with 6 month increments until you're ready. You gotta let me know what's good for you."

"Hmmm..." he came back with, "That sound like something that might work."

"You know what," I told him, "Let me get back with you tomorrow. I'll be in town for 2 days, then Nube and I will be headed for Atlanta. We can sit down tomorrow and work this all out."

"Aight cool," he responded, "How Lil Ms.Booji doing anyway?"

"Awww...fuck you nigga...she fine," I came back with, "Still doing what she do. Whas' wit' you and the new chick I saw at the party?"

"Maaan...that's so done wit," he said, "This female action is working me man...kinda off the wall wit' it right now. You know what I mean?" Actually I didn't know what he meant. In fact he kinda talkin off the wall his self.

"Yo Brick," I answered, "What the hell you mean by all that? Cause you lost me bruh."

"Man, just going thru shit and what not...ya know? Well naw...I guess you don't know. You got booji two-shoes and ya'll all up in paradise," he jokingly replied.

"Once again...fuck you nigga," I answered, "Don't concern yourself with nothing we doing. We good...we straight. In fact...paradise all to the left and right of us." We both started laughing.

"Oh...okay mu'fucka," he replied, "you got that one...you got it. But you need to know son...paradise lost is a mutha fucka."

"Is that right?" I questioned him, slowly thinking in the back of my mind, what is this all about? He obviously got something on his mind he's not speaking on. "Well listen," I told him, "I'm bout to go and collect Nube so we can get on back. I'll hit you up tomorrow so you can come thru and we can sit down and make shit happen."

"Cool," he said, "so then I'll see you tomorrow."

"Fa' sho', fa' sho," I answered him. Before he could hang up, I said, "Oh yeah B...remember one thing for me."

"Whas' dat," he answered.

"Paradise lost is paradise regained. Peace." I told him and hung up the phone.

Damn, Brick on some ole' twisted shit right about now. Some chick done got him hemmed up in the stress zone. That and the fact that he feeling the need to establish his own shit as a man. I can get with him on that . I mean Bryce and I are more than tight, he's like a surrogate father to me, but for some reason, he and Brick got some kind of slow beef that been cooking between them for a minute. Well, I guess the shit will all work out. I know Bryce ain't one to be blocking nobody's progress. He should be cool with Brick striking out on his own. Now getting back to me...I'ma go on and get this here lit. I came out to get myself mellowed out from this other nonsense. Hopefully Nube will be out in a minute, she should be just about done by now. Good, I said to myself as I saw the back door open, this should be her now and...nope...it was his fucking clown-ass. I just puffed and watched this mutha fucka as he approached me.

"How you doing brother?" he greeted me, and I reciprocated with a nod. "Well they're just about done in there and I was asked to bring the box of CD's to the truck," he said trying his best o get a response from me. Again I nodded, and just popped the back door to the truck, so he could slide the crate in. As he slid the crate in, he attempted another gesture of conversation.

"Our girl brought the house down today, did she not?"

"She always does," I kicked off, my voice monotone hoping he would catch my drift.

"Well I suppose you would know being that you her manager. You know Beena has always..."

"Listen up Trey," I cut into his sentence, "Let's get one thing straight. I ain't interested in making no talk with you here today or any day in regard to Nube. Unless you wanna talk about how you gonna stay the fuck out of our lives, then we ain't got nothing to say to one another." I looked at him and kicked back a nod like, "understand" as I closed the back door to the truck.

"Whoa," he answered back, "I just came out here as a favor to Beena so she wouldn't have to carry that heavy box being that your ass left the building. But you know what it's cool...it's not a problem...me doing her a favor. The fact is, I was first before you in doing favors and otherwise." I gave his ass a look, kinda like a warning.

"Otherwise?" I calmly inquired although I was about boiling under the surface.

"Otherwise," he kicked back smirking, "Beena used to love it when I..."

Now I don't know if he stopped because his senses suddenly returned to him to warn him, or if he was trying to prepare himself for what he knows was coming next. But whichever the case, he was not swift enough. Before he knew it I had granted him a quick elbow to the left side of his head and then grabbed him by the throat, placing my thumb and forefinger on his windpipe squeezing it shut. All the while I held my black in my left hand, and took a drag. I pulled off and turned and exhaled right in his face.

I just watched him gasping for air, and finally spoke, "Now...say what Trey? She loved it when you used to do what?" He wiggled and squirmed, gasping for air while I just watched. "Speak up mu'fucka," I taunted him, "I can't hear you. You was telling me that she loved it when you...when you what nigga!" His eyes started tearing, and I just twist my head to the side like "yeah...and what." All of a sudden I heard a scream.

"Oh my Lord...Oh God. He's killing him!" Nube and Ms.Dee had emerged from the back door and came across my choking session with Trey. "Oh...you let him go...you let him go!" Ms. Dee yelled.

Nubina

Oh shit...look at this here!! I can't believe this. Murad has got Trey by the neck choking him, while his eyes are all bugged out and tearing. What the??

"Let him go, let him go," Ms. Dee kept screaming the started hitting Murad with her bag. Oh see now wait a minute, she ain't gonna be just beating up on my man now.

"Okay Ms. Dee, I love you and all, but let's hold off

"But he's trynna kill him, he trynna kill him," she cried out hysterically.

"Trust me," I told her "If he wanted to kill him, he would have done it already. Just let me..."

"Ahhh noooo," she screamed hitting him in the head with her bag. Okay see...she done went too far. I stepped in and gave her a sharp push then played it off like I tripped.

"Oh man...I'm sorry Ms. Dee," I told her, "I was just trying to get in here so that I could stop this mess."

"Well I know my Trey...I know he didn't start this," she said to me.

"Well you know Trey and I know them both Ms. Dee," I responded, "and who started it could go both ways; there's really no need to establish fault at this point. Just let me get in here and stop this." She lowered her purse and stood back so I could get in.

"Rod," I started leaning in between them looking him directly in the eyes, "Let him go Rod...let him go." He eased the grip a little and took another drag on his black and mild.

"Nube," he said, "this bitch-ass here gonna try and give me an FYI on shit that went down between y'all."

"Down between us Rod, what are you talking about?" I asked.

"Down **between** y'all Nube," he threw back at me.

"Trey!!" I turned around appalled that he would go that route, "Tell me you didn't do that Trey?" I looked at him waiting for an answer, all the while Trey was starting to struggle and losing strength. Wait a minute I'm thinking...

"Murad," I quickly regained my reasoning, turning back to face him, "Let him go Bae...let him go." He looked at me and gave me that eye twinkle. Now I know that he was just making him sweat...but I'm sure this is not funny to Trey or his mother. "Murad...baby...you'd better...you know...you better let him go," I said between clenched teeth trying to subdue a smile from slowly creeping across my face. He just looked at me, his eyes still twinkling. "Come on Rod...baby please," I begged. He looked at me, gave me that lip twist and slowly released his hand from his throat and flicked him backward like an insect. Once he released him, Ms. Dee snuck over and whacked Murad again with her purse. "Aight now, go on Ms. Dee." I told her, putting myself between her and Rod, "That's enough of beating up on Murad. Go on over there and see to Trey. I think he could use your assistance."

"Murad," I got started, "What the hell is going on out here?"

"Look Nube," he answered me, "That was a real bitch move to sit there and try to feed me some shit on what happened between you all. Like the fuck I wanna hear that. That ain't no shit a real man would do...He lucky I didn't break his damn neck."

"You know what," I told him, "I'm not understanding this animosity thing between you two. He and I have been long over, and you and I are..." I was interrupted by a swish just past my ear, and I saw Murad duck, but still get hit with a blow to the base of his neck. I spun around to see Trey breathing like a mad-man having just exerted the last of his energy to sneak one off on Murad.

"Trey!" I cried out.

"Well he deserved it!" Ms. Dee yelled out, "He ain't had no business choking up on Trey."

"I don't believe this shit here," Murad started off, "You gonna fucking reach around Nube and sneak me?"

"Rod...look...let's just go," I said trying to stem anything else from jumping off.

"Naw," he started, "This nigga wanna reach around women..." And before I knew what was happening, he stepped off to the side, went around Ms. Dee and slammed Trey dead in his right eye. The force of the blow immediately caused his eye to start swelling profusely.

"Murad!" I now said turning back to him.

"Oh my Lord!" Ms. Dee cried out as Trey slumped over. I turned back to Trey and Ms. Dee and couldn't believe the sight before me. His eye was completely shut and was he was grimacing in pain leaning on someone's parked car.

"Oh my god...Trey...Trey...are you alright?" I fearfully asked. His eye was bubbling and blistering with alternating shades of red and white. Ooooo...that eye was gonna need medical attention for sure.

"Beena...Beena," he said breathing heavily, "I just need you to go right now. Just go on...I'll call you later." I looked at him, then to Ms. Dee who in turn just glared at me. I shrugged my shoulders then just climbed in the truck. Murad came around to close the door for me as he always does, and I just grabbed a hold of the door and slammed it shut myself. I guess he knew that I was angry with him, so he just threw up his hands, came around to the drivers' side and got in. When I looked out the window and didn't say anything to him, he just blew out a deep breath and pulled of.

Murad

After riding in silence for about 10 minutes, I made an attempt to reconcile with Nube. I know that she was aggravated with me and I don't like that feeling. It's not one that I have to contend with often...but I don't like it just the same. "So...we still hanging out at my house?" I asked her.

"Oh...I don't know Murad. Maybe you'd rather be alone. I'm saying...it ain't every day you get to turn a man's eye inside out," she responded.

"Oh come on Nube...that mutha' fucka snuck me," I responded pulling over, "He reached the hell around you...and snuck me. What kind of lame ass shit is that? He could have hit you!"

"Oh Murad...Murad...baby," she whined, "What is it between you and Trey? Why is it that you two are at each other's throats whenever you see one another?"

"Cause that mutha' fucka is desperate...and desperate mutha' fucka's can be dangerous," I told her, "First it's him popping up every chance he get and now it's his damn momma. Then they both gonna stand up there in the church and announce how much history you all got together and how she praying for ya'll to get back together, while the whole sista hood joining in offering prayers for the same. Why wasn't she fucking praying for him to get right when he was with you? Maybe her damn prayers would have been answered and then everyone involved would be happy. Then he standing there holding you tighter than he even wanna be and just gloating. And you know Nube...you know my tolerance is low for the nonsense. And on top of that, he think he gonna proceed to tell me some intimate details about you and him? I can't deal with the bullshit Nube...I can't...you know I can't." I took a pause from my volley of words to see how she was taking it all. She was just sitting there tight lipped, staring at me. "What?" I asked her all annoyed.

"You know Murad...you right," she said, "Trey and Ms. Dee are both acting out on some desperation. I came out for a positive community function and nothing more. They both took advantage of today to swing things their way and purposely slight you knowing that you were present. It was wrong, it was disrespectful and I'm going to let him know about it. But in the interim...we can't change the past and the future is every next tomorrow. I don't know why he keeps popping up, but he's here now and we just have to adapt. For whatever reason, he's destined to be included in our lives at this point and time and I believe this is something we can work through; in fact it's something we an overlook. Really...as a man, you can blow this off without a second glance or amuse yourself at his attempts. Sire...there is only one man that can capture the complete and total me and I sit here before him. You've got me Sire...I'm caught. I'm so out there on you, there's no way back...I wouldn't even know my way back if I thought about it. Not another man in this lifetime past or present could ever convince me that he coming better with it than you. And I know that it irritates you when you see brothers trying, but please understand...you got it all over them. And unless you let **me** go, I'm hooked to you Sire...forever."

I took a minute to take in all that she said and blew out a deep breath. Damn...as usual she's got me blown away. I mean...I guess I know she done with dude, it's just that I can just sense so strongly the desperation in his actions. Dude fucked up and now he trynna cash in on her kindness by using their history together.

"Babe," I told her, "I feel you on where you coming from and I appreciate everything we've got going for us. And I really didn't mean to upset you and all Nube, but he's been asking for a thrashing of that ass ever since our paths crossed," I told her.

"Murad...you know that I don't condone the violence. You gonna have to get some more control on that," she said, "But you were right in regard to them acting on desperation so I'm gonna try and understand your frustration about it all. But there's one thing I don't agree with you on."

"What's that?" I asked.

"Well I'm glad his momma never sent up prayers that he and I would stay together. Cause if she did and had been successful with it, I would never have been with you. And that right there would be a sin...and a shame," she finished off leaning in to get a kiss.

I obliged her and responded with a tender kiss laced with urgency as I asked her, "A sin Nube?"

"And a shame," she replied returning the kiss. I needed to ensure that her displeasure with me today melts away, and pave the way for some extra quality time tonight. I pulled back and watched her eyes and was happy with the message that was displayed there. The eyes were completely calm and pleading with me to just take her home, so that we could make use of our precious free time. I hit her off with 2 more urgent kisses, then put the truck back in gear and told her, "We on our way Nube...we on our way."

Chapter 35
Taking Matters Into My Own Hands

Murad

Since Nube had put shit in perspective, I was feeling some kind of way, as in needing to express some physical gratitude towards her. But that was gonna kind a have to wait a minute since we'd decided to stop off and pick up some take-out. I know she probably a little hungry since she hadn't eaten much before the event. Since Ambassadors was on the way I swung in there and scooped up 2 orders of fish and wings then got my ass back in the truck. As we laughed and talked on the continued ride home, I kept visualizing me trailing my tongue down that sweet neck of hers till I reached all them peaks and valleys she got going on. I mean each time I get skin to skin with her, she sets my ass off. Heart rate thumping like a club beat and shit. Yeah...I thought as we pulled up to my place...gonna make ample use of this down time.

I don't even know how I managed to make it thru the meal, cause at this point I was so ripe that just watching her chew was turning me on. If you ain't never heard of nobody that can make chewing sexy...then I'm here to tell ya...Nube got that shit on lock. I mean them little lips are just moving in slow motion, up and down and twisting in their own little rhythm...and then...ahhh...she licks them sexy lips. Maaannn listen...I wish she hurry up already, so we can get to dessert.

"So Rod," she said in between chews, "Despite the nonsense afterwards...what did you think of the presentation today?"

"On point as usual Nube. I mean I think it was well received by all in attendance. Anybody who wasn't a fan before today, is surely a fan now."

"Well yeah, that's all good but my main goal was to encourage women to empower themselves emotionally in their relationships by actually not letting their emotions rule," she replied.

"Well speaking of emotions," I came back with, "A brother got a little bit of emotions going on right now that he need to share with you." I got up from my seat at the table and extended my hand to help her from her chair.

"Oh...so you got emotions that you need to deal with...brother?" she asked lowering her tone as she rose from her seat wrapping her arms around my waist.

"Unh huh," I answered leaning down to lick whatever flavor I could taste off of her pretty lips, "Yeah...a brother feeling some kind of way."

"Well you know what that sounds like to me?" she asked me as she nibbled on my lips, then swiped her tongue across them.

"Ahh...what Butter?" I responded as shit turned itself up another notch.

"Sounds like brother need to work it out...yes?" she replied.

"Oh yeah," I answered, "Brother need to work it out...brother gonna work it out. Work it out all night."

As we both laughed lightly together, I picked her up and carried her upstairs to the bedroom and placed her down on the bed. I began delicate kisses to which she readily responded and before you know it we were caught up in our own mellow mood together. The mood was so nice, so sweet and unrushed that we just let it flow unconcerned with where it was going, or how long it was going to take to get there. All I know is that the sensation was so good, so good that you don't care if you stay right at this point forever and then....her cell phone went off.

"Oh damn," she said, "Who the hell could that be?"

"Who the hell cares?" I lustfully responded, "You can call em' back later."

"I don't know Rod...I don't like to leave my cell unanswered when I'm not at home." I looked down at her like...for real...let out a heavy sigh, then raised up so she could retrieve her phone. She sprinted over to her bag grabbed the phone looked at the number with a questioning glance before answering and said, "Hello?"

Oh damn, I thought as the response came thru, "Beena." Rod and I was about to be up in our favorite place and of all people to call.

"Trey," I responded, "What's going on...is something wrong?" I turned to face Murad and saw that his face had gotten mighty tight.

"Well besides the fact that I'll be out of work for the next week with an eye injury...then I guess everything is cool," he replied.

"Trey," I started, "You kind of brought that on yourself."

"How you figure Been?" he asked me, "Ole boy is over the top. Dude got an un-natural temper."

"Un-natural," I came back with, "Actually I believe that you got a natural response from him given what you were coming at him with. You of all people ought to know you can't challenge another man in that manner and expect a different response. It's no less than what you would have done." I turn back to Rod who was looking at me sideways and I knew that I needed to kill this conversation. "Well listen," I told him, "It's apparent that you've seen a doctor about your eye, and you'll be fine, so I'm kinda in the middle of something right now, and I'll have to speak to you another time."

"Wait Beena," he rushed out, "Don't hang up yet...please. Seeing you today...up on that stage...you speaking and delivering your message...it touched on something deep in me and brought to mind some of our better times together. I don't think I use to give you the credit that you deserved back then, and now it's evident that your credibility is overflowing. I really wish that I'd done things a lot differently Beena."

"Well I'm sure that in looking back, we all could have done things a lot differently," I told him, "But we are so here right now, and I've really got to get back to..."

"So come on Been," he cut me off, "After all that we been thru together, you ain't got time to hear me out...you just gonna leave me hanging?"

"Hold on," I said placing the receiver down on my chest as I looked back over at Murad trying to measure up how he was feeling about all this...I know he pissed. "Babe...listen...just give me 5 minutes," I asked even though I knew I was pushing it, "I promise...just 5 minutes Rod and it's me and you."

"You know what Butter...for 5...do you," he told me and went out on the balcony.

I exhaled with relief then took a deep breath and resumed myself on the line with, "I can give you 5 minutes Trey. What do you need to tell me, that I haven't already heard?"

"Well," he started, "I'm kind of wondering what's the true story with you and dude...you know...and this brother situation thing. I mean you really with him after that?" OMG...do he really think I need to explain this to him?

"Trey," I started, "Let me inform you on something. You don't get to question my choices on who I deal with. You are the last person that can call anyone out on anything about unsavory dealings. And another thing....."

Murad

Ain't this some shit right here. This mutha' fucka gotta be out his rabbit-assed mind fucking calling after the shit that just went down. Shady ass mutha 'fucka probably looking for some damn sympathy about his eye knowing damn well Nube soft-hearted and not gonna just blow him off since he supposed to be so injured and all. Sheeeiit...this nigga don't know... his ass got off light. Damn...let me exhale I thought as I turned and clutched the railing on the balcony. Let me stop and get myself together and think this thing out. We just talked about this in the truck on the way home...Trey is not a threat to me as far as she's concerned. Yeah and I believe her...he not a threat...but he certainly is a fucking aggravation. I'm saying come on...shit is over...accept that and move the fuck on. I mean, I can understand the grief over his loss, cause Nube is a fucking jewel, but sorry son...your ignorance on the value of rare gems is not my problem. In fact your ignorance is my blessing.

I made a point to check my watch and noted that 2.5 minutes had passed and noticed that she'd taken a seat on the bed, still very much in deep conversation. She did seem like she was annoyed herself and that right there kind of took it in another direction. I'm saying...that's my fucking lady right there, and I don't take kindly to nobody wearing on her nerves. But...she asked me to give her 5 and I'm gonna give her that cause she asked. I stood out on the balcony letting the time wind down before I returned inside and silently motioned to my wrist letting her know that time was up. She held up one finger in a motion to say 1 more minute. Yeah right...picture that...nigga on the phone blocking on my fucking time no less. The agreement was 5...and 5 only. I came over and sat next to her on the bed and leaned over and kissed her. She continued talking and so I kissed her again, then proceeded down her neck. I reached over and grabbed her legs from under her positioning her on her back as she continued to talk, "Trey...that is so not how I remember things at all. You know that you used to ..."

I took a deep breath, exhaled and continued on with what I was doing...like I said this, my fucking time right here. I continued to kiss her softly on her neck and unbuttoned her blouse as I proceeded to make my way down towards them peaks and valleys I'd envisioned earlier. Bingo...she had on a bra that had the closure in the front and I unsnapped it and released the restraints. I touched gently, slowly then kissed gently...slowly. Her breathing began to change and she began to lose focus on the words of the conversation.

"Trey...uhm...well...no...but then again..." I smiled inside as I continued to utilize my time and took the right nipple in my mouth. Her body jerked upward and she feebly raised her finger again as if to say...please...just 1 minute.

"Trey...listen...I really was...I mean really...in the middle of something...important. What...no...how you gonna take it there. I was not the one who constantly had distractions...you was the one...."

Okay...whatever he talking done recaptured her attention so I need to get this back to where it needs to be. Opportunity was definitely on my side today as she had on an elastic waist gypsy skirt that I slowly rolled down as I kissed licked and nibbled her abdomen. Once I got to the hipline, I scooped up the panties with the skirt and rolled away the whole kit and caboodle. She raised her eyebrows at me, yet continued to talk.

"Trey...going back and forth on events in the past is so irrelevant to today. You just need to..." With me freeing up the southern hemisphere, I reached down to lick and kiss her knees. She jumped a little, then tensed up. Oh no...we can't have that. I know just what to do to get her to relax. I let my tongue do a slow dance behind her knees, than brought it back around to her inner thighs. I kissed slowly, purposefully and accurately as her broken conversation informed me of my progress.

"Trey...okay...well just let me...uhm...well you...I'm trynna...." Look like this nigga got a hard time understanding she got shit to do. Guess I'm gonna have to help his ass out. I licked and kissed the inner thighs, teasing and nibbling, my tongue making its way slowly up to the treasure building the momentum along the way.

She tried to get a grip and excuse herself on the phone with, "I've...really...got to go...Trey..." He could have gotten his ass off the phone or she could have hung up...but since they didn't...wasn't gonna let them continue to impede on my time. I reached my destination and took my first swipe to which she let go an unmistakable moan. I took my second, my third, and my fourth swipe to which she flat out moaned in 3-D. I paused for a minute then went in deep for the nibble and nips to which she completely submitted herself with the all-out moans and calling my name. As her arms flailed to her side removing the phone from her ear, I reached up and took the cell phone from her hand. As I licked, sucked and teased her into the moans that I like to hear, I brought the cell phone right on down front and center to all the action and began to deliver some of my best work in sensor-round. I made sure to include all the special effects of the wet gushes of slurping, sucking, licking, splashing and the whole nine, all the while her intense moans served as the backdrop.

Once I knew that the full effect had been established, I paused, put the phone to my ear and said, "Yo Money...she busy." I rose up slid the phone closed and tossed it onto the dresser. I proceeded to lose my attire as she lay on the bed looking up at me like “how could you?” So I looked back down at her with my own look that said, “you had ya 5…this my time.” And now that we got that all out the way, I reached under her to cup them sweet checks, slid ole’ boy up inside of her and proceeded to knock that shit down …like there was no tomorrow.

Chapter 36
Bigger Than The Both Of Us

Dream

"Nigga please. You need to go and tell that shit to somebody that really cares, cause everybody in here knows you and your mama still waiting to get out of the 5th grade. She can't read no manual for a drivers' license...how she gonna apply with Transit as a bus driver Corey?"

A typical afternoon at the shop. Niggas hyking on each other, popping shit...talking game. Murad is in the chair with my cousin Bryce and I'm waiting for my cousin Brick to get with me. My father and his brother married sisters, my mom and my auntie. Ironically both women had 7 sons each from the brothers. My mom rounded her offspring to 10 with 3 girls, while my Aunt Kleesie, went for the uneven number of 11 by having 4 girls in her bunch. My uncle and auntie was a little older, so they'd had a few before my parents got started. My cousin Bryce is 46 and the oldest male offspring of the double Tillman clan. He tries to play his part with keeping us all in line...especially after my dad died. It's a big job to regulate 14 men, not to mention the sons of the sisters, sons of the brothers...testosterone just running rampant all down the family line. Some of us he was successful with and some of us...not.

There was an ensuing debate going on about the virtues or shall we say advantages of womanizing. It goes without saying that Murad was in the center of the conversation. Old man Walker who has been a barbershop fixture since forever just sat amongst the midst of it all half hearing and half seeing, but living for every minute of it.

"But check this Rod," Naim said, "You always had the hos' lined up waiting for a hit from you like feenin'crack heads. How you gonna be all of a sudden disagreeing?"

"Hey look," Rod said, "I ain't disagreeing with nobody, all I'm saying is that I'm on another page now...a new chapter. I ain't in to all that no more. I've just put things in perspective when it comes to physical contact"

"Oh so you plan on sharing that shit," Qwaim said, "or you gonna be stingy with it?"

"Yeah Rod...let me hear this shit," my cousin Lonnie said.

"Aight," Rod started, "Like I said...my perspective. When it comes to physical contact with a woman, I've broken it down to three categories. First off you have fucking...the plain... the basic, the simple, the pure act of it. Then you have the form of sexing...This is a step up from fucking as it is blended with an appreciation of the physical form at hand, i.e. person you're with at the time or the most convenient . And this sexing doesn't necessarily need an emotional attachment to it. Then of course in 3rd place is the genuine art of making love. Not to be confused with fucking or sexing. When you truly make love, you are physically and intimately communicating a deep expression of your emotional status and or commitment to a woman.

Now all 3 of these versions have a side B to them. Sometimes niggas just be out here fucking without a consciousness...just nasty and digging out everything moving. And sexing sometimes is done for the sweetness of it all or perhaps to satisfy an addiction you've come to develop to one particular sista's bedroom energy. And the split version for making love is that ultimate baby making love. When you love someone so that it surpasses all else that exists, and you make love on the basis that a precious life will be your end result. And my synopsis of it all is...with the exception of version B of fucking, if you are lucky enough to be with the right person...you can have them all."

"Oh check this nigga out, he done got him a new lady and all of a sudden, he talking all philosophical and shit," Naim said.

"Well sometimes a man gets to a point in his life where he knows what he wants," Bryce put in tilting Murad's head to the side to work on his sideburns.

"Yeah either that or she got his ass whipped," Naim threw back out there.

"Oh ya'll motha fucka's can go head with all that" Rod said, "If you know like I knew...you would be begging to get whipped."

"Oh don't be trynna rope us up into the same arena with yo' ass," Naim shot out. "I ain't never ....and say never... gonna be quote unquote whipped by no ass."

"Yeah man whatever," Rod said while extracting his phone that just vibrated on his hip. As he viewed the caller id box, a wide ass grin came over his face as he slid the phone to answer.

"Hey babe...what up? Yeah...I'm just about finishing up. Bryce is doing my side burns."

"Peace Nubina," Bryce hollered out, "What's going on there...how's the little lady doing?"

"Yo," Murad said laughing into the phone, "Did you hear Bryce...he wanna know how you doing? She said fine B...just fine. Yeah...what you like 10 minutes away. Aight...cool. I should be done by the time you get here...Just hit me up when you out front."

"Whoa...Nube coming by here?" Bryce asked. "How she gonna roll pass without stopping in to see one of her biggest fans?" I could see Murad hesitate slightly before he relayed that info to Nube.

"So you coming in...You sure? Aight...I'll see you when you get here. Later." he said disconnecting the call.

"Look at this nigga here," Naim said. "Little honey rolling around in his shit now...picking him up and what not."

"Oh daayuumm man....she out pushing the Escalade?" my cousin Sharief asked, "She sho'nuff got your ass flying under the radar. I mean we talking a bossed out 2008 ESV, spinning on 24's with every amenity going. That's a tall order for a dude to be rocking, let alone a female"

"Maaan....listen," Murad answered, "Y'all nigga's need to stop hawking me about what I'm doing."

"I'm just saying," Sharief responded, "shit must be awfully good if you got little honey pushing the big boy"

In response to the laughter throughout the shop Rod just replied, "All I got to say to that is....what the fuck ever...shit speaks for itself."

"You know what," Cory called out of the blue... all insignificant, his words just reeking of ignorance, "Ain't that Nubina girl, the same sister that used to be with your brother?"

The whole barbershop came to a stand still, clippers stopped buzzing in mid-air....combs left unattended, waiting to rake thru mounds of nappy hair. An anonymous voice whispered out, "That's what I thought." I quickly looked to check Murad for a reaction and saw his jaw click tightly.

"Now look," Bryce interjected, "That ain't none of ya'll business...stay out the man business."

"Naw its cool" Murad answered, "I knew the shit was bound to come up sooner or later. Yeah she and my brother was tight...but it wasn't the caliber of relationship that you thinking."

At that precise moment I wasn't sympathetic to him, cause although I declared that I would give him no more grief about it, I still couldn't hold favor to his decision to pursue a relationship with her. Besides every black man in the hood knows the first rule in Barbershop 101 - There are no exemptions on who gets ripped...on any given day that shit is up for grabs. You just gotta man up.

"Oh so you saying...they had one of them what you call it...poltanic relationships?"

As the whole barbershop bust out laughing, Murad just dusted the whole thing off with, "Mutha fucka...next time you wanna interrogate another man about his business...bring ya momma and ya fucking dictionary wit'cha...maybe the two of you can figure that shit out together." And with that the whole barbershop erupted in laughter again.

"Oh fuck you nigga," Corey shot back, "I don't need no dictionary to tell me..."

"Yo cut it," Bryce one again interceded, "There's a queen present," he indicated to Nube who had just walked in the door.

All heads turned, and once again the whole shop came to a full halt. As she stood in the doorway with a mode of innocence all around her, I couldn't help but to gawk with the others at her beauty. She had just had her hair done as well, and it was styled in beautiful loose curls that could rival Beyonce's. The one thing that put hers over the top was that these curls consisted of her own hair. She had on some blue pleated pants with a cuff and an ivory color silk sweater that stopped just at the waistband of the pants bringing attention to a very complimentary gold-toned link chain belt that fastened off to the side and dangled like an accessory to a set of banging hips. Somehow she had a deep navy blue suede jacket with fabulous detailed stitching that matched some fly-ass navy blue suede ankle boots and navy suede handbag. She accessorized in gold...nothing too elaborate, cause that much is true about Nubina...she doesn't get into materialism on a high level. In fact...I'm wondering if Rod bought that stuff for her. He on the other hand loves to shop. He's a clothes horse as well as a shoe monger. Not to mention he has more jewelry than a small jewelry store.

She looked dead on at Murad, and gave him that smile as if he was the only one there...and he did the same. I do have to say... the slacks were fitting her like they were custom made and accentuating her flawless shape. The simplicity of her look gave her a classiness that promoted within her sexiness beyond the average woman. I guess all them years that she'd been friends with my cousin Sumira...not too many of us took the time to notice...or at least I didn't. But today I had no choice but to admit that I see what Murad sees...that silent subdued sexy.

Bryce broke the silence with, "Oh you just gonna come up in here to grin at this nukka here? You can do all that later. Come on over here and show me some love."

She responded with laughter, "Bryce..you know I didn't forget about you. I came all the way up in here to especially give you love." She walked around to the chair and let him give her a big ole' bear hug. As she released herself from the hug, she turned and greeted everyone in the shop.

"Peace gentlemen," she started with then added on, "How are you Brick...Antoine...Sharief...Lonnie," giving acknowledgement to my cousins.

"Hey there Dream," she called out saving an extra special acknowledgement for me. A part of me felt like she was trynna win me over, while the other part of me was gloating with a big head that I got special attention.

"Hey Nube," the called out collectively.

"What's going on Princess?" my cousin Lonnie said.

"Oh just a little bit of this and a little bit of that," she answered. "We on our way uptown to meet with some big shots at PBS. I'm going to be writing a narrative for a documentary with them on social behavior."

"Damn girl," he responded, "You rolling with them white shirts huh?"

"Yeah...I can hold my own with them. The colors of the shirts don't matter too much to me. So what's going on up in Tillman's corner? Who you all ragging on today?"

"Well," Corey said, "We was just talking about you."

Nube spun around to question him. "Wow...did you say me?" she asked slightly amused, "I rate all that? Well...uh brother...I don't know your name."

"It's Corey," he interjected.

"Well okay then Corey," Nube replied, "How did I come to be the topic of your discussion?"

"It's just that...uh...some of us was...uh wondering," he started stumbling over his words.

"Naw...nigga...that was your nosey ass," Sharief called out. Bryce shot him a look and he recanted, "Oh excuse me Nubina for my profanity. But that was you being nosey Corey."

"Well Corey," Nube questioned him with a little devilishness about her, "What is it that **you** need to know?"

"Oh...well...I was just...you know like thinking...well like I had heard that... you used to be with the other brother...JT," he rushed out.

"Oh is that what's really important to you Corey...knowing whether or not I've had two brothers? Well if you chose to believe that ...then let me whisper something else in your ear," she said leaning over to whisper in his ear. I made a special note to watch Murad's reaction to this whole scenario and was surprised that he was not upset.

As Nube whispered in Corey's ear, his eyes got big and he said, "Word."

As Nube raised back she tipped Corey on the chin and said, "Close your mouth Corey," pushing his mouth shut. As the shop again erupted into laughter Nube broke out with, "Corey, trust me when I tell you...believe none of what you hear and half of what you see."

"You tell him Princess," Lonnie said co-signing to her cliché.

"Yeah well we gotta make this here move," Murad said as Bryce dusted him off and removed the cape. "Here you go B," he said paying for his cut, "I'll shoot back thru here once we get back from Cali. Nube is a shoe-in for a 6 episode spot on CSI-NY. We going out to do a final reading, and if them cats at CBS are satisfied, then it's a go."

"Whoa...now that's what I'm talking bout," Bryce responded, "Nubina making waves in waters everywhere."

"Yeah," Murad answered kinda in another zone, "she's definitely on the map. Aight...we gotta get outta here," he said breaking his reverie, "B...I'ma come thru once we get back, fellas...ya'll stay up. We gonna hook up and hang out once I get back."

"Oh man...go head with that," Brick answered, "we lucky we see you for a hair cut."

"Naw...I'ma get something going...on the real...something just for the fellas," Murad answered making his rounds dapping all the fellas up. "You ready," he said to Nube.

"Sure," she responded, "Gentlemen" she addressed the whole shop, "It was a pleasure...I leave you in peace."

"Okay...Later...peace to you..." the many greetings voiced throughout the shop.

And just as they turned to walk out, Nube turned back and called out, "And oh...by the way Corey," and blew him a kiss, "That's for you."

Once again the whole shop exploded in laughter, only this time, Corey couldn't do nothing but blush and laugh along with the rest.

Chapter 37

The Worst Day Of Our Lives

Murad

I had to continue to laugh as I stepped out of the barbershop taking Nube's hand as we made our way to the car.

"Nube...girl what in the world did you say to him?" I asked her.

"Oh, that's private information between me and Corey," she answered me laughing.

"Awww Nube...you gotta be careful what you tell his rusty ass, cause he silly enough to believe it."

"Well that would be on him then Rod...no lesson learned on his part," she responded.

"Girl...trust me," I said laughing, "He just ain't that deep. Now when he start calling your ass..."

"Rod please," she laughed back, "We both know good and well you ain't about to let that go down. Forget about him."

"Man...I'm about hungry. How bout you?" I asked knowing that we were having dinner first with the agent from PBS.

"I guess I'll be ready to eat once we get there," she replied, "I've been trying to mentally review my presentation, and just haven't given eating a thought. I'm sure that when we get up there, I'll be ready to eat. Did you hear anything back from Paul Rubenstein in regard to the deal on the sitcom?"

"Naw," I told her , "I'm gonna hit him up when we get in the truck...you know....try to knock that out before we go up here and wrap our minds around another set of dealings. I don't know Nube...we may have to get an assistant manager if offers keep presenting themselves like this."

She'd had to park like 4 doors down from the shop and as we approached the truck, I pumped the remote so that I could help her up into the front seat before closing the door. I walked around to the driver's side and got in the front seat. I turned the auxiliary, and lowered the windows so that we could get some air.

"I'm gonna get him on the phone right now and see what the deal is," I said reaching around to grab my CD case holder. "Nube see if my CD's are over there by you. I can't feel them on this side. As she bent down to check under the seat, I turned back to the front to see whether or not the phone was dialing, and immediately was met by a strange presence…then heard the click.

"Shit," I let out knowingly.

"That's right mutha fucka…you know what it is."

Dude was standing at my door with a gun cocked just behind my left ear.

"Murad I don't see…" I heard Nube stop short and I took a look over and saw that another one was on her side. He didn't have the gun in her face, but he had it pointing at her.

"Get out the truck," dude on my side ordered. I raised my hands slowly and opened the door and got out of the truck. Once I exited, homeboy made a point of looking me up and down. Yeah…I was dipped being that we were going uptown on business. He gave a nasty look then grunted out "UUNNNHHH" as he hooked off into the left side of my face, spinning me around; "I hate you pretty boy mutha fuckas," he said. I braced myself with both hands on the truck door sucking up the fact that my face was throbbing, cause now I was facing Nube. She was sitting in the passenger seat with her eyes larger than the moon, and this other cat was eyeing her like a Wendy's combo with cheese. I didn't even want to think the unimaginable, so I told her in a low voice, "Get out the truck Nube." She looked at me as if she didn't really comprehend, so I gave her the eyebrow raise I give her when I want her to know its okay. As she started to climb out, dude over here said, "Run me ur shit," snatching the blackberry out of my hand, " I want that jacket…that fuckin watch," he said as it came into view once the jacket was removed, "Yo…nigga…where da wallet?"

"It's in the jacket," I said slowly backing myself around the front of the truck so I could get on the other side next to Nube. As he searched the jacket to locate the wallet, he yelled "Yo Poo…git her shit."

By now I was on the other side and on the sidewalk, and I placed myself as a barrier against Nube as I backed us both up to the gate on the storefront behind us. Poo was just looking, staring at Nube as if he'd rather eat her than rob her. My fucking blood started to pump out of control as I didn't know what these niggas was gonna pop off with next.

"Yo... git her shit Poo...so we can bounce," the first dude said. Poo looked at me and the fact that I towered over him and then he raised the gun towards us.

"Hand over the shit," he said.

"Yo' Money," I started, "Why don't you all just take the truck and..."

"Yo Poo," the first dude yelled. Poo couldn't seem to make up his mind, and his partner pressing him presented him with the need to take action.

"Aight then...Shorty coming with us," he said reaching around me and grabbing a fistful of Nube's hair. That move right there put him at a disadvantage, and as she screamed out, I slammed my fist straight up into Poo's nose hearing the bone crack letting me know that I'd hit my mark.

"Oh shit," the first dude cried out. I saw him scrambling to squeeze off, so I grabbed Nube and slammed us both to the ground as he got off two rounds. "Yo Poo," he called out. When he didn't get a response he jumped in the truck and sped off.

As I heard the pealing of the truck tires competing with her frantic breathing, I turned to scoop her up and yelled out, "Nube...Nube...Are you okay... you okay?"

"I'm good Rod, I'm good," she answered me in a shaky voice that was not her own.

Poo was on the ground moaning and groaning with blood running down the front of his face, and I just lost total control. I got up and dragged his ass up off the ground and slammed him into the gate. I hammered him on the left side of his face, the right side of his face, and when he fell to the ground, I proceed to stomp this motherfucker clear thru the cement and straight to Hell without a passport. I was so in a whole nother zone consumed by my rage....I didn't hear Nube yelling for me to stop, nor did I see her run down the street back toward the shop.

"Yo' Dream...your brother is sho' nuff rolling a dime piece there," Naim said, "I hate to say it, but he was right...cause if that right there was my shorty...I'd be whipped like a mu'fucka." I really didn't have a response to his comment, so I just shrugged as if to indicate whatever. I saw Bryce take a glance at me, and I know that he had sensed my disapproval about the situation. I mean Brick, Sharief and all them are under the same pact being family and all but apparently no one really wanted to call Murad on his choice. In essence...they right...he's a grown-ass man...he's the one that has to live with his decision. Anyway...I'm next in the chair for Brick, and he's just about done with his current customer.

"I be with you in a minute cuz," he notified me.

"No problem," I answered, "It ain't like I got somewhere to be." Without warning we heard a pop-pop, as the sound of two rounds of gunfire filtered thru the open front door.

"Damn," Bryce said, "These nukka's can't find shit else to do than to be..." his voiced trailed off as the sound of a speeding vehicle came barreling past the shop. "Whoa," Bryce said, "Ain't that Murad's truck?"

As the blood in my veins began to freeze and before anybody had a chance to answer the question, Nube appeared in the front doorway in a disarray, and she weighed in with the final answer to the question when she let out a blood curdling, "LONNIIEE!!!"

Except for old man Walker...the whole shop emptied in a matter of seconds. When we got down the street Rod was stomping some dude into paste.

"Yo Rod...what the fuck," Brick yelled out.

"These bastards jacked me for my shit."

"Awwww...man," Lonnie interjected, "crack that niggas skull,"

"Done." Murad answered, still kicking the shit out of dude.

"Yo...yo...Murad...chill," Bryce intervened pulling Murad off of the guy. "Man...you got too much going for you to let this shit bring you down...you gonna kill him Rod."

"That mutha fucker deserve to be dead," Rod said. "He put his fucking hands on Nube," he bellowed as he paced back and forth, hands on his waist and steaming. "Yo...I'm scouting," he put out as an open invitation.

"Not a thing...let's roll," Brick said. "Lonnie...get the heat...I'ma go get the car."

I knew there was no way to stop Murad when he's been violated, so I just reasoned up that I'd be going with him on his mission. As Lonnie came back from the shop, and Brick pulled the car around the corner, Nube walked up and surveyed the scene. Fear and disbelieve portrayed itself across her face, and Murad seemed to wince as he remembered his obligation.

"Dream...take her home," he called out to me. I must have looked confused, so he answered my confusion and said, "My house...you know the code."

As he jumped in the car, Nube called out, "Murad?"

"I'ma call," he blew her off with. He wasn't beat to hang around and allow her time to reason with him. "Yo Dream...git her outta here," he said as the car pulled off with Brick, Lonnie, and Sharief in tow. Everyone else just stood around and just looked at dude on the street. I mean...exactly what was it that we were supposed to do about him. He took his chances trying to strong arm and he got dealt some consequences. Nube must have been on a different page cause she asked, "Bryce...what's gonna happen to him now?" indicating to the guy on the ground.

"Hey Dream...go get the car," he said to me, putting Nube in another big bear hug so that he could block her view of dude, "Don't you worry," he told her, "We gonna take care of it all...just go on home and wait for Rod." He sat there and held her in a hug until I backed my car up down the street, and when I got there he walked her over, opened the door and put her in the car.

"Everything gonna be fine little Tender," he said kissing her on the forehead, "Just fine." He tapped on the roof to let me know to go ahead and pull out, so I did just that...carrying us both to Murad's house.

Look at this shit of a mess here. Damn...why these little nukka's had to pick Murad to car jack? Man... "Well I guess ain't nothing else here left to see," I spoke.

"Yeah...mutha fucka got what he deserved," Naim said. "Guess he won't be out running up on people no time soon." As they all turned to walk away and head to the shop, I pulled out my phone to put in a call of necessity.

"Good evening...East Orange Police Dept. main desk," I heard after the 4th ring.

"May I please have Sgt. Machiah Tillman's line," I asked.

"One minute please."

"Sgt.Tillman...how can I help you," I heard.

"Yo Kye...yeah...looka here. Some knuckle heads done went and car-jacked Rod and assaulted Nubina over here by the shop," I told him.

"Damn...so what's the status?" he knew to ask me.

"Him, Brick, Lonnie and Reef went riding on them. I need you to call in his plates so you all can trace the truck; KMV 59Z. He got that Lo'Jack shit...I need you all to find that truck before they do. Rod got blood in his eyes, Brick on parole, and I'm sure Lonnie got a warrant or two on his ass," I said.

"Aight...I'll do that, then I'll call Jarod down in Newark so he can be on the lookout. Once they give a location on the truck, I'll meet Jarod over there. How many of them was it?" he asked.

"I don't know how you wanna do this...but one down already," I told him, "He laying over here...like a puddle of soup."

Chapter 38

Vengeance Is Mine

Murad

"Damn...Rod," Brick said. "You ain't had ya' shit on you?"

"How the fuck I'ma throw down in a gun fight and I got Nube with me?" I answered him highly irritated.

"Aight...Aight, relax," he replied, "I'm just amped...you right...you right. How fucking many of them was it?"

"Just 2," I answered him. "That nigga caught me out there, had his shit right up against my head, couldn't do nothing but go wit it. Besides the other dude was eyeing Nube like he at the buffet bar. All I was really trynna do was let em' take whatever and git on...I'da got the word on them later...but this Poo mutha fucka talking bout he was taking Nube with them and gonna reach around me and grab her by her hair."

"Oh fuck...no he didn't," Brick yelled out.

"Man...I'm telling you...I tried to push his fucking nose thru the top of his skull," I answered him, "I knew he had that shit on his mind the way he kept looking at her from jump.. B...I'm telling you...I don't know...I'm fucking telling you now...be ready to bail me. Every time I think about that nigga putting his hands on her" I had to stop and get a grip cause my blood was literally pumping like 50 miles an hour.

"Well I don't think his ass gonna be thinking too much about nothing, no time soon," Sharief said, "All we gotta do now is find homeboy with the truck"

"Oh we gonna find him," Brick said. "We gonna find him and give his ass a calling card from Tillman Inc."

"No doubt...no doubt," I answered, "That mutha fucka gonna pay deep in ass whup on this one. Besides I need to get my shit before he discovers it...I mean my shit is legit, but I don't want it out on the street linking me to fucking nothing. We gotta find the truck"

"Yo Rod," Lonnie piped in from the back seat, "Did you say one of them was named Poo?"

"That's what his boy was calling him."

"Well I know of a Poo...use to hang down on Chadwick. Matter o'fact...his ass just got out like last month. He run with this cat Frenchy and they known for running up on people."

"Well then Chadwick it is," Brick said turning the car south toward Newark, "I see he got one off on you."

"Yeah," I said rubbing my face on the spot of impact, "Nigga was fucking hatin, eyeing me up and down like a jealous bitch...yeah he got that shit off since he had the advantage, but I swear for God when we catch up to his ass...he gonna eat his fucking words."

"Well ain't you got that fucking Lo Jack," Sharieff asked.

"Yeah I do, but they ain't gonna act on it until I call it in," I answered, "I want to find his ass first and square shit up before the police show up."

"Well since you gotta call it in that gonna give us a jump," Lonnie said.

"Well...we ain't gotta worry about jumpin too far...there go his truck right there," Sharieff said.

Sure enough just out on 18th Ave my truck was parked outside the infamous Theodore's Lounge. Couldn't have been there that long.

"Yo Brick...box him in," I shouted, adrenaline back on the rise. This jack-ass got the nerve to be making stops and shit.

"I'm on it cuz," he said pulling up alongside the truck, "How we gonna do this?" he said as he set up his clips ready to pump if he needed to. Lonnie and Reef were in the back doing the same and made the first move to step out the car. As if on cue, homeboy came out of the spot and started advancing toward the truck.

By this time Lonnie and Reef were on the sidewalk and he just assumed they were the owners of the car.

"Uh...ya'll gonna have to move that fuckin car...I got somewhere to be," he shot off at them. By then Brick and I had gotten out of the car and advanced around to the other side. If I could've had a million bucks for the look on this nigga's face when he saw me.

"Oh shit," he called out as he attempted to run backwards reaching for his gun.

Lonnie, and Reef immediately drew on him and said, "Mutha' fucka…you got…don't even."

In his haste to get away, he stumbled over his own feet one door down from the club and fell backwards on his ass. Brick ran up on the right side of him and was about to crack his head open with the butt of his gun when I called out "Brick…hold up…this is fucking me right here."

"Aight," he said still holding the gun on him.

"Git his bitch ass up," I called out, as Brick snatched him up by the collar relieving him of his piece. "Ya'll check him," I continued to instruct as Lonnie and Reef came around to do just that.

In the mean time a couple of dudes came out of the club who happened to know him "What the fuck…" one of them said…reaching.

"Yo," Brick yelled out, grabbing Frenchy by the collar, "Hands up and 85 or ya' boy taking one thru the eye." Lonnie and Reef swung on him from different angles and as he realized he was out gunned he conceded.

"Aight…Aight," dude said raising his hands. After a slight pause he said "Yo Brick…is that you?" as he squinted in the dense light.

"Yo…who dat?" Brick threw back.

"It's me…Halim…from C15 down in Bridgeton."

"Hey Ha…what up dawg…what's good? Yo…this ya boy?" Brick questioned him.

"Yeah we cool and shit…whas' up?" Halim answered.

"Ya boy here jacked my cousin for his Escalade and some other incidentals," Brick said. "We came to collect."

"What the fuck is this?" I spit out fully frustrated, "Tea and crumpets? I don't give a fuck who knows who. Now he can lay down by himself or this can be a group thing…I really don't give a fuck…cause his ass is laying down tonight one way or another."

"Yo Rod, chill," Brick said, "Listen Ha...my cuz here is real upset tonight. He had his lady with him and they was real disrespectful to her...ya dude here gotta face it."

"Look," I stated, "Fuck all that...Halim...I give you my word a fair one going down between me and ya man." He looked at Brick as if to get an okay from him, and Brick nodded to let him know my word was bond.

"Aight then," I said "Hit me up...do the check so we can get this shit going." I obliged while Halim came and did a complete search.

"Yo Frenchy...he clean," Halim said. "Brick here is my boy and that's his people...you on ya' own for this one."

"That's shit's cool," Frenchy said, finding a sudden burst of courage, "I like bustin up them pretty niggas. I ain't even gonna break a sweat."

Great I'm thinking to myself. His ass is right where I want him to be...over confident. Niggas who over confident with themselves and underestimating me is just the incentive I feed off of.

"Let's go mutha fucka," I said advancing toward Frenchy, "Nix that talking...I'm bout to show you what this pretty ass nigga is working with."

"Let's go," he answered. As he threw up his hands and started his 360 rotation, I smirked inside acknowledging his typical jail house bullshit.

"Yeah pretty boy," he taunted, "I'm gonna enjoy..."

He didn't get to finish cause I tapped him straight in the mouth, splitting his bottom lip.

"Oh...oh...you got that one off," he said, "That's all you getting, cause I ruled when I was down in..."

He didn't even see the left I popped off straight into his right temple. One thing I learned in training thru my boxing and with my sensei...don't waste your energy and ability to strategize by talking thru your battles.

"Yo Frenchy," one of his people called out, "you down for two nigga. Whas up?"

He must have gotten ticked off by that comment cause he tried to charge me with a right hook that I sideswiped, and delivered him a sharp kick to the left kidney. He stumbled off balance, letting out a grunt then quickly tried to regain his step.

By now I think he knew his ass was gonna sweat and much more. At the same time he was trynna save face in front of his boys and the growing crowd that came outside to see the action.

"Awwww...shit," he said, "that's all the fuck I'm taking from you. That's it...that's it," he said all the while circling in his rotation, "Think ya ass better than somebody...you ain't shit. You lucky Poo real slow and shit, cause we was gonna take your girl and split that ass like..."

Wrong answer I thought as his words penetrated and brought back my kill along with a crashing right to the jaw. I heard the jaw pop, and kept on going. I was tired of playing with his ass and crashed a left into his chest. He stumbled, doubled over and came back up. Fine I thought as I crashed his face continuously with rights and lefts listening as the other jaw popped.

"Damn," his people called out. "That mutha fucka is whupping his ass something crucial"

"Yo...ain't somebody gonna stop it," somebody called out.

"It's a fair one," Lonnie responded, hand in his waist. "Ain't nobody stopping shit."

At this point I guess homeboy decided that he needed to take his last stand, and tried to charge me. Just before impact I delivered an upper cut to the abdomen and he doubled over grabbing me. I peeled his ass off of me and flung him up against the wall. And as he stood there now all bloody and lumped up looking worse than Martin after his fight with Tommy Hearns, he still felt the need to go out like a champ.

"So what mu' fucka," he slurred, "You still ain't shit." Enough of him I thought as I just up and gave his ass a round house kick straight to his mouth giving off a resounding "splish," as teeth, blood and whatever else flew thru the air.

"Daaayyumm," somebody called out as he hit the pavement face down. No sooner had he hit the ground, I heard police sirens in the background.

I stepped over to his ass and said, "Gimme my shit," as I rifled thru his pockets to get my wallet, my blackberry and my watch back. I guess the jacket was in the truck, and I prayed that my gun was still in the secret compartment. With the sirens in the background most people discreetly disappeared as most of them out there was in no position to see the police tonight.

"Yo Lonnie," Brick said, "You and Sharief ...take a walk. I'm staying here with Rod. I'll hit you up in a few."

With Brick being the oldest of the three they obeyed, and slipped away with the rest. Brick walked over to his car and put his gun in the trunk, just as the squad cars arrived. Three from Newark...and one from... East Orange? What the...as Brick and I both threw each other a questioning glance; we came to the conclusion at the same time as we both said out loud... "Bryce"

Chapter 39

Sitting With Jezebel

Dream

I wasn't exactly sure how to handle what just went down, so I let Nube do all the talking while I guided the car over to Murad's Maplewood townhouse.

"I don't understand why we as a people continuously pillage and plunder our own," she started, "I mean…how can you keep crying about what society does to you, yet you go out and bogard from the next man?"

"I don't know Nube," I offered my answer.

"Rod works hard for everything he's got," she said her voice starting to crack. Oh lord, I'm thinking, please don't let her start crying, I ain't good with females crying and whatnot.

"Well what happened?" I broke in with hoping to get her speaking as a distraction.

"Well we had just gotten into the truck, we were searching around for his CD case, while Rod was making a phone call, and then when we turned back around these 2 guys were up on the truck with guns drawn. The one on Rod's side ordered him out of the truck, and then he just up and punched him in his face…talking bout he hate pretty boys. Then he snatched his phone, took his jacket and his watch. In the meantime Rod told me to get out of the truck, which I did, and he came around to the other side to get me, and this other dude just kept staring at me, giving me the creeps. Rod tried to reason with them, and told them to just take the truck, but the first guy was demanding my things also. So the creepy guy, I guess was going too slow, and the first guy yelled at him, and then Creepy decided that not only did he want my things, but he was gonna take me with them and he reached around Rod and grabbed me by my hair. Next thing I knew, Rod hooked off on him…his face exploded…the 1st guy started shooting, and I was on the ground while the truck was speeding off. Rod went crazy Dream…he went ballistic on dude. I couldn't get him to stop, he wasn't hearing me."

Wow...I'm thinking, I know Murad...he's not going to rest until he spill blood from both them niggas. Damn...they tried to snatch up Nube? God only knows what them slimy bastards would have done if they'd succeeded. I didn't dare relay that to her, so I just answered, "Well, you did the right thing by coming back by the shop. Ain't no telling what shape dude would be in now if Bryce ain't pull Rod offa him."

"But yeah Dream," she replied, "How do we know now...how do we know?"

I just looked over at her, looking so small and scared, and all I could say was, "I don't know Nube...I don't know."

We got to the house, and I punched in the code and let us in. As I went to go take a seat on the couch, Nube made her way into the kitchen. "I'm gonna make me some tea Dream, would you like some," she asked me.

"Naw Nube, I'm straight," I answered. She put the water on, got a mug and a tea bag, then came back into the living room. She removed her boots and jacket, and set her bag in a nearby chair. I was taking it all into account how very much at home she seemed to be. Well what am I thinking...she and Murad was close like that before they hooked up...duh. She took a seat on the sofa and blew out a deep breath.

"I'm a little anxious Dream," she said, "Murad is really fired up. He's like in mad-man zone. There's no telling what can go down." I'm thinking...girl you don't even know the half. I'm sure she hasn't seen Murad at his worse.

"Don't worry about it Nube," I answered her, "He said that he'll call, so he will. He wouldn't leave you hanging like that. Besides Lonnie won't let things get too out of hand, he's more mellow minded."

"Dream," she started again, her voice shaking, "If something happens to him...if something goes wrong."

"Nube...Nube," I intercepted, "Don't...listen, just sit there, I'll get your tea. You want anything special in the tea?" I got up and went into the kitchen, cause I would be way lost if she starts crying.

"Umm...just some sugar and lemon," she answered, "Okay...I'm a get myself together. I don't wanna make you uncomfortable Dream. Just...I don't know...just worried."

"Well don't," I told her, "Worry that is. You know Murad can handle himself...no doubt on that. He'll be okay...trust."

"I suppose he'll call," she voiced softly, gazing towards the ceiling. "Thank you," she said as I came back into the living room handing her the cup of tea. As I sat down on the couch, she took a sip, and just sat staring at me from her spot on the couch.

"What?" I asked her as she looked.

"Just wondering. How do you handle being so drop dead gorgeous as a man...Do you find that people give you a hard time because of your good looks?"

"Who me?" I replied in confusion.

"Yes you Dream," she said lightly laughing, "I mean...you and Murad can be twins. You both have that beautiful cinnamon-brown skin, kinda glazed over in bronze, with that beautiful silky-wavy hair; an unbelievably handsome face, and a smile that can con anyone into believing whatever you've got to say. I don't know...it seems like people are constantly judging Murad because of his physical attributes in a negative manner. I was just wondering if you encounter the same."

"I guess I've never thought much about it," I told her, "The most problem that I've had, was keeping my head straight with all the attention from all the different women. Can't say I've really experienced much negativity. Nube, Murad is a different person. It's not just his looks, it's his unique flair, his steelo and his ability to succeed that makes him a target for haters."

"True, I agree," she said, "yet this guy here didn't know any of that about him, he just decided he needed to hit him based on his looks. And that shit right there is nagging me. Can you imagine the level of insecurities going on in people's minds?"

"Well that's just how dudes are Nube...very competitive. They can get easily intimidated by another man who's up on his game, cause it reminds him that he's not. And yeah...if you happen to look good, they hate on you even more. You know, now that you mention it, yeah...people do sometimes give me attitude for no reason at all."

"I thought so," she said, "You just walking around here all oblivious Dream. I see what Rod encounters all the time, so I know you get your share, whether you paying attention or not." She finished off her comment with laughter.

"Well what about you?" I asked her, "Do you get a lot of attitudes from other women. I mean you are definitely worth your weight in gold as well as beauty. How do you handle it?"

"Well Dream," she started, "I try to remain in a focused mindset. I feel that there's too many important things going on in the world for me to pay attention to female cattiness. I absolutely don't get involved on any level. If I happen to run across the attitudes, I brush them off, that's if I even take notice to them at all. Somebody else's attitude is so not my problem. I mean I had a lot of practice when Rod and I was on the road...you know...before we were together. Women would just be stalking him and pushing up on him left and right. Most of them thought there was something between us, so yeah I had to take some snide remarks. I just always handled myself in a positive manner, by letting them know there's no such day I would stand and argue with anyone over a man...you know. At the time I didn't know that would be preliminary practice for a reality that I have to deal with now that we're together."

"Okay," I stated, "but what about people just hating on you for always having an opinion, always having something to say. Do you find that people take it better from you because you're good looking, or unwilling to accept you because of your appearance?"

"Honestly Dream," she answered me, "I don't consider myself a great beauty...beauty is truly in the eyes of the beholder. I mean I know that I have desirable looks because I've been told so by others and not only that...I don't scare myself when I look in the mirror;" To that we both laughed, "But I am serious on the things that I speak about...I mean I really believe in the things that I have to say, and as I share them with others, I appreciate those who are able to connect to what I'm saying. For those who are not at the level to comprehend the true meaning, or either not willing to at least embrace it...I send up a prayer that some day they will. So the importance of people judging me for what I'm about is strictly on an individual basis. It all depends where they are in their life and how they come at me; I then make a point to respond or react accordingly."

Hmm…I never really had a true conversation with Nube; she's really about the positive issues she speaks about. That's cool, that's really a good thing. Perhaps I've been a little closed minded about her, thinking that she's a little shady to deal with one brother and then another. There's a vibe that I'm getting here today, that it is just not the case. I watch as she takes a sip of the tea, and then glances at the clock on the wall. We arrived here like 6:45; it was now 7:40 and time seemed to be dragging.

In an effort to keep her distracted, as well as quiet the burning question in my brain, I just jumped on in and asked her the ultimate, "Nube…what happened with you and JT?" She took another sip of her tea, set her cup down on the coffee table, and looked at me head on.

"Dream…I've known for a minute that you don't approve of my relationship with Murad…and I understand…believe me I do. And yes, it does look a little suspect from the outside looking in, but actually, JT was the one to end the relationship between us. He told me that he felt that my career and entertainment lifestyle did not fall in line with his religious beliefs and way of life."

"Really?" I responded to her.

"Yes…that's what he told me. But…I happen to know that Murad and JT spoke on us being together and it was revealed by Jayson that he felt I belonged with Murad," she said sending my brain into overload.

"Wait a minute," I started, "You telling me that Jayson made the decision that his women…his beautiful, gorgeous, sexy woman should be with his brother and not him?"

She looked at me and said, "Dream, people make choices based on where they are in their lives, and what they can mentally handle at the time. Trust me, your brother Jayson is a man of much spiritual wisdom and knowledge, and if he made that decision, he has it backed up with reasons that satisfy justification within him. So please don't judge him as a punk or a wimp or whatever you guys would classify him as. He is a man of solid mind…just not the man for me. I have nothing but love and respect for him."

"But Nube…I'm saying. Look at you girl…do you know how many eyeballs were popping out of their heads and I'm sure thinking unreal thoughts when you came into the shop earlier. As a man…how could Jayson let you go? On the physical alone…that's just too much to process," I told her.

I noticed that she blushed a little, but she remained true to the matter and said, "Dream…Jayson and I never slept together." At that given moment, I think my head spun around like the exorcist.

"Nube," I bust out all extra, "You guys were together for 2 years. What do you mean you never slept together?"

"Dream we never engaged in sex," she responded, "He was very much into his religion and felt that he was not at a personal level to engage in physical activity, so we abstained, and I supported him in his effort to obtain his level of self betterment. I mean, I wasn't involved with him when he was going thru his hurt and grief from Kane's mother, but I know issues like that can take anyone thru the loop."

"But you was his girl…his woman," I came back with, "And he's a man…how could he not want to?"

"Well I don' think that he never wanted to…like you said he is a man. One time we did get into some kissing and touching, but he shut it down, keeping us from crossing the line and that was that," she responded.

I just sat there with my mind spinning round and round. What the fuck is going on? … Jayson…no sex…Murad…in love…is it the "something else" is happening thing for real? It's truly beginning to look like something bigger than us all is going on. I guess my lack of responding to her last comment prompted her next statement.

"Dream…like I said before, I'm sure quite a few in the family is not happy with the decision Murad and I made, but I wouldn't change it for the world. I can now say I'm grateful that JT and I never crossed the line, cause it's makes the pill of them being brothers much easier to swallow. I love Murad, Dream…like it's nobody's business and I am not ashamed of that in any way. So for those who have a problem with it…Oh well…cause that right there is something that is never going to change."

As she got up to place her cup in the kitchen, I just sat there with my mind totally off base. Jayson had a stunner, a treasure, and he just handed her over to Murad? He and Murad have always had some kind of little tension thing going on between them; I guess because Murad has always been rough and tumble, and he always felt that Jayson was too soft, which is something that irks him. So I can't figure how Jayson...who you could say finally won something over Murad, would then turn around and give him the prize. What the fuck is truly going on?

"Dream," I heard her say breaking into my thoughts, "I'm going up to freshen up and change my clothes. Let me know if he calls."

"No problem Nube," I answered her.

As she trotted upstairs, I reached for the remote and turned on the TV. It was now 8:30 and instead of just sitting here, I decided to call Bryce and see if he'd heard anything. As I punched in the number, I flipped the channel on the TV and a report on News 12NJ caught my eye.

"*There were 2 men hospitalized in serious condition in connection with a car-jacking this evening that started on Sanford Ave. in East Orange, and ended up in Newark. Although the incident is still under investigation and details still sketchy, we do know that both men were not victims, but said to be the perpetrators behind the crime. We'll have more details on this twisted tale of events as the story develops.*"

Damn...I'm glad she upstairs and ain't hear this shit.

"Speak slick," I heard Bryce answer just as the newscaster switched to another story.

"Yo B," I answered, "Did you see the news? What's going on...where's Rod and dem?"

"They down at the precinct with Jarod," he said, "They giving statements, and the police are filing a report. Jarod got one of his boys taking the statement so that there is no connection of the Tillman name on the report."

"Yeah but what happened?" I voiced anxiously, "Jarod operating out of Newark, how did he get involved?"

"Well, I called Kye," Bryce answered, "I didn't want shit to get way out of hand, and I had him call Murad's plates in to that Lo-Jack shit, and they located the truck over on 18th Ave. By the time Kye and Jarod got over there Murad had that mutha fucka down for the count just like his partner. And really...I don't know which one is worse off...Kye said teeth and shit just spilled all over 18th Ave, and both of them bastards are unconscious. I don't know Dream...shit is looking critical."

"Damn B, that sure nuff ain't sounding good," I replied. "Well Jarod called your brother Jarrell, and he sent Aaron down there too. So far no charges are being filed against Rod, and Aaron is on the case making sure nothing is being misconstrued since somebody at the hospital has already leaked whatever to the media. Where's Nube? Is she alright?"

"Oh she upstairs right now," I said, "She trynna hang in there, but I think she bout ready to fold at any minute if she don't hear from Murad."

"Well if she ain't heard all the nonsense going on, I would leave it for Rod to fill her in," he said and I agreed. "Well try and hold it down over there, cause it might be a minute before they actually cut him loose. They're gonna be holding the vehicle as part of the evidence of a crime scene, and some other nonsense."

"Aight, no problem," I answered, "I'm here till Rod gets back."

"Cool," he replied, "I'll hit you up if I hear something new. Peace."

"Aight...later," I responded. "Oh...hey Dream," I heard him say just before I clicked off.

"Yeah B, what up?" I asked him.

"Thanks," he said and hung up. Yeah, I said to myself as I caught his drift.

I sat and continued to watch TV for a good little while. Nube never did come back downstairs, so I decided to go upstairs and check on her. It was like 9:30 pm and still no Rod. I went upstairs and she was sitting up on the bed rocking.

"Oh hey Dream," she said, "I was sitting up her trying to just relax and meditate, but I can't channel tonight. I thought about changing my clothes, but then I thought what if I have to go back out or something, and then I was thinking that maybe..."

"Nube," I interrupted her, "Why don't you come on back downstairs with me, and we'll watch TV together or play some music or something. You don't need to be sitting up here all by yourself...too much time alone to be thinking."

"You might be right Dream...I just didn't want it to seem like you had to be babysitting me," she responded.

"Aww come on girl...we all need a little babysitting every once in a while," I told her, "Don't worry, you can pay me back and watch little Dez for me some time. Anyway...I'm a little hungry. Come on down and I'll fix us something to eat."

"Oh now this I gotta see," she said laughing making her way up off the bed.

"Oh what you think, I'm all pretty boy with no skills?" I asked her, glad to see a smile on her face.

"Well we about to find that out...now ain't we?" she answered back laughing as we made our way back downstairs. Yeah...Jezebel and I.

≈

Well it took no time to figure out that the best I could whip up in the kitchen was the nearest take-out menu that delivers. We found a pizzeria that promised a half hour delivery, and put in an order for a cheese steak w/fries, buffalo wings, and a tossed salad. Well most of that was for me, the salad belongs to Nube. She promised that she'd share my wings with me. While we waited on the delivery man, I put on some music and we laughed and joked about back in the day when she first started hanging out with my cousin Sumira. She told me that she remembered how my Aunt Kleesie was always fussing around the house and how she remembers that Bryce was always the good guy and kind to her when he came by with his wife and kids. On the other hand she informed me that Brick kind of picked on her a lot. I never knew that, and wondered what that could've been about. Then she went on to tell me how she and Lonnie have always been cool and he'd defend her against Brick's comments. I do recall Lonnie always taking up for Nube...in fact he just about takes her side on everything now. Hmmm...I'm thinking. How is it that Murad never noticed her before...I mean, he Brick and Lonnie have been tight since they were rug-rats, and he was over at their house a lot. Even more so once he became old enough to go over by himself.

Well…Nube wasn't always the knock-out that she is now. She was more quiet, reserved, and a little afro-centric with a book-worm flair. So I'm sure she didn't possess enough flash at the time for Murad, who was the ultimate player. Who would've known that they would mature and come together at this point in their lives. I mean I think she and Rod are close in age, he's 33, so I guess she's somewhere in the same neighborhood.

The doorbell rang announcing the arrival of our food. I paid the man while Nube went in the kitchen to get us some plates and find us something to drink. We sat down at the kitchen counter and started in on the food. Damn, I hadn't realized how hungry I was, as I stuffed my mouth with the cheese steak. "Oh…I'm sorry Nube," I said between bites, "Did you want some?"

"Well I was gonna ask you for a couple of the fries, but you just slobbered all over them and..unh-unh," she answered me laughing.

"Ahh..stop it girl," I answered back, "You can have some off of this side. I didn't bite off of this one."

"Okay, let me get my plate ready," she said, "You want some of my salad?"

"Naw…I'm good with what I got. Go head though…get you one of them wings," I told her, "You promised you was gonna help me out with them."

"Alright, let me taste one. I don't usually do the wing thing," she said, "Besides, I don't wanna put too much food on my plate." She put some of the fries, the salad and a wing on her plate, then joined me in eating. "Oh, this is tasty. I didn't think that I'd really feel like eating, but I guess I'm a little hungry too," she said

"Yeah, especially if you haven't eaten all day. This is hitting the spot," I co-signed.

I proceeded to polish off the rest of my food while Nube started to slow down on hers. I saw her glance at the clock, and note that it was now 10:40. She let go a deep sigh, and gave me a look.

"What's wrong Nube?" I asked her, although I knew fully well what was tormenting her.

"Dream, it's been hours," she answered me. "I'm over here lost in déjà vue and going out of my mind. I'm sitting up here with you, in his kitchen, sharing food with you the way he and I do, and you over there looking like his twin, reminding me of him and how he ain't here. Dream…I can't sit here no more…I'm about to go out and start looking for him. Something ain't right Dream…something ain't right! He hasn't called. Why hasn't he called?" That question was immediately followed with her voice cracking again, and I had to jump into rescue mode or risk dealing with her inevitable waterworks.

"Oh…hey Nube…no, no…don't. He probably just got caught up handling some things. I'm sure he'll call or be home soon." I got up from my seat and went to embrace her.

"Dreeeaaammm," she whined deeply as I held her. "What if he caught up to them…and what if shit got ugly…Dream…"

"Ssshhh…ssshhh," I told her for a lack of anything else to say. I wasn't sure how to handle this delicate situation, so I decided to take the same approach that I take when little Dez is upset…have her take a nap. "Look," I told her, "Come on here in the living room. We'll watch some TV and you lay on the couch and relax. Come on," I told her leading her into the living room, "As a matter of fact…you take this pillow…I'll sit and you can just lay the pillow on my lap so you won't have to look at me and see him. Okay?" She gave me a weak smile, but she agreed.

"I guess Dream," she offered a reply, "But please…no watching any news. I don't want that negative energy to filter thru my mind right now. I already have enough negativity in my cipher going on." So I sat, and placed the pillow on my lap and she curled up on the couch and lay her head down. As I struggled with whether or not to tell her that he's at the precinct, she stated softly, "Dream…he hasn't called….he hasn't called."

I didn't know exactly what to do so I just patted her head like I do little Dez and said, "I know Nube…I know."

We sat together on the couch watching old re-runs of Good Times trying to remain distracted from the obvious. Whenever she got fidgety I would commence to rubbing her head or her back until she settled down. It was now 11:45. I sure hope Murad makes an appearance soon, cause Lil Bit here about to lose it. We sat, we watched, and laughed at some of the corny scenes, and then as fate would have it…a romantic moment with Thelma and that football player finance played itself out on the screen. Oh damn...that's all the hell I need right about now. She started fidgeting again, and sighing, I once again began to rub her head in an attempt to settle her down. As I rubbed I leaned over and noticed that tears were quietly running down her face.

"Nube," I started, "Everything's going to be alright, trust me. I'm positive..." I paused mid-sentence as I heard the light sound of the alarm being disarmed and the door swung open revealing Murad. As he closed the door, she sat up abruptly and for just a hot second stared as if she'd seen a ghost. One hot second only though, because the next thing I knew she was up off the couch and ran straight to him jumping up in his arms, Murad scooped her up on contact swinging her around as she wrapped her legs around his waist. She bust out in full fledged sobs, and Murad collapsed them both into the nearby club chair, and with his voice cracking he called out her name, "Nube," and then he lost it...and matched her sob for sob.

I was so intrigued, so mesmerized, I was stuck watching them like a movie. As she called out his name over and over like a frightened child, "Murad...Murad...Murad," he pretty much answered her in the same way, "Nube...Nube...Butter." She just buried her face in his neck holding onto him for dear life, as he rocked her back and forth. I heard him take a deep breath, and knew that he was trying to pull it together. He took his hand and wiped his tears from his face, then took her arms from around his neck.

"Nube," he said, "Nube baby...you okay? Let me see you Nube, let me see you. Did he hurt you, are you okay?" he said examining her arms, her neck, tracing his finger on her face, as she nodded yes that she was okay. He reached over and kissed her tears, her lips, her forehead.

She looked at him and said, "He hit you...Rod he hit you," she gently touched the welt on his face and started crying some more.

"I'm okay Bae...I'm okay. It's nothing Nube...stop crying," He told her.

"You didn't call...he hit you...and you didn't call," she started getting back into the deep sobbing again, "Rod...you didn't call...you said you'd call."

"Oh...hey Butter...don't...listen...shhhhh...shhhhh...I'm here now...I'm here. I'll never leave you that long again Nube...I promise baby...I promise. I'm here...stop crying."

In between sobs, she said, "I was...gonna come looking for you...I...what happened Rod...what happened?"

"We'll talk about it later Nube...just calm down for now. Okay? I'm here...I'm here forever Nube...forever," he answered her and hugged her up and started rocking her again, kissing her.

I guess they forgot all about me...forgot that I was even there. I stood up and got my jacket and my keys. Not wanting to really interrupt, I told them softly, "I'm gonna...just go on and go now."

He looked over to me teary eyed, as I reached over and dapped him "Thanks for looking out bruh," he said as I made my way to the door.

"No problem," I answered, "Anytime." As I opened the door, Nube said something that I couldn't hear as she was still hugged up against Murad's neck. I glanced at Murad with a questioning look and he translated, "She said thank you Dream."

"No problem," I answered as I turned to the front door. He indicated with the phone gesture, that he'd call me later. As I started out the door, they once again became lost in each other.

"Nube," he said, and she raised her head to look at him, he kissed her lips so tenderly, and with so much passion, I once again thought I was at the movies. She eagerly responded and I felt myself transfixed there watching this private tender moment.

"Murad," she finally said breaking free, wiping a stray tear from his face in the process, "I love you way too much to be without you...you didn't call... what if something had happened?"

"Nube...baby," he answered, "I love you too fucking much to **let** something happen to me. Ain't no way I'm trynna let you be without me. I love you Butter...I love you." And as they began to communicate that fact with more kisses, I finally exited quietly closing the door behind me.

Chapter 40

Out Of Control

Murad

Oh man...it feels so good to be home, holding Nube. I can't stop kissing her, hugging her. I mean...just seeing her is bringing back the whole ugly incident fresh to my mind. Damn I love her. If I never knew before...I definitely know now. I love her soooo fucking much...Man if something had happened to her!! I wanna just sit here and hold her like this forever, where I know she's safe. The world can just revolve right on around us...I don't care. All I care about is I'm home now...home with Nube and she didn't get hurt...well not physically anyway. She is pretty shook behind this. I really meant to call her, but the time just got away with all the nonsense down at the station. Damn...What was I thinking letting her come into the shop...if she had never stopped we would have just been on our way. Could've had a nice dinner, signed the release papers, gotten our itinerary and invoices in place; now I've got to get a hold of them at PBS and explain this and hopefully reschedule. We continued to sit, and I continued to hold her, running my fingers thru her hair for another 20 minutes before I told her, "It's been a long day Butter. Come on, let's go on up to bed."

She sat up kissing me once again, before she replied, "Yes...the longest day. You could have never convinced me that we have this many hours in one day. The time just seemed to crawl while I was waiting to hear from you. Rod..." she stopped with a strange look on her face.

"What babe...what's wrong?" I asked her as she appeared to be staring directly at me.

"Murad," she started breathing heavily, pulling open my jacket, "What..your clothes...Murad...whose? All that blood!!! Murad...what happened?"

"Nube," I tried to answer but she cut back in.

“Oh Rod…tell me…Oh my God…tell me you didn’t kill them. Murad…did you kill them?” I just looked at her cause honestly…I don’t know their status. All I know is they were transported to the hospital. She gasped and put her hand over her mouth in shock.

“Murad…you killed them…ooohh no…please no…you killed them Rod? Ooooohhhh…no Rod…baby noooo…Murad tell me you didn’t kill them. Tell me!” she demanded.

Again I was stunned with the ramifications her statement brought along with the not knowing what the fuck was going on with them clowns. Personally I really didn’t care…all I know is they had no business touching her, nor coming for my shit. Far as I’m concerned they got what they got. Still…for some reason…I just could not bring myself to answer her. Not getting an answer from me sent her into a brand new panic. She jumped up off of my lap and started pacing the floor like her pants were on fire.

“Murad…you gotta answer me Murad. I’m about to lose my mind…Oh no…this can’t be happening to us…Noooo Rod…tell me you didn’t kill them Rod…tell me you didn’t kill them,” she spewed out and then broke down crying again clutching her stomach. Damn, I thought jumping up to go to her side. I reached for her to embrace her and she gave me the hand stopping me in my tracks.

“Unh-unh Rod,” she said in between sobs.

I was immediately crushed by that gesture and reacted by breaking out with, “Nube…what the fuck…Oh…so you scared of me now?” She looked at me with teary eyes and just dropped down in place to the floor.

“Nooooo…” she whined. “I just…don’t want…that…I can’t,” she pointed indicating the bloody clothes. I didn’t realize the after effects of them ass whippings would be this deep, so I humbly took off my jacket and shirt and tossed it. I unbuckled my pants, letting them drop and stepped out of my shoes, then turned to her.

“Nube…baby,” I started, “Let me…can I hold you…please?” This shit here is spiraling out of control and it’s killing me. I eased my way over to her and sat down on the floor right next to her. I reached over to hug her and when she didn’t resist, I grabbed her up and put her back in my lap, letting go the deepest sigh of relief possible. Thank you God…thank you God…I would be so fucking lost if she was ever repulsed by me.

"Murad…" she said continuing to cry.

"Oh Butter…Butter…please don't…don't," I told her rocking back and forth.

"Then tell me Rod…tell me," she said.

"Aww man…Nube…I don't know," I finally spilled out, "I don't…fucking…know. Live…die…that's on them. They had no fucking business taking my shit and putting they hands on you."

"So…you saying that…the punishment…deserved…to be…so severe," she replied still broken up.

"Nube…them greasy mutha fuckas got exactly what they deserved. If they would have got that shit off in taking you with them…what Nube…what?" I told her putting it out there, knowing that she knew exactly what I meant without me saying it. She grabbed on to me and held me tighter as I rocked her until she settled down. We sat there for a few more minutes, and I guess the realization of what I just told her set in, cause she raised up, giving me a look that begged for help, as she once again grabbed her stomach.

"Rod…I," was all she said before she made an attempt to reach the bathroom…she didn't make it.

Halfway down the hall she lurched forward, falling to her knees and threw up. She looked down and appeared to be affected by the fact that she vomited and threw up again.

"Rod," she cried out.

"I'm here Nube…I'm here," I told her as I made my way down to her. I got right down on the floor next to her. "Aww Nube…you okay?" I asked her. She looked up at me, with her pretty brown eyes, searching my eyes for a rhyme and a reason as to why things went down as they did. I didn't have an answer for her. Her eyes held so much sadness there, that I almost started to cry again myself.

"Rod," she cried out again.

"What's the matter Nube…you feel another go round? Go head Nube…get it out," I told her. And she did. I backed up a bit, but it really wasn't too much else coming out. It seemed like she was done, so I got right back down with her and kissed her forehead.

"You good Nube...you alright?" I asked. She nodded and just sat there without speaking. I sat for a few minutes so she could get herself together, then I got up on my knees and started undressing her. She just sat right there and let me. I was extra careful not to track anything into the mess. I got her out of her clothes and just dumped them in a pile next to the mess. I'd worry about cleaning that up later. I bent down at the knees and just scooped her up and took her upstairs to the master bathroom. I kicked down the toilet seat and set her down. I turned on the water in the tub and as the tub filled up I got a bathroom cup and poured some mouthwash into it. "Here babe," I told her. She looked up at me and just got up and started rinsing.

While the water was running, I went back into the bedroom so I could get a rag from the closet and to find something to pin up her hair. I found one of her hair clips and came back into the bathroom. She was now brushing her teeth and I waited patiently until she rinsed.

"You done?" I asked her.

Again she just nodded. I went and stood behind her and took her hair and pinned it up out of the way. I reached over to shut off the water in the tub, then turned back and unhooked her bra. I removed it and tossed it to the side, then grabbed her panties at the waist and slid them down. She stepped out of them without a word, so I just scooped her up again, and placed her gently in the tub. I wet the rag, soaped it up, and just started washing her. I began with her face and continued downward. I washed every crack and crevice as gently as I could just like she was a newborn. I really wanted to climb in there with her, but I didn't press it, cause I'm not exactly sure what she got going on up in her head. Usually we pretty much in sync, but tonight...I can't catch her on the radar. I'm not used to her being this silent and withdrawn. Nube usually verbalizes everything...especially to me. Well tonight was one for the books, so I'll just leave her to herself. She'll open up to me when she's ready. Once I finished washing her, I let the water out; turned on the portable jet spray, and used it to rinse her off. I got the bath towel and helped her to her feet, she stepped out of the tub onto the bathmat, and I began to towel her down. After I finished I just wrapped her up in the towel and carried her into the bedroom and placed her on the bed. I unwrapped her from the towel and spread it out on the middle of the bed, and told her to lie down. She complied still without saying a word. I went to the closet in the dressing room and picked out some coconut lime body oil, then went back into the bedroom. I got up on the bed and begin to oil her, gently, carefully as if I was handling a piece of Swarovski crystal that I was scared to scratch. Once I finished, I went to the dresser and pulled out some nightwear from the drawer I keep stocked for her. She sat up, and I just went on and dressed her for bed.

"Wait right here," I told her as I went back to the dressing room to get a brush and comb. I went back in the room and attempted to wrap her hair. I mean...I've seen her do it a couple of times whenever she wears it straight. I parted it on one side and then made my way around like I was frosting a cake. I managed to get it wrapped around, just not as smoothly as she does.

"Be right back," I told her as I went over to her draw and got one of her head scarves. I came back and tied it around her head. I took her hand to help her up off the bed so I could pull back the covers and she climbed in. I pulled the covers up on her and knelt down o the floor next to the bed.

"Nube," I said. She looked at me, her pretty brown eyes reflecting tired pain. I kissed her tenderly, softly...she responded. Cool...she's still responding to my touch. "Get some rest Butter. I'm going to clean up and then I'll be right up...okay?" She nodded, then turned on her side and closed her eyes.

I blew out a deep sigh as I trekked downstairs to tackle this mess. My mind was congested with so much right about now. Just think...two fucking minutes brought about all this chaos. I had to sit up and be interrogated all night and Nube is all tripped out and shit. I made my way to the kitchen to get some garbage bags, and I guess I need to get the bucket and shit. Damn...this whole thing is a mess. Maybe I shouldn't have fed her that last piece of information. Nube always preaching the body is a temple, and I suppose the thought of someone purposely violating her just made her sick to her stomach. Shit...was I wrong? I don't know...Naw...she needed to know. Nube sometimes get stuck in the positive energy hemisphere and fail to realize that niggas out here don't give a damn that you Positive Polly, let alone trynna hear nothing you talking bout. They ruthless and out to get what they can and sometimes just do shit cause they can. I just should have never let her get out the truck and come into the shop. I filled the bucket with Pine Sol and hot water and went back to the hallway. I used some old newspaper to soak that ship up first before I even attempted to mop.

I walked back to the living room and collected my own clothes. Taking a look at them, they did look pretty disgusting...oh man...this was some of my good shit. Taking another look I just decided to toss them...I don't want nothing around that played no part in tonight's events. Different scenarios are still passing back and forth thru my mind now. I took them back into the hall and just put them in one of the garbage bags. I looked at her things; they were splashed up, but nothing that couldn't be cleaned. I took a second look and decided to toss them as well. I didn't want shit left as a reminder. I'll buy her some more if she wants me to. I proceeded to get the paper up, and put it in the trash, then went on to clean up the mess. I mopped the area like 3 times just to make sure I got it all. I poured the water out, then took the garbage bags out to the trash. I washed my hands, then went into the den to call Dream before I make my way back upstairs. I wasn't surprised at all when he picked up on the second ring.

"Yo Rod," he said, "I thought you might have called before now."

"Yeah, I probably would have," I answered, but after you left Nube took notice to my bloody clothes, and that shit touched off a mini tornado up in here. She was all hysterical and bugging cause she thought that I killed them."

"Well...she may not be too off base with it Rod. I spoke back to Bryce and he said that both them niggas in a coma. What the hell did you do over there on 18th Ave? They telling me that mutha fucka's teeth was laying all out on the ground."

"Puuuh," I blew out, "He lucky that's all that's wrong with him. Dez...I'm telling you...that mutha fucka gonna sit there and tell me him and his boy was gonna take Nube and split...." I stopped, I couldn't even bring myself to repeat it. Damn...now my damn stomach is gripping and shit. I took a deep breath and tried to pull it together. Dream just waited patiently giving me my moment. "Look Dez," I said getting back on solid ground, "I popped both his damn jaws, and after I lumped his ass real good, he gonna try to be brave and still talk shit. So I kicked him straight in his mouth and put his damn lights out."

"Damn Rod," he replied to my comments.

"Damn what Dez?" I asked him, "Now you sounding like Nube. She was over here tripping about whether or not I was too severe, till I told her what they pretty much planned to do if they would've got the chance to take her with them. She thought about that shit, and threw up all over the place."

"Wow," he answered, "That deep for her?"

"Yeah," I answered a little softer now, "She's real torn up about this whole night Dream. Oh man. I wish that I'd never let her park the truck and come in the shop. Bryce could have just seen her another time. What was I thinking Dream...what?" I had once again become overcome in anguish over my decision and the tone was laced in my voice.

"Yo Rod," he spoke, "You couldn't have known...it's not your fault. Scandalous mutha fuckas always out scheming and plotting without a reason. She had a right to come in and see her family; you can't stop living and analyzing every move you make cause of niggas out here with no purpose. I mean...as a man...you handled your damn business. Yeah...you intense with yours...but that was their tragic mistake. Moving forward, you just gotta take things one day at a time, and see how this all pans out. Consequences are gonna be there regardless, but whatever the case...I'm here for you Rod...whatever the outcome." I let his words filter thru and marinade. Dream was really beginning to mature, and I was impressed with his prospective on the current situation.

"Thanks Dez," I told him, "I appreciate you being there for me and sitting with Nube tonight."

"Ain't a thing," he answered me, "You've always been there for and supported me whenever I was going thru, it's the least I could do."

Whew…I blew out, “Well, I’m gonna go on and snatch a shower, get back upstairs and check on Nube, then try to get some rest too.”

“Alright then,” he said, “We’ll just keep a close watch on this, and deal with whatever.”

“You right…I’ll hit you tomorrow.”

“Aight, Peace,” he answered. “Yo Murad,” he called out before I hung up, “You got something real special there big brother.

He went on to hang up without waiting for a reply. I knew that was his way of apologizing for the shade he’d previously given to Nube and I on our decision to be together.

As I put the phone back on the base, I openly answered to the universe, “I know Dez…I know.”

Chapter 41

A Quick Decision

Murad

I climbed the stairs to with a heavy heart, still mentally displaced with all that went down tonight. Entering the bedroom, I saw that Nube was still lying on her side. I walked around to the other side of the bed just to check on her. She seemed to be resting and at ease, so I began to undress so I could get myself cleaned up. As I stood there undressing, I just watched her as she slept. Just laying there looking so damn beautiful, so sweet…so innocent. I slowly shook my head back and forth trying to fight back the demon of thoughts that kept filtering thru my mind. What if…what if? Come on…just shake it off Rod…it didn't…she's here, with you, safe Rod…she's safe. I turned to make my way into the bathroom so that I could just get in the shower, and take it down. I needed to rest my mind…my body. It's gonna take some time to get past this. Damn…I sure could use a blunt right about now.

I turned on the water as hot as I could stand it, and climbed in. As the steamy hot water assaulted my body, I reached over for the soap and got a nice foamy lather going. I washed, and buffed my body, then reached for the shampoo to work on my hair. As I cleansed my body, I tried valiantly to fight off the what if…and it could've been…and damn…that mutha fucka pumped off on us! It could have gone so wrong tonight I thought deeply as I tilted my head back to rinse my hair. As the warmth of the water spread across my skull, the seriousness of it all penetrated my mind and brought out an unsolicited sob from my throat. That shit scared me…as I didn't know where it came from…you know…all out of the blue. Next thing I know I was hit with a round of rocking sobs that shook me to the core of my soul. I couldn't seem to stop myself, couldn't get a grip as the thought of them planning to rape Nube refused to cease torturing me. I dropped to my knees in the shower as the thoughts overcame my senses to keep things in perspective. Why hadn't I listened to my gut, when Bryce first asked is she was coming in? I should've taken charge of that shit and told him no. Should've listened to my first mind...my first fucking mind.

I remained on my knees spilling out sobs that were as alien in nature as the sudden need for me to release them. I can't say that I have ever cried like this, not even as a child. I've always been the one to maintain control, always been able to stay on top of my game, no matter what. But this evenings events brought on the reality that everyone has to take a hit at some time or another...even the ones who are always so in charge of their every situation. This night also revealed to me how deep my attachment to Nube actually is and just how done I'd be if something were to happen to her. I turned off the water to help bring forth an effort in getting myself together. I slowly stood in the tub and reached for my towel. I vowed my mind to be still, and channel my thoughts to how I needed to restore order to our lives. I systematically dried my body and walked out to the bedroom. I was way too tired to rub on any oil, so I just grabbed some drawstring pajama pants and a wife beater and slipped them on. Before I got into the bed, I checked on Nube and she appeared to be sleep, so I slipped in gently from the other side and laid on my back, hands behind my head, deep in thought. As my mind tried to restore logic to the evening, I made a silent promise to myself to never let anyone ever get close enough to her to lay hands on her ever again. I went on with a tirade of thoughts running thru my mind and before long exhaustion set in...and I was out.

I don't know if it was an hour or 10 hours that passed, but I woke up in a fog as I heard Nube's voice crying out for me in the distance.

"Rod...Rod." As the fog started to clear, I saw that she must have been having a nightmare. I reached out and gently pulled her into my arms.

"Nube, Nube...baby," I whispered, "Its okay. I'm right here Nube."

"Rod," she cried out opening her eyes.

"I'm right here baby...I'm right here. It's okay...it was just a dream. It's done Nube...you safe...I'm here." She looked up at me, the darkness affording me a limited view of her eyes, but I could sense the fear was still there, so I just reached down and kissed her gently.

"It's all good Nube," I told her, "I'm gonna be right here...right by your side...from now until. Go back to sleep...get your rest."

She snuggled up to me and placed her head on my chest as I rubbed her back in an attempt to soothe her. She settled down, and we both attempted to go back to sleep. But every few minutes, it seemed that we would come to an impasse. She tossed...I turned. She rolled...I counter shifted. She fell asleep, yet cried out once more. Enough. I got up from the bed and went down to the den and turned on my laptop. I looked up a few things, went to the appropriate sites, then went back upstairs. At this point she was sitting up in the bed with her knees drawn up to her chest and her arms wrapped around them.

"Come on Nube," I told her as I flipped on the lamp, "Get dressed...we outta here."

She looked at me wide eyed and confused. "We got a plane to catch," I answered to the eyes.

"But I..." she started.

"Don't need nothing," I responded, "You got some extra clothes in the dressing room. Grab something to put on and let's go. We'll get whatever we need when we get there." She gave off another look.

"Costa Rica," I threw off and without another word...she got out of the bed and went to get dressed.

Chapter 42

Getting It Back To The Way It Was

Murad

The ride to the airport was pain stakingly silent and subdued. I'm sure that physical exhaustion played a big part in it, but for the most part we were traumatized and both sequestered within our own private thoughts of last night. I did notice that Nube seemed to cling to me as if afraid that if she let me out of her sight, the world would swallow her whole. I in turn manifested my torment by continually giving her kisses of consolation as you would a child that has fallen and scraped their knee. I have to say...we were truly a pair of emotionally wounded souls. She tossed and turned restlessly up under me on the plane, as I handled some business calls and other arrangements on the lap top. She responded once to an offer of some ginger ale, and then slumped back underneath me as if to burrow her self from the world. Once we touched down in Costa Rica the bright sunshine seemed to pull her out of her funk just a bit. I was grateful for at least that much.

After we were checked into our private bungalow, Nube insisted on getting her an all-over tan, so we got the sun-tan lotion, blanket umbrella and such and went on out to the beach. Each bungalow has their own private alcove of beach area surrounded by very thick bushes and posted fences. I had to let her know that she was on her own with this one cause I wasn't down for getting my soldier sunburned. I set up the chairs while she spread the blanket out on the sand. I opened the umbrella and set it on an angle so that she could lie out on the blanket and get her tan while I lay under the shade of the umbrella. She went to untie the sash on her robe and looked at me and gave me a shrug like "here goes." I shrugged back like, "go head." She took off the robe and placed it on one of the chairs, and lay down on the blanket. The sight of her was tantalizing as usual.

"Can you?" she asked.

"No problem," I said as she handed me the suntan lotion.

I started with her neck, and then branched out to her shoulders and arms. Even as I applied the lotion on her body, the events of last night kept rewinding themselves in my head. I finished up with the arms and absentmindedly went on to cover her breasts and then her stomach area. The touch of her full breasts kicked in a spark of a different nature, not a sexual one per say, but the touch of her sensual flesh did remind me of how wrong things could have gone. I reached over to get more lotion to do her thighs working my way down to her calves.

"Roll over," I softly told her so I could get the back.

I took a deep breath as I started at the back of her neck massaging ever so gently. She had not voiced one word to me since I started, and for some reason that shit was getting under my skin. I was starting to feel as if she was becoming detached from me, even though I knew better than that. I continued on in silence and just went on to cover her shoulder blades and then made my way down her back. Once I got to her waist, I poured some more out so that I could do her backside. I covered and massaged it expertly then went on to do the back of her legs. Once I got down to her cute little feet, I stopped mid-foot...I couldn't contain myself any longer. Her whole subdued persona was more than I could bear. The silence was killing me. I got rid of my swimming trunks, lowered myself down to the blanket and slid myself inside her from the back.

She trembled slightly as a whisper of a moan escaped her which was lost within my own deep moan. The soft velvet warm feeling that greeted me set off another set of emotions, and I just started moving gently, slowly, back and forth.

"Murad," she let out softly and started crying. That shit touched me so deep and tore me up to where I almost lost it again.

"Oh...Nube baby," I told her "I'm sorry baby...I'm sorry. I'm so damn sorry," I voiced to her over and over again, kissing her neck her head, the side of her face...kissing her tears, stroking inside her. "Don't cry Nube...oh man...don't cry Bae," I pleaded with her.

The only response I got was more sobs. "Nube...baby...stop crying Nube," I continued to plead. Again she wasn't hearing it. I needed to see her face, look into her eyes so that she could understand me.

"Nube...baby...turn over," I whispered in her ear.

I reared back and she complied raising her right leg up to her chest to turn and pivot so that I would remain inside her just as I taught her. Face to face was even more tormenting as her face was streamed with tears. I came back down to meet her bringing a long stroke with me and softly kissed her lips. I cradled her head in my hands and whispered in her ear, "Nube baby...I'm sorry...I'm sorry...forgive me baby please...please."

And with each please I stroked her as if our lives depended on it. She continued to cry and I continued to stroke. I stroked long, I stroked softly... yet I stroked deeply. I thought that I could stroke away her sorrow; I thought if I could stroke her deep enough she could feel how much I regret letting her park the truck and come into the shop. I guess I reasoned that I could regain her calm by stroking the pain away. Still she cried. I raised up on my elbows, and immediately felt a twist of pain in my chest.

"Nube," I called softly to her, "Nube baby...open your eyes bae...look at me...please open your eyes Nube." To my relief she opened them, and I decided right then and there I needed to get control of this situation.

"Nube," I started continuing to stroke, "Listen bae...you are my life...and I love you Nube...all day...everyday...and I know you feel me on that. I love you above and before anything else. We gonna make it Nube...we gonna be alright. Stop crying though, cause you crying is tearing my heart to pieces...and I need my heart whole Nube...I need it whole so I can love you entirely."

She slowed down some, but I was not quite satisfied, so I raised back on my knees, pulling her up with me by her shoulders and just impaled her upon me. She shuddered at the deepness of the penetration and wrapped her arms tightly around my neck with her feet crossed behind my back. I held her around the waist and guided her to meet my strokes as I continued to relay my regrets to her internally. I stroked as deep as I could go without hurting her and whispered how much I loved her in her ear. I tried to stroke my way into her soul so that she could merge it with mine, and comfort me as well. I thought that if I somehow stroked deep enough I could plant the feeling of security she needed deep inside of her like a seed. I needed her to know that she could trust that she'd always be safe with me, and not have to be looking over her shoulder everywhere she goes.

I stroked and I whispered, I whispered and I stroked till I got that vibe from her that she was ready to respond. "Nube...baby...I need you to talk to me...tell me you okay...Nube."

"Murad," she squeezed out.

"What Bae?" I asked her continuing to stroke

"I'm okay," she came back with.

"You okay Bae...you good?" I asked her again reinforcing with another deep stroke.

"Uh...yes," she answered in a quick breath and I knew that I was about to take her there.

"Okay...then I need something else from you Nube," I prompted her, giving her some extra long strokes.

"Give me what I need Nube...come on Bae."

"Ah...ah....," she replied.

"Tell me Nube...tell me," I urged her. I needed to hear it from her. I needed to know.

"I...I...ah...I...," she came back with.

"Ahhh yeah...Nube...tell me baby...tell me," I urged her on with the strokes getting deeper and deeper as I softly kissed her neck.

"I...Murad...ah...Murad...I...," she called out.

I gave her the last of the deepest that I could go as I whispered directly in her ear, "You what Nube?"

I felt her body tense and contract and she whispered back in my ear, "I... love... you... Murad," and then she released the sweetest fucking moan I ever heard in my life as she came, and took my ass right over the edge with her. I grabbed her so tight and held her so close as I spased, came...and released within her the gratitude that she was back and on her way to being the Nube that I know.

Chapter 43
This Is What It Is

Murad

I gently laid us back down on the blanket, sideways so that we would remain intact. For some reason I like to remain connected as long as possible afterwards. I looked into her pretty eyes and saw calm for the first time in the last 24 hours.

"I love you Butter," I told her, kissing her softly...tenderly.

"Oh baby...I know you do, I know you do," she answered, "You are so fucking good to me Murad, I don't think I would be able to handle ever being without you. I love you so much...and I just couldn't control my thoughts last night. I kept thinking what if...and what if...and they could have...are they dead...did he kill them...and all that."

"I know Bae," I responded, "Them same thoughts kept running thru my mind, torturing me. And now...it still ain't over." I wanted to tell her the truth on all that I know, but at the same time I wanted to be careful with what I revealed.

"Nube...listen," I started, "I want to keep you updated on this here situation. I spoke with Bryce on the plane and I found out that both of them fools are in the hospital. At first they were both unconscious, but one has come around since last night. The other one is a little more critical, he's in a coma. When I broke his nose some bone fragments passed thru his septum and pierced his brain. They trying to see if they can alleviate some of the swelling in the nasal passage, so they can go up in there and remove the bone fragments."

"Rod, baby...that's serious," she finally spoke, alarm returning to her eyes.

"Yes Nube...it is," I answered, "So far I haven't been charged with anything, but everything is still under investigation. Aaron and Jarrell are already on the case doing whatever they can out the gate. But yeah...there's gonna be some consequences on both sides of this." I watched her as she started to go into a whole nother zone. "Nube," I voiced. She directed her eyes back to mine and I continued, "Listen...I brought us down here to put all that to the side for now. Trust me...it will wait for us till we get back. I just want us to enjoy one another, and regroup after last night."

"You right Rod...you right," she answered, "I don't really want to think about all that right now."

"Great," I said bestowing another kiss to her lips, "But listen...one more thing I wanna run by you Nube. I want you to come stay with me when we get back. This way I can keep my eye on you and make sure that you're safe."

"Stay with you Rod," she asked, "For how long?"

"Forever Nube."

"Wow...Murad," she came back with, "We just openly started this relationship in July, and it's just now September and we gonna be moving in together? I don't know Rod. We supposed to be going slow with this thing, making sure everything is...you know...everything. Besides, what am I supposed to do with my place? I just can't break the lease."

"Nube, I had the contract for that drawn up as month to month with the option to sell...so you good," I told her. I personally handle all of our domestic finances from an exclusive cost of living account, so I know all the pros and cons of what we can financially juggle.

"Look Nube," I said, "I've had my eye on you since your first performance in Bryce's' backyard. Back when Kason was up in the mix. Once we hooked up as business partners we have been somewhat inseparable ever since. You've been the closest person to me in the last 2 ½ - 3 years and I'm feeling like everything is already everything. Us coming to terms with our feelings for one another was just the last mile to run in the race. If you wanna get technical about it...we've been together the whole time...we just didn't know it. I really don't see us moving in together as jumping the gun. Besides...I need this Nube...I need to know that you safe. I would never be able to sleep soundly again with you away from me. I mean...all I would do is stalk you and spend every night at your house anyway." She started laughing and I joined in with her.

"Rod," she said continuing to laugh, "Okay then…why is it that I have to give up my place and come and move in with you?"

"Cause baby," I started, "I've got more space. We talking what…3 floors, 3 bedrooms, 2 ½ baths, a yard, fireplace and balcony in the master bedroom and plenty of closets for sharing. Nube…you know I can accommodate you…and if you not satisfied with that, I'll go out and get us a whole new place."

"No Rod, that's not necessary," she replied, "I mean…you making sense…I just gotta think about it."

"Well look," I told her, "How bout this…we give it a 30 day trial run…we'll keep the lease running on your place, and if things turn out to be too much for you, you can go back to your own place. How does that sit with you?"

"Oh Rod…I don't know…I'm definitely gonna think on it…I promise. For now I just wanna lay here with you and soak up some of this sun."

"Aight cool," I told her flipping her up on top of me; I didn't want her to feel like I was pressuring her, "I'ma let you get your tan on for a little bit." As she lay up on my chest, I ran my fingers thru her hair and just savored the good feeling of her on top of me…me still inside of her. The ocean breeze felt wonderful, but the sun was direct and blazing. After about a half hour of sun tanning, she was ready to call it quits.

"Come on Bae," I told her my exhaustion setting in again, "It's a little hot out here; we can pick this up again tomorrow after we get some rest."

"Sounds good to me," she replied.

We got up, disconnecting for the first time and begin to gather our things and went back to the bungalow. Once inside I turned on the water for the shower and beckoned for her to join me. As she slowly advanced towards me, I grabbed her up and put us both in the steaming water.

"Rod," she cried out, "my hair's gonna…"

"Get wet," I finished for her, "I know Bae."

I took the shower gel and squeezed some out and just started lathering us both up. I just watched her as I touched certain places with the rag, and other places with my hands. Her eyes sparkled and danced with my every movement. She got a hold of the rag, and started washing and touching parts of me. I don't know if we ever got fully clean, but at some point of this wash fest, I pulled her to me and captured her sweet mouth with mine. I took my tongue and did a sweep around inside sending shock waves thru us both. The tub had some tiered landings inside and I took advantage by bracing my right foot up on the first landing. Anxious not to lose the moment I picked her up and just slid her back inside me partially on the lap of my hoisted leg, while she dangled the other one and braced her foot on the same ledge. As she held on to me, I braced my hands up against the shower walls and give her the sweetest upward strokes I could deliver.

As she started to sing out with her soft sweet moans, I broke out with my own declaration of pleasure. "Ahh...Nube...baby," I called out.

"Murad," she responded, "Don't talk baby...just listen...just listen."

So I did as she asked as we both refrained from talking and just listened to the sounds of pleasure we elicited from one another. It sounded like some off beat tune, yet at the same time sexy as hell. Before too long Nube started shivering and I knew she was once again near. I myself was trynna hold out and wait for her. I'm saying...ladies first. She broke her own request as she called out, "Murad...oh Murad."

"Yeah Bae...you ready?" I answered and asked her in a heavy voice. She simply nodded and I responded by picking her up. I turned us to the right putting us directly under the stream of warm steamy water as I tilted her back against the wall for support. And as I stared into her beautiful eyes, holding her in my gaze, I plowed in once...twice... three times deep and sent her back over the edge. She called out my name in that sexy way only she can do when we rocking it and I gave in to my sensations as well.

"Awwww Nube...Nube," I repeated like a lost soul. What the fuck you do to me girl, I'm thinking to myself...damn. She just don't know... I'm so out of my mind with her. It don't get no better than this. As I'm holding her up against the shower wall, I'm thinking how I've gotta convince her to come and live with me. I truly don't know if I can live day to day without her by my side now. I internally feel that we've crossed some milestone and this next step is just our destiny.

"Oh Rod," she gave off as I lifted her down. I reached down and once again captured her mouth with mine.

"What Nube," I responded, continuing to gently kiss her, "What you need Pretty?"

"Well, I think we may have to wash again…no?" she asked. I just bust out laughing at her as she looked up at me and said, "What? Well…don't we?"

"Not just yet," I told her as I turned around and led her to have a seat on the ledge of the shower stall. And as I got down on my knees and parted her legs, I told her, "We can…when I'm done. I don't want you to talk Nube…I just wanna listen."

As I took the first swipe with my tongue, I faintly heard the beginning of a low moan. Once I plunged in with a full thrust, and gently started to nibble and nip, I listened in ecstasy as the acoustics of the shower brought the sound of her moans to me in sensor round. And with the warm water massaging my lower back, hyping the sensations, I'm thinking…Damn…it don't get no better than this. Does it?

Chapter 44
Siesta-Siesta

Murad

Nube and I must have played around in the shower for another half hour before we finally got out and towel dried ourselves. Instead of taking the time to give one another body massages with oil, we used a spray on. For one thing we were both beat, and exempt of all energy. Number two, Nube insisted that we had to handle her hair immediately.

"Aww man, Nube," I peeled off, "Do you know how long this gonna take?"

"Well you should have thought about that before you wrangled me into the shower without a shower cap," she hit me back, "so come on…we gonna tackle this here together. You comb it out and part it and I'll grease and braid it."

"Awwww baby…can't you just blow dry it or something, and come to bed?" I asked.

"No I cannot," she answered, "Then I'll be looking all crazy tomorrow. Come on Rod…it won't take long."

So I got the comb and started to comb out. Her hair is a tangly mess of thick curls and waves when it's wet and I had to be careful. I combed starting with the ends and worked my way up. I used to help my mom with my little sisters hair when they were young so I had a little practice.

"Just six parts Bae," she called it in a sleepy tone herself, "That's all I've got the energy for." So I combed…parted and she greased and braided 6 cornrows going toward the back. This way when she takes it out, it will give her a crinkly wavy do to sport. By the time we were finished we were both hit like that. I could barely keep my eyes open as I made my way up off the bed. I went to the front door and put the Privacy sign on the outside. Although the sun was blazing hot outside, the inside was surprisingly cool with its high ceilings and breezy open space. I went to the balcony of the bedroom, and opened the French window paned doors to allow access of the fresh ocean breeze, while Nube climbed up in the canopy bed. I turned on the ceiling fan to medium then pulled back the netting and climbed in with her. I adjusted the netting to make sure it was closed and secured, then laid day next to her and pulled her to me.

"Rod," she called out softly, barely above a whisper, "I love you."

"Me too Butter...me too," I trailed off my answer as we both succumbed to our sleep depravation. And with the cool gentle breeze blowing in from the balcony and the swoosh of the ceiling fan overhead, we were both lulled into a much needed sleep. As time moved on we missed the beautiful afternoon sun as it blazed in the sky...and the beautiful orange sunset as it painted the horizon, cause we slept...and we slept...and we slept.

Chapter 45

Just What The Dr. Ordered

Murad

What a difference a day makes. Nube is absolutely glowing and just looking so relaxed. I'm glad I made the decision to get her away. That was some rough shit and I still feel bad she got caught up in it. I almost lost my damn mind last night. If something would have happened to her....

"Rod...did you hear me?" she said bringing me back to the moment.

"Naw bae, I didn't hear you. What's going on?"

"I was asking you if we should get some more dip for the onion rings. Or maybe I need to stop being so greedy," she replied.

"Nube go ahead and eat whatever you want. This here is a spontaneous vacation, calories don't count. Besides you good," I told her winking my eye at her. "Let me get a hold of this waiter and have him bring you some more. "Excuse me sir...uh...excuse me padre?" I said since he didn't respond the first time.

"Si Senor," he came over smiling and bowing.

"Can you bring us some more dip," I asked him.

"Si, si," he said and left to retrieve it.

While he was gone, I poured us both some more seltzer water. I don't trust the water in these foreign countries, so bottled seltzer is my choice of drink.

"I guess I'll try one of them when he gets back here with the dip," I told her. "Have you given any more consideration to what I spoke about earlier?"

"I guess you could say that," she answered. "I'm still thinking on it. That's a huge step we talking bout." She started moving stuff around as she saw the waiter returning, and I saw her give a confused look when he set down a stack of napkins.

"Oh no my man," I tapped him before he could leave, "We need more dip, not napkins."

"Que…dip?" he asked.

"Yes dip…for the onion rings," I said pointing.

"Si…si.Dip," he said again just standing in place smiling.

I'm looking at Nube like, what this guy don't understand.

"No sir…we…need…some…DIP. You know stick the ring in the dip," I told him making a hole with the fingers of one hand and using my finger on the other to stick in the hole for emphasis.

"Que?" he said.

"I don't even believe this," I said out loud, "Dude here don't even know what the fuck I'm saying."

"Well maybe if you explain it again a little slower," Nube piped in.

"Damn…how much slower do I have to go. They need to have people here that understand the damn language. All this fucking money I'm paying," I said getting a little annoyed.

"Senor…we need dip…do you understand? Dip?"

"Que?" he said.

"This mutha fucka," I keyed off while Nube raised her eyebrow, "Do you know… what the fuck…I am saying?"

"No fuck," he said.

Nube and I both did a double take, and I asked him, "What the fuck did you say?"

"I say no fuck," he answered getting upset.

"What the fuck?" I said aloud getting confused as to what this man meant.

"I no fuck…you fuck her on beach," he replied, and Nube spit her drink out all over the table.

I just sat there with my head swimming and looked at Nube. I asked her, "What did this mutha fucka just say?"

"Oh, I think he just said that you fucked me… on beach." she answered with a smirk.

"Yo my man…did you just say I fucked her…on beach?"

"On beach…you fuck on beach," he replied.

"Yeah…and… what the fuck that got to do with the dip?" I asked him.

"Que…dip?" he asked, "No my dip…you dip…you fuck!"

Nube and I just bust out laughing.

"Oh my god Rod, he must have seen us on the beach this morning. Oh my God this shit is too funny," she said laughing like a hyena, wiping tears from her eyes, "He must think you saying "dick." I couldn't answer her cause I was splitting my side laughing.

"Yo Senor," I started, catching my breath in between laughs, "I need some damn dip mutha fucka....DIP!!"

"You fuck on beach," he answered again. And this time we just tore the place down laughing. I guess the manager must have heard us howling and came over to see what the problem was.

"Good evening folks," he said, "Is there a problem?"

"Yo," I started again catching my breath, "your waiter here doesn't seem to understand that I would like some more DIP for the onion rings" And with that said, Nube and I bust out laughing again.

"Excuse me, I'll see what the problem is," he said.

The manager turned to the waiter and addressed him in Spanish. *"Pedro – what the hell is going on here? These people just want some more sauce for the onion rings...what they call dip. What is the confusion?"*

"Oh...I think he saying dick," Pedro replied.

"Why the hell would you think that?" his manager said, "Are you out here trying to practice your English again? I told you not to do that when you waiting tables alone."

"Well I see them this morning on the beach...and he give it to her good," Pedro said.

"You know we boast the privacy of the private beach here you ass-hole. What if they found out they were being watched?" the manager asked him, "What possessed you to practice your English if you did not know what he was saying? Listen... just go and get the damn DIP... and watch yourself."

As the waiter turned to finally retrieve the dip, the manager turned to us and said, "I do apologize, we are short staffed this time of the year, and Pedro is just filling in. He generally takes care of the grounds which includes cutting the bushes around the private beach area. I do apologize for the confusion, and he will be right back with your dip. Is there anything else that I can help you with this evening?"

“Naw padre…we cool,” I answered him.

“Then have a pleasant dinner,” he said turning to walk away.

“Oh my god Rod…you had my ass out there all exposed,” Nube said laughing.

“Yeah it was,” I shot back, “All hot, golden and tender.”

“Look at you,” she answered me, “Don’t even care if the whole world saw you tapping my ass out on the beach.”

“You know what,” I said swinging the conversation around to a more serious note, “After yesterday’s events, I could care less if the whole world watched as I made love to my lady…cause me needing to feel you, and the need to express my love for you was so imperative at the moment…that nothing else really mattered.”

“Murad Tillman,” she gushed as if ready to cry all over again, “I do believe I’m gonna have to love you forever.”

No sooner had she finished her sentence, the confused waiter came back with a small white bowl, and set it down in the middle of the table. He turned to me and gave a slight bow, and in perfect English he said, “Here’s your dip sir. But the dick…you give it to her good.”

As we sat there with our mouths open, he turned and walked away. I looked at Nube and she looked at me…and we tore the place down again with laughter.

Chapter 46
All Good Things Come To An End

Murad

Nube and I were consumed with sunning, funning, and relaxing for the next 3 days. We drank Pina Coladas, Mimosas, Mojito's...all that. We jet skied...did the paddle boat thing, took a midnight cruise to nowhere...feasted on exotic cuisine...and made love. I believe I detected an urgency in us both to drink up a sense of security from each other given the ordeal. I guess she was grateful that nothing happened to me in going after dude, and I know I'm more than grateful they didn't get to pull anything off with her. On our last night there we once again made love out on the private beach, under the moonlight with the wind kinda whispering in my ear; the sky sprinkled with stars and shit. I guess this is the kind of thing that goes on in them romance novels women be reading. And I tell you what...I'ma have to say...the sista's are on to something with it, cause that shit there felt right...a definite turn-on...no doubt. I guess if Pedro was watching, getting his nasty sneak-peek on...we damn sure done him proud.

I'd found a salon that was able to do Nube's hair before we left and when we touched down in Newark, her appearance was over the top blazing with her fresh hair do and stunning tan. Despite her million dollar appearance, I noticed that she seemed a little tense. Once we departed the plane, and went to retrieve our bags, I believe that the hustle and bustle along with the urban ambiance began to build on the reality that we were back into the mix. She stayed as close to me as my own shadow, looking everyone up and down as suspect. I had Dream pick us up from the airport, and he was waiting curbside when we stepped out of the doors. I placed Nube in the car and dumped our bags into his trunk. I hopped in and we pulled away from the curb.

"Hey Lil'Bit," he addressed Nube.

"Hey Dream," she answered.

I noticed the way that her smile picked up as well as the mellow flow between them both. I realized that the incident somehow brought a new dynamic to their relationship with one another, and I was glad that they were beginning to form a bond. Dez and I are close, and it would be un-natural for him and my lady to not be at peace with one another.

"Whas' good Dream?" she asked him.

"You Nube," he responded, "Girl you looking good...well rested. Got your tan going on and all dat. Damn sure better than the last time I saw..."

He stopped in his tracks, afraid that he'd said the wrong thing. As he glanced back in the rear view mirror to catch her reaction, a look of embarrassment on his face changed to surprise when she and I both bust out laughing.

"Thanks a lot baby boy," Nube answered him, "You know I was going thru a little something the other day, and you gonna put me on blast like that? Okay...I see how you do."

"Naw see...I was just observing the fact that...you know...that it look like my brother done took real good care of you. You know...that extra special attention," Dream laid out, trying to smooth over his previous comment.

"Nice try at a clean up...but you can save that Dream," she replied, "He takes real good care of me everyday." And when he gave her the raise of his eyebrow, she threw in, "Oh yes...that extra special attention."

"Aight Lil'Bit," he responded laughing, "Don't git ya little feathers all ruffled and fly away to the left. Hands down...Rod is the man. And I can vouch to that being that I taught him everything he knows." To that we all bust out laughing.

"So you the professor and Murad is the student?" Nube quizzed him.

"Yeah...now you got the clear picture," Dream answered.

"Well okay," Nube said, "Then I'm sure that he got an A in all subjects, cause while we were in Costa Rica maaan...Murad had me coming and going, just like a professional. I mean he was so on point that I was just feeling like..."

"Ah...ah...unh...unh...Hey!!" Dream burst out cutting her off, "Slow it up Lil'Bit...I don't wanna hear all that."

"But Dream," she said, "If you would have been there you would have been able to see how well your student performed on all that you taught him. I'm saying under his instruction, I just blossomed and was open and taking in everything Murad was bringing to me. Yeah...you would have been proud of the way he kept it coming and the way I took it all like a champ..."

"Nube," he screamed out appalled, "Girl...can you stop now...I mean like right now...or I'ma pull this damn car over." As Nube and I bust out laughing again, he turned and looked confused.

"Pull over for what Dream, "she said in between laughing, "It ain't that serious. I was just saying that I had shut down behind all that went down that night and Murad got me to blossom and open up by spiriting me away on this impromptu trip. While were there, he introduced me to jet skiing, paddle boating, and hazy, lazy tropic days of doing nothing. And although I had never done these things before, I took it all in...and benefited to the utmost. That's all I meant. What did you think I meant?"

He looked at me, and then he looked back at her before he responded, "Oh...I just...girl I don't know. I thought you was coming at me divulging some ole' freaky nonsense you two got into down there. I'm saying...a brother's ears are a little sensitive...don't wanna know no details like that."

"Aww...no Dream...never that," she replied winking at me, "Murad and I have more respect for you than that. Just the usual couple thang...just the usual. Right Bae?"

"Yeah Dream," I co-signed stroking my shadow in an absent minded gesture, "Just the usual bruh...just the usual."

As he looked back at her, then back over to me trying to decipher whether or not we were clowning him, she and I bust out laughing once more...throwing him back into uncertainty.

Chapter 47

Consequences...

Nubina

Wow...we've been back for just 2 days and the whirlwind of consequences have begun. Murad spent the first day answering phone messages and e-mails, while I worked on some new material. These early days of October have lent us some unusually cool temperatures, so I am perfectly okay with staying penned up in the house. Murad and Dream went over to my place yesterday and brought my most necessary things over, so I haven't been out since we've been back. I'm kinda feeling out of place because I want to...in some way...help Murad in this thing he's gotta face. I don't know if I'm feeling some kind of guilt or ownership to the incident because he got into this defending me, but I feel like I need to be doing something to rectify or absolve any penalties he may suffer behind this. It just seems a little unfair that I'm in here writing and reviewing new material, while he's conferring with legal counsel. I'm not eavesdropping or anything, but the door to the den is open and from the sound of the conversation...it don't sound like things are going too well. Rod sounds good and aggravated. Maybe I'll try and fix him a special dinner tonight, and try to put him in a good mood. I know that he has to go downtown to meet with the Essex County prosecutor's office with Aaron and Jarrell. That little Poo dude is still in a coma, and I'm feeling so torn when it comes to that. Yes...he was planning on doing a terrible injustice to me...and I know Rod was defending me and all...but damn...we bear to serve a huge brunt of the overall consequences behind Poo's actions. I don't know how all this could have been justifiably handled...I'm saying what does one do in the heat of that moment to protect what's his. Without a doubt Murad did what he felt he needed to do as a man...but wow...at what cost to our future together? This is a tough one.

"Look man...I'm just about thru with it for today," I relayed to Aaron, "I've got all the formal statements and documents you faxed over, this shit is starting to get redundant."

"Yo Rod," he answered me, "I just want your head right when go up in there tomorrow. You know...take it down a notch...relax, just let me and Jarrell do the majority of the talking."

I'm more than grateful that my brother Jarrell is a civil lawyer and his best friend Aaron from college is a defense attorney. Their legal combination of talents have worked a few miracles for the Tillman name in the past. Sure hope this will be one of those times, but in the meantime...I've had enough.

"Yeah...yeah...Ace...I got you...I'ma let you handle things." I offered, "I mean I'm so fed up with the whole nature of them mu'fucka's upsetting the balance of my day to day...I'm in a zone right now...can't think straight if I wanted to. So listen...I'll meet you downtown at 8:00 a.m. Cool?"

"Naw Rod," he came back with, "we gonna play this shit so straight...I'll come thru and pick you up, we need to arrive on a united front. We don't wanna give no room, or create a margin for any misconstrued or unsolicited statements and comments from no one... and to no one, especially if I'm not around. I know I don't have to tell you...black men with long paper ain't looked upon too favorably in the court system. And a good looking black man with money...a double indemnity. So together Rod...we going in together."

"Aight fine," I stated, "I'll be ready by 7:15, so whenever you come thru I'm good. Listen...I'll be home for the rest of the day...don't feel like going out, so if something pressing comes up...hit me up...I'll be in."

"Okay will do," he answered, "Rod...how's Nube doing?"

"She's good...not to anxious to go out herself, but we good," I responded.

"Is she coming tomorrow?" he asked.

"Not gonna happen Aaron," I came off with a little rough, "I don't want her mixed up or involved in anything else related to this bullshit. The shit went down, and as far as she's concerned, I want it in the past...don't want to take her thru reliving the foulness."

"Rod, a connection to a positive influence such as Nubina, could lend essential support to your case," he brought up.

"It could also lead to negative publicity for future projects for her that I'm not willing to sacrifice. No...She's got nothing to do with this. They stole my shit...I put their lights out. Me and me alone...that's what I'm running with. I don't want her name included in nothing," I spit out, then turned to check for her whereabouts. Lucky for me, she'd gone upstairs or to the bathroom or something.

"Murad...listen," he started.

"Aaron," I rudely interrupted, "Hear me good bruh...Nube is not to be involved in any way. I'm the one that let her park the truck when I should have stuck to my presence of mind, and she suffered deeply behind my decision. I'm not looking to put her thru anything else."

"But Rod, have you..."

"Yo Ace," I sharply stated cutting him off, "I'ma see you in the morning."

"Aight," he responded with a heavy sigh, "I'll be thru like 7:20ish...later."

As I hung up the phone I leaned over to massage my temples. He don't fool me none. I know as soon as he hung up he gonna call Jarrell, Bryce, Dream and anybody else he can get to listen. But it don't matter, can't nobody change my mind on this. Protecting Nube is my responsibility...that's mine right there...and it's my job as a man. I just sat holding my temples for a few till Nube came up behind me wrapping her arms around me and gently kissed my neck.

"Hey Rod," she said softly, "What say I make you something special to eat?"

"That sounds like a plan," I responded taking her from behind me and putting her in my lap. I just sat there holding her savoring the intense sensations I always feel when I've got her cuffed up. I was wrapped up in feeling so good at the moment, it's like...I could cry.

And I guess Nube was feeling the same exact thing, cause although I was able to hold my own, I could hear the tears in her voice as she stroked my head and kissed my face and let me know, "Everything's gonna be alright, Murad. Things will work out in our favor...I promise." I closed my eyes and leaned my head back thinking, I hope she vibing right this time...cause really...I just don't know.

Chapter 48
Weighing The Options

Murad

"I'm not too happy with you going this alone Murad. I want to be there...I wanna be with you," Nube informed me. She was sitting on the edge of the bed as I finished getting ready, pleading her case to accompany me. I mean it may seem as though I'm being selfish, but I just can't gamble the chance that she will get upset as she did that night. I wouldn't be able to handle her in that mode again, and honestly I don't even know what emotions may jump off on my part detailing this shit all day, so no...she gots to stay back. I need my focus and concentration on how I'm playing this out for me.

"Butter...listen," I replied, "This could be an all day thing...rehashing things over and over, and you don't need the negative atmosphere. Just relax, and take this time to finalize your project for the Atlanta collabo."

"I've got plenty of time for that Rod," she said, "I'd rather use this time today supporting you. I was there too...remember? This incident involved me as well."

"I'm well aware of that Nube, and that's why you gonna be sitting this one out," I told her as I secured my tie into place, "One time for you was enough of that go round."

"But we a team Rod," she came back with, "You going thru...I'm going thru. We work well on everything we do together...this will be no different. I want to be there for you."

"Nube baby," I stated to her as I came over and grabbed her up in my arms, "Can you trust me on this one? I need to be level-headed today, and if you're there I'll be distracted...concerned with your feelings, your level of comfort. I just really feel like I can focus better if you are here...safe...apart from all the negative fallout." She just looked up at me, kinda torn and confused. I know she didn't feel right to not be by my side today, cause that's how she is, but I also know that she wants to respect my decision as well. She put her head down a bit, as if she was pondering a new thought to hit me with, so I tipped her chin up with my finger and pleadingly nibbled on her lips. "For me Pretty...can you do me this one?" I asked her my eyes probing hers to understand.

She took a deep breath before replying, "Murad...baby...you sure?"

I gave her that side nod as I held her in my gaze, and I know she understood my response when she wrapped her arms around me. I returned the embrace, and told her "Thank you Nube...I love you." She just lifted her head and gave me a slow kiss laced with frustration.

The sound of Aaron's car horn broke into the moment, and I was thankful, cause I was getting soft. As I pulled away to get my coat I reassured her, "I'll call and keep you updated."

She looked at me sideways, and I threw in, "I promise Nube...this time I promise. And if I can't get the opportunity to get away, I'll make sure that somebody gets in touch with you. I promise." She just stood there looking so astoundingly beautiful, even though in a zone. For one second, I wanted to turn around and wrap her back up in my arms and stay with her...not contend with the nonsense awaiting me. But I had to go...face whatever was to be.

"I love you Murad,"she called out to me as I proceeded downstairs.

"I know Nube...I know," I replied as I made my way to the front door. In order to maintain my resolve and man up for what lay before me, I kept it moving. Didn't look back...didn't see the tears that slowly started to make their way down her cheeks.

Nubina

As I laid myself back across the bed, I tried to stem the rush of thoughts and emotions that flash-flooded my mind. This is big...this is serious, and I'm so out of element not being there to help him. Who could have known that 2 minutes of a negative mishap would engulf our lives in such chaos? I'm laying here crying while my man is going to face such uncertainty for responding to an act of violence against us. Will we ever as a people permit one another to relish in our own fruits of labor without envy? Damn...they had no good reason at all to be trying to relieve us of our things...our things!! Whew...I don't know what I'm going to do up in this house all day, worrying and needing to know what's going on. I have a good mind to get dressed and go on down there anyway, but no...I need to respect Murad's wishes. He feels that he needs to handle this alone, so...that's the way it's going down.

In the meantime...I need to talk to someone. I picked up the phone and dialed my mother's house, no answer. I hung up and called Lani's job and got the voice mail. Damn...where is everybody? Just out of habit, I dialed the next common person...Sumira.

"Good Morning...Sumira Johnson speaking," I heard after the 3rd ring.

"Hey Sumira," I responded, "It's me."

"Tania?" she said as if unsure.

"Yes, it's me." I answered. I could feel the tension thru the phone as a moment of silence followed my statement.

"Sumira," I said, "I'm sure Bryce and them told you what happened, and we just got back 2 days ago from Costa Rica. But now Murad's downtown under investigation and..."

"Tania, I've got to go," she said cutting into my dialogue.

"Oh...okay," I haltingly responded, a little stunned by her tone. "I guess I'll talk to you later?" I responded, to which I got the dial tone.

Wow...she still mad like that about me and Murad? Does it really mean that much to her? I put the phone back on the base a little dazed. You know...there's enough on my plate today then me concerning myself with Sumira's attitude. Guess I'll just try and relax and try to get things into prospective. No use shedding anymore tears for what already is. As I slowly assumed the lotus position while remaining on the bed, I couldn't help but shake the feeling that this may just be the start of a negative vortex which has the potential to spiral out of control. And as I closed my eyes to try and transfer my thoughts from negative to positive I got a fierce chill. Hmmm....

"It don't matter Ace, I'm not about to chance the negative spotlight on Nube by including her in this," I told Aaron for the 100th time, "We gonna have to come up with another resolution." We had been at this since 9:45 this morning. The prosecutor is willing to make some kind of deal if I will admit to an assault on Nube taking place, otherwise the case will be pushed forward to a grand jury and would most probably go to trial. The charges could be anywhere from assault and battery, attempted manslaughter or depending on Poo's outcome...manslaughter. Just as I'd suspected Aaron had called everyone that he could to support him in badgering me to be cooperative and not a one of them was making an impact. Jarrell, Jarrod, Lonnie, Bryce and even Dream had taken a half a day and come down.

"Ahhh...Rod," Aaron peeled off slowly, "You will be taking a huge chance letting this shit go to trial. You've no guarantee that you will be exonerated. I can tell you from experience how people can judge you for shit that you ain't even about just by your appearance. They might take one look at you and possibly link you to them cats as some kinda drug deal gone wrong."

"I understand all that," I responded, "I guess we gonna have to play it out, my mind is made up."

At that point the door swung open and Kye walked in. "Yo Chief," he came over and dapped me up, "What the fuck going on? They telling me you up in here trynna be Johnny Dangerously."

"Man Kye...I don't know why they interrupted ya day and roped you into coming down here," I told him.

"Cause somebody need to feed you the real on this here Rod. You know good and hell well you don't need no criminal record or catching no cases. You got some major shit going on for you, and this interruption of events right here is something that can be dealt with. What's it gonna hurt for Nube to make a statement on their attempt to abduct her? We could slap them nigga's with a kidnapping charge, which would all but absolve the charges on you. If we could prove self defense on the level of attempted kidnapping, I don' see it going to trial."

"You know what," I said, my voice winding down to tired exasperation, "Nube ain't in this. They took my shit, I went after them...that's all."

"Come on now Rod...ya ass ain't cut out for no damn jail...and you know it," Kye responded.

"What the fuck you trynna say," I came back with highly irritated.

"I think we all know what the fuck I'm saying," he shot back at me.

"And all ya'll know I can hold my own. Ain't no day in America I'll be playing the fucking Maytag. So you can get the fuck outta here coming at me with that shit there," I threw back at him.

"Yo...yo...come on now," Jarrell intercepted, " What we don't need is to be going at each other all twisted, that ain't gonna solve a damn thing."

"Yeah well...if people wanna call themselves fucking supporting me, they need not be talking out the side of they fucking mouth with the nonsense," I spit out, "I don't' need that shit right now."

"Then nigga...act like you know," Kye hit me with.

"Aight look," Aaron intervened, "Let's just take a break, get something to eat, and come back and coordinate our options. We've got till the end of the day to make a decision."

I took a deep breath in order to contain my anger and just replied, "Whatever."

My decision is gonna be my decision before lunch...after lunch...tomorrow...whenever. I pushed away and got up to leave the room, following Aaron to the cafeteria. I looked around checking for Dream, and didn't spot him. Maybe he went to call his job or something. Guess I'll take this time to give Nube a call as well. I don't want her freakin out like she did the last time. She was already uneasy about not being able to come down today. I absentmindedly scanned the menu as I waited while the phone rang. Okay...she not picking up. Maybe she in the bathroom I'm thinking as I slowly close the phone. I went on and ordered some Turkey Chili and went and found a seat thinking I'll give her another try before we take in back into the busllshit what...

negotiations???...for the lack of a better word. I sat and ate my chili while Aaron's and Jarrell's words floated somewhere between now and infinity.

Bryce nudged me with his elbow and said, "How you holding up Chief?"

"Man," I blew out, "I'm good...I'm good. Just want this thing over with no matter which way it's gonna float."

"Well you know I'm here just for support and not trying to knock your decision," he responded, "Just want you to make sure you as strong in the cause behind your decision as you are in the principle." I looked over to him and gave him a nod letting him know that I appreciated that input, and watched as he got up from the table.

"I'm gonna stop by the restroom and get back and see if I can catch Kye before he leave, " he said, "I'll stop by the room before I leave."

"Aight," I responded."Peace."

I sat there for a minute letting what he said marinade before I made my second attempt to contact Nube. That's strange...she still not picking up. I doubt very seriously that she ventured out the house by herself. Not so soon...well anyway...not today. Hmmm...guess I'll try the cell. Maybe she did feel the need for some fresh air or something, though I'd prefer she was not out alone. Damn...all these motha fuckas up in here call they self supporting me...I could've used one of them to stay back and support her at home. Okay...what's this now. She not answering her cell....I'm starting to feel some kind of way. We need to get back and get this thing over, cause I need to find out what's going on with Nube.

"Look y'all about ready," I peeled off to Jarrell and Aaron, "Let's get this going and done with. I got something I need to check on."

"Okay then," Aaron responded, "Let's get back to the drawing board."

We all got up and emptied our trays and headed back to the interrogation room. The room was empty when we first got back, and Jarrell looked at his watch and said, “Let’s get this shit cracking.”

I don’t know if that was a prompt or some kind of signal or something, but they all filed back in the room again. Bryce, Jarod, Lonnie, Kye and bringing up the rear Dream.

“Yo Dez,” I called out, “where’d you slide off to. I was gonna ask if you could do me a favor and go back to my house and sit with…” I stopped short with my tongue in my throat as Dream stepped to the side revealing….Nube.

“Aww damn…no you mu fucka’s didn’t,” I spit out, “Whose fuckin grand idea was this here? I told ya’ll niggas I didn’t want her involved in this shit.”

“Rod,” Jarod said, “Man…you not being reasonable. You excluding her is not benefiting anyone.”

“Who the fuck is speaking on benefits,” I yelled, “I’m looking out for her interests, not fucking beneficial effects.”

“Maan…why you gotta be so bull-headed,” Kye spoke out.

“Cause you niggas ain’t understanding me. She ain’t got nothing to do with this,” I yelled back.

“The fuck you mean,” Kye answered, “She got every fucking thing to do with this. If you would wipe that whipped juice up outta your eyes then maybe your ass could see shit a little more clearly.” Oh…this nigga here wanna try my patience I thought as I stood up to knock his ass out.

“Rod,” Dream broke in diverting my attention, “It was my idea. I called her and asked her to come down here.”

“Dez…what the fuck?” I turned and screamed on him, “You of all people know good and well my position on this. You was there with her that night. You know how shit went down.”

“Yeah…I was there,” he answered back his tone unwavered, “I was there with her for hours while she was up there losing her fucking mind over you. I know that shit affected her, but I also know how it affected her when she was without you.”

“It’s not your call Dream,” I answered back heatedly, “Not your damn call.”

“Well it may not be his call Rod,” Nube piped in, “But I’m damn sure glad he did call. Murad…we need to talk.”

I had just finished up my meditating when Dream called. Well at least my attempt to meditate. All the unsettling thoughts kept prompting uneasy vibes, and when the phone rang and Dream explained the status of the investigation I couldn't get my clothes on fast enough. He came and picked me up and I'm here…ready to handle this however it needs to be handled.

"Ain't nothing to talk about Nube," Murad answered, "We discussed all that we needed to back at the house."

"Well apparently the discussion was misguided, because there was no mention of my need to collaborate the chain of events of that day. You also never told me that you'd be presenting your version of how things went down as a solo attack. I was there Rod," I told him, "Hell if you gonna sit here and just omit that fact."

"Nube," he said heated, "What you coming down here talkin' ain't no different then what I've already heard. I'm not changing my position on this."

"Oh really," I quizzed him raising my eyebrows, "What I say above the others don't matter?"

"Nube," he spit out frustrated, his tone letting me know that I was putting him on the spot in front of the fellas.

"Murad," I gave him back just as irritated and frustrated.

"Look," he started off, "Yo…can you all excuse us," he told the guys. "I need to hear her out."

"Not a thing…no problem," they stated as they slowly filed out of the room closing the door behind them.

"Damn baby," he started again, "How you gonna come down here going against that I asked of you?"

"Going against you Rod? That's all that matters to you," I responded sitting my bag down on the table, "No…the question is…How you gonna singularly make a decision that could dramatically alter both our lives?"

"I'm making this decision cause I fucked up the first time Nube," he answered, "I should have never let you park the damn truck and come in the shop. I felt that shit in my gut when you said you was coming in, and I should have told you no…wait outside. None of this would have ever happened if I had made the right decision then. I didn't…so I'm making this decision now. You're out of it."

"I'm out of it?" I gave back, "You gonna make that decision when I can give a statement that will revamp the odds in your favor?"

"I don't want the negative aspect of this all disrupting your projects, nor taint your positive image and possibly interfere with future deals," he came back with.

"Damn them projects Rod. I ain't concerned about no projects," I told him, "My main project in life is maintaining what we've got together on a personal level. If I had to make a choice between the career and you….the career would be done cause you take precedence over it all."

"And I feel the same way," he answered, "You take precedence over anything else that I got going on. You have a beautiful dream and a special way of sharing it with everyone and my actions don't need to be the cause of any negative fallout on things you got going on."

"Murad…are you hearing me," I angrily stated, "Projects are not my concern…you are."

"Nube," he voiced so sharply I physically felt the slice, "My mind is made up."

"Oh…so your mind is made up," I replied, "The king has spoken and that's it?" He just looked at me with that "try me" attitude and gave me that damn head twist.

"Well okay fine Murad," I started out angrily, "You wanna sit here and leave me out here by myself. Fending for my damn self while you just locked up doing nobody no good?"

Again he just looked at me and twisted that head. I don't believe this man, all that we just went thru, so I so much as let him know, "Murad…all that we just been thru and you just gonna toss aside my opinion and my choices? Well it appears that you hell bent on getting you a bid up under your belt, so I guess you need to go on and do what you feel you gotta do. But let me let you know one thing, I don't do no fucking bids with no man…not on some bullshit like this. So if you so relentless on doing a bid…you'll be doing that shit by yourself…Sire."

I picked my bag up off the table and started for the door. I made it halfway across the room when he got up from his seat and called out, "Nube."

I stood trembling in place, consumed with anger, fear and frustration at this man, yet at the same time relieved that he'd finally said something. I turned slowly trying to will away the big tear drops from tumbling from my eyes. I was unsuccessful...once I faced him and raised my head they sped down my cheeks like an avalanche.

"C'mere Nube,' he said in a tone of redemption. I walked back over and set my bag back on the table as he pulled me to him. I could no longer contain myself as I cried out loud. He just leaned up against the table holding me in his arms, as I tried valiantly to stifle my sobs. In an effort to assist me, he leaned in and kissed me intensely. I looked up at him thru my tear stained eyes, and he spoke the words I wanted to hear.

"We gonna go your route Butter. We'll both give statements in regard to the attempted abduction."

I was so overwhelmed with relief a small sob escaped my lips anyway. He quickly remedied the situation by closing his lips upon mine, and I eagerly meshed my lips with his in response.

Dream

I'm glad I made the decision to go get Nube and bring her down here. Rod can be so damn stubborn sometimes...against his own good. She sure is letting his ass have it in a nice kind of way.

"Yeah...look at that nukka there," Kye spit off. Rod probably didn't know but once we left the room, we just went on the opposite side of a two-way mirror and we watched and heard everything anyway.

"It's all good," Lonnie said, "My little sis gonna set him straight. Princess got a good head on her shoulders."

"Well I hope so," Aaron put in, "I'm not comfortable with how this thing can swing if it has to go to trial. He would be taking a huge risk. Not to mention...dude still in a coma."

"Well we just gonna let the good of it all prevail. Lil Bit got a special place in his heart, if he gonna listen to anybody…it'll be her," Bryce added in his two cents.

"Aww shit…wait a minute," Kye said as Nube spoke her final piece.

"Murad…all that we just been thru and you just gonna toss aside my opinion and my choices? Well it appears that you hell bent on getting you a bid up under your belt, so I guess you need to go on and do what you feel you gotta do. But let me let you know one thing, I don't do no fucking bids with no man…not on some bullshit like this. So if you so relentless on doing a bid…you'll be doing that shit by yourself…Sire."

"Damn, she ain't playing," Kye said as Nube walked to the door. We all watched as Murad stood up and called out her name. We held our breath and watched as she turned around to go back to him. He reached out for her and she folded in his arms. And as he held her and told her they'd both give the statements we broke out with hoots and holla's.

"Ahh…I told you that nigga was sprung," Kye shouted out, "Ya'll should have went and got her from jump." And as Murad held Nube planting the kisses for life on her, with his arms around her waist he held out his right hand…and gave us the middle finger.

"Aww…this nigga here," Kye said as we all bust out laughing, "You got that one off Chief," Kye called out, "You the man Rod…you the man."

Chapter 49
'Ish Just Getting Started

Murad

We'd made a deal with the Essex County prosecutor's office. Nube and I both gave statements on the night's events and I was released without charges. We signed some papers and was informed that we still had to wait on a final determination. Two weeks had passed before we heard anything else. After some "probing" on Kye's part, 3 additional witnesses had come forth to vouch for that night's events. One was a little old Korean lady who had been peeking out the window of the closed store front where the assault took place. The other 2 witnesses were outside of Theodore's and could attest to Frenchy's statement of the plans he and Poo had for Nube, if they had gotten the chance to swipe her. With all that working in our favor the prosecutor's office still felt the need to impose some kind of reprimand on me. See that's the bullshit right there...I don't know, probably some fucking office is up for election this year and somebody trynna stack points on their political portfolio. I was exonerated of all of the serious charges, but still was hit with a probationary misdemeanor charge of vigilantism that required I do 100 hours of community service. I was also ordered to enlist the services of private security when travelling with Nube. With those two requirements in place the misdemeanor would be expunged from my files after 6 months. I don't know how I was gonna deal with the second option, cause I don't want or need no fucking body up in my business, as in no damn body guards. First off...I'm more than capable of protecting me and mine my damn self, and secondly...I ain't too keen on paying niggas to watch my back...yet at the same time be privy to some of my most private moments. I don't know how I'm gonna pull that shit off.

It's Sunday morning, and Rod and I are doing our most favorite thing, sitting in the bed eating breakfast and reading the paper. Rod deals in the New York Times being the financial guru that he is, while I the humanitarian stick to the Star Ledger. With this California king, it's just like our own private picnic area, playground, you name it. While I sit between his open legs, turned to the side, he flips thru his paper as I feed him from the bed tray in front of me, and flip thru my papers laid out to the side of me.

"Mmmm...Thanks babe," he says as I slide a forkful of veggie quiche into his mouth. I took a forkful myself before I turned back to checking out the section on the Essex county forum.

"Hey Rod, they've got a holiday festival coming up at the SOPAC theater. Wonder what the venue will be? Have you heard anything about that?" I asked in between chews.

"Naw," he answered, as I slid another forkful into his mouth. "Damn...remind me to double check my Sintron account later."

"Okay bae," I responded, "Rod...why you got this TV running on this paid program channel. You not even paying attention to it."

"Leave that channel alone girl," he called out to me as I reached for the remote.

"Are you serious right now?" I asked him with playful sarcasm.

"Hell yeah I'm serious," he replied, "I got some real good shit...I mean some very resourceful products from that channel."

"Good like what Rod," I came back with, "All them gadgets and what nots that just clutter up the place."

"Well you don't see no gadgets cluttering up nothing round here," he answered, "Everything I've invested in has proven to be worth it...so leave that TV alone lady."

"You know what? Fine," I told him laughing, "Big time financial analyst, business and entertainment manager, Mr. NY Times and Wall Street Journal subscriber, and you ordering off the "Saw It on TV" channel? Wouldn't the world like to know that lil tid bit of Murad Tillman."

"Maaaan listen," he responded, "You don't even know the half Nube...you don't know the half."

"I guess I don't know the half and not quite sure I wanna know," I told him plopping a strawberry into his mouth.

"Yo...you ain't got no whipped cream to go with that?" he asked me in regard to the strawberry.

"It's some up in the fridge, but I'm saving that for tonight," I told him.

"Oh really. What's going on tonight that we need whipped cream?"

"Wouldn't you like to know," I teased him getting up out of the bed.

"Stop playin Nube...what's the deal for tonight?" he asked my retreating back as I left room.

"You gonna have to wait until tonight and see," I answered heading down the stairs.

Once I hit the bottom step I turned around to find Murad at the top, feigning a menacing look.

"Oh...you gon' tell me about tonight, or I'ma have to..." he started and I cut him off with, "You gonna have to what?" As he leapt down the stairs two at a time, I made a mad dash to the kitchen with the tray laughing all the way.

"Stop...Rod stop...you gonna make me spill this stuff," I cried out giggling like a teenager.

"Oh naw missy...you gonna learn your lesson here today."

"No Rod...no," I ran giggling and screaming as he closed in on me. I slid the tray on the counter and dodged behind the counter to the left. He came for me on his right...so I switched to his left. He swept back around, so I ducked to the right.

"So you gonna make me work for this," he said grinning, "Wait till I get a hold of you...I'ma spank that ass just like you deserve."

"Rod...stop," I continued to laugh, "You not my damn daddy."

"I'm ya daddy today girl and soon as I get a hold of you I'm gonna..."

The phone interrupted his statement and I took that chance to yell out, "Get the phone, it's ringing."

"You get the phone," he said, taking note that him getting the phone would give me the advantage to escape.

"This your house," I kicked back to him while the phone was on its second ring.

"Oh you can kill that girl," he responded as the third ring went by, "You bout comin up on them 30 days, and you ain't going nowhere...so this our house."

"You'd better get it," I taunted him on the fourth ring, "Answering machine gonna pick up after the 5th ring. Could be important."

I watched as that registered with him and he slid off to the left to retrieve the phone. "Hello," he said as he grabbed hold of the phone. I didn't give him the option, I ran trying to make a mad dash for it, and he took off after me. I couldn't help but laugh and giggle, then scream at the top of my voice in the silliest school girl tone, "Muurraaad," as he semi tackled me and cuffed me up in his arms.

"Aahh...got you now," he called out laughing, "I'm bout to show you...bout to show you right now."

"Bout to show me what Murad," I said unable to control my laughing and giggling.

"I'ma give you that ass whipping you deserve," he said.

"Oh...okay," I said slowing down the laughter trying to catch my breath, "Is this gonna be the one I deserve...or the one that I like?"

"Mmmm," he answered me lightly kissing my lips, "Both."

As he began to put in some work on the kisses, I had to remind him that he was on an open phone line.

"Oh damn...I forgot. Hello," he said into the phone.

Murad

Nube play too much thinking she can outrun me...she know. "Hello?" I asked again into the phone when silence continued to greet me.

"Well...sounds like you two are all into it," a female voice responded.

"Yeah...who dis?" I asked not completely recognizing the voice, although something was very familiar.

"Oh so now you don't even know me," she responded in a huff. Ahh damn....fucking Jazmine.

"Yo...how'd you get thru...I had ya shit on block...you know what...that's all irrelevant...uh...I have nothing to say to you Jazz," I told her.

And before I could hang up the phone, she cried out, "Is that what you gonna say to your child?"

"My what?" I said, unsure that I'd heard right.

"That's right Murad...I'm pregnant," she added on.

"Okay...and you calling me up to tell me this because...why??" I asked.

"You know why Murad," she replied, "You're the father." You know this trick here is sure nuff on something. I can't remember the last time I was that in depth with her.

"Jazz," I peeled off laughing, "You need to come one better than that...that shit right there is impossible."

"Oh we shall see," she came back, "We shall see. You and your little "official girl" over there laughing shit up like you at the 3 ring circus...but play time is over...you gonna have to step up and take care of your responsibility. Our baby gonna be your new priority."

"Look Jazz I ain't trynna hear this yang you talking," I told her.

I knew the volume of her voice allowed her words free access to Nube's ears as I felt Nube go tense on me and start to pull away. I looked down at her and saw all the previous joy totally diminished, and a look of instant upset on her face.

"Murad...Murad," I heard Jazmine calling into the phone, "We need to get together and discuss how you gonna handle your responsibility."

"What?" I spoke into the phone. At this point Nube started to retreat from the room.

"Nube wait," I called out.

"Sound like you got some business to handle," she turned around and said in a flat tone.

"Babe listen," I responded, "This bitch is lying." Nube glared at me hard. She has always asked that I refrain from calling women bitches...at least not in her presence anyway. "What?" I glared back at her.

"Please don't use that name for her in my presence. She wasn't a bitch when you was with her," she replied.

"Actually...yeah she was," I came back with.

"Well then you had no business with her," she retorted.

"Look Nube...that's neither here nor there," I told her as she continued to walk away.

"It may not be here nor there, but it's "somewhere" up in there between you two, and I need to not be "here" right now," she said going up the stairs.

"Murad," I heard in a high pitch thru the phone.

"Yo...what Jazz?" I yelled back.

"How we gonna do this, how we gonna handle this all?" she asked.

"Jazz," I started, "I don't know what kind of games you feel you trynna play, but your little declaration of your impending pregnancy is not gonna break me and Nube up. I don't believe you coming at me with this 20 something year old bullshit. Did you not fucking hear about DNA...yeah...that's that little paternity test shit that's been into existence for a minute now. How you figure you pulling this nonsense off?"

"Oh don't you worry," she told me, "You gonna get your paternity test, but in the meantime, you need to let me know how you planning to support me and this child or I'm putting you on blast to the world. I ain't got no problem in letting them know how King Midas turned his back on his own child."

"Let me tell you something you little miserable trick," I peeled off, my temper starting to accelerate, "I will make sure that you pay deeper than a mu'fucka if you attempt to tarnish my name and reputation. You know good and well I can't possibly be the father of your child. I haven't fucked you since January heifer, and even then my shit was strapped up to the nines. What kind of sick math you doing?"

"Oh don't you worry bout it Murad," she came back with, "I'm good and pregnant. This ain't no recent shit here. I've been paying for all the pre-natal care myself since I couldn't get in touch with you, but now it's time for you to handle ya business. Our child don't deserve this."

"You know what," I started, "Let me present you with this here fact...don't fuck with me Jazz on some ole crooked bullshit. If you gonna come at me with something, it better be straight up and down like 6 o'clock. Anyway this here shit is on the fly...I'm gonna crush you. So if you trynna go toe to toe with me...you'd better be sure."

"Oh I've never been more sure Murad," she answered, "I've got an attorney to establish my rights and financial needs and we about ready to..."

"I'm warning you Jazz," I said cutting her off, "You don't wanna tangle with me on this."

"Well its too late for all that now Murad," she answered me in a huff, "Shit already tangled, and trust...you gonna straighten it out. Now we can do this the right way...or I can go the necessary route."

"You know what," I told her totally aggravated and not in the mood for shit else she had to say, "Do what you feel you gotta Jazz, I got something for everything you coming with. Now if you don't mind, I'm done."

"Okay Murad," she answered, "I'll do just that...all that I gotta do. We'll see what you got to say when the shit go down. Oh...and you know what...I know it's 3 days early...but you tell that bitch I said Trick or Treat...her fucking time bout to be up."

She hung up the phone in my ear and I had to take a few minutes to get my bearings. Fuck...what the shit is this girl trynna pull!!! I paced the floor twice before I headed upstairs to confront Nube. Damn...

Nubina

I know that I heard her correctly...she said she's pregnant and Murad is the father. I stood at the balcony doors in the bedroom looking out at the scenery as if it would help disengage what I'd just heard. As I watched the red and orange leaves fall into the yard below, her words played thru my mind again, "I'm pregnant and you're the father." She said that…I know she said that…I'm sure that's what I heard.

"Nube," I heard Murad say entering the room, "Nube…baby…"

"Did she say she was pregnant," I turned interrupting him, "cause I do believe that's what I heard. Did I hear her say she's pregnant Murad?"

"Yeah…she claims she is…but that's not my problem."

"It's not your problem?" I asked in a tiff.

"No Nube…it's not my fucking problem," he answered me.

"So she calling you cause what Rod…she looking for a godfather for the baby?"

"Okay look Nube," he started, "Jazz on some ole pranks and shit. If she actually is pregnant…it ain't by me."

"Well how far along is she?" I asked.

"Damn if I know," he responded, "I'm really not concerned cause I know it ain't mine."

"Well what…it's the end of October…and you all broke up like when…April that was. So how are you so sure you not the father Murad?"

"Cause Nube," he replied, "she and I ain't been down like that in a minute."

"In a minute you say?" I asked; my mind reverting back to our conversation in April, "I do believe I remember you saying things jumped off with you all that night after my engagement at Sarafins."

"Yeah…things did jump off, but it wasn't anything that could produce a child," he responded.

"Well then what happened Rod," I voiced angrily, "how you two kick shit off with sex and then just tell me she ain't pregnant?"

"Cause what happened that night did not involve intercourse Nube," he shot back at me.

"Well exactly what went down Murad…what went down?" I asked in distress.

"Ahh man Nube," he started, "It ain't really important…trust me."

"It's not important?" I asked pointedly, "She calling here announcing she's pregnant and it's not important?"

"Look Nube if you must know, she gave me some head work," he said completely aggravated.

"A blow job Rod?"

"Yes Nube...that's what it is," he responded.

"So you telling me she got pregnant orally? You saying you inseminated her thru her mouth?"

"I ain't saying nothing, cause she ain't pregnant by me," he answered.

"Well how she calling up here with her claims," I threw back out there, "What really went down that would give her the confidence to make that claim. She gotta know there's DNA now. How is she so sure?"

"Nube...I don't know," he began to explain, "We argued on the way to her house that night, I put her out the car when we got there. She asked me about coming inside to get some papers I asked her to get for me, and once I got inside she kinda just jumped my bones and went for my shit, insisting on doing me that favor."

"And you accepted Rod...you accepted the favor," I cried out.

"Aww c'mon Nube...I'm a man," he voiced back, "At that time I hadn't had any sexual contact in like 2 ½ months, and my desires got the best of me. It wasn't the best decision I ever made, but we wasn't together at that time Nube. Look I told you before, her coming at me like that just anchored the fact that I didn't need someone of such desperation up in my life."

"So you two argued, she invited you in, slobbed ya shit down, then you broke up with her and now she's pregnant?" I asked totally annoyed. This sounded like some complete bullshit.

"In a nutshell Nube...yeah," he answered.

In the nano second it took for him to answer me, a small epiphany filtered thru my mind and I thought about it...that little series of events does sound too ridiculous. And then knowing Jazz...I wouldn't put anything pass her. I took a deep breath then just went and took a seat on the settee. I looked up at him not knowing what else to say in regard to this nonsense.

Damn, I'm feeling so conflicted. I know that bitch is lying yet at the same time; I gotta see things from a woman's prospective. Nube has gotta be hurt and feeling some kind of way. She's been thru a lot of bullshit in her other relationships and this is probably adding on to her issues of trusting. I watched as she went and had a seat, and tried to see if I could read on her face just where she was at right now with this. I saw pain, hurt and confusion. I need to make this right....and now.

"Nube," I started going over to her, "I want to assure you this is not my baby. Jazmine is trying to pull the trump card in a game she playing without a full deck. I don't know how far along she's supposed to be and all, but in the end a test will bring out the truth."

"It's not like I don't believe you Murad," she answered, "I'm pretty sure Jazmine will do whatever it takes to stay in your life...it's just that anytime you have physical intimacy involved, the chance for a pregnancy cannot be ruled out."

"Butter...listen," I told her getting down on my knees in front of her, "I have not had sexual intercourse with Jazmine since January. So unless she about to drop that baby any day now...it ain't me. Not only that Nube...you know I don't ever have sex with anybody without using protection...never." She looked at me sideways and I knew where she was going with the look. "Well Nube...you ain't' just anybody...Bae you my life," I told her. She grabbed me around my neck, hugging me and holding on tight. I got off my knees and took a seat down on the floor bringing her down with me.

"Damn Rod...I don't know if I can do this right now. We just getting thru the carjacking and the boy still in a coma. Rod...uugghh!" she cried.

"I know Bae, I'm hearing you," I told her, "We got a lot on our plate to still contend with; the last thing we need is Jazz running some ole' bullshit like this. But Nube, we can't let her divide us with her nonsense."

"Oh...I'm not thinking bout going nowhere," she replied, "She gonna have to be a little more creative than that. In fact...I can't imagine anything she could tell me or do to make me leave you. I just could never give her that much power or energy."

"We just gonna take this day to day Nube," I told her, "She claim she's got an attorney looking into her interests, so I'll get Jarrell started on my behalf."

"An attorney Rod?" she asked alarmed.

"Yeah...so she says," I went on, "Who knows what that trick is up to. If she thinking her end result is money then yeah...I could see her taking this nonsense to an attorney. But on the real...I feel for dude if she roped him up into this cause like I told her, if this turns out to be straight up bullshit...I'm coming after her with all guns smoking and that would include him as well."

"Oh Rod...we so don't need this shit right now," she said hugging me up again.

"I know Butter...I know. But promise me...promise me you'll hang in there with me Nube. I can assure you that this is all some trumped up shit as retaliation for you and I coming together."

She looked up at me; her pretty brown eyes oozing love mixed up with uncertainty and said, "I'm in this until Rod...until."

Chapter 50

Hitting The Fan Hard

Murad

November 1st and Nube and I are down in ATL putting in the finishing touches on the rap callabo. She was so excited about working with Luda she could barely contain her excitement. For the most part the project was hot and shit was jumping off between them on point. He really seemed to appreciate her eagerness to work with him and she was flattered to be featured on his work. Nube has a special love for the rappers being that she started out in poetry. Well the ones of a true lyricist nature anyway. She is especially moved by those who are truly coming with a message or a lesson. I'm just sitting here watching her do her thing, interacting, working and lending that magical aura she possess to the ambiance of the room. She's a champ...a real go-getter. I wouldn't trade her for the world.

"Alright, that's a wrap," the production engineer proclaimed. They had just finished the 6th take and everyone seemed to be satisfied with the end result, so we were done. I watched as congrats were distributed and Nube and Luda exchanged hugs, before he walked her over to where I was.

"Just wanna give thanks," he told me extending his hand on the dap tip, "Your lady here is on the money...I really appreciate her style and I'm really honored that she came thru for me."

I just gave him the head nod, and topped it off with, "Anytime. This was a mutual opportunity of talents clicking and I'm sure that track will be a monster."

"Oh...no doubt...no doubt," he replied while Nube just stood there taking it all in. "Well listen," he said, "I'm bout to go get something to eat...got a new spot I just opened up. I would appreciate it if you guys would be my guest for the evening and join me." I hit Nube with a look that let her know it was fine with me, as long as it was fine with her.

“I think I’d like that,” she responded, “You done worked a sista…least you can do is feed me.”

“Cool,” he said laughing, “How bout I meet you all outside, and I guess you can follow me over.”

“That’ll work,” I replied reaching for my jacket. As he walked away to confer with his people, Nube leaned into me as she reached for her jacket as well.

“So what you think Rod? Is it gonna rock the charts or what?”

“Phew,” I blew out, “You know it. What I tell you Nube after the premiere? Everything you do is hot…nothing you do falls short. Wait till this comes out and starts blowing up on the radio…you gonna be busy Bae…extremely.”

“Alrighty then,” she responded, “If you say so…then I’ma go with that.”

For a brief second, I looked at Nube in a strange light, as her last set of words sank in. I don’t think that Nube believes in her own abilities. I think that perhaps she’s so busy out there just getting her messages across, utilizing her love of speaking that it never really sets in that she has something awesome going for herself. I guess she doesn’t realize the manifestations of her talents are admired by many. It seems as if she’s starting to second guess herself the deeper we get into this entertainment game. Hmm…I know that’s not where she wanna go with it all, and not into being in them “circles.” As far as I’m concerned, she can get out of the game now…we sitting on a good amount of paper right now, with only more to come. I prefer the real Nube, the true Nube, and if getting out before shit gets too hectic is what’s needed to preserve her sanctity…then so be it. We can break out now.

“Rod?” I heard her say as I’m thinking, “You ready?”

“Yeah,” I responded, “Let’s go.”

Nubina

Oh, this day has turned out to be one of the best in a long while. I mean with all that Rod and I have recently been thru, this day is putting a smile on my face. I just laid down my first rap callabo and I think it went very well if I must say so myself. Now we are here just eating, relaxing and having a good ole' time. One of the assistants on the projects was telling jokes and had us all doubling over in laughter. I'm truly happy to see Murad laughing and smiling. He's been going thru a lot lately and I sometimes worry about him. I mean how much can one person take. He's always been there for me, so strong, so in command. Yeah....he needs this good time right here.

"So Nubina," Clay the production coordinator asked, "Any new projects you got coming thru soon?"

"Well I stay busy, always out doing my thing," I answered, "Why do you ask?"

"Well I was really feeling your energy and kinda thinking about borrowing you again, after this single drops. I'm seeing some new things on the horizon that would really jump off with you involved."

"That sounds like an opportunity...of course it has to go before Murad," I responded.

"Oh for sure," he came back, "That right there is common knowledge. Don't nobody get at you without getting pass King Midas first."

"Just pure business bruh...pure business," Murad piped in laughing, "But let me know...we can sit down and discuss it when you ready."

"As soon as we get the single off and running, I'll do that," Clay said.

We sat around laughing, talking and just chilling for about 2 hours before people started to pull out. Luda stood up and thanked us once again, shook Murad's hand and gave me a hug.

"It was a pleasure," he whispered in my ear before he let go.

"Oh same here," I let him know as he released me. Murad and I gathtered our things and returned to our hotel suite.

"Wow," I said pulling off my jacket and stepping out of my shoes, "This was a productive, but long day."

"Yes it was," he added on, "I'm ready to hit the shower, and just take it down."

"Yeah, I'm feeling you on that," I absentmindedly spoke as I clicked on the TV while at the same time checking my phone. I had a text message from Lani. I retrieved it so that I could read it. It read, "Nube...whas goin on?"

"What is she talking about," I'm thinking in my head, flipping channels. Just as I was about to text her back, I came across the gossip show TMZ and who was up there on the screen but Jazmine, every bit of big and pregnant. "Rod!!" I yelled at the top of my lungs, turning up the volume, "Get in here!"

He stumbled into the living room from the bedroom just as Jazmine announced, "Yes...I have contacted him about the child, but he's denied it. And yes I know that he's with Nubina now, and that's all cool, but he can't deny what we had together and this child that was produced. Murad Tillman is a man of means, and he owes this child the same."

I turned to see how this was affecting him, as the TV droned on, "Ms. Meadows," one reporter asked, "It's apparent that you are well into this pregnancy, why is that you've decided to go public with it at this time?"

"I tried to contact Mr. Tillman numerous times but was unable to reach him," she answered.

I watched as Murad's skin tone turned to a fiery rust, and his jaw clenched tighter than a clam shell. "Ms. Meadows...Ms Meadows," another reporter called out, "Have you chosen this time to reveal this pregnancy because he and Nubina have gone public with their relationship? Is this an attempt to put a rift between them?"

"A what?" Jazmine responded, all irritated, "A rift? I don't know bout no rift, all I know is that she came in between me and Murad when we was together, and she was dealing with his brother first, so I could care less about her and how she feels, Murad and I...."

Her attorney seeing where she was headed interrupted with, "What Ms. Meadows is trying to convey is that she wants to let by-gones be by-gones. Regardless to the fact that her relationship with Mr. Tillman has gone awry, my client is merely seeking to establish paternity, and thus secure financial stability as well as the emotional support that her child deserves. This is not an effort to sabotage a relationship or revenge of a love triangle gone wrong. We are only seeking what is rightfully deserved."

"Ms. Meadows…Ms. Meadows," another reporter called out before Rod walked over and switched the channel.

As if that signaled a cue, his phone started ringing, then his side kick, and simultaneously my phone. "Here we go," he dejectedly remarked.

"Yo…what up?" he answered the first call, "Yeah…I seen the shit…hold on."

"Yeah…Lonnie…let me call you back…Aight."

In the meantime I answered my phone, "Hello…yes Lani. Well I had just gotten your message…then I turned on the TV and…Yeah…she claims he is…he said no…Yes I believe him….I dunno Lani. Well whatever…we gonna handle it…yes. Let me call you back…okay?"

In the interim, Murad was on the phone with Jarrell. "Man this shit here just don't ever stop," he voiced, "Well yeah…I guess she so called warned me. Said she'd take the necessary route…yeah…I couldn't tell you man. Unh-unh…not since January…strapped up, strapped down…yeah Rell, to the left, to the right, covered up as always. Okay…okay…naw…Thursday…we'll be back on Thursday. Yo Rell…I'm tired man…I'm fucking tired. Haters are coming at me left and right…I can't handle it. I'll wait to hear from you first…yeah…yeah Rell, I'm sure. Okay…later."

As he ended the call I just sat on the couch not knowing exactly what to do.

Murad

This miserable bitch. So…that's how she wanna go with this…she gon pay…her ass is gonna pay. I took a seat next to Nube on the couch and just threw my head back and closed my eyes.

"You know what Rod," I heard Nube say thru my fog, "I'm gonna go in here, and draw you a nice relaxing bath. I'll throw in some of my herbal bath salts that will ease your tension."

"Thanks Bae," I responded remaining seated.

She got up to go into the bedroom and entered the bathroom. I heard her wash out the tub before turning on the water to steamy hot. I sat there with my head swimming in disbelieve…yet at the same time believing that this was exactly what she meant she'd do. I swear if I never learned a lesson about tricks before, I sure nuff have learned one now. Not a cool option to be fucking with bitches strictly on the V-tip. That shit proves to be nothing but a headache. I can't even begin to think about all the bullshit I'm about to face behind this. She up here on national TV declaring I'm the father of her child. Damn....let me get a grip, I'm not in the mood to be all riled up. I'm just tired I thought as I walked across the suite to enter the bedroom. Once I got inside I saw Nube in the bathroom on her knees, throwing a heaping handful of salts into the tub.

As she swished them around with her hand, she turned to me and said, "Go head and get undressed Rod and get in."

"Can you join me?" I asked out of the blue.

"Are you sure Rod? Cause this is all about you tonight?" she asked.

"Nube," I voiced back tiredly, "If it's about me...then I want you... in the tub...with me. Can I get that?" She looked at me with such tenderness that I thought for a minute I might lose it.

"Not a problem Murad," she answered, standing up.

As the water continued to run we both just stood there lost in the melancholy mood, studying each others faces as we got naked. I climbed in first and settled myself against the back before I held out my hand for her to climb in and deposit herself between my legs. As she settled herself in with her back against me, I felt immediate comfort wash itself over me. If the rest of my life could feel as good as this moment, I'd sign up for that shit right now. If only...if only.

Nubina

Once we got back to Jersey on Thursday, our lives became consumed with utter chaos. We had anonymous calls as well as direct calls from media hawks for an exclusive or a rebuttal to Jazmine's accusations. Not only that...you know the word on the street was buzzing throughout the hood. Much talk flying around town about me, Rod and JT. I mean...it was to be expected, so it is what it is. That's the least of my concern in this all. I'm really not happy with the way Jazmine's trying to manipulate the situation. She's been calling talking about she has appointments to go to, and she needs "the father" of her baby there because there may be some medical condition happening, and oh…all kinds of nonsense. I told Rod to just swing with it for now. I reminded him that we didn't need the extra spotlight of attention especially since he was currently on probation. The last thing we want to do is substantiate her claims of him being callus and unconcerned. Jarrell backed me up on this, so against everything that is in him…he complied. He went when she called, he listened when he was around, and he asked all the questions that he could think of. So yeah…she sitting up in 7th heaven right about now knowing that Murad will be by her side during the remainder of this pregnancy. On the other hand…I don't know how I'm feeling. I mean…although hard I will have to accept this no matter which way the door swings. For one…Murad and I were not together when this supposedly took place, and the child is most definitely innocent. But having Jazz up in the mix for the rest of our lives…that would be a bit much.

Murad

This shit here is utter nonsense. I can't wait till she drops this damn baby…cause her math is definitely fucked up, or she's gotten her Doc in on the conspiracy. If my condom broke…this damn baby is over due, and if it did not…she got a couple of more months on this here PG thing. Shit ain't adding up, and despite all of our best efforts, this shit is taking a toll between me and Nube. I see that loss of fire from her eyes since this all came up, not to mention every time the phone rings with Jazz and her trumped up escapades, and I gotta go running to save face. Damn…never again…never in this lifetime or next…there will never be no fucking day in America I'll be dealing with some female on the strength of some pussy. It ain't worth it. If she ain't at least good enough to remain cool with you if things don't work about between ya'll….then she ain't worth dealing with period. Fuck if I done learned that shit the hard way. Nube is trying hard to be a soldier, but lately, she's become a little moody, grouchy and just going up to bed ahead of me. I mean we still get to do our thang…but we ain't maintaining…well not the way that we do. I mean I don't mind falling back from her, giving her some space cause this here is some true shit to deal with. But I would lose my fucking mind if she lost her desire or the need for my touch. I swear...I'd wanna be somewhere cracking skulls.

For a change we are relaxing in the bedroom watching a movie. It was one of them chick flicks that I really ain't beat for, but I figured I could compromise since she riding this baby thing out with me. Actually...it ain't all that bad. All was going good...Nube and I were snuggled up peacefully watching the movie when the phone rang. I reached over and answered it to be greeted by my brother Jarell. Now it ain't been but 2 ½ weeks since this chick went on TV and this has got to be about the 5th time she done had an issue. Jarrell told me her lawyer contacted him and said Jazz is in the hospital with some early contractions and she's requesting that I be present.

"Awww c'mon man," I voiced into the phone raising up from Nube, releasing her from my grasp, "You fucking kiddin me...please tell me you kidding me?"

"Afraid not Rod," he replied, "She down there performing and making enough noise for anyone interested in listening. You know Tricks in The Hood.com work all up in the hospital, and can't wait to scramble to the broom closet with they cells to dial My9 News or somebody. It's just better to play this all safe."

"Ahhh fuck!" I pushed out. I tried to keep my tone down when these calls started coming, but I'm bout to explode on this nonsense. I'm bout to go AWOL on this shit and let the chips fall wherever.

"Rod...Rod," my brother called out.

"What?" I replied heatedly.

"Keep it together man...come on. Keep ya head up. We gonna settle this shit in a matter of weeks, for real... we got science on our side. Just need to line up all our ducks in a row, then trust me...target practice gonna be on point. We'll shoot them down first time up. C'mon man...get a grip. I'll meet you down there. Park in the visitor's lot and I'll meet you so we can go in together. Aight?"

"Aight man?" he repeated when I didn't' respond.

"Yeah...yeah. I'll be there in a few...later," I told him and hung up the phone.

Needless to say Nube had slipped off into a zone, and I sure as hell couldn't blame her. "Bae, I gotta go," I sighed.

"Yeah, I kinda figured," she said, her tone flat and disappointed.

"Look, I don't know when I'll be back, so if you wanna go on to bed...you know...just go head, and I'll see if you still up when I get back. Okay?"

"Sure Rod," she answered with a weak smile.

I got up to throw on some sweats and my sneakers and grabbed my jacket. She looked up at me from the bed, and I leaned over and kissed her deeply. "Nube...you know I love you right?" I questioned her somber face.

"I know Murad...I know," she answered, her tone reflecting the look on her face. I pulled back and headed towards the door. Once again I didn't look back...knew that I wouldn't be able to digest the hurt and pain on her face. I trotted down the stairs and out the front door, never knowing that once I left, she drew her knees up to her chest, and as she wrapped her arms around her legs, she put her head down on them and cried like the devil had stolen her soul.

Nubina

I can't deal with this too much longer...I thought I could...but I can't. My head is throbbing and I'm just sick to my damn stomach over this. Every chance she get she wrangling him up into her arena. Okay...let me breathe...let me get up from her before I lose my mind. I've been sitting here up in my head for over 2 hours. I can't let this situation undo me...I've got to maintain my resolve...my common sense. I mean, I know Jazmine's type and know that she will try just about anything. I can't let her antics get the best of me. Maybe I can just take a trip to the supermarket and cruise the aisles, you know absorb the bright lights; pick up a few things on sale. Something about the supermarket always lifts my spirits. If I sit here I'll drive myself crazy. Just for a second...let me just get out of here. I jumped up from the bed, grabbed my jacket and the car keys and made my way to the front door. I wish that she would just go on and drop this baby...be it early or be she late...just drop the kid already so this can be settled once and for all. I jumped in the car and pulled off down to the end of the drive, turned right and headed across town to the store. I was lucky to get a spot close to the front door. I hopped out, grabbed a cart and pushed my way toward the entrance, tossing my hand back to hit the remote on the car. I slowed down once inside and cruised down the produce aisle. I saw a fresh fruit bowl, so I grabbed it and put it in the cart. I took my time going up and down the aisle just taking in the sights and smells of the market allowing the atmosphere to soothe my soul.

I spent a good 45 minutes in there before I headed to the checkout. As I began to put my stuff up on the belt, I looked up and saw the slew of gossip tabloids displayed for the picking. Such a shame how they feed on other people's misery in order to make a dime and....What!!! **Finance Mogul Denies His Love Child.** What the hell? I'm thinking in my head as I grab the paper. Story on page 7...I paused from putting my things on the checkout belt to turn to page 7. There on page 7 was a picture of Murad and I on the red carpet to my movie premiere with an embellished story about how he left a pregnant Jazmine to gallivant with me. And perfectly aligned to our picture was a recent picture of Jazmine just plump and all robust in her state of pregnancy. I can't believe this. First of all, I didn't know that I rated that much to be up in the Enquirer, and secondly...who did they speak with to get this concocted version of an article? *Budding actress Nubina who reportedly was engaged to the brother of the up and coming mogul started pursuing a romantic relationship with Murad Tillman while he was heavily involved with Ms.Meadows.* "What in the???" I'm saying out loud as I continue to abuse myself with reading this nonsense. *The poetess who is affiliated with civil and humanitarian causes doesn't seem to play fair in the matters of the heart. It was reported by Ms. Meadows that Nubina knowingly intervened in the relationship between she and Mr. Tillman in order to boost her career.*

"I can't believe this crap here," I exclaimed continuing to talk out loud.

"I can't believe it either," a voice called out, "Can you either buy the damn paper or put it back so we can keep it moving?"

I turned to face an irate man, all twisted with me for holding up the line. "You know what mister," I began all aggravated...then relented, "I apologize. I got something going on up here that you shouldn't be kept waiting for."

"Yeah, yeah...just move it lady," he gave back.

Okay now...see hold up. This shit here ain't fitting to be going down like that...and besides...today just ain't the day. "Excuse you?" I questioned him, "I willingly apologized and take accountability in causing a delay, so I don't think you need to be taking that tone with me Mister."

"Look lady...today...we all got things to do...today," he responded, "You need to deal with whatever's going on...on your own time."

"You know what..." I started again when I heard a male voice break in with, "Pardon me sir, I strongly urge that you re-think your tone...the lady has apologized already." I turned toward the direction of the voice to see... JT.

"Well I was just saying, people are busy," he responded.

"And she's already apologized Sir," JT responded with a little extra bass as well as determination in his voice.

Well...I didn't know he had it in him like that. The man simmered down as I proceeded to pay for my things. "Hey Jayson, thanks," I said to him as the cashier handed me my change.

"What are you doing out at this time of night?" he asked.

I was not in the mood to explain, nor put Murad in a bad light, so I just blew him off with, "A little last minute dessert idea came to mind, and I just had to have it." He looked at me sideways as if he didn't believe me.

"Are you sure Tania?" he asked "Cause I know that Murad wouldn't let you just venture out by yourself at this hour just to pick up some dessert. What's really going on?"

No sooner where the words out of his mouth, when the cashier said, "Miss...You forgot your paper."

"Oh that's not mine," I replied, "I don't feed into that nonsense, let alone support them by buying it."

"Well you were looking at it and put it down on the checkout with your order. Thought you wanted it and I rung it up, so it's yours," she said extending me the paper.

JT took the copy for me, and breezed over it...the blazing headline immediately caught his eye. "Aww Sweet," he said, "I sure hope you didn't let this upset you. You know this is all nonsense."

"Yeah it is," I replied, "But its nonsense that has somehow taken a life of its own and is beginning to plague Rod and I more and more each day. Everyday, every chance she gets, she's calling Murad to come be by her side for this pain or that pain. And this test...and that test. She is milking this thing for all it's worth. I just couldn't take it anymore....I had to get out for some air."

"Well come on," he said starting to walk, "Let's get your things in the car so that you can get back home. I'll follow you in my car. I'm still surprised that Murad let you come out by yourself."

"Rod doesn't know," I answered him, my voice quivering; "He's not home...again. Jarell called and said Jazz is in the hospital and her lawyer requested that he come down there. I don't know Jayson...I've had it with her pulling his strings like that and tormenting him so. I'm just so tired of it..." I stopped short as a rush of uneasiness came over me as I held my stomach and put my head down to take a deep breath. Damn I'm stressing much too much over this.

"Tania, are you okay?" he asked me .When I held my head up, the look of concern on his face gave me a scare and threw me into another state.

"Oh Jayson," I started, "I'm okay...I'm just tired and I just can't stand all the aggravation and the emotional ups and downs. I don't know how we gonna handle this if Murad is the father of Jazz's baby. I can't begin to think how I would handle consistent negativity for the rest of our lives. I just wish..." And instead of finishing my comments, I broke out crying.

"Ahhh no Tania no...don't cry," he said, "Everything will work out one way or another."

"But Jace you just don't understand," I replied all choked up.

"You know what, I don't understand," he answered, "But what I do know is that I'm not gonna let you drive home upset like this. We'll put this stuff in my car and you're coming home with me." I followed him as we proceeded to his car.

"But Murad will be worried when he comes home and I'm not there," I pointed out.

"Don't worry about it Sweet," he responded, "I'll give him a call and fill him in. In the meantime...just get in the car and relax."

As he unlocked the doors, I just did as I was told. I was tired of this damn roller coaster, and I just felt some relief in not having to think about the situation right now. I wanted to give up on thinking about Murad, Jazz and that damn baby. I just wanted a free mind from it all. He loaded my 2 bags into the trunk then climbed in and pulled off towards his house. He put the radio on to a jazz station as he let me have some space to get myself together. As I listened to the soft mellow sounds filter thru the car, I thought to myself how did I get here. How did I come to let this situation upset me so, and now I'm sitting here in the car with my man's brother, who by the way used to be my ex. How did I get here? I guess this baby thing is bothering me more that I want to admit.

"Well here we are," he announced pulling into his parking space.

I opened my eyes and proceeded to step out of the car. I wrapped my jacket around me snuggly as Jayson got the bags from the trunk. Wow...I haven't been by here in ages I'm thinking as I followed him inside once he unlocked the door. The place was neat and immaculate as always. I took a seat on the couch as he went to put my bags in the kitchen.

"Anything that needs to go into the fridge? Oh never mind...I see it" he called out.

As I sat, I just looked around taking in the atmosphere feeling the reminiscent vibes in the air. He walked into the living room from the kitchen and I looked up and smiled. He was so handsome...quietly handsome...in that good guy, good friend way. The one that I'd come to know all too well; and right now I wanted to recapture that camaraderie. Besides, he has a part in this ongoing scandal of hood gossip, so I asked him, "Jayson...I know you don't travel the same circles as Rod and I, or even Bryce and they, but...I know the word on the street hasn't passed you by totally...so how do you feel about all this going on?"

"All what Tania?" he responded.

"Well all the negative talk indicating you and I being together first, then you being passed off for Murad and the baby…possibly your niece or nephew, and…"

"Tania…it's not an option for me," he said cutting off my babble, "I trust in my faith and I am assured that somehow this chain of events are all part of God's process in getting us to where we need to be."

"Granted you're on point with that," I said, "But this is truly going to be one of the top 10 tests of believing in God's choices for me. I am seriously questioning whether or not I can sustain this."

"I'm surprised…I know that you have trust in a higher power, so what makes you say that Tania?" he asked.

"It's just that the way that Murad and I got together was so unconventional. I mean…you two are brothers, and dealing with two brothers was never something in the repertoire of my mind. But I love Murad so…a love so deep that I can't contest the reasons not to. He is my other half and I just don't know if I can share him in that way…I mean not like this JT…not with her. She's poisonous Jayson and I don't trust her to ever leave us in peace if this turns out to be his child."

"Tania," he said, "Listen to me when I tell you…you and Murad have something that exceeds the norm. I have never seen two people with such a parallel connection. I am sure that God will see you both over this hurdle. This is but one of many of life's obstacles and if you are going to succeed at this, you're going to have to stay strong in your faith."

I let his words marinade in the air above me before I allowed them to penetrate my brain…and I knew it was the truth that he was speaking, yet the truth just could not soothe me right now.

"Jace," I responded, "It hurts Jace…it just hurts so bad." And before I knew it I bust out crying again.

"Oh Sweet," he said wrapping his arms around me, "Hold on Sweet, it will be alright…just hold on."

Chapter 51
Rolling Over

Murad

Fucking home at last, I'm thinking to myself as I let myself in. As usual Jazmine was taking shit over the top and performing for an Oscar. I played myself real mellow the whole time. 4 damn hours down there with her. Now its bout 11:15, and even though it's not really late into the night…I'm beat. Hope Nube's in a better mood than when I left.

"Nube," I called out as I laid my keys on the kitchen counter. I opened the door to the fridge to grab me something to drink. Slipped out a can of gingerale and popped the tab. I wonder if she's sleep, I thought with my first gulp. She didn't answer me. Let me go on up here and check. I hadn't gotten 2 steps before my cell rang. "Aww hell no….no…no…this bet' not be. Oh…okay…its JT. Thought for a minute is was another Jazmine call.

"Hello," I answered thinking in my head what could JT be calling me for. He never calls me.

"Yeah Rod," he answered, "It's me, how did things go down at the hospital?"

"A stellar performance of her antics as usual," I answered, "She sure nuff gonna win an academy award before this is all over. I had to step out on Nube yet again tonight and I'm bout to go up here and check on her. I think she's sleep…I called out to her but she didn't answer me, but…" I stopped thinking…how does he know I was at the hospital.

"Murad," he started as if he was reading my mind, "She's not upstairs sleeping…she's here with me."

"Say what now," I said putting my soda down, "She over there with you? What's going on JT?" I asked starting to feel uneasy.

"Well I was out to the market this evening, and I bumped into Nube. She said she had come out to get some air;

she was upset about you and the whole baby thing. While she was in the check out line, she caught a glimpse of a blown up story in one of the gossip columns about you, her and Jazz, photos and all. Then to add on to that, some guy in line was shooting off his mouth about her holding up the line...and she was upset and out of sorts Rod, so I made her leave her car and come home with me. I didn't want her driving under them conditions."

"The fuck?...somebody was mouthing off at her?" I asked, starting to steam, "Who...where at... cause I'll go back down there and..."

"Rod," he broke in, "I took care of it, no harm done. Just a little misunderstanding."

"You took care of it?" I questioned him in doubt.

"Yes Murad," he answered, "I handled it."

"Well fine...fine," I said, "Good lookin JT, I'll be there in a few to pick her up."

"Well...she's tired and resting, so she's just gonna stay here with me tonight," he said.

"What you mean she gonna stay with you tonight? Aww hell naw. Her home is here with me...I'm coming to get her."

"Look Rod," he replied, "she's really worn out behind all this baby scandal. It's starting to make her physically ill."

"Aight cool," I answered, "Then I'll handle that all when I get her back home where I can take care of her."

"Murad, it's late," he responded, "Let her be, I'll bring her first thing in the morning or either you can come and..."

"I think not JT," I cut him off with, "Nube's well being is my job. I'll be there in 20."

"Murad...come on man...give her a break," he started, "She's at peace right now."

"Oh...so what you saying," I responded, "Her coming home with me right now is gonna cause her some stress?"

"Murad," he said, "I don't think you know just how much this thing is affecting her...in fact I don't think she truly realized that until this evening. Just let her take a break from the chaos this one time. Either way this thing turns out there stands to be many more nights that she's going to have to endure the impromptu phone calls and you'll have to leave her behind. Let her rest Rod…I promise I'll bring her home first thing in the morning."

Damn, I thought letting his words penetrate. For the first time, I really had to consider that JT had the better point of view on the situation.

Still I had to question something…anything, "So…what happened? I mean…she said she didn't wanna come home?"

"She didn't say that in so many words Murad," he answered, "But what she did say conveyed that a little escape would do her good right about now. She said she's in pain Rod…she's hurting. It's not that she doesn't want to be home with you…it's that being home with you makes her a prime witness to you constantly being put thru the ringer on this as well as leaving her alone with her feelings. She's just a little overwhelmed with the situation Rod. I'm thinking the gossip column and the jack-ass at the store just pushed her over the edge for a minute. I'm saying…she's good, you know our girl…she's gonna bounce back for sure…but just let her have these few hours Rod…please."

Wow…I never looked at it like that. I just always figured Nube was strong minded and solid in her thinking and that she'd find a way to handle this in the same positive fashion that she always does. "I don't know JT," I started, "Nube and I don't like being away…"

"Murad," he broke in, "Listen…I understand the intensity of your relationship and the strong feelings you have for one another…believe me I do. Trust me on this one…let her regroup, get things into prospective. To disturb her tonight would just reinvent the earlier thoughts of upset that transpired this evening. She loves you Murad…absolutely, so take my word for it, she'll still love you just as much in the morning." I thought about what he said…had to admit he was on point.

"Aight I guess," I answered, "Tell her to call me when she gets up. Aight?"

"You got it," he answered, "I'll see you in the morning. Good night Murad"

"Yo later," I responded. And just before he hung up I called out, "Jayson…she's all I got man…she's all I've got." Without looking for a response I hung up the phone.

Love should never have to be this hard, I thought as I stared blankly at the phone holding it responsible for my pain. No wonder I kept myself away from it all these years. I have never been in so much pain in all my life, and practically none of it by my own volition. Nube shouldn't have to feel like she needs to escape from her own home. This should be her place of peace, her safe haven. What I wouldn't give to turn back the hands of time on this one. Damn...I don't believe the nonsense behind it all. Phew...I'm at the fucking edge on this one...no...I have officially tipped the fuck over. Enough of this... I'm bout to medicate. I went into the kitchen to get out my stash of pre-rolled lai, and my Henny. I got a goblet out the cabinet, and headed back to the living room, plopped down on the couch and reached for the remote. Naw...forget about TV, I'ma listen to some music. I took the remote and clicked on my CD player.

"*Gotta stay sexy for your baby, tighten up my body, working on my ghetto pilates.*"

Yeah...just what I need, some Jaheim already loaded. I hit disc select and decided to start from the door with his first CD Ghetto Love. Cool, I thought as I poured my first shot, and lit up, leaning back I took a hit. Yeah...fucking sweet.

Chapter 52

Rolling Over Again

Murad

The sound of the phone ringing brought me out of my self induced coma. Aww shit…my head is banging…I must have laid here all night.

"Hello," I answered gruffly.

"Murad," I angelically heard, "Baby…what's going on? You sound…horrible."

"Nube," I pushed out, breathing at ease for the first time all night, "Whas' the deal Pretty? I get back home and you done flew the coop."

"Oh Rod, I don't know," she answered, "Last night I just felt so…hmm…I don't know…fed up. This Jazmine thing just got under my skin last night, and I couldn't contain myself. I mean, I just went out for some air and what not, then I had to go reading some more nonsense in the Enquirer and…"

"Oh yeah," I broke in with, "What the fuck JT talking bout, some nigga got in your face?"

"Not really Rod," she answered me, "I was holding up the line, and I did apologize, but then he got a little smart. And just as I was about to get him, JT stepped in and put him in check."

"So I heard," I told her, "I let him know that I appreciate that and all, but Nube…Bae you know I don't care for you being out by yourself…especially at night."

"I know Rod, but I just felt like I needed to separate myself from all the negativity, and you know how I love the supermarket," she replied.

"Listen Nube," I started, " I know this here is some tough shit to maneuver, but I wish you would have waited up for me and talked to me…you know let me know what's going on with you and how you feeling. I don't want you to ever feel like you have to leave your home…our home, in search of peace. That's something that should be afforded to everyone…no doubt."

"I don't know what came over me Rod," she said, "It's just that I've been stressing lately, more than I want to admit and I just was not feeling like myself last night."

"Well okay," I told her, "The last thing we need is shit to get so bad that you don't even feel like yourself. Come to me Nube. Whenever you feeling some kind of way, or you need some clarification, some comfort or some answers; just let me know Bae. I'm here for you...always. You ain't got to go nowhere else for nothing...I got you Nube...on whatever."

"Oh hey Rod...I know. I know you do," she kicked back, "I guess I was tripping. I've just been so out of sync lately, not even getting in my meditating as usual. I think being on the road, and trying to maintain the same schedule right now is just a bit much with all that's been going on."

"Well okay," I told her, "We can scale back on the appearances...your peace of mind comes first."

"No...no, Rod, I can handle it," she responded, "I just needed a minute to get things into prospective. I don't wanna fall off on what I do because we encountering some bumps in the road. I'm just gonna have to practice what I preach and pull myself together on this. There's no need to let this thing set precedence over me."

"Aight, now that's what I wanna hear from my baby...positive thinking," I stated, "So listen...I'll be there in like a half hour to get you."

"Oh no need for you to come out Rod," she answered, "JT's gonna drop me off on his way to work. We all set to go out the door."

"Well okay," I answered haltingly, "If ya'll ready to leave then...I guess I'll see you when you get here. I love you Nube...last night was rough without you."

"Aww Baby, it was rough for me too," she replied, "I don' like being without you...I missed you."

"Aight then," I started, "Go on and get ya' pretty ass in the car and bring it on home...I think I got a welcome home surprise for you."

"Oh do you now," she voiced sweetly, "well if it's what I'm thinking then you keep that right on tap, and I'll be right there. Got it?"

"Yeah girl…I got it…got it all and waiting to give it to you," I replied.

"Okay Rod," she hurriedly threw out, "JT's ready…I'll see you in a bit."

"Aight later," I answered and hung up the phone. Guess I'd better get my ass up and hit the shower and what not. Done laid down here all night in these clothes. Yeah…I thought as I headed upstairs to cleanse my physical and stimulate my mental with a steamy hot shower…today's gonna be a good day. My baby's coming home…and that shit right there is right in every way.

Jazmine

"You know I did Deena. I tried calling him and calling him for months."

"Well did you try stopping by his house?" she asked me.

"Naw," I told her, "he lives in a gated community. Anybody just can't get up in there. Besides, I wouldn't wanna have to run into that bitch and shit jump off between us. After all I am pregnant…but I owe her ass one from July. I ain't about to forget that shit she pulled at Sarafins."

"So yeah Jazz," Deena threw at me, "If I remember correctly, you said ole boy wasn't hitting you up like he used to. Not only that, you said you couldn't get him to ride strapless for nothing, so how did you get knocked up by him?"

"Oh girl you need to go on and stay out my damn business," I told her, "You such a nosey ass."

"Oh I ain't fucking nosey when you up in here giving me all the 411 on your sexscapades, and gloating bout your achievements."

"Well this here is gonna be my best achievement to date," I told her, "Especially if…" Aww damn, I think I said a smidgen too much. I know her birds' eye done picked up on that one.

"Especially what?" she asked.

Damn…I blew out a deep breath. "Especially if I hit the right mark," I answered.

"Hit the right mark with what Jazz? What you talking bout," she quizzed me, "Don't tell me this ain't Murad's baby…not and you all up on TV with lawyers and shit. Oh girl…don't be stupid…he gonna fry your ass on this one if…"

"Hey…look," I answered hotly, "This baby has a very good chance of being Murad's. Just as much chance as it needs."

"Okay bitch," she said, "What the fuck is you talking bout…spill it."

"Well," I started, "You know how I can give Superhead a run for her money. Well that night he was acting like he was done with me, so I kinda duped him to coming in the house. And once he got inside I jumped him and whipped that shit on him like somebody's A-list porno star. Girl I'm talking the best damn professional that I've ever given him…I mean swallowed and shit like a champ."

"Hold up," she interrupted, "Uh Nyasia…can you go in the back and bring up all the clean towels up front for me. Thanks." I had forgotten all about her little shampoo girl. Once she left to retrieve the towels, she pumped me for the rest of the story.

"So yeah," I continued, "Like I said, I swallowed and what not…made him feel real good. I thought he was gonna come out of his funk and stay the night. Well girl, he slipped himself out of my mouth, used one of my kitchen towels to get his self together and then he tossed me the towel and told me to lose his number."

"What!!" she said.

"Oh yeah," I told her, "And then that bastard walked up outta my house."

"Aww shit Jazz…you lying?" she asked me.

"Dee…why would I lie about some shit like that," I told her, "I'm telling you what went down."

"Damn girl, he played you," she came back with, "But that still don't explain how you wound up pregnant."

"Yeah…he did play me…but not as hard as he played his self."

"Okay how?"she asked.

"Cause once that mutha fucka left, I got up off my knees and pulled my drawers off. Then I took my hands and gathered all the cum from around my mouth and whatever was left that I didn't swallow and I took that shit and deposited it straight up in my coochie."

"Jazz," she yelled out all surprised.

"Deena what? His ass tried to play me, so I decided to give him something to play about."

"But Jazz," she came back with, "That right there is like far fetched and to the left. Ain't no guarantee that method would work. I'm surprised that you..."

"I know," I cut in with, "That's why I had a back-up to go with it."

"A back up?" she asked me, "Bitch...what the fuck else is you talkin bout?"

"Well about a week later I..."

"Uh wait a minute," she interrupted me again as the shampoo girl came back with the towels, "Nyasia, can you make a run to the corner store for me before my 2:20 gets here. Just get a couple a dollars out the tip stash and get me a turkey and cheese, a Pepsi and whatever you want."

She turned her attention back to me and said, "Now go head girl...."

Nyasia

OMG...I can't believe this shit I just heard here. I'ma walk real slow to the store cause I need to make this here phone call without any extra ears around. Aww come on Key...answer the phone.

"Yo...what up?" I heard.

"Yo Key, you ain't gonna believe what I just heard," I told him.

"Ny...what I tell you about calling me up wit ya' hood ass gossip. You know I ain't feelin you on dat," he blew me off with.

"But Key, this is mad serious," I told him, "It's about your Uncle Murad."

"What about my uncle Murad?" he asked me, all of a sudden interested.

"Oh so now you wanna hear it," I asked smugly.

"Girl...stop fuckin playin and break that shit to me."

"Well okay," I told him, so happy to have his full attention, "That bitch Jazmine is in the shop getting her hair done, and you won't believe what she just told Deena bout' how she got pregnant by your uncle. Well, what she had said was...."

JT

It seems like the days are getting shorter already. It's only about a week or more to Thanksgiving and the time seems to keep racing on. I've got to secure the final menu for the corporate campus as well as our offsite facilities. My company likes to do a real festive affair for the holidays, so I need to make sure everything is on board. Then there's the annual family dinner and...Oh yeah; I also have to meet with Sister Eleanor down at the church and make sure our soup kitchen is ready for the Thanksgiving dinner we prepare each year. Man...time is running short right along with these days. Guess I'll go in here and see if I can set things up on the computer. Oh man...I'm thinking as the phone starts ringing. Who else is needing something...did I forget anybody?

"Hello," I answered, unsure of the displayed number.

"Hello, Uncle Jayson," I heard, "This is me...Kiernan."

"Oh hey Key," I responded, "How are you? What's going on son? You and your mom at it again...has she been coming down on you?"

"Naw Uncle Jayson," he replied, "Nothing like that...we cool."

"So...to what do I owe this unexpected call? You need to come over for some more cooking lessons?"

"Naw...I'm good with that too. Actually I called because...well you know my girlfriend."

"Ah...no Key...which one?" I asked him.

"Aw come on Uncle Jayson," he laughed off, "Well okay...Nyasia...she work down at the hair salon over in Irvington. Uncle Jayson...she told me that girl Jazmine was in there...you know the one that Uncle Murad used to deal with before he got with Nubina. And she overheard some shit...oops...I'm sorry, I mean some things straight out her mouth that ain't cool Unc."

"Well Key...what exactly did she hear," I asked him setting down my papers and giving him my full attention.

“Well,” he started, “She said that....”

Chapter 53

The Shit Keep Rolling

Murad

Damn, it's starting to get real breezy these days. Only a few more days till Thanksgiving and Nube and I get to take a small break before we have head back to Chicago for another speaking engagement with the NAACP inner youth council. That Mr. Reagan was serious on Nube becoming a regular presenter in their program. We arranged a preliminary set up of 3 engagements within the next year, and the rest we'll play by ear. So we leaving out Monday, and returning on Tuesday. We have a small presentation Wednesday night in Union, and then we good for a minute. Thursday is our Tillman annual Thanksgiving dinner, so we'll be able to attend then just go on back to the crib and chill. I'm kinda looking forward to the get together...I mean with Nube and I on the go so much, I don't get to see my fam nearly as much as I'd like. I pulled the zipper up on my jacket a tad as the wind cut across my chest while making my way towards JT's front door. I got some business to handle, calls to make, so I sure hope this conversation with JT is gonna be short. All I know is he called and asked if I could stop by to discuss some issue that concerns me. He said he preferred not to deal with it over the phone, so here I am. Can't imagine what this shit could be about. As I ring the bell I figure...I'm about to find out.

JT

Wow... my mind is still swirling on the information my nephew revealed to me last night. It never ceases to amaze me how people can commit such acts of desperation without considering the consequences to follow, nor the fact that others than their intended party can be deeply hurt. I prayed about this thing all night and asked God to help me with the right way to present this to Murad. He'd been saying the whole time that he hadn't been with her in that way, and the mathematics to it was just not adding up. But given what Key told me last night, he just may be that child's father. Oh...there's the doorbell...I guess its show time. I made a small plea unto God, as I proceeded to the door and opened it.

"Murad," I greeted him.

"Yo JT...whas up?" he answered.

"Nothing...nothing...just getting ready for the food prep at the job, the church and our dinner thing. Uh...would you like a little something...or perhaps a drink?"

"Naw, I'm straight," he answered, "Nube got something back at the house she fixed last night, so when I get back we gonna tackle that." For some reason, I felt a slight pinch when he mentioned Nube waiting dinner back at the house for him. Was I jealous? "So what's this all about JT?" he asked taking a seat, "Something or somebody ain't coming correct if you calling me for a conference."

I should have known he would want to jump right in, so here goes. "Well, I got a call from Key last night," I began, "He called me with I would say, some disturbing information. He told me that one of his little girlfriends works over at the Evolutions salon in Irvington and yesterday Jazmine was in there getting her hair done."

"Well I know you ain't bout to hit me with no he say...she say shit," he interjected.

"Well no Murad," I replied, "It's more like she say...as in what Jazmine had to say. You know how you have been steadfast in your defense that you hadn't had intercourse with her in months?"

"Yeah?" he responded in a questioning mode.

"Well she revealed to her hair stylist in detail how she tricked you into coming in the house and then jumped on you and performed her best in oral sex. She said that she swallowed for you and everything, and then you cleaned yourself up, broke up with her and walked out on her."

"Uh...okay," he responded, "That's pretty much about the truth...so what's so ground shaking about that?"

"Murad," I started again, "You should never underestimate the desperation of a woman scorned. She told her stylist that she gathered all the remaining semen from inside and around her mouth with her hand and placed it up in her vagina."

"Say what now JT," he replied seemingly confused, "You say this bitch...did...what?"

"Uh...she inserted your semen into her vagina once you left the house," I repeated.

"The fuck!!!" he yelled out pounding the coffee table and jumping to his feet. "That grimey ass bitch...oh my god...you see...that's the reason I would never dip without wrapping my shit up. All these fucking years I played shit straight and then this trick here gonna go and...Oh man...the fuck!! You know what...you know what? She got that one off...her miserable ass got that one off. I would have never expected no shit like that. Ahh man...don't tell me...don't tell me she bout to make this all a permanent nightmare?"

"I don't know Murad," I told him watching him pace back and forth like a panther trapped in a cage. "There's a chance it could be."

"Damn Jayson," he came back with, "What the fuck if it is...what the fuck?"

"I don't have the answer to that Murad," I told him, "Just know that God doesn't make mistakes, and the child is a blessing regardless to the method of his conception."

"I don't wanna hear that shit," he vehemently replied, "Having a baby with Jazmine is not what I'm trynna do...let alone fucking hurt Nube like that."

"Oh it's already too late," I heard myself saying, "Tania has already been hurt by all this...and you gonna have to admit that your actions are the cause of her pain" I don't know where that statement came from. I guess it was something that I'd wanted to relay to him ever since I first heard of the scandal.

"Oh what the fuck you talking bout JT?" he angrily questioned, "You know hurting Nube is not on my itinerary...that shit right there happened before we got together."

"Well Murad," I told him a little heated myself, "I asked you not to hurt her, and you did. This should have been the ultimate occasion where you should have kept your infamous dick in your pants. Just this one time Murad...you couldn't have resisted this one time?"

"Oh yeah...that's real big of you," he said, "I guess you've got no problem in that department. You sat up there for 2 fucking years without expressing your physical desires for Nube, so I guess you an expert on abstaining. Yeah, I may have let the wrong head think for me that night, but you not exempt on hurting her either. You did a fucking job on her self esteem depriving her of sex while you claiming to be her man. Oh yeah...that's right...you forgot to let me in on that shit when I came to you about her and my decision." He's right, I did leave that out. Even though I knew that he would undoubtedly find out...that was just one indignity I didn't want to bare to him at the time.

"You know," I told him, "I may have deprived Tania of sex as you say, but at least I didn't jeopardize her and hurt her to the core with any wayward sexual behavior."

"Oh mu'fucka, you wanna go there," he replied to my statement, "Well I'll tell you what...if you wanna call being a man and having physical desires wayward...then wayward is one fucking thing you ain't ever got to worry about being called, with your dry ass, shriveled up neglected dick." I don't know what came over me, but the next thing I knew I let one go to the side of his face. Of course he came back at me with a searing left to the right side of my face, and a devastating upper cut to the body that damn near caved my chest in. As I fell backward over the coffee table, with the air knocked out of me, legs kicked back into the air, a sudden surge of sanity and reasoning resurfaced in me. I pulled myself up, got up on my feet and faced him.

"Look JT," he popped off, "Brother or no brother...you ain't about to be just hooking off on me like that. If we got to be scrappin' up in here all night...then so be it."

"Murad," I answered him humbly and short winded, "I don't...wanna fight you. This is insane...we both love Tania...yet we've both unintentionally hurt her. Look...I apologize for the things that were said here tonight. This was supposed to be an informative meeting with some possible resolution to the situation. I completely let insecurities prevail...once again...I apologize."

He let down his hands and plopped back down on the couch, and with a look of sincerity said, "Yo…JT…look…I'm sorry…too. It's just that I can't bear the fact that… yeah…I was irresponsible that night and yeah… I've hurt Nube to her heart, and possibly a hurt she'll have to endure the rest of her life…and that shit is eating me up Jayson. It's killing me to know I'm now a part of her collection of men who've brought her pain." I took a seat across from him and measured that he was valid in his sincerity.

"Murad," I started, "Sometimes things happen when we are not at our best mentally. It's part of life's balances and tests. Sometimes we rise above them, and other times we are caught up in the flow."

"Yeah well that don't seem to be a problem with you. You've always come off like the golden boy," he responded to my philosophy.

"Oh you think so?" I asked.

"Oh no doubt," he responded, "Jayson the Golden Kid…always the upholder of morality and thoughtfulness."

"Well," I stated, "you have no way of knowing that my gold, as you describe it, has been tarnished."

"Oh cause what…cause you didn't have sex with Nube?" he sneered.

I took a deep breath before I spoke, "Let me explain to you why I never entered into sex with Tania." He looked at me, gave me one of his approving lip nods, so I went on to continue, "A while back, I guess it's been about 3 years now, right after the time I found out that Kane was not my son. You remember how I fell off from the world, lost my job, my house and practically my sanity? Well it was during that time I'd gotten that little rusty apartment and just went thru my spell of drinking and ill-minded thinking. I let people come in and out of my place without question, and I let quite a few women come in and out as well. I wasn't very discriminate with the company I kept, and sometimes out of loneliness, I let myself become physically involved with women who in turn would ask me for money.

On one of these given days I was feeling particularly bad, and had been drinking most of the day. This woman Karina came by and asked me if I could let her have $20. I told her that I really didn't have it to spare and reminded her that she'd never paid back the $20 I previously loaned her. She started begging and cooing and I didn't really want to deal with her, so I just retreated to my room to lay down. Well after 15 minutes or so had passed, I heard her enter my bedroom and continue with her begging and whining then began to touch and caress my body. I was so not in my right mind, I decided to just lay back, close my eyes and not fight it. She touched, massaged and promised how she was gonna give me something ultra special…something I've never had before. Sounds familiar don't it? Well," I continued not waiting for an answer from him, "I lay there and let her strip me of my pants, and proceed to take me in her mouth. She licked, slobbed and worked me over so, that I became stiff and ready despite my drunken demeanor. She continued to promise me the time of my life and with my eyes still closed, I felt her climb on top of me. Rod…let me tell you…the feeling was so great…the sensation was nothing like I'd ever felt before. I twisted, I gyrated and gave it everything I got while she kept hyping me and calling out sexy innuendos. And I remember…just as I was about to come…I remember thinking that she has never felt so good before, so as I exploded with the most awesome orgasm I ever had, I opened my eyes to see that it was her 12 year old daughter riding on top of me and not Karina." For the very first time I could remember I witnessed a genuine look of sympathy from Murad.

"Damn Jay," he voiced in a low tone.

"Yeah," I continued, "I freaked Rod, I jumped up so hard and quickly I dumped the child off the bed and she fell onto the floor and broke her arm. Karina started yelling and screaming, calling me a stupid ass, and how I was gonna pay for it all. I took them down to the emergency room, where her Medicaid actually paid for it. I sat there in the hospital on pins and needles, yet ready for the authorities to come and arrest me for statutory rape…but it never happened. Karina didn't report it. Instead she came around routinely asking for money and favors and I just complied out of guilt. That went on for about 6 months and then she just stopped coming by. I summoned up the courage to ask one of her cronies and she told me that Karina was arrested and sent to jail for identity theft scams, and her daughter was sent down south to live with her mother. I pushed on to ask how the girl was doing, and was told that she was enrolled in school and seemed to be doing fine. There was no mention of a pregnancy, so I took that as I was safe and ran with it. But within my heart, I know I will never have the luxury of knowing the option of whether conception took place or not. And that weighs heavy on my heart Murad. I continued to freak until Kane...yes Kane sat me down and expressed his gratitude to me for being in his life and guiding him as the only man he will ever consider his father. And after that heart felt talk from a child...I got myself together and turned to the church. I prayed, studied and prayed. I asked God everyday to forgive me for my actions and to help me rebuild myself whole. And while I've come quite a distance...I can't shake that incident and the fact that I had sex with a 12 year old girl. I secretly fear that if I was to indulge fully in the act of sex, the whole ugly incident might resurface and set me back in my progress, and perhaps that dark period in my life.

So that right there Murad is the reason I couldn't enter into a physical relationship with Tania. My mind has not yet healed and my soul is still unhealthy. I don't know if or when I can mesh the two, but I had come to the decision that Tania should not have to pay any longer for my issues. God knows that I desperately wanted to get right and remain in a relationship with Tania. She's more than any man could ever want...and the fact that she agreed to give us a chance under the circumstances was more than I could ever hope for. I have never met a more giving and understanding person. Well...I don't have to tell you. But as I told you a couple of months ago...it was nothing but God in his infinite wisdom that brought you two together as business partners at the same time she and I started our relationship. I know now that he used that as a barrier to keep things in order and on the right track. I mean we were tested...God knows we were, but the right union prevailed...and she's where she's supposed to be. Hold on to her Murad...no matter what storms continue to come thru...you hold on to her...for she's a piece of heaven that comforts your soul, and few men get that in their lifetimes. God has hand picked you for his angel and rightfully so. You protect her like know one else can and you honor her for all that she is, and for that…I commend you.

Murad

Ouch…damn…fuck. Here I thought I had a rough situation to contend with, but his shit's got me beat by more than a mile. My heart truly goes out to him. I mean…I guess I can see now why he was gun-shy on getting into sex again. That shit right there would've fucked me up big time for sure, so yeah…I can understand. Damn…I sure didn't know.

"Yo Jayson…look," I started, "I apologize, I had no idea you was going thru like that. No idea what so ever."

"Well no one knew," he replied, "I told no one but God, that is until now. Tania doesn't even know. I kept telling her that my religious studying had priority over intimacy, and she made every effort to respect that. We slipped up one time and almost…"

"I know," I hurried to cut him off, "She told me. I was acting like a jerk that day and she was really put out with me and she was seeking comfort from her hurt."

"Murad, we never even…" he started again.

"I know JT," I stopped him again, "I know…she was straight with me on everything." Although Nube explained that one time to me, I sure as hell didn't need to hear it relayed to me again by him. Thinking of her and another man past, present or future just does not agree with me.

"Yeah, I should have known she'd be upfront with you," he replied, "Tania's one of the few who can give you that heart to heart truth, yet keep your feelings intact."

"Yeah," I absentmindedly replied shaking my head, "Nube is one of a kind." I was busy running thought in my second mind about how I myself, was gonna present this new found information here. JT must have been running in his second mind as well cause he came back with, "So…how do you think she'll handle this part of the saga?"

"I don' know JT…I can't say," I responded, "She can usually stand her ground, but lately, I don't know. She's been so edgy between the car jacking and then this pregnancy thing. In the meantime, she's trying to continue to uphold all her appearances. Hopefully she'll take it in and adjust, cause there's no way I'm gonna keep it from her."

"Well in the meantime," he jumped in with, "I think it may be a good idea to call Dy and get a professional opinion on this Jazmine thing. For all we know...Jazmine could have made the whole story up." What he said made perfect sense, our oldest sister Dylina is an OB-GYN and she would be able to shed whatever light on the situation. But somehow in my gut I knew...Jazmine did exactly what she said she did and my whole life could be changed forever.

"Yeah," I responded in another zone, as I pulled out my cell to dial my sister, "I could use some light...cause this is some dark shit right here."

Chapter 54

The Fan Done Broke

Dream

Ahh...yeah. This is whas up right here. Thanksgiving Day and our family dinner. Maaan listen...we be having some serious food going on every year. I mean with JT being a chef... and not to sleep on Bryce and his son, cause them 2 can give JT a run for his money. And like...my mom, my auntie and my sister Dy, they all can smoke some pots as well. I'd say we got that shit covered all the way around. I mean everybody else brings food as well, but I would say that group right there is the elite team when it comes to our affairs. But yeah...it's awesome each year. Our family is so big; we just rent out the Maplewood Women's Club and meet up there. You know with all of us together, shit be crazy...but fun. I'm really looking forward to it.

"So you hungry Sporty?" I asked my little man as we pulled into the parking lot. I make it my business to include him in all my family functions. His mama don't really have too much of a problem with it...I guess it's a chance for her to get one of her so called single mama breaks.

"I not hungry daddy," he answered back in his little 4 year old voice.

"What," I teased him, "You not hungry? Not even for some Honeycombs? Auntie Dy said she making you some Honeycombs?" That's his favorite thing to eat right now.

"No," he replied.

"No what Dez?" I asked.

"Don't want no Honeycombs. Mommy said I gotta eat Turkey. I don't want Turkey daddy."

"Well what you want?" I asked him as I climbed out the car and unstrapped him from his booster seat, "You want some chicken?"

"No" he stated.

"Well then," I said, "Some mashed potatoes?"

"No," he gave me again.

"Well let me see then," I told him as I took his hand and walked to the front door of the club, "What about some ice cream and cake?"

"Yay!!" he screamed out, "Ice cream and cake."

"Okay...slow ya roll Sporty," I told him, "You gonna have to do some chicken, mashed potatoes or something before we get you into the cake and ice cream. Deal?" He looked up at me with a pouting look on his face as we stepped inside.

"Hey what I tell you bout that sissy look. Fix ya face," I told him. I ain't going for none of that baby shit. "So deal or what?" I pushed back on him.

"Kay," he reluctantly replied.

"Aight...my man. Give me some," I told him, holding out my fist as he matched it with his little fist. No sooner had we stepped inside my mom ambushed me, grabbing little Dez up hugging and squeezing him.

"How Gramby little pudding doing? Huh...huh," she said kissing him all over his face as little Dez squealed and giggled with joy. In the interim she leaned over and said to me, "Think maybe you can call and give your brother the heads up before he gets here?"

"Heads up on what Ma? What's going on?" I asked her unzipping my jacket. She turned and nodded, and let I my gaze follow hers, "Oh daayuum," I spilled out.

"Yeah...exactly," she said walking away taking my laughing child with her.

Murad

Once I'd left JT's on Friday, I went home to fill Nube in on the latest. I explained to her that I had talked with my sister Dy and she told me that although not probable that method of conception would work, it was not totally impossible. So yes...there was a chance I could be the father. Initially she turned pale and got sick to her stomach. You know Nube got such a sensitive stomach which is easily upset on an emotional level. I guess that's why she tries not to operate day to day on emotions. But this here is enough to turn anybody's stomach. I couldn't do nothing but hold her and promise her that nothing would ever change between us. I made extra sweet love to her that night and then we fell asleep connected to one another just the way I like. I never go completely soft when I'm inside her like that. When we shift in the middle of the night, I instantly get hard again, and instinctively start stroking till we both fall back asleep. I took a glance over at her now as we riding over here to this dinner. She is absolutely beautiful…and so serene. We've decided that we were going to enjoy ourselves tonight and leave the negative situation in its place for the time being. It's Thanksgiving and I know I'm damn thankful today that I didn't hear a peep out of that trick Jazmine. I'd left all my phones home, and just walked with my Blackberry just in case some business that can't wait comes thru. As I pulled my car up into the parking lot, I was careful to park with enough surrounding space. I'd decided to get rid of the Escalade being that it was the catalyst for the upset that night. I've got an order in for a new one, but in the meantime, I'm pushing the 55 till the truck is ready. I got out the car and walked around to the other side to open the door for Nube. I helped her out of the car and turned back to pop the lock and set the alarm.

"You ready Pretty?" I asked her as I put her hand in mine and proceeded to the front door. She looked at me with them eyes and just nodded. "I love you Butter," I told her as I held the door open for her.

She stepped in and turned back to me and said, "I know Murad…I know."

Dream

Fuck…I tried reaching Murad on both of his phones, and I got no answer. Shit ain't been going right for him lately and this here ain't about to add up to nothing good. I sure hope that…too late, Nube just walked in the front door with Murad right behind her. And as always they were stunning in their appearance. Fur trimmed leathers and suedes, setting off the crisp look of fall just right. As they stopped to hang their coats up in the coat room, my sister walked up to them to greet them. She gave Nube a hug and in turn hugged Murad. She must have whispered something in his ear, because I saw his face grow tense. I saw her squeeze his hand in a comforting gesture then release it and walk away. He put his arm around Nube and gave her a reassuring hug, as he bent down to whisper in her ear. I saw her raise her eyes to his in surprise, then divert her eyes across the room to see Jazmine sitting so smug and comfortable at a table with my cousin…Sumira.

I walked over to offer my greetings, and arrived just as Murad said, "Look babe…we don't have to stay. We can make a plate and bounce."

"No Rod," she answered him, "She don't deserve to have that much power over us. We can handle it…we in this together…right?"

"Aight," he told her, "We'll give this a try."

"Hey Dream…what up son?" he said as I walked up hitting me off with a shoulder dap.

"Nothing good bruh…nothing good," I answered, letting him know that I was in allegiance with his problem.

"Hey Nube," I said grabbing her up for a hug.

"So no good huh Baby Boy?" she arbitrarily stated.

"Yeah sis…looks that way…looks that way," I responded.

"So where's little man?" she asked me pulling back.

"Oh, he somewhere around here. My mom scooped him up as soon as we walked in the door."

"Well…I'm gonna go and mingle…I haven't seen everybody for a good minute. Oh…yeah…I see Lonnie and Kiyma, I'ma go see whas up with them," she said over her shoulder as she left headed in their direction. Murad and I just stood silent as we watched her walk over, and approach Lonnie, who in turn scooped her up and twirled her around before setting her back down on her feet.

It was not until she reared back her head with laughter, that Murad finally spoke, "You know…Nube is really trying her best to keep it all together with this nonsense…I gotta give it to her. But what the fuck is this bitch trynna pull now?"

"Rod, I don't know," I answered him, "She was already here when I got here. Soon as I walked in the door, Ma told me to call you and give you the heads up…but I couldn't get you on either phone, and then you all just walked in the door."

"That's aight man…it's cool," he responded, "I purposely left my phones at home in order to avoid any trumped up calls from her ass. Now I know why she wasn't blowing my phone up all day. She knew from jump she'd be here today." As that thought settled in his mind, he couldn't help but think out loud, "Who the hell invited her…I mean who she up in here with anyway?"

"I don't know man." I responded to his question, "She's been sitting over there with Sumira ever since I got here."

"Hmmmm," he said drawling out a pondering thought, touching it off with a head nod. "Well, I'm gonna mingle for all that its worth and just steer clear of her and the bullshit."

"I feel you Chief…I feel you," I said as he walked away. As he went over to blind fold my little sister Brianna from behind, I couldn't help but lift my head to the sky and gave off the simple plea of "Please."

Nubina

"Hey Lonnie Youngblood," I gave off laughing as he spun me around and set me back down.

"Hey Princess, what's going on?" he responded.

"A whole lot Lonnie Blood… a whole lot," I replied. That was my special pet name for him from back in the day when he used to wear his hair braided. The braids on him reminded me so of a Native American. "Hey Kiyma," I offered leaning over and giving her a hug.

"How you doing girl?" she asked in an apologetic tone.

"I'm good…I'm good," I answered, "Doing my best to keep the negative in check. It's mighty powerful tonight, but I believe I can get thru it. Where's AJ? I haven't seen him in a minute…he's like what now?"

"He's 8 now," she answered.

"Wow…8…boy how time does fly. You blink and these kids grow up while your eyes are closed. I still remember me and Sumira giving you your baby shower."

"Me too," she said, "I still have my corsage up in the closet. AJ's over in the back with the other kids. They all playing that Wii game. So what you got new coming up next Tania? You such a big time star now…never home enough to hang with the girls no more."

"Oh I know," I whined, "I mean we do get a few stretch of days in between, but we just get so caught up with our private time with one another, or our laundry and market chores, we kinda just get lost with catching up with you all. That's why we were so excited about coming out tonight. Figured we could catch up with everybody and have a good time." The tone in my voice changed with the last 2 sentences, and they both noticed it.

"Princess," Lonnie said, "Don't you sweat nothing tonight…aight? I promise you I won't let nothing funky go down tonight. You my little sister…you used to always look out for me…so I'ma look out for you. Got it?" He cuffed me on the chin with the last of his remark, and it brought tears to my eyes.

I'm sure they both noticed as Kiyma grabbed me by the arm and said, "Come on girl. Let me take you in the back where all the kids are and just give your ass a review. You probably gonna have to pull out your wallet of pictures to tell whose who." We both peeled off some laughter as we headed toward the back.

Dream

We all socialized and munched for the next hour without incident. Murad and Nube stayed clear of the table area and everyone else kept a cool prospective, although the tension was evident. Some of the family had no issue with Murad and Nube being together, while others were not too cool with it. But for the most part, everyone was handling it…or so I thought. It is tradition that we all sit down together for the actual meal, and JT called us all together to do just that. He headed things off with a few words on how blessed we were as a family, and then he led us in united prayer. Once that was over, we made our way to the buffet table of foods to fix our plates. Murad and Nube had gotten their plates and went to sit at the table with my mother. The tables were set up in one huge horseshoe format, and the table to which my mother sat at was just to the left of Jazmine's table. As you would have it my Aunt Klessie had gone over to the table with Sumira and Jazmine with a disapproving look. She glared over at Murad and Nube who were busy into themselves and very unaware of my Auntie's displeasure. If they had known, maybe they would not have openly displayed their tight connection. Nube and Murad always taste tested and shared their food, and was in the process of doing that now. As Murad slid a forkful of food into Nube's mouth, my aunt let go a humph. And when Nube, buttered Murad's dinner roll, then handed it to him, she sucked her teeth and walked over.

"Murad," she announced, as she set herself in front of him, "Don't you think that you should be sharing your holiday with the mother of your child?"

"With all due respect Aunt Klessie," he replied, "I'm not trying to entertain that pending issue tonight."

"Pending issue...boy where are your morals?" she started, her voice elevating to the point that it caused stares and the volume in the room to dim. "You know there is no wrong child before God, and you are being ungodly to sit here in total disrespect of that woman."

"Okay...Auntie," Murad started, a twinge of annoyance in his voice, "It's been a quiet respectful night so far...can we keep it that way? I'm really not trying to evaluate any unsolicited opinions right about now."

"Humph," she blew out and stomped away. She made her way back over to the table and had a seat with Jazmine and Sumira, all the while glaring. I guess her failed attempt to move Murad emotionally got under her skin and wouldn't let her contain her displeasure.

"I tell you, it just don't make no sense," she bust out, stopping the whole room, "It's just plain blasphemy I tell you...just blasphemy. She start off with one brother, now she fornicating with another. It's just plain ungodly...ungodly."

"Come on now, Klessie," my mom said, "just let it go now. Thanksgiving is not the day for you to air your point of view."

"Thanksgiving is exactly the time," she answered back, "He should be respecting this woman that's bearing his child, rather than vampin' with that strumpet. The nerve I tell you, the nerve. She's a harlot before God"

"Yo Aunt Klessie," Murad started, rising from his seat, "You out of line to be calling Nube names."

"I call them like I see them. Only the likes of a common whore would share herself with 2 brothers," she answered him back. "But what would you care about running over JT...what do you know about loyalty...you always been the selfish one, walking round your whole life acking like you somebody special. Running thru women, thinking only of your self. Always did think you better than somebody else. Never caring who you hurting. Exactly...just exactly like your..."

"Uncle Quinn," Murad finished for her, "Yean...yeah...you've always thrown that nonsense in my face. All these years holding something against me, because I happen to look just like him. I personally have no bearing on the relationship that you had with him, and I'm tired of you imposing the hurt he delivered to you...on me. I am not to blame for what went wrong in your marriage. Perhaps if you weren't such a stiff ass prude, my uncle would have stayed around to be here for his family."

"Murad," my mother said in alarm, rising from her seat.

"Naw Ma...it's true," he said, "If she hadn't been so damn tight and always up under his collar, maybe he would have kept it home instead of taking it elsewhere."

"Murad," she angrily stated, backing it up with a slap to his face. At the same precise moment the two sets of sons from both women stood up, silently drawing territorial lines. "You know I done raised you better than to mouth off and disrespect your aunt like that," she told him in a tight voice. "Now I think...no...I know...you owe your aunt an apology."

Murad looked down at my mother, then over to my aunt, flexed his jaw and said, "Aunt Klessie, I'm sorry. I didn't mean no disrespect."

Then from nowhere...yet somewhere out of the blue Brick said, "Yo Rod, since when you going to the wall for some bitch over my mother?" For a hot second the room froze. What was wrong with Brick...what had gotten into him? Who knows...don't matter, cause in the very next second Murad had thrown the whole table over as he made a break across the room and got off a flying jump kick that came crashing down in the middle of Brick's chest spilling them both to the floor. Now I don't have to tell you, although Murad has trained professionally to be lethal and on point in his game of defense, Brick is just as expertly trained thru the school of hard knocks...aka the penitentiary. This here was gonna be some kinda of battle, and every one of us knew that and was thrown into action.

"Damn... this can't happen. Yo...break that shit up," Kye yelled out as Bryce, Lonnie Sharief and all the rest of us converged on the bundle of fury.

Nubina

I'm frozen here in my seat with my mouth open. I can't believe the attack Ms. Klessie just laid on me. I've been coming in and out of her house for years, hanging out and staying the night under her roof just like her own daughter. Did my choice really make her turn on me like that? I was in some kind of zone as I turned my head to face the table seating her, Sumira and Jazmine. Her face had the nerve to be contorted into fear and surprise as they were trying to contain the battle. Sumira just looked at me and glared, then turned her head. Surprisingly enough, Jazmine seemed utterly shocked and at a loss for words. Something in me had to know something...I had to satisfy something burning in my head. So in the midst of all the action, I got up to make my way over to the table. Murad's mom lightly touched my arm and asked, "Tania...honey...where you going baby?"

"Ms. Reeva," I started, "I've got to know...I just gotta know," I told her as I made my way over to Sumira's table as the clash of the Titans continued.

"Ms. Klessie, Sumira," I started, "All the years we've had together behind us and it comes down to this?"

"You know I ain't never liked no fast ass women," Ms. Klessie answered while Sumira continued to twist her face to the side ignoring me, "It' a sin before God that you would be with that man. You knew about Murad and his ways from way back when. Then you go and disrespect JT? That good God loving...God fearing Christian man. You have no right to bring such un-righteousness to this family."

"Klessie," I heard as Murad's mother came up behind me, "Right or wrong their choice is their choice, and only God can judge them on that."

Wow...I thought with her words, so Ms.Reeva doesn't approve of our choice either...or am I being extra sensitive?

"Her head done gone and got big with all that Hollywood attention, and she coming round here bringing scandal," Ms. Klessie shot back.

"So for me to love Murad is unrighteous and un-godly?" I asked.

"You slighted JT, a God fearing man, for the likes of Murad," Ms. Klessie answered.

Wow... I'm thinking again, what kind of sick twisted stories has she been listening to. Hadn't Sumira told her that JT was the one to break up...? I stopped in my thought and just looked at Sumira. I looked at her so hard and intent, that she had no choice but to turn and face me.

"And what Tania," she burst out, "Yeah...you wanna know...then yeah...it was me. I contacted Jazmine and invited her here. In fact...I picked her up."

"For what Sumira?" I asked her unable to believe my ears.

"Cause she's the mother of Murad's child," she answered hotly, "He need to be with his real family on Thanksgiving."

"And I'm your sister Sumira...your sister...your son's godmother. I used to be your real family," I argued feebly, "You saying all them years we invested together don't mean nothing to you?"

"You should have thought about that before you took up with Murad." she gave back.

"And me being with Murad is causing you what kind of distress Sumira? Explain to me exactly how that affects you. Because I love that man, you would choose to hurt me like this?" I asked her completely zoned out.

"Well if you hurting, then you brought it on yourself," she responded, "Murad ain't never been much, but he about to be this child's father, and you need to fall back and accept it." I stood there looking at her like she had 3 heads, as I faintly heard Ms.Reeva calling out to me.

"Tania...Tania..."

Jazmine

OMG!!! They are throwin down!!! Damn...I can't believe this is all because of me...or hmmm...I'm thinking...I guess in a way this is all over me. So with the fight going on and half listening to Sumira put Ms.Goody 2 shoes in her place, the sudden urge to gloat came over me, so I sat my ass right there...and I did.

Dream

Brick and Murad were locked in a dead heat of tussling. Not too many blows were being landed though, as Lonnie, Kye, Jarrod, Jarrell, Reef, all us were deep into intervening.

"Come on Yo," Reef spoke, "Ya'll got to quit...this shit ain't right."

"Yo Brick," Kye put in, "Let him go."

"Murad," Lonnie and I spoke, "Ya'll like brothers...come on now...yeah Rod...shit too tight between ya'll to be warrin' like this."

"Come on, ya'll upsetting ma and them," Jarrod said, "Besides its Thanksgiving, ya'll don't need to be doing this shit today." Neither one of them was hearing it, and it took a whole bunch of grips, grasps and pulls before we could separate them.

"Yo B, what's wrong with you?" Kye said.

"What you mean whas wrong with me; you ain't hear that nigga popping off slick to Ma?"

"Come on now Brick," Lonnie threw in, "That's Ma...you know how she can be...you lived with her all ya life."

"That don't give him the right to say whatever the fuck he want to her," Brick answered.

"No it don't," Bryce interjected, "And yeah Rod...you was wrong. That's your Auntie, my damn momma...and your elder. But by the same token B...you ain't had no business calling Nube no bitch. That was foul...she family too...regardless to who she dealing with, she family. She was family before she got up with anybody in this crew."

"Well I dunno," Sharief threw in, "Maybe Ma got a point after all, one girl...two brothers...it ain't right...look at all this coming from that there."

"That may be so," Lonnie said, "But Ma ain't had to put him on blast right here, right now, with her opinion about it."

"You know what," Rod finally spoke, "Being with Nube is my choice and my problem, nothing nobody in here got to contend with...not ever, so...you ain't got to worry about us fornicators tarnishing the Tillman name nor atmosphere, cause we out."

"Aww come on now Rod, don't be talking like you writing us off and shit," Kye said.

"Naw," Murad came back with, "People got a fucking problem with my decision, I'ma take my decision and we'll leave you all to yourselves."

He shook himself off, pulling away from the final holds of Jarrell and Lonnie and stormed across the room. Nube began to walk toward him but he kinda just marched straight past her toward the coat room.

"Murad," my mother called out trying to catch his attention. He wasn't hearing it. My little sisters ran up to him crying and pulling on him, begging him not to go. Murad treasured my little sisters and always showed them special attention and they in turn absolutely looked up to and adored him. But right now...he wasn't even moved by their tears and their pleas. He gently pulled their fingers off and kept walking.

As he crossed the threshold of the doorway and into the foyer he bellowed, "Nube!!!"

Nubina

Ahh...this night here is just a damn nightmare...I can't believe this here, I'm thinking as I began to follow Murad. I stopped mid-way to comfort Brianna and Tamira.

"Oh...hey come on ya'll," I told them, "Stop crying, it's gonna be alright."

"But he said we was gonna come home with ya'll tonight," Tamira said.

"Listen...tonight is not gonna be a good time. Don't worry sweeties, I promise, you guys can come and hang out with us on Christmas break. Okay?" They sullenly agreed, and I just hugged them both up. I released myself to go get my coat and check for Murad. When I got to the door, he had gone outside already, and instead Dy was there holding my coat.

As I took my coat from her and put it on, she looked at me and grabbed me up in a hug whispering in my ear, "So what you gonna do Tania...what you gonna do?"

I reared back to study her face...her eyes and answered, "I don't know Dy...I don't know.

Dream

Everyone just stood around kind of dazed after Murad and Nube's forced exit. My mother had gone to comfort my little sisters. They only 12 and 14 and don't really get too much exposure to drama like this, especially not involving their hero Murad. The rest of us guys started to slowly pick up the tables, chairs and food that had been strewn about during the rumble. I glanced over at Sumira and Jazmine and noted their smug looks of vindication.

I threw a glance over to Lonnie who had also peeped their actions and said, "If there's anybody up in here being bithcy, it would have to be them 2 right there. I don't know what's gotten into my sister. Her and Nube was tighter than gold and she go and play her like that for Jazmine."

"Man I don't know," I answered him, "Some kinda woman something going on I suppose."

"Perhaps a little prayer would be good right about now," JT announced, "We seem to have lost sight of the reason we're here today."

"We ain't lost our good reasoning," my Aunt Klessie began again, "That Jezebel of a heifer is the one came up in here causing all kinds of disorder."

"Aunt Klessie..." JT started.

"Naw boy...don't you go taking up for that floozy. If she can just up and be with your brother, then she never did deserve a God fearing man like you."

"Ma," Bryce intervened, "It ain't right for you to keep calling her names...let it go Ma."

"It is what it is Bryce," she screeched back, "God don't like ugly, and her fornicating with two brothers is ugly...so, so ugly."

"Let it go Ma," Kye kicked in.

"I'll let it go when she get her self up out of this family, so that we can have righteousness restored."

"Ma," Bryce once again stated.

"Ya'll not gonna tell me...," she continued to screech, "Ya'll not gonna make me...."

I stopped listening to all the comments as I stood and watched JT, he knows the truth; why is he just standing there allowing all this to go on. Now I see why Rod despises him...his soft ass. Oh enough already... "Would you all just shut the fuck up about some damn righteousness and fornicating. JT and Nube never slept together...they never had sex. So all you naysayers can just kill all that calling her names and judging them."

The room got deathly quiet, and the facial expressions froze, as all eyes became riveted on me. "Yeah...you heard what I said," I responded to the looks, "JT?" I threw out questiongly, expecting some back up.

He stood there for a few seconds then reacted, "It's true. The relationship was never consummated in that manner. I didn't want to deviate from my progress in my religious studies, and Tania respected my decision."

"Oooo...Ahh...Oh...What," came all the gasps and remarks.

"Now Jayson," my Aunt Klessie started, "What you saying now son? You don't have to go trynna smooth things over for the likes of her."

"No Auntie, it's true," he responded, "Tania is one gem of a woman with internal beauty that is only matched in it's entirety with her outer beauty. She has a creative, passionate soul, and Murad is the man for her. I gave them my blessings."

"Oh Jayson...Jayson, what kind of way is that...what kind of way?" she asked in a frenzy.

"It is the way God intended Auntie...exactly the way he intended."

Chapter 55
Love Don't Love Nobody

Murad

I can't believe this nonsense here. In fact…extra fucking nonsense by the hands of Sumira. I don't know what the fuck she got against me, but I'm sick'a her ass too. I guess she got the same damn problem with me as her momma. I wonder what is keeping Nube, I'm so heated, and I just wanna go home. I see her coming out the door of the Women's Club so I started the car. She got in and took a seat, securing her seat belt and just looked over at me.

"Babe, I'm so sorry," I told her, "I didn't know shit was gonna jump off like that. In fact I would have never expected that shit outta Brick."

"Well Rod," she responded, "You know Brick always felt some kinda way about me…thinking I'm stuck up."

"Yo listen," I told her, "He can think whatever the fuck he want…but what he ain't gonna do is sit there and blatantly disrespect you like that. No matter who or what broad he was ever dealing with…I have never called her out her name. He had no fucking right to do that at all."

"Oh Rod it don't even matter," she replied.

"The hell it don't," I responded still heated.

"They your family Murad…they gonna always be your family," she went on.

"Well…I really don't need no family like that Nube. Fuck em' all," I told her.

"Rod they gonna be there till…" she started.

"Fuck em' all Nube," I cut her off with, "Fuck em' all."

Nubina

Three days in and Murad was still hell bent on cutting us loose from his family. He says that has never felt such a betrayal in his life. I can say that I'm right on time with him on that one. I have been tight with Sumira since our college days. I spent so many days and nights up in her house and running with her family, it was just like my second home. But now...the specs have all changed, based on a decision Murad and I made on an emotional level. Our connection and sense of togetherness was just so strong, that we thought we could handle any fallout behind our decision. I'm not so sure right about now. In fact I've never been so conflicted ever in my life. Did we make a wise choice...or did we make a lustful mistake? It seems as though negative incident, after negative incident keeps revolving within our day to day existence. Our phone was ringing off the hook for the first 2 days. He answered only for his Mom and Dream and no one else. I was surprised when he ignored calls from Lonnie and Bryce. With all that he's been going thru lately with this baby thing, I think the sense of betrayal hurt him deeply and he doesn't want to have to acknowledge the option that they may be inclined to choose sides. I can certainly relate. The sense of betrayal by Sumira and her mom is so strong that I find myself analyzing if their opinions bear any truth. Right now...I'm on the fence.

Murad

We've gotten thru the holiday weekend and Monday morning has got me going into the city for some business. In fact, I've got to come back over again tomorrow as well as Thursday. Nube is still in a funk behind last Thursday, and had me cancel 2 of her engagements. She must really be bothered because she rarely takes that route. I moved everything over to the second week in December in order to allow her sufficient time to pull it together. In the meantime I've been trying to put in as much quality time with her that I can. I took her on a one day, all night escape to Cape May so that she could lie in bed and listen to the winter waves kiss the shore. She likes the essence and sounds of nature, and I figured it would help in soothing her. When we got back in on Sunday night, of course there was a message from Jazz. I just fucking deleted it. Didn't care what she had to say...if anything happened with her, the baby, nothing. At this point it's like...whatever.

Nubina

I'm sitting here rooted in my chair, completely in a zone. I've just been given confirmation to the fear that's been trying to suppress itself within me for a minute.

"So would you like me to schedule you?" I heard her ask.

"Yes," I answered.

"Well how soon would you like to come in?" she asked.

"As soon as possible," I responded.

"Well how about this Thursday at 11:00 am?" she asked me.

"That's fine," I answered in a hollow voice. I'm thinking that will give me time to speak with Murad on this.

"Well okay," she began, "Here's some material for you to read as well as instructions you're going to have to..."

I stared blankly at the space over her head as her words perfectly blended into the abstract painting on the wall. The various shades of gray's and blues seemed to reflect my very soul, and I wondered how long these colors would remain in control.

Murad

Nube has taken this down time to work on some new poetry for an engagement coming up after the New Year. We chilled Tuesday night into Wednesday. I did have to handle some business in the morning, but I took care of that at home in the den. Nube spent the morning in the kitchen working on some new recipe, and I worked diligently to finish up so that I could get some time going with her. Just as I was finishing up, she came into the den with a plate full of something. I don't know what it was, but it was smelling good.

"Hey Bae, you still busy," she said.

"Naw, I'm just finishing up. What you got there Butter?"

"Okay...see, this here is a new recipe I kind of mixed together," she answered, "It's like a West Indian chicken, veggie patty. And yeah...I added a little Feta cheese in there." She sat the platter down on my desk and came around the front of the chair and climbed up in my lap. "Aight Mister, you know what you gotta do," she said as she broke one in half and started blowing to cool the temperature. She offered it to me and I took a bite being careful not to burn my tongue. “How’s that Rod,” she asked watching me like a hawk as I began to chew.

“Uhmm..,” I uttered nodding my head.

“Yeah Rod…yeah,” she squealed, “You likes…you likes?” she asked.

“Banging Nube,” I finally spoke.

“Let me see,” she said taking a bite.

“Yeah…yeah?” I asked her smiling.

“Uhmm,” she answered in between chews, “I may be on to something here.” As she offered me a second bite, she looked at me and asked, “Murad…you know…we kinda never really talked about how you truly feel about possibly becoming a father right now. I mean…how do you really feel about the whole father situation?” I know this whole thing has been bothering her for a minute, so I figured that now was as good a time as any to set the record straight.

“Nube, listen,” I started, “I am at a point in my life where my priority is to work on building for myself. I’m trynna get my finances in order and secure the foundation for my future. I’m mean if this child proves to be mine, I’ll support it… no doubt, but I ain’t got time for changing no diapers, pushing no strollers , warming bottles and what not. I don’t mean to sound so disconnected, but having a baby is just not on the agenda for me.”

She just sat there for a minute, then said, “Well Rod?”

“What Nube?”

“Nothing Rod…nothing,” she replied.

“No…ain’t no nothing Nube,” I told her, “I know when something ain’t sitting right with you.”

“Well it’s just that sometimes the positive energy and the physics of life are presented to you at a time when you’re not able to foresee the logic and reason behind it.”

“You know Nube, I’m quite sure you are correct in your theory,” I answered, “But that right there is something I ain’t trynna do. A child coming to me at this present moment and time would be a huge setback to where I wanna be. I got a lot of plans in place that I still need to implement, and no matter how positive or beautiful the energy is…it would be a distraction.”

She seemed to be in a zone, so I leaned over and kissed her licking the crumbs from the patty off her lips, and told her, "Don't worry Nube, just like you once told me, things will all work out in our favor. Right?"

I gave the head twist to the side letting her know that I expected an answer. She looked me at me with them brown eyes so intently, I felt as if she was looking right thru me as she said, "I hope so Rod...I hope so."

Nubina

I can't believe that things have come down to this. Murad is in the city on business today, so today is as good a day as any. I'm sitting in the front seat of Dylina's car as we make our way to the offices of one of her colleagues out in Somerset. I had gone to the Millburn office for my initial visit, but we agreed that in order to afford me my privacy and anonymity, Somerset would be the better choice. Yeah...I guess Dy is as good at what she does for a reason, cause she spotted the changes about me, that I was not yet ready to admit were real. I explained to her my torment about it all, and she agreed to help me no matter which route I chose. Well I've made a decision, and true to her word, she's sticking by me on it. She told me that although Murad is her brother, she doesn't want to see me caught somewhere that I don't wanna be. I don't know...my mind seems to be made up but I'm still going back and forth in my heart. This could be such a beautiful thing if there was not so much ugliness surrounding it. Twice already, I started to pull out my cell and call Rod, but then I thought no...he's working and I don't wanna spring something so heavy on him right now. He has been going thru it for quite a while now, so I'll just handle this myself. Perhaps I should have been a little more responsible I thought as we pulled up into a parking space. I mean...just what did I expect would happen. Dylina turned to look at me as she turned the car off and asked,

"Tania...are you ready...are you sure?" I faced her and thought, it must be nice...a medical career, a husband, good family life with 2 kids.

"Yeah Dy," I answered, "Maybe the wisdom of time has me rescheduled in another time slot...you know when things are just not so chaotic."

"Now Tania," she started, "It's not too late, you can still change your mind."

"I know Dy, I know," I replied, "I just really think time is not on my side right now. Hopefully there will be a better time."

As we exited the car and headed to the front door, she threw her arm around me and said, "No such thing as a better time or a right time...Tania...just time."

Well...it actually took no time at all once I got inside. I was ushered to the dressing room where I undressed and left my belongings. I was then led into a surgical exam room where the staff was awaiting me. As I climbed up on the table, her colleague Dr. Patterson gave me a reassuring pat on the arm.

"Don't worry Ms. Baynes," she said, "I'm gonna take extra special care of you. Dylina has informed me on how precious you are to everyone. I promise that they'll get you back healthy and whole." I gave her a weak smile and just nodded.

"Are you ready?" she asked. Again I just nodded. The nurse came around and proceeded to run an IV line for the anesthesia. Once she was done Dr. Patterson stepped in again.

"Okay then, just lie back," she instructed, "The anesthesiologist will administer the dosage," as he moved in and injected a needle into the line, "and you can start counting back from 100, right about now and everything will...."

What did she say I'm thinking as my mind began to feel a dark warm fuzz at 99. At 98 I could have sworn that I heard my cell phone ringing... Murad ...I thought at 97, and then...all thought evaporated into total darkness.

Chapter 56

When The Bottom Drops Out

Murad

Wow...Nube ain't answering the phone. Let me see...its 2:30, I wonder where she at. Maybe she in the bathroom or something. I'll check back in a minute I'm thinking as I head cross town. I've concluded one meeting, but it touched off yet another. So now I gotta make this move cross town and kick some scenarios around with these other clowns. I'll check back once I finish up. She could be just resting...I mean she's been so moody lately...so at odds with this baby mess. Can't really blame her. Jazmine has spun a doozy here that could nail me to the wall for the rest of my life. Aaron has all the necessary paper work ready for court as well as a pending date for the DNA testing. I mean that shit is going down as soon as she drops her bundle. According to her doctor, late December, early January she should be sprouting. Ain't that some bullshit to start 2009 with? Yeah...happy fucking New Year.

Nubina

I awoke to a buzzing feeling, and opened my eyes to blinding bright lights.

"Ms. Baynes," I heard a pleasant voice, "How do you feel?" How do I feel, I'm thinking...what is she talking about. Oh...I suddenly remember as I'm hit with a small tug of pain in my pelvis.

"Huunnhh," I breathed out heavily, "I'm okay...a little crampy."

"Well that's to be expected," Dr. Patterson explained, "Everything went well, no problems at all. Generally the earlier this procedure is done, the less chance for complications. You should stay off your feet for the next 2-3 days and then you can resume your normal activity." I guess I just looked at her kind of strange and so she added on, "Oh...and no sex for the next 6 weeks. I'll also need to see you back in my office at that time for a follow-up. I want you to stay here and rest for at least another hour before I release you." That was just fine with me, cause suddenly I was so tired, mentally...physically...spiritually.

"Thanks for everything Dr.Patterson," I mumbled as I curled up on my side.

"No problem Ms.Baynes," she answered, "Now get your rest. I'll be back to check on you after awhile. Nurse Klein is right over there if you need her." I looked over to my right and saw the nurse seated at a small work station and just weakly nodded. As the doctor left the area, I closed my eyes, tuned out the smells and sounds of my environment and quietly cried inside.

After a solid, yet fitful hour and a half of sleep, I felt my eyes pulling themselves open. As I turned over, I caught the attention of the nurse.

"Hey there," she called out, "How you feeling?"

"I guess I'm okay."

"Well let me buzz Dr.Patterson," she said, "She asked me to let her know as soon as you wake." As she got the Doc on the phone, I pulled myself up in a sitting position. I looked at the clock on the wall and noted that it was 4:10 in the afternoon. Damn...I thought feeling empty...I know Rod's been looking for me, I know I heard my phone ringing just before...

"Well you're up," I heard breaking into my thoughts. Dr. Patterson had entered the room. "I'm just gonna check your vitals and then I'll be able to release you," she said strapping me up to the blood pressure band. "However we do have a small problem," she said throwing me into alarm. As I quickly searched her face for trouble she hurriedly said, "On no...nothing like that. It's just that Dylina was paged to an emergency call and won't be able to take you home. You're going to have to find someone to pick you up...and if not, you can hang out here for another hour or so, and I'll drive you back up." Oh man, I'm thinking. Who in the world could I possibly get to come get me...and who in the world could I even trust with this situation and information.

“Well I’m going to need to make a call and then I’ll be able to let you know my needs. Thank you Dr. Patterson,” I told her, “Am I able to get down now?”

“Yes sure,” she answered, “You can get dressed, make your call and then let me know. I’ve got 2 prescriptions waiting for you at the front desk. One is to help cease any bleeding and the other is an antibiotic as a precaution to infection.”

I got down off the bed and made my way back to the dressing room. I reached in my bag for the phone and sure enough…2 missed phone calls from Murad. I suddenly got weak in the knees and had to sit down in the chair and get my bearings. What the fuck did I just do…what did I just do, I asked myself in anguish. I love him…I love him so much…did I do the right thing? My initial reason for reaching for the phone reminded me that I needed to find a ride home. I hit the menu and started scrolling absentmindedly thru my phone book, when the ultimate name popped up…JT. I hit the tab and it started ringing. Yeah…I’m thinking as the phone rang, he works in Raritan I think or somewhere not too far from here. I sure hope that he hasn’t left work yet. He would be like the best choice I’ve got.

“Hello,” I heard touching off a flood of relief from me.

“Hello JT, it’s me Tania.”

“Yeah Sweet, I can see that,” he responded laughing, “What’s going on?”

“Well I had an appointment down here in Somerset, but I don’t have a way back home. I was wondering if you could swing by and pick me up?”

“You out here?” he asked, “Where’s Murad?”

“Well he had some business in the city, so we’re doing our own things today,” I answered.

“Well…okay,” he paused, “I’m about to leave now, so…sure, I can come get you. What’s the address?” I peeled off the info to him, and told him to call me on my cell when he was out front. I hung up feeling all kinds of ways, and just proceeded to put my clothes on so I could leave this memory behind.

As soon as I was fully dressed, I made my way to the front desk in the main office. Dr.Patterson was there signing some papers and she looked up as I entered the area.

"Here are your release papers, your home instructions, as well as your prescriptions. So I take it you've secured a ride?" she asked.

"Yes, my...friend works nearby, and he's coming by to pick me up," I answered.

"Okay then Ms. Baynes," she said, "Delores, please schedule Ms.Baynes for a 6 week appointment at the Millburn office. I've got to get back to my other patients, so...the best of luck to you Ms. Baynes and I'll see you in 6 weeks."

"Thank you again Dr.Patterson, "I'll see you then."

I waited as Delores scheduled me in for my appointment, then I walked over to the waiting room chair and took a seat. While I waited on JT, I couldn't stop my mind from thinking about how I was gonna tell Murad what just went down. I was most certain now that I should not have gone thru with it, but damn...it's too late now...far too late. I took a deep breath in, then blew out. What possessed me to put my mental...my physical thru this torture? Since when did I lose the ability to find reason and logic to my situations? Oh damn...damn. I need to be up outta here; the walls are beginning to feel as though they're gonna swallow me whole. Its 4:56, and I know...I just know Murad has got to be wondering where in the hell.... The sound of my cell ringing, startled me and I almost jumped out of my seat. I viewed the caller ID and saw it was JT.

"Hello," I answered.

"I'm out front Tania," he stated.

"Alright, I'm coming out now," I told him and hung up. I got up from my seat, waved to the receptionist and walked out the door. As I walked over to the car, I tried to get my sense of being together before I climbed in.

As I opened the car door and climbed in JT viewed me strangely, and asked, "Tania this is a medical facility. Are you okay...is everything alright?"

I looked at him, with his kind, understanding face and said, "No JT...I'm not okay. And I don't think things will ever be all right again. But what's done is done."

"Why...what's going on?" he jumped in with, "What can I do? Do you need me to..." And then as if a light switch flipped in his head he gasped. I turned away from him, lowered my head and the tears began to fall. "Aww no...Sweet," he voiced softly, "Tell me you didn't?" When the only response he got was my silent tears, he put the car into gear and drove off.

JT

No wonder she's been overly upset lately. I mean this would upset any woman, but Tania can generally handle such nuances without much ado. Damn...this is not good. This would explain her being so terribly upset at the market that day, and the strange way she looked when she grabbed her mid-section. And I thought she was looking extra busty at Thanksgiving, just thought maybe it was the outfit. From what she just said, I take it that Rod doesn't know. He' gonna definitely wild out on this one...he's already on edge. I wonder if she knows that his college girlfriend dealt him this same injustice years ago. Somehow I doubt it; Tania would never have done this knowing he's so against it. I waited a while before I attempted to say anything to her. Once we were on the Turnpike, I decided to begin my inquiry.

"Tania," I started, "How long have you known?"

"Oh I don't know Jace," she responded, "I've just been so caught up in what Rod's going thru and trying to stay on top of my appearances, that I just hadn't been paying attention. That is until the Thanksgiving Dinner...Dy brought it to my attention, and once she did, all the subliminal suppressions were released. She said she'd help me with whatever she could or whatever choice. Once we talked she stood by her word and hooked me up with one of her associates. She came out here with me today, but got called away for one of her patients. "

"So I assume that Murad's absence equates to the fact that he doesn't know?" I asked.

"You assumed correctly JT; he doesn't know," she answered."

"Aww Sweet," I shook my head in empathy, "That was not a good move. There are 2 things that emphatically carry a significant impact on a real man when it comes to children. One is to let a man believe that he's the father of a child when he's not, and the other is to terminate the life of his child without his knowledge."

"I know Jace...I know," she cried out, "That is so not like me. I've just been feeling so out of sorts with this whole Jazmine thing. It seemed like once I got a handle on it and would come to terms with it, something would crop up and put me back into confusion. I was doing so good with things until the dinner. Sumira and your Aunt Klessie's words and actions played so heavy on my mind Jasyon. For the first time I have been questioning if Murad and I should have entered into this taboo relationship. I mean...the words do hold an essence of truth. One woman...2 brothers; that's a situation I would have never thought I'd be a willing participant in. And look at me now...the so called Queen Nubina, operating on the actions of a strumpet, a Jezebel, a whore and a harlot. Oh and let's not forget a bitch. And these words are coming from the people I have known as my family for years. I guess they..."

"Sweet...no," I stopped her, "There was choice and purpose in the decision made between you and Murad to be together, and I happen to know personally that the choice was sanctioned by God. So don't you feed into any of the opinions and name calling of others. You and Murad have been selected to move forward and be one of the examples in our community on showing us how to get Black Love back to where it's supposed to be. Even with such extenuating odds against you, God is counting on you for a victory. So please don't let the primitive mind of others dissuade you from your goal or your love."

She sat silently for a minute, then she turned in her seat and said, "Jayson...you believe in Murad and I like that?"

"Tania," I offered her, "Take it from the man who once loved you as his own, and a man that still loves you for the woman that you are...God has great plans for you and Murad. You need to utilize everything you've got to bring his insight to the top. You're gonna win Tania...you're gonna win."

"I hope so JT," she replied, "I hope so."

Murad

Don't ask me why, but I'm feeling an uneasy tug in the air. Nube hasn't been answering me all damn day. It's fucking 6:30 and I'm just exiting the Lincoln, bout to hit this Turnpike and make my way home. As I rolled with the flow of traffic, my mind played in rewind, capping today's events. I'd had to meet with the CBS executives on scheduling dates, and salary negotiations. Fucking Rubenstein and his boy Jabowitz tried to run game on me but somebody should've told them who it is they were dealing with. They seem to be under the impression that they could snowball me into the low end of the ladder in regard to Nube's compensation for the 6 episodes. They gonna try and throw some 50G per episode on me. First off…I ain't like the way they were looking me up and down when I entered the conference room; as if I didn't have the right to be air tight in my Versace, but that shit is neither here nor there. We sat down and began to spin the negotiations and I let them know that 50G would not do.

"Well Mr. Tillman," Rubenstein kicked off, "Nubina is not quite what we would consider a seasoned actress. She doesn't have a whole lot of screen time under her belt."

"While that may be true," I told him, "Nubina is a natural talent and her many performances and national interactions lend value to her ability to deliver, no matter what the task."

They both leaned back in their chairs as if they needed to dig in for a battle, then Jabowitz stated, "The pitch is good, but we don't normally deal out numbers higher than that on a ringer, so to speak."

I sat up good and straight as I spoke, "I'm thinking ringer…is quite a poor choice in description of my client. She's proven her capabilities in her film debut. She has sustaining power in her performance. She's well worth whatever price requested."

"Mr. Tillman," Jabowitz kicked in again, "The fact of the matter is, we can cast call this part again, and get half a dozen other African American actresses, who would take 5G per episode."

"Not to mention taking a local that would save the network the expense of relocation fees," Rubenstein added, "So my advice to you is that you not run the risk of Nubina losing out on this introduction to perhaps...what could be a lucrative career."

Okay...these pasty mutha fuckas bout on my nerve here...fucking patronizing me. I'ma try to keep my cool and keep this shit in prospective, so...here we go, "Gentlemen...let me set the record straight here. Nubina in herself is not an actress, but as I previously stated...a natural talent. What she possesses is not something she studied for, it's an internal resource. Please know and understand that she has a lucrative career in spoken word, musical contributions as well as her writing; in fact she has written the theme songs for 2 other network sitcoms. In addition to her fictional writing, her narratives have been showcased and well received within the public access genre. She is not bound by financial need to take this spot or any other acting position. She happens to be an avid fan of Mr. Harper and his work outside of the series, as he is hers; and that fact is pinnacle to her agreeance to guest spot the show. He explicitly requested working with her. The request in turn substantiates the fact that the executive producer on the show as well as the executive writer have fashioned these 6 episodes in light of Nubina. They have the confidence that those episodes will appeal to a group of urban followers that will tune in on the strength of Nubina and raise the ratings to an all new high. So gentleman, if you feel as though you can't meet any numbers I present, we can end all said negotiations, and you can begin your new casting call for a poor substitute. Keep in mind that you will have to explain to the network higher ups, why the storyline will either be changed, or postponed thus deflating revenue from network sponsors as well as explain to the producers that their episodes will not garner the national attention, they were originally hoping for. So before you make any final conclusions... my advice to you is to weigh the facts carefully. But of course...the decision is yours gentlemen...all yours."

I intertwined my fingers in pyramid mode and sat back in a comfortable slouch in my overstuffed chair. Them pasty faces started to turn red, in spite of their efforts to remain aloof. They in turn, faced one another and then Jabowitz spoke, "Would you excuse us for a moment. We just need to hold a brief side bar."

"Not a problem," I told them standing up, "I'll just step over here to the far end of the room. I have a phone call to return, and I can get better reception over by the window." As I walked the 20 feet away, I instinctively pushed the button on my Stealth earpiece.

"Damn Ivan," Rubenstien said, "He's got us on that. I don't feel like going against Greg on any production hold ups, nor do I want to explain any loss of projected ratings."

"That's fine Jules," Jabowitz spoke, "But I don't care for the likes of Mr. Slick coming up in here putting the fucking screws to us. Like I said, she's a ringer. I myself have never heard of her before this."

"Well that's partly his point Iv,"Rubenstein replied, "she's up and coming in certain circles and starting to be noticed. We don't wanna piss Harper off, and get him all discombobulated. Besides...she is one hot cup of mocha latte. I'll be tuning in myself to get a look at that. Let's just see what number he's running with and cut it by 20. He'll never know."

Jabowitz shrugged and they relaxed back in their chairs ending their pow-wow which signaled to me to wrap up my fraud of a conversation. I played it off another 45 seconds, with "Yes....no...not a problem. I'll get back to you as soon as possible. Good Day."

"So Iv...Jules," I said returning to my seat, "Are we ready to drop the math on this?"

I had to laugh to myself I'm thinking as I took the exit for I78; after about 20 minutes more of bantering back and forth, I came off with double of what they offered plus the 20 they were trynna dupe me. I felt they needed to pay that extra 20 for labeling my baby a ringer, as well as making reference to her hotness. I mean...I know she hot, but I ain't looking for it to be brought to my attention by no perverted old white shirt. So we in good...all I'ma do is take that money and stack most of it into CD accounts and invest the rest. The fact is...we don't even need it right now...we straight. Now, if only I can assure that we straight every where else. I can't help but feeling uneasy as I pressed the button on the car phone to dial home. I need Nube to answer…I need shit to be alright. Somehow…somewhere I'm feeling…Not.

Chapter 57

Always Darkest Before Dawn

JT

Just before we took the exit off of 78, Nube announced the she was still feeling unsettled and not yet ready to go home. "Besides, I need to stop and get my prescriptions filled," she told me. I stopped on Morris Ave and went in to fill the prescriptions. I felt so torn with the whole situation. I used to love this woman...well...I still do, just in another capacity. And I know this choice wasn't easy for her, yet I'm somewhat surprised that she even considered it as an option. I'm not judging her...just wanting to understand. I pulled into my parking space and we exited the car to go in the house.

"I'm just so tired...spiritually and mentally," she said to me, "I guess I need to rest a minute before I do what I gotta do. There's simply no way around it." The words weren't out of her mouth 2 seconds before her cell phone rang...he had hunted her down.

She looked over at me, her eyes asking for support. I nodded my head with encouraging approval and told her, "Sometimes love needs to be harnessed Tania. Take the reins." As I walked away into the kitchen leaving her to herself, I silently prayed that she'd retain her resolve, her courage, and that Murad...would remember just how much he loves her.

Nubina

"Hello," I answered, scrambling in my mind as to what it was I was gonna say to him at this moment.

"Butter...finally you answered," he spoke, "I've been looking for you all day. What's going on...where are you?"

"I'm at JT's," I answered. "Ahh...here we go," he said, "The last time you was at JT's the end result was some kind of mishap. So what's going on this time?"

"Well it's just that..." I attempted to explain.

"You know what," he said cutting me off, "It don't matter. We'll resolve whatever when I get there. I'm on 78 now...so...like 10 on 5 Nube. Aight? "

"Yes Murad," I responded feeling like a child, "I'll see you when you get here." I hung up the phone so much past panic, till I was subdued. In those few short minutes I had settled up in my mind, that I was wrong in my actions, but I surely could not go back and reverse what I've done. The only thing I could do now is man up and deal with the consequences. I love him so much...god knows I do. Deep within, I could feel my heart fluttering around like a moth trapped in a jelly jar. As I closed my eyes and took a deep breath, I silently prayed that love would do her part and soften the inevitable hurt. Then again I'm thinking, love tends to be fickle, whimsical, and shady. Love may not hang around at all, since love doesn't care too much for confrontations. Most probably I'll have to stand up to this one on my own merit. And if he chooses to put me down after this...I'll just have to accept it...right after I die.

Murad

Damn...what is going on now? And how did she end up at JT's yet again? What the fuck am I walking into this time? I mean I know this here ain't on no creep shit. They were tight and had a relationship and all, but I know they both not of that mindset, so that's not what's bothering me. My thing is...I been there for Nube from the door, even when she and JT were calling themselves together. She know I got her on anything, so why does she somehow wind up going to him with her issues. Does she not trust me to resolve things for her? That can't be...she knows I'd move heaven and earth to alleviate anything stressing her. As I rolled off the exit, and made a quick right turn headed toward Springfield Ave, I thought maybe I was getting a little ahead of myself. Perhaps I should cool my heels till I get there, and just see what the deal is. JT lives over here in Union in I guess what you would call the Vauxhall section, so it's only a quick 7 minutes off of 78. I whipped the car around the next 2 lights, and pulled into his apartment complex. As I stepped out the car, that strange vibe hit me again, so I took a deep breath, trynna get my self together before I go up in here and face....What??

JT responded to the bell, and shoulder dapped me at the door before stepping to the side and letting me in. I turned toward the living room area, and there was Nube sitting on the couch, looking tired...very tired. I immediately became alarmed.

"Bae...what's going on," I asked making my way to her side.

"Just a little under the weather Rod," she answered.

"Well what's going on...what's the matter? Cause I could run you over to the doctors, or..."

"Rod...it's fine," she interrupted me, "I've seen the doctor already today."

"Well what did he say?" I impatiently asked her.

At this point, JT broke in with, "Excuse me guys. I'm gonna let you all speak with one another, I'll be in my bedroom."

Okay, I'm thinking, there's obviously something going on that I'm not up on. Hmmm.... "Nube," I simply stated giving her the side head nod.

"Rod," she started, "You know how I was asking you about the timing and logic of a child."

"Yeah...and?"

"Well I was asking because Dylina brought something to my attention last week at the dinner. Somehow she noticed off the bat, some changes in me, and she spoke on it"

"Nube," I cut in, "You talking in circles Bae. What?"

"Well I hadn't been paying attention with all that's been going on, and Dy figured out that I was pregnant."

"Pregnant...Nube...pregnant," I said in disbelief.

"Yes pregnant Rod," she answered me in alarm getting up on her feet, "Oh and I know Rod...I know what you said about it not being the right time. I'm sorry...things were happening to us left and right, and I was just so wrapped up in you...in us...and it was the last thing I was expecting and...."

Her words just became wonk-wonk-wonk, as the magnitude of what she said truly hit me. Pregnant...no wonder she's been so tired, so cranky and a little moody. I mean in spite of the Jazmine thing, I knew there was something else to her behavior. Nube usually keep it a hundred at all times, so I knew something was knocking her off point. As she continued to babble, I came up out of my mind and said, "Pregnant?"

"Yes Murad..." her unfinished response came as I picked her up and swung her around.

"Oh Nube...Nube. Pregnant...pregnant. Ah yes...my Butter gonna have a baby...my baby...our baby." I hooted spinning her and spinning her till I was about dizzy myself. I put her down and smothered her mouth with mine. I was feeling so emotional right now...so unexpectedly overwhelmed. I felt her pushing back from me; I suppose to come up for air.

"Rod," she said breathing heavy, "you said that you wasn't ready for no baby now...and that you weren't into the diaper changing and all that, and that a baby would be a distraction."

Oh...is that what she worried about. "Nube," I told her, "I was talking about that supposed to be baby of Jazmine's...not you. Never you. There ain't no day under the sun that I would never want a child from you. I've had that secret daydream since you were with JT." Oh damn...I ain't mean for that to come out standing up here in the man house...but fuck it...I'm being real.

"Aww Rod," she answered me almost in a panic, "I took it that you were speaking in general...you said you were still financially building and there was no time for a child now...you still putting plans in place, so..."

"So what are you flapping on about Nube?" I asked her stopping her babble once again, "A child from you...with you...is nothing but a blessing, and I can promise you that I'll be right here by your side for every little thing you need. Best believe I'll make sure you get the utmost in care. This pregnancy will be gravy in regard to your comfort...well...that's if it's anything within my control. But it don't matter cause whatever it takes, I'll make sure it gets done."

I scooped her up again and spun her around, on cloud nine, feeling like one of my best wishes has come true. It don't get not better than this. Then she let go in my ear, "Rod...I'm not pregnant anymore."

What the fuck am I supposed to do now…I'm thinking in my head as I feel his body stiffen against mine. I let out a deep breath as the inevitable pain began to make its way toward my heart. I couldn't even see his face at this point, and already my heart was breaking. He set me down and held me out at arms length.

"Say what?" he asked, the bass in his voice echoing the question throughout the room.

"I'm not pregnant anymore," I repeated, my voice quivering like I just stepped out of a tub of cold water. He let go of me, and just stood there looking at me. Perhaps he figured if he looked hard enough it would change what he'd just heard.

"Nube…look," he started, "I ain't about to stand here and believe what the fuck I just heard. Tell me I ain't hear that…tell me you on some emotional bullshit…and I'm misconstruing your words. Tell me Nube."

"Murad," I began my plea, "Sometimes things happen…and it's not the right time, you know and sometimes…."

"Nube," he stopped me, "Tell me something I wanna hear Nube…tell me something that makes sense to me…cause I'm bout to fucking lose it. Nube..," he trailed off, his voice escalating.

"Murad," I began again, "Things are just so chaotic right now, I mean…the media got you all up in the tabloids…and I really didn't want to bring anymore attention to that…cause you know Poo…he still in a coma, and you…you still on probation and everything."

"Nube," he bellowed and I continued.

"Rod you know…I was thinking about the things your family said…and I know you didn't need that stigma revisited on you…you know how they all think you were just a dog…and now you got 2 women pregnant at the same time and…"

"Nube," he bellowed again, the pain in his voice so deep that I wanted to run and hide rather than watch it consume him as it was.

"Rod, I thought that I was doing what was best at the time, I was confused… and I…I didn't want to put not one more thing on you," I told him as my voice started to catch in my throat, "You've gone thru enough, you've been..."

"Nube...what the fuck did you do?" he yelled grabbing me by my shoulders, "What the fuck did you do?"

"Murad...baby...I didn't want..."

"Nube," he screamed shaking me by the shoulders. JT ran into the room, and I held up my 4 fingers to indicate that I got this...it's alright. He reluctantly retreated back into the bedroom.

"Nube...what the fuck...Nube." he screamed.

My head began to throb and pound as the sound of the pain in his voice scratched against the reasoning in my mind like fingernails on a chalkboard. "Nube...Nube," he yelled his voice draining and becoming saturated with the pain.

I could no longer stand it...I couldn't bear to hear his pain anymore, so I belted out, "I'm sorry...I'm sorry...I was wrong. I was wrong...and so selfish...and I'm sorry. I know that I'm supposed to be wise, I know I'm supposed to be strong....I know that I'm supposed to carry a greater sense of being within me. Queen Nubina...Queen Nubina...everybody expects me to be a cut above the rest. But I'm just a woman...a woman Rod. A regular woman like any other you'll find out here....and **I** wanted to be the first to have your baby Murad...not Jazmine....I wanted it to be me having your first child. **Me** Murad...me...I wanted it to be me..." I finished off weakly.

"Nube," he continued to voice over and over as if in a trance, and then what seemed like an eternity of his soul ripping pain via my name, he slid to the floor, grabbing me around my waist resting his face against my empty womb and broke down. I cradled his head in my hands and just stood there so twisted, so weak, and so traumatized about it all, till I could no longer hold myself up on my own two feet. I slumped down to the floor, bringing his head down to my lap. And as he laid there with his head in my lap, and my tears falling like a waterfall down upon him, I stroked his head, stroked the tears on his face...stroked my tears that fell on his face and whispered, "I just needed it to be me Rod... I needed it to be me."

Chapter 58
A Light At The End Of The Tunnel

Nubina

We remained on the floor for what seemed like hours. I really don't know how long a time span passed before he parted his lips and said, "So...you came to JT with this, and he assisted you?"

I cleared the threat of stutter from my voice before I spoke and said, "No Rod. Dy took me out to one of her colleagues in Somerset. She got called in for an emergency, and I didn't have a way home. I remembered that JT worked out that way, so I called him for a ride home."

"So you saying he didn't know?" he asked me.

"No Rod," I told him, "He was in the dark until he picked me up and questioned the fact that I was coming out of a Medical Center."

"So my sister informs you that you pregnant, and then a week later takes you out of town to kill my child?" he threw at me.

"Rod baby...it wasn't like that," I told him.

"Then what was it like Nube," he came back with sitting up on the floor facing me, "You tell me what the fuck it was like for you and my sister to make the decision to kill my child and not let me in on it."

"She was just trying to help me Murad," I responded, "Just trying to help me out since I..."

"Since you what Nube," he chopped my response with, "Since you forgot how to be a fucking woman and come to me...me your man...the one who fathered the baby? Me Nube...the same man that been with you from the door, the one who supports you on any to everything. How could you not trust me Nube? How could you fuck me up like this Nube...fuck up my world?"

"Murad, I wish," I began.

"Save it Nube...fucking save it," he stated. And with that he got up off the floor, looked down at me like a blemish and walked out the front door. With the sound of the front door closing, JT once again emerged from the bedroom.

"Tania," he called out, coming to where I was on the floor, "Are you okay?" I just sat there mute, and rooted to the floor in a zone. "Tania...Tania," I heard just before I blacked out.

I woke up hours later on JT's bed with a blanket over me, and him sitting up next to me on the other side of the bed sleeping. "Jace," I called out, "Jace?"

"Oh hey Sweet," he responded, "You up?"

"Yes," I answered in a fog, "Murad?"

"I don't know Sweet...he left," he stated.

"How long ago," I sat up in a panic, "Where...well," I began, then I remembered, he told me to save it when I tried to explain myself. "Jace," I said, "Has he called...did you call him?" I asked.

"I tried Sweet, he's not answering," he told me.

"Well did he say," I started, "Nooo...? Do you think that...Jace," I finished off in alarm.

"Sweet listen," he told me recognizing my fear, "You need to relax...you need to rest. Your body has undergone a physical trauma today and you don't need to be stressing right now."

"How can I not stress Jayson," I told him, "He's never spoken like that to me before...I've never seen him so disgusted. Well...yeah I did...I guess that day when Trey and I bumped into each other back then. But that was different...Jayson...what if he don't want me no more...Jayson...what if he..."

"Sweet no," he answered me, before I could finish, "We not gonna do this tonight. It's been a long day...a rough day. Come let's get your medicine and get you ready for bed."

"But I gotta go home Jayson," I whined, "We don't like being apart from one another more than a couple of hours. He won't sleep well tonight without me and I know I won't. And Jayson...I gotta go home, he's upset...he's been thru so much lately."

"Nube I don't think it's a good idea for you to go home tonight. Besides, we don't even know if he went home...it's just best that you stay here. You're in no physical condition to handle anything else tonight but rest. I've spoken to Dy and she's gonna stop by first thing in the morning,"

"But Jayson," I pleaded, "I've got to make it right for him... Jayson...I've got to make it right."

"You will Tania," he told me, "Just not tonight."

Although I'd just awaken, I suddenly began to feel so tired and decided that he was right. I just need to get clean and go to sleep. I went into the bathroom and took a brief shower...it was all that I had the energy for. When I came out Jayson had left a sleep shirt for me, so I slipped it on. He knocked on the bedroom door and offered me a pair of his old boxers.

"Can you bring me my bag, I need my fem products out of there," I told him. I left for a few seconds and returned with my purse."Thank you," I told him as he stepped out of the room. I quickly hooked myself up with the necessities and crawled up on the bed. After a couple of minutes he came back and knocked on the door, entering with a cup of tea.

"Here you go Sweet," he told me, "I made you some tea and brought you some water to take your meds."

"Thanks JT," I said reaching for the cup. As I took a sip, I noted that it was Chamomile. "Yeah, I'm a need this tonight," I told him, "JT, I'm sorry to have gotten you caught up in all this. I originally thought I would just handle this all myself, and explain to Murad and take it from there. I never meant for you and Dylina to be all up in the middle. Rod was angry at the prospect that you two were involved...well until I explained that you were only pulled in at the end cause I needed a ride. But Jace...he's devastated...and all because I let my emotional mind have control."

"Tania," he responded, "I notice that you keep making reference to Murad, and all that he's been thru, and how you want to make thing easier for him. And I understand that you have a vast wealth of love for him, but you need to extend the same concern for yourself Sweet. You've been thru the same right along with him. You were carjacked right along with him, almost abducted, and then shot at just like him. You had to endure the prospect of him fathering Jazmine's baby along with all her antics. You had to pave your way thru daily while your personal lives where magnified in the media. Murad is not suffering thru this by himself…this whole thing is two fold. You need to recognize that not every thing is fixable…and certainly not by you. If you're going to fix that which you can…then you need to be fixing things together Tania. Life is too short to bear the burdens of the world."

I continued to sip my tea as I let what he said sink in. He's right of course; I guess I don't want to admit that I don't have control on everything in my own personal cipher. Circumstances will come up unexpectedly and throw things out of sync. I continued to sit and sip, just letting things roll around in my mind.

"Sweet?" Jayson asked interrupting my thoughts, "You need to go on and get some rest. Go on and take your pills."

As I swallowed them, I couldn't help but think that I was swallowing an anecdote for all the guilt that I was feeling. I set my cup down on the nightstand and looked at him. I studied his handsome, sweet, kind face. So understanding, always so comforting and thought that I could now understand his reason for celibacy. Sex is so powerful; the epicenter of many a volatile situation, and it should be entered upon with caution…much caution. Look at all the life changing incidents it's brought to my world. That thought suddenly overwhelmed me again, and I just slouched down in the bed pulling the covers over me. Jayson sat on the edge of the bed looking concerned. He don't know…I'm concerned about me as well. Concerned about what I'm going to do without Murad.

"You okay Tania?" he asked.

"No," I answered, "But what does that have to do with the price of tea in China." I closed my eyes welcoming the darkness of my eyelids and made the attempt to sleep.

I awoke the next morning to the smells of breakfast. Jayson pulled his seniority and cashed in on a day off to stay home and look after me that Friday. After breakfast Dy showed up to check me out and make sure that things were in order. She'd also stopped and picked me up some woman's underwear and more fem products at Jayson's request. Once she left, I sat on the couch wrapped up in JT's old sweats and a blanket and nodded in and out of a restless sleep all day. In between he cooked his illustrious meals to which I had no appetite, and relentlessly tried to keep my mind occupied, to which he couldn't. I was consumed with the fact that Murad had not reached out to me. Feeling this way was driving me up the wall and bringing back déjà vue to the days of Trey. I would get myself so worked up and crazy when he would take his seasons of putting me on the back burner while he pursued new attractions. I would remember how we'd be running hot, and operating so tight and then things would start to fall of as he became impatient with every little thing I did, and how every minor thing was made into a major problem. Then of course things would drop off sharply. He'd stop coming by, stop calling and I'd try to maintain and give him space until I could no longer bear it and pick up the phone. I remember the days of unanswered phone calls, cell phone going straight to voice mail and no response to my texts. For me, that is the worst feeling in the world...to be ignored by the man who holds your heart in his hands. I would torment myself with, who is he with...what are they doing...what is better about her...why does he need to do this...am I not enough...why do I put up with it...why don't he just leave me alone...Oh God, what if he leaves me alone. I mean just simply crazy. I had to put in so much work to elevate myself from that mindset...now here it is being unleashed from within once again, only this time from the man who has my heart and my soul. God help me cause this is one I don't know if I'll be able to make it thru. In between watching TV, reading and JT forcing me to eat, I intermittently called Murad, only to get no answer. And when I'd awake from one of my many cat naps I asked, "JT, did he call?"

"Not yet Sweet," he'd answer. My heart wanted to believe that he would, but by nightfall that first day, my gut knew that he wouldn't. As I got ready for bed, I couldn't help but to cry myself to sleep and pray that tomorrow would bring something positive to offset all of the negative.

Saturday morning I woke up praying to the Great One Divine as I watched the sunlight filter thru the slightly cracked blinds. I prayed that today would bring some peace to my soul. I prayed that Murad would put his hurt aside long enough to figure out that I'm hurting as well. I prayed that Wanka Tanka would forgive me on abusing one of his golden rules of life by destroying one. I prayed that the soul of my unborn child would also forgive me for my selfish decision, and I prayed that Wankan Tanka would once again bless me with the opportunity to bear life in the future. I lay in bed and prayed until I was repetitive and cock-eyed with concentration. My heart burned in my chest and my head was spinning although I was still lying down. I became frightened by my body's responses and began to cry. I sat up in bed to catch my breath and noticed JT sleeping at the end of the bed, same clothes from yesterday. My heart cried out in sentiment that he would sit guard over me, knowing that my emotional pain is for another man. I eased up on the crying and just sat there watching him and wiped my eyes. Alright now Tania, I told myself. You need to be grateful that you have people in your life that love, care and accept you for who you are. People who are pulling and rooting for you to excel in whatever you do. I had to acknowledge that this "situation" that I am currently under, I brought upon myself. So there is no one else to blame and no one that can make it right but me. I need to let go of all this self inflicted misery, and concentrate on building my way back to right. I know it's gonna be a chore...but I need to get to it.

"Jace," I called out softly, nudging him with my foot, "Jace...wake up."

He stirred, then rolled over opening his eyes responding with, "Sweet...what's up. Are you okay?"

"Yeah Jayson," I replied, "I feel better now...much better."

Jayson spent Saturday taking care of me just as he did yesterday, only this time, I participated. We ate a wonderful breakfast then went out for a ride. We stopped and picked up a couple of incidentals then returned to the house. He was not without prejudice to the fact that I was feening for Rod, and he checked twice to see if he could connect with him without success. The fact that Murad was still not answering pinched my heart something fierce, but I decided I had to suffer my consequences, and just let time do its thing. We stayed in the rest of the day and watched movies. Dream called at one point and asked JT if he knew where Rod was, and he just answered honestly that he didn't know. They talked for a few more minutes about nothing and everything and then he hung up. I slowly bided the time, and internally prayed for strength to make it thru whatever the outcome of this whole thing. Around 10:00 pm we dug into a German Chocolate Cake that JT had made yesterday during my sleep fest. I had 2 whole pieces...that is so not like me. I relished in my sweet gooey treat and washed it down with a big glass of milk. We watched some more TV before I decided to call it a night around 11:45 and retired to the bedroom. Although I was trying to instill calm within all day, the nights are a challenge, and in an effort to retain my resolve, I just prayed myself to sleep.

Sunday, the Sabbath day of many faiths. I awoke with a feeling...a vibe...something that I could not explain. As I washed my face, I took a look in the mirror and made a promise to myself to take hold of this situation and make a move. It's been more than 48 hours and that has always been our milepost for being apart from one another. Anything past 48 hours is surely cause for alarm. I got dressed and walked up into the kitchen to find JT once again preparing a meal.

"Good morning Sweet," he said as I took a seat at the kitchen table.

"Morning Jayson," I answered, "Doing your thang as usual." Whatever he was fixing smelled delicious, and I couldn't wait to sample it.

"Oh just some garden scramble wraps, and a little warm apple-blueberry compote with cinnamon crumble topping."

"Well whatever it is, I'm gonna devour it," I told him lightly laughing.

"Wow Tania," he said looking at me as if amused, "You're smiling...it looks good on you."

"Yeah," I answered as he set a plate before me, "I made a decision this morning to make an attempt to remedy this rift between Murad and I. I know you have a full schedule with church and all, so I figured I could call Dream to come and take me home."

"Hey listen," he responded, "I got this. You on my watch...I'll take you home after we eat and just go in for the afternoon program. I never use to devote the time I should have in the past, and this time...you come second to no one Sweet. I'll take you home."

"Awww JT, thanks," I told him my heart filled with pride, "You're the best. And I appreciate you being there for me lately. You're an all true man...a true friend."

"No sweat Sweet," he said, "I told you back then that I'd always be here for you regardless...and to that I hold my word."

We finished up around 11:30 am and I insisted on helping with cleaning up in the kitchen. I was nervous about not seeing Murad since Thursday evening, and I needed to keep my mind distracted. Afterwards I went into the bedroom to make a last minute effort to spruce up. I grabbed my hair up into a ponytail and applied some lip gloss and came to the conclusion that it would have to do. Jayson finished up a few phone calls dealing in some church business, and then went to get dressed. I took note that it was now 12:30 and a small panic began to rise within. I immediately pushed it down and told myself that this was something that I had to do...I had to know my fate. At 12:45, JT was all dressed and ready to go. I grabbed my things and followed him out the door. It was not a long drive from Union to Maplewood, so I hadn't had much time to come up with a strategy...guess I was going to have to wing it. As we pulled up to the gate, the guard out front recognized me immediately and smiled letting us thru. I don't know where I was gonna come up with the courage to walk thru the front door...but so help me God...this is the 13th hour.

Murad

I felt as though I'd died a thousand deaths since Thursday, so I started medicating myself early this morning. Couldn't really sleep ever since this shit kicked off. Phone ringing off the wall, cell phones going till I just shut em all off. Fuck it...fuck em all I'd told myself. I don't need 'em...I don't need nobody. So why does it feel like a damn freight train has rolled over my heart? I miss her...I love her...but she crushed me.

Something I never expected from her…not my Butter. I tried to reason that shit in my mind over and over…why did she just up and kill my baby? Why didn't she come to me? She call herself coming to me when she asked me about having kids, but how the fuck was I supposed to know she was talking about her? The only one pregnant at the time was Jazz, so I assumed she was speaking bout her. Ahh damn…I can't believe Nube would just up and do that without letting me know, I can't digest that shit one way or another. And she up there talking bout my family…my family said this about her and that. I don't give a fuck what none of dem mu'fuckas think. Their existence ain't paramount to me. Fuckin take em or leave em'…I don't give a damn. My thoughts and feelings started to get real loose as the Henny and weed started to saturate. I was feeling more and more like banning everyone to hell, you know…just cut the whole damn bunch of dem loose. Fucking Dy …my sister…my sister, gonna go take her somewhere and have it done.

Then she up over there with JT guarding her like she need some sympathy. Hell I'm the one needing the sympathy…I'm the one that was in the dark about it all…yeah…And then…that fucking Nube…gonna just keep her ass out and not come home…gone 2 whole days going on 3…she know I don't play that shit. Hiding ova there like a sick chicken…she know what she did…that's the guilt for ya'…she know. Stole my chance from me just like that bitch back in college…what was her name?…Aww fuck it…I forgot. But her ass was a sick chicken too…fucking goin round killing kids without telling somebody…give me the damn option…I should have a say so…I should have had a choice. But nooo…they gonna go and take my chance…kill my choice…kill my baby. I let my brain sit still on that realization right there….she killed my baby…she killed my baby. I became frozen in a zone and didn't even hear the alarm being released, didn't hear her footsteps as she padded toward the den, didn't notice the atmosphere in the room had changed until she spoke.

"I'm home Murad."

I'd told JT that I would be okay…just a feeling that I had. I told him that he could go on and pull off and if I needed him, I would call. I punched in the code and stepped inside feeling some kind of way. I mean on one hand, I was feeling the comfort of being at home while on the other, I was feeling unsure if this would still be my home. I closed the door behind me, and looked around. The living room welcomed me with it's usual demeanor of perfection, and I walked over to the couch to set my bag down. I lightly sniffed and detected the ever present scent of weed. I guess that's par for the course upset as he was. I surely can't blame him on this one. I took a deep breath and made my way toward the den…his spot, and there he was sitting in his over sized chaise, with a glass of Henny in one hand and a fat blunt in the other.

I stood in the doorway for quite a few seconds without being recognized, so I opened my mouth and announced, "I'm home Murad."

He broke his gaze and looked at me head on. I thought I saw a glint of relief in his eye, but he just gave me a lip nod, and nothing else. I took a few steps in, and attempted to make some conversation.

"Murad," I started, "I know that I've done the ultimate in disrespect that a woman could ever do to a man. I was absolutely wrong and selfish in how I handled what I felt was a problem. You have always been my rock…my savior…my protector. I let insecurities on my part cloud my usual resolve and caused me to use bad judgment. I should have been secure in the knowledge that you are a permanent fixture in my corner. If ever anyone is gonna be there for me Murad…it's you. I can't stress to you how much I regret discounting that fact, or how much I regret hurting you. I shouldn't have let insignificant words or name calling from others affect me to the point that I would make such an alteration to our lives as I did. I should have been able to trust all that you said in regard to this Jazmine thing and just continue to ride it out. I should have had faith that it would all succumb to our favor." I paused for a few seconds to see if I could gauge any reaction from him, but he seemed unmoved. I took a deep breath and jumped back in. “I know that I can’t undo what I’ve done Murad, and I beg you for forgiveness. I beg you to give understanding to the fact that I’ve been on an emotional roller coaster for the last couple of months. I beg you to not hold this against me and I pray that I am not diminished in your eyes behind it. It has to be the least proud thing I’ve ever done in my life, and I need you to know that I am hurting too. If it all believable...even more than you, because I know that I am the source of your hurt, and it’s killing me to have to live with that. Murad I love you more than I care to know and I can only pray that you still carry the same for me.” I paused once more, yet I still got no reaction, so I made my final statement, “I don’t know how I could ever make it up to you, cause an act of this severity can never be made up, but I want you to know that I deeply regret what I’ve done, and regret a thousand times over not entrusting you with understanding. I hope that you will consider what I’ve said here today, and please give me some feedback on where we’re gonna go from here.”

As I finished my statement I watched him for a response to which I got none. I stood there for a minute, just hoping that he would say something. Given the fact that he’d been administering, I couldn’t analyze whether or not he took in what I said, or whether or not he cared. So I just stood there becoming more and more anxious as the silence blended in with the scent of the weed and wrapped itself around my brain. I stood, he looked...he looked, I stood.

When it became apparent that he had nothing to say, I sucked in my breath and announced, “Okay Murad, I see that you don’t want me here, and I understand your disappointment in me, so I’ll just grab a few of my things and just go...I guess I’ll come back some time this week or next week and get the rest of my stuff. I don’t wanna put you thru anything else, and I’m thinking you wanna be to yourself, so I guess...”

“Nube,” he finally spoke in a tone that I’ve never heard before, but yet...thank God...I understood. Part of it said, “Kill the noise” while the other part said, “Come here.”

I double checked his eyes with mine and yes…that's what I saw there. I walked over to the chaise lounge and crawled up in his lap.

"You know I love you right Nube?" he asked me with a slight slur, "You know I love you and you know you hurt me…you cut me deep…but I love you Nube. And you know I'm intense with mine and I just gotta do…what I gotta do…till I get… my shit… together. But ain't nobody…leaving nobody. You ain't fucking leaving me…and I…ain't fucking leaving you. Ain't nobody…going… nowhere. We in this together right? Right Nube?" I shook my head yes like a little girl, and then laid my head down on his chest as the tears began to make an appearance.

"Nube," he called out again. I raised my face up to him and he placed a deep kiss upon my lips, I gladly returned the kiss and relished the touch of his lips upon mine. He pulled back and said, "We in this together right?"

"Together Rod," I answered, "We in this together."

With that I laid my head to rest back down on his chest and let the tears continue. And as I sat there crying from relief, guilt, shame…the whole nine, I gratefully inhaled the scent of the weed and just cried myself to sleep…laying in his arms.

Chapter 59

The Universe At Work

Nubina

I don't know when it happened or even what day it was...all I know is that I woke up in my bed...our bed, with Murad lying right next to me. I turned over and just watched this copper-bronzed, gorgeous specimen of a Nubian man, and thanked God for granting me the opportunity to be back home with him. I made a silent vow right then and there that I would do everything in my power to see this relationship stay its course and elevate to the levels and heights that JT assured me it would. Never again will I take it upon myself to make such a decision without correctly communicating all the necessary information. As I sat watching the beautiful blend of skin tones in his genetic make-up, I couldn't help but surmise that Murad could pass for several different ethnicities. Some days he looks Hispanic, then maybe Somali an or Egyptian. And of course he could also pass for Indian, both East and American. Let's not leave out Brazilian, Hawaiian and perhaps an Eskimo. Oh yeah and let's see...

"Hey Pretty," he said opening his eyes, stopping my racial interlude. "Wow...my head feel like it got an extra extension on it. Shit," he groaned as he rolled over.

"Yeah you were deep in your medicating when I got here," I told him. "Had a lot on my mind Nube...some heavy ass shit," he responded. "But that's all water under the bridge now," he stated in response to the guilty look that I could feel creeping across my face, "We ain't gonna re-hash nothing on that topic. What's done is done...we moving forward. Just take note that you need to trust in me that I'm gonna be the man I said I would be...and then let me do that Nube. Let me be the man I'm gonna be...cause the man that I am, will never do anything against your favor...never. I'm gonna always have your best interest at heart...cause the best is what I want you to have...and it's what you deserve." I looked at him and just melted all over again and started crying.

"Oh unh unh...enough of that Butter," he said, "There's been more tears than a little bit these last couple of months...we done with all that. From now on...we striving for the brass ring Nube, and we not gonna stop till we get it. Nothing...and no one is gonna ever come between us again. You with me on that?" he asked taking my chin in his hand and raising my eyes to meet his. He kissed me tenderly on my lips and I responded deeply. "Ahhh...you don't even understand how good that shit feels," he stated as he pulled back, "I missed you Butter...don't you ever stay away from me like that again."

"But Rod you..." I started.

"I don't care," he interrupted, "Next time...you'd better come after me." We both bust out laughing as he hugged me to him and we laughed till we couldn't no more.

Murad

Damn, it feels so good to have my Butter home. I mean...shit was rough, and it's still gonna take a minute for the ill feelings to completely blow over, but that's my heart right there, and I ain't putting her down for nothing. I had to take into account the things she said, and I had to admit that she's been under a lot of pressure with all that's been going on. And damn if Sumira and my aunt ain't had her shook with their nonsense...jumping all over her like she just some chick from the block. She been down with Sumira since they was like what...21 or 22? My Aunt Klessie just a miserable ass...probably jealous that Nube making moves while Sumira at her regular ass job, and divorced from her husband And then fucking Brick...gonna come out his face and call her a bitch. Maann...that shit right there still boils my blood. What the fuck is wrong with that nigga? He always did have some kinda cynical comments about her from back when. Who knows...maybe she had to check his ass a time or two in the past. I don't know...but I ain't got nothing else for him...I'm done. It's a good thing I pushed back Nube's engagements till next Tuesday. This will give her time to rest and for us both to regroup.

Dream hit me up last night and asked me what was going on, so I just told him we were trying to iron out some things, and just didn't answer the phone to avoid being distracted. I'm not quite sure he bought that but...it's true on my part. Didn't need no distractions at the time. Ever since Nube came home yesterday, I've been trying to make sure she's comfortable. Making sure she keeping up with taking her meds, and doing what she needs to do to heal properly. Sex ain't even on the horizon right now, and you know what...fine...cause sex has been the main antagonizer in both situations. Falling back from the sex right about now is cool. My sister Dy called to check on her, and I just handed the phone over to Nube. I'm still salty about all that. I'm saying...I can understand about all these woman's right and choices, the doctor confidentiality and what not...but you my sister...and that was my damn child. I don't know....its gonna be a good while before I can be at peace with that one. At any rate, we gonna take this time to heal...put all that we can behind us, and man up for the future. Jarrell had the order for the DNA testing to go forth upon the day of delivery. This way Jazmine will be responsible for her bills incurred should that prove not to be my seed. The order is signed by the judge and ready to go as soon as. That right there is a relief. He and I also have some other motions in the works, but we just gonna play it by ear for now. Nube and I are getting ready to get into some grub. I had gone out and picked up a take-out order from a new Caribbean spot in South Orange. It smells delicious and I'm bout to find out. Hmmm...bout to find out.

Nubina

Rod always finding these little places when it comes to food. But damn...this right here is good. Besides I'm grateful that I don't have to cook; probably anything he bring in right about now would taste good. I had gotten some Curried Tilapia with rice and veggies, while Rod got the Brown Stewed chicken. As usual we swapped and sampled our dishes and had us a marvelous ole time eating. Once we were done, we climbed up in the chaise chair in the den, and put on a movie. This time I let him pick and of course it was an action flick. Not a problem. A little action and chaos going on in someone else's life instead of mine, was definitely cool with me. We were about a half hour into the movie when the phone rang. Kye's number popped up along the bottom and Rod brushed it off with, "Not feeling him right now."

So it went unanswered. In about another 10 minutes, Jarrell's number popped up on the screen, and I looked up at him and said, "You not gonna get that?"

"Nope," he answered, "Whatever's going on can wait." I shrugged my lips and turned back around to continue watching the movie. Another 40 minutes into the movie...the intercom buzzed.

"Who the fuck?" Rod gave off. He picked up the phone and hit the security button, "Yeah," he responded.

"Mr. Tillman, I have your brothers out here, they say it's urgent," Carrington announced, in his light Jamaican accent.

"Aight, let em thru," Rod answered, "What the fuck is going on now? Urgent...what could be this damn urgent?"

He pulled up from me and proceeded to the door to intercept. I came up behind him, curious as well as a little scared as to what this could possibly be all about. He opened the door and waited as Jarrell along with Dream emerged from the car. The questions running thru his mind were reflected by the look on his face, and I knew that something was definitely wrong. Both Dream and Jarrell had very serious faces. I just stood frozen with my heart in my chest and wondering what now?

"Yo son...what up?" Rod greeted Dream as he stepped across the threshold, "Rell what's going on?" he asked once they were both inside.

"Look Rod," Jarrell spoke up, "I got word from Kye, followed up with a call from Aaron and Jazz's attorney; it ain't good."

"What ain't good?" Murad asked agitated and curious all at the same time.

"Jazmine's been in an accident. Her car was hit by a stolen vehicle down on Peshine Ave. Although the car was totaled, she survived with minor injuries; but she started hemorrhaging and it's believed that she lost the baby. I tried to call you, but I guess you was doing you. And I understand...I understand; but I don't have to tell you...we need to make our way down to the hospital."

I stood there transfixed in a state, unable to believe that this wave of negativity was determined to hold us in its grasp. I shook myself back to the moment to check on Murad's response. It broke my heart to see a look of concern, confusion and fear on his face. I know he didn't feel any kind of way about Jazmine, but just on the odds that the child was possibly his, this had to hurt. That would be the 2nd child he's lost in a matter of days. His face turned that ashy rust as he turned to me with a look in his eyes that said he didn't want to abandon me after all that he and I just went thru.

"Bae...listen," I told him, "It's fine...I know where you need to be now. It's not a problem. Go."

He stood there for a few seconds before he spoke, "Dream...I don't wanna leave her by herself. Can you..."

"You ain't even gotta ask Chief," Dream cut in, "I'm on it."

"Well...okay then," Murad spoke slowly as if he was in a daze. And I suppose he was. Talking bout what else could go wrong. He's definitely in a grey season. "Rell," he stated, "I be with you in a minute. Let me throw some clothes on."

"Take your time," Jarrell answered him.

As Murad went upstairs to get ready, Jarrell turned to me and asked, "So how you doing Nube?"

"I'm good Jarrell, I'm good," I answered.

It dawned on me at that moment that I hadn't spoken to anyone in the family since the night of the Thanksgiving fiasco. As if reading my mind he said, "Listen Nube, I just want you to know that I am in no position to judge anyone on their choices when it comes to happiness, and I'm really sorry about the way things went down at the family dinner. It would have been nice if you and Rod could have stayed and spent time with us all. So...not that you need my approval or nothing...I just wanted to let you know that, I'm cool with you and Rod being together. I think you're what he needs and I'm wishing you both the best."

I stood for a minute pleasantly surprised with what he'd said. I hadn't really heard many opinions from the family about us, except for Ms. Klessie and Sumira, so hearing a favorable one did me good right now.

"Well Jarrell," I replied, "Thank you very much for your honesty and the words of encouragement. I happen to love your brother very much or I wouldn't have even considered taking the chance I did having been with JT…but we gonna work on us and try to do this thing right…regardless."

"I'm glad to hear that…glad to hear it," he replied.

"Nube," I heard Murad call from upstairs.

"Excuse me fellas," I told them as I made my up to see what he needed.

"What's going on Rod?" I asked upon entering the room.

"C'mere Nube," he said his voice brandishing desperation. As I stepped over into his outstretched arms he lightly groaned in anguish, "I just need to feel you right now Nube…I just need to soak in your energy. Babe…I don't know what to do right now. I don't know how I'm supposed to feel right now…or even how I'm supposed to act once I get there. Damn…I wish you was coming with me." I looked up into his eyes and I saw that it was a semi-disguised plea for me to accompany him.

"Aww Rod," I replied, the tone of my voice laced with love and understanding, "And I would love to be right there in support of you, but that is so not my place right now. This is one of the steps you gonna have to handle on your own, and I know you'll do just fine. You handle everything from the sun and the moon for me, so I know you can integrate that expertise into dealing with this appropriately. Besides Jarrell will be there for any legalities…you'll be just fine…and I'ma be right here when you get back, and we'll take that next step together."

He slowly nodded his head in agreeance as he pulled me tight to him once again. "I fucking love you Butter…I love you," he said.

And as I hugged him back just as tight, I responded, "I know Murad…I know."

Murad

I can't believe this shit right here, I'm thinking as my brother whipped the car into the hospital parking lot. Aight…aight, breathe Rod…take this shit here like a dime a dozen… a dime a dozen. All this bout to come to an end one way or another. We stepped out the car and walked up thru the Emergency entrance.

“Let me,” Jarrell said. “Excuse me,” he addressed the receptionist, “I understand that you have a patient that was brought in as a result of a car accident. Ms. Jazmine Meadows...we are here on her behalf.”

“Are you family?” she nonchalantly asked as she continued flipping thru the papers on her desk.

“This is the potential father,” he answered indicating to me, “and I am his attorney.”

“Attorney?” she asked looking up and over to me. “Oh...oh yeah, you and Nubina...uhmmm ...oh yeah...uhh... I mean Murad Tillman...right?”

I just gave her quick head nod, and she said, “Hold on.” She picked up the phone and made a quick call to somewhere, “Yes...Stella...the father is here. Yes...he’s with his attorney. Okay...I will.” She hung up and said, “They’re expecting you. You will need to go thru those double doors and take the elevator to the 2nd floor and she’s about 6 doors down on the left...Room 1015.”

“Thank you,” Jarrell answered as we both pulled away from the desk. Speculation and shit bout to jump off now...I can feel it. Ole girl back up at the front desk all stuttering and shit. Damn...well it’s all bout to be a wrap, no matter what.

Rell and I entered the room to a hysterical Jazmine, just screaming all kinds of nonsense. Her mother, her 2 sisters along with 2 of her girlfriends was all congregated in the small room trying to placate her. “Where’s my baby...where’s my baby? Somebody get Murad...get him here...Now...I need him...I need him!!”

Upon our entrance her mother took one look at me and sucked her teeth hard. “Good Lord,” she called out, “You can stop ya screaming Jazz, he’s here.”

“He’s here? Where?” she pushed out, looking wildly across the room. She settled down for one hot second as her eyes settled upon me, then she put the theatrics back into play, “Muurrraad, Murad...I’m sorry...our baby...our baby. They took him...I don’t know where he is...they say he dead Murad....Murad.”

I took one look at her and although I wanted to hate her, I couldn’t be that spiteful right about now, not with what Nube and I just went thru. Not only that, her busted appearance projected a mode of sympathy to me on her behalf, so I sucked it in, took a deep breath and proceeded to be the "better" man on this.

"Jazz," I told her walking to the side of the bed and taking her hand, "It's gonna be alright. Things will fall in place."

"Fall in place where Rod...how?" she responded, back to her hysterics, "My son...our son is gone. Just like that Murad...he's gone. I want you to find them bastards that hit my car and make them pay...make them pay Murad."

I took a deep breath before I spoke, "Jazz, you know Jarod, and even Kye will pull whatever strings necessary to bring about justice on this."

"But they killed our child Murad...they killed our son," she continued hollering.

"So it was a boy?" I inquired.

"Oh yes Murad," she answered all extra, "Your first born...a son...but they won't let me see him. I haven't seen him. Where's my lawyer...I wanna sue this fucking hospital...they probably just stole my baby. I wanna see him."

"Jazz calm down," her mother told her, "You carrying on like a mad woman."

"I don't care...I need to see my baby...we need to see our baby. Murad...you get our baby here...make them bring us our child."

I looked over at Jarrell and it was just then that I noticed her attorney as well. Damn...this was becoming a delicate situation...I mean I don't know whose baby it was at this point, mine or not, but what I do know is that it was 100 percent her baby and she just lost it. So...I think I'ma see if can get a handle on this.

"Hey listen," I announced to the room, "Can you all give us some time to ourselves...please."

"Yeah sure, no problem," Jarrell answered.

"Jazmine?" her attorney questioned, "Is that okay with you?"

"Yeah it's okay...what you think?" she answered annoyed, "Murad gonna handle this all...he gonna make it right for our son...his first born."

Yo…what is all this need for the first born title? Must be some kind of woman shit…cause Nube mentioned something along the same line. Hmmm…

"Well we'll just be right outside," her mom answered as they all began to file out of the room. Once they all left, I took a deep breath and began to see what I could handle.

"So Jazz…first off…how you doing?" I asked.

"How you think I'm doing," she started back, of course all hyped, "I was in a car wreck. The car wreck that killed our child. What we gonna do now Murad?"

"Well first off, we gonna make sure that everything is investigated properly," I told her, "I mean…we gonna make sure that all attempts were made to save him, and then I'm gonna make sure that we get to see him and that all the proper arrangements are made."

"But he was my baby Rod…my baby. I can't be making no arrangements…I ain't come this far to do all that," she stated, the tears resurfacing.

"Well arrangements have to be made one way or another," I told her, "Being that no official paternity has been established, I do believe that responsibility will fall on you."

"How can you say that Murad…how can that be all that matters to you right now? He was yours and he's gone now, and it's too late for any damn DNA. How is that the first fucking thing on your mind Rod…how? Our child is dead." She sat up in that bed crying and heaving, and I thought to myself, Okay…she right…he gone, but it ain't never too late.

I'ma get this all figured out, but for now, "You right Jazz, what's important is what you want right now. So tell me, how do you want this done? Get whatever you need…don't worry about the cost." She stopped her crying and her eyes lit up…I swear I saw the little miniature words ka-ching shimmering and dancing on both her eyeballs.

"Oh Rod…Okay…well I was thinking that we could…"

Chapter 60

Keep It Pimpin

Nubina

Murad came home pretty much the next morning after going to check on Jazmine at the hospital. He said the doctor explained to him that the impact caused a blood vessel to tear in the uterus that apparently was already strained with the weight of the pregnancy, and that's what caused the hemorrhage. Jazmine was brought directly in and taken to surgery to try and stop the bleeding to no avail. She had awakened that morning to discover she'd lost the child and began her mission to find Rod. I mean wow...I feel so bad for her. She must have been like 8 months or so, and now she's childless just like that. Well...Murad is being a stand up guy and supporting her thru all this. He's made arrangements for the burial and all, and helping her out with all the insurance papers and whatever else that needs signatures. I have to say, I'm just a tad surprised that he's so cooperative. I guess with the child being taken suddenly like that, all the hard feelings previously felt don't matter. He's been thru so much...like I said 2 children in less than a week. I'm doing my best to support him however he needs me to on this. The burial will be next week in order to give Jazmine sufficient time to attend. I feel so bad for her...I mean, regardless to the circumstances, she was like 8 months pregnant and planning to have her child, then to have the child taken from you suddenly, thru such a violent act. I can't even imagine...the right to choice is one thing; your choice taken from you is another. Well whatever...I let Rod know that I'm here for him no matter what.

Murad

Aaron and Jarrell had put in some overtime in making sure that the DNA test would still be implemented despite the fact that the child was deceased. They argued the fact that if I was indeed the potential father, I had the right to respectively know of my loss, and if I was not the father, then I had the right to have my name and reputation reinstated. I'm sure glad that the judge was fair and objective on this or hell just woke up on the right side of the bed. But anyway you look at it, this whole thing is about to be resolved, and any obligations to Jazz will be done with. She's got nothing else to hold over my head. I sure gotta give it to Nube...she's been holding it down for me, supportive, understanding the whole nine. I got major plans for me and her once I put all this behind us.

Moving forward...I'm gonna make sure that shit get real lovely for us. I'ma tighten up on my business plans and financial arrangements and knock shit out the ball park. I need everything in place when I make the moves I need to make in regard to Nube. Hmm...in the meantime, I had to somewhat squash my little mood of insolence with certain family members, I mean...come on...Lonnie ain't do nothing wrong. I was just acting like a bitch...you know mad with the situation...so taking it out on the whole world. Nube has engagements next week that I won't be able to attend. Dream can't go due to work, so Lonnie would be my next best choice. In fact he's probably a better choice than Dream anyway. He's definitely more seasoned in dealing with niggas on the sly and he sure as hell ain't got no problem protecting her. Besides, she's his little pet...she can't do no wrong in his eyes. Them two been tight from day one...I never figured that one out...but it's all good. He and I spoke on the whole dinner thing, his momma, everything and we good. He don't have a problem taking a couple of days off from the shop and escorting Nube. That's good...that's good. I don't want any of her engagements compromised behind all this nonsense. I guess I need to admit, I was being a little defensive. For the most part...most of my family got my back on this here and well as with me and Nube. Guess I need to let go of unsettled feelings and make peace with it. But that shit with Brick, Sumira and my Aunt Klessie...I ain't ready to dissolve that. Them mu'fuckas left a bad taste in my mouth...Uhmm.

This is the first time I've ever been on the road without Murad. It's so surreal. I had two local engagements earlier in the week and now I'm down her in Maryland with Lonnie. He and Rod got back on track and Rod asked him to accompany me while he handles the remnants of Hurricane Jazmine and the situation with the baby. It's all cool. I love me some Lonnie. He's the best big brother figure I could ever have. Back in the day when I first met Sumira, he was so wild, so street, but for some reason he and I clicked. He would always compliment me and told me he admired me for pursuing a higher education. And when times got rough and hectic he would always encourage me to keep striving. I guess he was frustrated at the time with Kiyma, she was a little younger than him and not interested in much but materialism. He was on the block so yeah...she got whatever she wanted and then some. Then next thing you know, she became pregnant and all kinds of problems ensued. They broke up, they got back together, he cheated...she cheated, and God knows he just about died behind that. Whenever he was upset he would call me, and we'd talk about if for hours till he got himself straight with things. And that's how our special friendship started, and we've been tight and sharing love secrets and confidences ever since. Things went well this week, Rod's hanging in there, but today is Friday...the day of the funeral. I wish I could be there for him, but again...it's so not my place. This is another one of those steps he has to take alone. And I know he understands that, but it doesn't stop the feeling of imbalance we're both having being apart right now. Well...I don't wanna sit here in a down mood. Let me go see if Lonnie wanna go out to a few stores. It's only 11:00 am and the show is not until this evening. We should be able to do just a little damage and be back on time.

"Lonnie," I called out walking into the living room area of the suite, "What say you and I go out and hit a coupla stores?"

"What kind of stores you talking Princess?" he asked me warily, looking up from his magazine.

"Oh I don't know," I answered back, "I don't even know what's out there. I figured a little looking won't hurt."

"You know we got somewhere to be later. I ain't trynna have Rod get all in my ass if you late," he replied.

"Oh come on Youngblood," I responded, "Don't be like that, I'm not even gonna be that long. Just really want to get some fresh air and relax my energy. I'm a little wired up today. You know what today is right?"

"Yeah," he stated, "I know. My boy going thru...he going thru. I know he'll be glad when this is all over, so you all can get your lives back."

"Yeah," I offered, "He and I will finally be able to concentrate on us for a change...and that sounds like right."

"Well come on here Nube," he came back with, getting up from his seat, "Let's get going so that we can get back. While I'm out, I can probably get some of my holiday presents for Kiyma and AJ."

"See there," I told him, "I'm helping you out...putting you one up on things."

He cracked a smile as I began to laugh and said, "Yeah...I'm up on it aight. You know you picking them out right?"

"Yeah I know Youngblood...I know. Let's go," I said grabbing my coat and heading for the door. As we walked out the front door I felt a piercing chill. This time, not an eerie chill, but a definitive chill as if I was getting a message. I decided not to feed into it and just shrugged it off and thought...perhaps it was just the door to the negative portal finally closing. Yeah....

Murad

This whole morning has been nerve wracking. I have to admit that Jazmine is truly ripped up behind this. I guess it's hard to carry another human being inside you, and then have it snatched away. Yeah her tears and pain are real but...she also crying for the big payday she thought she was cashing in on. What she don't know is that I've got 2 sets of papers in my suit pocket. One set, in case I am the father, and another set in case I am not. I'm waiting on pins and needles now for a phone call from Aaron who is waiting on the follow-up call from the DNA lab on the results. They were instructed to relinquish the results to my attorney as soon as they were ready and he in turn would inform me. The funeral ceremony is just about done with now and Jazz is ready to go back up to view the body for the last time. This ain't what I wanna be doing, cause this shit here is heart-wrenching. He is a beautiful child...I can't say by looking if he's definitely mine or not, but a handsome little man nonetheless. I helped her up from her seat, and escorted her back up to the casket. Needless to say, she broke down hollering and screaming with her mom and her whole family joining in, escalating the effect. Once again...I ain't the one to be judging nobody on their grief, and since I'm torn with the unknown, I can let some of their grief supplement for what I'm unsure of.

I stood there with her and held her as she stroked the child's face and poured her eyes out. I'm trynna keep it together here, but this shit is rough...something I don't ever want to experience again. After about 10 whole minutes, the funeral coordinator signaled that we had to proceed. I gently pulled her away and led her back to her seat for the final eulogy. The minister came up and did his thing, and then the funeral director began to close out the ceremony. He informed everyone to the location of the burial site, and then he instructed us on the processional to the vehicle. Jazz was near hysterics by then, and I did what I could to console her. We proceeded outside and entered into the convoy of Escalade trucks and watched as the casket was put into an Escalade hearse. Jazz had heard of this over the top Black funeral home out of Westfield and she insisted on using them. They came with all the glitz and glamour you could ever imagine, so you know she called herself doing something with that. I let her have her way, after all what could I say...it's what she wanted for her child. We rode out to the cemetery without further incident as the cold air seemed to help suppress the unruly tension in the air. She held her own at the burial site until they lowered the little casket in the ground. Her knees began to buckle and I had to grab her up under the arms to support her balance. We stood there till the last rose was thrown and I waited there with her in my arms until she was ready to leave. I led her back to the car and opened the door and set her inside, glad that this part of the ordeal was over. Jazmine used her advantage points to lay all up under me on the somber ride back home. Despite the previous controversy between us, I didn't really have a problem letting her get that. After all, we had just experienced the loss of a child, possibly twice over for me. I tell you, this was most definitely one of the most severe moments of my life.

In all of about 30 minutes, we were brought back to the church where Jazmine's family was holding the repasse. I held it all together, smiling, shaking hands and what not. Every chance she got, Jazmine was pulling on me, clinging to me, introducing me to any and everybody that she could wrestle some sympathy out of. I broke away for a few minutes and went to the bathroom to relieve myself and run some cool water on my face. Damn...I haven't spoken to Nube since last night. I wonder how she's making out; I know she's got a few more hours before her show. I hope all of this doesn't affect her output in any way. She always gives 100 percent in all that she does, but with so much going on lately, and me not able to be there...you just never know. Maybe I can give her a call, I'm thinking as I leave the rest room. On my way back to the main reception room, I reached into my pocket to get my phone to giver her a buzz, when it began ringing. I checked the caller ID...Aaron.

"Yo Ace," I answered, adrenaline spinning.

"Yo Chief," he responded, "You Aight man...you good?"

"Yeah Ace," I told him, "It's all good, speak bruh."

"The verdict is in Chief...you're not the father."

My brain froze for a split second...I mean I was hearing what I always expected to hear, but her grimey trick did have me shook for a minute. "Ace...say what?" I questioned.

"You done Rod...99.9% not you," he kicked backed. I just stood there, with a conglomerate of thoughts running thru my mind, spinning and spinning like a non-stop merry go-round.

"Murad...Murad," I heard thru the phone, returning me back to the moment, "You gonna be okay? Do you need me to come down there?"

"Naw Ace...everything is cool," I answered, "I got this...I'm straight. Yo man...thanks. I got something to take care of. I'll hit you up when I get home. Later."

I ended the call somewhat in a daze and stepped back taking a deep breath. Damn...she took this shit there...all the way there knowing I was not the father. All that drama with my Aunt Klessie about taking care of my responsibilities, all the buzz around town, fucking media hype and word on the street. All the nights of running back and forth at her beck and call leaving Nube alone and isolated at a delicate time for her. My baby...my own baby lost in vain, cause this here is all the trumped up bullshit I knew it to be. Fuck...fuck!!! Let me breathe before I go back out here. Let me get it together...get myself in order. I walked back out to the main area on a mission. I scanned the room like a swat commander, seeking out my target; I spotted her and zoomed in for the hit.

"There you are Murad," she said as I advanced towards her, "This is my Aunt Glodene on my father's side. She was saying..."

"How you doing," I peeled off to the old squat, as I grabbed Jazmine by the hand leading her away. "I need to see you," I told her; the look on her face questioning my instant rude behavior. There really was nowhere to get her alone, so I just pulled her off to the side a few feet away from everyone.

"Murad...honey, what's wrong," she asked, "You look like...oh I know. It's still too hard to bear isn't it? I'm so glad you here with me...right by my side like I knew you would be."

She reached out and grabbed me up for a hug, her way of touching off her great performance and soliciting approval from her well constructed audience of family and friends. Okay...so this how she wanna play this, I grabbed her back up in a hug and swayed back and forth going with the flow before I gently pulled away. I reached into my right pocket and pulled out the "right" set of papers, envelope clean and crisp.

"Jazz," I told her placing them in her hand, "These are for you. A little something that you might wanna take your time and review first thing you get in the door tonight. Review them very carefully...and oh...have your boy, the legalese review them as well. I expect the required action on this by Monday morning. If all decrees are not put into place by the designated time, I promise you me Jazz, I will begin demolition on your life immediately.

"Murad," she gave off a little too loudly.

I moved in close and grabbed her chin between my fingers as if I was gonna kiss her. Once I got my lips close enough to hers that they brushed, I took my fingers and clenched on that chin in a death grip. All that she'd done, all that she'd put me thru and all that I'd gone thru behind her resurfaced my pain and I spoke to her in a measured tone, "Jazz...you have no idea all that I've endured and suffered behind this bullshit. Yeah...I get it...I hurt you...you wanted to hurt me...but you've hurt so much more than me behind this. Hurt that can never be repaired. And for that, I could snap your fucking jaw right here...right now."

I noticed her flinch as I added on the pressure. "You will...and I'll repeat that for you...you will do as mandated in those papers or regretfully live everyday that you get up and breathe. On top of that, shit is done with in regard to Nube...if you ever come at her again, if you ever fucking even look at her wrong...I'ma make sure shit is rectified. Do we understand one another?" I prompted her with a head nod.

And when she didn't answer, I clenched that chin a little harder. I threw her another nod, to which she responded a garbled, "Yes," as tears began to run down her face.

"Then we good," I told her. Looking down at her, tears coming down her face, I let my lips touch hers lightly before I pulled back and let her chin go. I stood watching her for a few seconds before I turned on my heels walked over to retrieve my coat, picked it up and walked out the door...didn't even think about looking back.

Part III

January 2009 – September 2009

Chapter 61
Come Monday

Nubina

My engagement that evening went off without a hitch and we rode back in late Friday night. The original plan was to stay overnight and come home the next day, but I was missing Rod, and told him that I needed to be with him. We got in like 1:00 am and I just fell into his arms once I got in the door. Since it was late, we told Lonnie to just stay over in the guest bedroom. After a beautiful shower together, we just lay in the bed wrapped up in one another. I listened as he gave me the run down of the day's events and the funeral. I mean...I tried to be supportive and listen to everything he was saying, cause God knows...he always listens to me, but with his arms around me, while I'm pressed up against his chest...his words echoing from within...that heavy bass tone...kind of hypnotized me and...began to...lull me...to sleep. I'm...so...tired. I couldn't help myself...I was hit. So I didn't hear him at all when he said, "Nube...it wasn't my baby."

Murad

"Nube...Nube. Did you hear me?" Damn...she sleep. I guess she's really tired. I kissed her on the top of her forehead and let my lips linger there for a minute. She feels so good...so right. I thought about my encounter today with Jazz, and I thanked God for this blessing of a woman I got right here. I mean...I know she made a mistake, being that she was rattled and all but, evil or scheming...it ain't in her. She's so damn real...so pure in her intent. I can't wait until we get pass all the fallout and press forward with our own lives. And as far as I'm concerned...that shit is starting tomorrow. And I can't wait for 2009...2009 looking like it's gonna be a good year...a very good year.

Saturday was a wonderful day. It started off with me, Rod and Lonnie going out to brunch, where Murad gave us the news that he was not the father of Jazmine's baby. In spite of myself I broke out in smiles from here to Japan. I mean…I was truly sorry that she lost her baby, I was just damn glad that it was not Murad's.

"Fuckin'sweet," Lonnie broke out with upon hearing the words, "I knew shit would prevail…I knew things would work out for you. That was some scandalous shit she pulled. She got her just desserts for that right there."

"Oh Lonnie," I whined.

"Oh Lonnie what?" he responded, "I ain't said nothing but right. Ole' girl tried to run mad game on my brother here, and game ran that shit back on her. You gotta come prepared to deal with consequences when you trynna play game without a clue. Can't nobody play game harder than game itself. On the real…her ass got burned. I mean…I'm sorry for the little guy…but Jazz got her due."

I looked over to Murad, and he just shrugged like…what?? I thought about it, then held my tongue. Just what would I be defending in regard to Jazmine and her actions anyway? She did pull a damn hemi, that which kind of lent to my insecurity and pushed me to my own off the wall decision. Aww let it go, I decided. Things worked out just as they should have…just the way the universe intended.

"Well you know what?" I said, "What's done is done and now Rod and I can finally move on. Right Bae?"

He give me a lip nod and said, "One last thing Nube…I got one last piece of unfinished business to see thru and then yeah…I can say we in the clear"

"Really?" I asked him genuinely stumped.

"Really," he responded. "Come Monday…6:30 pm…shit will be done for real"

I didn't have a clue to what he was talking bout, so I looked over to Lonnie, who looked back at me and just shrugged his shoulders and said, "He's in charge Princess…trust me…he got shit under control."

Murad

It's Monday, and I made sure that we adhered to a strict schedule. Nube did a speaking engagement at a senior citizen complex and then we had a brief meeting with some publishing executives' downtown at the Newark Gateway. They're interested in publishing one of Nube's poems formatted as a children's book, so we touched on some preliminary negotiations. We were done with all that about 3:00, so we stopped for a meal, and returned to the house by 5:30. We both showered, changed into our lounge wear, and was seated on the couch by 6:10. I had picked up some chocolate covered strawberries and some sparkling water yesterday, and I went to the kitchen and prepared a tray of them as well as two fluted glasses. Nube doesn't care for the taste of the strawberries that are laced in champagne, so in order to appease her I substitute the sparkling water to emulate that fizz effect. Whatever the little lady wants...the little lady gets. I took a seat next to Nube on the couch and flipped on the TV. Nube proceeded to babble on and on about a little of this and a little of that, so I just tuned her out while I channel surfed. At 6:30 I flipped to Fox5.

"Nube...kill it," I told her, "There's something I want to see on TMZ."

"Oh Rod please," she gave back, "Since when? You know good and well you don't..."

"Shhh..." I gently told her sliding one of the strawberries in her mouth, "I need to hear this."

A slender brunette reporter appeared on the screen giving off a greeting.

Good evening...we come to you this evening with a very special broadcast. A few months ago, we featured the pending paternity dispute of entertainment and financial manager Murad Tillman. We have been informed that a press conference exclusive to TMZ has been called by the mother of the child along with her attorney.

Nube turned to me wide eyed chewing on her strawberry, and hit me with a look that said... "What the fuck?" I hit her back with my own look that said... "You see it." We both turned back to the TV, as the reporter droned on.

I have been informed that they are just about ready to enter...Ah yes...they are entering from the left just now. We will now go live to the podium for this account.

We watched as Jazmine came in with an entourage of her mother, her 2 sisters and her attorney. I sat intent as she walked up to the microphone, papers in her hand and proceeded to speak.

"*Good evening. My name is Jazmine Meadows and I have an important announcement to make in regard to my paternity suit against Murad Tillman. I did appear on the show back in October at that time, to announce my pregnancy. Approximately 2 weeks ago after visiting family in Newark, I was involved in a car accident that resulted in the loss of my child.*"

At this point she began to sniffle, and her mom reached over and hugged her for support. She handed her a tissue to which she blew her nose, and then continued.

"*I'm sorry...but things are still fresh for me. But in regard to the child that I lost, it is with deep remorse that I inform you today...that Murad Tillman was not the father of my child. That fact has been substantiated by a DNA test, and I therefore bear no claim to any of his assets. I would also like to take this time to make a public apology to Murad Tillman and the whole Tillman family for my deceptive manner. In addition I'd like to publicly apologize to Nubina for my attempts to defile her reputation as well as her career and will keep all such future statements of a negative nature to myself. I also want it to be known that I alone bear the financial responsibility for my medical bills for my hospital stay as a result of the accident as well as previous pre-natal care. In regard to the funeral expenses, I will reimburse Mr. Tillman the full amount paid for monies he put out for the services for my child, as well as diagnostic fees for the paternity results. And I do so under the knowledge that should I renege on my responsibilities of said agreement, I as well as my attorney Jonathan Cantfield, will face criminal charges for deception with the intent to commit fraud, grand larceny as well as a liable suit for slander against Mr. Tillman and Nubina.*"

As she raised her eyes from the paper she was reading, a few of her crocodile tears streaked down her face, as several reporters started bombarding her with questions. As the TV droned on, Nube looked at me with a look I couldn't call. I don't know if she was happy…sad…confused…what?

"What Butter?" I asked her.

"Well," she started, "You don't think maybe you went a little hard?"

"Naw," I answered her cool and reserved, "Not after her antics instigated shit between me and my fam and then caused me to lose my true first born. Actually…I didn't go hard enough on her trifling ass."

I looked at Nube and she was quiet for a minute, then she picked up her glass of bubbly and raised it to me saying, "Here's to pressing on to a positive future, and may Jazmine and all the other Jazmine's of the world forever be removed from our lives."

"Here…here," I replied raising my own glass and clinking it with hers.

"Besides…she is such a bitch," she threw out.

I did a double take and just looked at her and smiled'

"Nube?" I questioned her…she know what I meant.

"What Murad," she answered me in a pseudo tone of surprise, "I know when to admit that my man is right…he knows how to call them…she's a bitch."

I laughed deeply as I raised my glass to clink hers again, "To the bitch then…and may she honor her contract."

"Yes…to the bitch," Nube answered clicking me back as we both began to laugh lightly. Sometimes you just gotta laugh to keep from crying. Now sooner than we had taken our next sip…the house phone…her cell…my cell…Blackberry…LG…all began a harmonious melody of ringtones. I looked at her…she looked at me and we both said, "Naaaahh."

Then she cuddled up under me and we just chilled and listened to the ringtones and ate chocolate covered strawberries and drank sparkling seltzer to our hearts content.

Chapter 62
Renovating

Nubina

I don't even have to tell you the next couple of days after Jazmine's announcement we were bombarded with phone calls. Family, friends as well as the media. Everyone was trying to get a first class scoop on the situation. Although Rod can be tough as nail, he's not into what he considers a bitch move like revealing Jazmine's attempt to impregnate herself with his sperm. Aside from the few people who were drawn into it like Dy and JT, we expressed her trifling deed to no one. Now, I can't speak for whomever else Jazz has told, or Key and his little girlfriend, but Murad and I both have more substantial issues on our minds to contend with. Any fallouts and opinions behind her actions will be on her alone. Time in the ensuing weeks passed quickly. I had a whirlwind of appearances in the third week of December, and then just one during the actual Christmas week. The Tillman family always gets together for Christmas Eve at Bryce's house from about 6:00 in the evening until. Murad was still feeling some kind of way from Thanksgiving and decided to pass on us going by there. I didn't press him with it because everyone's forgiveness and tolerance level is different. Instead we went by my mother's that day and stayed past dinner.

We spent our own quiet time at home that night and exchanged presents. We really didn't have much to exchange, cause for one...I am not into Christmas like that being that it is a religious based holiday. I do embrace the unity and ambiance of the joy and happiness it brings, as well as the family get togethers and the food. I know it's hypocritical of me, but I do have love for the season. The second reason our exchange is small is...what do you get for a man that already has everything he immediately wants or needs and provides the same for me? I mean actually...what else do we need. Rod spoils me terribly all year long, so Christmas is more so a day that we bestow gifts upon our families. However, this being our first year together, Rod gifted me with a custom made bracelet laced with intricate details and pink diamonds. It was the most exquisite piece of jewelry I have ever seen. It has the makings of ancient Egyptian royalty and I was truly impressed. At that point I had been reluctant to give him my gift as I thought it paled in comparison. Hopefully he will see the significance behind the gesture, or shall I say my attempted gesture. While Lonnie and I were out shopping in Baltimore, I came across a set of two baby ebony angels that were affixed to gold stems and had wings of 24kt gold. The bodies of the angels were composed of pure ivory and mother of pearl. The figures had been hand carved as well as hand painted. They were encased in a glass rectangle of about 6 by 8 and actually had a small pull chain to which you could turn on a light. It was almost like a mini curio. The wood was of fine dark cherry mahogany and not ply board. It ran me a couple of hundred, but money is not an issue. I thought it befitting at the time believing that he'd possibly lost two children. Now that we know he was not the father of Jazz's baby, I figured he'd still gone thru the pain, so the gift could still work. At any rate, I'd sat still holding my breath as he unwrapped it. I had taken the time to have a small plague engraved with an inscription that read... "The reality of you created the infinity they are."

Once he opened it and read it, he turned to me with tears in his eyes and said, "C'mere Nube." I went over to him and straddled him sitting on the couch. As he wrapped his arms around my waist, I reached over and kissed his lips.

"Murad," I started, "I know there is no replacing a child and you know how much I regret my actions; at the time I bought this, I thought there to be 2 that you'd lost. I saw this and thought that it somehow..."

"I love you Nube," he said interrupting me. I searched his face and saw nothing but total love and appreciation for what I'd given him, so I wrapped my arms around his neck and whispered in his ear, "I love you too Murad."

True to our word, we went and picked up Brianna and Tamira for the holiday break and spent that week entertaining them. We went to the movies, a Broadway play, a basketball game, shopping, the arcade, and Rod made appointments for us girls to get our hair and nails done. So by the end of the week... we were 3 beautiful chicks. On New Year's Eve, we got all dressed up and Murad took us out for dinner at an upscale restaurant in Weehawken over looking NYC. The view was magnificent and the girls enjoyed themselves immensely. We got back to the house around 11:00 p.m, just enough time to wind down and get our glasses ready with some Ginger ale for the girls, and some Cristal for us. Neither one of us are drinkers like that, but it was a present that had been given to us by Nuroscope, my record label and we figured this would be the appropriate time to utilize it. After all we were looking forward to new beginnings in the new year and trying things differently. Murad switched back and forth from 106 & Park Live for the girls, and Channel 7 from Times Square. We sat and watched, glasses poised in hand as the countdown came, till we got to 4, 3, 2, 1.... HAPPY NEW YEAR!!!!

"Happy New Year," I said leaning over and relinquishing a deep kiss.

"Happy New Year to you too Butter," he answered, "2009 is us Nube...2009 is us. I promise you that."

I looked at him, looking so at peace and so content and replied, "It's already us Murad...it's already us."

Murad

Things are running full steam ahead and Nube and I are scrambling to get things in order. We have an appearance at a Charter school up in Harlem, a spoken word engagement at a fund raiser for HIV, and we have to meet back with the book publishers. Not to mention that Poo dude finally emerged from his coma, so I had a few spontaneous meeting with Aaron in regard to that. All this and we gotta get ready to leave for Cali. The CSI episodes are being shot on location, so we'll be staying out there for the duration. It's already mid January, and we are due out there on the 19th. That works out fine since Nube has to get her 6 week check-up on the 15th. It's definitely been an experience being on this sexual hiatus, but it hasn't gone unappreciated. We've been connecting more and more mentally and besides…I'm a tad antsy about getting back into it right now. I have to admit, I'm still slightly salty about her choice in terminating my seed. I'm saying…what if she gets pregnant again. Or what…do I need to go back to wrapping shit up like I did before her? I don't know…how you start off with someone free stylin, then tell them you need to start protecting yourself? I mean I'm fucking talking bout Nube…my Butter…my heart. The kind of woman you wait all your life for to be able to splash up in. Damn…how did things get to here?

Well…I ain't gonna put too much energy into that right now, I have to wrap up the details on our transportation and accommodations. I'd had to get clearance from the probation department to go, as well as get the security issue waived. For one, substantial security would be provided on the set, and number two, CBS was not paying for any extra accommodations. Luckily for me, the initial hype of the case as all faded to black, and I was granted both requests from the County prosecutor's office. I probably have to admit that Aaron was probably right. Nube's popularity has grown, and her positive influences and civil efforts have not gone un-noticed. The DA ain't no fool either; any way he can get a positive plug in for any exposure riding on her status just might bring some light his way. But whatever the reason…we outta here.

Nubina

Wow…my good friend time has swept me up so fast and furious, I don't even know what day or week this is. All I know is we've been in Cali for 2 weeks now, and shooting and production is moving a little slow. I've shot 2 minor scenes so far, but I think there's been a snag or someone has a new angle they want to try out. In the meantime, Murad and I have been making our mark all up and down Rodeo Drive and Beverly Hills. We shopped a little, not too much; but we most definitely wined and dined. I told him he trynna get me fat so nobody would want me and he laughed.

“Butter please,” he said, “You don’t keep still long enough to get fat. Besides...a pound or two ain’t gonna hurt you. Actually it just might accentuate that one in a million baby ba-dunk you got going on.” Oh whatever...men always into body parts and what not. Yeah...I got a little bit of booty...nothing too overwhelming, but I guess he liking it. At any rate...I am so not my booty...if you wanna impress me deal with my mental. Cause I know I got quite a bit going on upstairs. Some cool and some a little eccentric, so yeah...you would be quite the champ to deal with me...LOL.

We went into over time on the set today, and it was like 9:00 p.m. before we got back in. The good thing about it was that we didn’t have to come in the next day. We had a light meal once we got in and then Rod had some business to handle. I took this time to take a bath, cause I sure could use the relaxation after today on the set. Shooting conflicts between directors, people spasing out and what not...geesh. Hill himself has been a gem, very patient and giving me helpful pointers. For the most part though, I’ve been holding my own. As I sit here soaking...what I’m thinking is that I really could use some attention, as in some loving. Rod and I haven’t got down that way since what...November or very early December? First I couldn’t, but since I’ve been medically cleared, we somehow have not gotten around to it. I mean plenty of hugs and kisses, but it’s about time for a sister to get thugged out in the bedroom. I don’t know though...he hasn’t really come at me like that. I wonder if he’s still hurting about the whole abortion thing or...wait...maybe the man just tired Tania...cut it out. He has other business ventures he has to maintain besides you. Cut him some slack. If you want some...go get it.

Murad

I’m glad I got that squared away I’m thinking as I hung up the phone. I traded some useless stocks, transferred some cash to open 2 new CD accounts, and sealed the final deal on some commercial real estate in Tennessee. Now I guess I can relax. We don’t have to go into the set tomorrow, so I’m thinking maybe we can hook up with my boy Stan while we out here. Our first year out on the road, I met Stan while Nube was doing a community event. He was a party promoter at the time that dibbled and dabbled in community affairs. He turned out to be real cool people, and we touch bases every now and again. I figured getting out with some real people could keep shit grounded while we out here in this Hollywood bullshit. I picked up the remote to flip on the TV when Nube came in the room. She was looking heavenly in this sexy ass bedroom set that I'd bought her. The robe was more than sheer, and the lingerie underneath was speaking all kinds of language to me. But even with all that going on...something, somewhere in the back of my mind was blocking. She came over to me and crawled up into my lap like she always does.

"Murad," she started, "We haven't in a minute, and I do think I'm feeling some kind of way." She leaned over and kissed me to which I responded.

"I mean...I need you to do what you do...cause I'm ready to hear myself calling your name Rod. Baby...I wanna be calling your name."

Sheeiiit...I wanna hear you call my name too; I'm thinking as I return the kisses and my hands start to wander all over them curves. I'd untied the sash on the robe and had my hands on her breast, massaging, teasing. And just as I was about to latch my lips onto one of her perfect nipples, the little Devil on my left shoulder said, "Yo...think about it Rod...she might get pregnant again...how you all gonna handle that situation this time around? It ain't been but a little over 6 weeks" I stopped and looked up at her beautiful face, eyes all steamy and ready. Damn...I wanna go there with her, sweet stroking and swapping juices all night long...but he right. I don't have no condoms, and if I did...how would I initiate my sudden need to use them with her now?

"Murad," she whispered, so hot and sexy that it brought me back to the here and now on the couch. Ole boy started stretching and growing in my pants, and I couldn't contain him if I wanted to...yet...I couldn't move forward with getting into Nube tonight. I was still on the fence about how I wanted to approach this. I mean...I never thought that I'd come up against this, truly thought I could get past it, but right now, I'm not willing to take any risks. I ceased the breasts squeezes and just hugged her up in my arms.

"Nube," I began my lame excuse, "I'm really kind of tired. I don't think I'm on board for the ride tonight." I felt her body go cold on me and the atmosphere in the room change immediately. She pulled back so that she could read my face and at that given second I could have died. I saw the hurt and humility so pronounced that I wanted to snatch my words back, but I also saw in her eyes that it was too late for that as well.

"Oh," she answered, her voice laced in personal pain, "Well I guess…I'll…you know…leave you to yourself…respect your space. It's kinda been a long day anyway, I'm just gonna go in here and go to bed. Nite Rod."

Before I could I think of something to say and make it right, she was up off my lap and on her way to the bedroom. I sat on the couch feeling like shit when the angel on my right shoulder said, "Now look what the fuck you done did…well I hope ya' ass is satisfied!!"

Nubina

I have never been so embarrassed in all my life. Here I am thinking I'm turning him on, and he's not even interested. Damn…I know this has everything to do with the baby. I mean we talked about it, and he claims he forgives me but…I don't think so. He don't…he can't…and I guess I can't really blame him. I made a bad choice and his resentment of my choice needs time to resolve itself. But okay…I'm hurting too. All this time we've been talking and he didn't feel like he could come to me and tell me he's feeling some kind of way about sex? Wow…I'm so disappointed…so hurt. Murad knows that our sexual connection means everything to me. How could he not think it would not come up sooner or later? Wow…what can I say. I guess I have to wait for time to intervene on this one…cause I doubt that I'll be the one to initiate sex again. Him rejecting me like that hurt like all else. And I'm not trying to feel that from him again…ever.

I can't believe that I just hurt Nube again with my actions. I mean...I didn't mean to hurt her feelings; I'm just not solid on where my mind is in regard to sex. I mean...6 weeks is no time for the shit to happen again, and I'm not ready to revisit no heavy decisions. And on the real that would kinda be like a slap in the face, cause if you gonna go and get yourself knocked up again in 6 weeks, you could have kept the first child. Awww...damn...I dunno. Fuck it...let me call Stan and see if he available to hook-up tomorrow. I pulled out my Blackberry and dialed him up. We talked for a good 45 before we hung up with plans to meet up tomorrow. Now I actually was tired, and decided to go on and get myself ready for bed. Maybe she'll be sleep and I can handle shit in the morning. I went in the bathroom and took an extra long shower, letting the hot water beat down on the tense muscles in my neck. I came out and went in the room to get dressed for bed. I sat down on the edge of the bed and looked over to check if she was sleep.

Well okay...she appears to be sleep. Good...I got time before I have to deal with this. I oiled up, put on my boxers and slid into bed. I leaned over for one last check and asked, "Butter...you sleep?" She laid there looking so perfect, so peaceful, and so damn beautiful, but she didn't answer me, I leaned over and gave her a kiss, "Love you Nube."

I rolled over and turned off the light as I tried to gain some analytical control of my emotional bearings. I knew that I had to fix this unexplained gap between us, and keep our shit on track. I also knew that I needed to do it right away, cause I knew in my heart that she was not sleep...just like I could feel in my soul the tears that I couldn't see. The ones that were rolling down her face ...as we lay there in the dark.

Chapter 63
Reconstruction

Nubina

I got up early and went to the kitchen to find something to fix for breakfast. I definitely was in need of some kind of comfort food, so I decided to try my hands at some Vanilla Pecan pancakes. I mixed up the batter, added the nuts and flavoring and started pouring them on the griddle. I don't eat sausage, but I pan broiled some turkey sausage for Murad to go with his pancakes. I put his food up on a plate and set it in the microwave while I sat and ate my food. As I chewed, I let my mind wander to all the possibilities as to why he brushed me off last night when he know we infamous in the bedroom. I'm missing it so...I'm missing him and I know he missing me regardless to what he says. I don't believe he didn't talk to me about it. I think today, he and I need to get this here straight. I'm thinking that... The phone to the suite rang suddenly putting my thoughts aside.

"Hello," I answered.

"Good morning Nubina," I heard the smooth sound of Hill's voice, "How are you this morning?"

"I'm good Hill...I'm good. What's up?"

"Listen...I know that today's a free day, but I was calling to see if you and Murad are available to roll with me today to check out one of my mentoring programs, at the Central Los Angeles Boys Club? I know that it's kind of last minute, but I thought I'd give you guys a little insight into one of my projects, and maybe possibly in the future, you can guest spotlight one for me?"

"Wow," I responded, "That sounds cool...cool. I would love to see you in action Hill...you know...see how you roll with yours." We both laughed, "But yeah, of course I'm interested. You can always count on me to assist in promoting the elevation of our youth. As far as I know we don't have any plans, so when Murad wakes up I'll fill him in."

“Okay then…cool Ms. Lady” he came back with.

“Well what time are we talking Hill?” I asked.

“I guess we should head out around 10:30. Is that too early?” he inquired. I turned to look at the clock. It read 9:20.

“I guess we can be ready by then,” I stated, “So where you wanna meet up?”

“Ah…no,” he said, “You guys are my guest. I did the invite…so I’ll come there and pick you up.”

“Well great,” I replied, “We’ll be ready. I’ll see you then. OK…bye.” Well that will work. A day we can be doing something constructive rather than out spending money or feeding our faces. I put the phone back on the base and got up to put my plate in the sink just as Rod walked into the kitchen.

“Hey Butter,” he said coming up embracing me from behind as I stood at the sink. He placed a tender kiss to the side of my neck and nuzzled there for a minute before asking, “Who was that on the phone?” This nukka here…acting like it ain’t no thing. My feelings are still hurt from last night…but I played it off.

“That was Hill,” I told him, “He’s gonna be here at 10:30 to pick us up and take us by one of his mentoring programs for the day. So you need to go head and eat, so we can be dressed and ready when he gets here. I left you a plate in the microwave.”

“Whoa…hold up,” he broke out with, backing up off of me. I turned around to face him and instantly felt some kind of way as his gorgeous face and dominant physique taunted me with the fact that he had me on knock-off, “He called up here…with some plans? Well…he should’ve ran that by me first cause we already got plans…we going out to my boy Stan’s house. Him and his wife are already expecting us to stop by and chill with them.”

“Oh is that right…and just when did you decide that?” I threw at him, “Oh…oh…wait…I know. It was probably around the same time you decided you didn’t want to be intimate with me anymore.”

Awww shit...I knew this was coming. "Look Nube...baby. I'm sorry about last night," I told her, "I've been having some thoughts about sex and us...and the birth control thing and I just haven't pinpointed where I'm at with all that."

She looked at me, kinda giving me that bobble head nod and said, "Sooo...you figured the best way to approach me with that was to wait until I was all hot in the ass and then reject me once I come checking for you?"

"Look Nube," I started, "You right...I was wrong. I should have told you how I was feeling so we could discuss what we wanna do in the future in regard to sex and preventing unwanted pregnancies." Did I just say that...was that the right thing to say...Cause something inside me said NOT... and looking at her face told me the same thing.

"Unwanted pregnancies? Wow Murad...wow. So you really didn't want the baby...did you?"

Aight see...now shit getting out of control. She done went and took that somewhere it don't need to be. Let me handle this...now.

"Nube...baby...nix the nonsense," I told her firmly, "Let's get this shit back in prospective right now. I was outta my fucking mind for 3 whole days when you dropped that shit on me that you got rid of my child...So **don't** come at me with that you talking right there. I would give **all** that I fucking got to push shit back to 2 months ago, where I would have paid attention to your moods, you being tired, your breasts all extra. I would have paid attention Nube to your upset stomach episodes, your low tolerance and you taking time off from appearances. And I would have most definitely listened to you a little more closely that night before...and saved my damn child. So don't Butter...don't come at me with that. Cause that shit you talking ain't got a leg to stand on." She stood there for a minute, and I could tell that she was stunned; her feelings were hurt behind what I just said. Oh well...that's what the fuck it is...and I mean that. She gonna have to deal with it.

"Murad," she finally said, "It's obvious that you still have some resentment towards me in regard to my mistake, and I guess you haven't fully dealt with it yet, so you know what? I'm gonna go on and spend the day with Hill...I think some time apart might do us something. So you go on and do your thing with...uh...Stan is it? And I'll just see you when I get back in."

"Nube," I said sharply, "They're expecting to see us **both** today."

She threw me off a lip nod and came right back, "And **so** is Hill."

We both stood there silent, defiant and mean-mugging. Was this a true fight, or were we avoiding the real shit that we needed to deal with? And where the fuck she get off throwing me a lip nod? That's what I do. After a few seconds of a stare down, she turned to leave the room and said, "Don't forget your breakfast in the microwave Sire. I made it especially for you." I watched as she retreated to the bedroom without hesitation. Fuck...There she go getting under my skin!! I wanna be mad at her...but I can't...I can't. I wanted to spend time with her today, so that I can explain what I've been feeling; but now she up and running with dude. How'd he get the damn number to the suite anyway? When I find out what, how and who slipped him the number... I'm knocking some fucking heads around. Shit...

Nubina

Despite the negative start to the day, it turned out to be one of the best I'd had in a long time. Hill came to pick me up right on time, and I was downstairs waiting. When he questioned me on Murad's whereabouts, I told him that some last minute business came up that was going to tie him up for the day. He said that he'd really wanted Murad to see the program as well, just in case he had any questions that he needed to consider as my manager. I assured him that I would fill him in, and maybe we would be able to check the program out again before we head back to the East coast. We spent the day speaking with the kids, Hill himself doing a lecture, and then playing board games, eating lunch and ended off with some of the kids performing some spoken word. I got so into it, and enjoyed myself so much that I hardly noticed that Murad had not called me not once today. Yeah...I hardly noticed it at all.

Murad

I had to do a damn solo today out to Stan's crib. When he asked me why Nube didn't come, I told him that she and Hill had some venture that had come up at the last minute, and she sends her apologies. His wife had been really looking forward to meeting Nube and was truly disappointed she didn't come. I told them that maybe we would get the chance to get back out there before we head home. We sat and chatted about this and that, touched on some things going on in the entertainment industry. He brought up some interesting ideas and I was hoping that I could retain it all, cause my mind was hopelessly preoccupied. It kept reflecting back to the fact that Nube was out by herself with her on screen love interest, while I was out here digging on Stan's boss family life with wifey and kids...all by myself. Being that I couldn't keep up the positive mood, I excused myself early and went on back to the suite.

As I entered the lobby, the desk clerk presented me with a manila package that had been delivered from the network. I'm sure it's some script changes, or scene revisions for Nube to review. I'll take a look once I get upstairs. Right now, I just wanna stretch out and put my feet up...settle my thoughts. Once I let myself into the suite, I went to the fridge and grabbed a bottle of Snapple, then plopped myself down on the couch. I picked up the remote and hit the TV...wasn't really interested in watching...just filling the void of Nube not being here. Let me see, it's 4:20, maybe I should hit her up, see how things going. I'm feeling some kinda way, and I'm damn sure missing her. She don't know...I would love to get back into it...I mean I live for sexing her, but...we do have to consider the possibility of pregnancy again. I guess I need to man up...apologize to her and sit us both down and have a discussion. It ain't gonna do nobody any good if we just... My cell phone buzzed on my hip, startling me. I unclipped it and checked...Lonnie.

"Yo...Lonz...what it do bruh?" I greeted him.

"Yo Chief...whas going on? How Cali treating you?"

"Man...Cali is Cali. Work...play and then some." I answered,

"Whas' kicking back home?"

"Man the same ole'...same ole," he responded, "Everybody cool, shop going strong...just Brick been on some kinda bull lately. I don't know whas' up wit him. Nigga act like somebody stole his fucking heart...but he ain't even into nobody right now. Well nobody that I know of."

"Yeah well," I started, "That's Brick and his shit. I still ain't got nothing for him. He went straight greasy on Nube."

"I can't blame you on that one Rod...I don't know where his head was that night," he offered, "But yeah...sound kinda quiet round there. Where my little sis at anyway?"

"Ya little sis ain't here. She out spending the day with her co-star," I told him.

"Who...Hill?" he asked in surprise.

"Yeah...Hill," I stated in a salty tone.

"Well why you not with her?" he inquired, "How'd that shit pop-off?"

"Maann...Lonz," I began to explain, "Me and Nube got into it a little bit and then our communication got crossed up...so...she wind up spending the day with ole' boy, and I went to check out my man Stan." The line was quiet for just a second too long, and I knew that something wasn't sitting right with Lonnie.

I was just about to ask him what the problem was when he asked, "So Rod...you doing right by Princess... feel me?"

"Aww come on Lonz," I replied, "I ain't even on no shit like that no more. I'm at the end of the fucking road on this one. I got big plans for Nube...that's my future. I ain't trynna lose her over nothing or nobody."

"Aight...cool," he came back with, relief in his voice, "I guess just sit her down and talk to her. You know you can get with Nube on anything. She not afraid to see shit for what it is."

"Yeah, that was my original plan," I told him, "Till dude snatched her up and spirited her away."

"Well I don't have to tell you to handle that as soon as she gets back. It ain't good to let things set to where they get out of control," he said.

"You ain't said nothing bruh," I replied, "I'm on it as soon as."

Lonnie and I peeled off conversation for another 20 minutes before we hung up. I checked the time and saw that it was well after 5:00 pm. Damn...I wonder how long he gonna keep her out...they do have to report back to the set tomorrow. He need to be bringing her back here. As I scrolled my phone and hit her cell number, I picked up the manila folder to check out what the changes would be. I listened as the phone was on it's 3rd ring, while my eyes slid down the first page. I came to the bottom which had an indication of the new change highlighted which read "Love scene upgraded to a bedroom scene: Assimilate nudity." What the fuck?? I ended the call just as I heard Nube's voice mail come on. What the...when the hell was this decided? I immediately hit Warren's number. He was the network liaison that was assigned to handle issues, concerns or correspondence in regard to production and shooting of the show.

"Hello," he answered after the 2nd ring.

"Yeah Warren...this is Murad Tillman. I just reviewed the script change, and I need to know when was this decided...and by whom," I pushed on him directly.

"Hey Murad," he responded, "I was expecting your call. Yeah...this came down last night...like 10 pm. Being that it was late, I didn't call last night, then today I got turned around. As soon as I saw your number, it him me that yeah...you'd be reaching out."

"So what gives? How did it become necessary to include a nude love scene?" I asked him.

"Man, I don't know," he replied, "The word is it was a last minute decision by someone up top. They claim the network put out a lot of money, so they wanted to make sure that the scene would be so captivating to the audience, that we would get a huge return audience for the following weeks and make the ratings soar. So yeah...a steamy bedroom scene would most definitely do it. Especially between those two. The network hasn't had such a hot looking couple on TV since like...when? Never as far as I know and...Oh...Hey man...I'm sorry," he broke out with, "I forgot that you're more than her manager."

"Hmm..." I uttered, not sure of how I wanted to respond. "Well tell me this," I started, "Wouldn't a significant change such as this be run by the person holding the part, as well as her manager first?"

"Sometimes they are," he answered, "And sometimes they are not. With most actors being members of SAG, most of their requirements or preferences are already in their profile and additional requests are presented to their agent. In Nubina's case, acting is not her tender, she's just guest spotting, so as with most guest spots, the network is running with the current level of popularity and the sense that the person will be grateful for the additional exposure to their career."

"Well I don't have no problem letting you know Warren...this right her don't sit good with me at all," I stated.

"I understand...I totally understand," he responded, "But I can assure you that it will be done tastefully. She will have on a gauze like mesh tape that will cover her breast area, and I believe a low cut bikini or thong for the bottom. The scenes will be shot to reflect the exposed skin only, after all this is still prime time TV. We only wanna give the impression of nudity...we're not allowed to shoot nude scenes."

"Yeah well...having her half naked in front of the whole set is not feeling like any kind of consolation to me," I told him.

"So Murad," he started, "What is it that you trying to tell me? Will Nubina be able to do this or not? It would not be a favorable move on her part to pull out at this point. If she wants to continue to do any acting, I would..."

"You can stop your campaign right there Warren," I interrupted, "Let's me and you get a clear understanding on this. Nubina does not have to do **anything**. She does not have to indulge in any program, TV show or movie to endorse her own popularity. She participates in these projects once she's been sought out and only if she feels it's of a positive nature. Not today...nor any day is she looking to solidify her roots in the acting profession. Trust me, this is just extra, and I do mean extra curricular activity that she does out of pure contention."

"Murad...Murad," he interceded, "I hear you, I hear you on all that you're saying. I however don't know what else I can say. It would not be a good thing to pull out now."

"Listen," I put to him, "In the interest of operating on a level of professionalism, I am more than prepared to review the change with her as my client, and get her feedback on it. I can guarantee you that the decision will be hers alone to make. I back and support her on whatever she decides to do. But know and understand this...anyway she does not want to expose herself and do this scene...we out on the deal. Consequences will be handled on our part accordingly."

"Wow," he came back with, "Okay...I appreciate your honesty. Well...the call for Nubina to the set tomorrow is not until 1 p.m., so that does buy us some time. I would appreciate if you could let me know if it's a go by at least 10:00 am...you know give me some time to keep my head off the chopping block so to speak."

"No problem Warren," I gave back, "No problem. I will discuss this with her and let you know the outcome first thing in the morning."

"Great," he responded, "I'll be looking forward to your call in the morning,"

"No doubt...no doubt. First thing." I responded.

"Talk to you then," he signed off.

"Hey Warren," I called out, thinking of something in the back of my mind.

"Yeah?" he asked.

"Shouldn't there be an executive signoff on the change or at least the request for the change," I inquired.

"Yeah...hold on," he told me, the sound of pages flipping in the background, "Okay...let me see. Here it is. Uh...it looks like Ivan Jabowitz."

Chapter 64
Completely Restored

Nubina

"Thank you Hill. Thank you for a wonderful day." We were headed back to the hotel suite after having grabbed some dinner. We ate at a cute little neighborhood place that specialized in healthy soul food. Have you ever? Only in Cali.

"No...Thank you," he stated, "The pleasure was all mine. Do you know how jealous my boy Carson's gonna be? He absolutely loves your spoken word, and even has a couple of your CD's. When I let him know that I actually spent the whole day with you...man...he gonna flip."

We both laughed it off as I asked, "Well why didn't you call and invite him to join us?"

"Ehh...he had to work today. Knowing him...if I had called him, he would've called out sick or something."

We both laughed again, "Oh...for real...he's into me like that?" I asked.

"Yeah, my man is way gone on you lady," he replied.

"Well that's good to know," I told him, "You tell him I said the next CD is on me. I really do appreciate his support."

"I will most definitely let him know," he replied as we pulled up into the circular driveway of the hotel.

"Guess I better go in and get settled so we can get back on the grind tomorrow," I presented, "And once again...thank you for a fantastic day. Just the right kind of stress buster I needed."

"Yeah, working on the set can be a little hectic at times," he answered, "but it's all good. You doing fine...these episodes are gonna raise the roof, I'm sure,"

"Well I hope so," I told him, "I would really hate to come on the show and compromise your fame with my lack of experience."

"Alright now Nubina," he replied, "Let's not even go there. You are a refreshing compliment to my rhetorical position on the show. I've been doing it so long its' become like tying my shoes.

Getting into a new groove on the set with you is a challenge. So I am the one who's grateful."

"Well...thank you Hill," I said opening the door, and stepping out of the car, "I can't wait to see our finished product aired...that's what it will take for me to be satisfied. Anyway...see you tomorrow...and we'll get back to the drawing board."

"Okay Ms. Lady...I'll see you tomorrow," he replied, "Tell Murad, I wanna get up with him real soon. Most definitely before you all leave town."

"Sure thing," I responded, "Will do...good night."

He pulled off waving, and I waved back before turning to go into the lobby. I wonder if he's even back yet I thought as I walked to the elevators, and I sure hope he's in a better mood. I feel like sharing the events of my day. I stepped off the elevator on our floor, and walked the hall to our room. I slid the card key thru the door and pushed on the handle once the green light flashed. I opened the door to the suite to find an empty living room. I walked in and set my bag down on the couch.

"Rod," I called out as my eyes swept over a manila envelope with the network logo, "I'm back." I picked up the envelope and slid out the contents. I guess this is a script change, and proceeded to read down the page. Love scene...upgraded to bedroom scene. Assimilate nudity. What??? I dropped down on the couch with my mouth open, just as Murad stepped in from the back. "Rod?" I asked, my mouth still hanging open.

"Hey Butter," he said, "So...you got a look at the new changes?" He came on in the room and took a seat in the chair.

"Murad," I uttered confused, "Nude bedroom scene? When did they come up with this...why is that necessary? I don't know Rod...I don't know. I didn't sign up for this. I respect Hill and his position on the show, but I can't work nude in front of him...cause we...well we... we like fellow activists in our community causes. How we gonna be naked together on TV? And forget about him seeing me naked, I don't wanna see him naked...I mean he's Hill Harper! I just saw him lecture young boys on the importance of male responsibilities...I can't look at him like that. I don't know Rod...and then...OMG...all the rest of the set will be present. Oh...Rod...I don't know...I just don't know if I can...."

"Nube," he voiced firmly. I stopped...took a breath. "C'mere," he said.

Murad

I watched as she got up from the couch and walked over to where I was, then assumed her natural position up in my lap.

"Listen," I told her taking her chin into my hand, "I've already spoken to Warren and let him know that any way that you are not comfortable with this, then we pulling out. If you ain't feeling this kind of scene, then so be it...you don't have to do it."

"Sheeesh..." she said taking a deep breath, "I don't know Rod. I mean I want to be responsible and mature and rise to the challenge and all but...naked?"

I did tell Warren that I'd discuss this with her on a professional level, so I let her know, "Nube...you won't really be nude. There is a flesh colored gauzed tape that covers the front of you and your breasts, and you will be wearing bikinis or a thong...your choice. They are only allowed to shoot the exposed skin, I guess your bare back, your thighs ...you know...like that. I'm assuming it's like the scenes you may see on the daily soap operas...you'll be wrapped in the sheets. So...it's totally up to you Butter." She looked at me, and I could see the confusion and the million in one questions on her face.

"Rod," she started, "What about you...I mean how you feeling about me doing a love scene?" I took a deep breath and decided to be nothing but honest.

"Nube, you know that I ain't feeling no man touching you...acting or not, but...this is business and I can handle it, as long as the dude is being respectful and honoring this as a job and nothing more. I have no choice but to understand that it's part of the territory."

"Murad, I don't know...I mean, I'm a big girl and all. It's just that...it will be awkward for me to interact with Hill like that. I mean kissing him, hugging him and the holding hands scenes are fine. But rolling around in the sheets...that kind of puts an incestual flava to it. He don't even think of me like that."

There she go, always selling herself short on the impact she has on men. I mean, I ain't got nothing against Hill...matter a fact...I don't think he would try to come at her like that either under normal circumstances, but...rolling around in the bed emulating sex with Nube...little man better hope he got a tremendous amount of self control, otherwise his shit gonna get real tight. Damn...now I'm bout to get a queasy stomach thinking bout this shit.

"Nube," I told her, "Bring it down a notch...it's not something you have to decide right now. We have until 10: 00 am to let Warren know our decision, so...no need to stress yourself...you can sleep on it." "I guess," she replied slowly. I could tell that mind of hers was still going.

"Well," she started, "On a whole nother note...let me tell you about my day. We started out at...." As she talked, my mind drifted off to our true matter at hand. Here it is, we ain't been handling our own bedroom issues, and now she gonna be rocking shit with Hill on screen. Damn...

Nubina

I'm laying here in bed, just thinking up a storm. I wonder if I can pull this one off. I mean...if this was anyone else but Hill. Okay...now what am I saying. I would have a problem doing this with anybody that I admire and respect. It kinda changes the way you view them. Hmm....I don't know. On the other hand, I wouldn't want to disappoint Hill and cause any kind of disruptions to the show on his part. He is the one that threw my name into the ring when they began scouting for a love interest for his character. Damn...I guess I can pull it together and do this. I don't know...Rod claims he's cool with it, as long as I'm comfortable. But I know him...I know him. This is going to be a mighty big pill for him to swallow. In fact...this is a choker.

Wow…just laying here next to Nube…a thousand and one things going thru my mind. I know how she is…she don't want to pull out on this cause she doesn't want to feel unaccomplished. I mean…I can understand…when you start something you don't want to come off as flaky and not finish whatever you're doing. But this here is huge…it's a whole nother level she ain't ever been on. I know that she wants to take on the challenge of it all…but perhaps this one is just out of her league. Well whatever she decides, I guess I'll be a man of my word and stick by her choice. But maaannn….listen…if it were up to me…she ain't gotta do nothing….and we'd be packing up our shit right now. I could feel that she wasn't sleep, just as I could feel that her mind was wandering around just like mine.

"Nube," I simply stated. She understood and she came scooting up under me throwing her leg over my thigh. Aight…that felt right…an instant Quaalude effect. Now maybe we can both go on to sleep.

"Murad," she spoke softly her voice implicating her need for reassurance.

"I'll be right there Butter…I'll be right there the whole time."

She gave me a sweet kiss on the side of my chest, squeezed me…hugged me…then went off to sleep.

I had gotten in touch with Warren at 10:00 o'clock that morning, so here we are 12:00 noon at the set a little early. Nube wanted to review with the production and directorial staff as to the exact process on this kind of scene. I have to admit that she is keeping it together so far. Well…at least she is trying, cause I know her…I can sense her underlying tension. I was talking some things over with Warren when I heard Hill come onto the set. I watched as he walked up to Nube and a group of staff and gave her a quick hug. She in turn hugged him back, and I guess he asked her of my whereabouts, because she turned and pointed over in my direction. He grabbed her by the hand and they both proceeded to my location.

"Murad," he said as he approached me giving off daps, "Listen…I just got wind of this change to the script, and I just want you to know that I will only do this on the condition that the two of you are both okay with it."

"Yo Hill…good looking…I appreciate that; but this here is Nube's call," I told him.

"We talked Hill," Nube said indicating she and I with a sweeping hand gesture, "It's not the most comfortable situation we've ever been in, but I'm going to do my best…no… we are both gonna operate as the professionals that we are."

"Listen Ms. Lady," he told her, "You don't have to do anything that you are uncomfortable with."

"What's life without experiences Hill?" she threw back at him, "How we gonna preach to the kids to take chances and meet adversity head on, and then back out when we get encountered with one of life's challenges? We're both respectable people Hill, I think we can make this work."

"Well okay Nubina," he came back with, "We most certainly can give it a try. I'm not sure the reason for such a drastic change, I feel like the scenes were going fine just as they are…but hey…the powers that be…their call. Now you sure you okay with this Ms. Lady?"

"As ready as I'm ever going to be for something that I've never done before," she answered him lightly laughing.

"Well, alright, I'm going to get prepared. I'll see you on the set," he told her. "Murad," he said turning to me, "I'll check you later."

I threw him a head nod in response. As he walked off to get ready, I looked at Nube and gave her that head twist she know, and she answered, "Well…we bout to see." She turned and left to go get prepped.

Nubina

OMG…I'm here, we're here…in bed, in the middle of the set. Lights…camera…action, and my stomach is butterfly city. The attire wasn't so bad; Rod was right... a very heavy adhesive flesh colored gauze was covering my frontal like wallpaper, and I chose for a very low cut bikini bottom, as opposed to a thong so that all of my bottom was not exposed. Hill was donning a pair of skimpy men's bikinis pulled slightly below the waistline to give that bare back effect. We were wrapped up in the sheets, with me kinda kneeling in his lap, facing him. As the director called out the cue, Hill started with his lines, and I somehow followed suit. Then the touching came...at first it was okay, but when he reached around to my backside ...I froze. I heard Hill call me by my stage name...

"Phoebe...Phoebe...baby...I been waiting for someone like you all my life...I need you."

I tried frantically to remember my lines, but all that kept running thru my mind was how long it's been since Murad has touched me, and here this man...and good friend of mine is groping on my ass.

I jumped and stuttered out, *"Sh..Sheldon,...."* And when the rest of my lines failed to follow the director yelled, "Cut."

"Aww damn...I'm sorry...I'm sorry Hill," I started explaining, "I just got a little mentally off balance. I'm so sorry Josh. Let's start again."

"Alright," Josh the director stated, "Let's take it from the top. In 3..2..1"

"Phoebe..Phoebe...baby...I been waiting for someone like you all my life...I need you." Hill started out again

"Sheldon...I need that to be the real you talking...the on point Sheldon. Not the...the.."

I froze mid sentence as his caresses sent waves of confusion over me. The energy was twisted. I've been on a sexual sabbatical so to speak, and can't get that inner me to cooperate. She knows this ain't the spirit that shadows her sexually...and she's blocking.

"Cut," I heard Josh call out again.

"Nubina," Hill said to me cupping me blow the chin turning me to face him, "Whas' up Lady...Is it too much for you...are you uncomfortable? Cause we can stop."

"No...no," I stammered, "I don't want to do that."

"Nubina," Josh came over to the bed, "Just relax...relax. It's your first time. Look...why don't we do this. Let's just try and run thru the whole scene…keep going and we can review it later and edit what we have to."

"He's right," Hill added, "For a first timer, it's best to do a dry run, you know, like a practice run and get the willies out of your system."

"Okay…okay," I answered nervously looking around for Murad. I saw him over at the production desk, his face kinda tight. I figured I'd better get a grip and get some of this right. Here it is, my man gotta watch something he really don't want me to participate in, and I got the nerve to be bombing. "Alright," I spoke up, "A practice run…let's try it."

"Okay…take it from the top," Josh announced retreating to his chair. "In 3 …2…1"

"Phoebe…Phoebe…" I heard Hill start off, and mentally kept track of my lines. I was able to pull thru the whole scene without missing a line…but my performance…it was flat. I was stiff, rehearsed and rigid, and I know it showed. I can't let Hill down like this…I just can't. Well tomorrow is another day…I've got to do better…gots to do better!!

Murad

Damn…it took everything in me not to get up and rescue Nube from her agony. I watched her struggle to deliver in her usual fashion…but it wasn't happening…she was crashing. Hill was trying to give her some pointers, and I guess she was trying to abide by them, but her self-consciousness must have gotten the best of her. They did 3 takes over and then one final wrap that they would consider for editing, with the possibility of a do over tomorrow. Once they disengaged the scene and Nube was released, I walked over to the taping area.

"Murad," she said…one word…one tone.

"Don't sweat it Nube," I told her, "Let's break outta here and regroup for tomorrow."

"Fine," she answered, "I'm just gonna go and get changed. I'll meet you out front."

She turned and went back to the dressing room, while I headed outside. Man…shit just ain't good like this. Nube all twisted and out of sync. I guess tomorrow is another day, she can get back at it then. I waited another 15 minutes before Nube came out, and I just took her by the hand and walked to the parking lot. We acknowledged a few greetings along the way, then just kept it moving. I placed her in the car and closed the door, then climbed in on my side. I know her mind was all over the place…so I just waited for…

"Rod," she started, "What the hell was that…what was I doing? I kept forgetting my lines…I couldn't concentrate…what? I mean…I did finally remember them all, but then I was all nervous and so not myself Rod. What…what is it? Hmm…maybe I might need to do it all again tomorrow…you know start from the beginning. I mean, I could go to bed early so that I can be well rested and ready to go. Rod…what you think?"

Wow…she finally took a break, "I don't know Nube," I responded. I didn't want her to think that I'm unconcerned, just don't want to overwhelm her confusion with my opinion. "Listen," I told her, "When we get back, maybe you can go get comfortable, and I'll see to our appetites. I need you to just relax for the rest of the evening."

"Well I'll tell you what," she started, "That sounds like the best plan I heard all day. I'm all sticky from all that tape…and that shit hurt when they gotta rip it off. And I think I'm gonna tell them to tone down on the make-up too. I don't think that I'm caring for all that stuff on my skin. But yeah Rod…back to the scenes. I know I could've been better…I know that we're gonna have to do it again. And I know…."

I let the rest of what she said breeze over my head as we headed back to the suite. There are times when I just let Nube babble…and this happened to be one of those times. I know that the love scene has got her thrown and she needs to release her nervous tension. Besides…I had my own babble going on up in my head. I mean…I dealt with it, but…dude's hands on her ass…touching feeling…that shit kept rewinding in my head in fucking hi-def. Things ain't sitting right with me on this. She outta sorts…I'm outta sorts. Things need to get back like right…and soon.

Once we got upstairs, Nube retreated to the bathroom for a shower while I went online to look up some local cuisine. I found a Tex-Mex place that boasted fresh organic ingredients and ordered us some chicken, fish and veggie tacos with yellow rice and extra trimmings. I got us some of the organic sweet tea and an order of organic non-alcoholic Pina Coladas. I tell you...they got everything out here in Cali. Once the order was in, I continued to handle other business on the laptop while Nube was in the shower. Hmmm...seems like she was taking an extra long time. I suppose she really needed to unwind. This acting and I guess this particular scene thing has really got her going. I don't know, I sure hope that she shakes it soon cause...

"Rod," she cut into my thoughts walking in the room wrapped in nothing but a towel, "I'm thinking I could use a rub down with some oil."

As she walked into the room holding the bottle...something inside me clicked. I don't know if it was the simple beauty of her hair pulled up in an updo, or the taunting moves in the way she walked wearing nothing but that towel but...the little devil on my left shoulder whispered, "Daaaayyyuumm...bruh...you let dude be all on that?"

I watched her as she came over to me, "Rod," she said extending the bottle towards me, "Please?"

I stood up from the chair, took the bottle from her, wrapped her up in my arms and started kissing her forehead. I proceeded to continue with the kisses to her checks, her nose, and then her lips.

"Rod...I," she started, but I squashed that with my lips. I took the bottle and tossed it as I backed her up against the wall continuing to kiss her, leaving the lips and trailing down the neck. She started to wiggle and moan, so I proceeded to the collar bone, peeling the towel away and slowly made my way down to the breast. Once I made contact...she started giving me her sing-song moans that sounded like a crossover single gone platinum. I showed her twins equal attention before I positioned myself on my knees making my way down to her stomach. On the way down and I tenderly kissed the smooth skin of her stomach giving her belly button a couple of teasing flicks of my tongue before I headed on to the V-spot. Once I was eye to eye with the V, I kissed it on the lips like a long lost relative, then French kissed the folds like I was in love and then…aahhh…inside to the honeycomb. I licked, sucked, teased and began to excite my own self as Nube began to have a sexual fit.

As it started to get good, her movements began to escalate, so she threw her left leg over my shoulder to keep her balance as I grabbed a hold of her by both her cheeks. I don't know what had come over me when she walked in from the bathroom. Somehow I had the urge to feel that body under me immediately, and I needed to watch it react to the taste test I was implementing with my tongue. I continued to give greetings to the V and show love to where I've been gone from way too long, while Nube continued to verbally express her extreme pleasure. One thing I know for sure…I ain't been gone that long that I can't recognize when my baby is ready. So just as she was about to get to "there," I put one hand under her butt and the other at her waist and slid her off her feet up the length of the wall. She instinctively threw the right leg up on my other shoulder as gravity forced her to slope her body at an angle, bringing her shoulder blades to rest against the wall for support.

So with the little devil on my left shoulder egging me on, "Yeah Rod…yeah boy…do it"…and the little angel on my right shoulder saying, "Thas' whas up…thas' whas up"….nothing could top the satisfaction my ego felt as I listened to the sound of my name spilling from her sexy ass lips, rebounding around the 4 corners of the ceiling… as I licked, nibbled and orgasmed that pussy into oblivion.

Nube came back blazing on the set the next day, and had that shit so hot…it was smoking like a California wildfire for a full 20 minutes. Dudes was pitching tents…while ladies were twisting in their seats and crossing their legs. All this on a one time take with she and Hill improvising a majority of the way. The shit was so believable that they got a standing ovation from the crew when the scene was done. Nube looked over to where I was and gave me a sexy wink, which I returned with a smile and a lip nod. My girl…back on track.

Chapter 65

101Black Men With Opinions

Murad

We finished up the CSI project and returned home after being in Cali for 7 weeks. In spite of our original misgivings, the love scene between Nube and Hill made the industry grapevine, and put speculation over the top with cause for a much anticipated air date. Yeah and...people was buzzing with other nonsense, Nube and Hill...Hill and Nube. But none of that was bothering me at this point. With all that Nube and I been thru, I felt as though we had passed another major milestone in our relationship, and was now on our way to other positive aspects to develop between us. It sure feels good to be back of the East coast. Cali is cool but, enough of that over the top pretentious atmosphere. Anyway...we have an engagement sponsored by the 100 Black Men organization. They are having a forum on Black Men vs. Black Women; in specific...their attitudes. A friend of some friend of Mr. Reagan out of Chi got wind of Nube and contacted us in regard to an appearance. It's all good...Nube can hold her own. In fact...my girl got it all under control.

Nubina

Awww man, Cali was the bomb. I had an awesome time. Once I got over the nude scene thing, the atmosphere on the set became magical. Well...Hill and I are so cool with each other that everything just kinda flowed. I truly admire him. And yes we did get to hang out with him once more before we left, as in Murad and I. We also went back out to Stan's house and had a BBQ dinner with him and his family. Really cool people...I could see us doing that again...time permitting. But now that we are back home, I've got a couple of other engagements to attend to. A forum on the topic of Black Men vs. Black Women is first on the agenda. It's taking place all the way up in the Bronx; not to mention that it's an all male audience. I don't know how they got the notion that I should be the one to address this. Oh well…not about to turn down any challenge…I'll just keep pressing on.

Murad

Damn…it's cold as hell out here today. Nube's was holding steadfast within the bend of my arm as I semi-drag her down the block trynna get out of this cold.

"Rod baby…you think you can walk just a tad faster," she said, "I'm only bout to fall on my face over here."

"Girl you better come on," I answered her laughing, "It's cold as shit out here."

"Well I don't know why you didn't let the car service bring us in instead of driving yourself. This way we wouldn't have had to park 3 blocks away," she hit me with, "You got me and Hassan out here doing a marathon in the cold."

I was still on probation and under the regulation of security when Nube and I travel the Tri-state area, so I had Hassan with us for this assignment. I guess I should have done the car service thing, but I guess I was just feeling like pushing my own whip today. I had gotten my new truck since back before we went to Cali, but I hadn't really had a chance to drive it. I think I just wanted to feel the power of the wheel. But right now, all I was feeling was the power of the wind cutting my ass. Thought I could sport this to the waist fur since I was driving, but I hadn't planned on having to walk.

"Well we here now," I said pulling open the door to the community center and holding it so that she could step in. I followed behind her as Hassan swiftly brought up the rear. He was a quiet guy…didn't talk much. Kye referred him to me. They started out in the academy together and now dude moonlights as security. This is only my 3rd time using him, and I ain't got no problems. A brother who ain't got a whole lot to say is fine with me. Once we got inside we were immediately greeted by Mr. Fuentes.

"Good day good people," he said extending his hand to which I took and obliged with a handshake.

"How are you sir," I offered, "We've spoken on the phone. I am Murad Tillman and this is Queen Nubina."

"Yes...yes. I've heard very positive things in regard to you both. I greatly appreciate your availability to present us with your talent here today Nubina."

"It's my pleasure Mr. Fuentes," Nube replied, "I absolutely love sharing thoughts and opinions. I just hope that they effectively touch on someone here today."

"I'm sure they will," he gave back, "We have about a half hour before we start so if you'd like to come on back to my office, I can offer you all some refreshments, coffee...tea."

"Thanks," I answered, "We'll take you up on that offer. I could use a little warm infusion...didn't know it was going to be this cold out today."

As we headed back to the office area, I noticed that a good little group of men were gathering in the main rec room and I wondered just how large of a turnout there would be today. I sure hope this was gonna be a peaceful venture...you know...no knuckle heads or thug wanna-be's trynna flex or nothing. If so, I guess Hassan and I will be able to handle that. Anyhow...All I'm ready to handle right now is some tea, hot chocolate or something.

Just as Mr. Fuentes said, the program was ready to go in the half hour. I do believe there was another event scheduled there to follow so time was of the essence. Before he introduced Nube to the group, I gave her a gentle squeeze of the hand and asked, "You okay with this...you ready Butter?"

"I got this Sire," she responded, and sauntered out to greet her audience.

"Good afternoon my brothers," she started off, "It is a pleasure as well as an honor to be here to share some viewpoints with you today. For those of you who may not know me, my name is Nubina, and I happen to have a lot of opinions."

The room burst out in small pockets of laughter, as one dude called out, "Yeah that's all we need is another Black woman with some more opinions."

"Oh...okay," Nube said, "I see we gonna have much discussion up in here today. So let's get to it. First off...I'm not here to argue any points, for you truly can't argue an opinion...and opinions are what we are engaging in here today. But just for the record gentlemen...be clear on what you wanna toss out at me...cause a sista don't hold no punches."

So with her standing up at the makeshift podium, she took her first challenge, and started an oracle tug of war.

"*Sister Nubina,*" a brother asked, "*Can you enlighten us on why most sista's are just a pain in the ass to deal with?*"

I can assure you brother that for every sister that you feel is a pain in the ass, there's a long laundry list pinned to her heart of dirt and grime that's deemed her nothing but injustices all her life. And that list can stem from an absentee father, a wayward lover and even trickle down to a trifling son. A good majority of sisters bear continual pain on a consistent basis, so yes...the pain can and does spill over to you men.

"*Okay, look,*" another guy said, "*You woman can't hold us to all kinds of expectations. We not mind readers...or God.*"

Well brother...you are not Gods in a biblical sense but truly God of your own emporium. It's high time for black men to stand up and step into their designated destiny. You hail from the most elite in power of the mind...yet you fall so far behind your other ethnic counterparts. While men of other communities are marrying and raising families in their 20's and 30's, a lot of Black men are still on the block, in the club, and practicing their never ending gaming technique.

"*Well you know what,*" a young dude called out, "*Females be out here trynna run game like brothers. They ain't innocent.*"

No...they not. But women are only following your lead...more so, what you've shown them. If they out here gaming, it's because you've taught them well with the emotional injustices that you've placed upon them. Now you can either pat yourself on the back for a job well done, or you can admit to the need for much work on your part to turn things around

"*But Nubina,*" another brother said, "*Even when we try to be understanding and accommodate you all, it seems like ya'll still gotta wild out on us.*"

When we coming off all extra, controlling, demanding and insecure...you gonna have to give understanding to it and wear that. I mean we've been left off the hook for so long that all you gonna hear from the black woman is a dial tone. We need you as black men to step up like you the Verizon network and get service restored so that we are all communicating on the same page.

"*Men and woman will never be on the same page,*" another young dude kicked off, "*Cause you women are stuck on the What Have You Done For Me Lately page. Always running that nonsense by us.*"

Oh young brother...let me address that. What you men fail to realize is that while we appreciate the time that you do give us, you need to understand that coming thru at the end of the day, after you've considered everyone else first, then sitting up on her couch eating up her snacks and drinking up her beverages, while she sits sleepy and unattractive in her night shirt and headscarf patiently waiting for some true attention. Then you fall asleep so she goes to the bedroom to retire since yes...she has to go to work in the morning, only to have you wake her up 45 minutes later tapping her on the shoulder to rock it out for another half hour, then you conk out to sleep, while you snore keeping her up till 3:00 am. All the while she's thinking about the thing going on with the car she didn't get tell you about, and the new outfit that she wanted to show you, or brag about the award she was presented with at work. You have no clue because you got what you came for...and in your selfishness...that's all that matters. It seems that most of you do whatever it takes to get your foot in the door, but once you're in, all you wanna do is lay up and put your feet up. That is not how a true man conducts a relationship with a woman.

"*Well I got something for you Nubina,*" another brother said, "*If he supposed to be ya man, what's wrong with chillin at the crib? You females always want hype and flash, and whining bout you wanna go out...you wanna do this and that. Why can't you all just be glad we there with you...and not out cheating or running with the boys?*

And I've got something for you as well. You just "being" there does not qualify as valid nutrition to a healthy relationship. For that matter, the TV is "there," as well as the furniture and although they bring a sense of comfort, the quality of comfort needed from you should be emotionally as well as physically tangible. Listening to her thoughts, ideas and concerns should be of extreme interest to you if you call yourself her true man. Being attentive to her needs, considerate of her dreams, respecting her wishes are the true precursors to foreplay...not just the little freaky gestures you display in the bedroom. Hugging, cuddling and kissing are merely the dessert like topper that secures things over to the next time around. It is my belief that man and woman together equates to a spirit of one, and you should always invest in the interest of your other half. It enables you to be cohesive in thought, actions and/or reactions, making for a much more pleasant aura to the relationship. And the other side to the coin is that, what you're not willing to do...another man will.

A mature man who seemed to be put together well stood and asked, "*I can certainly understand the frustration sister, but must black woman always have an adverse reaction to every situation.*"

That frustration is two-sided sir. We don't always want to react as we do...you know...as though we can't keep it together. That in itself is frustrating. And I hate to keep pointing the finger but...you as black men have created the monster. The so called "bitter black woman"...the one that all of society views us as. And I mean globally...all around the world the "angry black woman"...with the hands on her hips and neck twisting is how we are perceived. And sadly it's by the hands of our own men. You promoted the behavior by implementing less than, giving us less than, treating us less than and exacerbate it by passing us over for all the "others"...yes the other women of the world. Every other nation in the world is looking at our community like damn...you know black women ain't shit if they own men don't want them. You will be with anyone else beside your own kind, or shall we say the monster you created. Now the even sadder part is, you won't be with or commit to the monster, but you will sex and impregnate the monster. And when them little monster seeds we spit out grows up and turn into certified home grown monsters that's busting you in the head...stealing your shit and raping your family members...you need to remember that you...yes you black men have contributed a very integral part in it all.

"*You can't expect us to change the tradition of men. You all done read Uncle Steve's book,*" a dorky looking guy said, "*It's just what men do.*"

Sure it's what men do, but just because it's "what" you do, doesn't mean that "what" you do is right. Every time you make that statement you are supporting the fact that you have no ability to lead and instead take the easy approach of going with the flow. It also tends to reveal that you have no self control, as well as a lack of self progression. If you in the area of 26 years and upward, and you still holding on to that statement "that's what men do," then you are clearly the prodigy of immaturity. An answer like that mirrors that of a school boy who got caught pulling a prank, and when asked why he replies, "Cause."

And as a grown man you should know that to answer "cause" is just the end result of an unnecessary action.

"*Nubina...can I just say this,*" an intellectual looking dude said, "*In our community, the art of being a player has been handed down historically from generation to generation. My father taught me and my grandfather taught him. How do you expect it all to just stop now?*"

While that's all well and true...the time for that negative cycle in the black man's repertoire needs to cease. What your forefathers have failed to tell you is...You have to be careful...extremely careful in proclaiming yourself a player. First off playing games are most definitely for "children" so to speak. And okay, when you're young you get caught up in this love thing, and you may tend to play a game or two, I'll give you that. But just like life, the stakes are higher, and relationships are more complex as you accelerate in age. So keeping up with the game, and the odds of coming out as a winner decreases as you advance in years. Let's see...just like the childhood game of musical chairs. You may start of as a young man with your seemingly never ending supply of chairs and ever flowing music to go with them. But as time passes and life progresses, the number of chairs starts to dwindle and you find yourself with fewer places to sit. Some of you at that point become smart enough to take a final seat and get out of the game while you are ahead...and then there's always that ultimate all time player that just takes for granted that he will always walk away a winner. That is until that day when the music runs out, while his back or shall we say head is turned looking to see what else he can see and where else he can sit, and yes...the last chair is taken, leaving him standing...alone. So yeah...game over. Over at a point in time where abs are not stacking no more, biceps not flexing, knees and ankles groaning and creaking, and soldier boy used to fight much better battles. It's time that men...black men in particular understand that being a so called player is you...really...playing... yourself.

"*Sister Nubina,*" a righteous brother spoke, "*It's a known fact that the dynamics of a man vs. woman is structured with the man as the predator...the hunter so to speak. It is the natural order of the universe as well as his nature to hunt and conquer as many as he can. It helps to maintain and balance the energy between genders."*

Oh yes brother...I will agree with you on that one. Men are indeed predators by nature. And it is your natural instinct to hunt. But in his infinite wisdom, the Great One Divine has created us with the ability to process thought, logic and reasoning, and it is up to us to be in charge of our own accountability. In other words...you are equipped to decipher the difference between hunting out of necessity and hunting out of greed. Greed is a powerful destructive attribute that always...and I do mean always comes back to tumble your quick egotistical ascension or whatever structure you've built upon its basis.

"*Okay Sister Nubina*, another brother spoke up, "*If everybody gotta be accountable, then ain't it on the sisters not to swing with the game when we bring it? I mean...some of us got good game...yeah, I ain't trynna brag or nothing...but mine is on point. But that right there is on her when she fall for it.*"

Oh please...don't get it so twisted as to think that when a woman so calls falls for your bullshit and your egotistical gaming, that you are so on point with yours...cause the truth of the matter is she is doing what she does or making her choices to appease her ego and not yours. Just as you are approaching her to fulfill a void or smooth over one of your weaknesses or issues, she too is swinging with it for her own personal issues and albeit subconsciously...to appease her ego as well. So don't trick yourself into believing that you one up on her, cause in reality...you are both satisfying your egos by virtue of false means.

I got a phone call on my blackberry just as Mr. Fuentes, the sponsor of the session approached the stage. I quickly answered and passed off, "I'll call you back," so that I could stay tuned in to what was going on with Nube.

"Gentlemen, our time is just about up with the Queen," he announced, "and I'd like to thank her for her very poignant viewpoints and giving us as black men, some insight into this ongoing issue in our community."

The room kicked off into a round of applause as Nube responded, "Thank you gentlemen, thank you very much."

"Well hey," some guy shouted out, "When can she come back...cause she was making mad sense. And I would like an opportunity to bring her some more questions."

"Yeah...that was dope," someone else called out.

"Yeah...yeah.." a couple more chorused.

"Yeah...cause she don't understand. I still say a man gonna be a man...no matter," one slick-ass called out.

"Mr. Fuentes, may I address the audience with one final note," Nube spoke up.

"By all means; It would be my pleasure," he responded.

Nubina

"Gentlemen it has been a pleasure to share our opinions here today and I thoroughly enjoyed the opportunity, but I would just like to touch on one final note in regard to the last comment....A man gonna be a man...regardless. You know...that statement is open to interpretation and the context of it depends upon who's delivering it. A man is gonna be a man...and it is his responsibility alone to choose what kind of a man he wants to be. If he wants to be an insensitive, uncaring, disrespectful louse then it will reflect in his actions. The individual who wants to be a respectful, considerate and a consummate leader across the board will reflect that by his actions. So...again...it's all about choices. A man will be a man...but it's up to him alone what kind of man he chooses to be.

That brings me to my closing remarks of knowing and understanding the consequences of borrowing and lending. You see...it is my philosophy that a lot of men promise and emulate love as a means to coerce a woman into something less than promised. What you don't understand is that when you emulate or shall I say falsely simulate love, you are borrowing from one of the most powerful...the 5th Element...Love. Love in its truest form is so powerful, as it is a necessity needed to mankind. We are all born with our own reservoirs of Love that we are to utilize at the appropriate times. But when you pretend to love or use small fragments of love for manipulative gain, those withdrawals so to speak are being recorded. As you continue to knowingly borrow, with false intentions, you are unaware of the interest and fees that are steadily growing against your account.

Then finally the day comes when your trifling mind has concluded that your heart and soul needs to settle with a special someone. Well let me tell you, there's one of 2 things that will happen. One you will consistently reach out for, strive for and put in much effort to secure that one special someone who will in turn take love from you, without giving any back. No matter how much you extend or profess your love it will not be reciprocated, because love will not forget how much you borrowed from her and will not allow you to receive until your debt is cleared. Or 2...you will have borrowed so much from your reserve that when you do come across that special one you won't have the emotional resources or relationship skills to maintain them. Your Love account will be so overdrawn with indiscriminate souls and negative energy that has built up thru the years. Energy that equates to insufficient funds desperately needed to maintain a relationship. Instead of being able to step up to the challenge, you love account will be totally depleted and you won't be able to see your way clear to securing their heart, leaving you destitute and lonely. The Universe is very strict on preserving the 5th Element, and one way or another you will learn that, you cannot borrow from love without **ever** having to pay it back.

And for those of you who agree with the brother who feels that I don't understand, I'm gonna have to admit that I've pondered the very thought many a time. I mean...searched my mind many times over for some true understanding. So in regard to that dilemma I would like to drop this piece upon you. Its befitting title is "Understanding Richard."

Understanding Richard

I wonder what it's like to be the man behind the dick
Spittin game and talking slick
Back door pocket full of chicks

I wonder does he realize the consequence of game
Bastard kids without his name
Buck wild hoodrats hard to tame

Not sure that he can understand the pain that he inflicts
Out here making people sick
Doing damage with that dick

How good this manly feeling that he keeps coming for more
Losing brain cells that he stores
While he keeps a counting score

I wonder if it's worth it, all this dick he throws around
Making choices quite unsound
Humping booty pound for pound

I guess he feels it's worth it to betray a trust and bond
Taking scandal way beyond
Sentiments of being fond

Perhaps its pussy calling and she's twisting up his mind
As they do the bump and grind
While he's hittin from behind

Be nice if he would advertise for those who want to play
Dick games running on all day
For those looking for a slay

I hope his dick can handle rockin poo-tang all them years
Now he's living life with fears

And his crocodile like tears

He'll see there is no turning back for things he left behind
As his mind starts to un-wind
Inner vision left for blind

I wonder if he understands that life will now pass quick
As the clock goes on to tick
For the man behind the dick

Once she finished her delivery, the room was pin-drop silent till somewhere from the back a definitive clap started as one dude stood up started a chain reaction of a standing ovation. Every man in the place got on their feet and gave Nube a standing ovay, applauding Nube to the nines.

"Yo Chief," Hassan surprised me by saying as he stepped over to me, "She right as rain man...right as rain."

"Yeah man," I answered, "I'm so aware of that...so totally aware."

Chapter 66

An Offer I Couldn't Refuse

Nubina

It's been a couple of weeks since the presentation up in the Bronx, and Rods' phones have been ringing off the hook with all kinds of offers and requests. Other male organizations want me to come and do projects with them. The children's book publisher wants to do a possible spin off publication for a book in a different genre of their company. Not to mention Clay from Atlanta was ready to jump start a new project. So it looked like things were gonna be mighty busy for a minute. Murad and I are just so glad to be back on track with each other. Everything between us is going good, and I'm so okay with everything right about now. My good friend time has eased us into April, and I'm desperately trying to think about what I can do special for Murad's birthday next month. I mean this man has got everything and more...what else can I give him.

Right now he's up in Yonkers at a business meeting in regard to the Tennessee real estate deal, so I'm here making him some of his special dishes to ease the tension of the ongoing negotiations and rigmarole he'll be enduring all day. I'm putting in work on all of his favorites. I don't even know what I'm gonna do with all this food, but I just felt that I needed to make everything that he likes. It's about 11:45 am and I'm not even half way done on my menu. Oh...there's the phone...it's Rod.

"Hey Bae. How's it going," I picked up after the 2nd ring.

"Man Nube...things are intense. This one got something to say...that one doesn't agree. I tell you...that's the reason why I don't favor working in a group. There's too many other opinions, and viewpoints that have to be considered. When I'm flying solo, I don't have to get approval from no one else, nor deal with this type of nonsense. Anyway...what's going on with you Pretty?"

"Well, I kinda got a little buffet going on over here. Something I have been wanting to do for my man for a minute, so today's the day," I answered.

"A buffet?" he responded.

"Yeah... all your favorites. I figured that you could probably use a good taste or two after you handle your business today."

"From the way things are going you gonna have to make every favorite dish I've got," he said.

"You know that ain't no problem," I told him, "I've already started."

"So," he began, "You got the Salmon cakes?"

"Yes."

"And the cream style corn...the potato salad...BBQ chicken...Rice and Peppercorn gravy...uh... my mac-n-cheese?" he inquired.

"Yup," I answered, "Got all that as well as some Curry chicken with mixed vegetables, fried whiting, toss salad and even a Lemon rum cake."

"Butter...you got all that?" he asked me.

"Sure do...don't worry Bae," I responded, "I got it and it's all for you."

"Aww hell," he said, "I'm bout ready to agree to whatever these cats talkin, just so that I can get home and eat."

"Well don't rush now...cause I've got a few finishing touches I have to complete," I told him, "How bout you give me a heads up on what time you think you'll be home."

"That's kinda hard to say Nube," he replied, "It all depends on how soon we can get everyone to read on the same page. How bout I'll call you when were done and I'm on my way?"

"That'll work...you do that and I'll be sure to have everything ready and waiting," I told him.

"You sure Butter?" he tenderly asked me.

"As sure as the sky is blue," I answered, "It will all be waiting for you when you get here."

"Okay...cool. Look Nube...I gotta go," he said in response, "We bout to start rehashing the details again...I'll give a call back. Love you."

"Love you too Rod...later." As I hung up the phone I thought...damn....I'd better get back on the ball. I threw on some music, rolled up my sleeves and got focused. I worked until about 4:00 p.m. then I sat down to rest. I put my feet up put my head back and the next thing you know.....zzzzzzz.

≈≈

Wow…6:30 pm and Rod just called saying he's stuck in traffic on I-95. Who knows when he'll get here, that's at least an hour away without traffic. Man…I know he's going to be beat when he does get in. I'll do my best to keep this food warm and fresh. Hope he's not too late getting here. Hmmmm.....

Murad

Man look at this shit here. Fucking 8:30 and I'm just getting in. Mind you…I left there at 5:45. The only good part about it is that we finalized all the requirements of the deal and we are set to break ground next month. A brand new strip mall in a newly developed area of Clarksville Tennessee really didn't appeal to me at first, but once this cat Munford starting kicking the projections to me, it started to sound a little more promising in terms of financial turn around. So…I went on to take the gamble. Sure hope it pays off. As I parked the truck and set the alarm I realized how tired I was all of a sudden. Damn…I was planning on stuffing myself sick on Nubes' food, but the way I'm feeling, I'll be lucky if I get one plate under my belt. I unarmed the alarm and opened the door to a heaven sent aroma. Man…I can smell the testament of all her hard work all up in the place. It actually smells like a 5 star restaurant in here. I'm gonna have to man up and put in some work in on this food. She's gone thru the trouble of making it all for me, the least I could do is eat something.

"Nube baby," I called out, "I'm home."

"I'm in the den Murad," she answered me. I set down my briefcase and slipped out of my jacket, setting them both on the couch before I proceeded to the den. As I started undoing my cuff links, I walked into the doorway to…

"Hey babe…what's going on?" I asked her in regard to the candles placed around the room and a large basin set in front of my chaise.

"I've been waiting for you Sire," she told me as she approached me, taking hold of both my wrists and leading me to the chair. "Have a seat," she told me, "Just relax and let me handle this for you." As I sat down, she leaned into me and gave me a delicious kiss. "How did things turn out?" she asked me pulling back.

"It took all damn day, but we got everything squared away," I replied, "We'll be breaking ground next month."

"That's wonderful Rod, she said, untying my shoes and slipping them off my feet. "So... when's the next time you guys will have to meet again?" she asked removing my socks from my feet. "Stand up Rod," she instructed me.

"Nube babe...what you got going on?" I asked her complying with her request.

"I need you to take your pants off," she told me.

"Ahh...Nube baby...I'm kinda beat. I was hoping that I could just..."

"Relax Rod," she intervened, "I've got a special treat for you...and not what you're thinking. Just take the pants off mister, and lose the shirt while you at it. All I want you to do is sit back and relax."

I was too tired to ask or argue, so I just said, "Okay," and did as I was told. When I finished I sat back down in the chaise and was instructed to slide down to the end so that my feet would rest in the basin. She then went on to place some overstuffed pillows behind me so that I could recline. With my feet in the basin she proceeded to add a capful of what smelled like Vanilla as she started to explain.

"In many Asian countries it is an honorary custom to wash the feet of your dinner guest. And since you are my special guest of honor tonight, I would like to oblige." As she poured another capful of a different liquid, she continued to explain. "I am putting organic peppermint extract to energize and stimulate the senses in your feet, and a dash of vanilla to soothe the tension."She went on to pick up a thermal carafe with steaming water and poured it in the basin gently swishing around. Wow...this is different...really different...and relaxing. I never had anyone do this for me before. She then took a small natural bristled foot brush and began to gently scrub my feet with the mixture. I laid back and enjoyed it all; just breathing in the pleasant fragrance and enjoying the tingling sensation the peppermint was providing while I noticed to the ear my Pete Belasco CD was piping out a mellow vibe. Ahh...shit...this right here is sweet I'm thinking as I'm laid back on the pillows, feet tingling, the sensations truly relaxing my mind and my body. Nube went on quietly scrubbing and rinsing while I just laid there overwhelmed in relaxation. After a while she dried my feet off and lathered her hands with a home made balm of the same organic peppermint extract and vanilla and started applying it to my feet. As she took her time kneading and massaging, I think I literally lost consciousness and was floating somewhere in Nirvana. I was dreaming of ancient Babylonian slave girls, feeding me grapes, fanning me with huge palm leaves and kissing my feet...softly...gently...then licking...my toes. This was feeling way too real...what...I opened my eyes and caught the perpetrator... Nube.

"Oh...hey Butter. You don't have to..."

"Shhhh..." she clipped me seductively, "Relax Murad...relax." Oh...hey fine, I relented. I've got to admit this is the best side of heaven I've visited thus far. I'm not gonna complain. I laid back and relished the extraordinary sensations that were giving me pleasure as well as intrigue. She did an equally good service to both my dogs and then proceeded to slide her kisses upward. She made her way to the ankles, then upwards to the shin and knees. Just before she got to the thighs she reached out with her right hand and connected with ole'boy. Given all that sensuality that was enticed just moments ago, he twitched with awareness, slowly coiled himself up out of chill mode and jumped to attention.

"Nube," I softly called out, "You don't..."

"Murad," she clipped me again, as she began to softly fondle me and cause ole boy to throb with excitement.

"Here...help me out," she purred as she began to roll my boxers down. I complied and slid them down over my hips so she could finish relieving me of them. I continued to relax with my eyes closed as she massaged me back into Babylonia. It was all good...and then I felt a smooth cool wetness on my boys...and then a slight tingling.

"Ahhh...Nube," I lightly moaned.

She had applied some of the peppermint extract on her hands and was now giving personal attention to my jewels. I can't begin to tell you how good I was feeling right about now. She massaged, caressed, then embraced ole'boy and stretched him up to his fullest extension, then slid her hands back over and massaged his head.

"Uuuhhh," I let go without hesitation.

Daaayum...this shit here beats chiefing any day. Got me more blazed than I've ever been before. And just when I thought the shit couldn't get any better, she kissed ole'boy with them sexy ass lips. He jumped in surprise, and she licked him.

"Nube," I cried out this time.

She didn't wait for an addition to my outburst, she replied by taking ole'boy in her mouth. I moaned out loud and lost all reasoning after that. She licked him, kissed him and showed him love with so much sincerity, I couldn't object if I wanted to. All I could do was lay there as she took me on this exquisite journey. The peppermint extract was nipping and tingling and giving me that York Peppermint Patty effect. Man...I was consumed in sweet agony. I lay there as she put in sweet and tender work with ole'boy and took me to the highest high I have ever been. I was just about to the edge, when she went deep with ole'boy. I shuddered as she pulled back and went deep again, this time gagging. She pulled back and went back deep...gagged once...twice...and as I opened my eyes and called out, "Nuuuube..."she pulled back and cradled him between the crook of her neck and shoulder blade where he poured out his soul to her...every last drop.

Once ole'boy was done, she raised up, reached for one of the hand towels she had stacked, poured a little water on it from the carafe and cleaned us both up without a trace. I just sat and watched as she administered the task with such love and concern...she had my heart melted like Velveeta. She looked down at me and smiled, then threw the towel over to the side as she stretched herself out over my sated body and mind. I openly welcomed her and cuffed her up in my arms as she settled up on my chest.

"Nube," I mumbled, "The food."

"Don't worry Bae," she said, "I already made up 2 plates and put all the rest of it away. We can indulge later if we need to. You just go on and relax...you had a long day."

She didn't have to tell me twice...I was still somewhere in Nirvana. As we lay there quietly together she whispered softly, "I love you Sire."

I was so into my zone, all I could do was squeeze her in response. And I knew she understood the gesture when she reciprocated with a squeeze of her own. As I lay there drifting in and out of heaven, I couldn't help but think... Damn...It don't get no better than this. I can't wait to change her last name.

Chapter 67

Head ToToe

Murad

Bryce has been buzzing in my ear about family unity and mending fences for a minute now, so I've decided to allow myself 2 presents for my birthday. First one, I've agreed to meet up with the entire Double 7 plus and see the possibility of working things out. I guess maybe find out the true reason Brick came out his face like that on Nube...I don't know, I mean....we are blood...been tight...I mean like brothers, ever since knee high. At the very least he owes me an explanation to why he would offend me in that manner by disrespecting my lady. And I owe Bryce...he's always been my mentor, egging me on to stay positive and prosper. He really wants to see things mended throughout the family and I can understand where he's coming from. He used my birthday as the excuse to hook up, squash some things and celebrate all at the same time. So...we all supposed to meet up at his spot around 8:30. That's all well and cool, but I've got my own birthday surprise that I wanna implement myself before I swing with the fellas. Damn...I'm thinking as I finish getting dressed, we about to see...we about to see.

Nubina

Boy do I feel some kind of way. Today is Murad's birthday and he's going out to hang over at Bryce's. I mean...I don't want to begrudge him being with his family, but I wanted us to do something special together. The only thing about that...my silly ass don't even have a clue or an idea what to do with him or for him. I'm stuck on a glitch with that...so what could I say about him rolling with the fellas. He told me not to worry about it, because every day that we're together is like a birthday to him. He touched me so deep with that, I couldn't help but tear up. But he was adamant about celebrating with the guys so I'm just going with the flow. Oh well, I guess I'll find a way to make it up to him. For now I'll just sit here on the sofa and catch up on my reading. I hadn't gotten but 3 minutes in on the reading when Murad came downstairs dressed and ready to go. Man...he was looking and smelling good.

"Hey Butter," he said approaching the couch, "I'm just about getting ready to go. I really don't know how long I'm gonna be out so..."

"Soooo...what?" I asked putting the book down looking at him sideways.

"So come on and dance with me," he responded. "Dance with you?" I came back with.

"Yeah," he answered, "Dance with me. You wanted to know what you could do for me for my birthday...I want you to dance with me."

Aww...he's so sweet and thoughtful. Murad knows that I'd always wanted to slow dance and never got the chance to as a teenager cause I was so damn shy. He also knows that I was looking forward to my first slow dance at my high school prom...but that never happened, I never got a date and wound up going with my best girlfriend who was also dateless. Once I'd told him of those events in my life, he would make a point to slow dance with me every chance we'd get. How could I not love this guy?

"Okay," I said, removing myself from the couch.

"Hold on," he said, "Let me get some music going. Got any special requests?"

"No Bae. This is your day...you make the choice," I told him.

"True dat...true dat," he replied smiling. "Okay...here we go," he said as he came over and put me up in his arms. "You feel like singing for me Butter?" he asked.

"Rod...what is you talking? You know good and well I can't sing," I responded, laughing aloud to his request . He pressed start on the remote, then tossed it on the couch.

"Ahh....come on Nube," he gave me, "I'ma sing with you...yup...me and you...come on. It's my birthday."

"Well what are we..." I started, then paused as his song selection began to play. Oh okay...Remarkable...a duet with

Jaheim and what's that chick's name? Uhh...what's her name. Is it Terry...Dexter? I dunno.

"Okay...okay," I answered smiling, "I love this one...let's go." Of course I was up first.

"*I never quite told you babe, how much you meant to me. From first sight, that first night I knew instantly. That you'd be the one for me. Deep down in my heart baby.*" As I sang in my off tone to the beat, he just looked down at me and smiled.

"What?" I asked laughing.

"Aww come on now...you gotta keep up," he responded laughing.

"*Now all I can saaay...oooooo...head to toe...Credible,*" I interjected not wanting to miss that part. He looked at me, and we both bust out laughing.

"Okay...kay...now," I told him catching my breath, "You coming up...you coming up Rod. Hit it."

"*Girl I know I done put you thru some things. But I love you more each day and that ain't never gonna change, no. If you ever left me nothing would remain...you're part of me...no you're all of me.*"

You know actually... Rod don't sound too bad...not bad at all. My man got a little bit of skills going on. Why does that not surprise me?

"*Cause all I'll ever need to survive is right here in my eyes, it's you cause your love is so remarkable...girl you know...every thing about you from head to toe.....baby your girl you're so incredible...I just had to let you know.. .your love is so remarkable...can't afford to let you go. If you left I'd be so miserable,*"

Rod continued to sing. I looked up at him, a little surprised at his presentation and the intent look in his eyes. He is just too damn suave...I love him. Okay wait now...my part is coming up again...and yeah there he go throwing me that head twist as a reminder.

"*There's always sunshine when you're around, it's like my feet don't even touch the ground,*" I came in on cue. "*How my heart begins to pound,*" he met his cue, "*on one knee I will go down. Grab your hand and tell you now*" "*You will always be, all that I ever need,*" we sang in unison, "*Much more than my baby you're an angel heaven sent to me.*"

"Once was blind but now I see." "Never let your love get away from me," we sang accordingly. We continued to sing and laugh coming in on our respective parts.

"Girl I wanna spend my life with you." "I had to let you know." "It's something about you baby it's everything." "I'm never, never gonna let you go" "You're good for my heart...my mind...oooohhhh."

We continued thru the entire song hitting our marks on point, till we got toward the end, and Rod decided we needed to spin , so he laced my hands within his, and we continuously spun as we sang, "*Six carats of diamonds girl...a little bit of platinum too. Ain't enough cheddar in this world that I wouldn't spend on you*"

With that last line he raised our hands in the air, as the song played on, then brought our hands back down together in between us, ending the spin as he sang, "*Tell me...tell me you'll marry me?*"

And as Terry Dexter wailed on, "*Ooooo...yes I will,*" I just stood there muted and stared at the ring he'd somehow placed on my 3rd finger... left hand, while Ja belted out into the silence, "*You're good for my heart...my mind...my soul...oooo...you make me whole.*"

Murad

Man...I don't know. I'm standing here looking at her, she's stunned...I mean definitely surprised, but the silence is making me uneasy. She looked up at me and voiced softly "Murad."

I could tell by her tone that she was in need of reassurance, so I got down on one knee and sat her down on my other leg that was posted for support.

"Listen," I started, "I know that you were not expecting me to hit you up with this tonight, so in the interest of keeping anything from being misconstrued, let me clarify for you my exact intentions. Ms. Tania Baynes...will you marry me?"

I held my breath in nervous anxiety, searching her eyes for a signal or a sign that what I asked had penetrated. She sat for a minute, then searched my eyes for whatever she needed to see, and I suppose she found it...cause she leaned into me and blessed me with a decisive kiss, then pulled back and sweetly answered, "Yes."

Nubina

Murad has left the house to go on over to Bryce's and meet up with his family. I on the other hand am sitting up in the middle of our bed, marveling at my ring, my head still in a buzz over what took place tonight. Murad Tillman has asked me to marry him...marry him...And I said yes!! My ring is over the top exquisite, pink diamonds that happen to match the bracelet that he gifted me with this past Christmas. Wow...I mean, when did he decide this?... and then to go sneak me with that song. First of all, he know Jaheim can do **anything** for me, so that in itself was thoughtful. Then to propose to me, on such a classic...I am blown away. My, oh my, I don't know who shall I call first. Uhh...Lani...no...no...my mommy. As I reached for the phone, I pulled back as something inside me told me to wait...just savor this moment...savor it to myself...until.

Murad

"Hey Murad," Bryce's wife Shannon greeted me as she answered the door. I stepped in giving her a brief hug and a peck on the cheek.

"Hey there Shan," I responded, "How you been?"

"Been good...been good," she replied, "What you and Tania been up to lately...y'all home for a while?"

"Yeah...we here for like a week," I told her, "then we out to Chi for the Oprah show."

"Really," she came back in a surprised tone, "You guys just stay gone."

"I know Shan, I know...but I'm gonna get us some time off in the near future...trust me," I told her, "So, they here?" I asked walking toward the kitchen.

"Yeah, they all downstairs in the basement," she answered following me. "Go on down, and here," she stopped handing me a bucket of ice, "Take this down with you. Ole' big belly Bryce asked for this. If his butt don't quit all that beer drinking and eating everything in sight, I'm gonna have to take him in and get his round self a tummy tuck."

"Aww Shan…he cool…he cool," I said.

"No Murad," she stated, "you haven't seen him for a couple of months. Your boy is about to explode." She laughed, "Go on down there…you'll see for yourself."

I just responded with my own laughter and trotted down the stairs. As I came into eye view, the shout outs started.

"Rod" "Yo Chief…whas up?"

"Happy born day"

"Awww…nigga"

"What up son…happy birthday."

"King Midas…nigga what?"

I laughed and dapped my way thru the crowd, and like…wow. Bryce had everyone in attendance. I mean the 14 of us, then his 2 sons, his nephews, my nephew Key, our cousins on our pop's side…anyone that fell into the category of 18 and up was there. I walked to the back to Bryce's home grown pride and joy…his bar. He'd custom designed it himself with the help of Home Depot.

As I placed the bucket of ice on the counter I greeted him, "Yo B…whas' good?"

He gave me that slow deliberate nod before he answered, "Murad…glad you could make it. I appreciate it…really appreciate it. Like I've been saying, we all family, gonna always be family and as family we need to understand that…"

"Sometimes shit just happens," a voice broke in cutting him off. I turned around to confirm what I already knew…Brick.

"Whasup?" he kicked off to me.

I threw him a lip nod, replying, "S'all good."

I stood my ground…not wanting to be the one to initiate any physical greetings or contact. "Yo Chief, been a minute…been a minute," he gave me, "Listen…I know things jumped off a little foul between us the last time and…."

"And you what B?" I cut in, a low level of temper starting to break thru, "You thought I would be cool with you calling Nube out her name?"

"Yo...you think the fuck I'ma blow shit off the way you blasted on my momma?" Brick flashed back, his tone matching mine.

"Hey...hey," Bryce jumped in, as the room took a quick descent into silence, "I called everyone here to mend fences...not tear them down. We gonna sit down and discuss this...like grown men ought to. Ain't no room here today for nonsense and ego's. Brick...Murad, have a seat."

He walked over to the clearing and turned to motion us both to join him. Shit...I'm thinking as I proceeded to go take a seat, I ain't looking to be consumed in stress on my damn birthday, so if this turn out to be some shit I ain't trynna hear, I'm outta here.

"Brick," Bryce determinately repeated, since he hadn't made a move. He took one look around the room, and took in the vibe of expectedness, then lumbered his way over to have a seat.

"First off," Bryce started, "Nube has been a part of this family ever since she and Sumira were in college. Yeah while all of you were out slinging, balling, gaming, on the block...whatever, she's been right up in there giving respect to any and everyone regardless to your character. So I don't ever, and I do mean ever wanna hear her being disrespected like that again."

Brick mulled it over for a few seconds, then sullenly stated, "Yeah...yeah. She has, but Rod was mouthin off at Ma...that shit wasn't right either."

"Yo come on B," Lonnie interjected, "Ma always bumping her gums and getting into it with somebody. On the real, that ain't even the first time her and Rod got into it and you know it."

"Oh what the fuck is this," Brick responded, "Everybody need to gang up on me over her booji ass?"

Aight...my temper starting to rise into the danger zone. Before I could respond, Kye jumped in with, "Damn Brick...how fucking hard is your head? We trynna squash shit and you gonna come out ya face with another name.?"

"Oh don't run me that," Brick laid on him, "I said booji. What is booji? I ain't said nothing wrong. She booji and think she better than everybody."

I slid forward in my seat, and as Bryce noticed, he slid forward along with me. "Hold up Brick," he said trynna head shit off at the pass. "Ma has been Ma all her life, and always looking for a cause to speak on, but I've watched Nube grow from a special young lady to a phenomenal young woman and all this booji nonsense is just an excuse for something else you got going on with you. I don't know what your issue is, but whatever it is you feeling some way about should not be taken out on Nube, she has never..."

"She never what?" Brick yelled out, "She never what? She never...he never. Every thing is about fucking King Midas over here. And just cause she hooked up wit him, I'm suppose to congratulate 'em and buy they asses champagne or sumptin?"

"Yo Brick," Lonnie started.

"Yo Brick what?" he put out, "And you another one Lonnie. You fucking been taking up for her ass ever since. Ain't no surprise ...none at all. Princess this and Princess that. Ain't no wonder you'd be on his side bout this shit, cause thas' ya girl. Like what...is you fucking her too?" I stood up, and people started to peel back.

"Aww naw," Kye broke in, "We came here to work this shit out, we not gonna have another scene like we did on Thanksgiving. Brick you gonna have to..."

"What," Brick yelled out again, "I'm gonna have to what? Everybody here fucking trynna put me on blast. What about dis nigga here? His shit stink like every...fucking...body...else. All ya'll mutha fucka's bedazzled by him and his shit. Fucking Pretty Ricky got cars, houses, money and women. Always got a woman...every woman...all the women. Just like Ma said. He don't give nobody else a chance to get on. You know...leave shit open for somebody else to get thru...Noooo...It's fucking always about Murad. I could've got myself right with a girl like Nube...I would'a given her things and made her happy too. Niggas need to know my ass got purpose. I'da had my chance to show that I'm not just dumb ass Brick, the thugged out dude wit a pocket full of felonies." I just stood rooted in place, as did the whole room, silence engulfing the already stale air. Did this mutha fucka here just say what I think he trynna say? You know really…I think I need to sit my ass down on this one.

Bryce was the first to break the silence, "Brick…it's obvious that you got some kind of ill feeling toward Murad. When the hell did this all jump off? Ya'll been tight since the day you came out the womb. How you all of a sudden got a problem with him?"

"I ain't got a problem wit him," Brick barked back, "Well not really," he said his tone coming down a notch, "It's just that Rod got everything, all the shit that I've always wanted. The degree, the whips, the clothes, and the women."

"The women?" I finally voiced, "You had ya own female fan club B…always…just as fucking large as mine. So what women are you talking bout?"

"Nube," he stated in a flat yet concise voice, "I wanted to be with Nube."

I'm glad I was sitting my ass down, cause that right there caught me right in the chest taking my breath away. I sat for a minute before I responded.

"You wanted to be with Nube?" I asked him, the disbelieve evident in my voice, "Like…since when Brick? All you did was ever talk about her being stuck-up and booji, and how you needed a ride or die chick, and she just ain't it."

"Thas' cause I thought she would never wanna deal with me being who I was, and I guess I just resented her for it," he answered.

"Yo Brick," I threw at him, "How you gonna resent her for something she don't even know about? You gave her shade from day one. And what you thinking…like she gonna go for the dude that's always coming out his face about her?"

"I wasn't thinking all like that," he said, "All I knew was she was different…special and she ain't had the time of day for me."

"Time for you nigga," Kye interrupted, "How was she supposed to have time for you Brick when you was always in the street wilding out. And if that wasn't enough, any free time you had, you spent it locked up. So just when was she supposed to give your ass the time of day, when you ain't even give yourself the time of day?"

"When was she supposed to what?" Brick heatedly responded, "Man…fuck you Yo…fuck all you nigga's. All that shit don't matter no more, it is what it is. He got her…he had Jazmine, and neither one of them want me, so just fuck it…forget it."

"Jazmine?" I asked him totally confused, "What the fuck she got to do with any of this?"

"Yo look," he started, "Like I said before…things happen. A while back, I was out with Nasim and I bumped into your girl down at the Vanity. I bought her a drink being that she used to be cool wit you and all, and ole girl started pushing up on me. We had a few more drinks, and then she asked me for a ride home. I figured yeah…it was getting late and it won't gonna hurt nobody. Once I got to her house, she invited me in, just to chill she said. And then…I dunno, I guess one thing turned into another and we went at it."

"So you got with Jazmine?" I questioned him, background thoughts swimming in my head.

"Yeah Rod," he answered, "It ain't like I meant for that shit to happen. I mean, I left soon after, cause I knew that shit was wrong…you know going against the family agreement and whatnot, I figured that was that and I was done. But she called me the next day, and kept calling me, so I kept going over there, and before you know it, I was into her."

"You was into her?" I hit him with my second question. "Yeah Rod…into her," he came back with.

"So, let me get this straight," I put to him, "You been rocking shit with Jazmine, and you caught feelings, and now you into her?"

"Yeah, I'm into her," he replied, "But that shit don't matter none, cause she ain't thinking bout me like that. Truth be told…that shit is still all about you Chief."

"Yo B…listen," I started, "Ain't no thing at all between me and Jazmine…nothing. Ain't shit she can do for me, cept' owe me back that paper. She skanky as all hell. I don't know what she had on her agenda by pushing up on you, but you need to know that trick is dangerous Brick. Whatever the fuck it was all about...trust, her ass was up to no good. But you know what... if you feeling her, then by all means do your thing. Cause as far as I'm concerned, if you want to stick a pole up her ass and fly her on your porch like a flag, it truly makes me no never mind."

"Man...I know what she did wasn't right. Okay...yeah, on the real...she was grimey wit the whole thing," he started explaining, "But it's something bout her that kinda hooked me. And I don't even know if it's cause I really like her, or if I'm really feeling her cause she somebody you use to roll wit'."

"Damn Brick," Sharief said, "You sound like you all out over this chick."

"I dunno...maybe I am," he responded in a zone.

"Well damn," Dream piped in, "What the hell happened to the damn agreement?"

"Well shit"...

"Maan listen."...

"Son please." All kinds of statements of issue started flowing all around the room.

"You know," Bryce stepped in, "I'm glad that we all here. I think it's time we re-evaluate this agreement. Our numbers are getting out of hand, and paths are beginning to crisscross. Things may begin to get out of our control."

"That's all well and fine," Jarrell put in, "But I still feel there's a need for the agreement to remain intact."

"Yeah," Sharief piped in, "Cause we don't need to be having things going down like they did between Rod and Brick."

"Oh, that's more than true," Dream put in."

"Well let's say we keep the current rules," Bryce offered, "respect the boundaries as well as respect the present relationship, and just put a clause in place. Should we ever find ourselves drawn to someone who has had prior dealings with one of us, and if we for certain that we have **honorable** intentions, then be a true man, step up to the plate and clear things with whoever **before** getting into something. Agreed?"

"Yeah...Fine...That's cool," circled around the room.

"So Murad...Brick," Bryce said, "Can we say that things are all squashed between you two?"

I took a deep breath before I spoke; Brick's revelation had sprung some thoughts anew within me. I mean, me and Bryce used to rock rough and tear shit up all around the way back when, it don't feel right in my heart to just let that bond dissolve, I guess I got no qualms with letting shit go. But what I do know is, moving forward…I need to make shit understood….bond or no bond.

"Listen," I started, "I just need everybody here to know that I take my relationship with Nube very serious, that's my world, and I will by no means tolerate any disrespect of her regardless to whom you may be. Fam, friend or foe…it don't matter…take heed…think twice before you ever come out your face and disrespect my lady."

"Well you know…I'm cool wit dat," Brick offered, "And yo' Chief…I apologize. Thas' just some shit I been holding back for a minute and I was wrong for dat. We good?"

He stood and offered me his hand, I threw a lip nod, then stood and accepted his hand. We shook on it and gave up the love.

"So is everybody good? Bryce announced his inquiry around the room.

"Yeah…it's good….I'm cool….Not a problem," All came back in response.

"Then let's say we all have a drink on it. Here's to all honesty," Bryce stated.

"Here…here…" was the response.

"Anybody else got any admissions they wanna get out while we all here?"Bryce indiscriminately asked.

"Well," said Davon, my Aunt Nona's son, "Y'all remember that chick Sonia that used to be dealing with Dream…well we had kinda got into something at one time."

"Whoa…what?" Dream put out.

"No…long, long time after you put her down…long time," Davon defended.

"Well truth be known," Jarod said, "That little sweet thing that Kye brought to last years cook out slid me her number and yeah…we hooked up."

"Oh...oh...so it's like that," Kye responded, "Well ya'll remember ole'girl with the booty-do that was sweating Lonnie for years. All I could say is yeah...her damn booty do!!!"

"Aww shit," Lonnie called off laughing, "Yo' son you done crossed the damn line on that one. You know good and well if I wasn't with Kiyma, ole' booty-do was gonna be my wife."

As the whole room burst out in laughter Dream came out with, "Talking about greasy...all ya'll bout some greasy mu'fuckas. I don't see nothing but slick up in here today. So nobody...and I mean nobody here stuck to the agreement but me?"

"Ummm...Well...what...I'm saying...shit happens...nigga please," bounced around the room. He looked at me, and all I could do was shrug and give him a head nod. Poor Dream, just had his honorable bubble burst. Guess he don't remember how my dad use to always say, "A stiff dick ain't got no conscious."

"You know Dream," I started, "Don't even sweat the nonsense. It ain't nothing but a trade off of the chickens. When you come across that right one...that dove...you gonna know it, and there won't be no trade-offs of no type going on. Trust."

"I don't know Chief," he replied, "You may have gotten the one dove round these parts. Ain't a wonder none of these tell-all niggas' ain't try to get with her."

"Naw...we done had enough of that right there already. Long as nobody else up in here got a thing for Nube, the we good," I stated. The room got suddenly quiet. What the...

"So...ain't nobody else up in here wanted to be with Nube...right?" I asked.

"Well at one point...I kinda wondered...If you really wanna know...I'm saying... what... You know...Lil' Bit is hot...Maaan listen...you can't blame no grown man for that...I had always wanted a chance...To tell you the truth," came all the responses volleying around the room.

"Awww...you niggas' full 'a shit," I voiced with slight amusement in my voice, " But it's cool...ain't no thang...no thang at all...just keep in mind what the fuck I said at the top of the hour...friend, foe, fam...don't make a difference. Show any disrespect in regard to Nube...I'm looking to assassinate."

As the whole room burst into an explosion of laughter and remarks, I felt a vibe and looked over to my left to see Brick staring at me with some kind of look on his face. He peeped me checking him and throw me a head nod. Taking it for what I know was the final burying of the hatchet, I threw him one back with a smile.

Dream

Damn...my head is spinning after tonight. I'm just laying here on the bed sorting thru things before I shout out to Murad. I suppose he should be home by now, I decided as I reach for the phone dialing. All this time I'm thinking everybody on the up and up and Rod was the only one to break the agreement and ...

"What up Dream," I heard Rod's voice as he answered.

"Yo Chief," I replied, "Can you tell me what the hell just went down tonight?"

"Maaan listen," he came back with, "Niggas was out they minds tonight. All kinds of revelations being broadcast...I don't know."

""Yeah, who would'a thought," I told him, "I mean Brick secretly hating on you over Nube, amongst other things."

"You know," he responded, "I'm pretty much thinking it's just not all about me, but about me in the way in which he feels that Bryce looks at me...you know...I think shit don't sit right with him in regard to how Bryce always in my corner now matter what, yet always in his ass." I thought about it and concluded that he did have a point.

"Yeah Rod," I said, "You may be on point with that one there. Bryce is not too cool with Brick and his lack of...shall we say progress."

"Well you gotta look at it this way. Uncle Quinn was a good man, but not the best at setting examples. He was a little bit into himself, and that just didn't go over well with needing to raise responsible sons. Dad kinda mentioned that to me way back then," he told me.

"Wow...I sure wish I could remember more about Dad," I responded in a whimsical tone.

"Well moreover he probably made sure to drop them little seeds to me being that I looked just like Uncle Quinn," Murad said, "Probably trying to school me on the pitfalls of vanity. I mean they were brothers and I guess he watched him operate superficially all his life. Yeah...Uncle Quinn kinda went all out to the left with his...I guess sometimes being extremely good looking can be a detriment."

"Wow," I replied, "I'm glad that Dad had his head on straight although he was the younger of the two...kept our asses in line."

"Yeah that he did," Rod came off with."

"Yo Rod...check," I started, "All that Brick came out with tonight, you thinking what I'm thinking?"

"Oh no doubt," he answered.

"So that baby could've been Brick's?" I threw out.

"Yeah," he came back, his tone sounding remorseful, "Putting together all that he said, and knowing the way that Jazz maneuvers, there's a strong possibility...very strong possibility."

"Damn," I responded, "I guess we'll never know now huh?"

Before he could respond his other end beeped in, and he said, "Hold on." I turned to set the alarm on my clock as I waited for Rod to come back on the line.

Wasn't but a hot minute before he came back with, "Yo...that's him now. Said he need to kick around a couple of things on his mind...let me see wha's up with him, and I'll hit you tomorrow."

"Aight," I replied, "Later." As I hung up the phone, I couldn't help but think that the Tillman family had most probably suffered a loss. A loss never to be known...never to be replaced.

Chapter 68

Coming From Where I'm From

Nubina

Today I'm going on the Oprah show and I am well beyond excited. I mean, I was here like what...going on 3 years ago? But that was just a 15 minute spot highlighting my contribution to writing the theme songs for the sitcoms Just Us and Rainy Days. At the time both shows were very popular and I was merely being featured as the author to the then popular songs. Well this time around, I have my own segment on the show, and I am so impressed that I was summoned by the producers. Someone must have got wind of my work here thru the NAACP and put a buzz in the appropriate ear. However it's come about...I am ever grateful. This is so over the top. Murad is in the bathroom touching up his face. He doesn't bare an enormous amount of hair on his face, so it's easy for him to keep things in check.

"Nube, you just about ready," he called out to me.

I had just finished securing the second earring in place and answered back, "Yeah Rod...good to go." I gave my look the once over, hoping that I hadn't taken too much liberty. I have always admired Oprah's hair and wore mine similar to hers at times. Most currently, I'd been wearing it straight, but just so happen, I was in the mood to go it curly. Hope Ms.O don't have a problem with us sporting the same do today. Oh well...too late to change it now.

"Do me a favor then," he said, "Get my Blackberry and call the car service and let them know they can head out. It's under Distinct Transport."

"No problem," I called back as I went to retrieve the phone and place the call. I'm on my way to Oprah's....I'm so excited.

Murad

I'm sitting out in the audience anticipating Nube coming to the stage. She's still back in the green room while the last minute preparations are being set in place. I reached into my pocket to get my cell phone, and make sure it's turned off before her segment starts. Damn...I missed a call from Moms. How did that happen? Guess I'll give her a call back when we get thru here. Right now, I just wanna concentrate and feel this whole thing out.

Nubina

She's been here before, at the beginning of a budding career. This actress/poetess/humanitarian has now blossomed into an eclectic urban sensation and she's joining us today. Please welcome Queen Nubina. I followed the prompts and walked onto the stage to major applause. I approached Oprah and gave as well as was given the customary hug and cheek peck.

As I took my seat she opened up with, "Well...just look at you, all tan and sensational. You most certainly have blossomed. Love that hair."

"Why thank you," I responded slightly laughing at her acknowledgement.

"So Nubina, I understand since the last time you were here, you've chartered many new territories. I know that you've done remarkable work with the urban youth under a chapter of the NAACP right here in Chicago."

"Yes," I replied, "I've worked with Mr. Reagan and his staff at a facility for troubled teens and young women, and I've kind of established a growing repoire with the group. I enjoy the interaction that we have, and take pride in seeing some of them truly turn around."

"I have heard thru the grapevine that you have made a remarkable effort, and are graciously embraced at the home," she said, "So not only are you causing waves in the community, as we all know, you've had a role in the movie Finders Keepers, which grossed $39 million on its opening weekend. Tell us what that was like...your first acting role...am I correct?"

"Yes, that was my first acting debut, and essentially, it was a learning tool for me. All the seasoned vets were patient and I had such a wonderful time on the set," I told her, "I made note to observe the different styles and actions from each person and drew on their energy to create something of my own."

"And a successful creation of energy it was," she responded, "How many of you have seen the movie?" A substantial round of applause was given indicating the popularity of the movie.

"It was a small role, yet it had its significance," I stated.

"Significance indeed," Ms. O started, "It in fact gave way to your sophomore event with your role on CSI NY as the girlfriend of Dr. Sheldon Hawke. Tell us what that was like to work with Hill Harper."

"Well Hill and I have criss-crossed paths before," I told her, "And we share a common interest in giving back and building within the community, so when the opportunity came up to work together, it was a no-brainer. We had a great chemistry between us and it worked to bring harmony and reflect in our performance together. We have since become very close friends and I'd work with him again any day."

"So I've heard," she replied in a sly connotation, "I hear the chemistry was on fire in one specific episode, in fact capturing major ratings for CBS in the May sweeps. And we do have that clip here today for our audience." I turned and watched as the scene where the characters of Hill and I made illusionary magic consumed the screen. Wow…I was there and even so, this looks so…I can't explain it. Watching another me unfold right before my eyes…

Quaron

Fuck what nigga's be talking bout, rippin' me for watching the Oprah show. She got some good shit she coming with, besides it ain't like I got nuthin else to do up in this piece. Got another 18 months on this bid, so it gonna be a whole bunch more of these days. Damn, looka this here… they got that little honey Nubina from round the way on today. She tight…yeah she tight. As I switch up the size of the dumbbells, I peep these 2 fucking knuckle heads come up in the rec room. Shit...honestly I wish they carry they asses on elsewhere, I ain't looking to be dealing wit dey' shit today...

Nubina

"And speaking of chemistry," Ms. O said, "I hear that your personal chemistry is reaching new heights as well."

I felt a sudden urge to blush as I responded, "Well yes," I responded, "I'm in love with the most wonderful man in the world and he insures that our chemistry stays strong so that we reach new heights on a regular."

"I understand that he is your manager as well. Do you find that having a personal relationship with your manager to be undermining so to speak?"she asked.

"Quite the contrary," I replied, "Murad and I have a long standing history as extended family in a sense, so the combination works well for us."

"I have to ask," she started off; and I knew she was going in the direction of rumors and such, "I know that you have been thru quite a bit of controversy in regard to the paternity suit as well as a car jacking that you guys were involved in. What can you tell us about that?"

"Well as you know, it has been officially determined that Murad was not the father," I gave her, "but it was always common knowledge within our immediate cipher that it was biologically impossible due to the time of her conception. Their physical relationship had been long dissolved at that point."

"Okay," she said, "And to add pressure to an already tense situation, I understand that the allegations of paternity itself came upon the heels of the carjacking. I know that had to be overwhelming, can you just share with us your experience in particular with the car jacking."

"You know," I began, "That has been the worst day of my live thus far, and something I would never want to go through again. We were on our way to a business meeting, when they kind of ambushed us. They held us at gun point, robbed and assaulted Murad, and then tried to take me with them grabbing me by the hair. There was a scuffle as well as some shots fired upon us, and we were more than blessed to come out unscathed. Well...physically anyway. I'm certain that we both hold a small amount of residual trauma from that day."

"I also understand that Murad had to undergo an investigation, as both of the suspects were badly injured. Pray tell... how is it that the tables were turned on that set of events?" she said laughing out loud which started a domino laughter affect throughout the audience.

"Well Murad is quite skilled in self-defense, and somewhat over protective," I responded laughing myself. With my next response I took on a serious note, as I felt the need to set the record straight, "Most people have a preconceived notion about Murad and in some respect about me as well. We are both cut from the same cloth and share a mutual mindset stemming from our cultural territory. We both hail from the "hood" so to speak, and yes we are akin to those custom made ways and behaviors that are somewhat home bred in our community. But please understand... although we readily embrace the fact of "where we come from," we are by no means statistical by-products of our environment. Murad is a staunch businessman in addition to my manager. He owns properties as well as partnerships in real estate ventures. He has his degree in finance and is proficient in various investment venues. I mean, he is truly professional when it comes to business, and I would advise to never take that "business" persona lightly, as he does not feed into pretentiousness. He pardons no injustice, or instigative behavior from anyone, and people need to understand that he's real and therefore in the interest of "business"...devoid of games. A lot of times people see him and think he's all hype and glamour, or that he's slick or ghetto fab, and the fact of the matter is that he is just being himself...no holds barred. And yes...the customary patterns and behaviors that he has been accustomed to given his geographical up bringing, does manifest in his persona, but for the most part, he has not befallen the usual circumstances of growing up in the hood. He instead has used the exaggerated circumstances of urban life to graduate into his own productive, achieving black man."

"Wow," she gave off, "You giving up a mighty powerful word on this man. Is he really all that?"

"All that and more," I answered her with a smile, "He is truly the better part of me." With that last statement my gaze wandered out into the audience to where Murad was seated, and Ms. O followed my gaze with her own.

"Okay...let's get him on up here...let's meet the motivating man behind the lady," she said. I watched as the production staff prompted Rod to come up on stage and he rose from his seat setting off magnetic shock waves and applause...

Quaron

Just like I knew....these niggas intend to come over here and fuck up my day talkin bout, "Yo son...whas up?"

"What da' fuck it look like to you" I responded wishing these niggas disappear, "Pumping...watching my show."

"Oh yeah, he came back with, "Well what you watching? What...fuckin Oprah? Man ...this nigga here looking at...whoa! Thas' fucking dem! Poo...check this shit."

"Ahh yeah...Damn...that's that fly-ass goddess right there," Poo responded, "Damn shorty still sexy as hell, sure wish I could'a got her."

Wait...hole up don't tell me.... "Yo," I finally cut in, "Don't tell me that this here who you mu'fuckas car jacked?"

"Yeah thas fucking him," Frenchy said.

"Maann listen... you don't even know who you was up against," I put out, "That's fucking Murad Tillman. I went to school with his people and they aint no joke."

"Aww...they ain't all that...whas' so fuckin special bout dem?" Frenchy's dumb ass asked me.

"Well you obviously don't know... they got shit on lock round the way. It's like a bazillion of dem," I told them, "Some in law enforcement, they own some spots on the block, some of them mu'fuckas are lawyers and shit, and some of them just straight thugged. You can't do no shit by one of them without it being found out, them mu'fuckas got eyes and ears everywhere. Besides, I happen to know Murad Tillman is up on his game. He ain't got time for starting no trouble...just don't cross him tho'...cause he known for taking niggas down."

"Oh he ain't fucking all dat," Frenchy said.

"Oh really," I told him, "I heard he laid ya' ass the fuck out. Had you and ya' boy slipping in and out of darkness."

"Man...fuck you Yo," Frenchy gonna say, "I just was having a bad day, and then he caught Poo off guard."

"Man go head with that bullshit you talking," I told him, "You ain't know who the fuck you was runnin up on and you got what ya' ass deserve, most especially for putting your hands on his lady. Do ya'll know that's Nubina?"

"Who the fuck is she?" Frenchy asked.

"Queen Nubina," I came right back with, "She straight righteous with hers, real good people and always doing things for the community."

"Well I'on't know bout no damn Nubina," Poo said, "All is know is shorty git my dick harder than a mu'fucka."

This little fucking nasty pervert, I'm thinking. "Yo son...watch ya 'mouth," I told him, "She don't bear no disrespect from yur'ass..."

"Ahh...no...on the real," he answered with his stupid ass, "In fact my shit fuckin steel grid right now. Damn just look at her...I bet she got that good ass pussy...Yeah, I know she do...and it's probably sweet. Yeah...I think I smell her sweet juicy ass thru the TV, damn I wish I had another chance with her, I'd... "

See...this piece of shit here up on my nerve. Not only is he disrespecting one of our own...he fucking invading my space, and got me missing my show. You know what....

"Here nigga...catch," I told him tossing the dumbbells straight at his head. That shit caught him right between the eyes, and his ass folded like a bad hand going up against the 2 of spades. I looked over at his trife ass laying on the floor and took a seat blowing out a sigh of relief. Now I can watch the rest of my fucking show in peace...

I watched as Murad proceeded to the stage, and felt an immediate rush of pride. I could sense that he was aware of the private uproar he was causing in the audience, yet he held his usual suave demeanor. As he walked up on the stage, I saw Ms. O give a double take, and proclaim, "Yes indeed...yes indeed."

Murad came over and gave Ms. O the traditional hug and kiss on the cheek, then turned to me and gave me a romance filled kiss on the lips, immediately met by ooo's and ahhs' from the audience before he took a seat.

"Welcome...welcome," she started, "Yes indeed...yes indeed. You've certainly caused a reaction on the set today. So how's it feel causing such a stir everywhere you go?"

Rod smiled and answered, "It's something that I don't quite pay attention to much anymore. I learned early on in life that my physical appearance doesn't lend much validity to my true person."

"I guess that's a good attitude to take," she told him, "I can see how that would be essential in keeping you somewhat grounded, cause if you're only half the man she described in personality, this half right here would make up for any other deficiency."

Rod remained charismatic with a polite smile, and responded with a simple, "Thank you."

"So tell me," Ms. O asked him, "How do feel about Nubina and her burgeoning career? I mean it has to pose a few tense moments with you managing her as well as maintaining a romantic relationship."

"It has it moments of adversity," Rod replied, "But Nubina and I have a long standing history as friends and business partners that proceed the relationship component, and I truly believe that foundation is what keeps us in sync with work as well as play. So...we good...always." He followed that up with another of his magnetically brilliant smiles and the audience just ooohhh...aaahhhheed.

"Well yes indeed...yes indeed," Oprah said, "There can't be no other way but good when this is what you have to work with.

Right ladies?" To which the audience threw out "Yes…oh yes…amen" accompanied by deliberate applause.

She and I both laughed along to the response of the audience, then she turned to Murad and posed, "How does it effect you if at all, when Nubina has to play such a steamy role as she did on CSI? You know her guest appearance brought very high ratings to the show."

"Well," Rod started, "Her vision speaks for itself, but it is her persona which backs up the fact that she is the ultimate beauty. So yeah," he chuckled, "There's been a time or two my element of being secure was tested, but she is so good in letting me know in more ways than one, that no matter how big a star she may become…I will always play the role of her leading man."

"Ooooo…..aaawww…ooohhh," responded the audience.

"Well I must say," Ms. O proclaimed in a sassy tone, "You'se two are just each other's biggest fans huh?"

As Rod just smiled, I laughed and openly said, "The best arrangement that I know of."

"Well." Oprah came back, "Speaking of the leading man, my producers tell me that you just had a birthday 2 weeks ago, and it entailed something very special for you. They didn't reveal what, so would you like to share with us? "

"Yes…yes I did," Rod answered, "I decided that in order to make this birthday like no other, I would bestow upon myself the very special gift of asking Nubina to marry me. And she in turn topped my gift by presenting me with the best present that any man could hope for when she responded yes."

The audience went wild with gasps, comments, and applause as I instinctively held out my left hand and the camera zoomed in to let America marvel at my ostentatious pink diamond ring…totaling 6 carats.

Jazmine

"Damn girl" Deena had to say all loud and shit, "Did you see that fucking rock he got her?"

"Yeah, I seen it," I answered her hotly, "Why you fucking yelling for?"

Deena love the Oprah show, so she got the shit on and just my damn luck; I gotta watch Murad up on here with Nube. "Okay wait a minute now heifer," she came back with, "You the one tried to play science project and fucked everything up between you and him…so don't come at me like that."

Okay now…this bitch here getting on my nerve. She think cause she let me make a few dollars around here that I got to kiss her ass. I mean I'm grateful, since my company done went and let me go. After the thing with Murad came out, they started digging up petty shit, talkin bout I'm always absent, my lunch breaks are too long, oh and all kinds of bull. After like 3 warnings they went ahead and let me go. Now I gotta work wherever, so I can keep up my payments to Rod, or face criminal charges. Damn I had shit good until that little bitch up on that stage started buzzin in his ear. What I wouldn't give to wring her fucking neck! But shit…I know Murad ain't playing…If I wring her neck, I might as well wring my own, cause he straight sick over that bitch and would damn sure come after me. Oh well…I just kept pushing the broom sending the dust, hair and debris flying thru the air.

Chapter 69

Checkmate

Nubina

Rod and I are here at Sarafins tonight to do another community fund raiser. I came to give a performance where all proceeds would go to the YMCA of Orange to help send kids away to summer camp. The turnout was pretty good, so I'm hoping that we hit our mark in raising the needed revenue. I feel especially good about giving back to the community. It really feels good to know that you are making a difference in someone's life. I had just finished my last set, and was looking forward to getting home. Murad and I wanted to view the PBS segment to which I penned the narrative. There was an encore presentation coming on at 11:00 pm. If we get out of here in the next 15, we should be able to make it.

I left the stage and signed a few autographs and took a few pictures, before Rod stepped in to retrieve me. Just as we were preparing to leave, Minks sidelined us by his office to secure a signature from Murad pertaining to business.

"I'll be right back Bae, I promise," he told me as he followed Minks inside. I stood there for just a minute, then decided that I'd go on over to the bar and get something cool to drink. I had gotten no farther than the second booth nearest the bar, when a familiar figure emerged from the booth blocking my path. I looked up and...

"Trey," I said, "What are you doing here?"

"I heard that you were appearing, and I'm here supporting just like everyone else," he responded.

"Well okay," I answered, "That's good of you...did you enjoy the show?"

"Oh no doubt," he answered, "No doubt...but truly, I came because I really need to speak with you Beena. I'm going thru something right now, and it's imperative that I have your ear on this."

"Is that right?" I came back with, "So what is it that you needing to say this time Trey?" Before he could answer I felt a sense of déjà vue in the air as Murad slipped up behind me embracing me, and repeated me verbatim, "So what is it that you needing to say this time...Trey?"

Murad

What the fuck? Money here is like some fucking Saran Wrap and shit. He got a damn cling-on hold to the idea that he can keep running up on Nube. I stood there with Nube in my arms swaying back and forth for emphasis, and he just stood there hard-core hating.

Finally he opened his mouth and came off with, "What I need to say...doesn't concern you."

My temper flared immediately. I felt Nube grew tense as she begin to stand her ground in front of me, knowing that I was about to slide her to the side and go off on dude. "Nigga...you must be out'cha fucking mind," I started, my voice accelerating in volume, "**Anything** you got to say to her concerns me. Don't make the undisputed mistake of thinking I won't wipe the floor wit' ya ass this time around." All the while I'm trying to gently remove Nube from in front of me, but she's holding on steady, and I don't want to force it and hurt her.

"You was on some lucky shit last time bruh," he threw back at me.

"Really," I replied trying to pry Nube loose from me, "You wanna check my luck this time and see how you stack up mu'fucka?"

"Rod...Trey," Nube intervened, "We not gonna do this, not here...not tonight."

"Well it's apparent that Midnight here is persistent in trynna get his fucking dome split by stalking and shit. What's the purpose for all the unannounced encore appearances? What the fuck don't he understand about us being together?" I stated, this clown was getting on my last nerve.

"Whatever man," he came back with, "You ain't nothing but a high class thug, like I said that's been getting by on pure luck. Beena...I just need to talk to **you**...please?" This time I did grab Nube...much harder than I wanted to.

"Rod," she cried out more in alarm than out of pain as she knew my firmness with her meant I was ready to do damage.

I blew out a deep breath of air and stopped as she turned around to face me wrapping her arms around my waist.

"Murad," she voiced softly, "Please...please let me handle this. I promise you that I'm gonna make everything right. I promise everything will be handled here...tonight."

"Nube," I started back but she ambushed me with them beautiful eyes pleading with me, "Murad...baby...I promise. Just a few minutes, everything will be straight and then we outta here." I looked at her again, checking for validity and she replied with her eyes asking me to trust her.

"Fine," I said, "This is your thing...you handle it. I'll be at the bar."

I gave her a kiss, and proceeded to the bar stuffing my hands in my jacket pocket. Phew...I breathed out...his punk ass got that one off.

I'm trynna practice my patience, working on keeping my temper in check, but Midnight here feeling like he in a position to challenge me and...whoa...wait a minute...what is this I'm thinking as my hand comes across something in my pocket. I pull it out and realize that it's my Stealth hearing device that I utilize in my business meetings. The one I ordered from TV off the paid program station Nube rips me for watching. I remember now my last minute rush to get out the house on time and not really wanting to sport this jacket. The shit must have been in the jacket pocket since the last time I'd worn it...I guess that meeting with Rubenstein and Jabowitz. Wearing this last minute hook-up has now turned out to be a blessing in disguise. I know this shit ain't right, but desperate times call for desperate measures. It ain't so much as I don't trust Nube to handle her handle...I don't trust dude to be respectful and play fair. I walked over to the bar and took a seat, ordered a drink then turned around to survey the happenings. Nube was no dummy...she waited until I got my ass seated before she even invited him to have a seat in the booth and start their discussion. It was all well and good, cause as they sit down, I turned it on and put the earpiece in my ear prompt and ready.

"Trey," she started off, "What's going on? You up in here about to tangle with Murad...for what? Calling him names and such...a thug Trey...where is all this coming from?"

"Beena," he answered her, "I stand behind everything I said about him...he's volatile, he's crude and you talking bout marrying this man? Not only that...I gotta find out about it on TV?"

"Well I don't understand Trey...was I supposed to send you out a personal announcement?" she responded, "Since when did my private life need a security clearance from you?"

"Beena, come on," he dragged out, "I know his kind. This dude is so far from the man you used to tell me you wanted. So far from all that you stand for. He is so over the top on materialism, so flashy, and has had more than his fair share of women. He's all about flossing and frontin and living in the limelight. I don't know how he could possibly put it any kind of quality time or offer you the exploration of the true essence of life."

"And just how have you come to this conclusion Trey? Exactly what do you so call know to substantiate your claims?" she asked.

"Come on Beena," he replied, "This cat here walking around iced like Hov, wearing high end gear, and pushing luxury whips. His very existence screams exactly what he's about...game. He knows what he's doing to put a specimen such as yourself on his arm. That right there gives him accolades and props in his circle. Now...do you really think that marriage will quench the playa in him?"

She paused and took a deep breath before she replied, then got right into it, "Trey, I'm sorry that you have come to this conversation so misinformed. Yes Murad likes things of a material nature, and yes...woman have been a part of his past, but game has nothing at all to do with it. What he's worked hard for and what he's attained has nothing to do with any gaming. I've come to know that game can be brought on as well as played by anybody that harbors it in their mindset. Speaking from experience... you came to me dealing in nothing but game and you were living just as much from paycheck to paycheck as the next man. Your lack of material assets certainly did not limit your participation. So tell me...why does he have to fall into a category dictated by you simply because he has tangible possessions that convey his success? If you were listening when you saw our "announcement" on TV, you should be able to understand that he and I have both worked hard together as business partners to accumulate what we have. In fact he has done the burden of the footwork, while I had the easier part...to orate, and speak my mind. He saw my vision and believed in my dream; so much so that he went and took crash courses in what he needed to know so that he could operate efficiently in the entertainment business. He always has my best interest at heart and always secures nothing but the best deals and offers for me. And he participates Trey...unlike you...he gets involved in my research and willingly rehearses, or reviews or does whatever to assist me when I have an engagement. That man believes in me...in me Trey. So what do I care if he likes to look good, sport jewelry and drive nice cars. In fact...he does it rather well. So who am I to try and blanket his steelo?"

Ole boy seemed to hesitate on that, I guess he wasn't caring too much for the output he received. But I know a man of such desperation wouldn't stop there, and he supported my theory by coming back with, "You know what Beena...forget all that. All that is irrelevant when it comes to you and me. What is relevant is the bond that fails to cease between you and I. What about the way I used to make you feel Beena? How about all the times we grew apart, yet fell right back into sync once we caught up with each other? You ain't telling me this man can top that? There's no way that he can pull the responses out of you physically the way that I can."

Man...this mutha' fucka here...it took everything in me to contain myself from not going over there. I took a sip on my drink as a diversion...a slow sip. I promised Nube that I'd let her handle this...and I'ma try to be that bigger man right now. Bigger man...better man...I don't know...but this shit here is starting to wear thin right about now.

"Trey," I heard her say, "Please do not go there. That is sooo like you to pull the sex card as a resource."

"But you haven't answered my question Beena," he responded trying to put a seductive spin on it. Damn...I've got to get a grip immediately, before I turn this damn place out.

"Trey," I heard her reply, "You want an answer...do you really want me to answer that?"

"Yes Beena," he gave off smugly, "I would like an answer."

"Well okay Trey," she started, "For you I'll spill my guts. You've always had that way of pushing my buttons, so I'll enlighten you with all that I know. First off...yes Trey...you really know your way around the bedroom...you've got a lot of talent. And yes...you got me to respond in such a way that I never knew. But now...I do know. You may be talented, but Murad is gifted. He's gifted in the fact that he can make me respond physically thru his intimacy and desire for me. He's gifted because his physical overtures reflect the deep emotional feelings and respect that he harbors for me. He's gifted because he's established a mental connection between us that doesn't require words or physical contact. He's gifted Trey, because he understands the value of being together as "us" and not into putting notches on the belt of his ego. He's gifted because thru all this glitz, and glamour of this lifestyle, he has his eye on the true value of it all, and that is he and I surpassing whatever to be together."

"You know... it sounds like you're using all those "gifted's" as an acronym for lack of size and skills," he threw at her.

At this point she just looked at him for a minute. I was sitting there feeling rather taken with the things she just revealed about the way she felt about me, so I was kind of subdued at this point, and just sat still on the verge of what was next to come.

"Wow," I heard her breathe out, "Trey, you truly know not of which you speak, but since you wanna go there...you ain't got **nothing** on him Trey. Okay...in circumference...you about toe to toe, give or take a millimeter or so...but in length...he's got you Trey...by at least another inch and a half."

"Oh for real Beena," he said kind of annoyed, "How is that shit possible, when you used to have problems with all of me."

"Because Trey," she came back just as annoyed, "He not up in there tearing shit up and knocking things down. He's not trying to manufacture and solicit screams and hollers cause he "giving it" to me. Like I said before, he's gifted. He goes in with the pretense of building and expanding the love we have for each other thru intimacy. He takes his time and initiates skillfully until...before you know it...my body's internally adjusting and complying. He takes me somewhere new every time we are intimate and I love everywhere that we go. You may have gotten me to respond in a way I never knew, but he gets me to respond in a way that I have **never** known. When we're sexual, we are building on everything that impacts us on a regular, and we draw strength from one another to keep our daily balance. So don't judge the content or value of a package by its exterior. He's everything to me Trey. Everything in a man I've always wanted...I love him Trey."

"You love him Beena?" he asked her all cheesy.

"Yes Trey...I love him," she answered.

"How can you honestly say you love him Beena, when I still feel the love you have for me? I feel it Beena...you know how we used to vibe," his incessant reply was, "You can't deny that it's still there. That's why I'm wondering how you gonna marry this cat? How you gonna deny what I know we both feeling?"

"You right on your vibe Trey," she gave him, "There is a vibe of love there. I will always have love for you, you taught me a lot...although very unconventional, the lessons proved to be fruitful. In fact, I thank you for releasing me from your life, cause it helped me to build on my own self-esteem and confidence and it made the way clear for Murad and I to develop the tight relationship that we have. And for that I love you as well...so yes the vibe of love is there...just not in the mode of which you thinking."

"Beena," he answered her after a 30 second pause with the tone of his voice teetering on defeat, "Baby...I'm on the edge here. I have never in my life wanted something so badly. I understand that I fucked up. I understand that I put you thru such unnecessary nonsense...but I've come to realize that I love you

Beena, so much so that I can't bear to be without you...not another minute longer. I really Beena...no really... have no clue what I'm gonna do if you don't come back to me."

"Trey...listen...overall you're a good man," she fed him, "You're a handsome beautiful dark skinned brother with much going for you mentally. You can achieve anything you put your mind to, and I'm sure that some very nice woman..."

"Beena," he cut her off, "I don't want some nice woman...I need you."

"Trey," she responded, "You and I had our season, a long drawn out season. And now I'm with the man that I'm supposed to be with. He's my life partner. You're going to have to accept that and..."

"Beena," he once again cut her off, "I'm not gonna be able to accept that, I'm not going to be able to..."

"Trey," she now cut him off, "It really is not an option or choice for you. If you don't want to accept it, you're going to at least have to respect it. Just as I need to respect that Murad is being very patient about all this. I really need to get back to him and continue our evening."

She begin to rise from her seat, and he took a hold of her hand as she stood, stopping her retreat. For a split second, the thought crossed my mind to leap over there and annihilate his ass, but that thought passed quickly. I had just witnessed the most concise declaration of love for a man from a woman that I ever needed to hear, so I trusted that she would put this all into conclusion as she needed to.

"Beena...I love you," he said.

"Trey...I love him," she came back with.

"Beena," he started once again.

"I love him Trey," she interjected not waiting for him to continue.

"Beena," he tried once again.

"I love him Trey," she once again put forth.

"Beena...listen. Just listen..." he tried to get off.

"Trey," she said stopping him in his tracks, "I would take a bullet for him."

That statement seemed to shut down his quest of pursuit and an intense moment of silence passed as he released her hand.

"I really do wish you happiness Trey. I know in my heart that you are sincere in having changed your ways, so I'm sure all that you deserve will manifest itself in time," she relayed to him, "But my man...my king...is waiting for me, and he doesn't deserve to be kept waiting any longer. So you take care of yourself and be at peace...goodbye Trey"

Now you know that I've been working on myself. And I have come to understand all about the bigger and better thing, and the attributes of being a true man, but I just couldn't pass this one up. I stood as Nube walked over to the bar towards me, and I discreetly slipped the earpiece from my ear, welcoming her with open arms. I leaned against the bar in my best, playa stance, with feet spread apart, giving her nowhere else to go but between my legs. I drew her into me and gave her that ultimate...official...we are oh so sexing tonight kiss, then pulled back and hugged her to me as Trey sat observing it all, rooted in his seat. I purposely hugged her in a strategic fashion where my hand was placed ever so gently but securely on that beautiful golden ass...while my 30G diamond encrusted Rolex blinged a bright white spot that bounced off of his midnight face like a bull's-eye. As I hugged her to me looking over her shoulder I flashed him a definitive look and threw him the ultimate lip nod that said....Checkmate mutha fucka.

Not 10 seconds later, the DJ booth buzzed me on the cell to verify my special request. He was supposed to come with it a little earlier but I guess he got caught up. I really wanted to do something special for Nube, but I got a sudden change of heart.

"Yeah Slick," I answered him, "You right on time. I need you to hit me with Jaheim - The Making of a Man - track 10. Yeah...right now. Got it...Yo...good looking out."

As I slid the phone closed, I heard the beginning of the song come on, and thought damn that was quick. Just as well...Nube just lay up in my arms as the song played. I just stood there holding her until she looked up and said in a silky voice, "I can't wait till I get home."

"And I can't wait until I get you home," I replied, "You ready?" She just looked at me with them sexy brown eyes and shook her head. "Cool...well let's make this happen," I said raising up off the bar. I laid down a tip, took her by the hand and walked out stage right...into the rest of our lives.

Chapter 70

Take Us Or Leave Us

Murad

"Yeah Ma," I answered my mothers call.

"Boy don't you yeah Ma me," she gave me back, "Murad...you getting married? Getting married...since when...you and Tania?"

"Yes mom...of course to Tania," I told her.

"Well damn it, don't get smart...I know to Tania," she responded, "I'm saying..." Ah...here we go I'm thinking in my head.

"I tried to call you on your cell phone to see if you were going to be in town for the 4th of July holiday...you know so you can come on over to Bryce's cookout, and here I go see you up on the Oprah show talking bout you getting married. I gave Klessie a call and she don't know nothing about it, so I called Bryce and he don't know nothing bout it...I called Dream. Rod don't nobody know nothing about it! What's going on?"

"Ma," I said trying to line up my words, "I asked Nube to marry me, 2 weeks ago...for my birthday and she said yes."

"I know that boy, I watched the show. Heard every word the 2 of you said," she came back all agitated.

"Aw'ight then Ma," I released in a soothing manner, "Something ain't sitting right with you about this...what is it?"

"Murad," she voiced slowly, "Baby...marriage is serious. And on top of that, you all running in them circles, there's a lot of influence...a lot of pressure, and she steady getting more and more popular Rod. It's hard enough to maintain a normal relationship, let alone one with such flash and shine. And Rod...you know how you use to be with the women, this one, that one and another one...are you sure you done with all that?"

"More than done...listen Ma," I began, "Nube and I share something real...very real. We don't concern ourselves with what's going on around us, or what others have to say about who we are and what we doing. And yes...she's gaining in stardom, but that's all the more reason we're committed to remaining together. For one it keeps us grounded on a day to day basis, especially when we out in the midst of the chaos, and secondly our trust for one another mirrors all that we stand for, and that's something that's hard to come by Ma. Something like what you had with Dad. I don't worry about her sliding off with someone else, nor does she worry about me creeping. Mutual respect has us just that close. I know you can understand that can't you Ma?" She sighed deeply into the phone, and I knew that I'd touched her with mention of the relationship she shared with my father.

"Murad baby," she gave off a in a more mellow tone, "You sound like you have it all figured out. I'm glad I guess...but..?"

"But what Ma?" I questioned her hesitation.

"I just want you to be happy Murad, truly happy."

"Can I just tell you this," I came back with, "It don't get no better than this Ma...no better than this at all."

That was 2 weeks ago, the cookout is today, and Nube and I are getting ready simultaneously. I do believe this is the first time we'll be together again with the whole entire family. That right there gonna be a whole nother atmosphere. Squashing shit amongst the fellas is one thing, putting things to rest with the women...boy...I don't know. But fuck it...it's gotta be addressed, and today is as good a day as any. Nube and I are gonna be married, the shit is what it is, and hell if we gonna continue to separate ourselves over a few opinions. They gonna have to take us or leave us.

"Rod," she called out coming in from the dressing room, "Which outfit do you think I should wear?" I took a look at them both, one a sundress, nice but cute. The other was some classy capris' and a basic sleeveless collared shirt. What...

"Nube," I started, "It's gonna be like 90 degrees today. I know you got some shorts and what not in there."

"Well I've got some of the outfits I had last year from the Costa Rica trip, but they're too revealing."

"What?...go on and wear that stuff girl. Aint' nobody thinking bout you showing too much on a hot-ass day like..." I stopped mid-sentence as I realized her point of hesitation.

"Nube look," I told her, "You are a beautiful, creative, sexy-ass woman who works hard, and plays little. Don't let other people's opinions create a false perception of you. You are the most honorable and humble woman I know. If you wanted to wear cleavage split down to your navel, it wouldn't change the person that you are. Wearing the appropriate clothes for a summer BBQ is not gonna define what anyone else wants to think or say. You've got every right to wear whatever you want, around whoever you want. Bae...listen...your inner beauty precedes anything you could ever be wearing."

"Really Rod?" she asked me.

"Yes really Nube," I answered, "You go on and put the flyest thing you got going in that closet, and let that be they problem."

"Rod, I just don't want Ms. Klessie to have no reason..."

"Nube," I cut her off, "My Aunt Klessie has issues that will be there if you came stompin in with a turtleneck on, so nix it...put on what you feel like...and what I feel like seeing you in, the hell with anybody else."

"If you say so Sire," she kicked back to me as she returned to the dressing room. Yeah I do say so, I thought in my head.

In the next hour we were all ready and set to go out the door. Nube had settled on a pair of easy washed denim shorts that hugged on every inch of her spicy, yet petite set of hips. The length was kinda on the short side, but not overly; the shorts somehow made her shapely legs appear more robust in color than the usual. To compliment the shorts she had on this top that kind of had the back out, but yet had this criss-cross straps that crossed over the back high up enough to wear a bra with. It was sexy, yet simple and classy. The Ice Blue color, I have to say, had her looking hot in a subtle way. She topped it off with these Donald Pliner sandals I picked up for her. They're like a hi-end one of a kind sample shoe. Since it was hot as hell outside, she was wearing her hair straight, pulled back in a classic ponytail. She had found some kind of women's health supplements when we were out in Cali, that she's been taking ever since, and her hair has grown like 3 inches and shit. I couldn't help but take in her natural yet stark beauty. I was ever glad that she had taken my advice to wear what she wanted: She was rocking her Guggi bag, as well as rocking the bracelet that matches her engagement ring. What she don't know is I've got the necklace to match as well that I'm gonna present her with to wear for the wedding. Pink Ice...I'm really liking that color on her.

Nubina

Oh boy...we just pulled up to Bryce's. I can see all the cars outside signifying that most everyone is already in attendance. On one hand I'm feeling good about seeing everyone again; on the other hand, I'm not in the mood for any unpleasantries. I haven't spoken to Sumira or her mom since November. It's kinda hard to say how that will all jump off, but I'm not gonna concern myself with that. As Murad said, however they wanna feel about us is most certainly their problem. I'm gonna enjoy all that today brings. After thinking over what he said, I'm feeling A-okay with my outfit. I guess I'll have to admit that I let myself be a little more concerned with Ms. Klessie's thoughts of me than warranted; it's just that she played somewhat of an authorative role in my life when Sumira and I were back in college. But...I'm a grown ass woman now, and I owe allegiance to myself before anyone else, and I'm so glad that Murad has reminded me of that. I glanced up at him as he came around to my side opening the door for me. He's so real with me, always...never afraid to nudge me back on track whenever I derail...I love him.

"You ready Butter?" he asked taking my hand to help me out of the car.

"As long as it's me and you Sire...I'm ready for anything," I responded.

"Cool," he said, holding on to my hand, "Here we go then. Let's get this shit rolling."

As we rounded the side of the house and entered the back yard, we were greeted with a huge chorus of SURPRISE!!!! In spite of myself, I jumped and grabbed onto Rod. The backyard had been transformed to project a festive mood, decorated with silver and white decorations, with balloons and banners reading

Congratulations Murad and Tania, Happy Engagement, We Love You, Best Wishes...all that. I was so surprised and blown away, all I could do was cover my open mouth with my hand in awe.

"Wow," I heard Murad say as the whole family suddenly converged on us.

"Congratulations...you didn't tell us...we gonna kill you...hey let me see that ring...yo dawg that was slick...damn Lil'Bit, you got that nigga sprung," came all the comments and statements.

Jarod, Kye, Sharief, Brick, Jarrell...all dem surrounded us sucker punching and ripping Murad all the way.

"Damn...Yo Rod, you was at the house on your birthday and you didn't say shit. That's cold," Kye said.

"Ya'll mu'fuckas ain't got to know my every move," he responded laughing.

"You ain't tell us but you gonna go up on Oprah and tell the whole world?" Jarrell asked him.

"Yo...she asked...I ain't offer," he replied.

I couldn't even suppress the blush and smile I could feel on my face, I was so feeling good about the whole atmosphere. I took a quick glance around the backyard and saw that everyone if not more was there, just like all the years gone past. I saw Bryce over on the grill, just cooking and smiling over at us like a proud papa. I flashed him a smile back and at that moment I knew that he spearheaded this surprise thing. Let me go on over and give him some love. I broke loose from the family bundle, stopped to greet Kiyma and the girls, let them get a flash of the ring, and promised I'd be back to dish the details. First I gotta go over here and see Bryce. As I attempted to make my way over, I was ambushed by my second heart, Lonnie. He looked at me, I looked at him then he scooped me up like he always does swinging me around, calling me by his favorite pet name

"Princess."

"Lonnie Blood," I responded back. And as he swung me around, I hugged him tightly as I whispered in his ear, "He loves me Lonnie...he really loves me."

He set me down and pulled back looking at me and said, "No doubt Princess...like no other...you remember that...aight? He's that one we used to talk about...feel me?"

As I nodded my head yes in response like a little kid, he said, "Let me see that damn rock sissy. Word on the street flying high 'bout that ring."

I held out my hand for his inspection and he smiled at me nodding his approval and as I laughed, he said, "Bruh got class with his...got class. Damn...my brother...my dawg, gonna marry my lil sissy! Ain't that some shit."

"Yeah Lonnie B," I answered, "Who would'a thought Murad and I would be getting married...wow."

"Yeah...wow," we heard behind us and turned to come face to face with...Brick.

"Yo congrats Nube," he told me reaching in and giving me a huge hug. Wow is right...where the hell did that come from? Brick has never been that kind to me. Always challenging every thing I had to say, or just being straight mean. It had gotten to a point that I kept words with him to a minimum. Well whatever this is about...no skin off my nose...he family too.

"Thanks Brick," I told him returning the hug.

He pulled back from the embrace, giving me a look that I couldn't call, and said, "Murad is a very luck man. I gotta hand it to him. Not only can he appreciate what's right in front of him, son know how to take action on going for what he want. Gotta give him his due on that right there. Nube, can I just tell you...I apologize for calling you out ya' name back on Thanksgiving...that was really foul on my part. I guess I was kinda going thru something...but anyhow...that wasn't ya' problem...so...I wish you all the best...and I hope that you and Murad take real good care of each other. I know that's what I'd be doing."

"Oh, ain't no standing issue on that there B," I heard from the left, as Murad slipped up beside me wrapping his arm around my waist, "We always gonna do that...always." I looked up at him and he gave me that sexy-ass lip nod before he bent down and confirmed it with a light kiss.

"Yo Chief...whas good?" Brick greeted him giving the customary hand shake.

"It's all good B...all good," Murad responded.

"So you ready to do that huh?" Brick asked him, nodding in our direction.

"Been ready for a minute," Rod answered, "I was just waiting for shit to be right on my end...and everything's straight now, so...we gonna make it happen."

At this particular minute I realized that I was originally on my way over to Bryce, so I excused myself to go complete my mission. As I released myself from Rod, I waved at Bryce watching us from his perch by the grill, still smiling and cheesing and I started my trek over. I was about halfway when I felt a soft grip on my arm and turned to see...Ms. Reeva.

"Tania baby...come let me talk with you," she said in that I'm the momma voice. What could I do....I followed her over to a spot at the picnic table. Before I sat down I shot a questioning glance in Rod's direction, and saw that he had indeed noticed my second ambush. He shot me back a look that said... "I'on't know Nube," so I gave him a look that said, "Alright...I'll deal with it...don't worry."

"Tania," I heard returning my attention to the immediate.

"Yes m'am," I responded as I thought....here we go.

Mama Reeva

"So how's it been going?" I asked her, trynna start things off simple.

"Things are good Ms.Reeva...very good," she responded.

"You know you all threw us for a loop when we saw you all on TV announcing that you getting married."

"I'm quite sure that it did Ms. Reeva," she said, "Murad and I tend to hold onto things between us as long as we can so that we can draw a certain specialness from it; cause once information is revealed true or false, it tends to run rampant."

"Uh-huh," I told her, "I guess I can see your point with that. Honestly Tania, I was a little surprised, but then again, not really so surprised at all."

"I'm not quite understanding your last statement Ms. Reeva," she replied, "What is it that you mean?"

"Tania honey...I never really got the chance to sit and talk to you since you and Murad made a decision to be together, and I'm gonna have to admit that at first...I didn't like it not one bit...not one bit at all. But I've come to put trust in the fact that everything happens for a reason. As a matter of fact, I think that I kind of saw this thing coming on."

"How so?" she broke in with.

"Well for one thing, when you and JT decided to come together and try a relationship, I said good...he could use something positive in his life at the time. Then right at the same time, you and Murad made a decision to get into this entertainment thing together. All the working and spending so much time together brought you and Murad closer than you and JT. I took a look at the whole scenario, and thought...not a good thing. I could slowly see the attraction building between the two of you, I'm not sure if the two of you were aware of it yourselves. And I said to myself...this thing is not good. But as time went on I saw that you and Murad worked so well together, and that you and this whole thing was really starting to go places. I could also see that you were just a little bit too much of a spitfire for my JT. He has always been gentle and low key, and I could see that eventually you would leave him for someone else that could match your spirit. Now given Rod's past, I didn't think that it would be something that happened between the two of you either, but I began to see somewhat of a change, and his actions have shown me that he has changed for the better. And Tania...I do believe that has every thing to do with you."

"Well Ms. Reeva," she started, "I guess first off...I wanna thank you for being upfront with me, and secondly I'd like to thank you for seeing things for what they actually are. JT and I were the perfect companions in a peaceful kind of way, no hassles, no pressure. But Murad and I share great companionship along with a passion that guides us to reach beyond the normal limits of a relationship. I think we're both in love with the fact that we love each other and we can't seem to stop building on it. Let me tell you Ms. Reeva...I never in my wildest dreams ever thought Murad and I of all people would ever be together, let alone he turn around and become the Mr. Right in my life. I mean...I don't have to tell you that Murad has done his thing in the past in regard to women. Never thought that I would be someone he'd even consider...but now I do know...it was so meant to be."

I saw her looking off over to where he stood, and I felt without a doubt that this thing here between them was solid. She over here having a meltdown, and he over there...peeking over here, trynna act like he not looking and steady trynna see what's going on. I have never before seen Murad show that much concern for anyone else. Hmm...yeah...this here is a true thing.

"Ms. Reeva," she said, seeing that I was silent, "I apologize for any disruption within the family in regard to the Jayson, Murad thing, and I sincerely hope that you are not up in arms with me about it, as Ms. Klessie seems to be, because...no disrespect to you... but Murad and I are going to be married, regardless to anyone's opinion." No this little heifer didn't...but wait...I like her, I thought laughing out loud. She ain't afraid to speak for what's hers.

"Tania," I told her, "Baby...believe me, I have no problem with love when it's true. You and Murad most definitely have my blessing." I reached in and hugged her just as Dream walked up.

"Hey Nube...Ma. Whas' going on there Lil Bit? You and Rod done went and snuck one on us huh?" he asked bending down to place a kiss on her cheek.

"Something like that Dez," she answered him laughing.

"Well look," he told her, "Dy asked me to tell you to come up to the house and stop by the kitchen, she got something for you."

"Okay," she said rising from her seat on the bench, "I haven't seen her for a minute, let me go say hello. And Ms. Reeva thanks for your words...they mean a lot to me."

"Yeah girl...go on before Rod bust a gasket," I told her, "He over there looking like I'm gonna eat you alive."

She laughed and responded, "I suppose he thought you may have been upset with me."

"No darling," I replied, "The only thing I would be upset about is if you and he don't get started on making me some more gran-babies."

"Oh Ms.Reeva," she came back with, "I don't know bout all that. Murad and I are so not thinking bout babies right now."

"Unh-huh," I said to no one in particular while I watched as she walked over to where he was, "That's what she think...If I know my Roddy, he knocking that down every chance he get. Be pregnant 'fore she know it."

"Ma!!" Dream exclaimed in surprise.

Oops...forgot he was here. I turned at looked at him and said "What?...Well he do...don't he?"

Murad

We been here for a minute now, and so far so good. In fact most everyone is showing us nothing but love and support. I can't say bout my Aunt Klessie nor Sumira...cause really I ain't paying neither one of they asses no attention. I did notice Sumira sitting on the outside of the circle while Nube, and her sister Lani, Bree, Kiyma and all them was yakking away no doubt getting all gassed up behind the whole wedding thing. I got that all under control...all under control. As I took a seat in the far corner of the yard, Lonnie came over to join me taking a seat right next to me, and handed me a Heineken.

"Thanks Lonz," I told him.

"So do you guys have a date?" he asked.

"Well...I'm looking at September 12th," I responded taking a swig on the brew.

"September 12th?" he came back with in surprise, "Damn Rod...that's like less than 2 months."

"Yeah well...that would be the best time to avoid any schedule conflicts, and besides...it could be tomorrow and that wouldn't be soon enough for me. Yo Lonz...I'm way ready to make this whole thing official."

"You know,' he started, "In the beginning everybody thought that you were just taking on another conquest. I mean ain't nobody say nothing to you about it, cause at the same time they couldn't blame you. Look at her Rod...she's all that...she's everything. And I'm not talking bout just the outside. Princess has got a heart of gold and more than what's on the surface. I saw that back when, when she was in her Badu-mode and sportin the Peabody glasses and what-not."

"Yeah," I laughed out loud to his statement, "I used to see her running with Sumira and think, "whas up with lil ma?" First off she and Sumira seemed like they was on two different levels and Nube just kept herself so plain and serious all the time. I mean, she was never ugly...just hidden underneath a whole bunch of clothes and a little bit of attitude. But now...she has definitely blossomed...blossomed into a flower that I want in my garden forever."

"Aww nigga...look at you," he responded, "All shot out over my sissy."

"Can I ask you this," I inquired, "How is that you and Nube have been close all these years and nothing ever kicked off between you?"

"I can't tell you," he replied, "I've thought the same thing myself. Well for one...I have been so into Kiyma since and although I did my thing, something about Kiyma just settled in my heart. On the other hand...I just never had that set of feelings for Nube. Something about her clicked with me, and she had such an easy way of talking and understanding that I just became attracted to her personality and nothing more. And it's fine just like it is...she's the best man...that's my heart." I looked at him as I thought he's a good brother. Yeah he made his mistakes in life...but he got an even head on his shoulders.

"You know Lonz," I began, "I'm glad you feel that way about her...about us. That's why I would like if you would do me the honor of being my best man."

"On no doubt," he answered, "Nothing would make me happier."

"Aw'ight then, that's settled," I stated.

"You know Rod," he said looking out over the backyard, where Nube had gone on to join a volleyball game in progress, "That's my lil'sis...nigga take care of her. I mean...I know you do, and you my brother and all, but take care of her Rod. Watch out for her heart Chief...she's delicate. She try to front with all that braveness, but she soft."

"You know Lonz," I started, "I appreciate your concern and you looking out for her heart like that. I'm honored that you respect her like that...and trust me...as my brother, my fam, I promise you...I will never intentionally hurt her heart. I mean some shit popped off that did kinda get between us, but trust me...I'm not trynna be added to her collection of busters. I wanna see us grow old and grey together... you know raising grandkids and shit."

"Yeah," he responded, "That Trey mu'fucka really had her twisted, and then JT...maaann...I don't even know what to say on that one."

"Look...I can't tell you," I came back with, "Trey...I almost went up in that nigga mouth on more than one occasion. Only reason he was spared was because of Nube. And JT...I don't know...he was man enough to cut her loose since he felt he couldn't fit the entire bill as her man. Trust me he got his own set of reasons on that."

"Well you know," he began, "I never could see that right there working out. I mean Princess got a whole lot of opinions that just don't coincide with JT and what he talking. I was wondering how things were between them. I mean first off...just as soon as they supposed to be together, she out running the roads with you. Now you tell me...what man that's really into his woman is gonna let her stay gone more than not with another man, regardless that it's his brother. I kinda knew in my heart that JT wasn't hitting her off...not at all."

"Well hell," I told him, "I for one am ecstatic on that fact right there. Look at her Lonz...she is...damn she is..." I had to stop as I sat watching her jumping up and down playing the game and making my heart stop and my body yearn.

"Hey look," he replied, "Don't you be over there turning out my lil sissy."

"Turning her out?" I threw back at him, "You don't know ya lil sissy well bruh. Her little hot ass be the one turning me out." He choked on his beer as he let loose a laugh he couldn't contain.

"Damn Rod," he said, "You held the state MVP slot for all years running. You mean to tell me Princess whipping shit on you like that?"

I don't usually get into bedroom talk, not even with Lonnie, but all I could say was, "Mad whipping me on a regular son...mad whipping on a regular."

He bust out laughing as he said, "Oh is that why you always got to call me back when I hit you up?"

"Maybe," I responded with a smile leaving my answer elusive.

"Aww nigga," he came back laughing, "Princess got you wrapped around her finger."

"Yeah she do," I answered, "And wrapped around her finger is where I plan to stay forever."

His laughing ceased as he stopped to look at me slowly nodding as he gave me dap and said, "I feel you bruh...most definitely I feel you."

Chapter 71

Cruisin

Nubina

OMG...time is running by so quickly. Before you know it the wedding will be here. We got like what, maybe 5 weeks or so. And it seems now more than ever, I've been so busy. Offers have been coming in left and right since my television appearance on Oprah. I have a new script for a movie that Murad and I have to review, and now this invite to this weekend boat ride extravaganza. Cinque Jones and his brother Deek are like super moguls in the urban genre or dare I just go on and say it...hip-hop arena. I don't know but somehow I became of interest to him and his empire, and an invite was extended for Murad and I to attend this affair. The initial call came from his personal assistant who cited that Cinque was interested in meeting with me and discussing the possibility of working on future projects within his organizations. I mean Murad looked into it, and concluded that it could be a good power move career wise...but only if I was interested. He knows that I don't generally like to rope myself in socially with the hip-hop crowd as I tend to believe their power is misaligned in the messages they convey in our community. I was kinda reluctant at first, but you know...sometimes I gotta check myself. There are some very positive aspects in the hip-hop genre and some very intelligent and smart people as well. It would not hurt for me to associate...and I do mean associate myself to the experience. After all that's how we learn...that's exactly how we learn.

I was packing my essentials as my wardrobe for the weekend had already been taken care of by Nyla. I'd finally given in and consented to a stylist since my popularity has grown. I'm thinking yeah...I need to be on point at all times and no...we don't wanna entrust that chore to me. "God no," I laugh out loud. For the few occasions that Nyla coordinated my attire, I was pleasantly pleased. But this time...I don't know. All I know is that some kind of itinerary with a theme for the weekend was Fed-Exed and she's been on the move ever since. I don't even know what's been packed. I know that she and Rod bumped heads, in that playful, yet I do mean business kinda way, cause although there was a theme for the weekend, Murad Tillman was letting no one dictate to him what to wear. I do believe he reviewed the itinerary with her, and they came to some kind of compromise. She made a valid point to him that we most definitely were going to be surrounded by paparazzi and our looks should compliment one another in our presentation to the world. And then the wedding is right around the corner and then…

"Yea…yea…yea," he told her, "We'll talk Nyla…we'll talk."

So that was the end of that. I have no idea what, nor how I'm being presented this weekend with all these materialistic, over the top, trend following crowd of folk…but…Oh well…I'll take note and chart this one for future reference.

"Murad, I'm just about ready," I called out to him.

He called back up the stairs, "Aight…I'll be up in a minute to get all the bags and bring 'em down."

Murad

As I put the bags in the car, I'm mulling over in my head what I know about this cat. I had Dame check him and of course his profile came up clean. Well hell…pretty much that's to be expected from a man of his stature. He ain't get to where he is by being stupid. Anything he had on the off-set I'm sure he most definitely had that shit rectified, cause word on the street's been saying that Cinque is nothing less than ruthless. Along with being arrogant, self indulged and shaving deals to pad his pockets, he ain't nobody I'd really be giving favor to. But hey…I can't do nothing but respect him as a self-made business tycoon. I mean…I don't know everything this man has had to encounter, but apparently he's been on his grind and was able to not only stomp with the shirts, but surpass a couple of them on the way up. I ain't one for hating on shit like that, in fact, business wise…I applaud the brother. But the fact is…he ain't no different in my book in regard to anybody I do business with, or anyone else I do business with relating to Nube. Partna' better be genuine in his intent, cause his ass will go down just as easy as anyone else if he coming on some dirt and grime. I watched Nube as she set the alarm and exited the house pulling the front door behind her. Since the boat is leaving from the 43rd St Pier, I had Chuck taking us in as well as picking us up on the return.

"Hey Pretty," I said taking her hand to help her into the car, "You sure you got everything?"

"Yeah," she replied, "Got everything I'm gonna have. Anything I don't have, I'm just gonna have to be without. I don't have the energy to remember not another thing."

"Well don't even worry about it," I told her, "For all that I heard about dude, anything you may want or need will be on hand this weekend."

"Yeah," she responded, "I heard a few stories about him and his cipher. What do you think has peaked his interest in me?"

"I don't know Nube," I told her, "But on the real...whatever angle he coming at...he better be sure. He'd better be sure."

Nubina

We up in this cabin trying to get ready for this evening's welcome reception. Of course Murad is in the lead in regard to being more ready than I am. I did get a chance to shower and I was now unpacking the outfit Nyla labeled for tonight. As I unwrapped, I held up the garments scrutinizing all the way.

"What is this Nyla got me locked into?" I questioned out loud.

"Let me see," Rod said coming in from the sitting area. This was indeed a luxury yacht with stately cabins. I was informed that since I was the guest of honor on this weekend cruise that we were given the VIP cabin, only second to as well as right next door to Cinque's kingly cabin.

"Whoa Butter,' he kicked off, "It ain't looking like too much to this thing. Let me see."

I held up a kind of metallic green bra-ish kinda top if you will. It was complimented by these ankle length ...I think chiffon dressy pants with muted metallic stripes of greens, gold, coppers and bronze that pleated all the way down. They were hipsters that zipped on the side.

"Wait a minute now," I told him, "I think I know where she going with this...especially given the instructions and ornaments she gave me for my hair. She trynna play off the Queen Nubina title. Okay....I can see it."

"Well whatever she trynna do, you need to come on and make it happen. They got a starting time to all this...you know how I am about being on time."

"Alright Mister...I'm coming," I told him, "Are you gonna help me with my hair?"

"No problem," he responded, "Just go head and get the outfit on then call me when you ready for your hair. I've got a couple of calls to make."

Rod always got some damn calls to make. That man...alright, I'm not gonna complain. He has a lot of irons in the fire.

"Alright then, go ahead," I told him, "I can handle that much. I'll let you know when I'm ready."

As he walked back out to the sitting area, I proceeded to go on and get dressed. I had to admit, I was a little anxious to see just how this hook-up was going to look once completed. I pulled the rest of the accessories out and was more than surprised to see...

"Thongs?" I questioned out loud again, "See now, she don't know that I don't care for extra curricular activity between my ass in the form of underwear. I'm saying...who wants the effects of a permanent wedgie all damn day? Oh well, it is what it is. I'd better hurry up and get myself together. I don't want to be the one to have us late for the first welcoming event."

I quickly but carefully adorned myself in the dictated attire trying to make sure that I was representing correctly. Once everything was on I had to admit that the outfit was phenomenal. It was like I had an Egyptian princess or maybe like the I Dream of Jeanie look going on. I see now how the outfit correlated with Rod's. He was sporting a pair of fabulously detailed linen slacks that had an olive greenish-golden khaki hue to them, and a slightly form fitting ivory colored tee of silk and cotton that had a ribbed crew neckline which gave it such a distinct look. And then not to mention his foot gear. Rod is not the type to really wear any sandals, so as a compromise he had on these deep rich brown leather kind of sling back shoes that had a few slits on the side and intricate styling in the front. I don't know where this man finds these things, but hey...he's always on the mark, no matter what. Okay...now here we go, let me get started on this hair. Nyla sent me these 2 circular gold hair clips with instructions to part my hair down the middle then taking the front and clip it up on each side kind of criss-crossing it over each other. I'm looking at this paper she printed out and thinking what?? Where is Rod, I need help.

"Rod," I called out.

When he didn't answer, I took a peek out into the front; there he was deeply engrossed in a conversation. Oh forget him...we down to the wire, I'm just gonna wing it and take my chances. It's a good thing Nyla had deep conditioned, beveled and pin curled my hair. I parted, scooped and secured one side in a clip as best I could. I took the other side and scooped it up trying to do the criss-cross before I clamped it with the other clip. I took a look in the mirror and noticed that it was lopsided. Blowing out a deep breath, I made an attempt to straighten things out. I finagled with it for a minute and when I got to close to what I think Nyla is talking about, I just said forget it and went on to comb the back down so that it would hang. Oh boy...it has just a little too much of a curl on the ends for this Egyptian look, but oh well...we gotta go. I took the can of hair spay, gave it a quick spritz and proceeded out from the bedroom.

"Rod," I called as I grabbed my matching drawstring fabric wristlet, "I'm ready."

Murad

"Yeah...I would say about 10 to one," I answered. I was on a conference with my man Boswell comparing stock projections. He was one of the shirts I was able to remain cool with when I left Schwabs.

"Rod," I heard Nube call out, "I'm ready."

I took at look at my watch to check the time and figured that I needed to put this conversation on the back-burner.

"Well listen Boz," I started, "I gotta go. Show time is calling."

"No problem," he answered, "Give me a call when you get back in town and we'll review some new options coming down the pike. Talk to you later."

"Okay Boz," I replied, "Hit you soon as I get back...Later."

No sooner than I hung up the phone, it started ringing again. Oh man...we gotta get outta here. According to the itinerary, we need to be up on the main deck in like 6 minutes. I took a quick look at the caller ID and saw that it was Lonnie. As I hit the call button, I spun around in response to Nube, and as I answered the phone.

"What up?" The rest of my words took on an adhesive action in my throat as I glimpsed at Nube fully put together and ready to go.

"Rod," she said, "We gotta go Bae or we gonna be late. This is our first time up amongst these folk and the last thing we need to be is late. Besides...I am a little excited as well as nosey...I don't wanna miss nothing. Murad...did you hear me? I'm ready...why are you just looking at me like that?"

"Yo Chief...Chief," I heard thru the phone. Oh damn...Lonnie.

"Yeah Lonz," I answered unable to take my eyes off of Nube, "Whas' good?"

"You son...you," he replied, "I was calling to see how shit going so far."

"Well...uh...we gotta go Lonz," I stuttered as I continued to stare at Nube, "I'll hit you...uhmm... back tonight."

"Uh hunh," he stated laughing, "Tonight huh...aight...hit me later. Peace."

As I closed the phone, I continued to stare. The outfit indeed had Nube looking like some Egyptian or Middle Eastern royalty. The little bolero bra top fitted her shoulders just right and subtly accentuated her breasts. The pants rested just above her hips with the richness of the colors vertically flowing right along with the pleats. She had on a gold-toned belly chain with an emerald colored stone that came to rest perfectly at her navel. Her wrists were adorned with gold and copper toned bracelets with alternating stones of emerald and copper coins dangling. They were matched with a pair of tear drop shaped emerald earrings that dangled and highlighted the smokey green/brown shade of eye shadow on her eyes. Save for the eye shadow and lipstick, she had no other makeup on her face. That irresistible honey complexion of hers was doing its own magic. Her hair was parted in the middle and gathered up on each side with matching gold-tone hair clips that kind of criss-crossed the hair at the crown of her head and then merged into a cascading flow down her back.

"Murad?" she questioned stomping her pretty little feet that were strapped up in a unique pair of gold-toned leather sandals with just the right height heel.

It was only then that I noticed an ankle bracelet with the same emerald stones and copper coins. Damn...she don't even understand. We got somewhere to be in 2 minutes and she got me internally trynna keep ole' boy in his cage.

"Oh yeah...damn Bae," I finally responded, "You look...I mean...you look....Hell...you look like I need to be giving Nyla a raise."

"Well we can discuss her salary later," she said walking over towards the door, "Right now...we gonna be late."

"Aight...let's make our way," I said following her, my eyes glued to that baby ba-dunk sashaying out the door. Maaaan, I thought to myself pulling the door shut behind me, keep it together bruh...keep it 2-getha.

Nubina

Wow...this is so surreal. This yacht is huge...it's beyond huge. As Rod and I make our way to the main deck, we were instructed to wait in line in numerical order as we were going to be announced. Here we go, I'm thinking. This is part of the hoopla that really makes me no never mind. But I'm gonna suck it up and handle it and take it for the experience that it is. As Murad and I took our places, I took the opportunity to take in our surroundings and the others who were present on this extravaganza. I noticed a couple of well known people, other hip-hop moguls, as well as rap and R&B artists. There was a sprinkling of actors and actresses as well, but none on the level of

Hill or Will Smith or nothing like that. Well…I guess that was just as well, sometimes the hype can be exaggerated setting off a whole bunch of private attitudes and agendas throughout the atmosphere. Oh…here we go, we are advancing in line to be announced. Wow…I guess I'm slightly nervous. I've never done something like this…curious to see how this all pans out.

As we stepped up to the break way of the upper deck, Murad took my hand as the MC began his announcement, "Please join me in welcoming the newly engaged royalty hailing from New Jersey, Queen Nubina and King Midas."

We walked on to the main deck which was set up with numerous banquet tables. As we stepped into the forefront, we stopped and posed as the series of flashes captured our "in-crowd" debut, along with a smattering of applause. We were in that spot for about 45 seconds and then ushered over to a reception table where we picked up our name tags for seating assignments. Since Murad and I were supposed to be special guests we were seated at a table adjacent to Cinque's highly decorated table, center court. He was engrossed in a conversation and apparently not even paying us any attention. I guess its just as well, this here is so not us.

As we took our seats, Murad took my hand and traced the circles within my palm with his thumb. I turned and gazed directly in his eyes and without me having to say a word, he said, "I know Nube…I know."

Cinque

"Yo Deek," I leaned over to buzz in his ear, "This chick we supposed to be recruiting…what's her name?"

I poured myself another glass of Nouveau as he answered, "Nubina."

"And we want her cause…why?" I asked him.

"Yo Q," he answered, "She been getting mad accolades for her work."

"And what she do?" I cut him with.

"Damn Q, "he responded, "For someone running his own empire, you don't keep up with shit."

"Nigga, thas what I pay ya ass for," I told him, "Now what she do?"

"Well she does poetry, motivational speaking, community empowerment...uh lets see, she's done a movie, been on CSI. I mean quite a few things."

"Well I ain't never heard of the broad," I came back with.

"Well the publications staff thinks she would be a productive asset to the company, and so do I."

"Well that shit remains to be seen," I told him sitting my cigar down on the custom made rest. Fuck it...I'm hungry and when I'm hungry, I'm moody. Ain't trynna hear about some unknown trying get up on her 15 minutes of fame on my damn ticket. That shit ain't happening. "So when the fuck I'm gonna get to meet this chick, see whas trynna get in my pockets."

"Well actually," he said she's sitting at the next table to the right of you. Oh...and there she goes. They just got up to go to the appetizer bar."

I turned to the right to check out who he was talking bout and... "Deek," I said out loud, lust evident in my voice, "You kiddin me bruh."

"Kidding you about what?" he came back with.

"Yo...you ain't fucking tell me she was banging like that. Here I'm thinking she gonna be some dizzy bitch with glasses, dreads and some kente cloth or some shit. Damn...well who that nigga wit her?"

"That's her fiancé."

"Man where the fuck she get a fiancé from? We ain't recruiting his ass so why is he here?" I asked keeping my eyes on this gorgeous specimen before me.

"Q...you really need to get up on other shit outside of your labels. They was all up on Oprah 2 months ago and announced it to the world and what not," he responded.

"Man I ain't got no time for no fucking Oprah, nor her insignificant fiancé." I took another look and said, "Damn...how the fuck I miss that?"

"Yo bruh," he said, "you really need to expand your world. First off...Murad Tillman is hardly insignificant. He is a very well known businessman and manager. In fact...he's her manager, and they been tight with each other for a minute."

"A minute you say...how a long minute you talkin?" I asked picking up my imported Cuvee and taking a smooth pull. He gave me a look...that fucking look I can't stand.

"For a good minute," he finally answered.

Well it won't be for too much of a minute longer cause... "I could use a piece like that in my collection...yeah...I need to acquire that right there," I said out loud.

He just gave me that fucking look again, but I didn't care. As I watched that incredible sexy ass return to her seat, I couldn't help but picture me grinding that shit out as she lay up under me. Gotta make that shit happen...gonna make it happen I thought. As I turned away, I noticed Sanaiya sitting up here with her lips all fucking poked out like she lost her damn credit card.

I leaned over and whispered in her ear, "You got a problem?"

She looked back at me hard and gave me a tight, "No."

Then we good I thought cause I know good and well she ain't thinking I owe her ass nothing...but just in case I gave her that hard look back and told her, "Stay in your lane Ma...just stay in your lane."

I turned back around, pulled on my link ...and took a sip.

Murad

Somehow Nube and I made it thru the welcoming dinner without incident. I mean, for the most part, people were cool...nothing too much over the top. You know some of these hip-hop mega parties and how some crazy things go down sometime, but pretty much everything seems to be above board. Right after dinner Cinque and his brother Deek came over to greet me and Nube. Just seem like after the initial introduction and handshake, he held her hand just a little longer than necessary. Been trynna keep myself above all that, but I do believe I'm gonna have to keep my fucking eye on that one. We chatted for awhile about a little of this and that, and Deek explained how their organization was looking for a new creative edge, and they felt Nube could be the person they needed. We talked on for about 20 minutes or so with Deek and I agreeing to formally meet tomorrow afternoon. With the dinner event being over Nube and I mingled with a few of the other guests trying to get a vibe on this whole thing. I'm looking around and I tell you...this yacht here is a piece of work. It's got every amenity going for it like a 5 star hotel. There's a movie theatre, an indoor bar/lounge including a rec room. There is a large formal dining room that opens out onto a small deck area. The front of the boat has a large open area that is currently being used to host the outdoor deck festivities. In order not to get too hung up with anyone we decided to take us a little stroll down the length of the deck. We walked passed the many tables and chairs set up around the place for people to socialize and get their drink on and such.

As we slowed up to take a view of the night, she turned and asked me, "What do you think something like this cost?"

"Bae I don't know," I answered, "It gotta be a huge piece of change. I doubt anything I would ever spend...but to each his own."

"Well we all know that you certainly know how to make a dollar out of 15 cent," she told me laughing.

"Damn skippy," I told her, "One of the reasons why your portfolio is deep as hell in the black."

"Yeah...yeah...yeah," she told me, "But all that really don't matter to me, you know it don't. All that matters to me is you...and you being here with me right now."

Although it was mid August, the cool night breeze off the water swept across us giving Nube a shiver.

"If you cold, we can go inside," I told her.

"No, I think I wanna stay out here and take in the beauty of the stars and moon up against the darkness of the sky."

"Aight cool then," I responded.

As she leaned onto the railing, I embraced her from behind posting my foot up on the rung of the railing. Aww man...I silently savored the sensation of being this close to her. I don't know if she know, but this here outfit had Nube manufacturing all kinds of attention. The sista's were checking the uniqueness of it while the fellas were straight drooling. Me myself...no exception.

As I leaned into her, I spoke softly in her ear, "Butter...you know you got me going tonight."

"Really Rod," she answered me in a sly tone, "Going where?"

"Going outta my damn mind trynna keep ole boy in check. That outfit is causing all kinds of havoc on this here boat."

"It's not a boat Rod, it's a yacht," she said.

"Well boat...yacht...whatever. It don't matter cause we definitely gonna be rocking up in that cabin tonight."

"Rod," she looked up over her shoulder at me, "All this beautiful moonlight scenery and all you can think about is rocking out the cabin tonight?"

"No," I told her brushing her lips with a teasing kiss, "I'm also thinking about how much of a raise I wanna give Nyla. You know...being that it's a recession and all."

"Murad," she bust out laughing, "Still trynna make a dollar out of..."

"Yeah I know...15 cents," I finished for her as I closed my mouth on hers. She tilted her head back and returned the favor.

Cinque

Damn...I guess this is just one thing that got my ass tripping. I don't know what the fuck has come over me. Ever since I checked out this Nubina chick, I can't keep my damn eyes offa' her. Something about her is different, I can't say what it is, but somehow I feel like she all that I need to get by. Ahh here she come now taking a walk with her fiancé. And sheeit...that right there ain't nothing but a misdemeanor; as soon as I get a few minutes alone with her...it's all in the bag. I gotta admit though, dude here is nice with his...got a nice flow going. Been checking his gear, and that shit's tight, can't say I recognize the designer, but he doing his thing. Deek and I both gazed over in their direction as they stopped nearby and he wrapped himself up behind her.

As I gazed on, I heard Deek say, "Nice couple. They look real fly and all...but damn if Money don't keep her ass on a short leash."

"That he do," I responded while I shifted my Cuvee to my left hand, "I guess you gotta give the nigga credit for safeguarding his valuables. A diamond like that is bound to be scooped the fuck up if left unattended." Deek turned and gave me that damn look again...he know I hate that shit. Monitoring me like he my fucking mama.

"Seem like you got a problem," I prompted, "Is there a problem?"

"You tell me," he answered, "You tell me."

But maaannn...I didn't tell his ass nothing...I couldn't. I was too busy watching as they kissed and holding steady in my mind the promise of having Nubina on my plate. And from this point on...don't shit else matter.

Murad

Nube and I are back up in this cabin and ready to retire from this first day of events. She over there standing in the mirror in the foyer recapping some of the hi-lights of the night.

"Rod," she started, "Did you see the outfit that little Cee-Cee had on? I mean, if that's what you wanna call it. You could see straight thru it."

"Yeah I know," I answered her as I began to undo the buckle on my belt, "I know I'm about ready to get comfortable myself, it's been a long day, and I've got a mission of my own I wanna pursue tonight."

"Oh is that right?" she answered back. "Well I suppose you right. I'm ready to see how this fancy over the top bed on a boat sleeps myself."

"Oh...hey...don't get your hopes up too much on the sleeping," I told her, "Cause I'm about to fulfill a fantasy that's been haunting me all day."

"Look at you," she came back with, "Mind always somewhere where you want it to be. Who says I'm in fantasy mode tonight?"

"Butter...it don't matter," I told her, "Do you know how much work I had to put in tonight to not drag you in some hidden corner of this boat and have dem legs wrapped around me like a pretzel."

"Really," she said starting to unzip her pants. I took my shirt and pulled it over my head and stepped out of my shoes in the process. At the same moment, my cell phone rang. I checked the window…Lonnie. I'ma need to make this short.

"Yo Lonz, whas' good?" I greeted him.

"Nothing bruh…nothing," he replied, "I was calling to see how things going up on the floating extravaganza."

"Dude…this here boat is ridiculous. I mean they got…" I stopped right in the middle of my description because Nube had gotten the zipper down and was starting to slide her pants off revealing a pair of thongs. Thongs? Nube don't ever wear thongs…I need to be a participant in this historic event.

"Butter," I called out, "Hold up Bae…wait…let me help you on that."

She looked at me thru the mirror, her expression showing confusion as I told Lonnie, "Yo Lonz…I'ma have to hit you tomorrow. Yeah…no…I promise." I hung up without any further ado, and walked over to Nube with intrigue.

"Okay now Rod," she said still facing the mirror, "What is all this wait, hold up…what's going on?" I took a hold of the pants at the waist band and slid them down revealing the matching green thong which set off that ass-in- a million just right.

"Damn Butter," I said my voice heavy with desire, "I have never seen you sporting a thong. You putting shit with me way over the top now."

"Rod it's just a thong, nothing special. I really don't even wear them, but Nyla thought that it would go good with the style of pants, and she said…."

She stopped her sentence short as I trailed my middle finger along the length of the back string. Sometime Nube be talking too much and this was one of them times, but it don't matter, cause I really wasn't hearing nothing she was saying. I was much too mesmerized with the fact she had on a thong.

"Murad," she called out, her voice having came down to a sensual tone, as my finger found its way around to the front. I watched her in the mirror as she braced herself on the vanity table in front of the mirror as I started to pursue my fantasy with a finger dance.

"Ohhh Rod," she breathed out.

"Oh Rod what? I asked her, my tone matching hers in sensuality. I started nibbling and kissing on her neck, while I let my fingers dance around in the V spot. Yeah...I thought, looka there...like 2.3 seconds and she starting to get wet as hell.

"Murad," she called out again.

I lifted up from her neck to watch her in the mirror and again asked her, "What Butter?"

As we stood both facing the mirror with my hands working their magic up in the V spot, I watched silently waiting for her response. When she didn't respond, I decided to plead my case and fulfill my fantasy.

"Nube...baby," I started, "You know you had me going all day. You so over the top, I can't believe sometimes when I look at you, that you belong to me. Just look at you Bae...you are absolutely beautiful. And you even more beautiful when you feeling good."

"Uhh..ahhh," she began moaning as I played my best up in the V spot. She closed her eyes in pleasure and I marveled at her beauty still. I don't think she even knows how beautiful she is, so I think I need to remind her.

"Butter, open your eyes," I told her, "Come on...open them up...there you go. Look at you. Do you see how beautiful you are? That's the beauty I see when we all into us. Yeah Nube...check the beauty of it all. The you....the me...feeling so damn good."

"Ohhh Rod."

"What baby?" I asked her.

"Oooo...where we taking this...I mean...ahhhh."

I laughed softly as I whispered in her ear, "Don't' move...stay right where you are. I'm about to take it exactly where it needs to go." I reluctantly separated my finger from the V spot and relieved myself from my pants and underwear. Ole boy was talking to me like, "Bout time." I took a small step back and grabbed her by the cheeks and pulled her back to an angle of entry.

"Wait Rod," she called out watching from the mirror, "I still got my thong on...let me take it off."

"Unh-unh," I told her teasingly, "We gonna leave that on. We just gonna pull it over to the side and...."

"Ahhhh..." I called out as I introduced ole' boy to her for the first time tonight.

She moaned so soft, so sweet as she closed her eyes again. I felt the involuntary tremors of pleasure she gave off as we began to fall in sync with our rhythm. Damn...just look at her...so beautiful. I'm so over the top with the fact that she about to be my wife. Damn...

"Nube," I called out softly, "Do that for me Bae...open your eyes. I want you to see just how the beauty of you turns me on. Yeah...there you go."

"Ahh...Rod," she said lightly, watching us thru the mirror, "I feel so...weird ...looking...watching...but...it's different...it's...so good. Oh look at you Rod...look at us."

"It don't get no better than this Nube...no better," I responded. We continued to flow in our rhythm as we watched ourselves thru the mirror, till I got the notion to change things up before I lost it.

"Nube." I prompted her in the mirror, "Baby...come on and flip it for me Nube...gimme a 360 so that I can see your pretty face up close and personal."

"Rod...baby...you kidding me," she responded, "You...I can't...it's too high up."

"Naw...come on girl...you can do it," I told her, "Get that leg up high...just like you do when we practice our kick-boxing...just do like I taught you."

"Rod...but baby...that's higher than...I've ever kicked," she answered."

"Look...look," I coaxed, "I'ma help you out." I shifted our position and placed my arms on the hall table so that she would have some support.

"Come on baby," I told her pulling out just a little to giver her some space to maneuver, "Go on...bring that leg up...come on...you can do it."

"Damn Rod," she moaned out loud, "You got me up on this boat like we at Cirque du Soleil."

"Then come on and give me your best shot Ms.Soliel," I teased her, "Come on Nube…there you go."

She started to raise her leg up high and I supported her sides with my arms as she attempted to twist. As she got the leg to the height of my shoulder, I leaned back so that she wouldn't have to pivot all the way around and then just supported her as she twisted and slid her way around ole'boy. Damn…look at her…she doing it.

"Come on Pretty," I hyped her along the last couple of movements, "There you go…awww damn…that shit was tight."

"Murad," she called out now that we were face to face.

"What Nube," I answered lifting her up on the edge of the hallway table as I went in deep for the down stroke. She wrapped her sweet legs around my waist and sent my desire to a whole nother level as visions of my all day fantasy began to mesh with the reality of the moment; not to mention the déjà vue of our very first time. Shit…I'm thinking as I watch our reflection in the mirror, we truly are rocking shit out up in this cabin tonight.

"Murad….baby," she called out. As I continued to deliver my strokes keeping in sync, I chose not to respond but just watch the look of feel good on her face.

"Murad," she called out again.

I leaned forward and lightly licked then kissed her lips and whispered, "Nube baby…it don't ever stop feeling sweet baby…you got me going Nube…out of my mind all day when it comes to you."

"Murad," she gave me again, whining on just the right note.

"You so damn beautiful Nube…I been feenin for this all day…all damn day."

"Murad…Murad," she kept reciting as I picked her up from the table and we continued our dance in the upright stance with her legs wrapped around my waist. We rode it out, grinding to the left…to the right, up, down until her notes of pleasure started to change. She began to accelerate the recitation of my name, the tone getting deeper, stronger.

"Ahh.oh…ohhh…Sire" she sounded off leading the way into the melody of moans that I know best. And just as she began her

descent into her symphonic odyssey of pleasure, I called out "Ahhh....yeah Nube...blow. Yeah Butter....you blow."
And that she did....all up in that cabin.

Cinque

Got-damn...she called that mu'fuka Sire! I can't believe this shit here. Yeah...I keep my fucking eye on my friends and that same eye on my enemies even closer. That's the reason I got the VIP cabin hooked with security monitors...I don't trust nobody. But damn if I was planning on seeing this shit here. Well hell...it ain't my fault...they could've took that on up in the bedroom. Ahh man I'm thinking as I recline back on the bed, visions of it all still fresh in my head. Nubina...Nubina. She got a body like fucking gold and real secure with herself. I gots to get plans started on this acquisition here. Don't think I've ever come across one like her, but damn... I don't need to waste no time in finding out.

"Maaaannn," I thought out loud. I closed my eyes and let the vision of dude sexing her dressed in her top, her shoes and nothing but a thong, saturate my mind. I don't know how long I'd been laying there like that, but I heard Sanaiya call out, "Q?"

I opened my eyes noting that she had emerged from the shower and was looking down at me on the bed like she confused about something. I took a look to where she was looking ,and realized that I was holding my dick which was harder than a mu'fucka and throbbing like hell.

I slyly clicked the remote to turn off the monitor and played it off with, "Da' fuck you standing there looking at? You see it girl...git on it."

Chapter 72

I Sure Hope So

Nubina

"C'mon Rod get up," I said walking around the bed.

"Uhhnn...girl, kill it," he replied, "They said pajama brunch...we got until 12:00 o'clock."

"Okay and it's 10:45," I let him know, "You know I gotta follow Nyla's itinerary and get prepared. She'll kill me if I don't pull her little outfits off just right."

"Maaaannn listen," was all I got from him.

"Whatever," I said out loud, "I'm gonna go and start getting ready."

As I headed to the shower I thought, damn....I'm putting too much energy into this weekend societal affair. This is getting to be too much pressure...much too much.

Murad

Damn....I ain't feeling like getting up right now. Nube and I rocked this cabin out to the early morning. How the hell she all up and gung-ho after that? I guess it's the excitement of it all. This 3 day weekend cruise and this atmosphere is really new to her. Back when we first started going out on the road, she would stay back in the hotel while I went out to most of the after parties, so I guess she just a little out of sorts. Plus throw in the fact that she's supposed to be Cinque's special guest, and was asked to deliver a speech after Sunday's banquet. I know that for the most part, she can hold her own, but this crowd here is not her usual venue, so it's possible she's a little anxious. But whatever...I just need another half hour or so....won't take that long to shower and dress in some damn pajamas.

It's like 12:15 and Murad is still not ready. I told him to get his ass up...now we gonna be late. Oh boy....let me take it down a notch...it ain't that serious. I don't know why I'm in such a frenzy today. I know that I'm a little anxious about what I'm going to speak on tomorrow night. I mean, I haven't quite selected a topic yet. Hopefully it will come to me...I dunno. At any rate, I'm kinda hungry, perhaps if I get me something to eat, I can transform this mood I got going on.

"Hey Rod listen," I called out walking into the bedroom, "I'm feeling a little ahead of myself so I'm just gonna go on up and get me a cup of tea."

"Wow...you that much in a hurry?" he asked me, "I'm telling you Nube...I'll be ready in like 10 on 10."

"I'm getting a little cabin fever," I told him, "Could be the rocking of the boat, but I just wanna get me some tea to settle myself. I'll meet you up top."

"Aight," he responded, "I'll be right behind you."

I left the cabin pulling at the imaginary bottom of my pajama top. The workings of Nyla in affect...again, she's got my midriff out with a cropped pajama tee, matched with some cotton madras drawstring pajama pants. As I walked down the corridor and up to the open deck, I noticed that my French Pedi matched the subtle tones of mauve mixed in with the brown and gold tones of my pajama bottoms. Once I got upstairs, I recognized a few faces from last night and said my respective greetings. I also noticed the very beautiful and tall young lady who appeared to be Cinque's companion last night.

As she turned to look in my direction, I opened my mouth to say, "Hello, how you..." Oh damn....she gave me the "look" and turned her back on me. Okay...what is that all about? You know what...it don't even matter; I need to go find out if they have some herbal tea...I sure hope they do. I approached the coffee station and asked the attendant, "Excuse me...do you have any herbal tea available?"

"Oh, I'm not sure," she replied, "Let me find out. I'll just..."

"Is there a problem here?" I heard a male voice ask.

"Oh excuse me...Good morning Mr. Jones," the attendant said.

I turned around to see Cinque dressed in his pajama best.

"She was just asking about some herbal tea," the young lady continued, "and I was just about to go find out if we have any available."

"Well good morning or shall I say afternoon Mr. Jones," I offered, "Look it's really not a problem...I can make do as long as you have some decaf."

"And good morning slash afternoon to you Nubina. Just so you know...Mr. Jones is the dude that signed my birth certificate and bounced, and I hardly owe him that favor... so please, in your case Cinque or Q is fine. And being that you are my guest of honor this weekend, no such thing about you making do on anything...I happen to know of a stash of herbal tea in my private dining room...come...I'll take you down there and you can choose whatever you like."

"Oh, I don't wanna impose," I replied, "I can just drink the regular..."

"Nonsense," he cut me off, "Trust me...I got everything you could ever want, or need....herbal tea...not a problem...so after you."

He gestured with his arm and so I proceeded back down towards the stairs and back below deck. Once we got downstairs, he led us to a beautiful mahogany double door about 3 doors down from our sleeping quarters. I tell you this was truly a very impressive vessel.

"Here we go," he said leading the way inside, "There are cups and a hot water dispenser to the left and a variety of teas on the shelf just above."

As I walked into the elaborately decorated dining room I couldn't help but proclaim, "This is absolutely exquisite. Very private, quaint and elegant."

I walked over to the wooden buffet table and helped myself as he responded, "Yeah...came up from round the way, but I have a certain fondness for classy things as well as a classy environment."

"Well I must say," I said selecting an Orange Mint and Honey blend, "You've most definitely captured an elegant environment.

This has got to be the epitome of class that I have come across thus far."

I poured the water over the tea bag to let it stem and proceeded to turn around, and became startled as I turned around right into the arms of Cinque. What the....is this on purpose...did he just run up on me? I think I better....

"No," he said interrupting my state of being shocked and appalled, "It would be the utmost to capture you...cause you have been the epitome of class that I have come across thus far."

No this nukka ain't take this there, I'm thinking as he has the gall to continue holding me in his arms like he right. "Uh....excuse you," I stated calmly, "I'm finding it hard to believe that a man of your stature and being would even approach me in this manner."

He must have thought I was being cute, cause he came back with, "Oh I see that you have recognized my stature, so I'm sure you would be able to recognize all that I can give you. As I said...everything you could ever want...and everything you need."

And with his last statement, he leaned in close and kind of brushed our pelvises together, revealing evidence of a budding bulge. Oh no he didn't! Okay now I'm offended...just what makes him thing he can come at me like this?

"Q?" I asked, "Can you like...take a step back, so I can see what it is you think I need from you."

"Oh you want to see everything I'm coming with huh?" he replied.

"Oh yeah...yeah... wanna see everything you think I need," I said building it up as he released me and backed away. "Oh...back just a tad further," I told him and as he obliged I measured things up, took my chance and raised my right leg just as high as I did last night and delivered a calculated kick straight to the left side of his cheek right under his eye and took his ass down.

As he hollered "Fuck!" on his way down, I paced the floor heated, my mind in total frustration, scrambling and rambling. The fuck...I'm thinking...this slimy bastard here! Wait till I tell Rod...OH NO...what the fuck am I saying...I can't tell Murad. He would kill ...for sure this time!!! He said he'd kill anybody else that ever put their hands on me...yes he did...he'd kill them if they do and he know anything about it. Damn...what am I gonna do? Let me see...let me see. I looked over at him and he's got this purple welt starting to spread under his eye.

"Oh damn," I thought out loud, "Look what you made me do," I stated as I walked over and knelt down beside him in concern. "Are you alright?" I asked in a huff.

"Bitch," he said gruffly grabbing me by the wrist.

"Bitch-ass," I shot back just as gruffly, shooting daggers from my eyes, "Let me let you in on some very important shit," I told him, "It would be in the very best of interest for everyone involved if we just forget all about this right here."

"We ain't about to forget shit..." he started and I talked right over him with, "WE can and WE will...or there will be 2 other choices to make, you can either attend my wedding, or I can attend your funeral...and I'm letting you know, I ain't missing my wedding over your sorry ass."

"You out ya damn mind...you think your fiancé Dapper Dan gonna do me something," he came back with an evil snort, "Bitch...you must not know who the fuck I am."

"Then we got a problem," I told him, my voice laced in icy contempt, "Apparently you don't fucking know about **my** Dapper Dan. I would strongly urge that you go check with somebody...**immediately**."

He stared me in the eye and I stared right back without a flinch, giving him a side head nod to indicate that he needed to let my wrist go. He released me and I stood up watching him from his spot on the floor, as he glared at me.

I glared right back taking note to the blatant bruise on his face and told him, "You might wanna put some ice on that...spontaneous falls can be a bitch." I blew out a deep breath, then turned to walk away. Just as I was about to push the door, I remembered...my tea. I turned around and walked over to the buffet, retrieved my cup and said, "Thank you for the tea...I appreciate it Mr. Jones." I glanced back one more time as I walked over to the door, pushed it open...and walked out.

Yeah...here she come now. I watched as Nube cleared the top step, and noticed something different...she seemed to be bothered.

"Hey Pretty," I said to her brushing her cheek with a kiss, "Whas' goin on? You looked perturbed."

"It's nothing Rod," she answered, "I haven't had a chance to sip my tea yet...still a little unsettled."

"Well what was the hold up on the tea?" I asked her.

"Well...I asked around about some herbal tea, and our host insisted on taking me down to where he keeps his private stash, so it took a minute. I had to let it steep...flavor it and all. Actually...it's pretty good," she said taking a sip.

Hmmm....I thought, something ain't quite right, she looking a little flushed, "Nube," I started, "You sure you aight...you good?"

"Yeah Rod," she answered just as Deek came over to greet us.

"Good afternoon," he spoke indiscriminately.

"Good Afternoon," she answered, as I peeled off, "Whas" good?"

"Bout to tackle this brunch," he replied, "Would you guys like to join me? This might be a good time for us to get in on some pre-lim's Murad."

"Yeah, that sounds like a plan," I answered, "You don't mind do you Nube?"

"Oh not at all," she responded, "I could use something to go with this tea."

"Then let's do this," I said as Deek led the way to a reserved table. I gestured for her to follow him and I would follow in place behind her. As I placed my hand on the small of her back, I couldn't help but notice the energy...it was tainted. I leaned forward and whispered in her ear, "Nube?"

"No Murad," she answered, "Not a thing...I'm fine," she replied.

I shrugged it off for the time being, but don't think I didn't place that shit in the back of my head. Yeah right in the back under the file labeled...Shit That Ain't Right.

Nubina

I'm so glad that the brunch went off without a hitch. Murad and Deek chatted the whole time, yet I couldn't begin to tell you what the discussion entailed because I was still all discombobulated with my below deck encounter with Cinque. Whatever the case, I somehow managed to put it aside and make it thru. After brunch, everyone retreated back to their quarters to relax, then get ready for the BBQ that started at 5:00. Of course I would be sporting another of Nyla's outfits. This time it was pretty classic. She had me in some basic white jean shorts, with a custom designed cotton trapeze top in a beautiful soothing shade of lavender that criss-cross laced up in the back. I had packed my own Via Spiga leather slides and made a point to put them on. Nyla had wanted me to sport a sexy sandal with a heel, but I just wasn't feeling like walking a tightrope today. I also defied her and just parted my hair down the middle and sported 2 braids. Since my hair has grown a bit, I am able to pull that style off and used the gold coined hair clips for the ends to keep the braids in check. That in turn had me sporting some gold hoop earrings that Nyla included in my accessories. I'm more of a silver person, but what the hey...nothing about this weekend is par for the course.

Rod and I are sitting out in an open area of the deck as the BBQ is well under way. They have food stations set up in a horseshoe with an abundance as well as a variety of foods. In addition to that, they have three grilling stations, one for fish and poultry, then one each for beef and one for pork. You know...I can't believe folk still dining on Pork of all things. I'm reducing my consumption of meat more and more; I'm striving...I'm striving, but it gets hard sometimes when that cheeseburger craving hits you. But the one thing I do know...I sure as heck could never go back to the Pork. Yuk!!!

"Hey Rod," I said turning to face him, "Did you ever get the chance to call Lonnie back?"

"Naw," he responded, "Maybe I'll see if I can get a hold of him now."

No sooner than the words were out of his mouth, his phone started ringing. "Damn," he said, "Who this? Oh hold on…this Nyla. Hey what up Nyla? Yeah…she is. I guess pretty much. Say what now…the caterer can't find them? Well if they not gonna be able to do the job, then we may have to go with someone else. I need things to be right and exact. Nyla listen…"

At that point, I just got up and indicated to Rod, that I was going over to the bar to get something to drink. I asked him if he needed anything and he asked for a seltzer water.

"No problem," I told him as I proceeded in the direction of the bar.

I know that Nyla was helping him put together this wedding as a surprise to me. I did not have to lift a finger…his orders. He said that contrary to popular belief, he has dreamed of his wedding and his perfect bride since he was a little boy and now that the day is here, he wants to fabricate the day dream specific. He presented his request to me so earnestly and promised me it would be the most memorable, most extra special event of my life. I agreed and so he is off and running with his planning. The women in my life are all up in arms about that…said I have a right to have some input and say about my own wedding, yet I figure…this man gives me the world without my asking, does any and everything to keep my life and pursuit of my dreams devoid of complication; the least I could do is let him have the creative reins on something he's been dreaming of for a minute. More important than the venue, the colors of the gowns or the rings, is the fact that he and I made it to here…this place where love truly resides and we gonna stay here until.

As I made it halfway to the bar, I felt an uneasy vibe. I turned around to see Cinque stretched out in a lounger, and he appeared to be looking in my direction. I really couldn't tell since he had on a pair of dark shades. I suppose he probably over there feeling some kind of way, but you know what…I am so over him and this morning. I got more important things in my life to contend with.

Subconsciously, I threw him a lip nod, turned back around and continued on my mission for some cool refreshing drinks.

Cinque

Pshh..Look at this here. She gonna fucking throw me a lip nod. I can't believe this bitch, I don't know what the fuck it is that's stopping me from taking action on her ass...but I'm glad I told Deek to get me the stats on her and that fucking fiancé like yesterday. I don't know who he know or care how, but he got some info for me now. I took one last look at her as I leaned over, removed my shades and said, "Run it Deek."

"Well," he started, "Not that much on her. Nubina of course is her industry name, she legally goes by the name of Tania Baynes. Originally from Brooklyn, came to Jersey at the age of 21 with her parents and 2 siblings. Her father has since passed, so it's just her mother, sister and a younger brother. She attended Rutgers Newark campus from 1999 thru 2002 and graduated with a BA in political science with some kind of special concentration in urban studies. Previous to moving to Jersey, she attended Brooklyn College for 2 years. Uh...let's see...she met and became friends at Rutgers with Sumira Tillman, cousin to the fiancé, and kind of just blended in with the family. Started poetry and spoken word about 4 years ago, supposedly dated another brother briefly, but it never went beyond friends. Murad became her manager around the same time and secured her a whole lot of top-notch deals. Not to say that she didn't deserve them, cause word on the street got her noticed and requested. Like I said, she does a lot of community work across the country. She was in that movie Finders Keepers, and she played Hill Harper's lady on CSI last season pushing them ratings straight thru the roof. She's done some writing for PBS, uh...some motivational speakings and such for 101 Black Men, the NAACP. Oh yeah...she did a callabo track with your boy L, outta Atlanta, and she's scheduled to do another project with his label.

Now for ole'boy...legal name is Murad Tillman, he hails from East Orange, born and raised. He graduated from EO High and went on to Bowie State University. He graduated with a major in finance and a minor in accounting. He worked for 3 years at a local H&R Block, then went on to work for Charles Schwab as an investment analyst until the same 4 years ago, when he became her manager. The Tillman family runs deep Q. His pops and a brother migrated here when they were kids. Their blood line runs back to some ancient Indian tribe in the jungles of Panama. They were raised in Maryland with their parents where they met and married 2 Creole sisters outta Louisiana. One sister had 11 kids and the other had 10...each of them had 7 boys. More than half of them are grown now with kids of their own, multiplying the whole clan. They got a whole battalion of them and they strong on the male dominance. If you talking bout males aged 18 and up...they rolling about 40 deep right now. Their numbers include any and everything from lawyers, cops, business owners and mechanics to car thieves, hustlers, thugs and convicts. They got a couple of students as well and 1 college baller that's looking like an NBA sure shot. They've had their ups and downs, but for the most part they get mad respect around the way. Murad in particular has a take no shit reputation, and has no issue with backing it up. He's was a 3 time Golden Glove champion in high school, and he used that as a foundation to build on his martial arts. He studied to the level of 3rd degree back belt and kind of combined his trainings making him real swift. I heard that Money is real tight ....like on some Iron Ring UFC shit with his. Last November some unknowns carjacked him for an Escalade and tried to abduct Nubina, he beat both them niggas into a coma...one at the scene and one after him and his people tracked him down in Newark."

"So him and his people wore them out?" I asked. I was looking for anything to dilute this mu'fucka with.

"Naw Q...he took 'em out single handedly. In fact they were armed and actually popped off on them. One of them ran off with the truck, while the other ain't had no choice...he got the brunt of the ass whipping since he was the one to try and snatch Nubina."

"So what the fuck happen to them?" I asked.

"They serving time...or one of them," he responded, "Turns out, people in the hood are very loyal to them. Cat was in jail mouthing off in a sexual manner about Nubina, and some dude who know them, clubbed dude in the head with a pair of dumbbell weights for disrespecting her."

"So what happened to him" I asked, "They transferred him to the hospital?"

"No," he answered, "This time he went down...and never got back up. Yeah word is Q...Murad Tillman ain't nobody to take lightly...whether it be business or personal, he gonna protect down to the T. He's well known for dusting nigga's that run up on him wrong. I'm telling you, Money here is true story Q...swag and all."

"So what you saying...this nigga here is the fucking American Gladiator? What...can't nobody get next to him? I'm saying...can't nobody be all that strong. Every great warrior got a weak spot in they armor...he gotta have a weak spot." I vented.

"Well yeah," he said with a pause, "I would say his weak spot is Nubina. If you wanna get to his weak spot, you would have to get to him thru Nubina. And that right there is highly unlikely, for one he's pretty much with her all the time and holds her more closely since that incident. And number two...I heard that he schooled her on a little self-defense just in case something goes down and he's not around. I heard that she can take nigga's down herself if need be, in fact..."

He stopped mid-sentence and looked over to me and said, "Q...I sure hope she ain't the one that visited that knot up on your face, cause..."

"The fuck I tell you," I cut him off with, "I fell nigga. Don't bring that shit up again."

"Aight fine," he responded, his tone suspect, "Well that's pretty much their story. So... think you got all you need to know to make them an offer?"

It ain't the offer I'm getting at I realized as I failed to respond to him. Actually, I'm trynna justify why the fuck it is I'm still burning for her ass, and what I need to do to get her up under my wing. I took out another Cuvee and proceeded to light up.

As I sat running things thru my mind, I heard Deek call me, "Q..." I turned to look at him and was met by that damn look he keep giving me.

"Nigga what?" I threw at him.

He didn't answer me, he just kept looking at me sideways. So since he didn't have anything else to say, I just lit my Cuv, slid my shades back on and turned my attention back to scoping on her. Because of course, now...I want her even more.

Murad

Maaan listen...I wasn't prepared for nothing like this. Some brilliant mind went and trumped up a Cee-lo game and yeah...it didn't take too much persuasion to get me involved. I don't know what it is, but a got a penchant for the game. Gotta thank my Uncle Quincy for putting me down since I was like 12 year old. Ain't like I'm a champion or anything, but I can hold my own. But right about now...I ain't really holding too good at all. Still...I ain't about to fold. This singing cat Touraije rolling now, and I'm hoping he don't make a hit. Aight...there he go...damn....trips. I threw down another c-note as did the others. He rolled twice more and nothing so he passed the dice. This rapper cat De-phine supposedly out of Yonkers was up next, but he ain't hit on nothing either and he passed the dice on, as shit continued to get deep, a couple of cats pulled out the game. We was about down to 5 when Cinque scored heavy on the bank. Two more dropped out after that, leaving me, Cinque and the hype man Noopy. Man...listen, I had dropped a grip on this game and I wasn't about to fold now. Cinque was up now, so he rolled...did his thing and came up with 331. He looked me over and said, "Double or nothing."

I gave him a swift look topped with a head nod and replied, "Let's rock it."

Just as he passed the dice over to me, my blackberry went off. I took a quick look and saw that is was Nyla. "Excuse me for just a sec," I told them.

"Yo Nyla listen," I told her, "I'm kinda in the middle of something...I'll call you back....say what now....schedule conflict? Can't we get him to reschedule...the wedding is like 3 weeks away...what?"

"Yo Son," Cinque said interrupting, "You gonna roll or we calling this shit square?"

Damn I gotta handle this with Nyla...shit...I don't wanna miss my turn. "Aight...bear with me a sec," I told him. "Yo Nube," I called out across the deck, with a little more volume than I intended. She turned and gave me a questioning look, but made her way towards me just the same.

"Listen," I explained, "I'm up next, but I gotta handle this call, so I need you to hold it down for me a coupla rounds."

"'Uh...you want her to fill in for you?" Noopy asked.

"You gentlemen don't have a problem with that...do you?" I questioned.

They looked at one another and smiled, "Naw...we good," was the response.

I turned to Nube and gave her a head twist that said, "Are you good with this?" She gave a twist back that said, "It's been a minute Rod...but hey."

She took a deep breath, as I handed her my knot, then she turned in towards the game and said, "Aight...let's roll."

Nubina

Oh boy....what has Rod done went and got me into. I was across the deck chilling with a couple of the ladies who to my surprise were very open and friendly with me. I mean we were really hitting it off and getting into some good conversation on men and their expectations when Rod called me out of the blue to come and represent him in this game. Exactly...case in point. Well anyhow, I'm not about to leave him hanging. So here we go.

As Cinque tried to bore a hole thru me with his eyes, I gave him the straight poker face and said, "What's the bank?"

"Double or nothing," he responded his voice tight and his gaze locked onto my face.

You know what...I'm not gonna let this nukka rattle me...I ain't do nothing to him that he didn't deserve.

"Well alright," I said looking down at the bills laid out on deck. I added 10 c's to the pile and proceeded to roll. First roll out I hit 3 sixes. I did a double check at their faces, cause I think that means I get the pot. When they said nothing, I scooped down and claimed the money. I peeled off another 10 c's and laid it down.

"Still double or nothing," I asked.

Cinque did not answer, just fronted his paper, while Noopy hesitated, then threw his 10 down letting a "Maaaan," slide out the side of his twisted lips. This time I rolled a 325...damn...that I know don't amount to nothing. One more roll. A 446...so I'm up on 6. I passed the dice on to Noopy so he could continue the new round.

"Aight," he started, "I need to get loose right about now. Aight here we go...unnh."

He came out with a hit of 341.

"Damn," he said securing the dice to roll again. He tossed the dice against the deck and came up with a 642.

"Shit," he let out, "Gotta hit it just right this time...gotta spike it."

"Unnhh," he let go, revealing a 123. Oh no...I thought in my head...he's out.

"Daayuum," he proclaimed. "Yo Q," he stated throwing up his hands, "I'm tapped...y'all go head."

Cinque picked up the dice and looked at me sideways. After a few seconds, he dropped his gaze and released the dice. They feed him back a 312. He retrieved the dice and rolled again...236. Okay so...he go again. He took the dice for another spin and got a 226. Alright, now we both up on 6. That means we have to do a deal breaker. Is that what they call it? I don't know...but what ever it is...I'm up first. I scooped down to pick up the dice and shook them a little something, then tossed them...421. Okay, that's a great big ole nothing. Let me keep going...ahh...325. That ain't doing me nothing either. Again then, here we go again...114. Oh, that's it...his 226 beat out my 114. I stood up slowly and let my gaze meet his. I saw that little glimmer of vindication in his eyes, but you know what...I ain't mad at him. If he needs to dwell in the fact that he feels vindicated, I can let him have that all day.

"Well Mr. Jones," I stated, "Looks like the treasure is all yours. Great game, but I'm okay with being done."

As he continued to hold me under his gaze he stated, "Triple the pot...you wit' me?"

"Triple?" I came back with, "I don't know about all that. I mean we laid out some significant amounts here...and really what's the point. It's not like either of us are in dire need for money. Perhaps you just..."

"And so... you declining me again?" he cut in with.

"Again?" I came back with, while thinking to myself where is he trynna go with this.

I looked at him and saw a glint of evil in his eyes, as he told me, "Unwritten rule Nubina...it is considered an insult to decline the challenge of the man who holds the bank...I don't think your fiancé would appreciate you declining me twice in one day."

I suddenly felt a little hot flush of annoyance. Oh, so that's how he wanna go with this. I took a glance around at my surroundings...Murad was still MIA on his phone call, and the rest of the bystanders were doing just that ...standing by waiting for the "something" to jump off. Okay then....he got the wrong one right here. I don't like to be blindsided or challenged especially when there is an underlying ulterior motive.

"Swab your deck with paper Mr. Jones,' I told him, "You don't corner the market here on luck today."

He gave off the slightest of a grin and threw down 3G. I took a deep sigh, peeled of the same and placed it on the deck. Being that he had the last winning bank, he took the dice and rolled. 213...Okay...nothing to that. He rolled a couple more times hitting on nothing, then he rolled a 443. He raised from his crouched position, putting me in the mind of a sleek, yet sneaky feline, and handed me the dice as if he was delivering my fate into my hands.

I took the dice and thought, its all good, "Que c'era," I told him, stooped and swung my first roll. 512...its cool...I'll just keep it moving. I picked up the dice, stooped once more and let the dice go. 224...hey, well alright...that right there gets me the pot. Instead of gathering my treasure, I eyed Cinque, who I know was looking to extend his competitive pursuit.

"Quads on this?" I asked stoically.

In lieu of a verbal response, he raised his left eyebrow, and dropped 4 g's on the deck. I dropped my matching paper and proceeded to roll. I pretty much came up with nothing the first 3 times, finally rolling out a 335. Okay…it is what it is…I gotta go with it, I thought as I handed the dice over to him. He took the dice and blew on them…OMG…I haven't seen that in 99 years, that's so old school. He let 'em go, and came off with a 421. He took a quick glance in my direction before he let them roll again, and came up with 232. He continued on for 2 more rolls before he was delivered a 443 from the dice.

This time I looked at him with a slight grin, and I said, "Wanna roll to the 5th power with this?"

"We can roll this all night Lil' Pocahontas," he replied sarcastically.

Oh..okay…nukka wanna catch an attitude…fine. I proceeded to lay down 5 g's at the same moment as he and our hands brushed antagonistically against one another. At that he blew out a deep breath and so I answered him with a small hiss. Damn…look'a here…he got me behaving in a manner I try to avoid, but…I'm all in it now. I took the dice and rolled a 521, rolled a coupla more times and finally rolled out a 115.

As I passed the dice he glanced at me again and stated, "I'm bout to spank you on this Lil' Moccasins."

"Well then bring it Captain Q," I came back with, "Fake ass pirate without a patch."

That caught him off guard and he released that little evil grin of his.

"Aight," he said tossing the dice…352…nothing.

"Thas' okay," he said, "Thas'okay, cause I'm gonna take you out with this." He let the dice go to reveal a 613.

"Oh no," I called out facetiously, "613…Well shiver me timbers Captain…I'm shaking in my boots."

"Not as hard as you gonna be shaking, cause I'ma have ya' little ass walking the plank after I win this one," he told me. With that he came up high, swung his arm like Tiger Woods at the Masters and let them roll to get…662.

"Damn," he spit out as I let go a bubbling laugh…I couldn't contain myself. This was getting to be truly amusing. I guess others thought so as well, as we began to employ quite an audience.

"Aight, so you got that off ," he responded to my laughter, " You game to go 6 deep Lil' Feather?"

"As long as you take my place on the plank, then it's all good…let's go," I replied, as I put up the 6g's.

He returned the dice to me, and I thought in my head…damn I'm amped. He got me caught up in this unsolicited rivalry, but hey…I'm winning and it feels good. His arrogant ass self…well here goes. I let em' rip and the dice came back to me with a 213…ah…that means absolutely nothing.

"Watch out now there," he put out, "You may have to do one of them rain dances Lil' Hiawatha."

"Don't need no reminders from you Captain Q," I answered, "Did my dance to the elders this morning, and I'm sure they gonna represent like now…." I let them go once more and got a 224.

"Humph," he said as I passed him the dice, "Perhaps they ain't hear you. Looks like I best get my blindfold ready…you gonna have some serious walking to do."

"Yeah right," I gave off. He looked at me before he let the dice go, and came up with 432.

"Aight…aight," he said, "Thas alright…it's alright." I remained silent as he tossed the dice 3 times more before he secured a 522.

He looked up from his deck level crouch and I met him in the eye with, "7th Heaven Captain Q?"

"Yeah…we can go wit dat," he responded, "cause after this round, you gonna be calling me God, and if you act right….I'll let you be my angel."

"Oh never that Captain Q," I came back with, "Not enough room in heaven for our ambivalent status. You gonna have to recruit your angels elsewhere."

I took the dice and started to roll, the first 4 rolls got me nothing, then on my 5th roll, I hit with a 223. Ooo…scary. That's a low number, could easily be topped.

"Hoa…I don't hear no talking, Lil Mouth Running," he said taking the dice.

Damn...I done came this far into it, I can't get shook now, so I responded, "Just roll Captain...I'm getting a little hungry, so just before you walk the plank...I'ma need you to fix my plate."

"Picture that," he threw back as he slid the dice across the deck...145. Hmmm...okay let's keep this moving...I'm getting anxious. He scooped up the dice, blowing for good measure and tossed them again...614...Man....what's the odds that he'll hit what he needs...actually the odds are very good. He snuck one more look in my direction, then tossed the dice to hit 112.

"Ha," I called out, "112, ain't that the name of the group you tried to steal for your label back in the day?"

"It's all good...all good" he replied, "Let's go crazy 8 Ms.Nubina...crazy 8."

"Oh wow," I exclaimed, "Since you being all nice and decide to respect me by calling me by my right name...I say run it to the dime Q. We run it on 10 and we end it. Best hit wins ...aight?'

"You just don't wanna walk the plank," he told me.

"No...I don't," I told him, "But you still gonna fix my plate son. Let's go."

We both laughed as I gathered the dice and took my first shot....231.

"Hmmm," I said out loud. I scooped up the dice and rolled again...435. Alright now...I'ma try this one more time...224. Hmmm...not the best...not the worst.

"Here you go Sporty," I peeled off handing him the dice.

"Oh it's like that huh," he said smiling, "Okay...I'm bout to go on and teach you this lesson. This here is a mans' game...you should have stayed in your lane on this one." With that he let the dice roll and I be damn...he hit a 224.

"Well ain't that remarkable," I said, "We on the same vibe about something. Tie breaker Q...tie breaker."

"You right...you right," he answered, "Go head and give it your best shot, cause you bout to be blindfolded and doing your thang on the plank."

I took the dice and blew out a deep breath. Whatever way this was gonna end, I was so ready for it to be over and hell...I am hungry. I'm ready to eat.

“Well Mr. Jones,” I told him, poised to throw the dice, “When you fixing my plate, please know…I do not indulge in the swine.”

He looked at me, and we locked eyes for a split second, then I splashed the dice across the deck for the last time. As I held my breath, I watched the dice dip, dive and dance across the deck, then come to a stop, bringing to my favor…456.

The little crowd roared, “Whoa..damn…wow,” bringing my attention back to the fact that we’d been on display the whole time.

“Well whoop-whoop,” I called out pressing my palms to the heavens, “I do believe this is a done deal. Could you please have one of your peoples bring me a giant sized zip-loc so that I may store my winnings.”

He looked at me, smiled then stuck out his hand and said, “Congrats Shorty…you got me.”

I took his hand and shook it, then pulled him into me for a hug. As I held him in the moment, I whispered in his ear, “So we straight?”

He pulled back, giving me a look of sincerity and said, “Yeah…we straight.”

“Well then good,” I said releasing him, “Now go fix my plate.”

Nubina

Ahhh…man that was fun. Cinque did get me an extra large zip-loc and I dumped all my money into the bag. I thanked him and we proceeded over to the buffet table where true to his word, he made my plate for me. Handing me the plate he said, “So…you be up in the mix like that often?”

“Oh quite the contrae Mr. Jones, “I responded, “Only played with Murad and the rest of the family. Speaking of which…I need to go look him up. He done went and pulled a blank on me. So…I guess I’ll catch you around. And once again…thank you.”

I took the plate from his hand and walked toward the overhang. Just before the indoor lounge area, there was a bolted bench positioned right before the awning and there sat Murad. Can you believe it…still on the damn phone. Oh well… I marched on over, plate in one hand, holding on to my zip-locked treasure slid off my shoes and climbed right up into his lap, set the bag down next to us, crossed my legs and took a bite of my food.

"Whas'up Rod?" I stated, "Remember me?"

"Yeah...hold on Lonz, " he said into the phone.

"Oh...hey that's Lonnie," I voiced with enthusiasm, "Hey Youngblood," I called so that he'd hear me.

Rod leaned forward and kissed my lightly and said, "So whas' the deal Nube?"

"The deal on what Rod?" I countered, "You talking bout this?" I asked holding up the zip-loc stuffed to the brim with money.

"Damn Butter," he stated, "You cleaned up huh?"

"Oh you better know it," I told him, "I gets the job done."

As we both started laughing, I spoke out loud, "Whas' good Youngblood...you just now getting back to us?"

"Sound like it's all about you Princess," he answered as Rod had put us on speakerphone, "Heard you over there cleaning out the bank."

"Oh I did a little damage," I replied.

"It's a little more than damage up in this zip-loc Nube...daaayuumm," Murad chimed in,

"You hungry?" I asked him, "Here have a piece of my fruit, while I talk to Lonnie." I slipped some pineapple into his mouth and asked, "So Mr. Best Man, are you ready for this surprise wedding?"

"Don't even try it Princess," he responded, "You ain't gonna get me to talking and spill the beans."

"Awww Youngblood," I answered pretending to be taken aback, "That is so far from my intentions, just wondering if you ready and all...you know tux...bachelor party...oh...hey...let me holla at you about something. Here Rod...help me out with this plate...I need to talk to Lonnie."

As I handed the plate to him he readily surveyed it and began to make his way with it. "Now Lonnie," I said taking the phone off speaker, "What time do you want me up at the bachelor party?" We both released a chorus of laughter as Murad just shook his head joining in the laughter in between bites.

Cinque

Wow…just look at her so comfortable with it all. She just stepped out of her shoes and climbed up in his lap like it's the most natural thing to do. I'm still blown the fuck away with her and that damn dice game. She was able to hold her own fucking fair and square…got to admire that shit right there. Damn…if things ain't looking too good for me…the more I find out about her the more enticing she becomes. Damn…how is it that I passed over her? I watched as the vision of her screamed Indian Squaw meets Home Girl. How is it that I didn't come across her first? I stood there for a minute longer just watching as she sat up in his lap, taking turns eating and feeding him, talking on the phone and laughing without a care in the world. I thought to myself how difficult it's going to be to get past this shit. Damn…I need to stop standing here gawking, I'm feeling like I'm all assed out and open like the Holland tunnel. As I turned to head to the bar for something soothing, I thought to myself, that mutha fucka there better make sure to take good ass care of his self. I mean eat right, take his vitamins, get a flu shot and shit…all dat. Cause any way something happen to Money…best believe I'm making it my mission to tag her ass with a new last name.

Chapter 73
Who We Be

Nubina

Today is the last day to this 3 day cruise, and despite my original misgivings on this whole event…I have to admit, it's been a pleasure. I mean, I got to mingle and interact with several people that I would have never crossed paths with. More so, people that I may have been a little misaligned in my perception of them. At any rate, today it will be all said and done, and I've bonded and made a few connections. In fact, I think these new connections have inspired my speech that I'll be delivering in a few. Once again Nyla has proven her worth and had me in an exquisite gown; which fitted me everywhere that it needed to, yet gave me that old school movie star sophistication. It was a one shouldered shimmery vision of Apricot perfection that accentuated my weekend tan. I had to cheat on the hair thing since I'd sported the braids yesterday, which had given it a straight effect. I used those plug in steam rollers to get some of the body back, and then I had Rod assist me in securing an updo to die for. I took a look in the mirror at our work and was truly impressed.

"Well looka' here," I spoke as he came up behind me in the mirror to review our work, "If all else fails, perhaps we can go into the hairstyling business."

"Unh-huh," he mumbled wrapping his arms around me, nibbling my ear.

"Murad," I squeezed out, "Come on, don't get nothing started. I've got this speech to do, and I need to focus and be on point."

"Unh-huh," he replied continuing to nibble, "I'm feeling you on that focal point thing."

"Murad," I voiced gently, pulling myself from his embrace, "We've got to go; it won't be a problem for us to continue this later."

"Word is bond?" he asked.

“Word is bond,” I replied with a smile as I picked up my clutch.

“Then let’s make a move,” he said, “I need this here over and done with, so that we can get back and work on some continuation.” I looked at him sideways, then just shook my head walking to the door.

“Men.” I stated as I passed thru.

Murad

This has been an extraordinary weekend. All the apprehension we felt about coming on this cruise has vanished. Instead we gained some insight and valuable experience that we can possibly utilize in our future endeavors. In the meantime...I couldn’t help but chuckle at the look of surprise on Nube’s face when we came up on deck only to have her realize that Sunday’s event was an all white affair, and she was the only one dressed in another color. Nyla had thought it was good publicity, and got approval from the event coordinator, who also agreed that Nube sporting a different color would indeed signify her as Cinque’s special guest. All I know is she looks stunning tonight. In my heart I know that she will probably top that on our wedding day, yet at the same time I’m wondering how she could be even more than what she already is. She is so over the top gorgeous right now...man. I watched as she held the table captive thru dinner, her laughter peeling easily from within, as she and Cinque rehashed the sarcastic comments from yesterday’s cee-lo game. I also noticed that Cinque’s lady was a little stiff and kinda giving Nube the evil eye. In the midst of my observation, she changed her direction and glanced at me. With nothing more than a blink of the eye, she had changed her whole demeanor as well. She started batting her eyelashes, and rolling her tongue slightly across her lips. Well...whatever that’s all about, I ain’t feeding into her nonsense...nope. She ain’t the first lovely I’ve passed on, and won’t be the last. I gave her the whatever nod and turned my attention back to Nube and the rest of the table.

Deek

I can't believe this so called transformation that has come over my brother. Q ain't even the one to let by-gones be by-gones. He won't admit to it, but I know something went down between him and Nubina. More than likely he tried to come at her wrong, and she showed his ass a little some of what she know. I keep telling him, you can't skinny dip in your own pool of artists. When it comes to women, you don't shit where you live. Not to mention, business and pleasure ain't never mixed. I don't know...something strange is going down though, cause she laughing and talking with him like its all good. And Q sitting there hanging on to her every word like he caught up in the rapture, while her fiancé don't seem to be bothered by it at all. Maybe I'm just being paranoid...perhaps I've got shit twisted. Well I certainly hope that this time...things are different, and Q really has changed.

Cinque

Maaaannn listen...I could barely hold it all together at dinner. Nubina was doing all kinds of things to me in that dress. Shorty had me conjuring up all kinds of images like a love struck school boy. Damn...I ain't felt no shit like this since my crush on Danita Thompson back in the 8th grade! Fuck...I've got to pull my shit together...ain't no way I should be having no woman playing on my mental like this. In the meantime, her fiancé is on the phone...again...maybe I need to leave it all alone, but fuck it, any opportunity with her is an opportunity. I'ma see if I can at least get a dance out of the deal.

As the music blared in the background, I walked over to her and charmingly asked, "Does Lil Pocahontas have as much talent on the dance floor as she has in playing cee-lo?"

"Oh Lil' Pocahontas can hold her own," she replied, "Are you asking me to dance?" I just extended my hand and raised my eyebrows.

"No problem," she said, "Murad, I'm going to show Q up once again. I'll be back."

"So you gonna show me up?" I asked.

"Oh most definitely," she said laughing with that sexy ass voice of hers.

"Well," I told her, "let's say, I present you with this challenge...you dance the dance of my choice."

"Hey listen," she came back with, "Bring it...I'm game." I walked over to the DJ and put him down on my request, then walked back over to Nubina.

"Okay...so what's the deal Q...what's it gonna be?" she asked.

"Aight," I hit her with, "We gonna see what you got when it comes to ballroom dancing."

"Ballroom dancing," she repeated back to me completely taken by surprise. I watched as uncertainty crossed over her face, and then she slowly replied, "Alright...which one?"

"The Quick Step," I told her knowing that mastering that dance was rare, and one of the main reasons I made sure that I had it mastered. It gave me that feeling of being one step ahead of all the rest of the ordinary Joe's in this game...made me feel special...like I had more class about myself.

She smiled as the DJ announced our special dance, and as we took the floor, she turned to me placing her hands in the proper position and said, "It is so on...Captain Q."

Nubina

As the music started, I took a deep breath, smiled and let him lead. From the moment we started our first swirl, I think he knew I was with him all the way. By the time we did our first series of quick steps, I know that he was aware that I was definitely going to give him a run for his money. The one thing he didn't know was that I have always been intrigued with ballroom dancing, and a couple of year's back I went and took a class up in Montclair. The class taught all the basic ballroom dances, yet when we got to the Quick Step it gave me a fit. I couldn't seem to catch on for nothing. I started to feeling some kind of way, and decided that I couldn't let the dance get the best of me, so I kinda neglected all the other dances and concentrated solely on the Quick Step. I even went so far as taking secondary lessons after class in order to perfect it. Once I finished the class, you couldn't tell me nothing...I was the neighborhood Quick Step champ. Although I haven't danced it in a minute, the memory was engraved in my mind, and I let myself go and felt so light and free as I glided across the floor with Captain Q.

Murad

Damn....this wedding shit is a lot of work. Scheduling, ordering and what not. If I didn't have Nyla helping me with coordinating and all, I'd be up the creek without a paddle. But whatever...it's all worth it in regard to Nube. I need September 12th to be the most special day in her life ever. As I slid the phone closed, I turned my attention to the dance floor where Nube was dancing some kind of waltz or something with Cinque. I watched mesmerized as they performed step after step with precision. That shit was looking tight, I was truly impressed. As I felt myself slightly swaying to the rhythm, that impressionable feeling began to slowly fade to resentment. They were killing it on the dance floor, in a sophisticated sexy kind of way, and I remembered how Nube had tried to persuade me numerous times to come and go ballroom dancing with her, and I also remembered how I declined. Now as I watched as the image of her spinning and twirling, so utterly content in the arms of another man, I felt as I'd definitely done myself a disservice and had no one to blame for that shit but myself.

"Real cute couple huh?" I heard a seductive voice and turned to my left. Cinque's lady Sanaiya had taken a seat next to me.

Determined not to feed into her nonsense, I simply replied, "We all entitled to our opinions."

"Yes we are," she responded, "And some opinions become reality."

"Is that right," I stated continuing my effort to stay clear of the madness.

"Yeah," she began in response, "Q is pretty consistent in breaking in the new talent...if you know what I mean."

"Well basically...it really don't matter what you mean," I answered starting to get a little annoyed. I stood up to make my way to the bar and out of courtesy asked, "Would you care for something to drink?"

She looked at me with that something up ya' sleeve look and stood from the table and said, "I think I'll just join you at the bar...that is, if you don't mind." I looked at her trying to be extra, sending off messages with her body and shook my head thinking...here we go.

"Fine, it's not a problem," I told her extending my arm for her to lead the way. As she walked ahead of me, she put in every effort to enunciate the swish of her hips, tilting her ass at an unusual angle. I laughed internally as I reminded myself how them days are far gone....and that right there ain't done nothing for me...nothing for me at all.

Cinque

Fucking unreal...I am shook! Not only does she know ballroom dancing, but she got the Quick Step on lock. I thought for sure that I at least had this much over her. Damn...I'm so rattled behind it all that I'm the one scrambling to keep up. Not to mention the touch...the feel of holding her up so close after I've seen her and Murad getting it in. Maaan...that shit there got my heart racing at full speed. I hope that I can contain myself and make it thru to the finale. Ahhh....she is so damn beautiful, the color of her dress bouncing off the all white crowd. That shit is classic...just classy ass class. As we continued to dance I couldn't help but notice that at times her eyes were closed as if she was in the middle of a Calgon moment. Hell if I ain't wanna be Calgonated with her. In the very next moment she opened her pretty brown eyes and smiled at me sending me straight to the edge.

Damn...I started to tremble like I did back in the 5th grade when Raheim the bully used to whip my ass every Wednesday after school. I tried to keep in line with the music and hoped that she didn't notice how nervous I was. The dance was wrapping up and as we did our final pattern of steps, for some reason...I fucking froze. She did a quick nod, then improvised some little custom made steps of her own then rolled back into me and led us into the final rounds of swings and twirls ending it all on just the right note. As the whole yacht exploded into applause, she looked over to me with a knowing nod, and we both took a classic bow like we were professionals.

"Aww Captain Q," she began as the applause died down, " I had such a wonderful time that I do believe that I will bypass the fact that I won the challenge; I think I'll just chalk it all up to thank you...very much. This whole weekend turned out to be very much other than what I expected, so I would like you to know that I do appreciate you inviting us...it was an amazing experience. Well...I guess that I'll go on over and see if Murad is..."

"Nubina," I cut her off as I continued to hold on to the one hand that I hadn't released, "If you don't mind, I would like to talk to you...just need to be real with you." She looked a little skeptical, so I added in, "Okay, just one more dance...we'll dance and talk...please?" I saw her attitude change slightly, as she agreed and she allowed herself to be held within my embrace. As if he been over there reading fucking minds, the DJ slipped on some Luther...If Only For One Night.

As the first few notes of the song began, I started, "Nubina...for the most part, I want to apologize for my behavior yesterday morning. I mean...that's was so unlike me, and that's not generally how I approach a woman. I don't know what came over me and had me come at you that way...but I am sorry, and I would like to know if you can forgive me?" Deep down inside I knew exactly what it was...but I damn sure couldn't tell her that I'd peeped her and dude having sex.

She seemed to relax, took a deep breath and replied, "You know Q...I can forgive you and I suppose I do, but what I need you to check yourself on is getting caught up in the dynamics of this lifestyle and business. You are much too high in regard to position to let antics like that become the highlight of your reputation. I know that you are a smart man...you have to be, just look at all you've acquired. Don't let false images and perceptions mold you into less than a man, cause after awhile the ill thinking will transgress into less than desirable actions, leaving you vulnerable, as well as providing ammunition for those gunning for you to fail. You've come much too far to let ego, of all things dictate your destiny."

For the second time tonight, I froze, only this time mentally. First off...no one has ever told me about myself in this manner...and secondly...there wasn't too much for me to come back with, cause she was right and exact with it all. Damn....she making me nervous again...I'm starting to sweat. I need to say something...respond somehow.

"Well Nubina," I started, "I must admit that you may be the first one to put me in my place about myself and...you right. I like that...you wasn't mean with it, or trynna be boojie about it...just right. The only thing I can do is respect that...respect you."

"Well I can appreciate that Q,' she responded, "I don't have a problem with people making mistakes, it's when they know it and just remain obstinate about it. Wrong and strong all at the same time as my momma used to say."

"Well now that we have that out of the way." I changed up the subject, " Tell me how it is that a little round the way honey like yourself came to be all this."

"What do you mean Q...all what?"

"Well...let's see," I began, "I hear tell, you've had a television show, and done a movie."

"Okay...hear tell ain't good enough Captain Q," she told me, "I am insulted that you have not seen either one. What's up with you not supporting?" She looked at me smiling and I jumped to explain myself.

"Hey a brother be busy," I told her, "It's not easy you know...people only see the after affects, such as this boat, this party, the bling. But it takes a lot of me staying on point, and keeping one step ahead of the next man to maintain all this. So I apologize, sometimes I simply don't have the time. In fact, this weekend here is the first time off I've had in like 2 years."

"I guess I can relate," she answered, "Between my speaking engagements, guest appearances and writing, Murad and I have very little time for personal down time."

Hmmm, I thought, she so comfortable talking about dude, guess she truly all into him. Since she brought it up, I'ma take this chance to satisfy my curiosity.

"So…you and Murad real tight huh?" I asked.

"As tight as a button in a buttonhole," she replied laughing.

"Well it's not like I can blame him," I told her suddenly realizing that I may have been coming off too much like yesterday. So I immediately threw in, "I'm saying… I haven't had the reputation of having the best personality in regard to women, but if I'da had someone like you come into my life back when, I know that I'dve been a much different man then I am today."

"That's something that you cannot speculate on Q," she replied, "Just look how successful you are. You gained this all by taking the path that you took which did not include me."

"And I'm saying my path could'a been a little sweeter if I had someone like you by my side," I told her, "Look at you…you're bright, talented, smart and just a classic beauty. You positive with all that you coming with, and I'm saying…what more could a man ask for."

"But Q," she said, "what you failing to take into account is the fact that I have my own personal mission that I'm on, and dreams that I want to see manifest, and there's a great deal of sacrifice and effort that has to be put in on my part as well as the part of the person I'm with. With you and your ever growing empire, scheduling conflicts would abound left and right. You would not have time for me and all my needs, and I would've fallen victim to you filling your needs elsewhere."

"Wow…Lil Pocahontas," I responded, "You think that I would ever step out on you if you were my possession?"

"It would not be your choice…but your instinct," she replied, "You are a man who conquers, perhaps out of necessity or some internal need that's been with you since a child. Now incorporate that attribute into the industry that you dealing with on a daily basis, and it's becomes your inclination to harbor women like a fleeting natural resource. And now…throw in the fact that you're a very handsome man, and women will consort to anything to obtain just a slice of your life and viola…you all up in the mix of non-commitment. A one woman man…not your deal Q."

The music began to wind down, and so did our dance. And after all that she just said...trust me...I was in a zone. Somehow she just picked off everything right and exact about me, as if my life story was scripted on the flat screen TV located behind the bar.

I brought the dance to a stand still, thinking that I could not just end this conversation like this, so I came up with the best...or the best I could, so I thought at the time, "Nubina," I came off, "Just meeting me for the first time...not knowing all of me...my whole story, what makes you so sure that I couldn't be the man to give you all that you need?"

"Q," she said, looking at me with those beautiful brown eyes, "There was just one word you used which conveyed to me that; even with all that you have encompassed and with all the snazzy intellect and the junctures to closing your deals, you're still green when it comes to love. You are not yet ready young grasshopper."

I jerked my head back and gave her a questioning look, and she simply responded with, "Possession." She gave me a small curtsy, released my hand and made her way over to her American Gladiator.

Sanaiya

Well would you look at this, here comes little Ms. Royalty now. I guess she all done with Q for the time being and making her way over here to her fiancé. I don't understand what the big deal about her is, but I'm bout to show her that her man is just that...a man like all the rest. Just as she walked up, I made a point to pitch myself forward so that cleavage of my dress flapped open and revealed a good sight of my breast.

"Hey Murad," she addressed him, "Saniaya," she turned to me.

I smiled and said "Hello."

"So listen," she said turning back to him, "Did you get a chance to check out my fancy footwork?"

"Sure did," he answered, "Bae you nailed that, I was impressed."

"Well thank you Rod," she answered, "That's the very dance that used to give me a fit, remember? So I made sure to perfect it, and I'm so glad I did or Q would've come off golden with this one."

She followed that up with a little laughter as he stated, "Well I'll tell you what...I think I might have to reconsider your requests to learn this ballroom dancing...that shit was tight Nube...ya'll put it down."

"Oh that we did," she replied, "That we did. We'll I guess I need to freshen up and get ready to do my speech."

"Aight...cool," he told her, "Come on, I'll go back down with you. It will give me a chance to check on some messages."

They turned to walk away, oblivious to the fact that I was standing right there with my titty all hanging out for his benefit. And as he grabbed her by the hand, he turned as if he suddenly remembered that I was there, only to reach over to the bar to retrieve his blackberry.

"Wouldn't wanna separate myself from something so precious," he said to me, then threw me a lip nod and turned to walk away with little Ms.Royalty in tow.

Hmmm...I thought as I corrected my posture, closing down my exposed titty show. Damn...is this what complete shit feels like?...Cause that's how I feel right about now.

Deek

You know...I gotta say...watching Nubina up on the stage, that beautiful color dress setting her apart from the rest, her appearance is like commanding attention. And just about everyone is ready to do just that. She stepped up to the makeshift podium on the portable stage, gave a big smile then broke out in small laughter, and then broke out with:

You know, when I was first approached about an invitation to Cinque's weekend cruise, I have to admit that I hesitated. I thought, Cinque...he's that hip-hop mogul, I don't know...I'm kinda not into the cipher like that. Don't get me wrong, I think some of the best minds in the industry are centered in the rap game, I just don't personally agree with the portrait that some lyrics portray. And I guess in turn, I kind of let myself be falsely sueded that this weekend as well as this group of people would be immensely agitatating. I know...who the hell I am...putting forth judgment on what I know not. Well the one thing I can tell you is that instead of being annoyed or aggravated, I was given new insight into the raw energy of this creative faction of our community, and have come away with a new determination of who we truly be.

Well damn...this ought to be interesting. I looked over at Q who was sitting next to me and watched as he just pulled on his slim, all the while studying Nubina up on the stage. Sanaiya sat to the left of him, face fixed straight ahead as if she would as soon go home than continue to sit there. Oh well...it it what it is. I noticed a hush across the crowd, as Nubina continued....

I have laughed, talked and danced my way thru this weekend, and in between have come away with the notion that you and I are no different from one another. Yes...we all have our good moments, our not so good moments, but for the most part, those of us here have a considerate amount of success, so to speak. We have some of the so called "better" things in life, and some of us given extra opportunity simply because of who we are. And yes...we sure know how to floss the lifestyle and reap the benefits of it all...and we deserve it...we work hard for it. Yet we need to be reminded that this we have been granted with comes with a great deal of power for the most part that we highly underestimate. Hip-hop has become the pinnacle of urban trends on a global level, and surpasses that of any other genre. It has a certain magnetizing property to it that coerces elements in the human psyche and blankets a large population of cultures world wide.

This culture...whose creation is exclusive to our community garners us a great power, a power that we must come to understand and bear a responsibility for. The images, the vernacular behind this all cross-overs to all ethnicities, various age groups, as well as socio-economical classes. And while there is great diversity in the presentation of songs, and lyrics, the impact remains the same...phenomenal. Know your power... for more important than the image of the whips, woman and laid out cribs, are the words that suggest that women are instruments of sexual use, and that men bear no morality in honoring or respecting another's man union, by putting it on this woman so hard that she will leave her current man for him; only to let her know after the fact, that his pursuit of her stops at the acquisition of sex. More important than the image of the laid out crib, we should concern ourselves that a message is being portrayed to our youth leaving an indelible mark that it's all gravy, and does not allude to all the sacrifice and hard work behind it. We need to understand that our actions and images greatly influence a large and impressionable population. So my people...think what we could accomplish if we took that same creative energy and used it to promote positive messages.

And I know...you heard it all before, but I'm talking about taking it to the next level. Keep the same flava...you know keep them beats rocking...bust out them head bangers for the club, but let the lyrics convey something of a positive influence. Bring the game back around to dropping seeds in an informative and fly manner. Understand the power we have in our listening community and with such a following, we could set the stage to inform our youth to be ready to abolish the chains that hold us in mental bondage. We could educate them in a passionate manner that could provide them resources in which to flourish in this oppressive society. We could set the tone for redirecting the importance of the simplistic way of life through love and morality, making our youth the new age pioneers to restore humanity to the illustrious nature it was intended to be. We got that people...naturally...that power of intrigue and persuasion. We are innovative as well as creative trend setters, and we need to understand the power that we possess. We need to understand and utilize that power for the greater good of our community...our young ones. We need to understand who we be, and then build on the fact that we be the power. We are they...they are we. Know your power...understand your power.

As the whole yacht sat in awe of Nubina, I made a determination at that point that she was most definitely the new energy that we needed in our organization. I tossed a look over at Q, but he was inattentive to his surroundings, he had tunnel vision on Nubina. I don't know...I was feeling a strange vibe from him. I just don't know....

I generally like to close out my speaking with a little spoken word, and in this instance I want to give you some comparative thought on where we will continue to be, if we fail to know and understand our power. This piece is called Synonymous With We:

We *order food at White Castle*
Then **we** *stand at the counter staring*
Like it'll make the order come faster

We *get invited to a child's birthday party*
So **we** *go out and buy new outfits for our kids*
And put $10 in a card as the present

We *play hooky form work, while* **we** *still on our 90-day probation*
To take an unemployed man out to breakfast
And **we** *treat*

We *get the cable hook-up from the guy next door*
And when **we** *get caught*
We *turn the brother in to avoid paying reimbursement*

We *grieve at the death of a loved one*
Then turn around on Monday morning
And **we** *get a cell phone in their name*

We *drive the Lex Coupe, Beemer and the Benz*
Pay a grip on the note and insurance
Live at home with momma and **we** *2 months behind in rent*

We *crown in desire, convert to ignorance in our pain*
Co-sign to games of unregulated sensuality
Then **we** *pay with the possibilities of our lives*

We *hide our dreams*
With unprecedented success
Then **we** *turn around and sabotage our very existence*

We *fight strong for the wrong*
Many battles of an unnecessary cause
And then **we** *cry foul in defeat*

We live hard, we wallow long
Each day to the wire, our futures unintended
And in the end...we get buried on lay-away

Nubina stood still just for a second when the crowd started to applaud heavily, then got to their feet continuing the applause. I got to my feet as well donating my applause to the cause, only to have Q rise on my left and take a pull from his Cuvee.

Once he released he continued to stare her down as he told me, "Sign her. Whatever they asking...give them 30 percent more. Do whatever...I need her...got to have her in my empire."

I looked at him hard, intent, trying to see where he was going with all this. For once he didn't spase out on me for looking at him that way. He just returned the look for a minute, then turned his attention back to Nubina taking another pull.

This time he released and stated, "Masterpiece...fucking Masterpiece." As everyone continued to stand clapping, Saniaya pushed back from the table and retreated below deck. Q...didn't even notice at all.

Chapter 74
My Wedded Wife

Nubina

Wow...we got like 2 weeks before the wedding and still so much to do. Okay...what am I saying; nothing much for me to do except follow the script. My maid of honor and bridesmaids have gone for separate fittings than I in order to keep my dress and the color scheme to the wedding under wraps. Murad wants the actual wedding day to be the very first time I experience the visuals of it all. Soooo...I'm standing here now blinded folded mind you so that I don't get a premature peek at my wedding dress. When I say surprise...the whole day has been planned as just that. Nyla is the only one here with me in order to keep the leak factor under control, cause you know if Lani, Bree and Kiyma were all here, one of them would most definitely reveal it. The dress was custom made and Nyla was giving the last minute instruction on the fit.

"Okay," she said, "I need this taken in about ¼ inch on the right, and I also need this centered in the back just a little more evenly." I felt the seamstress flitting around me, nipping and tucking as she pinned, then said, "This is an awesome dress, you are most definitely going to be beautiful on your wedding day."

"Well thank you m'am," I answered her.

"Do we have the shoes on hand?" she asked Nyla.

"Here we go," Nyla replied.

"Alright then, you gonna have to help out here," the lady told her.

"Nube...take my hand and now slide your foot into the shoe," Nyla told me, "Okay, good...now the other."

"Hey," I said out loud to the air since I couldn't see, "I don't know about these, they feel a bit on the high side. Don't know if I'll be able to walk around in these all day."

"Well after all the picture taking, you'll probably be able to change your shoes," Nyla replied, "Just know that there will be a lot of picture taking."

I can only imagine. She and Murad have been working diligently on this wedding for the last couple of months and so far from what I know, it's going to be an extravagant affair. I tried to tell Rod, that we could just as well go to the islands and get married, but he insisted that this is what he wanted and that he was gonna make sure to do it the way he wanted it done. As the seamstress finished her alterations, they both helped me out of the dress and shoes, and then whisked the garment away, so that I could finally take off the blindfold. Wow, I thought again as I took a look around the bridal shop, mentally inhaling the whole ambiance of a wedding...I'm getting married...I am getting married!!!

Murad

Man...shit is down to the wire bout now. Me and the fellas just blew the tux spot in the city for our final fitting. Since I had just sprung this on them in July, I paid for all the tuxes so as to not put anyone in a financial bind. Cost is not a factor for me in regard to this wedding, and it's important to me to have my fam participate. I myself had mine custom made and was pleased with the finished product. So now that that's all out the way, I have to secure the transportation piece for the wedding day. Nyla and I found the ultimate spot down in South Jersey that will reflect my dream of a lifetime, and as soon as I laid eyes on it, I knew this was where I needed to make it all happen. Now given the location...and knowing my family; I hired two exclusive charter coaches to transport them. Number one, I wasn't relying on nobody to be on time in finding their way there, and two, they gonna be throwing drinks back like bar mongers, so I need that peace of mind that everyone will have a safe trip back home.

I listened as Lonnie, Brick, Sharief and Dream hyked on each other all the way back to Bryce's. The rest of the guys had gone in for their fittings the week before, so they were good to go. Once we arrived at the house I threw a quick shout out to Bryce and

Shan before I pulled out. I still had a couple of loose ends to tie up so I couldn't stay. As I headed home, I put on my Pete Belasco CD, cause I sure as hell needed some assistance in getting my mood mellow. Now I understand what them Bridezilla heifers be going thru...this wedding detail is a lot of work. I'm glad that I had been aggressive on stacking funds into an account for the occasion. That right there made things a whole lot easier. And of course, I hired Nyla who in turn used her resources and connections with A-list wedding coordinators to help me execute this dream. I finished up the ride home by track 6 on the CD and hummed the tune in my head as I headed into the house. I had talked to Nube before I left the city, so I know that she was over at her mother's and would be home later. I threw my keys on the kitchen counter as I went to the fridge in search of a snack. Let's see...what we got in here. I breezed past the grapes to whip out the bowl of cherries. Yeah...thas whas up. Some cherries and some seltzer water I thought as I grabbed the bottle. Just as I reached to pour some in a glass, the house phone rang. Damn...who is this calling on the house phone? As I took a quick glance I noted...Oh...JT.

"Yo" I answered after the 2nd ring.

"Hey what's the deal Murad?"

"Ain't nothing," I told him, "Just getting all the finishing touches on the details for the wedding."

"Yeah...what's that like 2 weeks away?" he asked.

"Two weeks too long," I answered, "Not only do I look forward to Nube being my wife...I'm looking forward to the honeymoon getaway. We've been on the move for quite awhile now, and we could use the downtime."

"I can understand that," he said, "I too am looking for the prophecy of this day to come to pass, and feel like I'm on a suspended high. But listen, the main reason that I've called you is...I well...I don't want to feel like I'm impeding my presence where it's not wanted, but..."

"What you trynna get at JT," I jumped in with at the end of his pause.

"I was hoping that you guys would do me the honor of letting me walk Tania down the aisle."

"Oh...hey man," I started, "Listen...that honor has already been fulfilled by Bryce. Nube asked him back at the cookout, and later on that night he called me and blubbered like a baby. Maaan...I can't take that away from him."

"Well I guess if things are already in place, then it is what it is," he responded.

"No doubt JT," I came back with, "I don't even know what to tell you...It's a done deal." Somehow the words seemed far too cruel for the man who had enough belief in us to not only step aside, but encourage us in our togetherness. But hell...it really is what it is. Damn!!

Nubina

The count down is over...today is here. I am in the bridal dressing room here at the most exclusive venue site I've known to date. The girls are all here buzzing around, eating fruit and sipping on sparkling cider. You know they all had something to say about that, especially Chanda, but Murad said he wasn't about to have no drunken maidens on our day. They can drink after the ceremony and picture taking. I had to laugh...he really had turned into a damn Bridezilla. But I can't help but beam with pride for him, he had a dream for this day, and he focused on getting everything the way he wanted. There's not too many men that would go that route.

"Wow Tania," said Bree, "You are absolutely the most stunning bride that I have ever seen."

"Thank you Bree," I told her, "And see...you all were on my case for letting Murad handle everything. I told you...he got me...all day...everyday."

"Oh boy," Lani said, "Do we have to hear another version of the Most Wonderful Man in the World?"

"Hell yeah," I answered as I laughed and the rest joined in, "You gonna hear about it for the rest of our lives...so get ready."

"Well I for one think it's just beautiful," Kiyma added, "That man knows exactly what he wants and it ain't take him no 10 years to make it happen."

"Yeah Boo," Chanda said, "You and Lonnie bout to qualify for that common-law action. You need to tell him to shit or get his ass off the pot." I looked at Kiyma and could tell that she was affected by what was said.

"Hey listen," I broke in with, "Love is not defined by a wedding...that is a personal dream based on an individuals own prospective. The situation of love cannot be forced and it knows the proper time to step in and make it right. Trust me Kiyma...Lonnie will make sure "it" happens when he's absolutely certain he can maintain it all."

"Well don't hold ya breath," Chanda had to throw out there.

"Okay...okay," Kira said putting up the barriers to prevent a scene, "This is Murad and Tania's day...so let's concentrate on that fact."

"Yeah," Donella added in her 2 cents, "It should be just about time to rock and roll."

As Bryce knocked on the door, all conversation ceased as heads turned to the door. He stuck his head in and simply said, "It's time."

As my girls stood to leave the room, they all stopped by me and gave me hugs and kisses, and I tried not to cry as they bestowed me with, "Congratulations...good luck...love you...you look amazing...see you on the other side."

As the last of them left the room, Bryce came over and gave me a great big hug. As he pulled back he held me at arms length and said, "Aight Lil' Bit, are you ready to become a true Tillman?" So overwhelmed by the moment, I just shook my head yes. "Well then," he said picking up my bouquet and offering me his bended arm, "Let's do this." I smiled...took my bouquet and his arm and we walked out the door.

Sumira

I'm not sure what kind of way I'm feeling, but Mama talked me into coming today. Not that she had to do that much talking ...cause truly...I wanted to witness this all first hand. You know...see Murad actually go thru with this...I mean...looking around...it seems like he went thru a lot of trouble and spared no expense. But he always been into flossin...this day is no different. I gotta say though...this place is laid out, and they claim he did the planning himself...well without any help from Tania. That in itself is a lot for any man to pull off...maybe he really does love her to do all this. Well...the music has started as well as the procession. All heads turned as Murad came down the aisle escorting my Aunt Reeva, followed by Lonnie escorting my mom, and then Tania's brother escorting her mom Mrs. Baynes. Once all the women were seated, Murad and Lonnie took their place at the altar, while Xavier took a seat next to his mom.

As a new tune began to play Lani made her way down the aisle solo as the maid of honor, followed in sequence by Dream and Kiyma, Brick and Bree, Kye and Chanda, Jarrell and Kira, Jarod and Donella, Sharief and Brianna and in last place, Aaron and Tamira. Well I don't know how much sense that makes putting Brianna and Tamira in the wedding without having somebody they own age to walk with, but it's all family...so I guess that makes it alright...I guess. I know I didn't have no kids in my wedding...kept it all grown and sexy. Once everyone had taken their places, a new set of lyrics started and Tania's descent began.

"*Promises you made me...All the things you told me... ...you said you'd never leave me...we'll be together for eternity. Now it's all in the past...now I know our love will last...Lady I will do all I can...lady I will be all I am...I'll give you all you've had before...so come on in and close the door. Let me show you what love could be...could you just please tell me. Will you believe in love...and the promise that it gives...I wanna love you for life...cause your love is why I live.*"

I watched in awe as Bryce sauntered down the aisle with Tania...she was the absolute image of perfection. She had on this one of a kind strapless ice pink gown that scalloped at the top of the bodice then look like it slanted toward the back. I can't really call it when it comes to the fabric, but it glimmered and fitted to her waistline like a second skin then blossomed out from the waist to a mid calf length. She wore a diamond studded tiara that gleamed and glittered against the color of her hair. Her hair was kind of an updo that swept to one side, yet had one side of loose curls hanging down displaying her true length. Around her neck was an outrageously gorgeous pink diamond necklace that matched the bracelet that I'd heard Murad had gotten her for Christmas. And hey...she rocking a set of matching pink diamond earrings...wow...she looks amazing. I watched as she maintained her smile as flashes continuously went off around her while my brother Bryce beamed like he was really her father. I couldn't help but watch with a careful eye as they approached me, I mean...I don't know how...or if she feeling some kind of way about me being here or not..so...oh...okay....she just passed by my seat without a glance in my direction. Humph...so that's how it is. I watched as she and Bryce passed me revealing the back view of her dress. The scalloped edges did wrap into each other and framed out a deep plunging keyhole cut in the back...I mean to the top of her lower back...damn. While I tried to sit there secretly hating on it all; I had to admit...the dress was tight...she looked hot.

Dream

As I stood next to Lonnie and Murad I watched as Bryce made his way down the aisle with Nube on his arm. This mansion was huge and the walk was gonna take a minute. I smiled deep inside to Murad"s choice of Love U 4 Life, as it somehow settled within as the perfect choice. I have seen my brother change from the ultimate ladies man to the most dedicated man in the western hemisphere. On the real...I would'a never thought Murad would be the first of us to get married...never in a million years. But here he is standing here...ready to make it all happen.

"*I want you to know that it' s for real...this feeling that I feel...I want you to know that it's so real...tell me ...reeaalll...yeah.* As Jodeci belted out the set of words I noticed JT...he stood up as Nube and Bryce were still quite a ways from the altar. Oh shit...damn...I knew things were running a bit too smooth...knew something foul was gonna kickoff. I couldn't do nothing but stand there and hold my breath as...what...Bryce stopped as he and JT bowed to one another, then he released Nube's arm and extended it to JT. Nube looked confused for a slight second throwing a quick glance to Murad who reassured her with a sly wink of the eye. Before taking JT's arm, she hugged him real quick then positioned herself to continue to make her way to Murad keeping the beat. Damn...I exhaled...as did a couple of others. I was so glad to see that love was still in control today.

Aight...that was slick...that was right. JT was the one that let her go and gave them the blessing and direction to be together. It's kind of fitting that he would be the one to officially give her away. That was smooth. *"Will you believe in love...and the promise that it gives...I wanna love you for life...cause your love is why I live,"* played on as JT and Nube made their way down the remainder of the walk, all the while flashes going off as select paparazzi, media and guests took pictures. I felt really warm inside as I thought of how I originally judged Nube before really knowing her, and now that I know...she is the best thing that happened to my brother...well...both of them. As they reached the altar Murad stepped forward and took Nube in his arms and slowed danced till the final verse of the song played a capella, *"Will you believe in love...and the promise that it gives...I wanna love you for life."* Then he spun her, brought her face to face with him as he sang out the last words in his own baritone... *"cause your love is why I live."* As the whole room sat silent he reached in and gave her a kiss to which she responded as if they were the only two in the whole wide world.

Cinque

Fuck...did I create my own hell by befriending the Royal Couple? I'm here at this wedding no less...couldn't turn down the invitation. She really did invite me herself as we said our good-byes at the end of the cruise. Quite honestly, she had an impact on me like I have never known and I wouldn't dream of doing anything else grimey or anything to hurt her. I plan to keep things sweet, keep things kosher and wait for my window of opportunity. And that's some shit right there, cause it ain't never been my practice to wait on nobody for no fucking opportunity, I'm all about going out and making opportunity bow down to me. But this here...well she...she's different. That one in a million that I know I gotta earn. I need her to want to come to me...and I don't care how long that shit takes...I'm ready to ride it out. Yeah...it means that much to me.

Dearly beloved, we are gathered here today to unite and bless the union of this man and woman as they have mutually decided to connect as one." I turned my attention to the officiator as he made his opening statement to start the ceremony, "The contract of marriage is not to be entered upon lightly and I take it that you two have given it considerable thought?"

"We have," they replied together.

"Well then...who gives this woman's hand in marriage?" he asked.

"I do," his brother replied.

Damn...ain't that some shit right there I thought in my head. I do believe this here the brother that she was supposed to be with first, but he moved out the way for Murad...fucking fool. As he took his seat, the Justice moved on with the ceremony.

"Murad and Tania have written their own vow's which they will now recite to one another, Tania," he continued.

I sat up straight in my seat as I listened to her sexy voice as she began, "*Murad...I stand here before you today as a very knowledgeable woman. And here before our friends and family I would like to admit I was not always as knowledgeable as I am today. I sought long...I sought hard to define for myself the meaning of love. I allowed situations and put my self thru misery at times in my pursuit only to find out that...love cannot be sought nor defined. Love is an unbridled entity that embraces you when your mind and soul come together in complete understanding of yourself. And when you can finally understand yourself...you can recognize love. I understand your strengths and your weakness, as well as your ability to put them aside when need be in an effort to build and fortify the belief we have in one another. With your efforts, I relinquished my doubts, and when your actions manifested your selflessness, I surrendered heart and soul. Murad...I have come to understand myself and the total sense of my being, and it is that fact which supports my belief that you are the consummate energy that shadows mine, and I am certain that nothing in this lifetime will deter me from basking within that energy until eternity.*"

As she finished her vows, I thought I heard a couple of sighs floating about, and I know ole' boy had to be moved by what she said...hell...I know I was. I continued to sit on the edge of my seat green with envy, wishing it was me as Murad started his vows. "*Tania...Tania Baynes, I just need you to know today...right here...right now...that you are not only the woman that my heart's desired...but the person that my soul has been searching for since I was old enough to entertain the idea of love. I understand that you have been sent to me to fulfill my childhood wish, and I intend to make every effort to validate my appreciation and gratitude for such a gift. Like an exotic flower, I understand the careful care and attention needed to sustain your unique beauty. Not the beauty that stands before me in the physical...but the internal beauty that exudes all else. I vow to you today that I will cherish as well as maintain your uniqueness, your beauty and the love that blossoms from it. I promise to remain true to our love and faithful to our union, all the while supporting your independence to remain the free and beautiful spirit that you are. From now...until always...I love you Butter.*"

I slid back on my seat once he was done feeling some kind of way as I observed a couple of sniffles and eye dabs going on around me. Yeah...I had to admit that this was the most pronounced admission of love between two folk that I've ever known. Just wish the hell it had'a been me...this should'a been me.

Dream

Damn, I thought as I tried to inconspicuously wipe away a tear. They tore it down with them vows. I know I heard Lonnie sniffing when Nube said hers, and now I'm sitting up here joining him now that Murad has finished his. I looked over at my mom and saw her trying to contain herself while all the while wiping away a steady non-stop stream. I guess it takes that real love to be able to express yourself so freely. I have to say that I am truly impressed by the whole affair thus far. That Jodeci song was smooth, then we strutted in on If I Knew by Jimmy Sommers...man that was tight as well. Now they just finished their own vows and we off to a solo.

My cousin Zaria has always been a songbird, and she took her place to the left of the altar to deliver us with song. She took the mic, announcing, "Good afternoon everyone...we are all gathered here today to witness the unity of my cousin Murad and my soon to be official family member Tania. Knowing and loving you both, I've hand picked this song for you by the artist Algebra because it seemed to mirror your love. SoMurad...Tania, this is for you.

She smiled out at the audience, bowed her head slightly then raised her voice in song.... "*At this time...and in this place, you are mine. And at this moment...in my life...you belong to me...to meee...ooooo. I don't think it's wrong...I can't help it...my mind asked my heart if she felt it...I did...I can only ask for so much please...I will settle for his touch. My arms brag to each bout how you feel...from conversations I know what they feel is real. The past it didn't last...the present went to fast...the future soon we'll be, I wish that far I could see but...At this time...in this place you are mine....aaannnd at this moment...in my life...you belong to me...oohhh to meee...oohhh.*"

I couldn't help but study Murad and Nube as they were being serenaded, and noticed that they were both under the spell of the song. I took another look around at the surroundings and all my family and guests and wondered if I too would one day find that special someone and celebrate with such a day as grand as this here. One could only wish...so like the song says, at this time...and in this place...I'm gonna take this moment to make my wish to one day be in this same time and place in my personal life. Yeah...make a wish.

JT

That song was so touching and so fitting in regard to Murad and Tania. Now that this day is finally here, I can't help but to acknowledge that I did what was right and exact in releasing Tania. The burden of the past seems to be truly lifted now that I see her soul is housed in true love, and starting a new beginning with a man that treasures her above all else. As my cousin finished the song she received a robust round of applause.

Once the clapping subsided the Justice went on with the ceremony by stating, "May I have the rings?" Lonnie reached into his pocket and retrieved the rings handing them over to Murad, who in turn handed them to the Justice. He held them both in the palm of his hands, then asked Murad to take the ring for

Tania, and place it on her hand as Murad continued with their custom vows, "*Tania, I place this ring on your finger as a symbol of my appreciation, my dedication and my love for you. With this ring may you always be reminded that as long as I live and breathe, you will never be alone, misguided or confused. The love and respect I have for you will remain solid and untarnished as this ring.*"

Nube looked up at Murad and you could see nothing but pure love in her eyes. She took the ring from the Justice's hand and placed it on Murad's finger as she cited, "*Murad...just as you feel the close fit of this ring on your finger, may you always feel the closeness of my love. May you know everyday in your heart that my heart will blanket yours, no matter how near or far in proximity we may be. Let this ring reflect the internal light of my soul, and if you should ever get caught out in the darkness, that light will suffice to guide you on your way back home. I shall never want, nor never need another love...this lifetime...next lifetime...I love you Sire.*

As she finished her declaration, a stray tear tiptoed from the corner of Murad's eye, and she reached up to catch it. Before she could complete the job, Murad took her delicate fingers in his hand and kissed the tips ever so gently as if to say, let them fall where they may. The Justice, broke the silence as he continued with the ceremony, "Murad and Tania...you have declared your undying love for one another before your family and friends on this day, with the promise to love, cherish and replenish your belief in your togetherness continuously. So with the blessings of all those here today, the solidarity of your love, and with the authority invested in me, by the state of New Jersey, I now pronounce that you are now husband and wife. You may kiss..." The statement went unfinished as Murad pulled her into his arms and solidified the vows, as applause rang out left and right throughout.

Chapter 75
A Lavish Affair

Dylina

Oh my gosh what a beautiful ceremony. I have got to say...my little brother has out done himself here today. We couldn't help but laugh as he jumped the gun and kissed Tania before the proclamation of husband and wife was even finished. I guess he was just that excited and anxious. To this day, I still marvel at the transformation he has undergone in regard to women, and if I weren't standing here today to witness it all, I wouldn't know any better. I guess he truly was waiting for that right one, and with all the circumstances surrounding their unorthodox relationship, I suppose Tania really is the one for him. He appears to be glowing more than she as they sway down the aisle exiting the atrium where the ceremony took place. I'm not sure, but I think that's a Jaheim song, well kind of a remake...I Choose You. I remember that from back in the day. I mean way back in the day...but anyway, look at them; so happy, so joyous...I love it.

Sumira

I can't help but to continue to wipe tears from my eyes as Murad and Tania make their way down the aisle as husband and wife. Oh My God...that was so beautiful. Well Tania has always been such a true person, such a beautiful spirit...I don't know what it was that had me acting all brand new with her. I have to admit that I have always associated Murad's actions with my dad's and the fact that he may have been trynna play my best friend just ticked me off. But now I see that he's for real about everything, and he truly loves her. Loves her the way my ex husband Bilal was supposed to love me, and the way my dad should 'a loved my momma. So who was I to judge and condemn them. I pushed them both away and all for what...they both proved to be on the up and up. More than I can say for my ex or my damn daddy. Then I had to go and make matters worse by befriending Jazmine out of spite, and he wasn't even the father...just like he said! What have I done I think as I watch them attempt to make their way back down the aisle, constantly being sidelined by so many people. As Murad turned to acknowledge one well wisher, Tania turned to her right and spotted me standing there in the aisle wiping my eyes. Can I just say...her eyes lit up like a child on Christmas, as she broke out into a smile, letting go of his arm and made her way towards me. Just watching my beautiful friend, face aglow and coming to embrace me...me who treated her so badly, put me back into the tears. Tears that I couldn't hold back anymore as she put her arms around me and said softly, "Sumira."

At the sound of her voice, I quietly broke down as she rubbed my back and shoulders rocking me back and forth.

"Tania...Tania," I tried to get out, but my words were all crossed up, "I'm sorry...so sorry...you see I...and then...I."

She simply continued to hold me rubing my back and said, "Sumira...honey...I know. It's gonna be alright...trust."

"But Tania," I started, "I didn't...you know...I was just being...and then Murad...Tania."

"Honey hush," she told me.

In another couple of seconds, Murad was able to free himself and caught up to our hug-fest. As soon as we felt his presence we both turned and looked right up into his face and just waited. He looked down for one minute and then gave me one of his you're forgiven lip nods, reached over and gave me a brief kiss to my forehead.

"Rod," I started, "I just..."

At that moment their wedding coordinator Nyla approached and motioned that they had to move on. Tania gave me one last hug then said, "We'll talk later...okay?"

I simply nodded my head in agreement as they moved on and continued the recessional as the rest of the wedding party followed in place.

Dream

Damn...we finally back inside finishing up on our cocktails, appetizers and drinks after being out in the garden for bout an hour and change taking pictures. We are in a separate wing from the guests, and about to go inside the ballroom for the reception and what not. Funny how you be around friends and family all your life and still never quite get used to all their antics. Good thing we about to hit the reception cause some of these here bridal party people are borderline wavy already. I just hope we can make it thru the entire affair without any unusual events taking place. Maybe so, cause their wedding coordinator Nyla is on the ball. She gathering folk up now and getting them in order. No more drinks till after the dance segments, she declared to the room as she noted there were a few who were well on their way to being wavy. As we all paired up and took our places, I saw Brick, Jarod, and a couple of the others checking Nyla out. Oh here we go...I'm thinking as I shook my head; new face in the place, tails wagging...niggas are too much. As we proceeded to make our way down to the ballroom, I couldn't help but notice Nube and Murad still in a world of their own. Man...I look forward to my turn at such a love.

As Nyla led us just outside the closed door to the ballroom, I heard the MC announce the presentation of the bridal party. The doors opened and the music started as we filed in beginning with Lonnie and Lani, the best man and maid of honor. As each pair of names were called we entered into the room amidst a barrage of applause and flashes from the cameras. After each couples' picture was taken, we were directed to our seats at the bridal table. No one was to be on the floor when the royal couple entered. With a mellow jazz tune playing in the background, the MC announced, " I would like to now present to you, New Jersey's royal couple, King Midas and Queen Nubina....better known as Mr. & Mrs. Murad and Tania Tillman."

As all heads turned to the closed doorway, they suddenly opened and Nube and Murad entered the grand ballroom to thunderous applause. Lights, camera action...you would 'a thought they was shooting a movie up in this place with all the cameras flashing and camcorders rolling. They leisurely walked in arm and arm, smiling, pausing for numerous photo shots. I guess they used to this kind of stuff, cause they really didn't seem bothered at all. Not to mention, they've both been looking forward to this day for a long time, and after some of the shit they been thru...I ain't even mad at them. If it was me, I'da been stone out of my head with pride that my day was finally here as well. They stood front and center on the dance floor as the hired videography crew went to work. Once they were finished with the pictures, the MC announced, "Tania and Murad have selected their own separate songs of dedication that they will dance to at this time. In keeping with etiquette we will go with the ladies choice first. So from our Queen we have..."

"Excuse me...may I make a special request?" JT broke thru with.

Oh boy here we go, I'm thinking. Nyla got into coordinator mode and took the mic stating, "Although we have a specific itinerary, we will be privileged to honor your request Jayson."

She approached him, he whispered in her ear, then nodded her head and walked to the DJ control booth to inform the music engineer. JT took this time to raise the mic and explain himself.

"My dear family and friends," he started, "I just want you to know here today that having been a part of this triangle of love since it's birth, I can say that I have witnessed many a dark situation for Murad and Tania. Days so dark that I continuously prayed that love would be on its most exemplary behavior and see them thru. I witnessed Love as she faltered once or twice on them, then watched as Love pulled thru, grabbed Perseverance by the hand and together delivered Murad and Tania across the finish line. Since I was the first to be informed by God on this prophecy of love, I would like them to honor their love by requesting this song as a reminder that you must work under the guise of togetherness in regard to true love and that a true belief in love will always be coveted by God."

And as he finished his impromptu speech, the opening bars of Marvin Sapp, filtered the room.

"Never would'a made it...never could'a made it...without you."

Yeah...I got to admit that JT is right on the money with this one. I know for a fact they would've never made it without one another. Shit was just too complicated; that belief they had in one another kept things going. I watched as did everyone else as they danced oblivious to the world around them, while my mom blatantly cried her eyes out. No doubt she was probably reminiscing back to the days of her and my dad. Sure wish my dad could've hung around but I guess it just wasn't meant to be. We all sat and watched as Murad and Nube flowed with the song till the end.

The room applauded as the song ended as they topped it off with a gentle kiss. Nube turned to locate JT and blew a kiss in his direction and said, "Love you Jayson...thank you."

The MC retrieved the mic and continued with the dedicational dance songs.

"That was a most touching dedication, and we will now move on with the song dedication from the Queen to her King." Flashes and lights continued to glare as Murad and Nube took position to the opening of her song.

"*Here we are together...in a place...in a space surrounded with love. Here to say YES I DO...love you...and I wanna be the only one...you...you are...you are just the one I want spend the rest of my life with. You are just the one to bring out the very best in me...you make me so happy...happy forever...and that's a mighty long time. We must be in love...we must be in love.*"

Not sure that I know this song, but it sure is catching. I watched my big brother as he held Nube within his gaze as he listened to the song. I do know that neither one of them knew each other's request, but I could tell that he was impressed with her selection for him. They danced on in simplistic beauty as the cameras continued to flash and capture the moment. Once the song was finished, they again obliged the picture takers as they sealed it off with a kiss. Damn that was tight...I liked that piece...liked it a lot. Wonder what Murad got that can top that...wonder what...yes indeed.

Nubina

"That was right on time Butter," he whispered in my ear as the song finished. I'm so glad that he liked it. Once I'd heard it, I knew it needed to be my selection. It conveys everything I feel about him...about us. I'm so...so glad that he liked it. I looked up into that gorgeous face in anticipation as to what was in store for me.

As we stood there cheesing and holding one another close, the reception host got on the microphone and announced, "We know have a special dedication from the King to the Queen in which he intends to personally serenade her with a song from one of their favorite artists. So King Midas...do your thing."

As the music began, I stretched my eyes in recognition as the room became after the snow fall quiet in anticipation of Murad singing. He sounded out the first word in his baritone voice, "*Forever,*" then continued on, "*The love I have for you will last forever. Loving you always. Forever...my love for you won't change...cause loving you's the best thing that I can do.*"

Damn Rod sounds good! So good I closed my eyes and placed my head on his chest to savor the rest of my song. As I heard "*Looking back,*" I thought in my head, hey...there's been a change in voice. As the voice sang on, "*On the times before you came....my life has changed.*" Upon recognition, I threw my eyes open and spun around to see...Jaheim...walking in from the garden patio singing my song...his song...damn it...our song! "*No more sleepless nights or lonely days...they're just a part of my yesterday...for you I've prayed.*"

I looked at Rod, he looked at me, and I just jumped up and down in a mini dance of joy...well for all that I could with these damn heels on. He picked me up and spun us around then put me down as Jaheim approached the dance floor. I turned to face him resting my back against Rod as Jah continued singing.

"*Forever...the love I have for you will last forever...loving you always...forever...my love for you won't change...girl loving you's the best thing that I can do.*" After that line I turned to embrace Murad so that we could dance out the song. "*You have taught me...and you showed me how to love again...yes you did...you are my best friend. So now I'm feeling so secure...gonna make sure that this love lasts forever...we will win...we will win.*"

Yeah…they will win I thought as I watched Rod, eyes misty as all hell. I know he having a hard time keeping it together. He has wanted this for so long. It didn't help none that the rowdy bridal party were up on their feet hooting and hollering like the hood personas that they are. Murad took it all in stride and just pumped his fist in the air then proceeded to hold Nube even tighter as Jaheim continued to sing.

"Yeah Chief…do it Chief…you the got-damn man," Brick yelled out. "Yeah Rod…Yo Son…you killing it today bruh…you and your Queen."

"You the man Rod…you know you the damn man," Kye followed in suit.

I started shaking my head, my hood ass fam; then thought no harm done as the dance played out without further incident. Of course at the end everybody gave a standing ovation, as Jaheim came over to greet the royal couple personally.

"Congratulations to the royal couple," he stated into the mic, "I just want to say that it has been a privilege to honor your request to sing at your wedding. Nyla contacted me and let me know that the two of you are my biggest fans, and on that note, I could not turn you down. It's good to see young love doing its thang these days, and most especially blossoming thru my music. So I thank you for the opportunity. Much love to you the royal couple, and I'm gonna hold you to this song request…Forever."

Nube not being able to help herself left Murad's arms to embrace Jaheim and give him a kiss on the cheek.

"You can stay for the rest of the reception can't you?" she asked.

"No doubt…no doubt," he replied.

Murad dapped him up, then Nyla led him off to a special table, while the royal couple took their highly decorated seats at the bridal table.

Man oh man...this is oh so awesome. My man...oops...I mean my husband did a damn good job with this wedding. First off, this estate is humongous and rich in sophistication with out being stuffy and overbearing. It's an old classic that they've renovated with a contemporary flair. The reception hall which probably was a grand ballroom at one time, had a huge atrium area added on that led out to glass enclosed patio doors. The patio doors in turn opened into a lovely garden area complete with the capacity for food serving stations and 2 bars. During the reception guests had the option of going outside in the fresh air atmosphere or staying inside within the AC. Rod and I tried to do a compromise and made several rounds indoor and outdoor in an attempt to greet all of our guests. I don't know if we got to greet them all, but we certainly tried. Some of them were straight feeling no pain. Murad likes to get down as the hostess with the most-est and had an open bar with top-shelf liquor. Needless to say...folks were getting his money worth for him. Not to mention the wide array of delectable foods.

For cocktail hour we had fresh baked bread and cheese stations as well as fresh fruit skewered to dip in a chocolate fountain, along with fresh veggies and gourmet crackers with various dips and spreads. There was another station that had macaroni salad, potato salad, cole slaw, fettuccine alfredo and veggie fried rice Then there was like a shrimp bar with cocktail shrimp, fried shrimp, Cajun shrimp, Hawaiian shrimp...you name it, about 10 different varieties of shrimp. We also had appetizers like mini beef, chicken and veggie patties, fried mushrooms, fried green tomatoes, catfish nuggets, fried onion blossoms, mini egg-rolls, mozzarella sticks and chicken fingers with fries for the kids. The entrees consisted of Natural Angus sirloin braised tips with wild mushroom sauce, Garlic chicken scampi with scallions and Parmesan encrusted baked Tilapia, all accompanied with your choice of mashed potatoes, oven roasted seasoned red potatoes, yellow rice, collard greens, string beans, yams and tossed salad. You had the option of choosing any or all sides if you so desired. And of course we had several choices in beverages including sodas, seltzers, flavored spritzers and spring water, home-made lemonade and fresh brewed tea that you could customize with 3 different flavorings of Strawberry, Raspberry or Peach. Then there was a choice of iced coffees, lattes, regular and decaf hot coffee as well as tea.

The dessert choices were astounding with more fresh fruit, mini Danish, a variety of cupcakes, mini peach and mixed berry cobblers and a collection of mini cakes of carrot, iced mocha, coconut and red velvet individually boxed with a flowered bow. There was also an ice cream station with vanilla, chocolate, strawberry, chocolate chip, butter pecan and pistachio hard ice cream flavors, 3 choices of sorbet that included mango, coconut and lemon, then soft custard flavors of chocolate, banana and vanilla. And you can trust and believe that every topping was available, from sprinkles, nuts, whipped cream, cherries, M&M's...you name it...we had it. I don't know how nor who consumed what but it was plenty to go around. I do know that Nyla coordinated a doggy bag station that was operated on a first come, first served basis. Murad wanted to make sure that all that was paid for to the caterers in food would be utilized and not thrown away. I guess if you looked at, he tried to go with his own unique selection of food than the traditional wedding fare. Most of our folk don't really care for that cutesy leave you hungry wedding food no way. I don't know nor do I care about anyone else...but I was definitely impressed.

Dylina

I sat watching as the festivities started to wind down. As I said earlier, this was truly an event to be remembered. I am still in awe at all the intricate details that Murad put into this wedding. The reception hall had been laced in a collection of exotic pink that complimented the Ice Pink shade of Tania's gown. In order to break up all the pink, as assortment of the most delicate white flowers where strategically placed within giving a much balanced ambiance. The tablecloths were of a rich white satin brocade and held glass vases of fresh water pink pearls with a mixture of the pink and white florals. The chairs had been adorned with the same fabric as the tables with beautiful ice pink bows tied around the back. After dinner the room had been offset with a soft pink lighting that produced a mellow mood. I laughed to myself as I remembered the earlier events of the toss of the bridal bouquet and the throwing of the garter. To my surprise there were more men who were eager to catch the garter than women who wanted the bouquet. I guess a lot of women just don't believe anymore. Either that or they just know better than to think that someone else's bridal bouquet will produce them a prince charming of their own. Of all people Brick caught the garter and was by far so gone when it came to placing it on the young lady's leg. He had to take it a little too far and tried to place the garter all the way up her thigh. She became immediately offended and smacked his face. Him and his drunken self just smiled, got up from the floor and leaned into her and kissed her. Most of the crowd was way past feeling no pain, and started hooting and clapping in amusement. I tell you...people. Anyway the young lady stormed off the floor in a tizzy yet was later seen huddled over in the corner with Brick as if she was now mesmerized with his intoxicated demeanor. I'm just so glad that the little set of antics amounted to nothing much, cause there are times when the people in this family get to drinking....it's more than a night to remember.

Murad

Clock ticking and me and Nube need to be up outta here. Nyla came over and stepped in to make sure that everything and everybody would be squared away, so that we could go on to began our nuptial festivities . It's about 1 a.m. and we got to catch a plane at 7 in the morning. As soon as we got the chance we slipped out the back door, and was led to a royal suite stowed away upstairs on the east side of the mansion overlooking the garden. I had arranged it so that we could get our rest on since we would have to leave so early in the morning to catch our flight. Didn't make too much sense to have to go back up the way and waste travel time that could be spared until morning. Besides, I want to hold onto this feeling as long as I can, and the ambiance of this place has got a brother feeling all blazed and whatnot.

Damn...I think as a look over at Nube, my wish has come true and today will be a day that I remember for the rest of my life.

"Murad," I heard breaking into my chain of thoughts, "We did it Rod, we did it," she said, We got past all the obstacles, we let the by-gones be by-gones and we made it to the beginning of the rest of our lives."

I walked over and scooped her in my arms as we both stood looking out the huge bay window at the spacious and beautifully lit garden.

"Yeah we did," I responded as I started to undo the fastenings on her dress.

"Ah yeah," she stated as I slid the dress down, "I'm tired as hell, don't know how I'm gonna do it, but we've got to solidify our vows tonight."

"Yes today was a very long day," I said kissing on her neck, "but we gonna top it off right."

I continued to kiss her neck and began to caress her body. She started to purr, then turned around to kiss me...deeply. I came back with it just as deep, as she started undoing the buttons on my shirt. I took my time, but wasted no time in removing my garments. This is the day I wished and dreamed of since I was a boy, and the day that I thought I'd never see. I so wished to be the man my father was, and held close in my heart the wish that I would get and appreciate a woman in my life such as he had. And right here...tonight...my wish has come true. As Nube and I began to fall into sync in our wedding night consummation, I felt in my heart that I needed some verbal confirmation to my wish.

As she began calling my name, I teased her to the exact sensual height then pulled back and softly quizzed her, "Nube, remember the day we decided to come together and we laid it down to each other who we are?"

"Yes Rod...I remember," she breathed out heavily.

"Well there's something else to add to your list of who you be...do you know?" I asked giving her another teasing probe.

Ahhhh...yes Rod, I am Tania Tillman," she smugly answered in a sexy voice .

"Ah...yeah bae...that you are, but that's not quite what I wanted to hear," I told her intensifying the rhythm.

"Uh...well...I don't know, Nubina...Nubina Tillman is it Nubina...Tillman...uh...ahhh...Nubina Tillman," she responded her breathing quick and sweet.

I laughed lightly and said, "No...that's not it." I began to move with a greater purpose.

"Ahhh..aahh...then Nube Tillman?" she came back with inquiry in her tone.

I pushed the rhythm up intensely, then brought it back down to sweet, as I let her know, "Naw...Butter that ain't it..."

"Buter Tillman...ahh..ahh..Butter Tillman," she cut me off as I slowly, sweetly teased her with the rhythm.

I laughed deeply this time as I continued my wishful tease. "Bae...I'm beginning to feel some kind of way...come on now...I know you know," I told her pressing on with the rhythm.

"Murad...Murad," she sang out.

"Okay...now we close," I told her rocking it a tad deeper.

"Mrs. Tillman...Mrs. Tillman," she cried out in frustrated pleasure. "Aaahh...ooohhh Murad...Murad...baby...I can't...I don't know..."she whined as I shook my head no to her last response.

"C'mon Butter," I coaxed, "Yes you can...you know. You're exactly who I've always wanted you to be."

I teased it up once more and she cried out, "Murad...Murad."

I know she was ready to explode, so I thought I needed to help her out, so I voiced softly, "Butter, look at me, let me see them beautiful eyes of yours. Yeah there you go...I'm looking into the eyes of my wife...my wife. The eyes that share a view of my soul...she knows me and I know her... cause she is?"

As I led off with the question, I took the rhythm over the edge and made my wish come true.

"Aaaahhh....Mrs. Murad Tillman," she sang out in a medley of moans, to which I promptly joined in behind her.

"Hell yeah...Mrs. Murad Tillman baby...forever...for life."

It don't even get no better than this. Last night was one of the sweetest moments of my life, or so I thought. We officially christened our marriage then took it down for the remaining time. The car service came and scooped us up about 6:20 am and whisked us up the Turnpike to the Teterboro Airport where a private luxury jet awaited us. Now I don't know how or when, because I was pretty much out for the count once we took off. Somewhere between last night and this morning I arrived in paradise as Mrs. Murad Tillman. I was lounging in a chaise on a spacious balcony of the most upscale resort suite, being feed fresh fruit by my husband Murad, as I basked in the sunlight enjoying the expansive and exhilarating view of the ancient seaside caves off the island of Symi Greece. Blue skies customized to the crystal blue waters and I thought that this right here...tops last night...and I now know that wishes do come true. This right here has got to be the sweetest moment of my life...cause it don't get no better than this...no better than this at all.

Part IV

2010

Epilogue

The day I punched the monster, turned into a rainy day.
I hit him and I punched him so that he would go away.
He's ugly and he's scary, and he's creepy like no other.
I really had it out with him; he scared my baby brother.

He came into our room straight thru the window like a fly.
He started jumping up and down as we just stood nearby.
I said, "Oh no, you've got to go, we're not afraid of you."
And he replied "Give me a try, just watch what I can do."

I thought we could ignore him and that he would go away.
But he just kept on stalking every time we tried to play.
I yelled, I begged, I pleaded, tried to bribe him with a quarter.
But that annoying monster went and doused me with some water.

I grabbed him by the collar tried to shake the thing away.
But all he did was laugh at me and turn a shade of gray.
My brother now was really scared and he began to cry.
I said, "you're gonna get it now," and punched him in the eye.

The monster stopped, and looked real sad, and said to me quite quickly.
"There's no harm done, just having fun, you didn't have to hit me."
His eyes got big, and watered up, and tears began to glisten.
I said "I'm sorry monster man, but you just need to listen."

He put his hand up to his head and said," I'm sorry too."
"But running round and scaring kids is really what I do."
And then he said, "Don't worry none; I'm off to scare another."
He swiftly left us standing there, me and my baby brother

Now once he left the air was still, the room got hot and dry
My baby brother turned to me and he began to cry
"You made him leave, I want him back, he only wants to play."
"It's too late now;" I said to him, "the monsters gone away."

The sky turned gray, and then to black, and then it turned to rain
The day I punched the monster, seemed to be the thing to blame
I should have let him have his way, and taken it all with stride
Cause now the rain is coming down, and we can't play outside.

As Nube finished reading the story, the whole assembly broke out into applause. The deal with the children's' publisher had come thru, and as per her agreement she was doing her first kickoff to the book with a reading at The Liberty Charter School in Newark. She said that although she welcomes all children to her fan base, she wanted to anchor her start in children's book within her own community first. She agreed to do additional book signings at the various Barnes and Nobles in the tri-state area once she fulfilled her round of urban schools first. She has another scheduled for Harlem, another in Jersey City, and last but not least her home town of Bed-Stuy. Yeah...Nubina about to be a household name all across the states. I can't even began to relay how damn proud I am of her. I have always been in tune with her ability for spoken word and her writings, but this spin-off into the children's venue is like a whole nother aspect of her talent that I'm getting to know. Her never ending talent never ceases to amaze me. I truly believe that her inner beauty and love for the essence of life itself gives her the ability to operate and express herself in just about any arena. Her love for the well being of others comes across in her demeanor as well as her actions. I appreciate the fact that she let me share the wonders of her life and I look forward to our future blessings. Her birthday is coming up next month, and I really want to do something special for her. Don't quite know yet what I'm gonna do...but trust it's gonna be special.

Nubina

Ahhh man...this is great. My first children's book is really jumping off. I wasn't sure if this was an area that I could tackle successfully, but my verses' have seemed to catch on and made the book a quick favorite. I guess it didn't hurt none that I had a beautiful jacket cover designed by none other than my sister Lani. She's always had an artistic eye and she offered her idea for a design on a whim. Well it turned out to be a gem of a whim, because the book is flying off the shelves. It took me a long time to be confident in my work, cause you know the workings of an artist are very personal; but if I had to make a choice I would say that this particular project has taken the top spot as my favorite. It feels good to see the sweet innocent eyes all wide with curiosity and interest to the story. And I really love all the oohs and ahhs at the colorful illustrations. Yes this book does me proud and I am truly looking forward to get started on the subsequent book projects. In the meantime, Rod's been trying to fish around and see what I want for my birthday next month. I don't know...I mean, not for nothing...there isn't one iota of any thing that I need in my life, so truly...good health and mental prosperity is enough for me. Speaking of, I've got to remember to keep my appointment this Wednesday; I've been feeling a little fatigued lately. Probably the consequences of this whirlwind schedule I've been juggling. Let's see... I got the book tours, I'm learning the script for an upcoming movie, not to mention 2 new projects that I'm working on for Q's company. Sometimes I wonder where all the energy comes from, and then at the times when I'm tired like this, I wonder what it would be like to just trade it all in and do the family thing. Yeah...me...Murad and a kid or two; I'm talking picnics in the park, celebrating birthdays and homemade movies like back in the day. Yeah...I wish.

About The Author

Tina Ray hails from Bed-Stuy Brooklyn and currently resides in Essex County NJ. She is a creative soul with many inticing novels and creations to come. Make A Wish reigns as her debut novel and she would expect nothing less than to hear your feedback. She awaits your correspondence and can be contacted at:

Tinaray684@gmail.com
Facebook page - Make A Wish

29342528R00313

Made in the USA
Middletown, DE
16 February 2016